· 1 ·

VENUS

VENUS

BEN BOVA

TOR®

A TOM DOHERTY ASSOCIATES BOOK
NEW YORK

VENUS

Copyright © 2000 by Ben Bova

Edited by Patrick Nielsen Hayden

A Tor Book
Published by Tom Doherty Associates, LLC
175 Fifth Avenue
New York, NY 10010

Tor® is a registered trademark of Tom Doherty Associates, LLC.

ISBN 0-312-87216-X

First Edition: April 2000

Printed in the United States of America

To D.H.G., J.L., and B.B.B.
with thanks, appreciation, and love

Heaven says nothing, and the whole earth grows rich beneath its silent rule. Men, too, are touched by heaven's virtue; yet, in their greater part, they are creatures of deceit. They are born, it seems, with an emptiness of soul, and must take their qualities wholly from things without. To be born thus empty into this modern age, this mixture of good and ill, and yet to steer through life on an honest course to the splendors of success—this is a feat reserved for paragons of our kind, a task beyond the nature of the normal man.

—Ihara Saikaku

VENUS

HELL CRATER

was late and I knew it. The trouble is, you can't run on the moon.

The shuttle from the *Nueva Venezuela* space station had been delayed, some minor problem with the baggage being transferred from Earthside, so now I was hurrying along the underground corridor from the landing pad, all alone. The party had started more than an hour ago.

They had warned me not to try to run, even with the weighted boots that I had rented at the landing port. But like a fool I tried to anyway and sort of hip-hopped crazily and bumped into the corridor wall, scraping my nose rather painfully. After that I shuffled along in the manner that the tourist-guide video had shown. It felt stupid, but bouncing off the walls was worse.

Not that I really wanted to go to my father's inane party or be on the Moon at all. None of this was my idea.

Two big human-form robots guarded the door at the end of the corridor. And I mean *big*, two meters tall and almost as wide across the torso. The gleaming metal door was sealed shut, of course. You couldn't crash my father's party; he'd never stand for that.

"Your name, please," said the robot on my left. Its voice was deep and rough, my father's idea of what a bouncer should sound like, I suppose.

"Van Humphries," I said, as slowly and clearly as I could enunciate.

The robot hesitated only a fraction of a second before saying, "Voice print identification is verified. You may enter, Mr. Van Humphries."

Both robots pivoted around and the door slid open. The noise hit me like a power hammer: thumping atonal music blasting away against wildly over-amped screeching from some androgynous singer wailing the latest pop hit.

The chamber was huge, immense, and jammed wall-to-wall with partygoers, hundreds of men and women, a thousand or more, I guessed, drinking, shouting, smoking, their faces contorted with grimaces of forced raucous laughter. The noise was like a solid wall pounding against me; I had to physically force myself to step past the robots and into the mammoth chamber.

Everyone was in party attire: brazenly bright colors with plenty of spangles and glitter and electronic blinkies. And lots of bare flesh showing, of course. I felt like a missionary in my chocolate-brown velour pullover and tan micromesh slacks.

A long electronic window swept the length of the cavern's side wall, alternately proclaiming "HAPPY ONE HUNDREDTH BIRTHDAY!" and showing clips from pornographic videos.

I might have known Father would pick a bordello as the site for his party. Hell Crater, named after the Jesuit astronomer Maximilian J. Hell. The gaming and porn industries had turned the area into the Moon's sin capital, a complete cornucopia of illicit pleasures dug below the dusty floor of the crater, some six hundred klicks south of Selene City. Poor old Father Hell must be spinning in his crypt.

"Hi there, stranger!" said a brassy, buxom redhead in an emerald-green costume so skimpy it must have been spray-painted onto her. She waggled a vial of some grayish-looking powder in my general direction, exhorting, "Join the fun!"

Fun. The place looked like Dante's Inferno. There was nowhere to sit except for a few couches along the walls, and they were already filled with writhing tangles of naked bodies. Everyone else was on their feet, packed in shoulder to shoulder, dancing or swaying and surging like the waves of some multihued, gabbling, aimless human sea.

High up near the smoothed rock ceiling a pair of acrobats in sequined harlequin costumes were walking a tightrope strung across the chamber. A set of spotlights made their costumes glitter. On Earth, performing that high up would have been dangerous; here on the Moon they could still break their necks if they fell—or more likely break the necks of the people they fell upon. The place was so tightly packed it would've been impossible for them to hit the floor.

"C'mon," the redhead urged again, pawing at the sleeve of my pullover. She giggled and said, "Don't be so twangy!"

"Where is Martin Humphries?" I had to shout to be heard over the din of the party.

She blinked her emerald-tinted eyes. "Hump? The birthday boy?" Turning uncertainly toward the crowd and waving her hand vaguely, she yelled back, "The old humper's around here someplace. It's his party, y'know."

"The old humper is my father," I told her, enjoying the sudden look of astonishment on her face as I brushed past her.

It was a real struggle to work my way through the crowd. Strangers, all of them. I didn't know anyone there, I was certain of that. None of my friends would be caught dead at a scene like this. As I pushed and elbowed my way through the jam-packed chamber, I wondered if my father knew any of these people. He probably rented them for the occasion. The redhead certainly looked the type.

He knows I can't take crowds, and yet he forced me to come here. Typical of my loving father. I tried to shut out the noise, the reek of perfume and tobacco and drugs, and the slimy sweat of too many bodies pressed too close together. It was making me weak in the knees, twisting my stomach into knots.

I can't deal with this kind of thing. It's too much. I felt as if I would collapse if there weren't so many bodies crowded around me. I was starting to get dizzy, my vision blurring.

I had to stop in the midst of the mob and squeeze my eyes shut. It was a struggle to breathe. I had taken my regular enzyme shot just before the transfer rocket had landed, yet I felt as if I needed another one, and quickly.

I opened my eyes and surveyed the jostling, noisy, sweaty throng again, searching for the nearest exit. And then I saw him. Through the tangle of weaving, gesticulating partygoers I spotted my father, sitting up on a dais at the far end of the cavern like some ancient Roman emperor surveying an orgy. He was even clad in a flowing robe of crimson, with two beautifully supple young women at his sandalled feet.

My father. One hundred years old this day. Martin Humphries didn't look any more than forty; his hair was still dark, his face firm and almost unlined. But his eyes—his eyes were hard, knowing; they glittered with corrupt pleasure at the scene being played out before him. He had used every rejuvenation therapy he could get his hands on, even illegal ones such as nanomachines. He wanted to stay young and vigorous forever. I thought he probably would. He always got what he wanted. But one look into his eyes and it was easy to believe that he was a hundred years old.

He saw me shouldering through the strident, surging crowd and for a moment those cold gray eyes of his locked onto mine. Then he turned away from me with an impatient frown clouding his handsome, artificially youthful face.

You insisted that I come to this carnival, I said to him silently. So, like it or not, here I am.

He paid no attention to me as I toiled to reach him. I was gasping now, my lungs burning. I needed a shot of my medication but I had left it back at my hotel suite. When at last I reached the foot of his dais I slumped against the softly pliable fabric draped over the platform, struggling to catch my breath. Then I realized that the strident din of the party had dropped to a buzzing, muted whisper.

"Sound dampers," my father said, glancing down at me with his old disdainful smirk. "Don't look so stupid."

There were no steps up the platform and I felt too weak and giddy to try to haul myself up beside him.

He made a shooing motion and the two young women jumped nimbly from the platform, eagerly joining the crowd. I realized that they were just teenagers.

"Want one?" my father asked, with a leering grin. "You can have 'em both, all you have to do is ask."

I didn't bother to shake my head. I just clung to the side of his platform, trying to bring my breathing under control.

"For Christ's sake, Runt, stop that damned panting! You look like a beached flounder."

I pulled in a deep breath, then stood as straight as I could manage. "And it's lovely to see you, too, Father."

"Aren't you enjoying my party?"

"You know better."

"Then what'd you come for, Runt?"

"Your lawyer said you'd cut off my stipend if I didn't attend your party."

"Your allowance," he sneered.

"I earn that money."

"By playing at being a scientist. Now your brother, there was a *real* scientist."

Yes, but Alex is dead. It had happened almost two years ago, but the memory of that day still scalded me inside.

All my life my father had mocked and belittled me. Alex was his favorite, his firstborn, Father's pride and joy. Alex was being groomed to take over Humphries Space Systems, if and when Father ever decided to retire. Alex was everything that I'm not: tall, athletic, quick and handsome, brilliantly intelligent, outgoing, charming and witty. I'm on the small side, I've been sickly from birth, I'm told that I tend to be withdrawn, introspective. My mother died giving birth to me and my father never let me forget that.

I had loved Alex. I truly had. I had admired him tremendously. Ever since I could remember, Alex had protected me against Father's sneers and cutting words. "It's all right, little brother, don't cry," he would tell me. "I won't let him hurt you."

Over the years I learned from Alex a love for exploration, for seeing new vistas, new worlds. But while Alex actually went out on missions to Mars and the Jovian moons, I had to stay cocooned at home, too frail to venture outward. I flew an armchair, not a spacecraft. My excitement came from streams of computer data and virtual reality simulations. Once I walked with Alex on the red sands of Mars, linked by an interactive VR system. It was the best afternoon of my life.

Then Alex was killed on his expedition to Venus, he and all his crew. And Father hated me for being alive.

I left his house for good and bought a home on Majorca, a place all my own, far from his dismissive sarcasm. As if to mock me, Father moved to Selene City. Later I found out that he'd gone to the Moon so he could take nanotherapies to keep himself young and fit. Nanomachines were outlawed on Earth, of course.

It was clear that Father went for rejuvenation treatments because he had no intention of retiring now. With Alex dead, Father would never leave Humphries Space Systems to me. He would stay in command and keep me exiled.

So Father lived some four hundred thousand kilometers away, playing his chosen role of interplanetary tycoon, megabillionaire, hell-raising, womanizing, ruthless, corrupt giant of industry. I was perfectly content with that. I lived quietly on Majorca, comfortable with a household staff that took excellent care of me. Some of my servants were human; most were robots. Friends came to visit often enough. I could flit over to Paris or New York or wherever for theater or a concert. I spent my days studying the new data about the stars and planets that were constantly streaming back from our space explorers.

Until one of my friends repeated a rumor she had heard: My brother's spacecraft had been sabotaged. His death was not an accident; it was murder. The very next day, my father summoned me to his moronic birthday party on the Moon, under the threat of cutting off my stipend if I didn't show up.

Looking up at his youthfully taut face again, I asked my father, "Why did you insist that I come here?"

He smiled down sardonically at me. "Aren't you enjoying the party?"

"Are you?" I countered.

Father made a sound that might have been a suppressed laugh. Then he said, "I have an announcement to make. I wanted you to be on hand to hear it directly from my lips."

I felt puzzled. An announcement? Was he going to retire, after all? What of it; he would never allow me to run the corporation. Nor did I want to, actually.

He touched a stud set into the left armrest of his chair and the stupefying noise of the party blasted against my ears hard enough to crack my skull. Then he touched the other armrest. The music stopped in mid-beat. The tightrope-walking acrobats winked out like a light snapped off. A holographic image, I realized.

The crowd fell silent and still. They all turned toward the dais, like a sullen horde of party-dressed schoolchildren forced to listen to their principal.

"I'm delighted that you could come to my party," Father began, his low, modulated voice amplified and echoing across the crowded chamber. "Are we having fun yet?"

On that cue they all cheered, clapped, whistled, and yelled lustily.

Father raised both hands and they all fell silent again.

"I have an announcement to make, something that you hard-working representatives of the news media out there will find particularly worthwhile, I think."

Half a dozen camera-carrying balloons were already hovering a few meters from the dais, like glittering Christmas ornaments floating buoyantly. Now several more drifted out of the farther reaches of the chamber to focus on my father.

"As you know," he went on, "my beloved son Alexander was killed three years ago while attempting to explore the planet Venus."

A collective sigh swept through the throng.

"Somewhere on the surface of that hellhole of a world his spacecraft lies, with his remains inside it. In that terrible heat and pressure, the corrosive atmosphere must be slowly destroying the last mortal remains of my boy."

Somewhere a woman broke into soft sobbing.

"I want to offer an inducement to someone who is bold enough, tough enough, to go to Venus and reach its surface and bring back what's left of my son to me."

They all seemed to stand up straighter, their eyes widened. An inducement?

My father hesitated for a dramatic moment, then said in a much stronger voice, "I offer a prize of ten billion international dollars to whoever can reach my dead son's body and return his remains to me."

They gasped. For several seconds no one spoke. Then the chamber filled with excited chatter. Ten billion dollars! Reach the surface of Venus! A prize of ten billion dollars to recover Alex Humphries's body!

I felt just as stunned as any of the others. More, perhaps, because I knew better than most of those costumed freeloaders what an impossible challenge my father had just offered.

Father touched the stud on his chair arm and the babble of the crowd immediately was cut down to a muted buzz again.

"Very nice," I said to him. "You'll be named Father of the Year."

He gazed disdainfully down at me. "You don't think I mean it?"

"I think you know that no one in his right mind is going to try to reach the surface of Venus. Alex himself only planned to coast through the cloud decks."

"So you think I'm a fraud."

"I think you're making a public relations gesture, nothing more."

He shrugged as if it didn't matter.

I was seething. He was sitting up there and getting all this pub-licity. "You want to look like a grieving father," I shouted at him, "making the whole world think you care about Alex, offering a prize that you know no one will claim."

"Oh, someone will try for it, I'm certain." He smiled coldly down at me. "Ten billion dollars is a lot of incentive."

"I'm not so sure," I said.

"But I am. In fact, I'm going to deposit the whole sum in an escrow account where no one can touch it except the eventual prize winner."

"The entire ten billion?"

"The whole sum," he repeated. Then, leaning slightly toward me, he added, "To raise that much cash I'm going to have to cut a few corners here and there."

"Really? How much have you spent on this party?"

He waved a hand as if that didn't matter. "One of the corners I'm cutting is your allowance."

"My stipend?"

"It's finished, Runt. You'll be twenty-five years old next month. Your allowance ends on your birthday."

Just like that, I was penniless.

DATA BANK

She glows so bright and lovely in the night sky that virtually every culture on Earth has called her after their goddess of beauty and love: Aphrodite, Inanna, Ishtar, Astarte, Venus.

Sometimes she is the dazzling Evening Star, brighter than anything in the sky except the Sun and Moon. Sometimes she is the beckoning Morning Star, harbinger of the new day. Always she shines like a precious jewel.

As beautiful as Venus appears in our skies, the planet itself is the most hellish place in the solar system. The ground is hot enough to melt aluminum. The air pressure is so high it has crushed spacecraft landers as if they were flimsy cardboard cartons. The sky is perpetually covered from pole to pole with clouds of sulfuric acid. The atmosphere is a choking mixture of carbon dioxide and sulfurous gases.

Venus is the nearest planet to Earth, closer to us than Mars. At its nearest approach, it is slightly less than sixty-five million kilometers from Earth. It is closer to the Sun than Earth is; Venus is the second planet outward from the Sun, while Earth is the third. Venus has no moon.

It is almost the same size as Earth, slightly smaller, so that the gravity at its surface is about 85 percent of Earth-normal.

There the similarities end. Venus is hot, with surface temperatures well above 450 degrees Celsius (nearly 900 degrees Fahrenheit). It rotates so slowly that its "day" is longer than its "year:" the planet makes an orbit around the Sun in 225 Earth days—a Venusian year, yet it rotates around its axis in 243 Earth days—a

Venusian day. And it rotates backward, clockwise as viewed from its north pole, while Earth and the other planets rotate counter-clockwise.

Venus's atmosphere is so thick that atmospheric pressure at ground level is equal to the pressure of an earthly ocean more than a kilometer below the surface. That atmosphere is more than 95 percent carbon dioxide, with less than 4 percent nitrogen and only negligible traces of free oxygen.

The thick layers of clouds that perpetually cover Venus from pole to pole reflect some 75 percent of the sunlight that hits the planet and make it very bright and beautiful to look at. The clouds, though, are made of sulfuric acid and other sulfur and chlorine compounds; there is practically no water vapor in them.

There are mountains and volcanoes on Venus, and evidence of plate tectonics that have shifted vast sections of the crust. There must be Venus-quakes, as well.

Imagine trying to walk on the surface of Venus! The very ground is red-hot. The atmosphere is so thick that it warps light like a fisheye lens. The sky is perpetually clouded. Yet there is no real darkness: even during the long Venusian night there is an eerie, sullen glow from the red-hot ground.

Because Venus is moving in its orbit around the Sun while it slowly rotates on its own axis, if you stood on one spot on the surface it would take 117 Earth days from one sunrise to the next—if you could see the sunrise through those thick, all-pervading clouds. And the Sun would rise in the west, set in the east.

Looking up into the grayish-yellow clouds you might see patches of darker areas hurtling across the sky, forming and dissolving against the murky background nearly fifty kilometers overhead, scudding from horizon to horizon in about five hours. Now and then you might see a stroke of lightning flashing down, or hear the threatening rumble of a distant volcano.

No place in the inner solar system is so challenging, so dangerous. By comparison, the Moon is easy and Mars a picnic.

Could life exist on Venus, either high in the clouds (where temperatures are cooler) or deep underground? There is *something* in Venus's atmosphere that absorbs ultraviolet light; planetary scientists are not certain what it might be. Could there be bacterial forms that live underground, as there are on Earth and presumably on Mars and Jupiter's moon Europa?

If there are any creatures living on the surface, they must be capable of withstanding heat that melts aluminum and pressures that can crush spacecraft.

Formidable monsters indeed.

SELENE CITY

t should've been you, Runt!" he howled. "It should've been you who died, not Alex."

I awoke with a start, springing up to a sitting position in the darkened hotel room, both my fists gripping the bedsheets tightly enough to rip them. I was soaked with cold sweat and trembling from head to foot.

The dream had been too real. Too totally real. I squeezed my eyes shut, sitting there on the bed, and my father's enraged face burned before me like the wrath of some ancient god.

The party at Hell Crater. His announcement of the Venus prize. His notice that he was cutting me off without an income. It had all been too much for me. By the time I made it back to my hotel in Selene City I was near collapse, the carpeted hotel corridors swimming dizzyingly, my legs weak as tissue paper even in the low lunar gravity. I got to my room, went straight to the lavatory, and fumbled with my hypospray syringe. At last I injected a full dose of the enzyme medication into my arm, then tottered off to bed and fell almost instantly asleep.

Only to dream. No, it wasn't actually a dream; it was a reliving of that terrible day when we learned that Alex had been killed. A nightmare. I relived every agonizing moment of it.

When we got the news that there was no possible hope left, Father had blanked his phone screen and turned to me, his face distorted with fury.

"He's dead," my father had said, his voice cold and hollow, his gray eyes like ice. "Alex is dead and you're alive. First you killed your mother and now you're still alive while Alex is dead."

I just stood there while he glared at me, grim and bitterly angry. At me. At me.

"It should've been you, Runt," he snarled, his fury mounting, his face going from white to red. "You're worthless! Nobody would miss you. But no, you're here, you're alive and breathing while Alex is dead. It should've been you, Runt!" he howled. "It should've been you who died, not Alex."

That was when I moved out of the family home in Connecticut and bought my place on Majorca, as far from Father as I could get. Or so I thought. But he went me one better, of course, and moved to Selene City.

Now I sat in a hotel bed, shaking and cold with midnight sweat, alone, totally alone.

I got up and padded barefoot to the lavatory; tottered, actually, that's how weak and wretched I felt. The light went on automatically and I fumbled with my hypospray syringe until I finally got a plastic cylinder preloaded with the proper dosage of enzyme clicked into place and pressed it against my bare arm. The faint hiss of the medication squeezing through the microneedles and into my bloodstream always reassured me. But not that night. Nothing could calm me, I thought.

I was born with a rare form of pernicious anemia, a birth defect caused by my mother's drug addiction. It could be fatal if not controlled by injections of a cocktail of enzymes that included vitamin B12 and a growth hormone that prompted my body to create new red blood cells. Without that medication I would weaken and eventually die. With it I could lead a perfectly normal life—except for the need to take the injections at least twice a day.

If anyone ever tells you that nanomachines could cure any medical condition, if only they weren't outlawed on Earth, don't believe him. The best labs at Selene City—the capital of nanotechnology research—haven't been able to program a nanobug that can build millions of red blood cells every few hours.

I went back to the bed with its tangled sweaty sheets and waited for the medication to take effect. With nothing better to do, I called out for the video news. The wall screen immediately glowed to life and showed a scene of terrible devastation: another raging hurricane had swung all the way across the Atlantic and was pounding the British Isles. Even the Thames Barrage—the high-tech dam across the river—had been overrun and large sections of London were underwater, including Westminster Abbey and the Houses of Parliament.

I leaned back against my pillows and watched, hollow-eyed, as thousands of Londoners poured into the streets in the lashing cold rain to escape the rising floodwaters. "The worst cataclysm to hit London since the Blitz of World War II, more than a century ago," the news announcer intoned in a crack-of-doom voice.

"Next channel!" I called. Death and destruction were not what I wanted to see. But most of the channels were showing London's agony, live and in full color. I could have watched it all in three dimensions if I'd called up the hologram channel. There were flotillas of boats chugging down the Strand and Fleet Street, rescuing men, women, children—even pets. Workers were struggling to protect Buckingham Palace from the encroaching waters.

Finally I found a channel that was not showing the flood. It was a panel discussion by self-proclaimed experts on the global warming that was causing such storms and flooding. One of them wore the green armband of the International Green Party, another I recognized as a friend of my father's—a sharp-tongued corporate lawyer who clearly loathed the Greens. The rest were scientists of various stripe, no two of them agreeing on anything.

I watched, glassy-eyed, hoping their quiet, mannered deliberation would lull me to sleep. As they spoke, the screen displayed animated maps that showed how the icecaps in Greenland and Antarctica were melting and how much sea levels were expected to rise. Half the American Midwest was in danger of being turned into a huge inland sea. The Gulf Stream was going to break up, they said, freezing Britain and Europe into an extension of Siberia.

Just the perfect lullaby to soothe me to sleep. I was about to turn the wall screen off altogether when the yellow message light began blinking. Who would be calling me at this time of night? I wondered.

"Answer," I called out.

The entire wall screen turned a milky grayish white. For a moment I thought there had been some malfunction of the video.

Then a synthesized computer voice spoke to me: "Mr. Humphries, please excuse my not showing my face. It would be too dangerous for you to see me."

"Dangerous?" I asked. "For whom?"

The voice ignored my question, and I realized this was a prerecorded message. "We know you have heard the rumor that your brother's ship was sabotaged. We believe your father was responsible for his death. Your brother was murdered, sir, and your father is his murderer."

The screen went dead. I sat there in the darkened hotel bedroom, stunned, shocked, gaping wide-eyed at the faintly glowing wall screen. My father had Alex murdered? My father was responsible for his death? It was a terrible, awful accusation, made by someone too cowardly even to show his or her face.

And I believed it. That's what staggered me the most. *I believed it.*

I believed it because I remembered the night before Alex left for his ill-fated expedition to Venus. The night he revealed to me why he was really going.

Alex had told everyone that he was going to Venus to study the planet's runaway greenhouse. Which was true enough. But he had a hidden agenda as well. He told me about it that night before he left. There was a political motive behind his scientific mission. I remember Alex sitting in the cozy, quiet library of the Connecticut house, where we lived with Father, and whispering his plans to me.

Earth was just starting to feel the effects of greenhouse warming, Alex told me. Glaciers and polar caps melting. Sea levels rising. Global climate changing.

The International Green Party claimed that drastic steps must be taken before the whole American Midwest is turned back into the inland sea it once was and the permafrost in Canada melts, releasing megatons of frozen methane into the atmosphere and driving the greenhouse effect even further.

"You're one of them?" I whispered in the dark to him. "A Green?"

He chuckled in the shadows. "You'd be too, Little Brother, if you paid any attention to the real world."

I remember shaking my head and muttering, "Father would kill you if he knew."

"He knows," Alex said.

He wanted to use his mission to Venus to show the world firsthand what a runaway greenhouse can do to a planet: turn it into a dead ball of rock mantled in poisonous gases, without a drop of water or a blade of grass. It would be a powerful icon, a picture branded into the consciousness of the world's voters: This is what Earth will become unless we stop the greenhouse warming.

Powerful political forces opposed the Greens. Men such as my father had no intention of letting the IGP gain control of the international organizations that regulated environmental protection measures. The Greens wanted to triple taxes on multinational corporations, ban all fossil-fuel burning, force the evacuation of major cities, redistribute the world's wealth among the needy.

Alex's expedition to Venus, then, was actually a mission to help the Greens, to give them a powerful image to use against the entrenched political power of the Establishment, against our own father.

"Father would kill you if he knew," I had said.

And Alex had replied grimly, "He knows."

My fear of Father's reaction was merely a metaphor, kids' talk. Now I wondered if Alex had understood it that way.

I could no more sleep than I could lift Gibraltar. I prowled through my suite in the long shuffling strides that the Moon's low gravity demands, by turns angry, frightened, desperate.

Like all the lunar communities, Selene City is underground, dug into the ringwall mountains of the giant crater Alphonsus. So there is no dawn creeping through your windows, no sunrise to announce when a new day begins. The lights out in the corridors and public spaces turn up to a daytime level, bang, that's it. In my suite the lights turned on automatically as I paced, the switches activated by my body heat.

After several hours I finally realized what I would do. What I had to do. I ordered the phone computer to contact my father.

It took several minutes. No doubt his disgusting party was still going on in high gear. At last, though, his face appeared on the wall screen in my sitting room.

Father looked tired, but relaxed, smiling lazily at me. I realized he was in bed, leaning back on glistening silk-covered pillows. He was not alone, either. I heard muffled giggles from beneath his bedcovers.

"You're up early," he said pleasantly enough.

"So are you," I replied.

He huffed. "Don't look so disapproving, Runt. I offered these ladies to you, remember? It would be a shame to waste such talent."

"I'm going to take your prize money," I said.

That popped his eyes open. "What?"

"I'll go to Venus. I'll find Alex's body."

"You?" He laughed.

"He was my brother!" I said. "I loved him."

"I had to twist your arm to get you to come up here to the Moon, and now you think you're going to Venus?" He seemed enormously amused by the idea.

"You don't think I could do it?"

"I *know* you can't do it, Runt. You won't even try, despite your brave talk."

"I'll show you!" I snapped. "I'll take your damned prize money!"

Smirking, he answered, "Of course you will. And elephants can fly."

"You're forcing me into it," I insisted. "That ten-billion prize is a powerful incentive to a man whose income shuts off next month."

His smirk faded and he turned thoughtful. "Yes, I suppose it would be, wouldn't it?"

"I'm going," I said firmly.

"And you assume that you'll win my prize money, eh?"

"Or die trying."

"You don't think you'll be the only one trying to grab my ten billion, do you?"

"Who else in his right mind would even think of going?"

With a sneer, Father answered, "Oh, I know someone who'll try. He'll try damned hard."

"Who?"

"Lars Fuchs. That bastard's out somewhere in the Belt right now, but as soon as the word reaches him, he'll head for Venus without blinking an eye."

"Fuchs?" I had heard my father speak of Lars Fuchs often, and always with hatred. He was an asteroid miner, from what little I knew of him. Once he had owned his own corporation and had been a competitor of my father's, but now he was nothing more than an independent miner scratching out a living in the Asteroid Belt, a "rock rat," in my father's genteel phrasing.

"Fuchs. You'll have to wrestle my prize money away from him, Runt. I don't think you're man enough to do it."

I should have realized at that precise moment that he was manipulating me, he was *forcing* me to jump through his hoops. But to be perfectly honest, all I saw was a life of destitution unless I could take that prize money.

Well, that wasn't quite all that I was thinking about. I still saw Alex's handsome, determined face from that last night he had spent on Earth.

"Father would kill you if he knew," I had said.

"He knows," Alex had replied.

WASHINGTON, D.C.

This is the opportunity of a lifetime," Professor Greenbaum groaned like a creaking hinge, "and I'm too old to take advantage of it."

I had never actually seen an elderly person before, not close up, in the same room. I mean, poor people probably aged, but with everybody who could afford it getting telomerase treatments as soon as they reach adulthood, and rejuvenation therapy for adults who had aged before telomerase was approved for general use, no one grew old anymore.

But Daniel Haskel Greenbaum was *old*. His skin was all wrinkled and spotted. He was stooped over and looked so frail I was afraid his bones would shatter when I shook hands with him. Actually, his grip was rather firm, even though his eyes were pouchy and the skin of his face sagged and was filled with lines and creases, like a worn old arroyo eroded by centuries of weathering.

Yet he was only seventy-something.

Mickey had warned me about Greenbaum's appearance. Michelle Cochrane had been one of his graduate students. Now a full professor herself, she still worshiped Greenbaum. She called him the greatest living planetary scientist in the solar system.

If you could call his asthmatic, arthritic, painfully slow pace of existence *living*. He had refused rejuvenation therapy, for some obscure reason. His religion, I think. Or perhaps just pure stubbornness. He was the kind who believed that aging and death were inevitable, and should not be avoided.

One of the last of that kind, I might add.

"He has the courage of his convictions," Mickey had told me years earlier. "He's not afraid of dying."

"I'm scared to death of dying," I had joked.

Mickey hadn't seen the cleverness of my *mot.* Yet I knew she had taken telomerase treatments when she finished puberty as a matter of course. Everyone did.

Greenbaum was the world's leading authority on the planet Venus, and Mickey had pleaded with me to meet with the old man. I had agreed without giving it another thought. The next thing I knew, she had arranged a meeting in Washington, D.C., not only with creaking Professor Emeritus Greenbaum, but with an angry-looking black bureaucrat from the space agency named Franklin Abdullah.

My father had immediately trumpeted to the news media that his other son—me—was going to try to recover Alex's remains on the surface of Venus. Like a proud parent, he assured the reporters that if I came back with Alex's body I would be rewarded with the ten-billion-dollar prize. I became an instant celebrity.

Fame has its advantages, I've been told, but I have yet to discover any of them. Every scientist, adventurer, fame-seeker, and mentally unstable person in the Earth-Moon system sought me out, begging for a chance to go to Venus with me. Even religious fanatics had insisted it was their destiny to go to Venus and I was God's chosen method of transporting them there.

Of course, I had willingly invited a half dozen of my closest friends to come on the voyage with me. Artists, writers, videographers, they would make valued contributions to the expedition's history and be good company as well: more so than dull scientists and wild-eyed zealots.

Then Mickey had called me from her office in California and I had agreed to meet with her and Greenbaum without even asking myself what she might be after.

At Abdullah's insistence the meeting took place in the space agency's headquarters, a musty, dreary old building in a run-down neighborhood of downtown Washington. We met in a windowless little conference room; the only furniture was a battered old metal table and four unbelievably uncomfortable stiff, hard chairs. The walls were decorated—if that's the proper word—with faded old photographs of ancient rocket launches. I mean, some of them must have gone back a century or more.

Until that afternoon, I had never seen Mickey in person. We

always communicated electronically, usually through an interactive virtual reality link. We had first met—electronically—several years earlier, when I'd begun to get interested in Alex's work in planetary exploration. He had hired her to tutor me. We worked together every week in virtual reality sessions, she from her office at Caltech, I in the family home in Connecticut, at first, then later from my own place in Majorca. Together we roamed Mars, the moons of Jupiter and Saturn, the asteroids—even Venus.

Seeing her in the flesh was a bit of a shock. In our VR sessions she had apparently used a much younger, slimmer image of herself. Sitting across the conference table from me, she was a rotund little thing with mousey brownish hair that hung limply down to her earlobes. Telomerase treatments could keep you physically young, but they could not overcome years of sitting in a university office eating junk food and not getting any exercise. Mickey wore a black pullover sweater and black athletic slacks, the kind that have loops for your feet. Yet her round chubby face was so full of good humor, so sparkling with enthusiasm, that it was easy to forget her dumpy appearance.

Franklin Abdullah was something else altogether. He sat across the conference table from me, wearing an old-fashioned three-piece suit of charcoal gray, his arms folded across his chest, and scowled as if everything in his life had always gone wrong. Believe me, he didn't give the appearance of the stereotypical "faceless bureaucrat." He had an *attitude*. I didn't know why, but he actually seemed angry that I was preparing to go to Venus. A strange point of view from someone in the space agency.

"Since you asked for this meeting, Professor Cochrane," Abdullah said, "why don't you tell us what you have in mind." His voice was deep and rumbling, like the growl of a lion.

Mickey smiled at him and wiggled a little in her chair, as if trying to get comfortable on the iron-hard plastic cushion. Clasping her hands on the tabletop, she looked at me—a bit apprehensively, I thought.

"Van is putting together a mission to Venus," she said, stating the obvious. "A crewed mission."

Professor Greenbaum cleared his throat noisily, and Mickey immediately shut up.

"We are here, Mr. Humphries," the old man said, "to plead with you to bring at least one qualified planetary scientist to Venus with you."

"With a full complement of proper sensors and analytical systems," Mickey added.

Now I understood what she was after. I should have seen it coming, but I'd been too busy looking over the design and construction of my ship. And fending off all the other crazies who wanted a free ride to Venus.

I felt a little embarrassed. "Um . . . you see, this isn't a scientific mission. I'm going to Venus—"

"To win the prize money," Greenbaum interrupted, cranky and impatient. "We know that."

"To recover my brother's remains," I said firmly.

Mickey hunched forward in her chair. "But still, Van, this is an opportunity to do terrifically valuable science. You'll be beneath the clouds for days on end! Think of the observations we'll be able to make!"

"But my ship is designed strictly for the pickup mission," I explained to them. "We find the wreckage of my brother's ship and take back his remains. That's it. We won't have the space or the capacity to carry a scientist with us. The crew is at a minimum."

That wasn't exactly the truth, of course. I had already invited those friends of mine to come along on the expedition, the writers and artists who could immortalize this expedition after we returned. The engineers and designers naturally took a dim view of carrying what they considered to be nonessential personnel. I was already fighting with them over the size of the crew. I couldn't go back to them and ask them to add still another person, plus all the equipment that a scientist would want to bring along.

"But, Van," Mickey coaxed, "to go all the way to Venus without making any scientific studies of the planet . . ." She shook her head.

I turned to Abdullah, sitting at the head of the little table, his arms still folded across his vest.

"I thought that the scientific exploration of the solar system was a responsibility of the space agency's."

He nodded grimly. "It was."

I waited for more. Abdullah just sat there. So I said, "Then why doesn't the agency send an expedition to Venus?"

Abdullah slowly unfolded his arms and leaned them on the tabletop. "Mr. Humphries, you live in Connecticut, isn't that right?"

"Not anymore," I said, wondering what that had to do with anything.

"Any snow there this winter?"

"No, I don't think so. There hasn't been any snow for several winters in a row."

"Uh-huh. Did you see the cherry trees here in Washington? They're in bloom. In February. On Groundhog Day."

"Today is Groundhog Day, that's right," Greenbaum agreed.

For a moment I thought I had fallen into Alice's rabbit hole. "I don't understand what—"

"I was born in New Orleans, Mr. Humphries," said Abdullah, his deep voice like the rumble of distant thunder. "Or what's left of it, after the floods."

"But—"

"Global warming, Mr. Humphries," he growled. "Have you heard about it?"

"Of course I have. Everybody has."

"The space agency's limited resources are fully committed to studies of the Earth's environment. We have neither funding nor approval for anything else, such as exploring the planet Venus."

"But the Mars expeditions—"

"Are privately funded."

"Oh, yes, of course." I had known that; it had just never occurred to me that the government's space agency *couldn't* participate in the exploration of Mars and the other planets.

"All studies of the other bodies in the solar system are privately funded," Greenbaum pointed out.

Mickey added, "Even the deep-space work that the astronomers and cosmologists are doing has to be financed by private donors."

"Men like Trumball and Yamagata," said Greenbaum.

"Or organizations such as the Gates Foundation and Spielberg," Mickey said.

Of course I already knew that the big corporations backed the mining and manufacturing operations off-Earth. The competition for raw materials out in the Asteroid Belt was something that Father had often talked about, heatedly.

"Your father is financing this mission to Venus," Abdullah said. "We are—"

"I am raising the money for this mission," I snapped. "My father's prize money will be awarded only when and if I return safely."

Abdullah closed his eyes for a moment, as if thinking over what I'd just said. Then he corrected himself. "No matter what the ultimate source of the funding may be, we are appealing to you to allow this private venture to include a scientific component."

"For the good of the human race," Greenbaum said, his raspy voice actually quavering with emotion.

"Think of what we might discover beneath the clouds!" Mickey enthused.

I sympathized with them, but the thought of battling with those designers and engineers made me shake my head.

Greenbaum misunderstood my gesture. "Let me explain something to you, young man."

My brows must have gone up. Mickey tried to hold him back; she literally tugged at the sleeve of his pullover shirt, but he shrugged her off. Surprising vigor for a rickety old man, I thought.

"Do you know anything about plate tectonics?" he asked, almost belligerently.

"Certainly," I said. "Mickey's taught me quite a bit about it, actually. The Earth's crust is composed of big plates, the size of continents, and they slide around on top of the hotter, denser rock below the crust."

Greenbaum nodded, apparently satisfied with the state of my education.

"Venus has plate tectonics, too," I added.

"It did," Greenbaum said. "Half a billion years ago."

"Not now?"

"Venus's plates are locked," Mickey said.

"Like the San Andreas fault?"

"Much worse."

"Venus is on the verge of an upheaval," Greenbaum said, his eyes fixed on mine. "For something like five hundred million years the planet's plates have been locked together. All across the planet. She's been building up internal heat all that while. Sometime soon that heat is going to burst out and totally blow away the planet's surface."

"Sometime soon?" I heard myself squeak.

"Geologically speaking," Mickey said.

"Oh."

"For the past five hundred million years Venus's surface has been virtually unchanged," Greenbaum went on. "We know that from counting meteor impacts. Below the surface, the planet's internal heat is blocked. It can't get through the crust, can't escape."

Mickey explained, "On Earth, the planet's internal heat is vented out of volcanoes, hot springs, that sort of thing."

"Water acts as a lubricant on Earth," Greenbaum said, peering intently at me, as if to determine if I was understanding him. "On Venus there's no liquid water; it's too hot."

"No liquid water," Mickey took up, "means no lubrication for the plates. They lock in place and stay locked."

Nodding, I mumbled, "I see."

"For five hundred million years," Greenbaum said, "the heat's been building up below Venus's surface. It's got to go somewhere!"

"Sooner or later," Mickey took over, "Venus is going to erupt cataclysmically. Volcanoes everywhere. The crust will melt and sink. New crustal material will well up from below."

"It's going to be *wonderful!*" Greenbaum actually cackled with glee.

"And this might happen while I'm down on the surface?" I asked, suddenly fearful that they might be right.

"No, no, no," Mickey said, trying to soothe me. "We're talking geological time frames here, not human."

"But you said—"

Greenbaum went from cackling to gloom. "We'd never be lucky enough to have it happen while we're actually on the scene. The gods aren't that generous."

"I wouldn't call it luck," I said. "The whole surface suddenly melting and blasting out volcanoes and all that."

Mickey said, "Don't worry about it, Van. It won't happen during the few days you're below the clouds."

"Then what are you so worked up about?" I asked.

Abdullah piped up, in his bass register. "Not every scientist agrees with Professor Greenbaum."

"Most planetary scientists disagree with us," Mickey admitted.

"Damn fools," Greenbaum grumbled.

By now I was thoroughly confused. "But if it's *not* going to go through this cataclysm, then what are you so excited about?"

"Seismic measurements," Greenbaum said, staring at me again. "That's what we need."

Mickey explained, "The whole issue depends on whether Venus has a thick crust or a thin one."

It was starting to sound like a pizza contest to me, but I kept my mouth shut and kept on listening.

"If the crust is thin, then the upheaval is more likely. If it's thick, then we're wrong and the others are right."

"But can't you measure the crust with robot sensors?" I asked.

Mickey replied, "We've had some measurements over the years, but they're inconclusive."

"Then send more probes," I said. It seemed so obvious!

They both turned to Abdullah. He shook his head. "The agency is not allowed to spend a penny on studies of Venus, or anything else that isn't directly related to Earth's environmental problems."

"But private donors," I said. "Surely it wouldn't cost that much to send out a few probes."

"We've been trying to get funding," Mickey said. "But it's not easy, especially when most of the specialists in the subject think we're wrong."

"That's why your mission is a godsend," Greenbaum said, with the fervor of a missionary. "You can carry dozens of seismic sensors to Venus—hundreds! And a scientist to handle them. Plus a lot of other equipment."

"But my spacecraft won't have that capacity," I insisted. Perhaps pleaded is a more accurate term.

"It's the opportunity of a lifetime," Greenbaum said again. "I wish I were thirty years younger."

"I can't do it," I said.

"Please, Van," said Mickey. "It's really important."

I looked from her earnest face to Greenbaum's to Abdullah's and back again.

"I'd be the scientist," Mickey added. "I'd be the one going to Venus with you."

She looked so intent, so beseeching, as if her entire life depended on going to Venus with me.

What could I tell her?

I took a breath and said, "I'll talk to my people. Maybe there's a way for us to carry you along."

Mickey jumped up and down in her chair like a kid who'd just opened the biggest Christmas present in the history of the world. Greenbaum half-collapsed back in his seat, as if the effort of this meeting had drained all the strength out of him. But he was grinning from ear to ear, a lopsided, gap-toothed jack-o'-lantern grin.

Even Abdullah smiled.

GREATER LOS ANGELES

Tomas Rodriguez had been an astronaut; he'd gone to Mars four times before retiring upward to become a consultant to aerospace companies and universities doing planetary explorations.

Yet what he really wanted was to fly again.

He was a solidly built man with an olive complexion and thickly curled hair that he kept clipped very short in almost a military crew cut. He looked morose most of the time, pensive, almost unapproachable. But that was just a mask. He smiled easily, and when he did it lit up his whole face to show the truly gentle man beneath the surface.

Unfortunately, he was not smiling now.

Rodriguez and I were sitting in a small conference room, just the two of us. Between us floated a holographic image of the spacecraft that was being constructed for my flight to Venus. Hanging there in midair above the oval conference table, the ship looked more like an ironclad dirigible than anything else—which it was, almost. Of course we were using the latest ceramic-metal alloys for her exterior, rather than iron.

With a slight frown creasing his brow, Rodriguez was telling me, "Mr. Humphries, we can't hang another gondola under the gas envelope without enlarging the envelope by a third or more. Those are the numbers from the computer and there's no way around them."

"But we need the extra gondola to accommodate the crew," I said.

"The friends you want to bring along are not crew, Mr. Humphries," Rodriguez said. "The working crew can be accommodated in the single gondola, as per our original design."

"They're not just my friends," I snapped, feeling testy. "One of them is a top planetary scientist, another is a writer who'll be doing a book about this expedition . . ." My voice trailed off. Except for Mickey, the others were indeed nothing more than friends, acquaintances who wanted the thrill of flying to Venus.

Rodriguez shook his head. "We can't do it, Mr. Humphries. Not at this late date. We'd have to scrap everything that's been built and start all over again from scratch."

That would be too expensive, I was certain. Even with a ten-billion-dollar prize in the offing, the banks were already nervous about financing the construction of my ship. International lending officers I had known from childhood wrinkled their brows at me and talked about risks and the inability to get insurance coverage for their exposure. We had to design the ship as frugally as possible; adding what would actually be a separate module for nonessential passengers would be unacceptable to the money people.

The trouble was, I had already invited those people to come along with me. I couldn't disinvite them now, not without enormous embarrassment. And I had promised Mickey that she could come along, too.

Rodriguez took my silence for assent. "Then we're agreed?" he asked.

I said nothing, desperately running different schemes through my mind. Maybe a second ship? A backup. That might work. I could present it to the bankers as a safety precaution. What did Rodriguez call that kind of thing? A redundancy, that's right. A safety redundancy.

"Okay," he said, and resumed his painstakingly detailed briefing of every single component and system of the ship. I could feel my eyes glazing over.

I had named my vessel *Hesperos*, after the ancient Greek name for Venus as the beautiful evening star. Alex's ship had been almost identical in design and he had called his *Phosphoros*, the old Greek name for Venus as the morning star, the light-bringer.

"And here," Rodriguez was droning on, "is the descent module."

A little spherical metal object appeared beneath the ship's single gondola, sort of like a bathysphere. It was attached to the gondola by a line so thin I could barely make it out.

Rodriguez must have seen my brows hike up. "That's a Buckyball cable. It'll take kilotons of tensile stress. One of 'em saved my life on Mars, during the second expedition."

I nodded and he went on and on, in infinite minutiae. Rodriguez was wearing what he jokingly referred to as his "consultant's suit:" a sky-blue collarless jacket with matching slacks and a crisp open-necked saffron shirt. The color of the shirt reminded me of the clouds on Venus, a little. Me, I dressed for comfort: salmon-pink sport shirt, authentic blue jeans, and tennis shoes.

I knew it bothered Rodriguez that we were going with virtually the identical design as Alex's ship, which had somehow failed and killed its entire crew. Rodriguez believed in caution; he claimed you didn't live long enough to be an ex-astronaut unless you knew how to be careful. But by using Alex's basic design we could save a ton of money; it would have cost a good fraction of the prize money to design a new vessel from scratch.

"That's the basic design and layout of the bird," Rodriguez said at long last. "Now I'd like to go over the modifications and improvements we're going to put in."

I felt my lips curl slightly. "You mean that some of the modifications won't be improvements?"

Rodriguez broke into a grin. "Sorry. Sometimes I slip into corporate bafflegab. Every modification will be an improvement, I promise you."

So I leaned back in my padded swivel chair and tried as hard as I could to pay attention to his earnest, plodding review. It was tedious to the point of paralysis, especially when I could see through the room's only window the wide Pacific glittering in the afternoon sun. It was so tempting to call an end to this interminable briefing and spend the rest of the day on the man-made lagoon behind the seawall.

This high up in the hills it was hard to realize that once there had been beaches and surfing and homes strung all along the ocean-front. Malibu, Santa Monica, Marina Del Rey—their beaches had all been drowned when the Antarctic icecap started melting down. Even now, on this balmy, sunny afternoon the waves were pounding the new seawall and spraying the road that ran behind it.

While Rodriguez droned on, my thoughts drifted back to that anonymous phone message I'd received in Selene City. Father had murdered Alex? It sounded too terrible to be true, even for him. And yet . . .

But if my father had anything to do with Alex's death, why had he cooked up this mission to recover his son's body? Some form of atonement? Guilt? Clever public relations to throw the suspicion off him and quiet the rumors?

Such thoughts scared me. And depressed me terribly. It was too much for me to deal with. All I really wanted out of life was to live quietly in my home on Majorca, have a few friends drop in from time to time, go visiting when the mood struck me. Not take a risk-filled flight to another world. Not listen to Rodriguez going on and on with his endless details.

I'm doing this for Alex, I told myself. But I knew that was nonsense. Alex was dead and nothing that I or anyone else could do was going to change that.

"Are you all right, Mr. Humphries?"

With an effort, I focused my attention back on Rodriguez. He looked concerned, almost worried.

I ran a hand over my face. "I'm sorry. What did you say?"

"You seemed far away," Rodriguez replied. "Are you okay?"

"Um . . . I've got to take my injection," I said, pushing my chair away from the table and the hologram floating above it.

Rodriguez got to his feet as I did. "Okay, sure. We can finish this later."

"Right," I said, and headed for the door.

I didn't really need the injection right at that moment. I even could have taken it there in the conference room; it's no big deal, just press the microneedle head of the syringe against your skin and squeeze the activator button. But I told everyone that I had to do it in my private quarters. It was a convenient fiction, a way of getting out of worrisome or boring situations, such as this dreary briefing.

So I went to the suite of rooms I was using as my private quarters in the building up atop the Malibu hills. Once it had been a research laboratory, but when the sea started rising the local government wanted to condemn the building, for fear the hills would erode so badly that it would go sliding into the ocean. Humphries Space Systems bought the complex for a pittance, then got the condemnation procedure legally stopped—with a generous application of money to the appropriate officials.

Now the former laboratory was owned by my father's corporation. More than half its space was rented to other corporations and the harried engineers and administrators of the Greater Los Angeles Seawall Project, who were working against time and the tides to keep the rising Pacific Ocean from inundating more of the city.

My quarters were on the top floor of the central wing, small but decently furnished. As I opened the door I saw that my phone screen was blinking MESSAGE WAITING in bright yellow letters.

"Play my messages," I called out, heading for the bathroom and my syringe.

The mirror above the sink flickered briefly and then my father's stern face appeared. "I warned you about Lars Fuchs, remember? Well, my people have found out that he's cobbling together some kind of ship out in the Belt. He'll try for my prize money, all right, just as I thought."

The idea that I'd have competition for the prize didn't bother me very much. Not at that moment. From the way Father described it, Fuchs wouldn't be much of a threat. Or so I thought.

Then Father delivered his bombshell. "By the way, I've picked a captain for your expedition. She'll be arriving at your quarters there in Malibu in an hour or so. Her name is Desiree Duchamp."

Father's image winked out and I was staring at my own slack-jawed reflection. "But Rodriguez is going to be my captain," I said weakly.

The door buzzer sounded.

Laying the syringe on the countertop, I went out into the sitting room and called, "Enter."

The door unlocked itself and swung open. Standing there was a tall, slim, dark-haired woman of indeterminate age, wearing a skintight jumpsuit of glittery black faux leather. Her eyes were large and luminous. She might have been beautiful if she would have smiled, but the expression on her face was hard, bitter, almost angry.

"Come in," I said, then added. "Ms. Duchamp."

"*Captain* Duchamp, thanks to you."

She marched into the room on long-legged strides. With the outfit she was wearing I expected her calf-length boots to have spike heels, but instead her heels were sensibly low. Otherwise she looked like a video portrayal of a dominating sex symbol. All she needs is a whip, I thought.

"Thanks to me?" I echoed. "This is my father's idea, not mine."

"You're the one going to Venus," she said, her voice low. It would have been sultry if she weren't so obviously displeased.

"I have a captain already signed up," I said. "Tomas Rodriguez. He's been—"

"I know Tommy," Duchamp interrupted. "He'll be my Number One."

"He's my captain," I said, very firmly. "We've already signed a contract."

Duchamp went to the long couch on the other side of the room and sat down as if she owned the place. For a long moment I just stood by the door, staring at her.

"Close the door," she said frowning.

I called out, "Shut." The door swung and its lock clicked.

"Look, Mr. Humphries," Duchamp said more reasonably, clasping her hands together. "I don't like this any more than you do. But Hump has decided he wants me to captain your spacecraft and we're both stuck with that decision."

Her fingers were long and the nails colored fire-engine red. I walked over toward the couch and sat on the armchair facing it.

"Why did he pick you?" I asked.

She frowned again. "To get rid of me, why else?"

"Rid of you?"

"This is his idea of a kiss-off. He's tired of me; he's got a couple of new tarts to chase."

"You were his mistress?"

She actually laughed. "Christ, I haven't heard that term since I was reading novels under the blankets after lights-out at boot camp."

I shook my head. I was starting to feel giddy, a sure symptom, so I got to my feet. "Excuse me," I said, heading for the bathroom.

It took less than a minute to administer my shot, but when I returned to the sitting room she was at the desk by the window and the wallscreen displayed her biographical résumé. She was a qualified astronaut, sure enough, a veteran of eleven flights to the Asteroid Belt and three to the Jupiter system. On four expeditions she had been mission commander.

"How long have you known my father?" I asked, keeping my eyes on the screen instead of her.

"I met him about a year ago. We were bedmates for three months. Something of a record for Hump."

"He was married to my mother for six years," I said, still studying the data on the screen.

"Yeah, but he was sleeping with a lot of other kids. She was out of it half the time with her habit—"

I whirled on her, furious. "You don't know anything about it! You might think you know, he might have told you a lot, but it's all lies. Lies! Vicious, self-serving lies!"

She jumped to her feet, as if to defend herself from assault. "Hey, don't blame me."

"That's my mother you're talking about," I snapped. "If she got hooked on narcotics it was *his* doing."

"Okay," Duchamp said placatingly. "Okay."

I took a deep, deliberate breath. Then, as calmly as I could manage, I told her, "I don't want you on my mission. Not as captain. Not in any capacity at all."

She shrugged as if it didn't matter. "You'll have to straighten that out with your father."

"It's not his decision."

"Yes it is," Duchamp countered. "Remember the golden rule— he who has the gold makes the rules."

MAJORCA

threw a sort of party of my own, a disastrous affair with just a dozen or so of my close friends. They flew in from all points of the compass obligingly enough, all dressed in the latest "in" fashion: neo-Victorian dinner clothes for the men, the women in low-cut evening gowns rich with artificial feathers and real gems.

Style is an ephemeral thing. I'm told that once, young adults such as myself and my friends dressed in grungy military fatigues and camouflage shirts. A generation later the youthful set was piercing their navels, eyebrows, even their sex organs, and wearing metal studs through their tongues and lips. Their children spent their rebellious years in plastic jackets that imitated samurai armor and tattooed their faces like Maori warriors.

The "in" style for my group was sophistication. We dressed extravagantly in vintage dinner jackets and sequined gowns. We pretended to smoke faux cigarettes of harmless organics. We glittered with jewels and bracelets and earrings of precious metals from asteroids. We spoke in the elegant tones of cultivated boredom, affecting the witty cynicism of Oscar Wilde and Bernard Shaw. Profanities and crude language were far, far beneath us.

Yet even though we dressed so elegantly and spoke so genteelly, my gathering was a fiasco. It was terribly embarrassing to have to tell them that I couldn't take them with me to Venus. I stammered through the reasons, and was surprised to see looks of relief on some of their faces.

But only on some of them.

"Do you mean to stand there and tell me that you made me fly all the way here from Boston just to tell me you're reneging on your invitation?" demanded Quenton Cleary. He looked quite splendid in a crimson Hussar's uniform, with loads of gold braid and a chestful of ribbons and medals. Something of an athlete, Quenton starred on the international volleyball team that he had organized. They had even competed on the Moon against the amateur team that Selene City had put together. And they had almost won, too, despite the totally different conditions there.

"It can't be done," I said, feeling miserable. "I even had to tell Professor Cochrane that there will be no room for her on the vessel."

When I tried to explain it all again, Quenton took the whole tray of crystal champagne flutes from the table and heaved them across my living room. They smashed against the stones of the fireplace into a thousand shards.

That was Quenton: given to physical expression. But he was no fool. No one was standing within five meters of the fireplace when he gave vent to his temper. No one was scratched. He didn't damage the Vermeer hanging over the fireplace, either.

"Really, Quenton!" said Basil Ustinov.

"Well, I had to fly all the way here from Boston, you know," Quenton said heatedly.

"And I flew here from St. Petersburg," Basil riposted. "What of it? I'm just as disappointed as you are, but if Van can't do anything about it, there's no reason to get violent over it."

They had all come from long distances, all except Gwyneth, who was studying in Barcelona at the time. Of course, with Clippership rockets no major transport hub on Earth was more than an hour away from any other hub. It took more time to drive from the airfield at New Palma to my home up here in Majorca's hills than it did to fly from Boston. I had often considered putting in a landing field for copters or jumpjets, but the thought of battling the townspeople and their dreary little community council kept me from even proposing it.

I could see the town's point of view, I suppose. It truly was lovely up here in the hills, away from the thundering rockets and screeching helicopters. Not even tourist buses could get through the town's main street, so this part of the island stayed tranquil and relaxed.

As I sat back in the silky comfort of my favorite couch and gazed through the sweeping windows at the Mediterranean, I realized how much I loved this home of mine. The sea was calm, its long gentle waves touched with the pink of approaching sunset. The hillside marched down to the water in a series of terraces that still held vegetable gardens and vineyards. Hannibal had seen those terraces. This land had been under human cultivation since long before history had begun to be written.

The rising sea level had inundated the beaches, of course, as well as much of the old city of Palma. Even the gentle Mediterranean was swallowing up its seacoasts. Still, Majorca was as close to paradise as I could imagine.

And I was going to leave this all behind to live in a metal cell for months at a time so that I could risk my life and limb trying to be the first person to set foot on the red-hot surface of Venus. I shook my head at the absurdity of the position I had put myself in.

But Quenton was getting pugnacious. "I don't like having promises broken," he said petulantly. "Van, you've gone back on your word."

"There's nothing I can do about it," I said.

"I don't believe you."

My cheeks burning, I got to my feet. "Are you accusing me of lying to you?"

Quenton glared at me. "You made a promise and now you've broken it."

"Then get out of my house," I heard myself say. It surprised me, but I realized that I was suddenly quite thoroughly angry.

Francesca Ianetta huffed, "Really, Van!"

"You, too," I snapped. "All of you!" I swept the room with an outstretched hand and shouted, "You can all get out! Now! Leave me alone!"

For a moment there was nothing but shocked silence. Then Basil pulled his rotund body from the armchair he'd been sitting in. "I suppose I should get back to my work," he said.

Basil's idea of work was to smear colors across a display screen. He was a very talented artist, everyone said, but he was extremely lazy. He could afford to be; his patroness was extremely wealthy.

Nodding curtly, I said, "Yes, you should."

"I shall go back to Rome," Francesca said grandly. "I have an opera to finish."

"Good," I said. "Maybe if you put some real work into it you'd actually finish it."

"Really!" she said, appalled.

"Go on, all of you," I repeated, shooing them toward the door. "Go!"

Shocked, astonished at my outburst of poor manners, they left my house. Still hot with anger, I watched them from the window of my entertainment room, a procession of flamboyantly bright-colored automobiles, their electric engines making hardly a hum on the winding brick road that went down the hillside switchbacks and connected with the motorway.

"There they go."

I turned from the window. Gwyneth was standing next to me. She hadn't left, and I was glad of it.

The word that always popped into my mind whenever I thought of Gwyneth was *alluring*. She had a way of looking at me, a side-long glance through those long lashes of hers, that told me she wanted me as much as I wanted her. In earlier years she would have been called a courtesan, a kept woman, or worse. To me, she was a companion, a friend who shared her body and her mind with me. Gwyneth was serious, quiet, as steady as you'd want a companion to be. She had a wicked sense of humor, which she rarely let anyone see. She was slim, tiny, almost elfin, with long auburn hair that billowed beautifully in the breeze when we sailed together. Her face was to die for, with chiseled high cheekbones, luscious full lips, and almond-shaped eyes that were a golden, tawny brown.

"You're not angry with me, too, are you?" she asked, with a coy smile.

I felt my anger dissolve. "How could I be?"

She gave me an odd, quizzical look. "The way you told them off . . . you're starting to let the others know how strong you really are."

Surprised, I asked, "Strong? Me?"

"Real strength," Gwyneth said, her eyes studying my face. "Not the silly tantrums Quenton throws. You have real steel, Van, deep inside you."

"You think so?"

"I've known it since I first met you. But you keep it hidden, even from yourself." Then she added, in a murmur, "Especially from yourself."

Suddenly I felt uncomfortable. I turned away from her and looked out at the cars disappearing down the hillside road.

"You'd think they'd double up," Gwyneth said, coming closer to stand beside me. "Not one of them offered to ride with any of the others."

I hadn't thought about that until she mentioned it. They could have driven together if they'd wanted to; the automated cars could find their way back to the airport rental lot just as well unoccupied.

We walked together back into the broad expanse of the living room. The robot cleaners had already swept up the shattered glassware.

"I suppose I'll never see them again," I said.

She smiled coolly. "They'll forget about your temper tantrum . . . as long as you have money."

"Don't be cruel," I said. I didn't like to think that they tolerated me only because I helped them in their chosen fields. It was true, of course, that I was a major backer for Francesca's unfinished opera, and—come to think of it—Quenton had asked me for a loan to keep his team going. That had been more than a year ago; not a word from him about paying it back.

What would they do when they realized I was broke? I hadn't found the courage to tell them that my income had been cut off. I was living on loans reluctantly advanced by banks against the ten billion prize dollars. Even though many of those bank officers were longtime friends of mine or the family's, they grew more nervous with each passing month. As if it were their own money they were playing with! I hadn't told any of the bankers about Lars Fuchs and apparently they were not as well informed about Fuchs as my father was.

Gwyneth and I walked wordlessly out onto the terrace to watch the last moments of the sunset. The sky turned flame red, flecked with purple clouds. The sea glittered crimson. From this high up the gentle waves lapping against once-dry terraces sounded like a distant sigh.

Gwyneth looked lovely in her graceful floor-length gown of gold lamé. She leaned her head against my shoulder. I slipped an arm around her waist.

"I depend on your money, too," she said, almost whispering. "Don't you forget that."

Two years ago, when I had first met Gwyneth, she had been a ballet student in London. Then she decided to major in art history at the Sorbonne. Now she was studying architecture in Barcelona. I was letting her use my apartment there. In the two years I had known her, we had never used the word *love*. Not even in bed.

"That's not important," I said.

"It is to me."

I didn't want to know what she meant. I enjoyed her company;

in a way, I suppose, I needed her. Needed her common sense, her emotional support, her quiet strength.

She pulled away from me once the sun had dipped below the horizon. I gestured toward the French doors and we went back inside.

"You realize," Gwyneth said, as we sat together on the couch beneath my one and only Turner, "that most of them are glad they're not going with you."

With a nod I replied, "Yes, I thought I saw relief on their faces. Not Quenton's, though."

She smiled. "Quenton's simply better at disguising his real feelings."

"But he was so eager to go."

"At first," she said. "Over the past few weeks, though, his ardor cooled considerably. Didn't you notice?"

"No. Why do you suppose . . . ?"

Gwyneth lifted her slim shoulders slightly in a miniature shrug. "I have the feeling that the closer you got to actually taking off on your expedition, the more Quenton—and the others, too—realized that they were frightened."

"Frightened?"

"Of course."

"Were you frightened, too?"

"Of course," she repeated.

I sank back onto the cushions and thought about that for a moment. "Yet they all agreed to go. You, too."

"It sounded exciting at first. Going to Venus and all that. But it *is* dangerous, isn't it?"

I nodded. And before I realized what I was saying, I admitted, "I'm frightened, too."

"Ahh," she said.

"I don't want to go through with it. I really don't."

"Then why do it?"

"I need that prize money."

Gwyneth sighed. "It always comes down to the money, doesn't it?"

"I've made an idiot of myself."

"Not if you go through with it," she said. "When you return you'll be financially independent of your father for the rest of your life. That's worth something, don't you think?"

"I could get killed."

She gave me an odd look. "Yes, there is that."

We sat there in silence for some time as the shadows of twilight deepened and the room grew dark.

At last I said, "You know, it was Alex who turned me on to science. To planetary astronomy and all that."

"Really?"

I could barely make out her face in the shadows. "Yes. He was ten years older than I. As far back as I can remember, whatever he did, I wanted to do."

"Including scientific exploration."

Nodding, I remembered, "He started showing me where he'd been on Mars. I did virtual reality trips with him. It was fascinating! A different world. So much to see, so much to discover."

Gwyneth sat there beside me in the dark and let me babble on.

At last I said, "It's not the money! It's not. I'm going to Venus to find my brother. I'm going for Alex."

She kissed me lightly on the cheek and whispered, "Of course you are, Van."

Was it really true? Were either one of us speaking the truth? I wanted it to be true. With a pang of guilt, I recognized that I *needed* it to be true.

Then she said, "About the flat in Barcelona."

"What about it?" I asked.

She hesitated a long moment. "Well, it's only . . . you see, if you don't come back from your expedition, I have no legal right to remain there. Your father will boot me out, won't he? Or his lawyers will."

No, I thought. Father wouldn't evict you. He'd take one good look at those promising eyes and lithe figure and take you for himself.

But I didn't tell her that. Instead, I said, "I'm having a will drawn up. The apartment will be my bequest to you. Will that be sufficient?"

She kissed me again, this time on the lips.

We never spoke about love, or gratitude either, but we understood each other perfectly well.

LIFTOFF

odriguez was almost pleading with me. "Look, Mr. Humphries, you've got to make a decision. Who the shit's going to be in command of this mission?"

It startled me to hear him use even a minor profanity. He's really upset about this, I realized. The expression on his face showed how distressed he felt. He looked almost desperate.

We were in my office at the launch complex on Tarawa. A Clippership was being serviced out on its pad, scheduled to lift us into orbit in an hour. Rodriguez sat across the desk from me, tension in every line of his body.

My desk chair was supposed to be stress-free. The very latest design. Soft pseudoleather padding. Adjustable headrest. Fully reclinable. Heat and massage units built in. But stress isn't merely physical, and I was feeling the muscles and tendons of my neck and shoulders tightening up like torture racks.

Rodriguez was already in his light tan flight coveralls, ready to go. But he demanded my decision before we lifted off.

"It's her or me," he said, with real bitterness in his voice. "One of us is named captain and the other goes home. Which one will it be?"

I'd been putting off the decision for months, avoiding both Rodriguez and Duchamp as much as possible. I had the perfect excuse: I was cramming as much planetary astronomy into my brain as I could. Mickey had decided that if she couldn't come along to Venus, then I would have to be her surrogate. I would handle the seismic probes and other sensors that we would carry aboard *Hesperos* while she directed my work from California.

All through those months of preparation Desiree Duchamp had been acting as if there were no possible doubt that she was captain of *Hesperos*. She lorded it over the other crew members and treated Rodriguez as if he were her assistant. Rodriguez was entirely right. I couldn't put off this decision any longer.

Before I could say a word, though, the door from the corridor swung open and Duchamp stepped in, uninvited. She wore the same dun-colored flight coveralls as Rodriguez, but on her they looked crisper, sharper, almost like a military uniform.

"You're both here. Good," she said.

Rodriguez shot to his feet. "It's just as well you're here, Dee. We've got to—"

Duchamp pointed a long, manicured finger at him like a pistol. "Tommy, I don't mind you speaking informally to me in front of the owner, but don't you *ever* call me Dee or anything else except Captain Duchamp in front of the crew."

"Who says you're the captain?" Rodriguez snapped.

"The man who's paying for this expedition, that's who."

"I take my orders from Mr. Humphries, here."

A thin smile curved her lips. "I take my orders from Mr. Humphries, *there*." She gestured toward the ceiling. My father was still living at Selene City.

They both turned toward me. I got slowly to my feet, wondering which way to go. Decide! I railed at myself. Make a decision and stick to it.

"If you'll look at your incoming mail," Duchamp said coldly, "you'll see that he will get the banks to cut off all funding for this expedition if I'm not the captain. You'll have to go home and lose the prize money."

"My ass he will!" Rodriguez growled. Turning back to me, close enough almost to touch noses, he said earnestly, "Let your father threaten all he wants. Once we're in orbit he can't touch us. Go on to Venus, carry out the mission and you won't need his frigging money. When we get back home you'll be a hero, a celebrity! Without your old man."

Duchamp countered, "Do you think for one instant that the crew will undertake the risks of this mission knowing that their pay has been cut off?" She laughed harshly. "You'll never get off the ground!"

I felt nausea welling up in me. I was confused, torn in a dozen different directions. I clasped my hands to my head and shouted at them, "Why can't you two work something out between yourselves? Why do you have to put me in the middle of this?"

"Because you're the owner," Duchamp said.

At the same time Rodriguez said, "You're the head of the expedition."

"Whether you like it or not," Duchamp went on, "you're in charge here. It's your responsibility. You're the one who has to make the decision."

That's not true, I thought. My father's still in charge. He's making the real decisions. I'm just his puppet, dancing at the ends of his strings. He's forcing me to decide the way he wants me to.

"Well," Rodriguez demanded. "What's it going to be?"

I let my hands drop to my sides. My stomach was churning. My knees felt rubbery.

"She's right," I heard myself say. Totally miserable, I admitted, "If my father cuts off the money the crew won't even get aboard the Clippership out there."

Rodriguez began, "But I could—"

"No, no." I cut him off. I felt like sobbing, but I held myself together as best I could. "She's got to be captain. I can't risk destroying this mission. My hands are tied."

Duchamp allowed herself a smug smile. "Thank you," she said, then headed for the door. As she reached for the knob she turned halfway and said, "By the way, there's been a crew change. Nunnaly is out. I've put a biologist in her place."

She opened the door and left my office. I just stood there, relieved that the decision had finally been made, worried about how Rodriguez would react, and stunned about Duchamp adding a biologist in place of our astronomer. A biologist? What for? Nothing could possibly be living on Venus.

Rodriguez snapped me back to reality. "Okay, that's that."

His fists were clenched at his sides. He looked as if he wanted to hit somebody. Maybe me.

"Don't quit," I said. "Please take the second-in-command position. Please."

He was fuming, that was clear to see.

"I'll double your pay," I said.

He was staring grimly at the closed door, I realized.

"I'll add a bonus out of my own money. Please don't quit on me. I need you."

Slowly Rodriguez turned back toward me. "The bitch knows I couldn't turn down the chance to go to Venus. She knows I'll go no matter what rank you give me. She was counting on that."

"Then you'll go?" I asked, almost breathless. "As second-in-command?"

"I'll go," he said bitterly. "Even with *her* as captain. I can't turn my back on this. It's going to be an experience money can't buy."

I sank back gratefully into my stress-free chair. "Thanks, Tom," I said. "Thanks."

He grinned mirthlessly. "But I'll still take that doubled pay, boss. And the bonus. I'll swallow her crap and be your second-in-command. But I want the money you promised."

I nodded, feeling weak, and he left the office.

An experience money can't buy. That's what Rodriguez had said. But he'll take the money just the same. Why not? Money is the universal lubricant. You need money to buy everything you want, every single thing. And as long as my father's money is paying for this expedition, I thought, he'll be making all the real decisions.

Meanwhile, I couldn't find any information about what Lars Fuchs was up to. Not even my father could. The man seemed to have disappeared entirely.

"He's up to something," my father warned, time and again, in his messages to me.

I asked Father's image on my screen, "But what can he do if he's all the way out there in the Belt?"

"I wouldn't be surprised if he's left the Belt and is heading for Venus," my father replied sourly. "His fellow rock rats are covering up for him, keeping silent no matter how much pressure my people put on them."

"But he'd have to register his ship with the International Astronautical Authority, wouldn't he?" I asked.

Father nodded. "Sooner or later he'll have to . . . or be declared an outlaw vessel. I'm not giving my prize money to an outlaw."

We lifted off in the Clippership with no problems. In ten minutes we were on orbit, approaching rendezvous. I started to feel queasy in zero-gravity; my stomach went hollow and I felt as if I were falling even when I could see that I was safely strapped into my seat. If I moved my head I got dizzy and nauseous, so I just sat there quietly, tying to keep myself from upchucking, while the Clippership went through its docking maneuvers.

It seemed like hours, but as soon as we were docked a feeling of weight returned and I started to feel all right again.

My ship *Hesperos* was designed specifically for the Venus mission; she was too small and cramped for the long flight from Earth. To ferry *Hesperos* out to Venus we leased an old factory ship from the Asteroid Belt, named *Truax,* and refitted her for the task. The two vessels were connected by a Buckyball cable and rotated around their common center of gravity so there was the equivalent of a regular Earthly gravity aboard.

We didn't do that just for comfort. The gravity on Venus is only a few percent less than Earth, and if we had coasted out to Venus in zero-gee, our muscles and bones would have been deconditioned during the two-month flight. This way, with artificial gravity induced by spinning, we'd be ready for diving into Venus's clouds as soon as we parked in orbit around the planet.

Once we were cleared to unbuckle, I went straight from the Clippership to my stateroom aboard *Truax.* It had been the captain's quarters when *Truax* had plied the ore route between the Asteroid Belt and the Earth/Moon system. I saw that it was adequately furnished, although a bit shabby. Still, the foldout bed felt comfortable enough and the wall screens all worked. There was enough room to avoid the feeling of being cooped up. No windows, but the wall screens could be programmed to show any view I had in my video library.

I checked the closets and the lav. All my clothing and personal toiletries were in place. Good. The medicine cabinet was fully stocked with my enzyme supply, and three syringes were laid neatly in the drawer beside the sink. Fine.

Still, the stateroom had the faint odor of strangeness about it. The lingering residue of someone else's presence. I never got to feel completely at ease there. Certainly the built-in desk and other furnishings weren't in a style I would have picked.

That couldn't be helped now. I gave myself an injection and then went to the desk. There was business to be attended to. Duchamp was the captain, very well. But how dare she kick our astronomer off the mission and substitute someone I hadn't even met? A biologist, no less.

I asked the intercom system to locate her. In a few seconds her lean, sharp-featured face appeared on my screen.

"I need to speak with you, Captain," I said, laying just a hint of stress on the last word.

"We're in the midst of a systems check," she said, her expression flinty. "I'll be free in one hour and . . ." Her eyes flicked away for a moment ". . . eleven minutes."

"In my quarters, then," I commanded.

She nodded and the screen went blank.

I waited in my stateroom. I could have gone out to the bridge, it was hardly ten paces down the passageway. But I decided it would be better to make her come to me. Establish the authority. She'd been named captain, she'd won that battle. But I'm the owner, I told myself, and she's not going to run roughshod over me.

I hoped.

One hour and twelve minutes later she knocked once on my door, opened it, and entered my stateroom. Her coveralls still looked crisp and fresh. If the systems checkout had strained her in any way it certainly didn't show in her appearance.

I stayed seated at my desk. With a gesture I invited her to sit in the nearest chair. She sat and crossed her legs, but for the first time since I'd met her she looked tense. Good, I thought.

"About this new crew member," I began. "It's not your place to make personnel substitutions."

"I'm aware of that," she said.

"Then what do you mean by displacing our astronomer with a biologist, of all things? You can't—"

"The fact that she's a biologist was not uppermost in my decision," she said sharply, cutting me off.

"What?" I must have blinked several times. "What do you mean?"

"Her name is Marguerite Duchamp. She's my daughter."

"Your daughter!"

"My daughter."

"That's rank nepotism! We don't need a biologist. I don't want a biologist! You can't bring your daughter on this mission!"

Duchamp merely raised an eyebrow and said, "My daughter comes with me."

"It's impossible," I said, as firmly as I could manage.

"Look," Duchamp replied, with ill-concealed impatience, "your father wants me out of his way, okay. But I'm not going to leave my daughter on the same planet with that humper. Not with him! Understood?"

I gaped at her. Beneath that icily cool surface she was burning with rage. And I understood why. My father had dumped her because he'd become more interested in her daughter. And she was furious about it.

They say that hell has no fury like a woman scorned. But what about a woman scorned because the man wants her daughter?

Then I wondered how the daughter felt about it. Was Duchamp protecting her daughter against my father's unwanted lechery? Or was she dragging her away, kicking and screaming?

Either way, it looked to me like a nest of snakes.

We left Earth orbit the following day and started on the two-month-long trajectory to Venus. We had to burn more propellant than the minimum-energy trajectory would use, but I figured that cutting the transit time in half was worth the expenditure.

I hardly felt the thrust when we broke orbit. I was standing off in one corner of the bridge doing a media interview while the working crew attended to their jobs. Off to Venus! It was a good news subject. Fine human interest: Van Humphries setting out to recover his dead brother's remains from the hellhole of the solar system. Later that evening, when I saw the network's broadcast, though, they showed more computer simulations of what Venus's surface might look like than they showed of me.

But my father kept worrying about Fuchs, bombarding me with tension-riddled messages Where was he? What was he up to? It made me worry, too.

No matter. We were on our way to Venus. That was the important thing.

DREAM

knew I was dreaming but somehow it didn't matter. I was a mere child again, a toddler just learning to walk. There was a grown man looming in front of me, holding his arms out and calling to me.

"Come on, Van. You can do it. Walk to me."

In my dream, I couldn't make out his face. His voice sounded kind, friendly, but his face was somehow hidden from me.

"Come on, Van. Take a step. Come on."

It was enormously difficult. Much easier to hang on to whatever piece of furniture my chubby little fingers were clutching. Or just plop down and crawl on all fours. But his voice beckoned to me, half encouraging, half pleading, and I eventually let go.

I took a teetering step, then another.

"Good boy! Good boy, Van."

I saw his face. It was my brother Alex. He was only a child himself, nine or ten years old. But he was helping me, encouraging me. I tried to reach him. Step by labored, dangerous step I tried to get to his welcoming arms.

Instead, my legs buckled and I plopped onto the floor.

"You're hopeless, Runt. Absolutely hopeless." Suddenly it was my father towering over me, a disgusted look on his face.

"The ancient Greeks would have left you on a mountaintop to feed the wolves and crows."

Alex was no longer there. He was dead, I remembered. I sat there on the floor and blubbered like a baby.

IN TRANSIT

had met the crew several times before we left Earth, of course. The crew of my ship *Hesperos,* I mean. *Truax* had its own crew—an even dozen of grizzled, experienced men and women—but I had practically nothing to do with them. Captain Duchamp handled that part of the mission. It was my crew, the crew of *Hesperos,* that I cared about.

In addition to Duchamp and Rodriguez there were only four others: three technicians, for communications, life support, and sensor systems, and the physician. The comm and sensor techs were women about my own age, rather nondescript techies who talked in jargon and kept pretty much to themselves. Same for the life support guy, except he was chubby and rather surly—the kind who always gave the impression that the least little technical problem was the end of the world.

They had to be good, though. They had been okayed by both Rodriguez and Duchamp. Naturally, all our systems were actually run by the ship's mainframe; the human techs were needed for repairs and maintenance work, mostly. For a while I had thought about using robots instead, but Rodriguez convinced me that the humans were more versatile and handier. And cheaper, too.

The one crew member I dealt with on an almost daily basis was the physician, Dr. Waller. He kept tabs on my anemia and made certain that I was in good general health. He was quite a bit older, about Duchamp's age, and claimed he had never used any rejuvenation therapy for himself. Yet he looked suspiciously young to me; the only sign of his age was his thinning hair, which he kept pulled

back into a short ponytail. He was black—from Jamaica—and for
some reason I usually found it hard to judge the age of black people.
He always looked solemn, even grave. His eyes always seemed to
be bloodshot.

"There's really not much for you to do around here, is there?" I
asked him once, while he was running me through the diagnostic
scanner.

His red-rimmed eyes focused on the readouts, Dr. Waller
answered, "Be glad of that, Mr. Humphries."

Even though his face was somber, he constantly hummed to
himself, so low I could barely hear it, a tuneless background
buzzing. His voice had a sort of singing lilt to it. If I kept my eyes
closed I could imagine him smiling happily instead of the dour
somber face he actually wore.

"You can put your shirt on," he said as the scanner yoke lifted
up and slid back into its niche in the infirmary bulkhead.

"Will I live, Doctor?" I kidded.

He nodded briefly, but said, "Your triglyceride count is rising.
Too many sweets. Must I put a block on the dispensing machines?"

I laughed. "I'm the owner of this vessel, remember? I could
remove any block that you code into the galley's computer."

"Then we shall have to rely on your good sense. You need more
exercise and less fatty foods."

I nodded. "Right."

"Otherwise you are in excellent condition."

As I sealed the Velcro front of my shirt I asked, "With everyone
in good health and no accidents to deal with, how do you fill in your
time?"

His normally solemn expression brightened a little. "I am writing my Ph.D. thesis. I took this position so that I would have the
time to write it. And no distractions! No interruptions. No excuses
to put it off."

"What's the subject of your thesis?"

"The underlying similarities among the organisms of Mars, the
Jovian moons, and Earth."

"Well," I said, "maybe we'll find some organisms on Venus to
broaden your scope."

Dr. Waller actually smiled, a bright flashing smile full of white
teeth. "I hardly think so, Mr. Humphries. I chose this mission
specifically because I do not expect any new data to come up and
cause me added complications."

*   *   *

During the first week of our flight I met Marguerite Duchamp exactly twice. The first time was shortly after we broke Earth orbit.

Once we were safely through the keyhole and on the proper trajectory toward Venus, Captain Duchamp left Rodriguez in charge of the bridge and asked me to come with her to the captain's cabin, as she called it. It was a compartment off the bridge, only a few paces along the passageway from my own quarters.

"I want you to meet the expedition's biologist," she said over her shoulder as she slid open the compartment door.

"Your daughter," I said as I entered the cubicle.

It was quite a small compartment, barely room enough for a bunk and a foldout table. She was at the bunk, taking clothes out of a travel bag that lay open atop it. She did not turn around when she heard the door open.

"Marguerite, I want you to meet the owner of this vessel."

She turned, looking slightly surprised. I suppose I looked surprised, too. Stunned, actually. Marguerite was a duplicate of her mother. Younger, of course, not so taut or intimidating, yet so physically alike that I thought she must be a clone. The same tall, slim figure. The same sculptured cheekbones and strong jaw. The same jet-black eyes and raven hair.

Yet where her mother was demanding and dominating, the daughter seemed troubled, uncertain of herself. The mother wore her shoulder-length hair severely pulled back; the daughter's flowed softly, and was considerably longer.

"This is Mr. Van Humphries," Duchamp said. Then, to me, "My daughter, Marguerite."

"Martin's son," she murmured, taking a step toward me. Out of the corner of my eye I saw her mother bristle.

I extended my hand. "Pleased to meet you, Ms. Duchamp."

She touched my hand briefly. Her fingers felt warm, pulsing.

"Marguerite has a doctorate in biology from Oxford," Duchamp said, flatly, as if it were a challenge, not a trace of parental pride in her voice.

Then she added, "I thought you two should meet."

"I'm happy to make your acquaintance," I said to Marguerite. Glancing at her mother, I added, "although I'm afraid there won't be much for you to do on this mission."

She did not smile back. Very seriously, she said, "Perhaps I can

help with some of the other scientific observations, then." Her voice
was low, soft, resigned.

The cabin seemed cold enough to start a glacier.

"We'll find something useful for you to do, don't worry," Captain Duchamp said.

"Yes, Mother. I'm sure you will."

I decided it was time to get out of there. The bitterness between
mother and daughter was thick enough to cut with a chain saw.

Dr. Waller said I should exercise, so I started jogging through the
warren of passageways and cargo bays of *Truax*. The old factory
ship's major cargo hold, which once carried huge tonnages of asteroidal ores, was like a vast cave made of metal. Our expedition's
crated supplies hardly filled one corner of it. The outgoing crew had
worked hard to clean up the holds for us; they had even opened the
bays to the vacuum of space for several days on end. Still the metal
bulkheads were dingy with dust. I could feel it crunching on the
soles of my running shoes. When I ran a hand along a bulkhead the
metal felt gritty; my fingers came away stained with dust.

It made me grin, though. I was touching the dust of other
worlds. Instead of sitting at home and staring at virtual reality simulations I was actually out here, touching other worlds, planetoids
that had floated in the silent emptiness of space for billions of years,
since the time when the solar system had been created.

Then I discovered the bay that held the old smelter, silent and
unused now. Yet I could sense the heat of the big nuclear-powered
ovens as they melted down the ores in the first step of the refining
process. Pulverized chunks of asteroidal rock were ruthlessly lique-
fied here, all their minor elements driven out to be collected by the
mass separators, purified into the metals and minerals that were
building the human race's expanding civilization.

For the first time I got an inkling of what my father's corporations actually did. They were converting ancient leftovers from the
creation of the solar system into habitats and factories and spacecraft for the men and women who were living and working in space,
on the Moon and Mars, in the armored modules floating on the ice
of Jupiter's major moons.

From the catwalk high above the smelter I drank in the heat that
seemed to still hang in the air like a living presence. I could hear in
my mind the growling roar of the rock crushers, the shuddering

rumble of the conveyor belts that carried the pulverized ore into the white-hot fury of the smelter. When I closed my eyes I could see the glowing streams of man-made lava flowing into the separators in the next huge bay.

All silent now, except for the soft echo of my running shoes padding against the metal grillwork of the catwalk. All stilled, unused, because I had decided in a reckless, angry moment to take up my father's challenge.

As he knew I would! That understanding came to me as I jogged along the catwalk, hit me so hard I stopped and gripped the handrail, feeling almost dizzy. He maneuvered me into this! He knew I'd take up his challenge. Or did he merely hope that I would? Either way, I rose to his bait and snapped at it.

Why did he do it? Why did he set all that up, the party, the announcement, the prize? Just to get me off my butt and send me to Venus? To get me out of his way? To kill me, the same way Alex was killed?

Why?

COMPETITION

I was walking along the passageway toward my stateroom, cooling down from my run, sweaty and smelly in my running suit, when I saw Marguerite Duchamp coming up the passageway from the other direction.

I had seen her exactly once since her mother performed that awkward, anger-edged introduction on the day we left Earth orbit. Marguerite had kept pretty much to her quarters and—to tell the truth—I kept pretty much to mine, except for my daily exercise runs. Come to think of it, she might have been poking around the big old ship or working on the bridge as much as her mother and I wouldn't have known it.

I couldn't get over how much she resembled her mother, like a younger twin or clone. The same dark hair and eyes, the same slim supple figure. She was slightly taller than me, but then almost everybody was slightly taller than me. Father called me Runt because I am small, there's no getting away from that fact.

She was wearing standard dun-colored coveralls, with flat-heeled shipboard slippers. No matter how much she looked like her mother, though, Marguerite was obviously younger, fresher, without her mother's brittle armor of haughtiness, more—approachable.

I saw that she had sewn a bright green armband on the left sleeve of her coveralls. And as she approached me, I noticed that her thick dark hair was tied back with a green ribbon that matched the armband.

"You're one of them?" I blurted.

Her onyx eyes flashed at me. "Them?" she asked.

"The Greens."

She seemed to visibly relax. "Of course," she answered casually. "Isn't everybody?"

"I'm not." I reversed my course and fell into step beside her.

"Why aren't you?" she asked, apparently not noticing that I was sweaty and smelly and must have looked a mess.

Her question puzzled me for a moment. "I guess I've never paid that much attention to politics."

Marguerite shrugged. "With your money, I suppose you don't have to."

"My father's very involved," I said. It came out sounding defensive.

"I'm sure he is," she said scornfully. "But he's not a Green, is he?"

"No," I admitted with a little laugh. "Definitely not a Green."

She was headed for the galley, and I went along with her, smelly running suit and all.

"How well do you know my father?" I asked, realizing as the words came out of my mouth that I was being just about as tactless as a class-A boor.

She cast me a sidelong glance as we walked along the passageway. "I only met him once. With my mother."

"Only once?"

"That was enough. More than enough."

The way she said it made me wonder what had happened. Father can be quite suave and winning when he wants to be. He can also be demanding and vicious. From the ferocity of her mother's reaction, Father must have hit on Marguerite very blatantly.

Although it had been refurbished along with the rest of the ship, *Truax*'s galley looked scuffed and hard-used. No amount of spit and polish could make the dispensers' dulled, worn metal surfaces gleam like new again. Marguerite helped herself to a tall mug of fruit juice. No one was sitting at the tables, so I poured a chilled mug of the same for myself and went over to sit beside her. She didn't seem to mind the company. And what if she does, I told myself. I'm the owner of this vessel. This is *my* ship. I'll sit where I damned well want to. But I was glad she didn't get up and move away.

"So, what do people call you? Marjorie?"

"Marguerite," she said stiffly.

"Marguerite? Nothing else?"

"That's the name my mother gave me."

I suppose she realized she was being curt, almost rude. Softening a little, she said, "I can't abide being called Marjorie or Margie. And Maggie . . ." She shuddered with distaste.

I had to laugh. "All right. Marguerite, then. I'm Van."

We talked, mainly about politics. No further mention of my father. Marguerite was an ardent, dedicated Green, devoted to the ideals of stopping the Earth's warming by drastically changing society. Solar energy instead of fossil or nuclear fuels. Taxation to redistribute wealth and shrink the gap between rich and poor. Stronger international controls on trade and information commerce.

I tried to make her see that nuclear power would help to wean the world off fossil fuels much better than solar energy possibly could.

"Especially with helium-three for fusion generators," I told her, with growing enthusiasm. "We could triple the world's installed electrical power capacity and cut greenhouse emissions by seventy percent or more."

She frowned slightly. "Your father has a monopoly on helium-three, doesn't he?"

"His corporation owns a large chunk of the helium-mining operations on the Moon. I wouldn't say he has a monopoly. Besides—"

"And he controls the lunar raw materials that are needed to build solar power satellites, doesn't he?"

"He doesn't *control* them. There's also Masterson Corporation. And Astro Manufacturing."

Marguerite shook her head. "Mr. Humphries, your father is one of our most implacable enemies."

"Yes, I know. And my name is Van."

She nodded and we continued talking. I forgot about my enzyme shot, forgot about Marguerite's hard-driving mother and Rodriguez and the rest of the crew. I even forgot about Gwyneth, living in my apartment in Barcelona. I was enjoying talking with Marguerite. As we chatted on I commented on how strikingly she resembled her mother.

"Why not?" she asked, very seriously. "I'm a duplicate."

"A clone?"

With a brief dip of her chin, Marguerite said, "Mother's always said she's never met a man she'd trust to father a child with her. So she cloned herself and had the embryo implanted in herself. Eight and a half months later I was born."

I shouldn't have felt as staggered as I did. Duplicates were nothing new; people had been cloning themselves here and there for years. The procedure was outlawed in many nations and moralists railed against the supposed inhumanity of it. But here was a perfectly lovely, lively young woman who happened to be a clone of her mother.

"When did all that happen?" I asked.

Her eyes widened for a flash of a second and I felt suddenly embarrassed.

But Marguerite just laughed. "I haven't needed any rejuvenation treatments yet."

"I mean . . . I suppose I was really wondering about your mother's age. My father's past a hundred, and . . ."

I cursed myself for a fool even while my mouth blabbered on. I could easily look up their ages in the mission's dossiers.

Marguerite let it pass and our conversation drifted on, relaxed and friendly. Until we began to talk about the mission.

"Don't you think it's strange," Marguerite asked, "that no human expedition was sent to Venus until your brother went?"

"The unmanned probes scoped out the planet pretty well. There's been no need for human missions."

"Really?" Her brows hiked up. "I thought you were a planetary scientist. Aren't you curious about this planet?"

"Of course I am. I'll be running a series of seismic probes for Professor Greenbaum, you know."

"No, I didn't know."

"He has a theory about the planet's surface overturning," I explained. "He thinks the surface will get so hot it'll begin to melt."

"Fascinating," Marguerite murmured.

I waved a hand in the air. "It's not a very attractive planet."

"Attractive?" she snapped. "Are we talking about exploring a world or starting a resort hotel?"

"I mean, it's a hellhole. Hot enough to melt aluminum and all that."

"But that's just what makes it so interesting! A planet almost the same size and mass as Earth and yet with a totally different global environment. A runaway greenhouse effect. Where Earth's atmosphere cycles carbon dioxide, Venus cycles sulfur compounds. It's fascinating."

"It's a desert world," I said. "Utterly lifeless. There's nothing for a biologist to study."

"Are you certain it's dead?"

"No water," I pointed out. "Unbreathable atmosphere. It's hot and dead and dangerous."

"On the surface, I grant you. But what about up in the clouds? The temperatures are cooler there. And there's *something* in those clouds that absorbs ultraviolet energy, much the way chlorophyllic plants absorb infrared."

"None of the probes ever found living organisms or even organic material. Nothing could live in temperatures more than twice as hot as boiling water."

"Absence of proof," she said loftily, "is not proof of absence."

"Venus is dead," I insisted.

"Is it? What about all that sulfur in the atmosphere? Sulfur's an important component in the Jovian biochemistry, isn't it?" she demanded.

"Well, perhaps so . . ."

"And sulfur metabolism was present in Earth's earliest organisms. It's present today, in the hydrothermal vents at the bottom of the oceans."

"Nonsense!" I spluttered. Why is it that when you don't have any facts on your side you tend to talk louder and solidify your position into concrete?

Quite seriously, Marguerite asked, "Why do you suppose that there were more than a dozen missions to Venus before the year 2020, but since then, hardly any?"

I hadn't the foggiest notion, but I said, "The earlier probes told us what we needed to know. Oh, I admit there're lots of unknowns remaining, but the planet's so terribly uninviting that no one even thought about sending out a human team."

"Until your brother went."

"Yes," I said, my insides suddenly clenching. "Alex went."

"We have permanent research stations on Mars and the Jupiter system," she went on, relentless, "and mining operations in the Asteroid Belt. Yet nothing for Venus. Not even an orbiting observatory."

"The scientific community lost interest in Venus," I said. "It happens. With so much else to study—"

"The scientific community lost *funding* for Venus," Marguerite said firmly. "Funding that comes mainly from wealthy patrons of universities, such as your father."

"He paid for my brother's expedition," I said.

"No, he didn't. Your brother paid for his expedition out of his own funds."

I blinked with surprise. I hadn't known that. I had just assumed . . .

"And your brother died on Venus."

"Yes," I said, my guts churning. "That's right."

"Do you think the rumors are true: that your brother's craft was sabotaged?"

"I don't know." I felt perspiration beading on my brow and my upper lip. I was annoyed, irritated at the turn our conversation had taken.

"They say your father didn't want his mission to succeed. They say your brother and he had a terrible argument about it."

"I don't know," I repeated. "I wasn't there."

"Didn't your brother tell you about it?"

"Obviously not!" I snapped. I realized that, except for that last night in Connecticut, Alex had told me very little about his plans, his hopes, his fears. He'd been almost a stranger to me. My own brother. We might just as well have been born into two different families.

Silence stretched between us uncomfortably.

Then it was broken by the comm screen on the galley's bulkhead. It glowed orange and the communications computer's voice said, "Incoming message for Mr. Humphries."

"Display," I called out, glad for the interruption.

Until I saw that it was my father's face on the screen, larger than life. He was scowling with displeasure.

"I've just found out where Fuchs is," he said without preamble. "He's registered his ship and planned trajectory with the IAA, at last. He's heading for Venus, all right. The sonofabitch is on a high-gee burn that will put him in orbit around Venus days before you get there."

TRANSFER

I took one last look at my stateroom. When we had boarded *Truax* the single room had seemed rather cramped and decidedly shabby to me. Over the nine weeks of our flight to Venus, though, I'd grown accustomed to having my office and living quarters all contained within the same four walls—or bulkheads, as they're called aboard ship. At least the smart wall screens had made the compartment seem larger than it actually was. I could program gloriously wide vistas, videos of almost any spot on Earth. I usually settled for the view of the Mediterranean from my hilltop home in Majorca.

Now we were ready to transfer to the much smaller *Hesperos*. At least, the crew was. I dreaded the move. If *Truax* was like a tatty old freighter, *Hesperos* would be more like a cramped, claustrophobic submarine.

To make matters worse, in order to get to the dirigible-like *Hesperos* we were going to have to perform a space walk. I was actually going to have to seal myself into a spacesuit and go outside into that yawning vacuum and trolley down the cable that linked the two vessels, with nothing between me and instant death but the monomolecular layers of my suit. I could already feel my insides fluttering with near panic.

For about the twelve thousandth time I told myself I should have insisted on a tugboat. Rodriguez had talked me out of it when we'd first started planning the mission. "A pressurized tug, just so we can make the transfer without getting into our suits?" he had jeered at me. "That's an expense we can do without. It's a waste of money."

"It would be much safer, wouldn't it?" I had persisted.

He looked disgusted. "You want safety? Use the mass and volume we'd need for the tug to carry extra water. That'll give us an edge in case the recycler breaks down."

"We have a backup recycler."

"Water's more important than a tug that we'll only use for five minutes during the whole mission. That's one piece of equipment that we definitely don't need to carry along."

So I had let Rodriguez talk me out of the tug. Now I was going to have to perform an EVA, a space walk, something that definitely gave me the shakes.

My jitters got even worse whenever I thought about Lars Fuchs.

Once my father told me that Fuchs actually was racing for the prize money, I spent long hours digging for every byte of information I could glean about him. What I found was hardly encouraging. Fuchs had a reputation for ruthlessness and achievement. According to the media biographies, he was a merciless taskmaster, a driven and hard-driving tyrant who ran roughshod over anyone who stood in his way. Except my father.

The media had barely covered Fuchs's launch into a high-velocity transit to Venus. He had built his ship in secrecy out in the Belt—adapted an existing vessel, apparently, to his needs. Unlike all the hoopla surrounding my own launch from Tarawa, there was only one brief interview with Fuchs on the nets, grainy and stiff because of the hourlong delay between the team of questioners on Earth and Fuchs, out there among the asteroids.

I pored over that single interview, studying the face of my adversary on my stateroom wall screen, in part to get my mind off the impending space walk. Fuchs was a thickset man, probably not much taller than I, but with a barrel chest and powerful-looking shoulders beneath his deep blue jacket. His face was broad, jowly, his mouth a downcast slash that seemed always to be sneering. His eyes were small and set so deep in their sockets that I couldn't make out what color they might be.

He made a grisly imitation of a smile to the interviewers' opening question and replied, "Yes, I am going to Venus. It seems only fair that I should take this very generous prize money from Martin Humphries—the man who destroyed my business and took my wife from me, more than thirty years ago."

That brought a barrage of questions from the reporters. I froze the image and delved into the hypertext records.

Fuchs had an impressive background. He had been born poor,

but built a sizable fortune for himself out in the Asteroid Belt, as a prospector. Then he started his own asteroidal mining company and became one of the major operators in the Belt, until Humphries Space Systems undercut his prices so severely that Fuchs was forced into bankruptcy. HSS then bought out the company for a fraction of its true worth. My father had personally taken control and fired Fuchs from the firm that the man had founded and developed over two decades.

While Fuchs stayed out in the Asteroid Belt, penniless and furious with helpless rage, his wife left him and married Martin Humphries. She became my father's fourth and last wife.

I gasped with sudden understanding. She was my mother! The mother I had never known. The mother who had died giving birth to me six years afterward. The mother whose drug addiction had saddled me with chronic anemia from birth. I stared at her image on the screen: young, with the flaxen hair and pale blue eyes of the icy northlands. She was very beautiful, yet she looked fragile, delicate, like a flower that blooms on a glacier for only a day and then withers.

It took an effort to erase her image and go back to the news file. Fuchs had taken off for Venus in a specially modified ship he had named *Lucifer*. The Latin name for Venus as the morning star was Lucifer. It was also the name used by the Hebrew prophet Isaiah as a synonym for Satan.

Lucifer. And Fuchs. After a high-gee flight, he was already in orbit around Venus, more than a week ahead of me. Sitting there in my stateroom, staring at Fuchs's sardonic, sneering face on the wall screen, I remembered that the time had come to transfer to *Hesperos*. There was no way to get out of it. I still wished I were home and safe, but now I knew that I had to go through with this mission no matter what the dangers.

But my thoughts went back to my mother. I had never known that she was once Fuchs's wife. My father hardly ever spoke of her, except to blame me for her death. Alex had told me that it wasn't my fault, that women didn't die in childbirth unless there was something terribly wrong. It was Alex who told me about her drug dependency; as far as my father was concerned she was faultless.

"She was the only woman I ever really loved," he said, many a time. I almost believed him. Then he would add, cold as liquid helium, "And you killed her, Runt."

A single rap on my door startled me. Before I could respond, Desiree Duchamp slid the door open and gave me a hard stare.

"Are you coming or not?" she demanded.

I drew myself up to my full height—not quite eye to eye with my captain—and forced my voice to be steady and calm as I answered, "Yes. I'm ready."

When she turned and headed down the passageway I squeezed my eyes shut and tried to conjure up a picture of my brother. I'm doing this for you, Alex, I said to myself. I'm going to find out why you died—and who's responsible for your death.

But as I headed down the passageway after Duchamp, the image in my mind was of my mother, so young and lovely and vulnerable.

We had done simulations of the EVA procedure a dozen times, and I had suited up each time. I thought it was silly, like children playing dress-up, but Duchamp had insisted that we pull on the cumbersome suits and boots and helmets and backpacks even though we were only going to play-act in the ship's virtual reality chamber.

Now the crew was gathered at the main airlock, busily getting into their spacesuits. It looked to me like some athletic team's locker room, or a changing booth in a beach-side cabana. I paid intense attention to every detail of the procedure, though. This time it would be for real. A mistake here could be fatal. Leggings first, then the thickly lined boots. Slide into the torso and wiggle your arms through the sleeves. Pull the bubble helmet over your head, seal it to the neck ring. Then work the gloves over your fingers. The gloves had a bony exoskeleton on their backs, powered by tiny servomotors that amplified one's muscle power tenfold. There were also servos built into the suit's joints: shoulders, elbows, knees.

Duchamp herself hung the life support rig on my back and connected the air hose and power lines. The backpack felt like a ton weighing on my shoulders.

I heard the suit's air fans whine into life, like distant gnats, and felt cool air flowing softly across my face. The suit was actually roomy inside, although the leggings chafed a little against my thighs.

Marguerite, Rodriguez, and the four other crew members were all fully suited. Even Dr. Waller was frowning slightly with impatience as they waited for me to finish up.

"Sorry I'm so slow," I muttered.

They nodded from inside their fishbowl helmets. Marguerite even managed a little smile.

"All right," Duchamp said at last, once she was convinced my suit was properly sealed. "Radio check." Her voice was muffled slightly by the helmet.

One by one the crew members called to the EVA controller up on the bridge. I heard each of them in my helmet earphones.

"Mr. Humphries?" the controller called.

"I hear you," I said.

"Radio check complete. Captain Duchamp, you and your crew are go for transfer."

With Duchamp directing us, they went through the airlock hatch, starting with Rodriguez. Then the doctor and, one by one, the three technicians. I followed Marguerite. Duchamp grasped my arm as I stepped carefully over the sill of the hatch into the blank metal womb of the airlock.

Once she swung the inner hatch shut I felt as if I were in a bare metal coffin. I started to breathe faster, felt my heart pumping harder. Stop it! I commanded myself. Calm down before you hyperventilate.

But when the outer hatch started to slide open I almost panicked.

There was nothing out there! They expected me to step out into total emptiness. I tried to find some stars in that black infinity, something, anything to reassure me, but through the deep tinting of my helmet I could not see any.

"Hold one." Rodriguez's familiar voice calmed me a little. But only a little. Then I saw the former astronaut—now an astronaut once again—slide into view, framed by the outline of the open hatch.

"Gimme your tether," Rodriguez said, extending a gloved hand toward me. It looked like a robot reaching for me. I couldn't see his face at all. Even though the bubble helmets gave us fine visibility from inside them, their protective sunshield tinting made them look like mirrors from the outside. All I could see in Rodriguez's helmet was the blank fishbowl reflection of my own helmet.

"C'mon, Mr. Humphries. Gimme your tether. I'll attach it to the trolley. Otherwise you'll swing away."

I remembered the drill from the simulations we had gone through. I unclipped the end of my safety tether from its hook at the waist of my suit and handed it mutely to Rodriguez. He disappeared from my view. There was nothing beyond the airlock hatch that I could see, nothing but a gaping, all-encompassing emptiness.

"Step out now, come on," Rodriguez's voice coaxed in my earphones. "You're okay now. Your tether's connected to the trolley and I'm right here."

His spacesuited form floated into view again, like a pale white ghost hovering before me. Then I saw the others, a scattering of bodies floating in the void, each connected to the trolley by thin tethers that seemed to be stretched to their limit.

"It's really fun," Marguerite's voice called.

We were not in zero gravity. The two spacecraft were still swinging around their common center of gravity, still connected by the Buckyball cable. But there was nothing out there! Nothing but an emptiness that stretched to the ends of the universe.

Shaking inside, my heart thundering so loudly that I knew they could all hear it over my suit radio, I grasped the edge of the outer hatchway in my gloved hands and, closing my eyes, stepped off into infinity.

My stomach dropped away. I felt bile burning up into my throat. My mind raced. He missed me! Rodriguez missed me and I'm falling away from the ship. I'll fall to the Sun or go drifting out and away forever and ever.

Then something tugged at me. Hard. My eyes popped open and I saw that my tether was as taut as a steel rod, holding me securely. But the trolley seemed to me miles away. And I couldn't see any of the others even when I twisted my head to look for them.

"He's secured," Rodriguez's voice said in my earphones.

"Very well," Duchamp replied. "I'm coming out."

I was twisting around, literally at the end of my tether, trying to find the rest of us.

Then the massive bulk of Venus slid into my view. The planet was huge! Its tremendous mass curved gracefully, so bright that it was hard to look at it even through the heavy tinting of my helmet. For a dizzying moment I felt as if its enormous expanse were above me, over my head, and it was going to come down and crush me like a ponderous boulder squashing some insignificant bug.

But only for a moment. The fear passed quickly and I gasped as I stared at the overpowering awesome immensity of the planet. Tears sprang to my eyes, not from its brightness, from its beauty.

I felt someone tugging at my shoulder. "Hey, you okay, boss?" Rodriguez asked.

"Wha . . . yes. Yes, I'm all right."

"Don't freeze up on us now," the astronaut said. "We'll be ready to move soon's Duchamp gets herself connected to the trolley."

I couldn't take my eyes off Venus. She was a brilliant saffron-yellow expanse, glowing like a thing alive. Goddess of beauty, sure enough. At first I thought the cloud deck was as solid and unvarying

as a sphere of solid gold. Then I saw that I could make out streamers among the clouds, slightly darker stretches, patches where the
amber yellowish clouds billowed up slightly.

I was falling in love with a world.

"I'm secured. Let's get moving." Duchamp's terse order broke
my hypnotic staring.

Turning my entire body slightly, I saw the seven other figures
bobbing slightly around the trolley, which was nothing more than a
motorized framework of metal struts that could crawl along the
Buckyball cable.

I looked down the length of the cable toward *Hesperos,* which
seemed to be kilometers away. Which it was: three kilometers, to be
exact. At that distance the fat dirigible that was our spacecraft
looked like a toy model or a holographic image of the real thing. At
its nose the broad cone of the heat shield stood in place like a giant
parasol, looking faintly ludicrous and totally inadequate to protect
the vessel from the burning heat of entry into those thick yellow
clouds.

"All right, by the numbers, check in," Duchamp commanded.

Nothing happened. Silence.

"I said, by the numbers." Duchamp repeated, her voice taking
on an edge. "Mr. Humphries, as owner of this vessel, you are number one. Or have you forgotten *everything* from the simulation
runs?"

I twitched with surprise. "Oh! Yes, of course. Number one,
secured." As I said the prescribed words I yanked on my tether to
make certain they were true. It held firmly.

Rodriguez answered next, then Marguerite. As the other crew
members checked in I thought again of what a farce Marguerite's
"official" title of mission scientist was. But I was glad she was with us.
I could talk to her. She didn't lord it over me as her mother did; even
Rodriguez made it clear, without realizing he was doing it, that he
regarded me as little more than a rich kid playing at being a scientist.

"All right, then," Duchamp said. "Captain to *Truax.* We are
ready for transfer."

"Copy you ready for transfer, Captain. *Hesperos* main airlock is
cycled, outer hatch open and waiting for your arrival."

"Systems check on *Hesperos?*" Duchamp asked.

"All active systems in green except for APU, which is off-line."

The auxiliary power unit was off-line? My ears perked up at
that. But neither Duchamp nor any of the others seemed to be worried about it.

"The main airlock is green?" Duchamp asked sharply.

"No, sir," came the immediate reply. "Main airlock is blinking red."

"That's better," she said. The airlock indicator should blink red when its outer hatch is open. I could sense Duchamp's bitter smile at catching the EVA controller in a minor slipup.

"Activate trolley," she commanded.

"Activating."

I felt a very slight tug on my tether, and then all of us were moving toward the distant *Hesperos,* accelerating now, sliding down the long Buckyball cable like a small school of minnows flashing across a pond. *Hesperos* seemed to be coming up at us awfully fast; I thought we'd crash into her, but I kept silent. Sometimes you'd rather die than make an ass of yourself.

Sure enough, the trolley smoothly decelerated, slowly coming to a stop as the seven of us swung on our tethers like a trained team of acrobats in a silent ballet until we were facing down toward *Hesperos.* I marveled that we went through the maneuver without bumping one another, but Rodriguez later told me it was simple Newtonian mechanics at work. My respects to Sir Isaac.

The trolley stopped about ten meters from the open airlock hatch, with us hanging by our tethers with our boots a mere meter or so from *Hesperos*'s hull. As we had done in the virtual reality simulations, Duchamp unhooked her tether and dropped to the hatch, her knees bending as her boots hit the hull soundlessly.

She stepped into the airlock, disappearing into its shadowed depths for a moment. Then her bubble helmet and shoulders emerged from the hatch and she beckoned to me.

"Welcome aboard, Mr. Humphries," she said. "As owner, you should be the first to board *Hesperos.* After me, of course."

VENUS ORBIT

've tried to contact him a dozen times, Mr. Humphries," said the communications technician. "He simply doesn't answer."

It was the longest sentence the comm tech had spoken to me since I'd first met her. Her name was Riza Kolodny. She was a plain-looking young woman with a round face and mousey brown hair that she kept short, in the chopped-up look that had been fashionable a couple of years earlier. Like the other two technicians, she was a graduate student picked by Rodriguez and okayed by Duchamp. According to her dossier she was a first-rate electronics specialist. She certainly did not look first rate in any way, not to me.

I was bending over her shoulder, staring at the hash-streaked communications screen. Riza was chewing something that smelled vaguely of cinnamon, or perhaps it was clove. She seemed apprehensive, perhaps afraid that she was displeasing me.

"I've tried all the comm freaks," she said, lapsing into jargon in her nervousness, "starting with the frequency Captain Fuchs registered with the IAA. He just doesn't answer."

Hesperos was not built for creature comforts. The tubular gondola that hung beneath the vessel's bulbous gas envelope housed a spare and spartan set of compartments that included the bridge, galley, a single lavatory for all eight of us, work spaces, infirmary, supply lockers, and our so-called living quarters—which were nothing more than slim, coffin-sized berths partitioned off for a modicum of privacy. There was no room aboard *Hesperos* for anything but utilitarian efficiency. We all felt crowded, cramped. I had to fight off incipient claustrophobia whenever I slid into my berth; I felt like Dracula coming home for a good day's sleep.

The bridge was especially cramped. The comm center was nothing more than a console shoehorned in a bare few centimeters from the captain's command chair. I had to twist myself into a pretzel shape to get close enough to Riza's chair to see her screen. I could feel Duchamp's breath on the back of my neck; she was ignoring me, her dark eyes intently focused on the EVA displayed on the main screen before her. Rodriguez and the two other techs were outside in their spacesuits, clambering over the heat shield, checking every square centimeter of it.

"Maybe Fuchs's ship has broken down," I thought aloud. Wishful thinking, actually. "Maybe he's in trouble."

Riza shook her head, fluttering her butchered hairdo. "*Lucifer* is telemetering its systems status back to IAA headquarters on the regular data channel, same as we are. The ship's still in orbit with all systems functional."

"Then why doesn't he answer our call?" I wondered.

"He doesn't want to," said Duchamp.

I turned to face her, not exactly an easy thing to do in the jammed confines of the bridge.

"Why not?"

She gave me a frosty smile. "Ask him."

I glared at her. She was making a joke of my effort to contact Lars Fuchs. There were only the three of us on the bridge; Rodriguez's chair was empty.

"I could relay our call through IAA headquarters," Riza suggested. "He might reply to us if the request came through them."

"He won't," Duchamp said flatly. "I know Fuchs. He's not talking to us because he doesn't want to. And that's that."

Reluctantly, I accepted her assessment of the situation. Fuchs was going to remain silent. The only way we would learn of what he was doing would be to access whatever data he was sending back to the International Astronautical Authority in Geneva.

"Very well," I said, squeezing between Duchamp and the display screen she was watching. "I'm going to the observation port to do my news broadcast."

"Stay clear of the airlock," Duchamp warned. "Tommy and the others will be coming back in less than ten minutes."

"Right," I said as I ducked through the hatch. The main passageway ran the length of the gondola; it was so narrow that Rodriguez joked that a man could fall in love squeezing past someone there.

Before we left Earth the question of news coverage had come up. Should we bring a reporter along with us? Back when I thought I'd be bringing some of my friends along on the journey, I had been all in favor of the idea. I thought the nets would *love* to send a reporter to Venus, and I had several friends who could have qualified for the role. For a while I even considered asking Gwyneth to be our reporter/historian.

Live broadcasts from the mission couldn't fail to get top ratings, I figured. Unfortunately, the net executives saw it differently. They pointed out to me that newscasts from *Hesperos* would be interesting the first day or two, but they'd quickly become boring on the long voyage out to Venus. They admitted that once we got there, live reports from Venus would be a sensational story—again, for a day or two. But afterward the story would lose its glamour and become nothing but colorless, tedious routine.

"It's science stuff," one of the junior executives—a sometime friend of mine, in fact—told me. "Science stuff is boring."

They certainly were not willing to pay a reporter's expenses and insurance. It was Duchamp who suggested that I serve as the expedition's reporter, the face and voice of the *Hesperos*'s mission. "Who better?" she asked rhetorically. I liked the idea. It eliminated the need to carry an extra person along with us. I would file a personal report on the expedition's progress every day. I would become a household figure all around the Earth/Moon system. I really thought that would be terrific. Even if the nets wouldn't feature my broadcasts every day, people could access them whenever they wanted. I often wondered, as I went through my daily report, if my father ever watched me.

Duchamp was no fool. Removing the need to bring a reporter with us, she also removed any possible objections I could raise about her replacing our astronomer with a biologist. Her daughter. Fait accompli. She had manipulated me beautifully and I hardly even minded it, although we both knew we didn't need a biologist aboard. Duchamp did it for personal reasons.

Yet I didn't mind. I was actually pleased that Marguerite was with us. Except for my daily news report I had no real duties aboard *Hesperos*. Time hung heavily as we coasted out to Venus and then established orbit around the planet. Marguerite had little to do, also, as far as ship's duties were concerned, although she usually seemed busy enough when I went looking for her.

Often she was in the little cubbyhole that had been converted into her laboratory. After leaving the bridge and heading for the observation port in the nose of the gondola, I naturally passed by her lab. It was smaller than a phone booth, of course.

The accordion-fold door was slid back, so I stopped and asked her, "Are you busy?"

"Yes," said Marguerite. It was a silly question. She was pecking at the keyboard of a laptop, one of several she had propped along the compartment's chest-high shelf. There was no room in her lab for a chair or even a stool; Marguerite worked standing up.

"Oh. I was on my way to do my news report and I thought I'd stop in the galley for a few minutes . . ." My voice trailed off; she was paying no attention to me, tapping at the keyboard of one laptop with a finger while she clicked away on a remote controller with her other hand, changing the images on one of her other screens. The images looked like photomicrographs of bacteria or something equally distasteful. Either that or really bad primitive art.

I shrugged, conceding defeat, and continued down the narrow passageway to the galley. It was nothing more than a set of food freezers and microwave ovens lining one side of the passageway, with a single stark bench on the other side, where one of the gondola's oblong windows showed the massive, curving bulk of the planet below, gleaming like a gigantic golden lamp.

I slumped down on the bench and gazed out at Venus's yellowish clouds. They shifted and changed as I watched. It was almost like staring into a fire, endlessly fascinating, hypnotic. The clouds' hue seemed to be slightly different from one orbit to another. At the moment they looked almost sickly, bilious. Maybe it's just me, I reasoned. I felt like that, sad and sick and alone.

"Mind if I join you?"

I looked up and there was Marguerite standing over me. I shot to my feet.

"Pull up a section of bench," I said brightly.

She sat next to me and I caught a scent of perfume, very delicate, but a wonderful contrast to the metallic starkness of the ship.

"I'm sorry I was short with you back there," she said. "I was running the latest UV scans of the atmosphere. Sometimes it gets pretty intense."

"Oh, sure. I understand."

Marguerite was still wrapped up in her work. "*Something* down in those clouds absorbs ultraviolet light," she said.

"You think its biological? A life-form in the clouds?"

She started to nod, then thought better of it. As if she were a long-experienced scientist, she buried her enthusiasm and answered noncommittally, "I don't know. Perhaps. We won't know for certain until we get down into the clouds and take samples."

Without thinking I argued, "What about all the sampling the unmanned probes did, years ago? They didn't find any evidence of living organisms."

Suddenly Marguerite's dark eyes snapped with annoyance. "They weren't equipped to. They all carried nephelometers to measure droplet size, but not one of them carried a single instrument that could have detected any biological activity. A Shetland pony could've flown by and those dumb-ass robots would never have noticed."

"There weren't any biological sensors on any of the probes?"

"Not one," she said. "Venus is a dead planet. That's the official word."

"But you don't believe it."

"Not yet. Not until I've looked for myself."

I felt a new respect for Marguerite. She could be just as much a tigress as her mother in matters that she cared about.

"How much longer will we stay in orbit?" she asked.

I hunched my shoulders. "We're scanning the equatorial region with radar, looking for any sign of the wreckage of my brother's ship."

"Wouldn't it be all smashed into small pieces?"

"Probably not," I answered. "The atmosphere's so thick that his ship would've gone to the bottom like a ship sinking in the ocean, back home. I mean, the pressure down at the surface is like our oceans, a kilometer or more below sea level."

She thought about that for a moment. "So it wouldn't be like a plane falling out of the sky on Earth."

"Or like a missile hitting the ground. No. More like the *Titanic* settling on the bottom of the Atlantic."

"You haven't found anything yet?"

"Not yet," I admitted. *Hesperos* was in a two-hour equatorial orbit; we had circled the planet thirty times, so far.

"How much of a chance is there that you'll spot something?"

"Well, we know where he first entered the atmosphere, the latitude and longitude. But we can only guess where he might have drifted while he was in the clouds."

"He didn't have a tracking beacon?"

"Its signal broke up a lot once he went into the cloud deck, so we've got to scan a pretty wide swath along the equator."

Marguerite looked past me, out at the clouds swirling across the face of Venus. She stared at them as if she could get them to part by sheer willpower. I watched the profile of her face. How much she looked like her mother! The same face, yet somehow softer, kinder. It made me think about how little I looked like my father. Alex resembled Father. People had often exclaimed that Alex looked like a younger replica of Martin Humphries. But I resembled my mother, they said. The mother I never knew.

Marguerite turned back to me. "Are you really a planetary scientist?"

The question surprised me. "I try to be," I said.

"Then why aren't you working at it? There's your planet, right out there, and yet you spend your time wandering around the ship like a little lost boy."

"I've got a complete set of instruments taking data," I said. It sounded weak and defensive, even to me.

"But you're not doing anything with the data. You're not analyzing it or using it to change the sensors' operating parameters. You're just letting everything chug along on their preset programs."

"The data goes back to Professor Cochrane at Caltech. If she wants the instruments changed, she tells me and I make the changes."

"Like a graduate student," Marguerite said. "A trained chimpanzee."

That stung. "Well . . . I've got other things to do, you know."

"Like what?"

"I send in my news reports every day."

Her lips pulled down disapprovingly. "That must take all of ten minutes."

Strangely, I felt laughter bubbling up in me. I normally don't take kindly to criticism, but Marguerite had hit me fairly and squarely.

"Oh no," I answered her, chuckling. "It takes more like half an hour."

Her expression softened, but only a little. "Well, then, let's see. I'll give you eight hours for sleeping and an hour and a half for meals . . . that leaves fourteen empty hours every day! If I had fourteen hours on my hands I'd build a whole new set of biosensors for when we dip into the clouds."

"I could help you," I said.

She pretended to consider the offer. "Uh-huh. Do you have any background in cellular biology?"

"I'm afraid not."

"Spectroscopy? Can you take apart one of the mass spectrometers and realign it to be sensitive to organic molecules?"

I must have been grinning like a fool. "Um, do you have a manual for that? I can follow instruction manuals pretty well."

She was smiling now, too. "I think you'd better stick to your own specialty."

"Planetary physics."

"Yes. But get active about it! There's more to science than watching the readouts of your instruments."

"I suppose so. But so far the sensors aren't showing anything that the old probes didn't get years ago."

"Are you certain? Have you gone through the data thoroughly? You mean to tell me there's *nothing* different? No anomalies, no unexplained blips in the incoming data?"

Before I could think of an answer, Duchamp's voice came through the intercom speaker built into the overhead. "Mr. Humphries, radar scan has picked up a glint that might be wreckage. Could you come to the bridge, please?"

RECONNAISSANCE

odriguez was back on the bridge when we got there, and with all three chairs occupied, the bridge was simply too small for both me and Marguerite to squeeze in. I ducked halfway through the hatch and stopped there. Marguerite stayed behind me, in the passageway, and looked in over my shoulder.

The bridge felt hot, stuffy. Too much equipment jammed in there, humming away. And too many bodies radiating heat. The air seemed soggy, murky, and yet at that moment it fairly seethed with suppressed turbulence.

The main screen, in front of Duchamp's command chair, showed a frozen radar image: dark shadows and jumbled shapes of landforms with a single bright glint at its center. Rodriguez was leaning forward in his chair, studying the image, perspiration beading his brow.

"That could be it," he said, pointing to me. "It's definitely metal; the computer analysis leaves no doubt."

I stared hard at the blob of light. "Can we get better resolution? You can't tell what it is from this image."

Before Riza could reply from the comm console, Duchamp snapped, "We've magnified it as much as we can. That's the best we can get."

Rodriguez said, "It's within the footprint that your brother's craft would be expected to have, knowing what we know about when and where he went down. Nothing else metallic has shown up in the region."

"We'll have to go lower for better resolution," Duchamp said. "Get under the cloud deck and use optical sensors."

"Telescopes," I muttered.

"Yes."

"What region is that?" Marguerite asked, from behind me.

"Aphrodite," said her mother.

"It's a highland region, more than two kilometers higher than the surrounding plains," Rodriguez said.

"Then it must be cooler," I said.

Duchamp smiled humorlessly. "Cooler, yes. The ground temperature is down to a pleasant four hundred degrees Celsius."

The lowland surface temperature averages above four hundred fifty degrees, I knew.

"Are we set for atmosphere entry?" I asked.

"The heat shield's been checked out," Duchamp replied. "Propulsion is ready."

"And still no word from Fuchs?"

Riza answered from the comm console, "He entered the cloud deck two hours ago, halfway around the planet. I got his entry position from the IAA."

"Then he hasn't seen the wreckage?"

Duchamp shook her head. "If we've seen that glint, he has, too."

"The plane of his entry was almost exactly equatorial," Riza said, almost apologetically. "He'll most likely come out of the clouds in the same region as the glint."

I felt a dull throb in my jaw and realized that my teeth were clenched tight. "Very well then," I said. "We'd better get under the clouds, too."

Duchamp nodded, then touched a stud on her chair's left armrest. "Captain to crew: take your entry stations. Stand by for atmospheric entry in ten minutes." She lifted her hand and looked directly at me. "Clear the bridge of all nonessential personnel."

I took her unsubtle hint and backed out into the passageway. Marguerite was already striding away.

"Where are you going?" I called after her.

"To my lab. I want to record the entry."

"The automatic sensors—"

"They're not programmed to look for organic molecules or other exotic species. Besides, I want to get the entry process on video. It'll look good for your news report."

I started to reply, then sensed Rodriguez standing behind me.

"She threw you off the bridge, too?"

He grinned at me. "My entry station is up forward with the life support technician." He squeezed past me and started along the passageway.

The trouble was, I had no official entry station. If we went strictly by the rules I should've slid into my berth and stayed there until we jettisoned the heat shield. But I had no intention of doing that.

"Is there room for a third person up there?" I asked, trailing after Rodriguez.

"If you don't mind the body odors," he said over his shoulder.

"I showered this morning," I said, hurrying to catch up with him.

"Yeah, well, it's gonna get a little warm up there, you know. You'd be more comfortable in your berth."

I lifted my chin a notch. "You don't have to pamper me."

Rodriguez glanced over his shoulder at me. "Okay, you're the boss. You wanta be in the hot seat, come on along."

Striding down the passageway behind him, I asked, "How are you and Duchamp getting along?"

"Fine," he said, without slowing down or looking back toward me. "No problems."

Something in his voice sounded odd to me. "Are you sure?"

"We've worked things out. We're okay."

He sounded strange . . . cheerful, almost. As if he were in on a joke and I wasn't.

We passed Marguerite's tiny lab. The accordion-pleat door was folded open and I could see her standing in the cubicle, her head bent over a palm-sized video camera.

"You'll have to strap down for the entry," Rodriguez told her. "It's gonna get bumpy for a while."

"I'll help her," I said. "You go ahead and I'll catch up with you." Mr. Gallant, that's me.

Rodriguez looked uncertain for a moment, but then he nodded acceptance. "The two of you have got to be belted in for the entry. I don't care where, but you've got to be in safety harnesses. Understood?"

"Understood," I assured him. Duchamp had made us practice the entry procedures at least once a day for the past two weeks.

"ENTRY BEGINS IN EIGHT MINUTES," the countdown computer announced.

Marguerite looked up from her work. "There. The vidcam's ready."

She pushed past me and started down the passageway to the observation blister, the camera in her hand.

"Aren't you going with Tom?" she asked.

"I was," I said, "but if you don't mind I'd rather stay with you."

"I don't mind."

"Rodriguez gave me the feeling I'd just be in his way up there."

"I'm sure he didn't mean it that way."

"I know when I'm being condescended to," I insisted.

"Tom's not like that."

We reached the blister, a metal bubble that extended outward from the gondola's main body. Three small observation ports studded its side, each window made of thick tinted quartz. Four padded swivel chairs were firmly bolted to the deck.

"You won't see much through the tinting," I said.

Marguerite smiled at me, and went to a small panel beneath the port that slanted forward. Opening it, she snapped her camera into the recess. Then she shut the panel again. Three tiny lights winked on: two green, one amber. As I watched, the amber light turned red.

"What's that?" I asked, puzzled. "I thought I knew every square centimeter of this bucket."

"God is in the details," Marguerite said. "I got Tom and my mother to allow me to build this special niche here. It's like an airlock, with an inner hatch and an outer one."

"They allowed you to break the hull's integrity?" I felt shocked.

"It was all done within the standard operating procedures. Tom and Aki both checked it out."

Akira Sakamoto was our life support technician: young, chubby, introspective to the point of surliness, so quiet he was almost invisible aboard the ship.

I was still stunned. "And the camera's exposed to vacuum?"

She nodded, obviously pleased with herself. "The outer hatch opened when the inner one sealed. That's why the third light is red."

"Why didn't anybody tell me about this?" I wasn't angry, really. Just surprised that they'd do this without at least telling me.

"It was in the daily logs. Didn't you see them?" Marguerite turned the nearest swivel chair to face the port and sat in it.

I took the chair next to her. "Who reads the daily reports? They're usually nothing but boring details."

"Tom highlighted it."

"When? When was this done?"

She thought a moment. "The second week out. No, it was the beginning of the third week." With an impatient shake of her head, she said, "Whenever it was, you can look it up in the log if you want the exact date."

I stared at her. She was smiling impishly. She was enjoying this.

"I'll fry Rodriguez's butt for this," I muttered. It was a phrase I had often heard my father growl. I never thought I'd say it myself.

"Don't blame Tom!" Marguerite was suddenly distraught, concerned. "My mother okayed it. Tom was only doing what I asked and the captain approved."

"ENTRY IN SIX MINUTES," came the automated announcement.

"So you asked, your mother approved, and Rodriguez did the work without telling me."

"It's only a minor modification."

"He should have told me," I insisted. "Breaching the hull is not minor. He should have pointed it out to me specifically."

Her roguish smile returned. "Don't take it so seriously. If Tom and my mother okayed it, there's nothing to worry about."

I knew she was right. But dammit, Rodriguez should have informed me. I was the owner of this vessel. He should have made certain that I knew and approved.

Marguerite leaned over toward me and tapped a forefinger against my chin. "Lighten up, Van. Enjoy the ride."

I looked into her eyes. They were shining like polished onyx. Suddenly I leaned toward her and, reaching a hand behind the nape of her neck, I pulled her to me and kissed her firmly on the lips.

She pushed away, her eyes flashing now, startled, almost angry.

"Now wait a minute," she said.

I slid back in my chair. "I . . . you're awfully attractive, you know."

She glared at me. "Just because my mother's letting Tom sleep with her is no reason for you to think you can get me into your bed."

I felt as if someone had whacked me with a hammer. "What? What did you say?"

"You heard me."

"Rodriguez and your mother?"

The indignation in her eyes cooled a bit. "You mean you didn't know about them?"

"No!"

"They're sleeping together. I thought everyone on board knew it."

"I didn't!" My voice sounded like a little boy's squeak, even to myself.

Marguerite nodded, and I saw in her expression some of the bitterness her mother exuded constantly.

"Ever since we left Earth orbit. It's my mother's way of solving personnel problems."

"ENTRY IN FIVE MINUTES."

"We'd better strap in," Marguerite said.

"Wait," I said. "You're telling me that your mother is sleeping with Rodriguez to smooth over the fact that she's captain and he's only second-in-command?"

Marguerite did not reply. She concentrated on buckling the seat harness over her shoulders.

"Well?" I demanded. "Is that what you're saying?"

"I shouldn't have mentioned it," she said. "I've shocked you."

"I'm not shocked!"

She looked at me for a long moment, her expression unfathomable. At last she said, "No, I can see that you're not shocked."

"I'm accustomed to men and women enjoying sex together," I told her.

"Yes, of course you are."

Then a new thought struck me. "You're angry at your mother, is that it?"

"I'm not angry. I'm not shocked. I'm not even surprised. The only thing that amazes me is that you can live in this crowded little sardine can for week after week and not have the faintest inkling of what's going on."

I had to admit to myself that she was right. I'd been like a sleepwalker. Or rather, like a clown. Going through the motions of being the owner, the man in charge. All these things happening and I hadn't the slightest clue.

I sagged back in my padded chair, feeling numb and stupid. I started fumbling with my safety harness; my fingers felt thick, clumsy. I couldn't take my eyes off Marguerite, wondering, wondering.

She looked back at me, straight into my eyes. "I'm not like my mother, Van. I may be her clone, but I'm nothing like her. Don't ever forget that."

"ENTRY IN FOUR MINUTES."

ENTRY

Orbiting Venus's hot, thick atmosphere at slightly more than seven kilometers per second, *Hesperos* fired its retrorockets at precisely the millisecond called for in the entry program.

Strapped into the chair in the observation blister, I felt the ship flinch, like a speeding car when the driver taps the brake slightly.

I leaned forward as far as the safety harness would allow. Through the forward-angled port I could see the rim of the big heat shield and, beyond it, the smooth saffron clouds that completely shrouded the planet.

Except the clouds were no longer smooth. There were rifts here and there, long streamers floating above the main cloud deck, patterns of billows like waves rolling across a deep, deep sea.

Marguerite was turned toward the port also, so I could not see her full face, only a three-quarter profile. She seemed intent, her hands gripping the arms of her chair. Not white-knuckled, not frightened, but certainly not relaxed, either.

Me, I was clutching the arms of my chair so hard my nails were going to leave permanent indentations in the plastic. Was I frightened? I don't know. I was excited, taut as the Buckyball cable that had connected us to the old *Truax*. I was breathing hard, I remember, but I don't recall any snakes twisting in my gut.

Something bright flared across the rim of the heat shield and I suddenly wished I were up on the bridge, where I could see the instruments and understand what was happening. There was an empty chair up there; I should have demanded that I sit in it through the entry flight.

The ship shuddered. Not violently, but enough to notice. More than enough. The entire rim of the heat shield was glowing now and streamers of hot gas flashed past. The ride started to get bumpy.

"Approaching maximum gee forces," Duchamp's voice called out over the intercom speaker in the overhead.

"Max gee, check," Rodriguez replied, from his position up in the nose.

It was *really* bumpy now. I was being rattled back and forth in my chair, happy to have the harness holding me firmly.

"Maximum aerodynamic pressure," Duchamp said.

"Temperature in the forward section exceeding max calculated." Rodriguez's voice was calm, but his words sent a current of electricity through me.

The calculations have an enormous safety factor in them, I tried to reassure myself. It would have been easier if the ship didn't feel as if it were trying to shake itself apart.

I couldn't see a thing through the port now. Just a solid sheet of blazing hot gases, like looking into a furnace. I squeezed my eyes down to slits while the battering, rattling ride went on. My vision blurred. I closed my eyes entirely for a moment. When I opened them cautiously, I could see fairly well again, although the ship was still shuddering violently.

Marguerite hadn't moved since the entry began; she was still staring fixedly ahead. I wondered if her camera was getting anything or if the incandescent heat of our entry into the atmosphere had fried its lens.

The ride began to smooth out a bit. It was still bumpier than anything I had ever experienced before, but at least now I could lean my head back against the padded headrest and not have it bounce so hard it felt like I was being pummeled by a karate champion.

Marguerite turned slightly and smiled at me. A pale smile, I thought, but it made me smile back at her.

"Nothing to it," I said, trying to sound brave. It came out more like a whimper.

"I think the worst is over," she said.

Just then there was an enormous jolt and an explosion that would have made me leap out of my chair if I weren't strapped in. It took just a flash of a second to realize that it was the explosive bolts jettisoning the heat shield, but in that flash of a second I must have pumped my entire lifetime's supply of adrenaline into my blood. I came very close to wetting myself; my bladder felt painfully full.

"We're going into the clouds!" Marguerite said happily.

"Deceleration on the tick," Duchamp's voice rang out.

"Heat shield jettison complete," Rodriguez replied. "Now we're a blimp."

Rodriguez was inaccurate, I knew. A blimp has a soft envelope; ours was rigid cermet. It wasn't often I could catch him in a slip of the tongue. I threw a superior smile to Marguerite as I popped the latch on my safety harness. The instant I stood up, though, *Hesperos* shuddered, lurched, swung around crazily, and accelerated so hard I was slammed right back into my chair.

The superrotation.

The solid body of the planet may turn very slowly, but Venus's upper atmosphere, blast-heated by the Sun, develops winds of two hundred kilometers per hour and more that rush around the entire planet in a few days. In a way, they're like the jet streams on Earth, only bigger and more powerful.

Our lighter-than-air vessel was in the grip of those winds, zooming along like a leaf caught in a hurricane. We used the engines hanging outside the gondola only to keep us from swinging too violently, otherwise we would have depleted our fuel in a matter of hours. We couldn't fight those winds, we could only surf along on them and try to keep the ride reasonably smooth.

Truax, up in a safe, stable orbit, was supposed to keep track of our position by monitoring our telemeter beacon. This was for two reasons: to stay in constant communications contact with us and to plot the direction and speed of the superrotation wind, with *Hesperos* playing the same role as a smoke particle in a wind tunnel. But *Truax* hadn't deployed the full set of communications satellites around the planet by the time we got caught in the superrotation. Without the commsats to relay our beacon, they lost almost half our first day's data.

And if anything had gone wrong, they wouldn't know it for ten, twelve hours.

Fortunately, the only trouble we had was a few bruised shins as *Hesperos* lurched and swirled in the turbulent winds. It was like being in a racing yacht during a storm: you had to hold on to something whenever you moved from one place to another.

It was scary at first, I admit. No amount of lectures, videos, or even VR simulations can really prepare you for the genuine experience. But in a few hours I got accustomed to it. More or less.

I spent most of those hours right there in the observation blister, staring out as we darted along the cloud tops. Marguerite got up and went back to her lab; crew members passed by now and then, stumbling and staggering along the passageway, muttering curses every time the ship pitched and they banged against the bulkhead.

At one point Marguerite came back to the blister, a heavy-looking gray box of equipment in her hands.

"Shouldn't you be checking the sensors up forward?" she asked, a little testily, I thought.

"They're running fine," I said. "If there were any problems I'd get a screech on my phone." I tapped the communicator in the chest pocket of my coveralls.

"Don't you want to see the data they're taking in?"

"Later on, when the ride settles down a little," I said. It had always nonplussed me that many scientists get so torqued up about their work that they have to watch their instruments while the observation is in progress. As if their being there could make any difference in what the instruments are recording.

Marguerite left and I was alone again, watching the upper layer of the cloud deck reaching for us. Long, lazy tendrils of yellowish fog seemed to stretch out toward us, then evaporate before my eyes. The cloud tops were dynamic, bubbling like a boiling pot, heaving and breathing like a thing alive.

Don't be an anthropomorphic ass, I warned myself sternly. Leave the similes to the poets and romantics like Marguerite. You're supposed to be a scientist.

Of sorts, a sardonic inner voice scoffed. You're only playing at being a scientist. A real scientist would be watching his sensors and data readouts like a tiger stalking a deer.

And miss the view? I answered myself.

We were dipping into the clouds now, sinking down into them like a submarine sliding beneath the surface of the sea. Yellow-gray clouds slid past my view, then we were in the clear again, then more mountains of haze covered the port. Deeper and deeper we sank, into the sulfuric-acid perpetual global clouds of Venus.

The ride did indeed smooth out, but only a little. Or maybe we all became accustomed to the pitching and rolling. We got our sea legs. Our Venus legs.

It was eerie, sailing in that all-enveloping fog. For days on end I stared out of the ports and saw nothing but a gray sameness. I wanted to push ahead, to go deeper, get beneath the clouds so we could begin searching the surface with telescopes for the wreckage of my brother's vessel.

But the mission plan called for caution, and despite my eagerness I understood that the plan should be followed. We were in uncharted territory now, and we had to make certain that all of *Hesperos*'s systems were performing as designed.

The mammoth cermet envelope above us had been filled (if that's the right word) with vacuum. Its hatches had been open to vacuum all the time of our flight from Earth orbit, then sealed tight when we entered Venus's atmosphere. What better flotation medium for a lighter-than-air vessel than nothingness?

Now we were slowly filling the envelope with hydrogen gas, sucked out of the clouds' abundant sulfuric acid through our equipment that separated out the wanted hydrogen and released the unwanted sulfur and oxygen. On Earth hydrogen's flammability would have been dangerous, but Venus's atmosphere contained practically no free oxygen, so there was no danger of explosion or fire. The envelope itself was a rigid shell of cermet, a ceramic-metal composite that combined toughness and rigidity yet was lighter than any possible metal alloy.

To go deeper, we would vent hydrogen overboard and replace it with atmospheric gas: mainly carbon dioxide. When the time came to rise again, we intended to break down the carbon dioxide into its component elements of carbon and oxygen, vent the carbon overboard, and let the lighter oxygen buoy us upward. Higher up we intended to dissociate the sulfuric acid molecules of the clouds again and refill the envelope with hydrogen.

We had tested the equipment for splitting the carbon dioxide and sulfuric acid molecules before we ever took off from Earth, and now, inside the globe-girdling cloud deck of Venus, we put it to work to fill the gas envelope with hydrogen.

Eager as I was to go deeper, I was perfectly happy to see that the equipment worked in Venus's clouds. I had no desire to be stuck down at the surface with no way to come back up.

So we coasted along in the uppermost cloud deck, patiently filling the big shell above us and testing our equipment. Once in a while it seemed to me that we weren't moving at all, that we were stuck in place like a ship run aground on a reef. All we could see out the ports was that perpetual yellowish-gray sameness. But then some strong current in the atmosphere would grab us and the gondola would tilt and groan like a creaking old sailing ship and my insides would flutter just a little bit.

I was constantly worried about Fuchs, of course, but the IAA reports on his activity showed that he was also moving cautiously.

He had entered the atmosphere several hours before we did, but so far had not gone much deeper than we had. Like us, he was floating in the upper reaches of the top cloud deck, pushed around the planet by the superrotation winds.

"He's no fool," Duchamp told me as we sat together in the spartan little galley. It was the only place aboard *Hesperos* where two or three people could sit together, other than the bridge.

"Lars takes risks," Duchamp said, "but only when he's certain the odds are in his favor."

"You know him?" I asked.

She made a thin smile. "Oh, yes. Lars and I are old friends."

"Friends?" I felt my brows hike up.

Her smile faded. "I first met him just after he had lost his business and his wife. He was a pretty desperate man then. Hurt and angry. Bewildered. Everything he had built up in his life had been snatched away from him." She exhaled a puff of air through her nostrils, something between a grunt and a sigh.

The expression on her face told me she knew perfectly well that the man who had destroyed his company and taken his wife was my father. She didn't have to say it; we both knew.

"But he pulled himself up again, didn't he?" I snapped. "He's done fairly well in asteroid mining, hasn't he?"

Duchamp looked at me for a long silent moment, the kind of look a university professor gives to an especially dense and hopeless student.

"Yes," she said. "Hasn't he."

IN THE CLOUDS

At least, during those first days coasting through the clouds, I had an excuse to stay close to Marguerite. I was supposed to be a planetary scientist, I kept reminding myself, and even though she was a biologist we began to work together, sampling the clouds.

Marguerite's lab was too crowded for both of us to use it at the same time, and it would have been impossible for us to work together in either her quarters or mine; each of us had nothing more than a narrow berth with a privacy screen shuttering it. We could have both fit in either berth, but no scientific research would have been done. Indeed, I found myself wondering what it would be like to have Marguerite cupped beside me in my berth. Or hers.

But she had no romantic interest in me, that was clear. Instead, we turned the observation post up in the gondola's nose into a makeshift laboratory where we took samples of the cloud droplets and analyzed them.

"There really is water in the clouds!" Marguerite exclaimed happily, after a long day of checking and rechecking the results of our spectral analyses.

"Thirty parts per million," I grumbled. "It might as well be zero for all the good—"

"No, no, you don't understand," she said. "Water means life! Where water exists, life exists."

She was really excited. I was more or less playing at being a planetary scientist but to Marguerite the search for life was as thrilling and absorbing as Michelangelo's drive to create great works of art out of rough slabs of marble.

We were sitting cross-legged on the metal decking up in the gondola's nose section because there was no room for chairs and nobody had thought to bring any cushions aboard. The transparent quartzite nose itself showed only the featureless yellowish gray of the eternal cloud deck; it might just have well been spray-painted that color for all that we could see out there. Two mass spectrometers sat to one side of us, half a dozen hand-sized computers were scattered on the deck plates, and a whole rack of equipment boxes—some gray, some black—hummed away along the bulkhead beside me.

"The presence of water," I pointed out, "does not automatically mean the presence of life. There is a good deal of water on the Moon, but no life there."

"Humans live on the Moon," she countered, with mischief in the lilt of her voice.

"I mean native lunar life, you know that."

"But the water deposits on the Moon are frozen. Wherever there's *liquid* water, like under the ice crust on Europa—"

"The water vapor in these clouds," I interrupted, jabbing a finger toward the observation port, "hardly constitute a supply of liquid water."

"They do to microscopic organisms."

I had to hold back a laugh. "Have you found any?"

Her enthusiasm didn't waver one iota. "Not yet. But we will!"

I could only shake my head in admiration for her perseverance.

"This proves that there must be at least some volcanic activity down at the surface," Marguerite said.

"I suppose so," I agreed.

The reasoning was simple enough: Any water vapor in Venus's atmosphere quickly boiled up to the top of the clouds, where the intense ultraviolet radiation from sunlight broke up the water molecules into hydrogen and oxygen, which eventually evaporated away into space. So there had to be a fresh supply of water constantly replenishing the droplets. Otherwise they would have all been dissociated and blown off the planet ages ago. The source of the water most likely came from the planet's deep interior and was vented into the atmosphere by volcanic eruptions.

On Earth volcanoes constantly blow out steam, sometimes in explosions that tear the tops off the mountains. But the water vapor they vent into the atmosphere stays in the atmosphere, on Earth. It's not lost to space because Earth's atmosphere gets cold at high altitudes and the water condenses and falls back as rain or snow. That's why Earth has oceans and Venus doesn't. Earth's upper atmosphere is a "cold trap" that prevents the water from escaping the planet. Hothouse Venus doesn't have a cold trap in its upper atmosphere: at the altitude where on Earth the temperature dips below freezing, Venus is almost four hundred degrees Celsius, four times hotter than water's boiling point. As a result Venus can't build up any appreciable water content in its atmosphere.

I wondered what this meant for Greenbaum's theory about Venus's whole surface erupting into a planet-wide upheaval. There must be *some* volcanic activity venting at least a bit of the planet's internal heat into the atmosphere.

"We'll have to go deeper to find life-forms in the clouds," Marguerite said, as much to herself as to me. "The UV absorber isn't that much further down."

I was still thinking about volcanoes. "We've been watching Venus for more than a century and no one's seen a volcanic eruption. Of all the spacecraft that we've put in orbit and landed on the surface, not one sensor's picked up a volcano in the process of erupting."

Marguerite poo-poohed me. "What do you expect? We've only sent a few dozen robot spacecraft to orbit Venus and even fewer landers. We've ignored the planet terribly."

I had to agree. "Still, if Professor Greenbaum is right and there isn't that much active vulcanism . . ."

"Maybe we'll catch an eruption," Marguerite said. "That would be a first, wouldn't it?"

She was all enthusiasm. But I thought of the ancient Chinese maxim: Be careful what you wish for; you might get it.

Fuchs still worried me. Apparently he was still sailing in the clouds, as we were. But aside from his position I could get no information about him from the IAA. For a good reason: He was giving out no information, nothing but his tracking beacon and the standard telemetering data that showed his basic systems to be operating in good order. When I tried to get details about the design of his ship or the array of sensing systems he carried, I drew a blank. *Lucifer* was his ship, his design, built out in the deep darkness of the Asteroid Belt, equipped according to his specifications and no one else's. He reported the minimum required by the IAA and kept everything else to himself.

One thing I was able to do during those first days in the clouds was to begin to build up a map of the superrotation wind pattern. By recording our position from the ship's inertial navigation system I was able to generate a three-dimensional plot of where those winds blew, a sort of weather map of Venus's jet streams. Every time a powerful gust buffeted us and made me grab for a handhold, every time a sudden upwelling bounced us or a cold spot made us drop until my stomach crawled up into my throat, I thought to myself that at least I was getting useful data.

The winds fanned outward from the subsolar point, of course. That was where the Sun was directly overhead, blazing down on the planet's atmosphere like a blowtorch. Venus turns so slowly, once in 243 Earth days, that the subsolar spot gets blasted remorselessly. The atmosphere rushes away from there in a gigantic heat-driven flow, setting up currents and convection cells that span the girth of the planet. I measured wind speeds of nearly four hundred kilometers per hour: We were setting a Guinness speed record for lighter-than-air vessels.

Deeper down, where the atmosphere gets thicker and so much hotter, the winds die to almost nothing. At a pressure similar to that of an Earthly ocean a kilometer or so deep, there could be nothing that we would recognize as winds, only sluggish tidal motions.

At least, that's how the theory went.

My map of the superrotation winds was coming along quite nicely after a few days, and it made me proud to realize that I was making a real contribution toward understanding Venus. When I tried to extend my data down to a slightly lower altitude, though, in an effort to see how far down the winds might extend, the computer program glitched on me. Insufficient data, I thought, peering at the display screen.

I had coded the map with false colors, each color indicating a range of speeds. There they were, a network of jet streams all rushing out from the subsolar point, in shades of blue and green. With my VR goggles on, I saw it all in three-dimensional motion. But there was the damned glitch, a swath of red and a few kilometers below our present altitude. Red should have indicated even higher wind velocity than we were in now, but I knew that was wrong. The wind velocities had to get lower as we went down in altitude, not higher. Something was wrong with the program.

I mentioned it to Duchamp and Rodriguez when we met to decide on when we would start down toward the surface.

Our conference center was the observation blister, the only place in our cramped gondola where three or four people could sit comfortably. Duchamp and I sat side by side, our chairs swiveled away from the observation ports. Rodriguez sat on the floor facing us, his back against the far bulkhead.

"All systems have performed well within their design range," Duchamp said, tapping a manicured fingernail on the screen of her handheld computer. "Unless I hear otherwise, I declare this phase of the mission completed."

Rodriguez nodded. "No complaints about that. It'll be good to get out of this wind and down to a calmer altitude."

"Calmer," Duchamp said, "but hotter."

"We can handle the heat."

She smiled at him as if they had some private joke going between them.

I spoke up. "My map of the wind system keeps throwing this glitch at me." I had brought a handheld, too, and showed it to them.

"The red indicates even higher wind velocities than we're in now," I said.

"That's an extrapolation, isn't it?" Rodriguez asked. "It's not based on observational data."

"No, we haven't gone down that far, so we don't have any data from that altitude."

"A computer extrapolation," Duchamp said, like an art critic sniffing at some child's lopsided attempt to draw a tree.

"But the extrapolation is based on pretty firm meteorological data," I pointed out.

"Terrestrial meteorological data?" asked Duchamp.

I nodded. "Modified to take into account Venus's different temperature, pressure, and chemical regime."

"An abstraction of an abstraction," Duchamp said, with a *that's-that* wave of her hand.

Rodriguez was staring at the smear of red at the bottom of my map. He handed the palm-sized computer back to me and said thoughtfully, "You don't think there could be some kind of wind shear down at that altitude, do you?"

"A supersonic wind shear?" Duchamp scoffed.

"It's not supersonic at that pressure," Rodriguez pointed out.

She shook her head. "All the planetary physicists agree that the superrotation winds die out as you go deeper into the atmosphere and the pressure builds up. The winds get swamped by the increased pressure."

Rodriguez nodded thoughtfully, then said slowly, "Yeah, I know, but if there really is a wind shear it could be a killer."

Duchamp took a breath, glanced from him to me and back again, then made her decision.

"Very well," she said. "We'll rig for intense wind shear. Check out all systems. Make everything secure and tightened down, just as we did for atmospheric entry." She turned to me. "Will that satisfy you, Mr. Humphries?"

I was surprised at the venom in her reaction. I swallowed once and said, "You're the captain."

"Good." To Rodriguez she said, "Tommy, this means you'll have to go outside and manually check all the connectors and fittings."

He nodded glumly. "Yeah. Right."

Then, smiling coldly, Duchamp turned back to be. "Mr. Humphries, would you care to assist Tom?"

"Me?" I squeaked.

"We could use the extra hand," she said smoothly, "and the inspection is actually at your behest, isn't it? You and your computer program."

You bitch, I thought. Just because my computer program showed a possible problem she's blaming me for it. Now I've either got to risk my neck or show everybody that I'm a coward.

Rodriguez leaned across the narrow passageway separating us and grabbed my knee in a rough, friendly way.

"Come on, Mr. Humphries, it won't be so bad. I'll be with you every step of the way and you'll be able to tell your grandchildren about it."

If I live long enough to have grandchildren, I thought. But I swallowed my fear and said as calmly as I could, "Sure. It ought to be exciting."

It certainly was.

Basically, our task was to check all the connectors that held the gondola to the gas envelope above us. It was a job that a plumber could do, it didn't call for any special training. But we'd be outside, in a cloud of sulfuric acid droplets that was nearly a hundred degrees Celsius, more than fifty kilometers above the ground.

Rodriguez spent two intense hours briefing me on what we had to do in the virtual reality simulator. Six main struts had to be checked out, and six secondary ones. They connected the gondola to the gas shell; if they failed under stress we would go plunging down to the red-hot surface like an iron anvil.

Akira Sakamoto, our dour life support technician, personally helped me into my spacesuit. It was the same one I had used when we transferred from *Truax,* but now its exterior had been sprayed with a special heat-resistant ceramic. The suit seemed stiffer to me than before, although Sakamoto insisted the ceramic in no way interfered with limb motion.

Without a word, without any discernible expression on his chunky broad face, he slipped the safety harness around my waist and clicked it in place, then made certain both its tethers were properly looped so they wouldn't trip me as I tried to walk.

Dr. Waller helped to check out Rodriguez, who got into his suit unassisted. But you had to have somebody go around to make certain all the seals were okay and the electrical lines and life support hoses hooked up properly from the backpack.

Marguerite came down to the airlock, too, and watched in silence as we suited up. I was trembling slightly as I wriggled into the ungainly suit, which was now sort of silvery from its new ceramic coating. But I realized with some surprise that my trembling wasn't so much fear as excitement. I knew I should have been scared out of my bleeding wits, but somehow I wasn't. I was going to *do* something, something that had to be done, and even though it was dangerous I found myself actually looking forward to it.

In the back of my mind, a jeering voice was saying, Famous last words. How many fools have looked forward to the adventure that killed them.

But with Marguerite watching me I didn't seem to care. I thought I saw a hint of admiration in her eyes. At least, I hoped it was admiration and not amusement at the foolish machismo I was exhibiting.

OUTSIDE

Okay, we do it just the way we did in the sim." In my helmet earphones, Rodriguez's voice sounded harsh and tight, definitely more tense than his usual easygoing attitude.

I nodded, then realized he couldn't see me through the tinted fishbowl helmet, so I said, "Right." Just like a real astronaut, I thought.

He went into the airlock ahead of me, cycled it down, and then went outside. Once the outer airlock hatch closed again and the 'lock refilled with ship's air, the inner hatch indicator light turned green.

My spacesuit was definitely stiff. Even with the servomotors at my elbow and shoulder joints grinding away, it took a real effort to move my arms. Before I could reach the airlock control stud with my gloved hand, Sakamoto pressed it, his beefy face dour as usual. But he made a little hissing bow, the first sign of respect I had ever seen from him.

"Thanks," I said as I stepped into the airlock, hoping he could hear me through the helmet.

As the airlock cycled down and the outer hatch slid open, I had to remind myself that this was going to be different from an EVA in space. This would be more like doing steelwork at the top of a tremendously tall skyscraper. If I made a false step I wouldn't simply float away from the ship, I'd plunge screaming to the ground, fifty kilometers below.

"Take it slow and easy," Rodriguez told me. "I'm right here. Hand me your tether before you step out."

I could see his spacesuited form clinging to the handgrips set into the gondola's outer hull, beside the hatch. Both his tethers were clipped to its rungs.

I handed him one end of my right-hand tether. He clipped it a rung beside his own.

"Okay now, just the way we did in the sim. Come on out."

The good thing was we were enveloped in the cloud, so I didn't have to worry about looking down. There was nothing to see out there except a blank yellow-gray limbo. But I could feel the ship shuddering and pitching in the currents of wind.

"Just like rock climbing," Rodriguez said, with an exaggerated heartiness. "Piece of cake."

"When did you do any rock climbing?" I asked as I planted one booted foot on a rung of the ladder.

"Me? Are you kidding? When I get up more than fifty meters I want an airplane surrounding me."

I had never gone rock climbing, either. Risking one's neck for the fun of it has always seemed the height of idiocy to me.

But this was different, I told myself. There was a job to be done. I was making a real contribution to the mission now, not just cowering in my quarters while others did the work.

Still, it was scary. I suppose Rodriguez could've done it all by himself, but long decades of experience dictated that it was far safer to have two people go out together, even if one of them was a neophyte. Besides, with me out there we could cut the time for the inspection almost in half; that in itself made the whole job a lot safer.

In a way, the pressure of the Venusian atmosphere helped us. In space, with nothing outside a spacesuit's fabric but vacuum, a spacesuit tends to balloon up and get stiff. That's why we had the miniature servomotors on the suits' joints and gloves, to assist our muscles in bending and flexing. Even at this high altitude, though, the atmospheric pressure was enough to make it almost easy to move around in the suits. Even the gloves flexed fairly easily; the servomotors of the spiny exoskeleton on the backs of the gloves hardly had to exert themselves at all.

One by one, Rodriguez and I checked the braces and struts that held the gondola to the gas envelope. All the welds seemed solid, to my eyes. Neither of us could find any sign of damage or deterioration. One of the hoses that fed hydrogen from the separator to the envelope seemed a bit looser than Rodriguez liked; he worked on it for several minutes with a wrench from the tools clipped to his harness, dangling from a support strut like a monkey in a banana tree.

As I watched Rodriguez working, I checked the thermometer on the wrist of my suit. To my surprise it read only a few degrees above freezing. Then I remembered that we were still fifty-some kilometers above the ground; on Earth we'd be high above the stratosphere, on the fringe of outer space. Here on Venus we were in the middle of a thick cloud of sulfuric acid droplets. Not too far below us, the atmosphere heated up quickly to several hundred degrees.

Dangling out there in the open reminded me of something but I couldn't put my finger on it until at last I remembered watching a video years ago, when I'd been just a child, about people hang gliding off some seaside cliffs in Hawaii. I had burned with jealousy then, watching them having so much fun while I was stuck in a house almost all the time, too frail to try such an adventure. And too scared, I've got to admit. But here I was, on another world, racing in the wind fifty klicks high!

"That's done," Rodriguez said as he returned the wrench to its place on his belt. But he fumbled it and the wrench dropped out of sight. One instant it was in his hand, then, "Oops!" and it was gone. I realized that's what would happen to me if my tethers failed.

"Is that it?" I asked. "Are we done?"

"I ought to check the envelope for any signs of ablation from the entry heat," Rodriguez said. "You can go back inside."

Without even thinking about it I replied, "No, I'll go with you."

So we clambered slowly up the rungs set into the massive curving bulk of the gas envelope, with that hot wind gushing past us. I knew the atmospheric pressure was too thin up at this altitude to really push us, yet I felt as if I were being nudged, harried, shaken by the wind.

It was slow going, climbing one rung, unclipping one tether and snapping it on a higher rung, then stepping up again and unclipping the other tether. Just like mountain climbers, we never moved a step until we had both tethers locked on safely. I could hear Rodriguez's breathing in my earphones, puffing hard with each step he took.

Duchamp was listening in on everything, of course. But I knew that if we got into trouble there was nothing she or anyone else could do about it in time. It was just Rodriguez and me out here, on our own. It was frightening and kind of exhilarating at the same time.

At last we got to the long catwalk that ran along the top of the envelope. Rodriguez knelt down and activated the switch that raised the flimsy-looking safety rail that ran the length of the metal mesh walkway. Then we fastened our tethers to the rail; it stood waist-high all the way down the catwalk, from nose to tail. A row of cleats projected up from the edge of the walkway, like the bitts on a racing yacht where you tie down the lines from the sails.

"Top of the world," Rodriguez said cheerfully.

"Yeah," I said, my voice definitely shaky.

Together we walked to the bulbous nose of the envelope, where the big heat shield had been connected. I could see the stumps of the rods that had held the shield in place, blackened from the explosive bolts that had sheared them off. Rodriguez bent over and examined the nose region, muttering to himself like a physician thumping a patient's chest during a checkup. Then we walked slowly back toward the tail, him in the lead, our tethers sliding along the safety rail.

I saw it first.

"What's that discoloration?" I asked, pointing.

Rodriguez grunted, then took several steps toward the tail. "Hmm," he mumbled. "Looks like charring, doesn't it?"

I suddenly remembered that these clouds were made of sulfuric acid.

As if he could read my mind, Rodriguez said, "Can't be the sulfuric acid, it doesn't react with the cermet."

"Are you sure?" I asked.

He chuckled. "Don't worry about it. It can't even attack the fabric of your suit."

Very reassuring, I thought. But the charred stains on the cermet skin of the gas envelope were still there.

"Could it be from the entry heat?"

I could sense him nodding inside his helmet. "Some of the heated air must've flowed over the shield and singed the butt end of the envelope a little."

"The sensors didn't record a temperature spike there," I said.

"Might've been too small to notice. If we expand the graph we'll probably see it."

"Is it a problem?"

"Probably not," he said. "But we oughtta pressurize the envelope to make certain it doesn't leak."

I felt my heart sink. "How long will that take?"

He thought before answering. "The better part of a day, I guess."

"Another day lost."

"Worried about Fuchs?" he asked.

"Yes, of course."

"Well, he's likely got problems of his—*Hey!*"

The safety rail alongside Rodriguez suddenly broke away, a whole section of it flying off into the yellowy haze, taking one of his tethers with it. He was yanked off his feet, flailing his arms and legs, the remaining tether anchoring him to the still-standing section of rail, the other one trying to pull him off the ship.

I lunged for him but he was already too far away for me to reach without taking off my own tethers.

"Pull me in!" he yelled, his voice bellowing in my earphones.

"What's happened?" Duchamp asked sharply in my earphones.

I saw him unclip the one tether from his belt. It snapped off into the clouds. I grabbed the other and began hauling him in.

But the railing itself was wobbling, shaky. It was going to tear away in another few seconds, I realized.

"Pull me in!" Rodriguez shouted again.

"What's happening out there?" Duchamp demanded.

I unclipped one of my own tethers and fastened it onto one of the cleats set into the catwalk. Then, with Duchamp jabbering in my earphones, I unclipped Rodriguez's remaining tether before the railing broke off and he went sailing into oblivion.

"What the hell are you doing?" he yelled.

His sudden weight almost tore my arms out of their sockets. Squeezing my eyes shut, I saw stars exploding against the blackness. With gritted teeth, I clumped down onto my knees and used all my strength to clamp the end of his tether to the cleat next to mine.

I saw that the broken end of the railing was fluttering now, shaking loose. And my other tether was still hooked to it. Instead of trying to reach its end I simply unsnapped it from my belt and let it flap loose, then turned back to hauling in Rodriguez's line.

He was pulling himself in as hard as he could. It seemed like an hour, the two of us panting and snorting like a couple of tug-of-war contestants, but he finally planted his boots back on the catwalk. All this time Duchamp was yelling in my earphones, "What is it? What's going on out there?"

"We're okay," Rodriguez gasped at last, down on his hands and knees on the catwalk. For an absurd instant I thought he was going to pull off his helmet and kiss the metal decking.

"You saved my life, Van."

It was the first time he'd called me anything but "Mr. Humphries." It made me feel proud.

Before I could reply, Rodriguez went on, in a slightly sheepish tone, "At first I thought you were going to leave me and go back to the airlock."

I stared at the blank fishbowl of his helmet. "I wouldn't do that, Tom."

"I know," he said, still panting from his exertion and fear. "Now," he added.

DAMAGE ASSESSMENT

Captain Duchamp and Dr. Waller were waiting for us when we came through the airlock. I could hear her demanding questions, muffled by my helmet, directed at Rodriguez.

"What happened out there? What was that about the safety rail?" And finally, "Are you all right?"

Rodriguez started to explain as I lifted my helmet off. Waller took it from my trembling hands and I saw Marguerite hurrying up the passageway toward us.

While we both worked our way out of the spacesuits, Rodriguez gave a clipped but thorough explanation of what had happened to us. Duchamp looked blazingly angry, as if somehow we had caused the trouble for ourselves. I kept glancing at Marguerite, standing behind her mother. So much alike, physically. So strikingly similar in the shape of their faces, the depth of their jet-black eyes, the same height, the same curves of their figures.

Yet where the captain was truculent and demanding, Marguerite looked troubled, distressed—and something else. Something more. I couldn't tell what it was in her eyes; I suppose I subconsciously hoped it was concern for me.

Duchamp and Rodriguez headed for the bridge. Waller went without a word back toward his cubbyhole of an infirmary, leaving Marguerite and me alone by the racks of empty spacesuits.

"Are you all right?" she asked me.

Nodding, I said, "Fine. I think." I held out my hand. "Look, I'm not even shaking anymore."

She laughed, a delightful sound. "You've earned a drink."

We went down to the galley, passing Waller's closet-sized infirmary. It was empty, making me wonder where the doctor might hide himself.

As we took cups of fruit juice and sat on the galley bench, I realized that I did indeed feel fine. Was it Churchill who said that coming through a brush with death concentrates the mind wonderfully?

Marguerite sat beside me and took a sip of juice. "You saved Tom's life," she said.

The look in her eyes wasn't adoring. Far from it. But there was a respect in them that I'd never seen before. It felt terrifically good.

Heroes are supposed to be modest, so I waggled my free hand and said merely, "I just reacted on instinct, I guess."

"Tom would have been killed if you hadn't."

"No, I don't think so. He—"

"He thinks so."

I shrugged. "He would've done the same for me."

She nodded and brought the cup to her lips, her eyes never leaving mine.

I had to say something, so I let my mouth work before my brain did. "Your mother doesn't seem to have a molecule of human kindness in her. I know she's the captain, but she was practically chewing Tom's guts out."

Marguerite almost smiled. "That's the way she reacts when she's frightened. She attacks."

"Frightened? Her? Of what?"

"Tom nearly got killed! Don't you think that scared her? She is human, you know, underneath the stainless steel."

"You mean she really cares about him?"

Her eyes flashed. "Do you think she's sleeping with him merely to keep him satisfied? She's not a whore, you know."

"I . . ." I realized that I had thought precisely that. For once in my life, I kept my mouth shut while I tried to figure out what I should say next.

The speaker in the ceiling blared, "MR. HUMPHRIES WANTED ON THE BRIDGE." Duchamp's voice.

Saved by the call of duty, I thought.

I sat scrunched down on the metal deck plate of the bridge between Duchamp's command chair and Rodriguez's. Willa Yeats, our sensors specialist, was in the chair usually occupied by Riza, the communications tech.

The four of us were staring hard at the main display screen, which showed a graph of the heat load the ship had encountered during entry into the atmosphere.

"No blip," Yeats said, with an *I told you so* tone. She was on the chubby side, moonfaced and pale-skinned, with the kind of dirty-blond hair that some people charitably call sandy.

"There was no sudden burst of heat during the entry flight," she said. "The heat shield performed as designed and the sensors show all heat loads well below maximum allowable levels."

Duchamp scowled at her. "Then what caused the charring on the envelope?"

"And weakened the safety railing?" Rodriguez added.

Yeats shrugged as if it weren't important to her. "I haven't the faintest idea. But it wasn't a pulse of heat, I can tell you that."

She had a very proprietary attitude about the ship's sensing systems. As far as she was concerned, if her sensors didn't show a problem, no problem existed.

Duchamp obviously felt otherwise. The captain looked past me toward Rodriguez. "I suppose we'll have to go out there again and see just what those charring marks are."

Rodriguez nodded glumly. "I suppose."

"I'll go with you," I said. Before either of them could object I added, with a pinch of bravado, "I'm an experienced hand at this, you know."

Duchamp did not look amused, but Rodriguez chuckled and said, "Right. My EVA lifesaver."

"You don't have to do that," Yeats said, obviously disappointed at our obtuseness. "If you simply pressurize the envelope the sensors will tell us if there's a leak."

"And what if we rip the damned envelope wide open?" Duchamp snapped. "Where are we then?"

Yeats looked abashed. She didn't have to answer. We all knew where we'd be if the envelope cracked. There was a set of emergency rockets hooked to the bathysphere; in theory it could serve as an escape pod. But none of us wanted to test that theory. The thought of all eight of us crammed into the tiny iron ball and rocketing up into orbit was far from comforting.

"Inspect the charring," Duchamp said with finality. "Then we can pressurize the envelope."

"Maybe," Rodriguez added, morbidly.

Gripping the arms of their two chairs, I pulled myself up to my feet. "Very well, then, we'd better—"

Marguerite burst into the bridge, nearly bowling me over.

"Life!" she exclaimed, her eyes wide and shining. "There are living organisms in the clouds! Microscopic but multicelled! They're alive, they live in the clouds . . ."

She was babbling so hard I thought she was close to hysteria. Her mother snapped her out of it with a single question.

"You're sure?"

Marguerite took a deep, gulping breath. "I'm positive. They're alive."

Rodriguez said, "I've gotta see this."

I took Marguerite's arm as gently as I could and maneuvered her out into the passageway. Otherwise there was no room on the bridge for Rodriguez to get up from his chair.

We trooped behind Marguerite to her cubbyhole of a lab. As we stopped there I realized Duchamp had also left the bridge to accompany us. We stared at the image from the miniaturized electron microscope displayed on the wall screen. I saw some watery-looking blobs flailing around slowly. They were obviously multicelled; I could see smaller blobs and dividing walls pulsating inside them. Most of them had cilia fringing their outer edges, microscopic oars paddling away constantly. But weakly.

"They're dying in here," Marguerite said, almost mournfully. "It must be the temperature, or maybe the combination of temperature and pressure. It's just not working!"

Straightening up from the microscope's eyepiece, I said to her, "By god, you were right."

"It's a major discovery," Rodriguez congratulated.

"Send this to the IAA at once," Duchamp commanded. "Imagery and every bit of data you have. Get priority for this."

"But I've only—"

"Do you want a Nobel Prize or not?" Duchamp snapped. "Get this data to IAA headquarters *this instant.* Don't wait for Fuchs to get in first."

Marguerite nodded with understanding. For the first time since she'd burst into the bridge she seemed to calm down, come back to reality.

"I'll get Riza to establish a direct link with Geneva," Duchamp went on. "You bang out a written statement, two or three lines will be enough to establish your priority. But do it *now.*"

"Yes," Marguerite said, reaching for her laptop computer. "Right."

We left her there in her lab, bent over the computer keyboard.

Duchamp headed back toward the bridge. Rodriguez and I went toward the airlock, where the spacesuits were stored.

"RIZA," we heard Duchamp's voice over the intercom speakers, "REPORT TO THE BRIDGE AT ONCE." She didn't have to repeat the command; there was no room for doubt or delay in the tone of her voice.

"Bugs in the clouds," Rodriguez said to me, over his shoulder. "Who would've thought you could find anything living in clouds of sulfuric acid?"

"Marguerite did," I answered. "She was certain she'd find living organisms."

"Really?"

I nodded to his back. I had just witnessed a great discovery. Duchamp was right, her daughter would get a special Nobel for this, just like the biologists who discovered the lichen on Mars.

She expected to find living organisms on Venus, I told myself again. Maybe that's the secret of making great discoveries: the stubborn insistence that there's something out there to be discovered, no matter what the others say. Chance favors the prepared mind. Who said that? Some scientist, I thought. Einstein, most likely. Or maybe Freud.

We commandeered Dr. Waller and Willa Yeats to help us into the spacesuits. With his bloodshot eyes watching me intently, Waller hummed quietly as I pulled on my leggings and boots, then wormed into the torso and pushed my arms through the sleeves. I found myself wondering how Marguerite's discovery was going to affect his thesis. I almost laughed aloud, thinking how the doctor's quiet voyage without interruptions had backfired on him.

Two meters away, Willa chattered like a runaway audio machine as she watched Rodriguez get into his suit. They checked out our life support backpacks and made certain all the lines and hoses were properly connected. Then we sealed our helmets.

Rodriguez stepped into the airlock first. I waited for the lock to cycle, my heart revving up until I thought Riza at the comm console on the bridge must be able to hear it through the suit radio. Relax! I commanded myself. You've been outside before. There's nothing to be scared of.

Right. The last time Rodriguez had nearly gotten himself knocked off the ship. I had no desire to go plummeting fifty-some kilometers down to the rock-hard surface of Venus.

The airlock hatch slid open and Rodriguez stepped back among us.

"What's the matter?" I asked. "What's wrong?"

This close, with the ship's interior lighting shining through his bubble helmet, I could see the puzzled, troubled look on his face.

"Got a red light on my head-up." The suit's diagnostic system, which splashed its display onto the helmet's inner surface, showed something was not functioning properly.

"What is it?" I asked.

"Gimme a minute," he snapped back. Then, "Huh . . . it says there was a pressure leak in the suit. Seems okay now, though."

Dr. Waller grasped the situation before I did. "But it went red when you cycled the air out of the airlock?"

"Yeah. Right."

We spent the better part of an hour pumping up the pressure in Rodriguez's suit until it started to balloon. Sure enough, there was a leak in his left shoulder joint. The suit fabric had a resin compound that self-repaired minor leaks, but the joints were cermet covered with plastic.

"It looks frayed," Dr. Waller said, his voice brimming with curiosity. "No, more like it was singed with a flame or some source of heat."

"Damn!" Rodriguez grumbled. "Suit's supposed to be guaranteed."

I remembered the old joke about parachutes: If it doesn't work, bring it back and we'll give you a new one. It was a good thing the suit's diagnostics caught the leak in the airlock. Outside, it could have killed him.

So Rodriguez unfastened his helmet and wriggled out of his suit and put on one of the backup suits. We would have to repair his suit, I thought. We only carried four spares.

Finally he was ready and went through the airlock. No problems with the backup suit. I heard him call me in my helmet earphones, "Okay, Mr. Humphries. Come on through."

I went into the airlock and got that same old feeling of being locked into a coffin when the inner hatch slid shut. The 'lock cycled down—and a red warning light started blinking on the curving face of my helmet, flashing into my eyes like a rocket's red glare.

"Hey, I've got a problem, too," I yelled into my microphone.

The entire EVA excursion was a bust. Both our original suits were leaking and Duchamp decided to scratch the EVA until we could determine what the problem was.

I thought I knew.

BUG FOOD

don't know," Marguerite said, frowning with puzzlement. "It's too soon for me to tell."

Her voice was low, tired. The excitement of her discovery had worn off; now I was presenting her with its horrifying consequences.

We were walking down the passageway from her lab to the galley, where we could sit together in comfort. I was leading the way, for once.

"It can't be a coincidence," I said over my shoulder. "There's got to be a connection."

"That's not necessarily true," she objected.

We reached the galley and I punched the dispenser for a cold cup of juice, then handed it to her. After I got one for myself, I sat beside her on the bench.

"There are bugs out in the clouds," I said.

"Microscopic multicellular creatures, yes," she agreed.

"What do they eat?"

"I don't know! It's going to take some time to find out. I've spent most of the day jury-rigging a cooler for them to live in!"

"What's your best guess?" I demanded.

She ran a hand through her thick dark hair. "Sulfur oxides are the most abundant compounds in the cloud droplets. They must metabolize sulfur in some way."

"Sulfur? How can anything eat sulfur?"

Marguerite jabbed a forefinger at me. "There are bacteria on Earth that metabolize sulfur. I would have thought you'd known that."

I had to grin. "You'd be surprised at how much I don't know."
She smiled back.

I pulled my handheld computer from my pocket and punched
up a list showing the composition of the fibers of our spacesuits. No
sulfur.

"Would they eat any of these materials?" I asked, showing her
the computer's tiny display.

Marguerite shrugged wearily. "It's too soon to know, Van. On
Earth, organisms metabolize a wide range of elements and compounds. Humans need trace amounts of hundreds of different minerals . . ." She took a deep, sighing breath.

"It's got to be the bugs," I said, convinced despite the lack of
evidence. "Nothing else could have eaten through the suits like
that."

"What about the railing? That's made of metal, isn't it?"

I tapped on the handheld. "Cermet," I saw. "A ceramic and
metal composite." Another few taps. "Contains beryllium, boron,
calcium, carbon . . . several other elements."

"Maybe the organisms need trace elements the way we need vitamins," Marguerite suggested.

I went back to the list of suit materials and displayed it alongside the list of the safety rail's composition. Plenty of similarities,
although only the cermet had any measurable amount of sulfur in it,
and not much at that.

Then I realized that both suits had leaked at joints, not the self-
repairing fabric. And the joints were made of cermet, covered with
a thin sprayed-on layer of plastic.

"You've got to find out what they digest," I urged Marguerite.
"It's vitally important!"

"I know," she said, rising to her feet. "I'll get on it right away."

I thought about the charring along the tail end of the gas envelope. "They might be chewing up the shell, too."

"I'll get on it!" she fairly shouted, then started up the passageway back to her lab. She looked as if she were fleeing from me.

So I'm pushing her, I thought. But we've got to know. If those
bugs are eating our spacesuits and the ship itself we've got to get
out of here and fast.

I stood there for a dithering moment, not certain of what I
should do next. What could I do, except prod other people to do the
things that I can't do myself?

I decided to go up to the bridge, but halfway there I bumped into Yeats, who was hurrying down the passageway in the opposite direction.

"Anything new?" I asked.

"All bad," she said as she squirmed past me. Her body felt soft and actually pleasurable as she pressed by. I wondered how a man's gonads could assert themselves even when his brain was telling him he's in deep trouble.

"What is it?" I called after her.

"No time," she shouted back, hurrying even faster. I'd never before seen her move at anything more than a languid stroll.

Shaking my head, in exasperation as much as disbelief, I made my way to the bridge. Duchamp and Rodriguez were both there. Good, I thought.

"We can't pressurize the gas envelope until we can determine its structural integrity," Duchamp was saying, in the kind of stilted cadence that I knew was meant for the ship's log. "The leak rate is small at present, but growing steadily. If it's not stopped it will affect the ship's trim and cause an uncontrollable loss of altitude."

She looked up at me as I stopped in the open hatchway. Jabbing a finger on the chair arm's stud that turned off the recorder, she asked impatiently, "Well?"

"We've got to get out of these clouds," I said. "The bugs out there are eating the ship."

Duchamp arched her brows. "I don't have time for theories. We've developed a leak in the gas envelope. It's minor, but it's growing."

"The shell's leaking?" My voice must have gone up two octaves.

"It's not serious," Rodriguez said quickly.

I turned to him. "We've got to get out of these clouds! You were out there, Tom. The bugs—"

"I make the decisions here," Duchamp snapped.

"Now wait a minute," I said.

Before I could go further, she said, "With all deference to your position as owner of this vessel, Mr. Humphries, I am the captain and I will make the decisions. This isn't a debating society. We're not going to take a vote on the subject."

"We've got to get out of these clouds!" I insisted.

"I totally agree," she said. "As soon as we can repair the leak in the envelope, I intend to go deeper and get below this cloud deck."

"Deeper?" I glanced at Rodriguez, but he was saying nothing.

"Have you forgotten Fuchs? The IAA just sent word that he's descending rapidly toward the clear air below the clouds."

The prize money didn't look all that enticing to me, compared to the very strong possibility that we would all be killed if the bugs chewed away enough of the ship.

Rodriguez spoke up at last. "Mr. Humphries, we can't make an effective decision until we know how badly the gas envelope's been damaged."

"It's really very minor," Duchamp said. But then she added, "At present."

"But it's getting worse," Rodriguez said.

"Slowly," she insisted.

"As long as we stay in these clouds we're going to have colonies of Venusian organisms feasting on our ship's metals and minerals," I retorted hotly.

"This is no time to panic, Mr. Humphries," she said.

I thought it over for half a second. "I could fire you and appoint Tom captain."

"That would be tantamount to mutiny," she snapped.

"Wait," Rodriguez said. "Wait, both of you. Before anybody goes off the deep end, let's repair the envelope and get back in proper condition."

"Do we have time for that?"

Duchamp said coldly, "May I point out that Fuchs is diving deeper while we fiddle around here. If your bugs are eating our ship, why aren't they eating his?"

"What makes you think they're not?"

"I know Lars," she said with a thin smile. "He's no fool. If he thought he was going into more danger by descending he wouldn't go down."

I glanced from her to Rodriguez to Riza, sitting wide-eyed at her comm console, then back to Duchamp.

"All right," I said finally. "I'm going back to the bio lab to help Marguerite determine if the bugs caused the damage to our suits. How long will it take you to repair the leak in the hull?"

"Several hours," Duchamp said.

"Yeats is suiting up now, with Akira. They're going to start the work from inside the shell," Rodriguez said. "It'll be safer that way."

"But they'll still be exposed to the bugs, won't they?" I asked. "I mean, if the outside air is leaking into the shell, the bugs are coming in with it."

Duchamp said flatly, "That's assuming you're right and it's the bugs that damaged your suits."

"You can't let them stay out too long," I insisted. "If the bugs do eat the suits—"

"The fabric is self-repairing," Duchamp said.

"The joints aren't," I pointed out.

There was one quick and dirty way to test whether the bugs were eating the suit material, Marguerite and I decided. I hacked off a small section of the cermet knee joint to my damaged suit to serve as an experimental guinea pig. It wasn't easy; the cermet was tough. I had to scrounge an electric saw from the ship's stores to do the job.

Then I brought it to Marguerite's lab, where she had set up a spare insulated cooler as an incubator for the Venusian organisms.

But when I brought the cermet sample to her, she was downcast.

"They're dying," Marguerite said, as miserable as if it was her own child expiring.

"But I thought—"

"I've tried to duplicate their natural environment as closely as I can," she said, as much to herself as to me. "I've kept the temperature inside the cooler just above freezing, right about where it was in the clouds. I've lowered the air pressure and even sprayed it with extra sulfuric acid. But it's not working! Every sample I take shows them weakening and dying."

I handed her the ragged little square of cermet I'd cut out. "Well, here, get this into the cooler with them and let's see what happens before they all die."

She had done a remarkable job of jury-rigging what had once been a spare cooler unit into a laboratory apparatus. The lid was sealed against air leaks, although there were half a dozen sensor wires and two small tubes going through the sealant into the cooler's interior.

All-in-all, it looked very much like the makeshift contraption that it was, the kind of thing that scientists call a kloodge. I once heard of such devices being named after someone named Rube Goldberg, but I never found out why.

Looking worried, Marguerite deftly sliced my cermet sample into hair-thin slivers with a diamond saw, then inserted half of them into the cooler through one of the tubes.

"What are you doing with a diamond saw?" I asked.

That made her smile. "What are you doing without one?" she countered.

"Huh?"

"I had hoped we'd pick up samples of Venusian rock. The saw can slice thin specimens for the microscope."

"Oh, of course," I said. I knew that; I simply didn't think of it at that moment.

"I would have thought," she went on, "that a planetary scientist would have this kind of equipment with him for geological investigations."

I felt my brow furrow. "Come to think of it, I believe I do."

She laughed. "I know you do, Van. I stole this from the equipment stores that you had marked for your use."

She'd been teasing me! To hide my embarrassment, I bent over and peered into the narrow little window in the cooler's lid. All I could see inside was a grayish fog.

"That's actual Venusian air inside there?" I asked.

"Yes," she replied, frowning slightly. "I was drawing it off from the main probe we've been using for the nephelometers and mass spectrometers."

I caught her accent on the past tense. "Was?"

She made an irritated huffing sound, very much like her mother. "The probes have been shut down. Captain's orders."

"Why would she . . . ?" Then I realized, "She doesn't want to run the risk of having the bugs break loose inside the ship."

"That's right," Marguerite said. "So I've got this sample and that's all. No replacements."

"And yet she acted as if she thought I was crazy when I told her the bugs ate the suits and the railing."

Marguerite shrugged as if it weren't important to her. But it was to me.

"She's a first-class hypocrite, your mother," I said, with some heat.

"She's the ship's captain," Marguerite answered stiffly. "She might think your idea's crazy, but the safety of this ship and crew is her responsibility and she's decided not to take any unnecessary risks."

I could see the logic in that. But still . . . "She's sent Yeats and Sakamoto out to repair the shell."

"That's necessary. There's no getting around it."

"Perhaps," I admitted reluctantly. "But she shouldn't let them stay out too long."

"How long is too long?"

"How long were Rodriguez and I outside? Both our suits were damaged."

Marguerite nodded. "I'm sure she's watching their readouts."

The timer on the cooler chimed, ending our conversation. Marguerite drew out a sample of the Venusian air, rich with sulfuric acid droplets and the organisms that lived in them. Quickly she prepared a microscope slide and put the display onto the screen of the laptop computer she had plugged into the electron microscope.

"They're recovering!" she said happily. "Look at how vigorously they're swimming around!"

"But where's the suit material?" I asked.

She turned from the laptop to stare at me. "It's gone. They've digested the cermet. It's food for them."

DEADLY DECISIONS

raced along the passageway to the bridge. Duchamp was in her command chair, as usual. I could hear Yeats's voice, puffing with exertion:

". . . going a lot slower than I expected. This is tough work, let me tell you."

"You've got to bring them back inside!" I said to Duchamp. "Now! Before the bugs kill them."

Rodriguez was not on the bridge. Riza Kolodny, at the comm console, looked at me and then the captain and finally turned her face resolutely to her screens, not wishing to get involved.

Before Duchamp could reply, I said, "The bugs eat cermet. It's like caviar to them, for god's sake!"

She leveled a hard stare at me. "You have proof of this?"

"Your daughter has the proof in her lab. It's true! Now get those two people back inside here!"

Duchamp looked as if she would have preferred to slice my throat, but she touched the communications stud on her chair arm and said crisply, "Yeats, Sakamoto, come back inside. Now. That's an order."

"Okay by me," Yeats said, with obvious relief. She was not accustomed to much physical exertion, clearly.

"Yes, Captain," said Sakamoto, so even and unemotional that the words might just as well have come from a computer.

Duchamp called Rodriguez back to the bridge and Marguerite came up from her lab. She and I crowded the hatchway as she displayed her experiment's results on the main screen. Within minutes, Dr. Waller, Yeats, and Sakamoto came up, making a real crowd in the passageway. I could feel them pressing me, pushing their sweaty bodies against me. My heart was racing; I felt queasy and breathless at the same time.

"I'm still checking air samples for the signature of the cermet materials," Marguerite was telling her mother, "but so far there is none. The organisms seem to have digested every molecule."

If this information rattled our steely-eyed captain, she did not show it. Turning to Rodriguez, she said, "What do you think?"

Rodriguez's brow was already deeply creased with worry. "We've got a catch-twenty-two situation here. We need to repair the shell or sink, but if we go outside the bugs will degrade our suits so badly we'll be at risk of total suit failure."

"You mean death," I said. "Someone could get killed."

He nodded, a little sheepishly, I thought.

Marguerite added, "Meanwhile the organisms are eating away at the shell. They could damage it to the point where . . . where . . ." She drew in her breath, realizing that if the shell failed, we would all go plunging into the depths of the atmosphere.

Is this what happened to Alex? I wondered. Was his ship devoured by these hungry alien bugs?

Then I realized that the organisms weren't alien at all. This was their natural environment. We were the aliens, the invaders. Maybe they were instinctively fighting against us, trying to drive us out of their world.

Nonsense! I told myself. They're just bugs. Microbes. They can't think. They can't act in an organized way.

I hoped.

Duchamp looked straight at me as she said, "This is what we're going to do. Each of us will take turns at repairing the shell. None of us will stay outside longer than Tom and Mr. Humphries did."

"But our suits were damaged," I objected.

"We will keep the excursions shorter than your EVA was," Duchamp said. "Short enough to get back inside before the bugs can damage the suits."

From behind me Yeats grumbled, "Then it's a race to see if we can plug the leaks faster than the bugs can eat through the shell."

Duchamp nodded. "In the meantime, I intend to go deeper."

"Deeper?" Riza blurted.

"There's a layer of clear air between this cloud deck and the next, about five kilometers below us," Duchamp said.

Rodriguez grinned humorlessly. "I get it. No clouds, no bugs."

I could feel Yeats start to object, but before she could the captain went on, "Willa, I want you to estimate the maximum time we can work in the atmosphere out there before we run into danger of suit damage."

"Yes, Captain," Yeats said glumly.

"Tom, you take the conn. Mr. Humphries and I will take the first shift. Everyone else will take a turn at the work," she hesitated a moment, looking past me. At her daughter, I supposed. "Everyone except Dr. Waller," she said.

I felt the doctor's gusting breath of appreciation on the back of my neck. He was in no physical condition for an EVA, true enough. But I worried about Marguerite; she had no training for this sort of thing. Or did she?

Duchamp got up from her command chair. Everyone in the passageway flattened themselves out to make room for her to pass by. I followed her, fighting down the fears that were shaking me.

In a sense, of course, none of us had any training for this sort of EVA. Virtual reality simulations were all well and good, as far as they went, but nothing could prepare you for being outside in those clouds, with the wind gusting against you and the ship shuddering and bucking like a living animal. Add to that the knowledge that the bugs were chewing away on your suit . . . it scared me down to my bladder. I felt jittery, almost light-headed.

But it had to be done, and I wasn't going to back away from my share of the responsibility.

It wasn't easy, that's for certain. Even though we worked inside the shell, grappling along its curving bulkhead, dangling from the structural support beams by our suit tethers was far more demanding than climbing mountains.

And it was dark inside the shell. Outside, even in the clouds, there was always a yellowish-gray glow, a sullen twilight that was bright enough to see by, once your eyes adjusted to it. Inside the shell we had to work by the light of our helmet lamps, which didn't go far. Their glow was swallowed up by the yellowish haze pervading the shell's interior. It reminded me of descriptions of London fogs from long ages ago, groping along in the misty gloom.

"Riza," I heard Duchamp call over the suit radio, "get Dr. Waller to put together as many lamps as he can take from stores. We need working lights in here."

"Yes, Captain," came the comm tech's reply.

Despite everything, I had to smile inside my helmet. Duchamp wasn't allowing our ship's doctor to sit idly while the rest of us worked.

We sprayed epoxy all across the shell's enormous interior. And it was huge in there; the vast curving space seemed measureless, infinite. The darkness swallowed the pitiful light from our helmet lamps. I began to think about Jonah in the belly of the whale or Fuchida exploring the endless caverns inside Olympus Mons on Mars.

There was no way to know precisely where the leaks were; the shell wasn't instrumented for that and the leaks weren't so big that you could see daylight through them. We concentrated our spraying on the aft end of the envelope, naturally, because that's where we had seen the charring.

Duchamp and I spent an exhausting half hour in the shell, then Rodriguez and Marguerite replaced us. Duchamp would have had the entire crew in there at once and gotten the job over with, except for the fact that we had only two epoxy spray guns aboard.

So, two by two, the crew worked hour after hour on sealing the leaks in the gas envelope. Exhausted as I was, I took another turn, this time with Sakamoto. Rodriguez actually went out three times. So did Yeats, grumbling every inch of the way.

When my second tour was over, I half collapsed on the deck just inside the airlock, too weary even to think about peeling off my suit. I simply lifted off my helmet and sat there, not even taking off my backpack. It wasn't only the physical exertion, although just about every muscle in my body was shrieking. It was the mental strain, the knowledge that the ship was in trouble, serious trouble, and we were all in danger.

Sakamoto, standing above me, pulled his helmet off and gave me a rare smile. "Work is the curse of the drinking man," he said, then started to get out of his suit. I couldn't have been more surprised if he had sprouted wings and flown back to Earth.

Finally it was finished. I had crawled into my berth to inject an enzyme shot into my arm when the intercom blared, a scant six centimeters from my ear, "MR. HUMPHRIES TO THE BRIDGE, PLEASE."

Bleary-eyed, I finished the injection, then slid out of the berth and padded in my stocking feet toward the bridge, not even bothering to smooth out the wrinkles in my coveralls. Somewhere in the back of my mind I knew I was sweaty and far from sweet-smelling, but I didn't care.

Duchamp was in her command chair, as flinty as ever. Rodriguez must have been grabbing a few winks of sleep. Yeats was at the comm console.

As soon as I ducked through the hatch, Duchamp said to Yeats, "Tell him, Willa."

Looking far from jocular, Yeats said, "I have good news and bad news. Which do you want to hear first?"

"The good news," I snapped.

"We stopped the leak," she said. But her face did not show any sign of joy. "The ship is back in trim and we've broken out of the clouds into the clear air."

"We're pumping out the air we took in during the descent through the cloud deck," Duchamp added, "and replacing it with the ambient air, outside."

I nodded. "Good."

"Now the bad news," said Willa. "Every one of our suits is damaged, at least slightly. Not one of them would pass a safety inspection. They all leak."

"That means we can't go EVA?"

"Not until we repair them," Yeats said cheerlessly.

"All right," I said. "That's not as bad as it might have been."

"The question is," Duchamp said, "will there be more bugs in the deeper cloud decks?"

"It gets awfully hot down there," I said. "More than two hundred degrees Celsius. And that's thirty, forty kilometers above the surface."

"So you don't think we'll have any problems from the bugs?"

"We should ask Marguerite. She's the biologist."

Duchamp nodded. "I've already asked her. She said she doesn't know. No one knows."

I heard myself say, "There can't be anything living at such high temperatures! It gets up to four hundred degrees and more at the surface."

"I wonder," she murmured.

From being a total skeptic about the bugs, the captain had swung to suspecting them to be lurking in the next cloud deck, waiting to devour us.

Then another thought struck me. "Where's Fuchs? Has he gone down into the second cloud deck yet?"

She nodded. "No. He appears to be hovering in this clear area, just as we are, according to the latest word from the IAA."

"I wonder if he : . ." Duchamp and the bridge wavered out of focus, as if someone had twisted a camera lens the wrong way. I put out a hand to grasp the edge of the hatchway, my knees suddenly rubbery.

I heard someone ask, "What's the matter?"

Everything was spinning madly around me. "I feel kind of woozy," I heard my own voice say.

That's the last thing I remember.

COLLAPSE

opened my eyes to see Dr. Waller, Rodriguez, and Marguerite bending over me. They all looked grim, worried.

"Do you know where you are?" Waller asked, the lilt in his voice flattened by concern.

I looked past their intent faces and saw medical monitors, green worms crawling across their screens. I heard them beeping softly and smelled antiseptic.

"The infirmary," I said. My voice was little more than a croak.

"Good!" Dr. Waller said approvingly. "Full consciousness and awareness. That's very good."

Marguerite looked relieved. I suppose Rodriguez did too.

It didn't take much mental acumen to see that I was lying on the infirmary's one bed. Located back at the tail of the gondola, the infirmary was the only place on *Hesperos* with space enough for people to stand at bedside. Our bunks were nothing more than horizontal closets.

"What happened?" I asked, still not feeling strong enough to do anything but lie there on my back.

"Your anemia came up and bit you," said Dr. Waller.

I glanced at Marguerite. I had never mentioned my condition to her, but apparently Waller had told her everything while I was unconscious. She looked concerned, but not surprised. Rodriguez had known about it, of course, but he still looked very worried, his forehead wrinkled like corduroy.

"But I've been taking my shots," I said weakly.

"And engaging in more physical exertion than you have ever

done in your life, I should think," said the doctor cheerily. "The hard work caught up with you."

"A few hours . . . ?"

"It was enough. More than enough."

Talk about depressing news. Here I thought I was doing my share, working alongside Rodriguez and even Duchamp, facing the same dangers and duties as the rest of the crew. And my god-cursed anemia strikes me down, shows everybody that I'm a weakling, a useless burden to them all. Father was right: I'm the runt of the litter, in every imaginable way.

I felt like crying, but I held myself together as Waller fussed around me and Rodriguez left, half apologizing that he had to get back to the bridge.

"We're getting ready to enter the next cloud deck," he said. "We decided just to skim in and out, take some samples of the cloud droplets and see if there are any bugs in 'em."

I nodded weakly. "Good thinking."

"It was Dee's idea—Captain Duchamp's."

I turned my head slightly toward Marguerite. "It's a good thing we brought a biologist along with us," I said.

She smiled.

Rodriguez grabbed my hand and said, "You take care of yourself now, Van. Do what the doc tells you."

"Sure," I agreed. "Why not?"

He left. Marguerite remained at my bedside.

"How long will I have to stay here?" I asked Dr. Waller.

"Only a few hours, I should think," he replied, his face as somber as ever. "I'm running diagnostics on your red cell count and oxygen transfer to your vital organs. It shouldn't take very long."

I pushed myself up to a sitting position, expecting to feel my head spin. Instead, it felt fine. Marguerite hurriedly pushed up my pillows so I could sit back against them.

"You make a good nurse," I said to her. I actually felt pretty good. My voice was coming back to its normal strength.

"You scared the wits out of everyone, collapsing like that."

"How should I have collapsed?" I joked.

"Humor!" said Dr. Waller. "That's good. A certain sign of recovery."

"There's nothing really wrong with me," I said, "except this damned anemia."

"Yes, that's true. Except for the anemia you are in fine physical condition. But as Mercutio says to Romeo, the wound may not be as deep as a well or as wide as a church door but 'tis enough, 'twill serve."

Marguerite understood. "You have to be careful, Van. Your condition could become serious if you don't take proper care of yourself."

There was a part of me that was perfectly happy to be lying on a sickbed and having her looking so concerned about me. But how long would that last? I asked myself. I've got to get up and be active. I don't want pity. I want respect.

"What you're telling me," I said sharply to the doctor, "is that if I have to do any serious physical exertion I should take extra enzyme shots."

He nodded, but pointed out glumly, "We only have a fixed amount of the enzyme supply in our medical stores. And we do *not* have the equipment or resources to make more. Your supply is more than adequate for normal usage, with a healthy additional amount in reserve. But still—you should pace yourself more carefully than you have today, Mr. Humphries."

"Yes. Of course. Now, when can I get up and back to my work?"

He glanced at the monitors lining the infirmary's wall. "In two hours, more or less."

"Two hours," I said. "Fine."

I was actually on my feet much sooner. I had to be.

Marguerite brought me a handheld computer to work with while I sat in the infirmary bed, waiting for Dr. Waller to finish his diagnostics. He left the infirmary for a while, humming to himself as usual. I checked with IAA headquarters back in Geneva and, some ten minutes later, got a reply that Fuchs had entered the second cloud deck more than an hour earlier.

He was ahead of us again. And apparently he had suffered no damage from the bugs that had attacked our gas envelope. Why not? Was his *Lucifer* made of different materials? Had he been damaged and then repaired his ship more quickly than we had been able to do?

Sitting there staring at the printed IAA report, I began to wonder what would happen if Fuchs actually did get to the surface first and recovered Alex's remains. He'd get Father's ten billion in prize money and I'd be penniless. Totally cut off. I wouldn't even be able to afford my home in Majorca, let alone the apartments I maintained here and there.

I wondered what my friends would do. Oh, they'd put up with me for a while, I supposed. After all, it would be egregiously impolite to just drop me immediately because I'd lost all my money. But sooner or later they'd turn away from me. I was under no illusions about that. They were my friends because I was their social equal or—many of them—because I had the money to support their operas and plays and dabbles at scientific research.

Penniless, I would also become friendless quite quickly. Gwyneth couldn't afford to stay with me; she needed someone to pay her bills.

What would Marguerite do? I asked myself. I couldn't see her abandoning me because I'd become poor. On the other hand, I couldn't see her supporting me, either. We didn't know each other that well, really, and besides, I doubted that she had the kind of money it would take to support me.

That's what was whirling through my mind as I sat on the infirmary's lone bed, waiting for Dr. Waller to come back from wherever he'd disappeared to and give me permission to get—

The ship lurched. I mean, *lurched*. We had bounced and shuddered when we were in the superrotation winds up higher, but once we'd sunk down to the clear region between the first and second cloud decks the air pressure had become so thick that the winds were smothered and our ride had become glassy smooth.

But now everything suddenly tilted so badly that I was nearly thrown off the bed. I clutched its edges like a child riding a coaster down a snowy hillside.

Through the closed hatch of the infirmary I could hear alarm bells blaring and the thundering slams of other hatches swinging shut automatically.

The infirmary seemed to sway. For an instant I thought I was getting dizzy again, but then I remembered that I was in the tail section of the gondola and it was the gondola itself that was swinging beneath the gas envelope. Somewhere an alarm siren started shrieking.

I jumped out of bed, glad that Waller hadn't stripped off my coveralls. The floor beneath me tilted again, this time pointing downward like an airplane starting to dive. Something behind me crashed to the floor.

"ALL HANDS STRAP IN!" the intercom blared. Great advice.

I had to clutch the bed to keep from sliding down to the infirmary hatch.

The hatch swung outward and banged against the bulkhead. Dr. Waller was on the other side, his red-rimmed eyes wide with terror.

"We're sinking!" he screamed. "The gas shell has collapsed!"

SINKING

For what seemed like a century and a quarter I just hung there, clutching the bed while alarms hooted and wailed all along the gondola, staring at Waller as he held on to the hatch frame with both his hands. In the hollow of my stomach I could feel the ship dropping.

"ALL HANDS TO THE AIRLOCK," the intercom speakers blared. "GET INTO YOUR SPACESUITS. *NOW*."

It was Duchamp's voice, sharp as a surgeon's scalpel, not panicked but certainly urgent enough to make me move.

"Come on," I said as I stumbled past Waller. He seemed frozen, mouth gaping, eyes goggling, unwilling or unable to let go of the hatch frame and start downhill toward the airlock.

I grabbed his shoulder and shook him, hard. "Come on!" I shouted at him. "You heard the captain. That means everybody!"

"But I can't breathe in my spacesuit!" he said, nearly in tears. "The one time I had to use it I nearly suffocated!"

"That doesn't matter now," I said, yanking him free. "Come with me, I'll show you how to do it."

The ship seemed to straighten out somewhat as we staggered and weaved down the passageway. We had to manually open hatches every few meters. They automatically slammed shut behind us. At least the alarms had been silenced; their wailing was enough to scare you into cardiac fibrillation.

Rodriguez was already at the airlock, helping Riza Kolodny into her suit. The other two technicians crowded behind him, getting their own suits on.

"Where's Marguerite?" I asked him.

"I don't know. Maybe up at the bridge with her mother," he said, without looking up from his work.

"These suits are all damaged," I said, holding out the sleeve of my own. The elbow joint was obviously blackened, as if singed by a flame.

"You want to go with no suit at all?" Rodriguez snapped.

Waller moaned. I thought he was going to faint, but then I saw a growing stain across the crotch of his coveralls. The doctor had wet himself.

"What's happened?" I demanded. "What are we going to do?"

Still checking Riza's backpack, Rodriguez said, "Damned shell cracked open. We're losing buoyancy. Can't keep the ship in trim."

"So what—"

"We're going to the descent module, use it in the escape pod mode. Ride it up to orbit and hope *Truax* can find us."

"Then why do we need the suits?"

"Whole front section of the gondola's leaking like a frickin' sieve," Rodriguez said, his voice edged with fear-driven tension. "If the leaks reach the bridge before we can get everybody into the pod . . ."

He didn't have to finish the sentence. I got the picture.

I helped Dr. Waller into his suit before starting to put mine on. The ship kept dipping and then rising, making my insides feel as if I were on an elevator that couldn't make up its mind. Waller seemed almost in shock, hardly able to move his arms and legs, his eyes staring blankly, his mouth sagging open and gasping like a fish. It flashed through my mind that he had the only undamaged suit on board; all the others had developed leaks, even the spares.

By the time I got my own suit on, Marguerite and her mother were still nowhere in sight. I clomped down the slanting passageway toward the bridge.

"Where're you going?" Rodriguez yelled after me. "I gotta check you out!"

"I'll be back in a few minutes," I called back, shouting so they could hear me through the helmet. "Get everybody to the escape pod. I'll catch up with you there."

Checking out the suit was nothing more than busywork at this stage of the game. They all leaked to some degree, we all knew that. But we only needed them for the few minutes it would take to clamber into the bathysphere and dog its hatch shut.

I wasn't going without Marguerite, though. What was she doing? Where was she?

Her lab was empty. The ship seemed to straighten out again; the passageway even angled upward a little, for a moment.

I pushed on to the bridge. There they were, both of them.

". . . can't stay here," Marguerite was saying, pleading really.

"Someone's got to keep the ship on as even a keel as possible," Duchamp said, her eyes fixed on the main display screen. Sitting in her command chair, she had a laptop across her knees, her fingers working the keys like a concert pianist playing a cadenza.

"But you'll—"

I broke into their argument. "Everyone's suited up and headed for the escape pod."

Duchamp looked sharply at me. Then, with a single curt nod, she turned her gaze to her daughter. "Get into your suit. Now."

"Not until you come with me," Marguerite said.

The picture is etched in my mind. The two of them, as identical as copies from a blueprint except for their ages, glaring at each other with identical stubborn intensity.

"Both of you, get your suits on," I said, trying to sound commanding. "The others are waiting for you."

The ship lurched and heaved wildly. My stomach tried to jump into my throat. I grabbed the hatch frame for support. Marguerite, standing beside her mother, staggered and fell into Rodriguez's chair with an ungainly thump.

Duchamp turned back to the main screen, banging on the laptop's keyboard again.

"We're losing the last bit of buoyancy we have," she said, not taking her eyes off the screen. I saw that it displayed a schematic of the ship's maneuvering engines.

"Then we've got to get out!" I snapped.

"Someone's got to keep the ship from diving deeper," Duchamp said. "If I don't work the engines, we'll sink like a stone."

"What about the regular trim program?" I demanded.

She barked out a single harsh "Hah!"

I said, "The computer should be able—"

"There's no way the computer can keep this bucket on a halfway even keel without manual input," Duchamp said. "No way."

"But—"

"I'm only barely managing to hold her at altitude now."

As if to prove her words, the ship dipped down again, then popped sharply upward. I thought I could hear moaning from up forward, where the rest of the crew was waiting for us.

"It's the captain's duty," Duchamp said, glancing at me. Then she smiled thinly. "I know you didn't want me for the job, but I take the position seriously."

"You'll kill yourself!" Marguerite shrieked.

"Get her off the bridge," Duchamp said to me.

Still clinging to the rim of the hatch, I thought swiftly. "I'll make you a deal."

She arched one brow at me.

"I'll get Marguerite suited up and bring your suit here to the bridge. Then you suit up and come forward to the escape pod."

She nodded.

"Come on," I said to Marguerite.

"No," she snapped. Turning to her mother, she said, "Not without you."

Duchamp gave her a look I'd never seen on her face before. Instead of her usual stern, flint-hard stare, the captain's features softened, her eyes glistened.

"Marguerite, go with him. I'll be all right. I'm really not suicidal."

Before Marguerite could reply I grasped her wrist and literally hauled her out of the chair, off the bridge, and down the slanting passageway to the airlock where the suits were stored.

"She'll kill herself," Marguerite said in a throaty whisper, as if talking to herself. Over and over, as I helped her into her spacesuit, she repeated it. "She'll kill herself."

"I won't let her," I said, with a bravado I didn't really feel. "I'll get her into her suit and up to the escape pod if I have to carry her."

I only said it to make Marguerite feel better, and I'm certain that she knew it. But she let me help her put the suit on and check out the backpack.

I took the least-used-looking of the remaining suits and we staggered back up the passageway toward the bridge again. The ship's pitching and reeling seemed to calm down somewhat. Maybe we had hit a region of calm, stable air, or we were finally in equilibrium with the air pressure outside.

We got to the bridge and I offered to run the auxiliary engines while the captain got into her suit.

She gave me a pitying smile. "If I had a few days to teach you . . ."

"Then let's get Rodriguez up here," I suggested.

"I'll go get him," Marguerite said.

Raising her hand to stop her daughter, Duchamp said, "The intercom still works, dear."

"Then call him," I commanded.

She seemed to think it over for half a second, then tapped the intercom stud on her chair arm. Before she could say anything, however, the message light on the comm console flashed on.

Duchamp called out to the computer, "Answer incoming call."

Lars Fuchs's heavy, jowly face filled the screen, glowering angrily.

"I picked up your distress call," he said flatly, with no preamble.

Hesperos's command computer was programmed to beam out a distress call when safety limits were exceeded. The instant the alarms began going off and the compartment hatches were automatically shut, the computer must have started calling for help. In ten minutes or so, I realized, we would be getting inquiries from the IAA on Earth: standard safety procedure for all spaceflights.

"We're preparing to abandon ship," Duchamp said. "Buoyancy's gone."

"Stand by," Fuchs said, the expression on his face somewhere between annoyed and exasperated. "I'm approaching you at maximum speed. You can transfer to *Lucifer*."

Strangely, Duchamp's expression softened. "You don't have to do that, Lars."

He remained irritated. "The hell I don't. IAA regulations require any craft receiving a distress signal to render all possible assistance, remember?"

"But you can't—"

"If I don't come to your aid," he snapped, "the IAA will hang me out to dry. They'd love to make an example of me. And they won't hang me by my neck, either."

I studied his face there on the bridge's main display screen, at least two times bigger than life. There was anger there, plenty of it. Bitterness deeper than I'd ever seen before. Lars Fuchs looked like a man who'd been forced to make hard decisions all his life, iron-hard decisions that had cost him all hope for ease and joy. Joyless. That's was it. That was what made his face so different from anyone I had ever seen before. There was no trace of joy in him. Not even a glimmer that a moment of happiness would ever touch him. He had abandoned all hope of joy, long years ago.

It took all of two or three seconds for me to come to that conclusion. In that time Duchamp made her decision.

"We only have a few minutes before the gondola starts breaking up, Lars."

"Get into your suits. *Lucifer* will be within transfer range in . . ." his eyes shifted to some data screen out of camera range . . . "twelve minutes."

Duchamp drew in a deep breath, then nodded once. "All right. We'll be ready."

"I'll be there," Fuchs said grimly. Strangely, I thought I heard just a hint of softening in his voice.

CATASTROPHE

Rodriguez came back to the bridge and took over the conn while Duchamp struggled into her suit. She had to step out into the passageway, there was no room on the bridge to do it. Marguerite and I both checked her out. The suit had several slow leaks in it but would be good for at least an hour.

"We'll be aboard *Lucifer* by then," Duchamp said from inside her helmet. We were close enough so I could see her face through the tinted bubble. She wore the same hard-edged expression she usually showed. No trace of fear or even apprehension. If any of this frightened or worried her, it certainly did not show in her face.

"We'd better be," Marguerite said, barely loud enough for me to hear her. All our suits leaked a little, thanks to the bugs. I was grateful that we didn't have to pressurize them; Venus's atmospheric pressure at this altitude was slightly higher than Earth's.

It seemed to me that the ship's pitching and bobbing smoothed out somewhat under Rodriguez's hand, but that may have simply been my imagination—or the fact that I liked him a lot better than our hard-bitten captain.

Even so, the metal structure of the gondola began to groan and screech like a beast in pain. I stood out in the passageway and fought down the urge to scream out my own terror.

Marguerite didn't seem to be at all afraid. In fact, she knotted her brows in puzzlement. "Why are the bugs attacking just the one area of the gondola and not the entire structure?"

"What makes you think they're not?" I managed to gulp out.

"The only part being damaged so far is the section between airlock and the nose area," she said.

"How can you be sure of that?"

She jabbed a gloved thumb back toward the bridge. "Look at the life support display. That's the only section that's lost air pressure."

She was right, I saw as I peered at the life support screen. Now I furrowed my own brows. Was there any difference between that section and the rest of the gondola? I tried to remember the schematics and blueprints I had studied long months ago, when we were building *Hesperos*.

That entire section was designed around the airlock. Maybe the bugs were chewing on the plastics that we used as sealant for the outer airlock hatch?

"Is the inner airlock hatch sealed shut?" I called in to Rodriguez, who was still in the command chair.

Without stopping to think why I asked it, he flicked his eyes to the "Christmas tree" display of lights that indicated the status of the ship's various systems. Most of the lights were bright, dangerous red now.

"No," he said, shaking his head inside his helmet.

"Seal it," I said.

"It won't do any good," Marguerite said. "If the bugs have eroded the outer hatch's sealant, they'll do the same for the inner hatch."

"It might buy us a few minutes' time," I countered.

Duchamp, fully suited up now, agreed with me. "Every second counts."

She went into the bridge and repossessed her command chair. Rodriguez came out into the passageway with us. He had to squeeze a little to get through the hatch with his suit on.

"All right," Rodriguez said. "Helmets sealed. Let's go up forward with the others."

"What about her?" Marguerite asked.

Duchamp replied, "I'm needed here. I'll leave the bridge when *Lucifer* starts taking us aboard."

"I'll stay here with you, then," Marguerite said.

"No," I said. "You're coming with us."

She had to turn her entire body toward me for me to see the flat refusal in her eyes. The same rigidly adamant expression I had seen so often on her mother's face; the same stubborn set of the jaw.

"Captain," I called out, "give the order."

"He's right, *ma petite*," Duchamp said, in a voice softer and lower than I had ever heard from her. "You've got—"

The message light began blinking again and Duchamp stopped in midsentence. "Answer incoming call."

Fuchs's bleakly somber face filled the comm screen. "I'll be maneuvering beneath your ship in four minutes. I won't be able to hold station for more than a minute or so. You'll have to be prepared to jump."

"Not below us!" Duchamp cried, startled. "We're breaking up. Debris could damage you."

Fuchs glowered. "Do your suits have maneuvering propulsion units?"

"No."

"Then if you can't fly, the only way to get from *Hesperos* to *Lucifer* is to drop." His wide slash of a mouth twitched briefly in what might have been the ghost of a smile. "Like Lucifer himself, you'll have to fall."

Jump from *Hesperos* onto *Lucifer?* The idea turned my innards to water. How could we do that? How close could Fuchs bring his ship to ours? I should have added maneuvering units to the spacesuits, I never thought of it back on Earth. We weren't planning any EVA work except for the transfer from *Truax,* and we had the cable trolley for that. Rodriguez should've known that we'd need maneuvering jets in an emergency. Somebody should've thought that far ahead.

"Three minutes, ten seconds," Fuchs said. "Be prepared to jump." The comm screen went blank.

"Come on," Rodriguez said, nudging my shoulder to point me up the passageway.

Marguerite still hesitated.

"Go with them," Duchamp commanded. "I'll hold this bucket on course for another two minutes and then come along."

"You won't do anything foolish?" Marguerite asked, in a tiny voice.

Duchamp gave her a disgusted look. "The idea that the captain goes down with his ship was a piece of male machismo. I'm not afflicted with the curse of testosterone, believe me."

Before either of them could say anything more, I put my gloved hand on Marguerite's backpack and shoved her—gently—along the passageway.

I never found out if shutting the inner airlock hatch slowed down the bugs' destruction or not. As it turned out, it didn't matter, one way or the other.

The rest of the crew, Dr. Waller and the three technicians, were up in the nose section, already inside the descent module. As far as they knew we were still planning to use the 'sphere in its escape pod mode and rocket up into orbit, to be picked up by *Truax*.

As we hurried up the passageway toward the hatch that opened onto the airlock area, Rodriguez again ordered us to seal our helmets. "Air pressure's okay on the other side of the hatch," he said, "but there's probably a lot of Venusian air mixed in with our own. You wouldn't enjoy breathing sulfuric acid fumes."

I checked my helmet seal six times in the few steps it took us to reach the closed hatch.

Meanwhile, Rodriguez used his suit radio to tell Waller and the techs to get out of the pod and into the airlock section. They asked why, of course.

"We're going to transfer to Fuchs's ship, *Lucifer*," he said.

"How?" I heard Riza Kolodny's adenoidal voice in my helmet earphones.

"You'll see," Rodriguez said, like a father who doesn't have the time to explain.

We got the hatch open and looked into the airlock section. It seemed safe enough. I couldn't see holes in the structure. But the metal seemed to be groaning again, and I could hear thin, high-pitched whistling noises, like air blowing through a lot of pinholes.

Rodriguez stepped through the hatch first, then Marguerite. I followed. The ship lurched again and I put out my hand to rest it on the sturdy metal frame of the airlock hatch, to steady myself.

Just then the hatch on the opposite end of the section swung back. Four spacesuited figures huddled there, anonymous in their bulky suits and reflective bubble helmets.

Duchamp's voice crackled in my earphones, "Fuchs is about a hundred meters below us and moving up closer. Connect your tethers to each other and start down to his ship."

Rodriguez said, "Right," then pointed at me. "You first, Mr. Humphries."

I had to swallow several times before I could answer him, "All right. Then Marguerite."

"Yessir," Rodriguez said.

There was no need to cycle the airlock. I just slid its inner hatch open and stepped inside, then punched the button that opened the outer hatch. Nothing happened. For a moment I just stood there like a fool, hearing the wind whistling around me, feeling trapped.

"Use the manual override!" Rodriguez said impatiently.

"Right," I answered, trying to recover some shred of dignity.

I tugged at the wheel and the outer hatch slowly, stubbornly inched open. Rodriguez handed me the first few tethers, clipped together end for end. He and Marguerite were hurriedly snapping the others onto one another.

"Attach the free end to a ladder rung," he told me.

"Right," I said again. It was the only word I could think of.

I leaned out the open airlock hatch to attach the tether and what I saw made me giddy with fright.

We were scudding along high above an endless layer of sickly yellowish clouds, billowing and undulating like a thing alive. And then the huge curving bulk of *Lucifer* slid in below us, so near that I thought we would crash together in a collision that would kill us all.

"*Lucifer* is on-station," I heard Duchamp's voice in my ear-phones.

Fuchs's ship seemed enormous, much bigger than ours. It was drawing nearer, slowly but noticeably closing the gap between us. Gasping for breath, I clicked the end of the tether on to the nearest ladder rung. Then I realized that Rodriguez was right behind me, feeding tether line out the hatch, past my booted feet. I watched the tether snake down toward the top of *Lucifer*'s bulbous shell, dropping like an impossibly thin line of string down, down, down and still not reaching the walkway that ran the length of the ship's gas envelope.

I suddenly realized that I hadn't taken any of my enzyme supply with me. Even if we made it to *Lucifer* I'd be without the medicine I needed to live.

Then *Hesperos* dipped drunkenly and the gondola groaned again like a man dying in agony. I happened to glance along the outer surface and saw that the metal was streaked with ugly dark smudges that ran from the nose to the airlock hatch and even beyond. I could see the thin metal skin cracking along those dark streaks.

Marguerite and Rodriguez were behind me, the four other spacesuited figures—Waller and the technicians—stood huddled on the other side of the airlock hatch. They were all waiting impatiently for me to start the descent toward *Lucifer* and safety. I stood frozen at the lip of the open hatch. Clambering down that dangling tether certainly did not look at all safe to me.

The groaning rose in pitch until it was like a screeching of fingernails on a chalkboard. I pulled my head back inside the airlock chamber, panting as if I'd run a thousand meters.

"She's breaking up!" Rodriguez yelled, so loud that I could hear him through my helmet as well as in my earphones.

Before my eyes, the front section of the gondola tore away with a horrifying grinding, ripping sound, carrying Waller and the technicians with it. They screamed, terrified high-pitched wails that shrieked in my earphones. The front end broke entirely free and flashed past my horrified eyes, tumbling end over end, spilling the spacesuited figures out into the open, empty air.

"Save me!" one of them screamed, a shriek so strained and piercing I couldn't tell which of them uttered it.

I saw a body thump down onto *Lucifer,* below us; it missed the catwalk and slid off into oblivion, howling madly all the time.

I could hardly stand up, my knees were so watery. Rodriguez, pressed in behind me in the airlock, whispered, "Jesus, Mary, and Joseph."

The screams went on and on, like red-hot ice picks jammed into my ears. Even after they stopped, my head rang with their memory.

"They're dead," Rodriguez said, his voice hollow.

"All of them," said Marguerite, quavering, fighting back tears.

"And so will we be," Duchamp's voice crackled, "if we don't get down those tethers *right now.*"

The ship was bucking violently now, heaving up and down in a wild pitching motion. The wind tore at us from the gaping emptiness where the nose of the gondola had been. A ridiculous thought popped into my mind: We didn't need the airlock now; we could jump out of the ship through the jagged open end of the gondola.

I could hear Rodriguez panting hard in my earphones. At least, I assumed it was Rodriguez. Marguerite was there, too, and I thought Duchamp had to be on her way down to us by now.

"Go on!" Rodriguez yelled, as if the suit radios weren't working. "Down the tether."

If I had thought about it for half a millisecond I would have been so terrified I'd have frozen up, paralyzed with fear. But there wasn't any time for that. I grabbed the tether with both gloved hands.

"The servomotors will hold you," Rodriguez said. "Loop your boots in the line to take some of the load off your arms. Like circus acrobats."

I made a clumsy try at it, but only managed to tangle the tether around one ankle. The servomotors on the backs of the gloves clamped my fingers on the line, sure enough. All I had to worry about was making a mistake and letting go of the blasted line with both hands at the same time.

Down I went, hand over hand.

FALLING

t was hard work, clambering down that swaying, slithering line of connected tethers. Drenched in cold sweat, my heart hammering in my ears, I tried to clamp my boots around the line to take some of the strain off my arms but that was a clumsy failure. I inched down the line, my powered gloves clamping and unclamping slowly, like an arthritic old man's hands.

Lucifer seemed to be a thousand kilometers below me. I could see the end of the connected tethers dangling a good ten meters or more above the catwalk that ran the length of the ship's gas envelope. It looked like a hundred meters, to me. A thousand. When I got to the end of the line I'd have to jump for it.

If I made it to the end of the line.

And all the while I crawled down the length of tethers I kept hearing the terrified, agonized screams of the crewmen who fell to their deaths. My mind kept replaying that long, wailing, "Save meee!" over and over again. What would I scream if I missed the ship and plunged down into the fiery depths of inescapable death?

"Send the others down." It was Fuchs's heavy, harsh voice in my earphones. "Don't wait. Get started *now.*"

"No," Marguerite said. I could sense her struggling, hear her breathing hard. "Wait . . ."

But Rodriguez said firmly, "No time for waiting. Now!"

I looked up and saw another figure start down the tethers. In the spacesuit it was impossible to tell who it was, but I figured it had to be Marguerite.

She was coming down the line a lot faster than I was, her boots gripping the tether expertly. Had she told me she'd done mountain climbing? I couldn't remember. Foolish thought, at that particular moment.

I tried to go faster and damned near killed myself. Let go of the line with one hand, then missed my next grab for it while my other hand was opening. There's a delay built into the servomotors that control the gloves' exoskeletons; you move your fingers and the motors resist a little, then kick in. My glove's fingers were opening, loosening my grip on the tether, when I desperately wanted them to tighten again.

There I was, one hand flailing free and the other letting go of my grip on the tether. If I hadn't been so scared I would've thrown up.

I lunged for the line with my free hand, caught it, and closed my fingers as fast and hard as I could. I thought I heard the servomotors whining furiously, although that must have been my imagination, since I'd never heard them before through the suit and helmet.

I hung there by one hand, all my weight on that arm and shoulder, for what seemed like an hour or two. Then I clasped the tether with my other hand, took the deepest breath I'd ever made in my life, and started down the tether again.

"Where's my mother?" I heard Marguerite's fear-filled voice in my earphones.

"She's on her way," Rodriguez answered.

But when I looked up I saw only their two figures clambering down the tether. *Hesperos* was a wreck, jouncing and shuddering above us, falling apart. The gas envelope was cracked like an overcooked egg. The gondola was half gone, its front end torn away, new cracks zigzagging along its length even as I watched. The bugs from the clouds must have made a home for themselves in the ship's metal structure.

Well, I thought grimly, they'll all roast to death when she loses her last bit of buoyancy and plunges into the broiling heat below.

Then I caught a vision of *Hesperos* crashing into *Lucifer,* and wondered how long Fuchs would keep his ship hovering below us.

"Hurry it up!" he called, as if he could read my thoughts.

Marguerite was sobbing openly; I could hear her over the suit radio. Rodriguez had gone silent except for his hard panting as he worked his way down the tether. They were both getting close to me.

And Duchamp was still in the ship. On the bridge, I realized, working to hold the shattered *Hesperos* in place long enough for us to make it to safety. But what about her safety?

"Captain Duchamp," I called, surprised that my voice worked

at all. "Leave the bridge and come down the safety tether. That's an order."

No response.

"Mother!" Marguerite sobbed. "Mama!"

She wasn't coming. I knew it with the certainty of religious revelation. Duchamp was staying on the bridge, fighting to hold the battered wreck of *Hesperos* in place long enough for us to make it to safety. Giving her life to save us. To save her daughter, really. I doubt that she cared a rat's hiccup for the rest of us. Maybe she had some feelings for Rodriguez. Certainly not for me.

And then I was at the end of the tether line. I dangled there, swaying giddily, my boots swinging in empty air. The broad expanse of *Lucifer*'s gas envelope still seemed an awfully long way off. A long drop.

All my weight, including the weight of my spacesuit and backpack, was hanging from my hands. I could feel the bones of my upper arms being pulled slowly, agonizingly, out of my shoulder sockets, like a man on a rack. I couldn't hang on for long.

Then I saw three spacesuited figures climbing slowly up the curving flank of the massive shell. They looked like toys, like tiny dolls, and I realized just how much bigger *Lucifer* was than *Hesperos*. Enormously bigger.

Which meant that it was also much farther away than I had first guessed. It wasn't ten meters below me; it must have been more like a hundred meters. I couldn't survive a jump that long. No one could.

I looked up. Through my bubble helmet I saw Marguerite and Rodriguez coming down the line toward me, almost on top of me.

"What now?" I asked Rodriguez. "It's too far to jump."

Before he could answer, Fuchs's voice grated in my earphones. "I'm bringing *Lucifer* up close enough for you to reach. I can't keep her in position for long, so when I say jump, you either jump or be damned. Understand me?"

"Understood," Rodriguez said.

"Okay."

The broad back of *Lucifer* rose toward us, slowly moving closer. The three spacesuited figures were on the catwalk now, laying out long coils of tethers between them.

We were getting tantalizingly close, but each time I thought we were within a safe jumping distance *Hesperos* bobbed up or sideways and we were jerked away from *Lucifer*. My arms were blazing with pain. I could hear Rodriguez mumbling in Spanish, perhaps a prayer. More likely some choice curses.

I looked up again and saw that *Hesperos* was barely holding together. The gondola was cracked in a hundred places, the gas shell above it was missing pieces like an uncompleted jigsaw puzzle.

The only thing in our favor was that the air was thick enough down at this level to be relatively calm. Relatively. *Hesperos* was still jouncing and fluttering like a leaf in a strong breeze.

Marguerite's sobbing seemed to have stopped. I supposed that she finally understood her mother was not coming and there was nothing she could do about it. There would be plenty of time to mourn after we had saved our own necks, I thought. When your own life is on the line, as ours were, you worry about your own skin and save your sentiment for everyone else for later.

"Now!" Fuchs's command shattered my pointless musings.

I was still dangling a tremendous distance from *Lucifer*'s catwalk, my shoulders and arms screaming in agony from the strain.

"Now, dammit!" he roared. *"Jump!"*

I let go. For a dizzying instant it felt as if I hung in midair, not moving at all. By the time I realized I was falling I thudded down onto the curving hull of *Lucifer*'s envelope with a bang that knocked the breath out of my lungs.

I had missed the catwalk and the men waiting to help me by several meters. I felt myself sliding along the curve of the shell, my arms and legs scrabbling to find a grip, a handhold, anything to stop me from sliding off into the oblivion below. Nothing. The shell's skin was smooth as polished marble.

In my earphones I heard a sort of howling noise, a strangled wail that yowled in my ears like some primitive animal's shriek. It went on and on without letup. I couldn't hear anything else, nothing except that agonized howl.

If *Lucifer* had been as small as *Hesperos* I would have slid off the shell and plunged into the thick hot clouds kilometers beneath me. I sometimes wonder if I would have been roasted to death as I fell deeper into the blistering hot atmosphere, or crushed like an eggshell by the tremendous pressure.

Instead, Fuchs's crewmen saved me. One of them jumped off the catwalk and slid on the rump of his suit to my side and grabbed me firmly. Even through the yowling noise in my earphones I could hear him grunt painfully when his tether stopped us both. Then he looped the extra tether he carried with him around my shoulders.

I was shaking so hard inside my suit that it took me three tries before I could control my legs well enough to follow Fuchs's crewman back up to the catwalk, where his companion already had his arms wrapped around Marguerite. I found out later that she had dropped neatly onto the catwalk and not even lost her balance.

I was on my hands and knees, gasping from the efforts of the last few minutes. My shoulders felt as if someone had ripped my arms out of them. I was beyond pain; I was numb, wooden.

The catwalk seemed to shift beneath me, tossing me onto my side. I looked up and saw *Hesperos* breaking apart, big chunks of the envelope tearing away, the gondola splitting along its length.

Marguerite screamed. I saw the line of tethers flapping wildly, empty.

Raising myself painfully to my knees, I looked for Rodriguez. He was nowhere in sight.

"Where's Rodriguez?" I demanded.

No one answered.

I looked directly at Marguerite, who had disengaged herself from the crewmen who'd held her.

"Where's Tom?" I screamed.

I couldn't see her face inside the helmet, but sensed her shaking her head. "He jumped after me . . ."

"What happened to him?" I climbed to my feet shakily.

Fuchs's voice answered in my earphones. "The third person in your party jumped too late. I had to jink the ship sideways to avoid the debris falling from *Hesperos*. He missed us and fell into the clouds."

LARS FUCHS

That was the long, terrified scream I heard in my earphones: Rodriguez falling, falling all that long way down to his death.

I stayed there on my knees until two of the crewmen yanked me up roughly by the armpits of my suit. I could hardly breathe. Every muscle and tendon in my body was in agony. And Rodriguez was dead.

Marguerite said softly, "My mother . . ." She sounded exhausted, as drained physically and emotionally as I felt.

I looked up. *Hesperos* was gone. No sign of the ship. Nothing above us but swirling sickly yellow-gray clouds. Nothing below us but more of the same. Duchamp, Rodriguez, Waller, and the three technicians—all dead. Venus had killed them. But then I realized that was not true. It was my fault. I had brought them to this hellish world. I had made them intrude into this place where humans were never meant to be. I had killed them.

And myself as well, I thought. Without my medication I'd be dead soon enough.

Tethered together like mountain climbers, we slowly, painfully, climbed down the ladder rungs set into the curving hull of *Lucifer*'s gas envelope to an airlock hatch set into its side. My heart lurched in my chest: I saw dark streaks smearing the length of the envelope, just as they had stained *Hesperos*'s shell.

The bugs were chewing on *Lucifer*'s hull, too. It was only a matter of time before this ship would break up just as *Hesperos* did. We were all going to die. There was no way around it.

"Move it!" Fuchs's voice snarled in my earphones. "Stop your dawdling."

What difference did it make, I thought as I ducked through the airlock hatch.

My eyes widened with surprise when I saw that the inner hatch of the airlock was wide open. I hesitated a fraction of a second, only to be shoved unceremoniously by the crewman behind me through the inner hatch and into the compartment beyond it.

"I'm sealing the lock in ten seconds," Fuchs snapped. "Whoever's still outside will *stay* outside, understand me?"

As I stumbled into the compartment beyond the airlock chamber I half turned and saw, beyond the crewman's shoulder, Marguerite's spacesuited figure. The crewmen's suits were different from our own; their fabric was a dirty grayish silver, the suits looked bulkier, stiffer, and their helmets were the old-fashioned kind, mostly opaque with a faceplate visor, instead of the fishbowl bubbles that we wore.

The crewman behind Marguerite turned and pulled the airlock hatch shut.

"Stand by for emergency dive," Fuchs commanded. "Prepare to fill forward buoyancy tanks." Then he lapsed into a guttural foreign tongue; it sounded oriental to me, not Japanese but something like it. He was talking to someone on his bridge, obviously. Or perhaps to a voice-activated computer. Not to us.

One of the crewmen dogged the airlock's inner hatch shut while the other clomped in his heavy boots to what looked like a pump. I heard it start chugging, but then its noise faded. And my spacesuit stiffened and ballooned noticeably. Finally it clicked into place. They had used this compartment as an adjunct to their airlock, so we could all get into the ship quickly rather than squeezing through the regular airlock chamber one at a time. Clever.

But as we waited for the compartment to fill with normal, breathable air, I realized that there were only two crewmen with us. I had seen three when we were descending toward *Lucifer*. Did they deliberately leave the other one outside? Even if Fuchs was ruthless enough to give such a command, what kind of men were these to obey it?

The pump's chugging grew louder again, which meant the compartment was filling to normal air pressure. At last the crewman near it checked a readout on the wrist of his suit, then bent awkwardly and shut off the pump. He and his partner raised the visors of their helmets. They were both Asians, I saw.

I unsealed my helmet and lifted it off my head. Marguerite just stood there, unmoving, so I went to her and took off her helmet. Her eyes were dry now, but they were staring, unfocused, seeing into the past, sorrowful beyond telling.

I almost told her not to regret her mother's death because we would be dead ourselves soon enough. But I didn't have the guts; actually I didn't even have the strength to open my mouth.

"Get your suits off," Fuchs's voice commanded, "and toss them out the airlock. They're contaminated. Get rid of 'em, quick."

I blinked with surprise. Apparently Fuchs was not resigned to dying.

With the crewmen helping, Marguerite and I slipped out of the backpacks and peeled off our spacesuits. The crewmen were silent, blank-faced, and quite efficient. They got rid of our suits quickly.

"Follow the crewmen up to the bridge," Fuchs said, as soon as our suits went out the airlock. I realized he must be watching us, although I couldn't see a camera anywhere in the blank-walled compartment.

One of the crewmen opened the hatch and gestured us through into a long passageway. We were still inside *Lucifer's* gas envelope, I knew. Apparently the vessel had no gondola dangling below; the living and working quarters were built inside the envelope.

The vessel was at least double the size of *Hesperos,* that was easy to see. Marguerite and I, escorted by the two silent, impassive crewmen, walked down the long passageway to a ladder. Peering up and down its well, I saw that it went two decks down and two more up.

We climbed up. One of the crewmen went before me, the other stayed behind Marguerite. I got the unpleasant feeling that they were behaving like guards escorting a pair of prisoners.

The bridge was spacious, with four crew stations and a commodious command chair. Which was empty when we arrived there. All four of the personnel present were Asians, three of them women. No one said a word.

"Can any of you speak English?" I asked.

"When they have to," came Fuchs's voice, from behind me.

I turned. He was standing in an open hatch off to one side of the bridge, framed by its metal edges.

Lars Fuchs had a thick, wide physique, built low to the ground. A barrel chest, short heavy arms and legs, but those arms looked as strong as a gorilla's. He seemed powerful, ferocious, like a black bear or some other wild animal with strong, sharp claws and a short temper. His face was set in an unpleasant, sardonic scowl, almost a sneer.

"So you're Martin Humphries's son, are you?"

I nodded as he stepped closer to me. Surprisingly, he was slightly shorter than I, only a hair or so, but definitely shorter. Yet he seemed enormous to me. He was wearing a black collarless shirt with short sleeves, and black baggy trousers tucked into calf-length black boots that hadn't been polished in a long time.

He came up to me, looked me up and down as if I were a specimen in a zoo, his wide thin lips turned down in an expression of pure loathing. I tried to meet his gaze, but what I saw in his eyes made me shudder inwardly. His eyes were like ice, cold and Arctic blue. This man would kill me if it suited him. Or anyone else.

He looked past me, toward Marguerite, and for just the flash of a second his expression changed completely. I saw surprise on his face, shock, really. His jaw dropped open, his eyes went wide.

But only for a fraction of a second. He closed his mouth with a click of his teeth and let out a long, snorting breath. But his eyes remained fixed on her.

"Marguerite Duchamp, is it?"

"Yes," she said in a voice barely strong enough to be heard.

"You look just like your mother did, twenty years ago." Fuchs's own voice was lower, softer.

"You knew her then?" Marguerite asked, trembling.

He nodded wordlessly.

"She . . . she's dead," Marguerite said.

"I know." He turned back toward me. "This idiot killed her."

Neither Marguerite nor I said a word of objection.

Fuchs clasped his hands behind his back. "Or rather, his father did." He stepped closer to me again, like an inquisitor examining his prisoner. "This was all your father's idea, wasn't it?"

Anger flared through me. "You jumped at the chance to take his prize money quickly enough," I said.

Fuchs grinned at me mirthlessly. "True enough. I certainly did."

For a long moment we stood almost touching noses while Marguerite and the silent crew members watched us.

Fuchs pulled away. "Very well," he said, pointing a finger at Marguerite. "You'll be my guest aboard this vessel. Welcome, Ms. Duchamp."

He made a ludicrous little bow, with a smile that—on his heavy, fleshy face—was little less than grisly.

Then he turned back to me again. "And you, Mr. Humphries, can replace the man I lost rescuing you."

"Lost?" I blurted. "You lost a man?"

With a disgusted look, Fuchs explained, "My first mate was overcome by an unexpected burst of courage. When your vessel began to break up and the third man on your line started to fall away, my heroic first mate tried to reach him."

"What happened?" Marguerite asked.

"What do you think? He jumped off the catwalk and grabbed the falling man's ankles, trusting that his own tether would keep him safely anchored to my ship."

"Those tethers are supposed to be able to take tons of stress," I heard myself say.

"And so they do," Fuchs said, sarcastically. "But the railing it was clipped to doesn't. It ripped away and the two of them fell out of sight. Damned fool!"

That was Rodriguez that the first mate tried to save. The two of them plunged screaming to their deaths.

Fuchs jabbed a stubby finger at the technician sitting to the right of his command chair. She was a large, bulky woman with a round, flat face that looked to me almost like an Eskimo's.

"So you, Amarjagal, are now first mate."

He pointed again, this time at the wiry young man sitting next to her. "Nodon, you take over as propulsion engineer."

Both of them nodded. Don't they ever say anything? I wondered. Has Fuchs hired a crew of mutes?

He turned back to me. "I have a vacancy now for the position of communications technician," he said, almost politely. "You are now my comm tech, Mr. Humphries. That's an undemanding job, just right for someone with your lack of skills."

"Now just a minute, Fuchs, I'm not—"

He kicked me in my left shin, so hard that my leg exploded with pain. As I howled and bent over to clutch my leg I saw his right fist swinging at me. There was nothing I could do. He punched me in the kidney, my body spasmed upright and his left fist smashed into the side of my face. I crashed onto the deck so hard my vision went double.

Fuchs towered over me, fists on his hips, a leering smile on his jowly face. "Hurts, doesn't it?"

I couldn't speak. All I could do was writhe and groan from the pain.

"That's your first lesson in ship's discipline," he said, his voice flat and hard. "You will address me as *sir* or *Captain Fuchs*. And you will follow my orders quickly and correctly. Understand me?"

I was seeing flares of pain flashing before my eyes. I couldn't talk, couldn't even breathe.

Fuchs kicked me in the ribs. "Understand me?"

I nodded. Weakly.

He grunted, satisfied, and strode away. "Find a berth for our new comm tech," he ordered the crewmen.

I was awash with pain. But what hurt most was that Marguerite had just stood there, immobile as a statue. Even as I lay there on the deck she made no move to come to my aid.

I was losing consciousness. I could hardly breathe. As the world faded, the last thing I saw was Fuchs crooking a finger at Marguerite.

"You come with me," he said to her.

She followed him.

Everything went dark.

NIGHTMARE

I was walking in my garden outside the house on Majorca, Gwyneth at my side. She was wearing something light and so filmy that I could see her naked body beneath the sheer fabric. It billowed when the breeze blew in off the sea.

A mosquito whined past my ear. I became very annoyed. Genetic controls were supposed to have eliminated insect pests from the island. What had happened? What had gone wrong?

I turned to ask Gwyneth but it wasn't her anymore. It was Marguerite walking beside me in her spacesuit, of all things, carrying its helmet in her gloved hands. Wearing a spacesuit in my beautiful garden by the Mediterranean on a sunny springtime afternoon.

I smiled at her and she smiled back. But then I felt the sting of an insect on my bare arm and slapped at it.

"You've got to get into your suit," she said to me, and it was her mother instead of Marguerite.

"But you're dead," I said, not believing my eyes.

"So will you be if you don't get into your suit!" she replied urgently.

"But I don't have a suit," I said. "Why would I keep a suit here?"

Instead of answering she pointed a gloved hand out to the Mediterranean. The sea was boiling away, bubbling and gurgling with a mad hissing roar as immense clouds of steam rose into a sky that suddenly was no longer blue, but a grayish sort of sickly yellow. An immense glowering light was burning through the clouds, the Sun so close and huge and hot that it was like an all-devouring god come to destroy everything it touched.

"Quickly!" she yelled. I couldn't tell if it was Marguerite or her mother. She was putting on the helmet of her spacesuit.

I turned frantically, searching the garden for my suit. All I found was the beautiful flowers and vines, withering, browning, bursting into flames all around me.

And the insects were crawling all over me, biting, eating my flesh, burrowing into my skin, and chewing on my innards. I could feel them gnawing away inside me and when I tried to scream no sound came out. They had devoured even my voice.

But I heard others screaming. The long, screeching, terrified wails of men and women falling, falling through the boiling hot air, wailing, "Save me! Save meeeee!"

DEATH SENTENCE

My eyes snapped open. I lay on the bunk they had put me on, stiff and sore from the beating Fuchs had given me. My quarters consisted of a tiny section of a larger compartment, screened off from six other bunks by a thin plastic shoji-type sliding door.

How long I lay there, I don't know. I was unconscious much of the time. I could hear people moving about and talking in a low, guttural foreign language on the other side of my screen.

I felt terribly weak. Without my regular enzyme shots my red cell count would fall until I sank into a coma and died. Maybe that would be for the best, I thought as I lay there, miserable and alone. No one would care if I died. No one would mourn my death. I meant nothing to anyone. It would make utterly no difference to the world if I left it forever.

"Van?" Marguerite's voice, calling softly from the other side of the shoji screen. I could see her silhouette against the white squares of plastic sheeting.

"Van, are you awake?" she called again.

"Come in," I said, surprised at how strong my voice was. I certainly didn't feel strong, not at all.

She slid the screen back. My bunk was flush against the bulkhead, so she simply stood where she was, out in the common area of what I took to be the crew's quarters. I could see no one else in the compartment; the crew must all be on duty, I thought.

Marguerite was wearing an ill-fitting gray jumpsuit that bagged over her trim frame. She had turned the pants and sleeve cuffs up; they were far too long for her. Her eyes were red; she had been crying. But she was dry-eyed now, and her hair was neatly combed and pulled back from her beautiful face.

"How do you feel?" she asked, almost timidly.

As I looked up at her, I realized that my right eye was swollen almost shut. She bent over me and for a moment I had the inane idea that she was going to kiss me.

No such luck. I reached out to her and she took my hand tenderly in hers. But that's as far as she was willing to go.

"Are you all right?" she asked.

"What difference does it make?" I heard myself say. Whine, almost. "I'll be dead in a few days."

Her hand tightened around mine. "What do you mean? You weren't hurt that badly."

"My enzyme shots. Without them my anemia will kill me."

"Ohhh," she actually groaned. "I had forgotten about your condition."

"My medical supplies were aboard *Hesperos*," I said. "Unless there's an olympic-class biochemist aboard and a warehouse full of pharmaceutical supplies, I'm a dead man."

Marguerite looked truly distressed. "We don't even have a ship's doctor. Fuchs didn't include one in his crew."

"Then he might as well have killed me instead of just humiliating me."

"There must be something we can do!"

"You're a biologist," I said, the faintest tendril of hope flickering within me. "Could you . . . ?"

I let the question dangle between us. Marguerite stared down at me for a long, silent moment. I could see it in her eyes. There was no way she could synthesize the growth hormone I needed. I realized that I didn't know the hormone's chemical formula or even its technical name. I always had people around me like Waller to take care of those details.

God is in the details, I remembered hearing somewhere. Death is in the details, I told myself.

Marguerite broke into my thoughts. "He wants to see you," she said.

"Wants to see me?"

"The captain. Fuchs."

I actually managed to bark out a bitter laugh. "Why? Does he need more punching practice?"

"He sent me to bring you to his quarters. He said you've been resting long enough."

I growled, "So he's making medical diagnoses now. That's why he doesn't need a physician in his crew."

"Can you get up?" Marguerite asked.

"Sure," I said, propping myself on an elbow and then gripping the bunk's edge with both hands to support myself in a sitting position. My head thundered with pain.

Marguerite grasped my shoulders to steady me as I got to my feet. I wanted to slide an arm around her waist but thought better of it.

"I can stand on my own," I said, working hard to keep from moaning. Or collapsing.

Someone had taken my slippers. Marguerite checked the drawers built in under my bunk while I stood there and concentrated on standing erect. The slippers were gone.

So I headed for the hatch barefoot. The metal deck felt reasonably warm.

"See?" I said as we ducked through the hatch and out into the passageway. "Nothing to it."

In truth, I felt better than I had any right to expect. A little woozy, but that might have been nothing more than my imagination. Plenty of aches and stiffness, and my head throbbed with pain. But I made it down the passageway under my own power.

As we reached the ladder that led up to the bridge level I caught a glimpse of myself in the blank face of a display screen set into the bulkhead. My right eye was swollen and discolored, my hair a disheveled mess. I stopped and smoothed my hair into place. I had to hold on to some shred of dignity when I faced Fuchs again.

Up the ladder we went, down another passageway. Then we stopped in front of an accordion-pleated door labeled CAPTAIN.

I squared my shoulders as best as I could and rapped on the metal door frame.

"Enter," came Fuchs's muffled voice.

His quarters were a shock to me. It was only one compartment, but it was spacious enough to contain a real bed, a desk, several comfortable chairs, cabinets, and one entire bulkhead lined with shelves of books. There were even old-fashioned paper books, thick and battered from long use, alongside the cyberbook chips. The floor was carpeted with a large, colorful oriental rug.

Wearing a loose-fitting black tunic over charcoal-gray trousers, Fuchs was standing by what looked like a long picture window, gazing out at the stars. Actually, it was a wall screen, of course.

"The universe," he said, gesturing with one hand toward the panorama of stars. "I never tire of gazing at heaven."

I was gaping at the books, I suppose, because he took a couple of steps toward the shelves and said, "When your ship is your home, you bring the comforts of home along with you."

"Books?" I asked, stupidly.

"What better?" Fuchs countered. "The memory of the human race is there. All the hopes and fears, all the vice and glory, all the loves and hates."

There was one book on his desk, a leather-bound volume that looked as if it were centuries old. I tried to make out the title on its spine, but the lettering was too cracked and faded.

"Now then," Fuchs said crisply, "I want you to spend the rest of the day familiarizing yourself with the communications gear. That's going to be your post from now on."

He spoke as if I had been a member of his crew since day one. As if the beating he had given me on the bridge had never happened.

"It's a fairly standard setup, the comm computer does all the real work," Fuchs went on, digging his hands into the pockets of his tunic. He pulled something out of his tunic pocket and popped it into his mouth. Pills of some sort. Narcotics? I wondered.

"Being comm tech won't put too much of a strain on you," he said, with a sneer. He had forgotten nothing. Neither had I.

"For as long as I live," I said.

His eyes narrowed. "What does that mean?"

"He's ill, Captain," Marguerite said.

"Ill?"

"I have a pernicious anemia that was being controlled by enzyme injections that generated red-cell proliferation," I said, all in a rush. Then I added, "Captain."

Fuchs glanced from me to Marguerite, then back again.

"My pharmaceutical supplies went down with *Hesperos*," I went on. "Unless we return to orbit and rendezvous with *Truax* I'll be dead in a few days."

He huffed. "Really."

"Really," Marguerite said.

Fuchs looked at me intently, chewing on his pills, then paced over to his desk.

"How do I know this isn't some crackbrain fraud that you've cooked up to keep me from winning your father's prize money?"

I almost laughed at him. "Wait a few days and watch me die."

With a shrug, Fuchs said, "Okay. That's what I'll do, then. In the meantime, you'll work the comm console."

"You can't!" Marguerite blurted.

Fuchs leveled a stubby finger at her. "Don't presume that my feelings for your mother will allow you to behave disrespectfully to me. I'm the captain of this vessel and you will *not* tell me what I can and cannot do."

Marguerite drew herself up to her full height, several centimeters taller than either Fuchs or I. Her eyes blazed.

"If you allow Mr. Humphries to die, Captain, I will bring charges of willful murder against you as soon as we reach Earth."

Strangely, he grinned at her. A mirthless, sardonic grin, almost a grimace. "You've got your mother's spirit, sure enough," he said.

Then his normal scowl returned and he said to me, "Report to the comm console. Now!"

Marguerite started to object. "But you—"

Fuchs silenced her with a wave of his hand. "You bring up all the charges you want. We're a long way from Earth, and as long as we're on this vessel my word is the law. Understand me?"

"But he'll die!" Marguerite wailed.

"What of it?" Fuchs said.

Neither Marguerite nor I had an answer for him.

COMM TECH

So I dutifully followed Fuchs to the bridge and sat at the horseshoe-shaped communications console. What choice did I have? I ruefully wondered which hurt more, my bruised face or my bruised ego.

Marguerite came to the bridge also, and just stood near the hatch staring at Fuchs unwaveringly. If she made the man uncomfortable, he gave no outward sign of it. I called up the operations manual for the comm system and concentrated on studying it.

There were two others on the bridge, both silent, stocky, dour-faced Asians. Fuchs had apparently recruited his crew exclusively from the Orient. I started to wonder why. Are they more loyal? Less likely to resent or resist his tyrannical ways? Perhaps they're willing to work for less pay. Or, more likely, they're simply more docile and obedient. I was totally wrong in each of my surmises, but I didn't know it then.

Fuchs had been right about the communications system. If the operations manual was to be believed, the system was quite simple and logically set up. Its own internal computer did most of the work, and it interfaced with the ship's central computer very easily.

I saw on one of the console's screens that there were dozens of messages from *Truax* that had gone unanswered. The communications technicians up there in orbit kept trying to get some answer out of Fuchs, but he refused to speak to them. The messages became demanding, even *Truax*'s captain angrily complaining about Fuchs's silence.

The screen began to blur slightly. I squeezed my eyes shut and when I opened them everything seemed normal again. But I knew that symptom well enough. It was the first sign that I had missed an enzyme injection. Soon there would be others.

Then I heard Fuchs say, "You're not needed here on the bridge. Go to your quarters."

I looked up from my screen and saw that he was speaking to Marguerite, who was still standing by the hatch.

"You have to do something about Mr. Humphries," she said, without taking her eyes off him.

Fuchs glanced at me, his frown deeper than usual. "There's nothing that can be done," he said.

"What about a blood transfusion?"

"Transfusion?"

"If we can't produce the hormone that promotes his red-cell production, then perhaps transfusions of whole blood will keep him alive."

They were discussing me as if I weren't there, as if I were some experimental animal or a specimen in a laboratory. I felt my face burning, and I knew my cheeks must be flame red.

But neither of them was looking at me.

Fuchs barked out a rough laugh. "Do you seriously think any of my crew has a compatible blood type?"

"Perhaps I do," Marguerite said. "Or you."

To my shame, I didn't dare turn around to look at him. I was afraid of him, pure and simple. I expected him to laugh Marguerite's idea to scorn. Or to get angry. Instead, I heard nothing but silence. Neither of the other two crew members raised a murmur. For long moments the only sounds on the bridge were the inescapable background hum of electrical power and the faint beeps from some of the sensor systems.

Marguerite broke the lengthening silence. "I can call *Truax* for his medical records."

"No!" Fuchs snapped. "There will be no communications with *Truax* or anybody else."

"But why?" she asked. "You're beaming your telemetering signal back to the IAA on Earth. Why not—"

"Every vessel is *required* to report its status to Geneva," Fuchs interrupted. "But I'm not required to communicate with anyone else and I'm not going to do it. Nobody's going to get any claim on my prize money. Understand me? Nobody!"

"You can't be serious," Marguerite protested.

Fuchs replied, "The ship's computer has complete medical dossiers on all the crew. There's a medical diagnosis system in the sick bay; it may not be state-of-the-art, but it'll do. When Humphries is finished his watch here on the bridge you can run him through the medical scanners and determine his blood type, then see if anyone aboard matches it."

Marguerite said, "Thank you, Captain," in a tone that was far softer than her previous words.

"Now get off the bridge," Fuchs snapped, as if to make up for the small concession he'd just granted her.

As I returned my full attention to the screens before me, I realized that Fuchs had made his concession to Marguerite, not to me. He actually didn't care if I lived or died, but he had a much different attitude toward her.

A full watch on the bridge was eight hours long, under Fuchs's command. On *Hesperos,* watches had been the more normal four hours, and Duchamp had been lenient about even that, since the ship was so heavily automated.

Lucifer carried a crew of fourteen, I eventually found out. All of them Asians, two-thirds of them men. Only Fuchs's iron discipline kept order among the crew. They did their jobs with a silent efficiency that was almost eerie. There must have been some sexual relationships among them, but I never caught a hint of any. Of course, they were wary about me. I was definitely an outsider among them.

I tried to work the full eight-hour shift at the comm console, tried as earnestly as I could. It wasn't just that I was afraid of Fuchs, although I certainly was terrified of his brutality and strength. But there was something more: my own pride. I hated being considered a weakling, a Runt. I was determined to show Fuchs and all the rest of those silent, watchful Asians that I could do a man's work.

But my body betrayed me. Hardly a full hour into my watch, my vision began to blur again and no amount of blinking or knuckling my eyes could help. It's all right, I told myself. You can still do your job. Stick with it. Hang tough. Futile words. After another little while I grew light-headed, dizzy. The screen before my blurry eyes began to spin around and around. No matter how I commanded my body to behave, things just got worse. I felt weak and nauseous. I knew that I couldn't get up from my chair if I wanted to.

I couldn't breathe. My chest felt as if someone had clamped a vise around it and I couldn't lift my ribs to get air into my lungs. I gasped like a hooked fish.

I swiveled the chair around a little, my vision going gray. The last thing I remember was saying, "Captain, I'm not . . ." Then I slumped out of the chair and sprawled on the deck. Darkness overwhelmed me.

I heard voices from a long, long distance away. They echoed hollowly, as if coming through a tunnel.

And I felt a sudden, sharp, stinging pain on my face. Again. And again.

My eyes cracked open slightly.

"See? He's coming out of it."

It was Fuchs leaning over me, slapping me. Quite methodically he slapped my face, first one cheek, then the other.

"Stop it! Stop it!" someone was yelling. Not me. The only sounds I could make were faint groans.

I tried to raise my arms to protect myself but couldn't. Either I was too weak or my arms were strapped down. I couldn't tell which.

"I'm not hurting him," Fuchs said.

"He needs a transfusion right away." It was Marguerite's voice, concerned, determined.

"You're certain he's not faking?" Fuchs asked. I was trying to open my eyes all the way but the effort was too much for me. I let my head turn and tried to see Marguerite but she wasn't within the range of my vision.

"Look at the monitors!" she said sharply. "He's dying."

Fuchs exhaled a long, sighing breath from deep in his barrel chest, almost like the warning growl a dog makes just before it attacks.

"All right," he said at last. "Let's get it over with."

They were going to let me die, I thought. They were going to stand over my prostrate body and watch me die.

I realized at that moment that no matter how much I philosophized or tried to justify the end of my existence, I did not want to die. Maybe I deserved death. Certainly no one would miss me or grieve over me. Not my father. Not Gwyneth or any of my so-called friends. No one.

But I did not want to die. With every atom of my being I wanted to survive, to be strong, to get up and live.

Instead, my eyes closed again and darkness returned to envelope me totally.

* * *

I must have dreamed. A weird, mixed-up dream it was. Alex was in it. But sometimes he was Rodriguez. Both of them were dead, killed on Venus.

"Don't give up," Alex told me, with his carefree grin. He tousled my hair. "Don't ever give up."

But I was falling, plummeting like a stone through dark roiling clouds that flashed lightning like the strobe lights at a concert. Rodriguez was beside me in his spacesuit, screaming that last primal scream that I had heard when he died.

"Don't give up!" Alex called to me from afar.

"He's already given up," my father's disdainful voice answered. "He's got nothing to live for."

"Yes he does," Alex insisted. "He's got me. And he's got himself. Find me, Van. Find yourself."

I woke up.

I guessed that I was in the sick bay. I was on a thin mattress atop what seemed more like a narrow table than a bed. Medical monitors beeped and clicked all around me. The metal overhead curved low above my eyes.

I felt strong and clear. No blurred vision. No dizziness. I took a deep breath.

"You're awake."

Turning my head, I saw Marguerite standing beside my table. She looked fresh, newly scrubbed. She was wearing a crisp jumpsuit of deep blue that fitted her much better than the shapeless bag she'd been wearing before.

"I'm alive," I said. My throat was dry, but otherwise my voice was almost normal.

"Do you think you can sit up?"

I started to nod, but instead I pulled myself up to a sitting position, no hands.

"How's that?" I asked, marveling that I felt no giddiness at all.

"Fine," said Marguerite. She touched the foot of the table with one finger and the mattress inflated behind me to form a pillow that I could sit back against.

"Would you like something to eat?"

I realized that I felt hungry. Starving, in fact. "Yes, thank you," I said.

Her smile beamed at me. "I'll fix you a tray."

She ducked through the hatch behind her. When I flexed my arms I saw that a plastic bandage had been sprayed onto my left inner elbow. She must have done a blood transfusion.

I looked around. The sick bay was the size of a small closet, crammed with medical sensors. There was no room for a desk or even a chair, only this table I was sitting on. I touched my right cheek. The swelling was down. In the glassy reflection of the nearest display screen, my face looked almost normal.

Marguerite came back with a tray of cold cereal and fruit juice.

"You did a blood transfusion," I said, rather than asked.

Standing beside me, she nodded.

"Who gave the blood?"

"Captain Fuchs did," Marguerite said. The expression on her face was unfathomable: quite serious, like a judge about to sentence a felon to a very long term. But there were other things in her eyes as well.

She looked away from me. "He's the only person on board who has a blood type similar enough to yours."

I chewed on a mouthful of cereal, then swallowed. It tasted bland, pointless. "Maybe it'll give me some of his personality," I muttered.

Marguerite did not smile. "No," she said, "I wouldn't want to see that happen."

Before she could say anything more, Fuchs himself pushed through the hatch. Suddenly the sick bay was overcrowded. I felt distinctly uncomfortable.

But I lifted my chin a notch and said, "Thank you, Captain, for saving my life."

He sneered at me. "I couldn't afford to lose another crewman." Then, gesturing toward Marguerite, he added, "Besides, it wouldn't do to have Ms. Duchamp here accuse me of murder while I'm claiming your father's prize money. It would be just like your father to renege on the prize because I let his son die."

I shook my head. "You don't know my father."

"Don't I?"

"He wouldn't care about my death."

"I didn't say he would," Fuchs corrected. "I said he'd use your death to renege on giving me the prize."

He stressed the word *me* ever so slightly, but enough for us both to hear it. I glanced at Marguerite. She wouldn't meet my eyes.

"How soon can you resume your duties on the bridge?" Fuchs asked gruffly.

Before I could reply, Marguerite said, "He should rest and—"

"I'm ready now," I said, pushing my tray aside.

Fuchs made a sardonic little smile. "My blood must be doing you some good." He looked at his wristwatch. "Jagal's on the comm console at the moment. You can relieve her in two hours."

Before either of us could say anything, Fuchs turned to Marguerite and asked with mock beneficence, "Will that be enough rest and recuperation time for your patient? Never mind answering. It'll have to do."

Looking back at me, he said, "Two hours."

Then he grasped Marguerite's wrist and led her out of the sick bay. He held her possessively, like a man who felt he owned her. Marguerite glanced back over her shoulder at me, but she went with Fuchs without a word of resistance, without a moment of hesitation.

Leaving me sitting there, hot anger welling up in my gut.

WAVERIDER

I served my eight-hour watch on the bridge under Fuchs's sardonic eye. No sign of Marguerite. I should have eaten a bigger meal; I was ravenously hungry, but I gave no outward sign of it—except for an occasional growl from my hollow stomach.

One of the burly, blank-faced Asians relieved me at the end of my stint. I got up and headed for the passageway, determined to find the ship's galley.

But instead Fuchs called to me. "Wait right there, Humphries."

I froze in place.

He shouldered past me and through the hatch. "Follow me," he said, without turning back.

He led me to his quarters, the compartment stuffed with books and comfortable furniture. The bed was neatly made. I wondered where Marguerite was.

"How do you feel?" he asked.

"Hungry," I said.

He nodded, went to his desk, and spoke into the intercom in that Asian language that might have been Japanese.

"Sit down," he said, gesturing to one of the leather-and-chrome chairs in front of the desk. He himself took the creaking swivel chair behind it.

"I've ordered dinner for us. It should be here in a few moments."

"Thank you."

"I wouldn't want you to starve to death on my ship," he said, with just the hint of a malicious smile.

"Where's Marguerite?" I asked.

The hint of a smile disappeared. "Where's Marguerite, *sir,*" he corrected.

"Sir."

"That's better. She's in her quarters, resting."

I began to ask where her quarters were, but before I could get the first words out he jabbed a thumb over his shoulder. "Her quarters are next to mine. It's the most comfortable compartment on the ship, except for this one. And it allows me to keep a close watch on her. Several of the crew members are very attracted to the young lady—not all of them male, either."

"So you're protecting her."

"That's right. None of them will dare try anything as long as they know she's mine."

"Yours? What do you mean?" I saw his face cloud again and quickly added, "Sir."

Before he could reply the door slid open and one of the crewmen carried in a large tray filled with steaming bowls. He parceled out the food between us, putting Fuchs's dinner on his desk and dropping legs from underneath the tray to turn it into a table for me.

I shook my head inwardly at the contradictions I was seeing. Fuchs ran a tightly disciplined ship, yet there were touches of . . . well, luxury was the only word I could think of. He liked his creature comforts, obviously, although he didn't care to extend the same level of amenities to the rest of the crew.

I looked around at the books that filled his shelves: philosophy, history, poetry, fiction by old masters such as Cervantes, Kipling, London, and Steinbeck. Many of the volumes were in languages I did not know.

"Do you approve?" he asked, with a pugnacious air.

I nodded, but heard myself answer, "I prefer more modern writers, Captain."

He snorted with disdain. "I suppose we can dispense with the formalities while we're alone in here. No need to address me as 'captain' or 'sir'—unless someone else is in the room."

"Thank you," I said.

He grunted, almost as if embarrassed by his small concession. Then he pulled a small vial from one of the desk drawers, shook a few tiny yellow pills into his hand, and tossed them into his mouth. Again I wondered if he was a narcotics addict.

I tried to make out the lettering on the spine of the old book on his desk. Its leather cover was cracked and peeling.

"Paradise Lost," he told me. "John Milton."

"I never read it," I confessed.

"Very few have."

That made me feel rather uncomfortable. Fishing around in my memory, I came up with, "Isn't there a line in it that goes, 'Better to reign in Hell than serve in Heaven'?"

Fuchs grimaced. "Everybody knows that one. I prefer:

> Infernal world! And thou, profoundest Hell,
> Receive thy new possessor—one who brings
> A mind not to be changed by place or time.
> The mind is its own place, and in itself
> Can make a Heaven of Hell, a Hell of Heaven."

He spoke with such fervor, such a dark deep-rooted passion, that I was totally taken aback. I didn't know what to say.

"You may borrow it if you wish."

"What?"

"The book. You may borrow it if you'd like to."

My brows must have hiked up to my scalp. Fuchs laughed harshly, "You're surprised at a show of generosity? You're surprised that I'm pleased to have someone aboard with whom I can talk about philosophy or poetry?"

"Frankly, I am surprised, Captain. I had thought that you'd want nothing to do with Martin Humphries's son."

"Ah, but you forget, you have *my* blood in you now. That's an improvement. A vast improvement."

I had no reply for that. Instead, I began, "About Marguerite—"

"Never mind her," he snapped. "Don't you want to know about my *Lucifer*? Aren't you curious about why my ship survived and yours broke apart? Aren't you wondering about where we are and how close we are to your father's prize money?"

"Is that all that interests you, the money?"

"Yes! What else is there? Your father took everything else from me: my career, the company I founded, my reputation, even the woman I loved."

I could see we were moving into dangerous territory, so I tried to change the subject to a safer ground.

"Very well," I said, "tell me about your ship."

He stared at me for a long, wordless moment, gazing blankly, those cold, ice-blue eyes of his seemingly looking through me into another dimension. What was going through his mind I have no way of knowing. His face went as blank as a catatonic's. He must have been revisiting the past, reminding himself of what he had lost, how he had reached this point in space and time. At last his broad, heavy-jowled face regained life; he shook his head slightly, as if clearing it of painful memories.

"Overdesign," he said at last. "That's what you learn when you stake your life on a vessel that's got to carry you across interplanetary distances. Overdesign. That's the lesson I learned out in the Asteroid Belt. Bigger is better. Thick skin is better than thin."

"But the weight penalty—"

He snorted again. "Your problem is that you had that astronaut guiding your hand."

"Rodriguez," I said.

"Yes. He spent his life on scientific excursions to Mars, didn't he? Rode out there on elegant, state-of-the-art spacecraft designed to be as efficient as possible, slimmed down to the least possible gram, worried about every cent of cost and every newton of rocket thrust."

"That's the way spacecraft have to be designed, isn't it?"

"Oh, certainly," Fuchs answered sarcastically. "If you're working with academics and engineers who've never moved their own carcasses farther than the vacation centers on the Moon. They produce highly refined designs, so highly refined that they use the very latest materials, the most sophisticated new systems and equipment they can conceive."

"What's wrong with that?" I asked.

"Nothing, if you're designing the craft for someone else to use. If you're worried about spending the boss's money. If your design philosophy is to give your master a vessel that has the very latest of everything *and* is built at the lowest possible cost. An impossible contradiction, don't you see?"

"Yes, but—"

"But if you're prospecting out among the asteroids," Fuchs went on, overriding my objection, "then you learn pretty quickly that your ship has got to be strong, powerful, with as many redundant systems as you can pack onto it. You're a billion kilometers from anywhere out in the Belt; you're on your own. You can't expect somebody to come out and repair you or bring you a fresh pot of coffee when you run out."

He was enjoying this lecture, I could see. He was smiling with unfeigned pleasure.

"So here we are, you and me, both determined to get to the surface of Venus. You allow your astronaut to design as dainty a vessel as he can, sleek and slick and pared down to a hairsbreadth in every detail. Why? Because that's the way he's always operated. Because his attitude, his training, his whole life has been spent in demanding the most elegant designs the engineers can create."

And we failed, I admitted silently. *Hesperos* broke up and crashed. And *Phosphoros* before her, I finally realized.

"Now me," Fuchs tapped his chest with two fingers of his right hand, "I'm not elegant. I'm a prospector from the Asteroid Belt. A rock rat. I was out there with Gunn and the other pioneers, before your father even dreamed about sticking his grubby fingers into asteroidal mining.

"I saw that the ships that succeeded were the overdesigned, overbuilt, overequipped clunkers that could take a beating and still bring their crews back alive. Now which type of vessel do you think would do better against the . . . uh, *rigors* of the Venusian environment?"

I asked, "Did you suspect that there would be metal-eating organisms in the upper clouds?"

"No. Not for a minute. But I knew that my ship had to have a skin thick enough to take whatever Venus could dish out. Not a cockleshell like yours."

"The bugs are eating away at your hull, too, aren't they?"

He waved a hand. "Not anymore. We're so deep into the second cloud deck that the outside temperature is rising to well over a hundred degrees Celsius: the boiling point of water." He made a sardonic smile. "The bugs are roasting nicely."

"And there aren't any other organisms at this level?"

"I've assigned Marguerite to sample the clouds. So far, no signs of bugs. I suspect that the hotter it gets out there, the less likely that anything could live in it."

I nodded agreement. He spoke on and on about the superior design of *Lucifer* and how well the ship was holding up to the constantly increasing pressure and high temperature of the atmosphere outside the hull.

"In another ten or twelve hours we'll break out below the clouds into clear air. Then we can begin the search for what's left of *Phosphoros.*"

"And my brother's body," I mumbled.

"Yes," he said. "I'm looking forward to seeing your father's face when he has to hand me that ten billion. That should be something worth waiting for!" He chortled with unalloyed glee.

His laughter was cut short. The ship lurched as if some giant hand had slapped it sideways. My dinner bowls clattered off the tray-table and onto the carpeted floor. I nearly slid off my chair. An alarm started hooting.

Fuchs gripped the arms of his swivel chair, his face turning into blind rage. He pounded a fist on the phone keyboard and roared something in that Asian language the crew used. I could not understand the words but easily recognized the tone: "What the hell's happening?"

A high-pitched, frightened voice replied in a rapid staccato over the keening of the alarm.

Fuchs jumped out of his chair. The deck was slanting noticeably as he came around the desk. "Come with me," he said grimly.

We staggered along the passageway, walking uphill the few steps it took to reach the bridge. The alarm's wail cut off, but the deck beneath our feet continued to buck and toss.

Fuchs went straight to his command chair. The other crew stations were occupied, so I stood by the hatch, holding on to its rim. Marguerite came up behind me, and I slid an arm around her waist to steady her without thinking about it.

The bridge's main screen showed a bewilderingly rapid flow of graphs, sharply curving lines in many different colors laid out over a gridwork of lines.

Fuchs spat out an order and the screen cleared momentarily. Then a computer-enhanced image came up that made no sense to me. It showed a circle with a dot off to one side and pulsing rings of light flowing outward from it, like the ripples made in a pond when you throw a stone into the water.

"Subsolar point," Fuchs muttered. "Even down at this level."

I understood what he meant. Venus turns so slowly on its axis that the spot on the planet directly beneath the Sun stays at "high noon" for more than seven hours at a time. The atmosphere beneath that subsolar point heats up tremendously, as if a blowtorch were blazing away at it hour after hour.

That terrible heating is what drives the superrotation winds, high up in the Venusian atmosphere, where the air is thin enough for winds of four hundred kilometers per hour to race around the planet. Lower down, where the atmosphere is much thicker, such winds are damped down.

But not completely, we were finding. Like sluggish ripples in a thick, soupy pond, there were waves flowing out from the subsolar point even at the depth to which *Lucifer* had already penetrated.

We were being tossed along that wave front, like a surfer caught

on a gigantic curl, driven across the planet like a very tiny leaf
caught in a very large, deliberate, slow but inexorable wave.

While I stood there, gripping the hatch frame with one hand
and Marguerite with the other, Fuchs battled to right the ship and
break it free of the wave that was blowing us halfway around Venus.

The crew, for once, were not impassive. As Fuchs rattled out
orders, their faces showed grim intent, even the wide eyes and gaping mouths of fear.

Fuchs took his eyes off the screens for a moment and saw Marguerite and me standing there, hanging on while *Lucifer* bobbed
and pitched in the grip of the massive wave.

"The engines are useless," he said to us. "Like trying to stop a
tsunami with a blowgun."

The two technicians glanced at him when they heard *tsunami,*
but one glare from Fuchs and they got back to their work of trying
to hold the ship in trim.

"The only thing we can do is ride it out until we get to the night
side again," Fuchs murmured, thinking aloud. "It ought to damp out
over there."

Yes, I thought. It ought to. But we had believed that the subsolar wave would be no problem at this depth into the atmosphere.
Venus believed otherwise.

Now we were in the grip of a mammoth wave of energy that
pushed us along at gale-force velocity, flinging the ship headlong
across the planet like a frail dandelion tuft at the mercy of the inexorable tidal wave.

"Deeper," Fuchs muttered. "We've got to go deeper."

MUTTERINGS

stayed at the hatch, clinging to Marguerite, for what seemed like hours. The ship kept bucking and shuddering, riding the massive wave that was driving us halfway across the planet.

But although my body was still, my mind was working furiously. This subsolar wave was like a moving wall that pushed us away from the daylit side of Venus. If the wreckage of *Phosphoros* and Alex's body were on that side of the planet it was going to be next to impossible to reach them, unless the wave truly did peter out at lower altitude. If it didn't, we would have to wait a month or more for the planet's ponderously slow rotation to swing the Aphrodite region to the nightside.

I doubted that Fuchs had supplies enough for us to dawdle down here for several weeks. I know that *Hesperos* certainly hadn't. I wondered if *Lucifer,* overdesigned though it was, could physically survive in Venus's thick, hot atmosphere for a month.

We must have stood there at the hatch for hours. It wasn't until the next watch showed up and pushed past us that Fuchs looked sternly at me and said, "Get back to your quarters, Humphries. You too, Marguerite."

The ship's motion had smoothed out considerably, although *Lucifer* was still pitching up and down enough to make my stomach uneasy.

"You heard me!" Fuchs snapped. "When I give an order I want it obeyed! Move!"

"Yes, sir," I said, and led Marguerite down the passageway toward her compartment.

She slid her door open, then hesitated. Turning to me, she asked, "How are you feeling?"

"Fine," I said. Beyond her I could see the compartment Fuchs had given her. It was spare, utilitarian, probably the quarters for the first mate who had been killed trying to save Rodriguez. It was next to Fuchs's more luxurious quarters, but there was no connecting door, I saw.

"No problems with the anemia?" she asked.

"We have more immediate problems to worry about," I said. As if to emphasize my point, the deck lurched, throwing her against me. I held her with both arms.

She disengaged herself, gently, perhaps even reluctantly, I thought. But she did pull away from me.

Yet she seemed genuinely concerned about me. "We have no way of knowing how long the transfusion will help you. . . ."

"Never mind that," I said. "What's he doing to you?"

Her back stiffened. "What do you mean?"

"Fuchs. What's he doing to you?"

"That's not your concern," Marguerite said.

"Isn't it?"

"No, it isn't."

"You're trying to protect me, aren't you?"

"By sleeping with him, you mean?"

"Yes."

For an instant I thought I was looking at her mother; her expression went cold, hard as steel.

"Don't flatter yourself," she said.

I felt anger flaring through me. "Then you're sleeping with him to protect yourself."

"Is that what you think?"

Exasperated, I shot back, "What else can I think?"

Icily, Marguerite said, "I am not responsible for what goes on in your mind, Van. And what is happening between Captain Fuchs and me is our business, not yours."

"You don't understand," I said, "I—"

"No, *you* don't understand," she said, her voice venomously low. "You think that I'll flop into bed automatically with the highest-ranking male aboard, don't you?"

"That's what your mother did, isn't it?" I spat.

For a moment I thought she was going to slap me. She drew back a bit, and I must have inadvertently flinched.

Instead, she hit harder with her words. "You're jealous, aren't you? My mother picked Rodriguez over you and now you're jealous that Fuchs is the top dog in this pack."

"I don't want you to be hurt," I said.

"Worry about yourself, Van. I can take care of myself."

With that she turned on her heel, stepped into her compartment, and slid the folding door shut. She didn't slam it, but it banged into place quite firmly.

"I thought I told you to go to your quarters."

I whirled and saw Fuchs standing just outside the hatch to the bridge, no more than ten meters away. How long he'd been standing there, I had no way of knowing.

"Now!" he snapped.

Right at that moment I wanted to leap at his throat and strangle him. Instead I slunk away toward the crew's quarters, docile as the defenseless Runt that I was.

Even through the self-absorbed funk that I was in, I could sense the tension in the crew's quarters. None of the burly Asians paid the slightest attention to me as I crawled into my bunk and slid the shoji screen shut. They were all huddled around the long table in the middle of the compartment, bending their heads together and muttering to one another in their Asian tongue.

I could hear their tone through the flimsy screen: heavy, dark, foreboding. It didn't sound at all like the jabbering I had heard earlier. I tried to tell myself it was nothing more than my imagination at work, yet I couldn't overcome the feeling that the crew was definitely unhappy. Something was bothering them, and they were talking about it with grim intensity.

At least, while I lay there trying to get some sleep, the ship's plunging and lurching smoothed out. We must be on the nightside, I told myself, or deep enough into the atmosphere for the subsolar wave to have damped out.

I fell asleep at last, with the crew's guttural mutterings serving as a rough sort of lullaby.

I dreamed, but my memory of it is hazy. Something about being weak and sick, and then somehow overcoming it. I think I was sitting up on a dais, like my father did at his birthday party. Marguerite was in the dream, I'm pretty sure, although sometimes she was someone else—maybe her mother.

Whatever, when I woke I trudged out to the galley and put

together a meal from the selections in the freezer. Then I showered and pulled on a fresh set of coveralls from the storage drawers built in beneath my bunk. Strangely, my old slippers had reappeared. There they were, in the drawer with the underwear.

There was precious little privacy in the crew's quarters. I pulled my screen shut when I dressed, but that meant bending and twisting like a contortionist in the narrow space between my bunk and the shoji screen.

I thought I'd have several hours to myself before going back on duty, but the ship's intercom speakers put an end to that idea.

"MR. HUMPHRIES, REPORT TO THE CAPTAIN'S QUARTERS IMMEDIATELY."

It was Fuchs's voice. He said it only once; he expected me to hear it and obey. Which is precisely what I did.

Marguerite was there, sitting in one of the chairs in front of his desk. Fuchs was on his feet, hands clasped behind his back, pacing slowly the length of the compartment, chewing on something; those pills of his, I thought.

"Have a seat," he said to me.

I took the chair next to Marguerite.

"We've lost the better part of a day because of the subsolar wave," he said, without preamble. "I propose to make it up by diving below the last cloud deck and making best speed back to the Aphrodite region."

I glanced at Marguerite. She seemed aloof, distant, as if none of this had anything to do with her. Fuchs's bed was still neatly made up, I saw, but I knew that didn't mean much.

"The crew seems unhappy with my decision," he said.

I wasn't surprised that he had sensed the crew's tension. "Do you have the entire ship bugged?" I asked.

He whirled on me, fists clenched. I quickly added, "Captain."

Fuchs relaxed, but only a little. He went to his desk and touched a key on the phone console. A large section of the bare metal bulkhead turned into a display screen. I saw the crew's quarters from a vantage point up in the ceiling. Several of them still sat huddled around the central table, muttering.

"They're speaking in a Mongol tribal dialect," he said, with a disgusted smirk. "They think I can't understand what they're saying."

"Can you?" Marguerite asked,

"I can't, but the language program can."

He jabbed a stubby finger on the keyboard again, and the mumbling, guttural voices were overlain by a computer's flat, emotionless translation:

"... he is determined to get down to the surface, at all costs."

"He will kill us all."

"He wants the prize money. Ten billion dollars is an enormous incentive."

"Not if we all are killed."

"What can we do?"

"Take the ship and get the hell out of here."

I looked from the screen to Fuchs, still standing with his hands clasped behind his back. His face was as unemotional as the computer's translation.

"But how? He is the captain."

"We are twelve, he is one."

"There are the other two."

"No problem. One woman and one weakling."

I felt my face redden.

"The captain is no weakling."

"And Amarjagal will not go along with us, now that she is first mate."

"Who else would be against us?"

"Sanja, perhaps."

"I can convince Sanja to stand with us."

"But if we take the ship and head back to Earth, we won't get the prize money."

"To hell with the prize money. My life is more important. You can't spend money when you are dead."

Fuchs clicked off the display and the computer's translation.

"Don't you want to hear more?" Marguerite asked. "The details of what they're planning?"

"It's all being recorded," he said.

"What are you going to do about this, sir?" I asked.

"Nothing."

"Nothing?"

"Not a thing. Not yet. So far, they're just griping. Our little joyride on the wave shook them. If things settle down, if we don't encounter any more scares, they'll forget about it. Their share of the ten billion overrides a lot of complaints."

Marguerite said slowly, "But if we run into more trouble . . ."

Fuchs snorted. "They'll try to kill us all. After raping you, of course."

BELOW THE CLOUDS

Whatever possessed you to hire such a gang of cutthroats?" I demanded.

Fuchs gave me a humorless grin. "They're a good enough crew. All of 'em learned their trade out in the Belt. They're rough and unpolished, but they know how to run this ship—and survive."

I said, "And should we run into any more difficulties—"

"Which we will," Marguerite interjected.

"They're going to take over this ship and kill us all," I finished.

Fuchs nodded somberly. He sat heavily in his desk chair and let out a gust of air that would have been a sigh, had anyone else breathed it. From him, it sounded more like an animal's growl.

"I suppose a little demonstration is in order," he said at last.

"A demonstration, sir?" I asked.

He eyed me disdainfully. "Yes. A calculated show of force. Something to make them more afraid of their captain than they are of Venus."

"What are you going to do?" Marguerite asked, genuine fear in her voice.

Fuchs made a grisly smile for her. "Something aggressive, I imagine. They'll understand that. They'll get my message."

"What do you mean?"

"You'll see." Then, as if he'd made his decision and didn't have to worry about it anymore, he pressed his hands flat on the desktop and pushed himself up out of the chair. "I should be on the bridge. You two, attend to your duties."

"I'm off watch, sir," I said.

"Yes, but you're the closest thing we have to a planetary scientist here. We'll be poking out below the clouds soon. Get to the observation station up in the nose and make certain all the sensors are recording properly."

The first thing that flashed through my mind was that I had done my eight-hour stint on the bridge. He had no right to ask me to pull double duty. Almost instantly, I remembered that he was the captain and there was no court of appeals here.

"Yes, sir," I said, getting to my feet.

Marguerite got up, too. "I'll go with you," she said. "I wouldn't miss this moment for the world."

The view through the observation port up forward was still nothing but blank yellowish-gray clouds. Fuchs's so-called observation center was little more than a jumble of sensing instruments packed in around a bank of thick viewing ports. The ports themselves had been shuttered when Marguerite and I first got there. Heat shields, of course. It had taken me several minutes to figure out how to raise them.

"It's warm up here," Marguerite said. Her face glistened with a sheen of perspiration.

"Not only here," I replied. "The deeper we go, the hotter it gets."

She touched the thick port with her extended fingertips, then jerked them back quickly.

"Hot, eh?" I asked needlessly. "You can't run coolant through the ports, it would ruin their transparency."

I pulled up the schematic of the ship's cooling system on the computer terminal built into the bulkhead below the ports. Coolant was piped through the entire hull and carried back to the heat exchangers for recycling. The heat exchangers dumped the accumulated high-temperature fluid into the engines that controlled our flight. The heat of the Venusian atmosphere was helping to drive *Lucifer*'s steering engines. We had built the same type of system into *Hesperos*, naturally. It not only cooled the ship, it helped run the engines.

Still, it was getting hotter. I felt sweat trickling along my ribs, felt my coveralls sticking to my damp skin.

Marguerite made a nervous little laugh. "At least it's a dry heat. The humidity outside must be zero."

I glanced at the sensor displays. The air temperature on the other side of our ports was climbing far past a hundred degrees Celsius. And we were still more than thirty kilometers above the surface. Sure enough, there wasn't enough water vapor in the atmosphere to measure. For all practical purposes the humidity out there was zero.

"He said we'd be breaking out of the clouds," Marguerite murmured, staring out into the endless yellow-gray haze.

"Yes, but there's no way of knowing how—"

"Did you see that?" Marguerite cried.

For just the flash of an instant the clouds had thinned enough to see what appeared to be solid ground, far, far below us. But then the mist had closed in again.

"We must be close," I said.

Then the clouds broke and we were beneath them. Marguerite and I stared down at the distant landscape of barren rock. It was utter desolation, nothing but bare hard stony ground as far as the eye could see, naked rock in shades of gray and darker gray, with faint streaks here and there of lighter stuff, almost like talc or pumice.

"We're the first people ever to see the surface of Venus," Marguerite said, her voice low, breathless.

"There've been radar pictures," I said. "And photos from probes . . ."

"But we're the first to *see* it, with our own eyes," she said.

I had to agree. "Yes, you're right."

"Are all the instruments working?" she asked.

I swiftly scanned their displays. "All recording."

She stared down at the scene of bleak devastation as if unable to pull her eyes away. The ground down there looked hot, baked for aeons, blasted by temperatures hotter than any oven.

"We'll be passing into the nightside soon," Marguerite said, more to herself than me.

I was starting to recognize geological formations on the surface. I saw a series of domes, and the wrinkles of a pressure-deformed region. There seemed to be mountains out near the horizon, although that might have been a distortion caused by the density of the thick atmosphere, like trying to judge shapes deep underwater.

"Look!" I pointed. "A crater."

"It must be fifty kilometers across," Marguerite said.

"It looks new," I said.

"Do you think it is? Pull up the map program and check it."

I did, and the display screen on the bulkhead showed the same crater on the radar map.

"There's not much erosion going on down there," I remembered. "That crater will still look new a hundred million years from now."

Marguerite looked dubious. "In all that heat and that corrosive atmosphere?"

"There's chemical weathering of the rock, but it goes very slowly," I told her. "And the heat is steady, constant. There's no hot-then-cold cycle to make the rocks expand and contract. That's what erodes rock on Earth, that and water. It just doesn't happen on Venus."

Nodding, she asked, "Are the telescopes recording all this?"

For the tenth time I checked the instruments and the computer that monitored the sensors. They were all toiling away faithfully, recording every bit and byte of data: optical, infrared, gravimetric, even the neutron scattering spectrometer was running, although we were much too high above the ground for it to capture anything.

We stayed there for hours, watching the landscape unfold beneath our straining eyes. When *Lucifer* drifted across the terminator and into the night-shadowed side of Venus, we could still see the ground perfectly well. It glowed, red-hot.

"It's like looking down into hell," I muttered.

Marguerite said softly, "But there aren't any doomed souls to see."

"Yes there are," I heard myself answer. "We're the doomed souls. We'll be lucky to get out of here. It might take a miracle to save us."

We stayed in the observation center for almost exactly eight hours. As the time drew to a close, the ship's intercom blared in its computer-generated voice: "ALL THIRD WATCH PERSONNEL REPORT TO YOUR DUTY STATIONS IN FIFTEEN MINUTES."

I realized that I was ravenously hungry. Still, Marguerite and I left those viewing ports reluctantly, as if we were afraid to miss something that might show up, despite the fact that we knew there was nothing to see down there but more heat-blasted bare rock.

Except for the wreckage of a spacecraft.

We were too high to see the wreckage of *Phosphoros* with our naked eyes, but I was hoping the telescopes and their electronic boosters would pick it up. Then I realized that we might also find what was left of *Hesperos*. Maybe even Rodriguez's spacesuited body was waiting for us somewhere down among those glowering rocks.

We stopped at the galley for a quick snack, then I headed up toward the bridge and dropped Marguerite off at her quarters.

"I'm still hoping to find something biologically interesting down at this altitude," she told me, "although I doubt that anything could live in such heat."

I had to grin at her. "Your last biological discovery nearly killed us."

She didn't see it as funny. Her face fell, and I mentally kicked myself for reminding her of her mother's death.

Fuchs was not on the bridge when I reported for duty, but he showed up shortly afterward, looking grim. I wondered what he was planning as his "calculated show of force." I remembered how he had punched me and wondered if the violence he had spoken of would be something of the same.

All through my eight-hour stint the bridge was quiet and tense. *Lucifer* was cruising lower and lower as we sailed around the night-side of the planet, scanning the surface below with all our sensors, including the radars. We knew Alex's last reported position; he was drifting along the equator when his beacon stopped transmitting. The last word he had transmitted was that his ship was breaking up and the crew was getting into their escape pod. We calculated that he must have gone down somewhere near the equator, or close enough to it so that our sensors could spot his wreckage as we sailed purposively around Venus's middle.

The man at the life support console was one of the leaders we had seen conspiring in the crew's quarters, a sizable Asian named Bahadur. He was a full head taller than I, with broad shoulders and long, well-muscled arms. He kept his head shaved, but a thick dark beard covered his jaw. His skin was sallow, almost sickly looking, and his eyes gave the impression that he was thinking secret thoughts.

Fuchs spoke hardly a word to any of us during the watch. But when we were replaced by the next shift, he stepped out into the passageway after us.

"Humphries," he called out, "follow me." Almost as an after-thought he added, "You too, Bahadur."

He marched us to the sick bay and told Bahadur to stand by the table. There wasn't enough room in the bay's narrow confines for the three of us, so I stayed out in the passageway by the open hatch.

"Bahadur, you look unhappy," Fuchs said, in English.

"I, Captain?" The man's voice was low and deep, almost a basso. I was surprised that he could speak English, but then I remembered that English was the standard language among space crews.

"Yes, you. Any complaints? Any problems you want to speak to me about?"

Bahadur blinked several times. He was obviously thinking as fast as he could. At last he said, "I do not understand, Captain."

Fuchs planted his fists on his hips, then switched to the Asian language he used on the bridge. He must have repeated his question.

Bahadur swung his head slowly from side to side. "No, sir," he said in English. "I have no problems to speak to you."

Fuchs considered his response for a few silent moments. Then he said, "Good. I'm glad."

"May I go now, Captain?" With Fuchs standing a hand's breadth in front, of him, Bahadur was pinned against the sick-bay table.

"Are you certain everything is okay?" Fuchs asked, his tone openly mocking now. "I don't want any member of my crew to be unhappy."

Bahadur's brows knitted. Then he replied, "I am happy, Captain."

"That's fine. And the rest of the crew? Are they all happy, too?"

"Yes, Captain. Happy."

"Good. Then you can tell them for me that I would be very unhappy to see them frightened like a bunch of cowardly rabbits."

Bahadur jerked back as if he'd been slapped in the face.

"Remind them that I explained to each and every one of you that this would be a dangerous mission. Do you remember that?"

"Yes, Captain," Bahadur said slowly. "You said there would be dangers."

"And a great reward at the end. Do you remember that, also?"

"A great reward. Yes, Captain."

"Good!" Fuchs said, with conspicuously false cheer. "Remind the rest of the crew. Danger, but a great reward afterward."

"I will do so, Captain."

"Yes." Fuchs's expression became iron-hard. "And tell them that I don't want my crew to be weeping and wailing like a pack of old women. Tell them that."

Bahadur's shaved head was bobbing up and down now like a puppet's. Fuchs stood aside and the man scuttled past him, through the hatch, and rushed by me like a schoolboy running from the wrath of the headmaster.

I turned from the crewman's retreating back to Fuchs, still standing there with his fists planted on his hips. So this was the captain's "calculated show of force." He had cowed the man completely.

"Surprised?" Fuchs asked, sneering at the awe that must have been clearly written on my face. "What did you expect me to do? Beat him to a pulp?"

SPYING

have to confess that that was exactly what I had expected Fuchs to do: unleash the same kind of furious violence on the crewman Bahadur that he had vented on me the first time we met face-to-face.

But he was far cleverer than that. He had cowed the big Mongol with moral superiority and a caustic, withering tongue. Would it be enough, I wondered as I started back to the crew's quarters. Would the big technician stay cowed?

"I wouldn't go back there just now," Fuchs said to me as I started down the passageway.

I turned back toward him. "Sir?"

With a sardonic little smirk he explained, "They probably think you're spying on them."

My eyes nearly popped out of my head. "Me? Spying?"

"How else would I know about their grumbling?"

"Don't they realize you have cameras watching them?" I asked. "Microphones listening? Computers to translate their language?"

Fuchs actually laughed, a harsh, bitter barking. "They're tearing their quarters apart right now, searching for my bugs. They won't find any."

"Why not?"

"Because they've crawled away on their built-in wheels, down along the air shaft and into my compartment." He looked smugly pleased with himself. "Want to see 'em?"

Without waiting for my reply he headed down the passageway. He didn't bother to look back. I followed, as he knew I would.

"I'm sure they're doing an especially good job of ripping your bunk apart," he said as we reached the door to his quarters. "When they find nothing, they'll be certain that you're the spy in their midst."

"That's why you had me come with you when you braced Bahadur!" I realized.

Fuchs's only reply was a sly grin.

We entered his compartment. He went to his desk and pulled a slim flat black object from the top drawer. He pressed a thumb against it and several tiny lights winked green on across its top.

"Remote controller," he explained. "Set to operate only when it's activated by my thumbprint. Otherwise, it runs the wall screen."

The wall screen stayed blank, though. Fuchs aimed the remote at the ventilation grid in the overhead. The lights blinked briefly, and then a pair of miniature metallic objects crawled through the grid and along the metal overhead toward him.

No bigger than my thumb, they looked like minuscule metal caterpillars. Midget-sized wheels lined their lengths. Looking closer, I saw that they were actually ball bearings.

"Magnets hold them against the overhead," Fuchs said, almost as if speaking to himself. "Nanomotors provide propulsion."

"But nanotechnology is outlawed," I said.

"On Earth."

"But—"

"This is the real world, Humphries. My world."

"Your world," I repeated.

"The world your father exiled me to, more than thirty years ago."

"My father exiled you?"

Fuchs turned off the remote and sat heavily in his desk chair. The two bugs clung to the overhead, inert.

"Oh, the old humper didn't have me officially driven out. I still have the legal right to return to Earth. But I could never build my own company there. Your father saw to it that I'd never be able to raise a penny of capital. None of the major corporations would even take me on as an employee."

"Then how did you survive?" I asked, taking one of the chairs in front of the desk.

"It's different off-Earth. Out on the frontier you're worth what you can accomplish. I could work. I could control other workers, supervise them. I could take risks that nobody else would even think of taking. What did I care? Your father had stolen my life, what difference did it make?"

"You built your fortune off-Earth."

"What fortune?" he snorted. "I'm just a derelict, a man who's captained ore ships and run prospecting probes out in the Belt. One of thousands. A rock rat. A drifter."

My eyes turned to the battered book on his desk. "'Better to reign in Hell than serve in Heaven,'" I quoted softly.

He laughed bitterly. "Yes. The original sour-grapes line."

"But you'll be a very wealthy man when you come back from Venus."

He stared at me a moment, then said, "Satan sums it up neatly:

> All is not lost—the unconquerable will,
> And study of revenge, immortal hate,
> And courage never to submit or yield."

I had to admire him. Almost. "That's how you feel?" I asked.

"That is precisely how I feel," he said, with fervor.

"All these years you've nursed a hatred against my father because he beat you in business."

"He *stole* my company! And stole the woman I loved. She loved me, too."

"Then why did she—"

"He killed her, you know."

I should have felt startled, I suppose, but somehow I had almost expected that from him.

Seeing my disgust, Fuchs leaned forward intently. "He did! She tried to be a good wife to him but she still loved me. All that time, she still loved me! When he finally understood that, he murdered her."

"My father's no murderer," I said.

"Isn't he? He killed your brother, didn't he?"

"No, I can't believe that."

"And now he's killing you, as well."

I shot to my feet. "I may not be on very good terms with my father, but I won't listen to you making such accusations."

Fuchs started to frown, but it turned into a sneering, maddening chuckle.

"Go right ahead, Humphries. March off in righteous dudgeon." He waved a hand in the general direction of the door. "They ought to be finished tearing your bunk apart by now. Be careful what you say to them. They're convinced you're spying on them for me, you know."

* * *

The atmosphere in the crew's quarters was as thick and venomous as the Venusian air outside the ship. They all stared at me in sullen silence.

My bunk was torn to shreds. They had ripped apart my sheets, my pillow, even the mattress. The drawers beneath the bunk were pulled out, thoroughly rifled. Even my shoji screen had been slashed, every single pane.

I stood beside my bunk for a long moment, my heart pounding in my ears. It felt hot in the crowded compartment, oppressively hot and sticky. Hard to breathe.

I turned to face eight hostile Asian faces staring at me, eight pairs of hooded brown eyes focused accusingly upon me.

I licked my lips, felt sweat trickling along my ribs. Their overalls looked stained with sweat, too. They must have been working very hard to find the captain's bugs.

I looked directly at the tall and broad-shouldered Bahadur, his shaved head rising above all the others.

"Bahadur, you understand English," I said.

"We all do," he told me, "but most of us do not speak it well."

"I am not the captain's spy," I said firmly.

They did not reply.

"He has planted electronic bugs in the air shaft. He uses the computer to translate your language."

"We searched the air shaft," Bahadur said.

"His bugs are mobile. He takes them away when you search for them."

One of the women pointed at me and spoke in a rapid, flowing tongue.

"She says you are the bug," Bahadur translated. "You spy on us."

I shook my head. "Not so."

"The captain likes you. He shares meals with you. You are the same race as he."

"The captain hates me and my father," I said. "He is watching this scene now and choking with laughter."

"The punishment for spying is death," said one of the men.

"Go ahead and kill me, then," I heard myself say. "The captain will enjoy watching you do it." I had no idea where such foolish courage came from.

Bahadur raised a hand. "We will not kill you. Not where it can be seen."

Whatever shred of courage I had in me evaporated with those words. It took a real effort of will to stand there facing them all. My knees wanted to collapse. And a voice in my mind was screaming at me, *Get away! Run!*

Before I could say anything aloud, though, the captain's voice blared through the loudspeaker, "EMERGENCY! ALL HANDS TO EMERGENCY STATIONS! THE PRIME HEAT EX-CHANGER HAS FAILED. THE SHIP IS DANGEROUSLY OVERHEATING. ALL HANDS TO EMERGENCY STATIONS!"

OVERHEATING

They all raced past me and out the hatch, leaving me standing suddenly alone in the crew's quarters. My bunk was a mess and the others had just threatened my life. But I found myself ridiculously worried over the fact that I hadn't the faintest idea where my emergency station was.

The captain would know, of course. So I trotted down the passageway to the bridge. All the stations were occupied, I saw.

Fuchs looked up from the display screens. "Mr. Humphries. So pleased you decided to join us."

His sarcasm was like acid. I simply stood at the hatch, not knowing what I should be doing.

"Take over the comm console, Humphries," he snapped. Then he spat out a harsh command to the woman already seated there.

She got up and quickly left the bridge. I took over the comm console. I saw that, despite the emergency, the communications systems were running quite normally. Our automated telemetering beacon was functioning as it should. Intercom channels within the ship were filled with jabbering voices that I couldn't understand.

"Should I send out a distress call, sir?" I asked.

"To whom?" he snapped.

"IAA headquarters in Geneva, Captain. At least, we should let them know what's happening to us."

"The telemetering data will give them the full picture. We will maintain silence otherwise."

I knew that a distress call wouldn't help us one iota. We were ninety million kilometers from any possible rescue. Not even

Truax, up in orbit above us, could enter the atmosphere and come to our aid.

We sat in tense silence on the bridge for hours. I was sweating, and not merely from the rising heat. I was frightened, truly frightened. A nasty voice in my mind told me with biting irony that if the crew was able to repair the heat exchanger and save the ship, their next action would be to murder me. Maybe it would be better if we all went down, I thought.

It had been madness, every millimeter of the way, this insane expedition to Venus. What had ever made me do it? I racked my brain, seeking answers for my own foolish behavior. It wasn't the money, I told myself. It wasn't even my feeble hope of earning some respect from my father. It was Alex. All my life, Alex had been the one person I could rely on. He had protected me, encouraged me, taught me by his example how a boy should grow into manhood. He had been all that a big brother should be, and more.

I'm doing this for you, Alex, I said silently as I watched the communications screens. I could see the faint reflection of my own face in the main screen in front of me. I didn't look at all like Alex. No two brothers could look less alike.

But Alex had loved me. And I was ready to give my own life to be worthy of that love, that trust. It was a vain, self-serving excuse, I told myself. But it was also true.

"Let me see the heat exchanger bay," Fuchs commanded.

I roused myself from my thoughts and punched up the ship's inboard schematic, then tapped the area marked HEAT EXCHANGER BAY. The screen filled with an image of four crew members stripped to their waists, sloshing in sweat, as they labored over the malfunctioning exchanger. Bahadur seemed to be their chief. With something of a jolt I realized that two of the bare-chested crew were women. Their comrades paid no attention to their nudity.

Fuchs began to speak to Bahadur in his own language, growling and snarling at him. I slipped a phone plug into my right ear and activated the translation program.

I might as well have listened to their native tongue. They were using such heavy tech-talk jargon that I barely understood anything. Apparently there was a blockage in one of the main tubes that resulted in a growing hot spot that threatened to erode the high-temperature ceramic that coated the inner walls of the tubing. Fuchs spoke sarcastically of "hardening of the arteries" to the laboring crew.

"We must take the main exchanger off-line to make the necessary repairs," Bahadur said. I got that much clearly.

"For how long?" Fuchs asked.

"Two hours. Maybe more."

Fuchs tapped swiftly on the keyboard built into his armrest, then stared hard at his main display screen. It showed a graph that was meaningless to me, except that it shaded from light blue through a bilious pink to a blaring fire-engine red. A single curve arched across the gridwork, with a blinking white dot hovering on the edge of the blue-shaded region.

"All right," Fuchs said. "Take it off-line. You've got two hours, no more."

"Yes, sir," said Bahadur.

It took more than two hours, of course.

Fuchs gave orders to lift the ship to a higher altitude, where it was slightly cooler. I realized that we were dealing with a few tens of degrees now, desperately hoping that we could tolerate two hundred degrees Celsius for a bit longer than two hundred and fifty.

The ship rose slowly. Our altitude readings inched higher, but the temperature outside the hull did not fall more than a few degrees. And it was growing constantly hotter inside.

We sat at our stations on the bridge, literally sweating out the repairs to the heat exchanger. The temperature rose steadily. I watched that blinking white cursor travel along the graph's curve from the blue into the pink, heading inexorably toward the red area that marked danger.

Marguerite called from the sick bay. "I have a man here suffering from heat prostration, according to the diagnostic program."

I could see past her worried face one of the crewmen lying flat on the table, eyes closed, his face bathed in sweat, his coveralls soaked.

"Baldansanja," Fuchs muttered. "I need him at the pumps. We have to climb out of this soup, get up to a cooler altitude."

"He's totally exhausted."

"Give him a couple of salt tablets and get him back to the pumps," Fuchs commanded.

"But the diagnostic program says he needs rest!" Marguerite pleaded.

"He can rest after we've repaired the heat exchanger," Fuchs snapped. "I need every joule of work those pumps can give us, and Sanja's the man who knows those pumps better than anyone else. Get him on his feet! Now!"

Marguerite hesitated. "But he—"

"Inject saline into him, give him a handful of uppers, do whatever you have to do to get him back at those pumps," Fuchs demanded. It was the first time I had seen him appear to be worried.

The man on the table stirred and opened his eyes. "Captain," he pleaded in English, "please forgive this weakness."

"On your feet, Sanja," Fuchs said, in a more conciliatory tone. "The ship needs you."

"Yes, sir. I understand, sir."

Fuchs punched off the channel from the sick bay before Marguerite could say anything more. In a few minutes Baldansanja reported from the pump station, back at the aft end of the ship. He sounded weak, but Fuchs seemed satisfied to have him on duty again.

After nearly three hours Bahadur called in. In English he reported, "The heat exchanger is back on-line, Captain."

The man looked happy: grimy, his bald head glistening with perspiration and rivulets of sweat trickling into his beard, but a big toothy grin spreading almost from one dangling gold earring to the other. I had seen that kind of expression on people's faces before. It was the exhausted yet triumphant smile of an athlete who has just broken a world record.

I looked from his image to the graph. The white cursor was blinking on the edge of the red zone.

Fuchs gave no congratulations. "How long will it stay on-line?"

"Indefinitely, Captain! For as long as we need it!"

"Really?"

"If we step up the maintenance routine," Bahadur amended. "Inspect and clean one tube at a time, every twenty-four hours, sir."

Rubbing a hand across his broad jaw, Fuchs replied, "Yes, I think that's in order."

He pointed at me. "Get me the pump station, Humphries."

"Yes, sir," I said.

Baldansanja was back there, sitting grimly in front of a maze of dials. His face was dry, his eyes wide, pupils dilated. I wondered what medication Marguerite had given him.

"Sanja," said Fuchs, "we're going down again. The emergency is over. Report to sick bay."

"I will monitor the pumps, Captain," he said doggedly.

"Report to the sick bay. Don't make me repeat my order again."

The man's eyes went still wider. "Yes, Captain. I will go."

It took a while for the bridge to cool down to a relatively comfortable level. Fuchs called off the emergency, but by then it was time for my normal watch so I stayed at the comm console. Fuchs gave me a ten-minute break to get something to eat and relieve myself. I was back on duty in nine minutes and thirty seconds.

"Have you ever heard of Murphy's Law, Humphries?" he asked from his command chair.

"If anything can go wrong, it will," I replied, then hastily added, "Sir."

"Do you know the reason behind Murphy's Law?"

"The reason behind it, sir?"

He gave me a disdainful huff. "You think of yourself as something of a scientist, don't you? Then you ought to be interested in the reasons behind phenomena. Root causes."

"Yes, sir," I said.

"Why does the air-conditioning system break down during the hottest weather of the year? Why did our heat exchanger fail when we needed it most?"

I saw where he was heading. "Because that's when the maximum strain is put on it."

"Exactly," he said, leaning back in his chair. "Now tell me, what else is going to fail? Where will Murphy strike next?"

I had to think about that. We needed the heat exchanger to keep us from cooking to death as we descended deeper into Venus's atmosphere. We also needed the life support systems, but no more so now than we did the day the crew came aboard, back in Earth orbit.

"Well?" Fuchs goaded.

"The pumps," I guessed. "The pumps keep the gas envelope filled with outside air so we keep descending."

"And stay in trim," he added.

"And when we're ready to go up again," I reasoned aloud, "we'll be dependent on the pumps to drive the air out of the envelope and lighten us."

"Very good, Humphries," Fuchs applauded mockingly. "Very astute. As soon as you end your watch, I want you to go to Sanja and start learning how to run the pumps."

"Me?"

"You, Mr. Humphries. Your talents are wasted here at the communications console. That's much too simple a task for a man of your brilliance."

He was jabbing at me; why, I had no idea. The two other technicians on the bridge were as blank-faced as usual, although I thought I saw their eyes meet briefly.

"Yes, Humphries," Fuchs went on, "it's time you got those lily-white hands of yours dirtied a little. A bit of honest work will make a man of you, mark my words."

I definitely saw the glimmerings of a smile on the navigation technician's lips before she could mask it. I was the butt of Fuchs's scornful humor. But why?

Fuchs left the bridge shortly afterward, and Amarjagal, the first mate, took the conn. She gave me a sour look, but said nothing.

When I finished my watch, I left the bridge, intending to find Baldansanja and start learning about the pumps. But I only got as far as the open door to the captain's quarters.

"Take a look at this, Humphries," he called to me.

That was an order, not a request, I knew. I stepped through the doorway and saw that his big wall screen showed the ground below us, glowing hot in the darkness of the Venusian night.

"Like Milton's lake of fire," he said, staring grimly at the bleak barren rock.

He touched a control on his desk and the overhead lights went out. There was no illumination in his compartment except the eerie hellish glow from those red-hot rocks more than thirty kilometers below us. Their fiery light made his face look evil, satanic—and yet exultant.

"A dungeon horrible," he quoted,

> "on all sides round
> As one great furnace flamed; yet from those flames
> No light, but rather darkness visible . . ."

He turned to me, still smiling devilishly. "Have you ever seen anything like it?"

I stared at him.

"No, of course not," he answered his own question. "How could you? How could anyone? Look at it. Just look at it! Terrible and magnificent. Awesome and beautiful in its own ghastly way. This is what hell must have looked like before Lucifer and his fallen angels were condemned to it."

I was speechless. Not so much with the view of the ground, but with Fuchs's obvious fascination.

"A whole world to explore," he said, still staring at the screen. "An entire planet, so much like our own in size yet so utterly, confoundedly different from Earth. How did it get this way? What made Earth into paradise and Venus into hell?"

Despite myself I stepped closer to the screen. It truly was awesome, beckoning in a terrifying, grotesque way, like the old horror tales of vampires luring their prey to them: a vast plain of bare rock glowering sullenly, so hot that it glowed. There's never darkness on Venus, I realized. Despite the clouds it is never dark down there.

That's where we were going. That's where we had to go, down there, into that infernal red-hot hell. Alex was down there; what remained of him, at least.

And Fuchs was fascinated by it. Absolutely enthralled. He stared wordlessly at the searing-hot rocky landscape below us, his lips pulled back in an expression that might have been a smile on any other human face. On him it looked more like a snarl, a look of defiance, the face of a man staring at his archenemy, his nemesis, a foe so powerful there is no hope of overcoming it.

Yet he dared to face this enemy, face him and battle against him with all his might.

How long we stood there staring at the blistering scorched landscape I can't tell, but at last Fuchs tore his gaze away and turned on the overhead lights. It took a real effort of will for me to turn away from the screen and look at him.

For once, Fuchs was silent. He dropped down into his desk chair, his face somber, thoughtful.

"I could have been a scientist," he said, looking back at the scorched surface of Venus again. "My schooling wasn't so good, though; I never had the grades to make it into a university. Or the encouragement. I went to a technical college, instead. Got a job before I was twenty. Earned my living instead of earning a PhD."

I had no reply for him. There was nothing I could say.

His eyes finally met mine. "Well, once I've got your father's money in my fist, then I can take all the schooling I want. I'll come back to Venus with a proper scientific mission. I'll explore this world the way it deserves to be explored."

He's entranced by Venus, I finally understood. I pretend to be a planetary scientist, but he's truly enthralled by this horrible world. In a strange and bizarre way, he's in love with Venus.

Yet this was the man who had casually set me up for the crew's suspicions, who had cruelly badgered me on the bridge less than half an hour earlier.

"I don't understand you," I murmured.

He cocked a brow at me. "Because I'm fascinated by this alien world? Me, a rock rat, an asteroid bum, excited by the mysteries and dangers we're facing? You think that only certified scientists with the proper degrees in their dossiers are allowed to become enraptured by the new and unknown?"

"Not that," I said, shaking my head. "It's the contradictions in you. You're obviously a man of intelligence, yet you behave like a barroom tough most of the time."

He laughed. "What would you know about barroom toughs?"

"Just a little while ago you were ridiculing me in front of the crew."

"Ah! That hurt your feelings, did it?"

"I just don't understand how you can do that and still invite me to share your feelings about exploring this planet."

He clicked off the display, frowning. "We're not here to explore. We're here to find your brother's remains and go back to claim your father's prize money."

I must have blinked with surprise a half dozen times before I could find my voice again. "But just now, only a few minutes ago, you said—"

"Don't mistake dreams for reality," he snapped. Then he seemed to relent slightly. "Someday, maybe," he murmured. "Maybe someday I'll come back. But we've got to live through this mission first."

I shook my head. There was much more to this man than I had realized.

"As for my ragging you on the bridge," he said, "all I was doing was trying to save your life."

"Save my life?"

"The crew thinks you're my spy among them."

"Thanks to you!"

He whisked a hand through the air, as if brushing away an insect. "Now they might have some doubts. I'll probably have to kick your butt a few more times to convince them."

Wonderful, I thought.

"And I shouldn't invite you into my quarters, of course. That makes them really suspicious. So don't expect this kind of treatment anymore."

"I understand . . . I guess."

"Yes. I shouldn't have asked you in right now, but I just couldn't sit here alone watching the planet unfolding below us. I had to share it with somebody, and Marguerite's sleeping right now."

It wasn't until I was halfway up the passageway to the crew's quarters that I wondered how Fuchs knew Marguerite was asleep.

MUTINY

That session with Fuchs brought home something important to me. I was supposed to be a planetary scientist, yet I had done precious little to live up to the claim.

The instruments that I had put on board *Hesperos* to satisfy Professor Greenbaum and Mickey Cochrane had done their work automatically. I hardly needed to look at them, much less do actual scientific work. And now even they were gone and I was little more than a captive among Fuchs's crew.

I mean, Alex came to Venus to find out how the planet had turned into a greenhouse hell. He wanted to determine what had happened on Venus to make it so different from Earth, and whether our own world might take the same disastrous turn. Sure, there was plenty of politics involved. The Greens trumpeted Alex's mission and were all set to use his findings to bolster their own pro-environment, anti-business programs.

But beyond all that Alex was genuinely interested in learning about Venus simply for the sake of knowledge. He truly was a scientist at heart. I know my brother, and I know that he was using the Greens—accepting their money for his mission to Venus—as much as they were using him.

And me? I had sworn to follow in Alex's footsteps, but I had done precious little about it. Here was Fuchs, of all people, embarrassing me with his passion about exploring the planet while I stood there like a tongue-tied dolt, a dilettante who's merely pretending to play at being a real scientist.

No more, I swore to myself as I cleaned up the mess the crew had made of my bunk. I said not a word to them, and they watched me in silent hostility. As I tacked a ripped sheet onto the torn shoji screen, I told myself that I was going to find out as much about Venus as I could and everyone and everything else could be damned, as far as I was concerned.

The trouble was that I didn't have any of the equipment we had carried aboard *Hesperos*. Still, *Lucifer* bore its own battery of sensors. I resolved to tap their data and begin a comprehensive investigation of the atmosphere. After all, we had an excellent profile from the sampling we had done. Marguerite had her airborne, metal-eating bacteria to study; I was going to learn everything I could about the Venusian atmosphere.

And, in a few days, when we finally reached the surface, I was determined to collect samples of those scorching-hot rocks and bring them back to Earth.

A fine and noble intention. But then my damned anemia began to gnaw at me again.

I ignored the symptoms, at first. Tiredness, shortness of breath, occasional dizzy spells. Forget them, I told myself. Concentrate on your work.

I tried to convince myself that I was merely working harder than normal, between my new duties learning about the pumping systems and my studies of the data Fuchs had accumulated on the Venusian atmosphere. But at heart I knew that my red-cell count was sagging; hour by hour I was growing worse.

Marguerite noticed it. She had turned the sick bay into something of a biology lab, where she pored over the data she had amassed on the Venusian aerobacteria. She had not been able to bring any samples aboard when we had jumped the failing *Hesperos,* and Fuchs would not have allowed samples on his ship anyway, I knew.

"I'm trying to figure out what kind of container we could use to hold them," Marguerite told me, "so we can collect samples on our way back up and bring them to Earth."

The little display screen on the sick bay partition showed a chemical analysis of the aerobacteria's protoplasm, a senseless hash of chemical symbols and numbers as far as I was concerned.

She was biting her lower lip as she studied the screen. "If only I'd had the time to do a DNA workup," she murmured.

"Assuming they have DNA," I said. I was sitting on the table, legs dangling. The bay felt slightly chilly to me, but considering the hot atmosphere just on the other side of the hull, I felt no urge to complain.

"The Martian bacteria have helical structures in their nuclei. So do the lichen."

"And if the Venusian bacteria do too, does that prove that helical structures are a basic form for all living organisms, or does it show that life on all three planets must have come from the same origin?"

Marguerite looked at me with a respect in her eyes that I had never seen before.

"That's a very deep question," she said.

I tossed it off nonchalantly. "I'm a very deep fellow."

Her gaze became more intent. "You're also a very pale fellow. How have you been feeling?"

I started to put up a brave front, but instead heard myself say, "It's coming back."

"The anemia?"

"Yes."

"The transfusion didn't work, then."

"It worked fine, for the past few days," I said. "But getting a transfusion of whole blood doesn't cure my anemia. *My* DNA doesn't make enough red blood cells to keep me alive."

She looked terribly concerned. "You'll need another transfusion, then."

"How often can he give blood?" I wondered aloud.

Marguerite cleared her display screen with the jab of a finger and called up a medical reference. "No one can donate a half-liter of blood every few days, Van. We'd merely be killing the donor."

"He won't be that generous, believe me," I said.

She looked up sharply at me. "How do you know?"

I answered, "Fuchs has a much more active sense of self-preservation than that."

"Then why did he give you his own blood in the first place?"

"Because you said you'd accuse him of murder if he didn't, remember?"

"That's right, I did, didn't I?" she said, with the hint of a rueful smile touching her lips. "I had forgotten that."

"I don't think it would work again."

"It won't be necessary," she said.

"Why not?"

"He'll donate his blood voluntarily."

"Really?"

"Really," she said, with great certainty.

"How can you be so sure?" I asked.

She looked away from me. "I know him better now. He's not the monster you think him to be."

"You know him better," I echoed.

"Yes, I do," she said defiantly.

"He's sleeping with you, isn't he?" I demanded.

Marguerite said nothing.

"Isn't he?"

"That's none of your business, Van."

"Isn't it? When you're going to bed with him to keep me alive? When you're doing this for my sake?"

She looked truly stunned. "For your sake? You still think I'd pop into bed with him for your sake?"

"Isn't that . . . I mean . . ."

Marguerite's dark eyes held me like a vise. "Van, don't you realize that what I do, what he does, even what you yourself do, is strictly for our own individual benefits? We're all trying to stay alive here, trying to make the best of what we've got to deal with."

Now I was completely confused. "But . . . you and Fuchs," I stammered. "I thought . . ."

"Whatever you thought is wrong," Marguerite said firmly. "If I were you I'd stick to the real problem: how to get enough blood transfusions from the captain to keep you alive without killing him."

I glared at her, feeling as hotly angry inside as the fiery red-glowing ground below us.

"You don't have to worry about him," I growled. "He won't risk his neck for me, and he knows you can't accuse him of murder if giving me more transfusions will kill him."

Before she could reply, I pushed past her, out of the sick bay, and up the passageway toward the observation center in the ship's nose.

I never got that far.

As I passed the open hatch of the crew's quarters, Sanja called out to me, "Mr. Humphries, come in here, please."

He was the one crew member who had shown something more than suspicious hostility toward me, the man in charge of the ship's pumping systems, my direct superior.

I stepped through the hatch and saw that Bahadur and two others—including one of the women—were standing along the bulkhead on either side of the hatch.

Sanja looked distinctly uneasy. He was slightly built, almost birdlike, with darker skin than the others, sort of a cocoa brown.

The other three eyed me in grim silence. Bahadur especially seemed to be glowering menacingly.

"Mr. Humphries, we must go to the secondary pump station," Sanja told me.

"Now?" I asked, looking around at the others. They seemed like a death squad to me.

With an unhappy nod, Sanja said, "Now. Yes."

My pulse was thundering in my ears as we trooped down the passageway, past the bridge, heading for the aft end of the ship. Fuchs was not in the command chair when we passed the bridge, I saw; Amarjagal had the conn. The doors to both the captain's quarters and Marguerite's were tightly closed as we went by.

Fine, I thought. They're in bed together while the crew murders me. Bahadur has timed his move perfectly.

I didn't know what to do. My knees started to shake as we approached the secondary pump station. My palms felt sweaty. Neither Bahadur nor any of the others had spoken a word to me, except for Sanja. For a ridiculous instant I remembered old Western videos that I had watched as a child. This certainly looked like a lynching party to me.

With each step we took Bahadur seemed to grow larger. He was a big man, taller than anyone else aboard, broad in the shoulder and narrow in the hips. His shaved head and bushy beard gave him an appearance of savagery. Baldansanja looked slim and weak next to him, a harmless man driven by the stronger Bahadur. The other man and the woman were both solidly built, a bit taller than I and much more thickly muscled.

The secondary pumping station was two ladder-flights down, at the tail end of the passageway, nothing more than a pie-slice-shaped chamber with a pair of backup pumps housed in hemispherical metal covers.

"Sit there," Bahadur said, pointing to one of the hemispheres.

"I know you think I'm a spy for the captain," I started to say, "but that's entirely wrong. I'm not—"

"Be quiet," Bahadur said.

But I couldn't keep my mouth shut. Fear loosens the bowels in some men. In me, apparently, it loosened the tongue. I babbled. I couldn't stop talking. I gave them chapter and verse of how Fuchs hated my father and me and would congratulate them for murdering me, how they couldn't get away with it, how the IAA and the other authorities would find out about this when they returned to Earth and investigate my death and—

The woman slapped me hard across my face. I tasted blood in my mouth.

"Be silent, Mr. Humphries!" hissed Bahadur. "We have no intention of harming you unless you force us to."

I blinked, the whole side of my face stinging as I swallowed salty hot blood. The woman glared at me and muttered something in her native tongue. I understood the tone: "Shut your mouth, foolish man."

I sat there in silence. But I couldn't help fidgeting. My hands refused to stay still. My fingers drummed along the thighs of my coveralls. Every nerve in my body was jangling, quivering.

The others took flat little black boxes from their pockets and scanned the bulkheads, overhead, and deck. Looking for bugs, I figured. The woman grunted and pointed to a plate in the metal overhead. While Sanja stood beside me, looking downcast, they unscrewed the plate and removed a tiny piece of plastic. It looked like nothing more than a speck of dust to me, but Bahadur frowned at it, threw it to the deck, and ground it beneath the heel of his boot.

I looked up at Sanja. "What's this all about? What are they going to do?"

He shushed me with a finger to his lips.

So I sat there in terrified silence for what seemed like hours. Sanja stood irresolutely beside me, obviously miserable, while the others arrayed themselves on either side of the compartment's hatch and occasionally peered up the passageway that ran along the keel of the ship.

At last the woman hissed something that sounded like a warning and they flattened themselves out against the bulkhead. Sanja seemed to be trembling just as hard as I was, but he whispered to me, "Be absolutely silent, Mr. Humphries. Your life depends on it."

Sitting there on the pump housing, a prisoner in a makeshift cell, I leaned over slightly so I could see up along the passageway. Fuchs was striding toward us, his face a thundercloud, his hands balled into fists.

Bahadur pulled a knife from his coveralls. I recognized it as a steak knife from the galley. The other two drew the same weapons.

I glanced up at Sanja. He seemed paralyzed with fear, biting his lip, staring up the passageway at the approaching captain. I could hear Fuchs's footsteps now, treading along the metal decking swiftly, firmly.

They meant to kill him, I finally understood. I was nothing more than the bait. This trap had been set for him.

So they kill him, I thought. And we pull out of Venus and go home. If I keep my mouth shut I can survive this. I can back up their story. I can convince them that if they kill me too the authorities will know they'd committed murder, but if they let me live I'll corroborate whatever story they concoct about Fuchs and we'll all get out of this alive. After all, Venus is so damnably dangerous almost any story they invent would be believable.

We can live through this! I won't get Alex's remains, but I can always come back. What we've learned on this mission will allow me to build a better, safer vessel for the return trip.

Fuchs was a few strides from the hatch. Bahadur and the two others stood on either side of the hatch, out of his sight, knives drawn.

If our positions were reversed Fuchs would let them kill me, I told myself. He set me up for this in the first place, making the crew think I was spying for him.

They could hear his footsteps too, I realized. They were waiting, poised to strike. Sanja stood frozen beside me, unwilling or unable to utter a peep.

I leaped off the pump housing and dove out the hatch, screaming, "It's a trap!" at the top of my lungs.

I barreled into Fuchs, who simply pushed me aside. As I climbed to my feet, Bahadur and the two others pushed through the hatch, roaring with frustrated rage.

Bahadur reached Fuchs first, and the captain leveled him with a single powerful punch. The other crewman staggered back as Bahadur slumped to the deck. Fuchs kicked Bahadur in the head, then stood waiting in a semi-crouch, his lips pulled back in a ferocious grin.

The crewman slashed with the knife but Fuchs ducked under it and punched up into the man's midsection so hard it lifted him off his feet. I heard the air gush out of his lungs and he dropped to his knees. Fuchs smashed a rabbit punch to the back of his neck and he fell atop the prostrate Bahadur.

All this happened in the time it took me to get to my feet. The woman stood in the hatch, amazed and confused, knife in hand, glancing from Fuchs to the inert bodies of her fellow conspirators.

Fuchs was still grinning terribly. The woman hesitated, wavered. Sanja hit her from behind with a karate chop that knocked her senseless.

It was over. Fuchs bent down and took the knives from them. Bahadur was moaning, his legs twitching slightly, the other crewman still on top of him, still unconscious.

Turning to me, the three knives in one hand, Fuchs said, "Well, that's over."

"Captain," Sanja said, his voice shaking as he stepped over the woman he'd knocked out, "I was forced by them . . . I would not betray you, I was—"

"Quiet, Sanja," said Fuchs.

The man closed his mouth so quickly I could hear his teeth click.

"That took some nerve, warning me," Fuchs said to me.

I was panting, my legs felt weak, my bladder full.

"I knew what was going on, of course," he went on. "Clever of them to use you as bait. They would have slit your throat afterward, of course."

"Of course," I managed to choke out.

"Still, it took some guts to bolt out like that and try to warn me." His face was almost devoid of expression; neither pain nor pleasure showed; not relief; certainly not gratitude.

"It made it easier to take them, bringing the fight out here to the passageway," he went on, almost musing, reviewing the brawl like a general going over the after-action reports from a battle.

"They would have killed you." I heard my own voice quavering.

"They would have tried," Fuchs said. "It would have been a tougher fight inside the pump station, I admit."

I was starting to feel almost angry. He was acting as if nothing much out of the ordinary had happened.

Bahadur moaned again and tried to sit up. Fuchs watched him struggle to get out from under the other crewman. He leaned his back against the bulkhead and held his head in both hands, eyes still closed.

"Hurts, doesn't it?" Fuchs taunted, leaning slightly toward him. "Not as much as a knife in the ribs would hurt, but still I imagine your head's pretty painful right now."

Bahadur opened his eyes. There was no defiance in them, no hatred, not even anger. He was whipped and he knew it.

"Sanja," the captain commanded, "you and Humphries take these three mutineers back to the crew's quarters. They are confined to their bunks until further orders."

"Mutineers?" I asked.

Fuchs nodded. "Attempting to kill the ship's captain is mutiny, Humphries. The penalty for mutiny is summary execution."

"You're not going to kill them!"

Fuchs gave a disdainful snort. "Why not? They were going to kill me, weren't they?"

"But . . ."

"You want to give them a fair trial first, don't you? All right, I'll be the prosecutor, you can be the defense attorney, and Sanja will be the judge."

"Here and now?"

Ignoring my question, he leaned down and slapped Bahadur smartly on the cheek. "Were you going to kill me?"

Sullenly, Bahadur nodded.

"Speak up," Fuchs said. "For the record. Did you intend to murder me?"

"Yes."

"Why?" I asked.

"To get away. To leave this place before all of us are killed."

Fuchs straightened up and shrugged at me. "There you are. What need have we for further witnesses? Sanja, how do you find?"

"Guilty, Captain."

"There," Fuchs said. "Neat and legal. Put them in their bunks. I'll deal with then later."

DEATH

anja and I led a trio of very cowed would-be mutineers back to the crew's quarters. None of them spoke a word as they shambled along the passageway. In the crew's quarters, the other off-watch personnel stared silently as Bahadur and the other two slumped onto their bunks. No one said anything; it wasn't necessary. They all had known what Bahadur was planning, I thought. They all were content to stand back and let it happen.

I couldn't stay in the crew's quarters, not anymore. I saw to it that the three mutineers were in their own bunks, stiff and sore from the beating they had taken, then I headed back toward Fuchs's compartment.

Marguerite was in his quarters, spraying a bandage around his left biceps.

"Come in, Humphries," Fuchs called from the chair where he was sitting with his sleeve rolled up to the shoulder.

"You're injured," I said, surprised.

"Bahadur sliced me with his first move," Fuchs answered easily. "My vest didn't protect my arms."

He gestured with his free hand to a mesh vest that was draped over one of the other chairs. I went to it and fingered the mesh: cermet, light but tough enough to stop a kitchen knife.

"You didn't go into the fight unprepared, did you?" I said.

"Only a fool would," he replied.

Marguerite finished the bandaging and stepped back. "You could have been killed," she said.

But Fuchs shook his head. "Sometimes the captain has to bring things to a boil. Let the crew simmer in their complaints and fears for too long and they might cook up something you can't handle. I saw this coming from the moment we were blown off course by the subsolar wave."

"You knew this was going to happen?" she asked.

"Something like it, yes."

"And you used me to set it up for you," I said.

"You played your part."

"They might have killed me!"

He shook his head. "Not until they'd got to me first. You were perfectly safe as long as I was still alive."

"That's your opinion," I said.

He gave me a tolerant grin. "That's the fact of the matter."

Before I could reply, Marguerite changed the subject. "Van is going to need another transfusion."

Fuchs's brows rose. "Already?"

"Already," she said.

"Too bad we cleaned up the blood from my wound," he muttered.

"I'm worried about this," Marguerite said. "If Van's going to need a transfusion every few days—"

"We'll only be here a few days more," Fuchs interrupted. "Either we find the wreckage or we pack it in and leave."

"Still . . ."

He silenced her with a wave of his hand. "I'm good for another liter or two."

"No, you're not. You can't—"

"Don't tell me what I can and can't do," Fuchs said, his voice ominously low, threatening.

"If I could call back to Earth," Marguerite said, "and tap into Van's medical records, perhaps—"

"No."

"It's for your own good," she said, her voice almost pleading.

He glared at her.

"I might be able to synthesize the enzyme Van needs from your blood. Then you wouldn't have to give any more transfusions."

"I said no."

"Why not?"

"There will be no communication between this ship and Earth until we've recovered Alex Humphries's remains," Fuchs said, with steel in his voice. "I will not give Martin Humphries any excuse to renege on his prize money."

"Even if it kills Van?"

He glanced at me, then turned back to Marguerite. "I'm good for another liter or two of blood, over the next few days."

I spoke up. "*Truax* has my complete medical records in its computer files. You could get the full description of the enzyme from them."

Fuchs started to shake his head, but hesitated. "*Truax,* eh?"

"In orbit around this planet," I pointed out. "Nowhere near Earth."

He mulled it over as he rolled his sleeve down and closed the Velcro seal at its wrist. "Okay," he said at last. "Access *Truax's* medical computer. But that's all! You're not to speak to anyone. Not a word, do you understand?"

"Yes, I understand," Marguerite said. "Thank you."

Then she looked over at me. It took me a moment to realize what she expected.

"Thank you, Captain," I mumbled.

He brushed it off. "You're still going to need a transfusion, though, aren't you?"

"Until I can synthesize the enzyme," Marguerite said.

"Assuming you can," Fuchs pointed out. "*Lucifer* isn't equipped with a biomedical laboratory, you know."

"I'll do what I can," Marguerite said.

"Okay." Fuchs got to his feet. "Let's get down to the sick bay and get this damned transfusion over with."

Marguerite made me lay on the table and had Fuchs sit on a chair that she wedged into the sick bay's cramped space. He seemed perfectly relaxed, chewing on a mouthful of those pills of his. I couldn't stand to watch the needle go into my arm or Fuchs's; I had to close my eyes.

As I lay there, I remembered my other problem.

"I can't go back to the crew's quarters," I said.

"Why not?" Fuchs asked calmly.

I opened my eyes and saw that damnable tube sticking in his arm, filled with bright red blood. Suppressing a shudder, I focused on Marguerite, standing over us with a concerned expression on her beautiful face.

"After what happened with Bahadur and those others," I began to explain.

"You've nothing to be afraid of," Fuchs said.

"I'm not afraid," I answered. And it was true. It surprised me, but I really wasn't afraid of them.

"Then what?" Fuchs demanded.

"I just can't sleep in the same room with people who would've murdered me."

"Oh," Fuchs said condescendingly, "you're uncomfortable with ruffians as your bunk mates."

Marguerite chided, "It's not a joking matter."

"I'm not joking," Fuchs said. "Tell me, Humphries, just where do you think you can bunk, if not in the crew's quarters?"

I hadn't given that any thought at all.

"There's no place else aboard," Fuchs said, "unless you want to sleep on the deck someplace."

"Anywhere—"

"And then you'd be sleeping alone," he went on. "Unprotected. At least, in the crew's quarters there are some loyal souls nearby: Sanja, or Amarjagal, for example. Nobody will try to slit your throat while one of them is around to witness it."

"How can I sleep when people in the other bunks want to slit my throat?" I demanded.

Fuchs chuckled. "Don't worry, you'll be perfectly safe. They've shot their bolt."

"I can't sleep there."

His voice hardened. "This isn't a cruise ship, Humphries. You'll follow my orders just like all the others. You go back to your bunk. Put some iron in your spine! At least you can pretend you're not afraid of 'em."

"But you don't understand—"

Fuchs laughed bitterly. "No, *you* don't understand. You're returning to the crew's quarters. End of discussion."

He has my life in his hands, I told myself. There's nothing I can do. So I shut my mouth and squeezed my eyes shut when Marguerite slid the transfusion tube out of my arm.

"Let my blood circulate through you for a few minutes," Fuchs said, amused. "That ought to give you enough courage to crawl into your bunk and go to sleep."

I was furious with him. But I said nothing.

Not even when he draped his beefy arm on Marguerite's shoulders as the two of them left the sick bay for their quarters.

No one said a word to me when I returned to the crew's quarters. They wouldn't even look in my direction. Not even Sanja, who was off duty when I got there.

Amarjagal, the first mate, must have been up on the bridge. Fuchs was in his quarters. With Marguerite, I knew. The two of them, together. I tried to shut the images out of my mind.

Despite everything, I fell asleep. Perhaps Marguerite had slipped a sedative or tranquilizer into my veins along with the transfusion. I slept deeply, without dreams. When I woke up I actually felt refreshed, strong.

I swung out of my bunk and padded barefoot to the lavatory. Two crewmen were washing up. When I entered they hastily rinsed themselves off and left.

A pariah. They were treating me as an outcast. Very well, I shrugged to myself. At least I get the exclusive use of the toilets and showers.

I always wrapped a towel around my middle when I went back to my bunk from the lav. Most of the others were not so modest. Even the women apparently thought little of nudity, although I must say that none of them stirred my interest at all. It wasn't racism; some of the most exciting, erotic women I've ever known were Asians. But the women aboard *Lucifer* were either dour and chunky or dour and so gaunt you could count their ribs from across the compartment. Not my type at all.

At any rate, as I went back to my bunk with my hair still wet from the shower and a towel modestly knotted around my waist, I saw that several crew members were clustered around one of the other bunks. They didn't seem to be doing anything, just standing there with their backs to me.

I thought little of it as I slid my sheet-covered shoji screen shut and pulled on a fresh set of coveralls. It was the last clean pair in the drawer beneath my bunk. I'd have to either find more in the supply locker or find out if the ship had a laundry unit aboard.

The crowd was still standing in the same spot as a few minutes before, their backs still to me. I recognized Bahadur's tall form and shaved head.

I was curious, but they obviously didn't want to have anything to do with me. It seemed to me, though, that they were clustered around Sanja's bunk. At least, I thought that's where his bunk was.

What was going on? I wondered. But I decided it would cause trouble if I asked or tried to push in among them to see what was going on.

I didn't have to. They melted away from the bunk, each of them seemingly going in a different direction. Bahadur walked slowly toward the intercom unit set into the bulkhead by the hatch, shaking his head and muttering in his beard.

I could see Sanja's bunk now. The privacy screen was open. He was lying on his back, eyes staring blankly upward. His throat was ripped open, caked with blood.

I threw up.

PUNISHMENT

Fuchs stared down at Sanja's dead body. No one had touched it. Bahadur had called the captain. One of the women had handed me a tissue to clean my face. Another handed me a wetvac to clean the floor of my vomit.

Fuchs prodded the corpse, flexed Sanja's wrists and ankles.

"He's been dead several hours," he muttered, more to himself than the rest of us.

Turning, he spotted me trying to mop up my mess. He gestured bruskly and rattled off some commands in the Asian dialect that the crew spoke. One of the men grabbed the buzzing wetvac out of my hands, his face surly.

"Come here, Humphries," Fuchs called.

Reluctantly I stepped closer to the bunk. My stomach heaved and I tasted burning bile in my throat.

"Control yourself!" Fuchs snapped. "What happened here?"

"I . . . I was asleep."

Fuchs seemed more irritated with me than concerned about Sanja's murder. I was convinced it was murder.

He looked across the compartment. The other crew members were sitting on their bunks, or huddled around the table in the open area in the center. A few were standing near the hatch, clustered around Bahadur.

Fuchs gestured to the tall, bearded Bahadur. He walked slowly, with as much dignity as a man can muster when he's sporting a blackened, swollen eye.

"Well?" Fuchs demanded.

Bahadur answered in English. "He committed suicide."

"Did he?"

Bahadur pointed to the knife resting on the bunk at Sanja's side.

Fuchs asked more questions in their Asian language. Bahadur gave answers. From their tone I gathered that Bahadur was offering no information at all.

At last Fuchs heaved a heavy, deep sigh. "So Sanja slit his own throat because he was ashamed of betraying your mutiny," he summarized.

"Yes, Captain. That is the truth."

Fuchs eyed him with utter disgust. "And who's going to commit suicide next? Amarjagal? Or maybe Humphries, here?"

I nearly threw up again.

"I cannot say, Captain," replied Bahadur. "Perhaps no one."

"Oh?"

"If we lift ship and leave this evil place, then no one will need to die."

"Maybe you're right," Fuchs said, his ice-blue eyes colder than ever. "Maybe you're right. Come with me."

He started for the hatch, Bahadur following him. "You too," he said, crooking a finger at the man with the wetvac. He'd been one of the mutineers back at the pump station. "And you," he added to the woman who'd been there also.

The three mutineers glanced at one another. The rest of the crew hung back from them, as if afraid to be contaminated by their presence.

"And you, Humphries," Fuchs said. "Come with me."

He paraded the four of us up the passageway, toward the nose of the ship, and then down a ladder to a hatch set into the lower deck.

"Open it up," he commanded Bahadur.

I watched, puzzled, as the man tapped out the standard code on the electronic control box set into the heavy metal hatch. It sighed open a crack and Bahadur pulled with both hands to swing it open all the way. It must have been heavy; he grunted with the effort.

"There's one of *Lucifer*'s three escape pods," Fuchs said in English, pointing downward with a blunt finger. "Plenty of room for the three of you and several others. You can ride it up to orbit and make rendezvous with *Truax* up there."

Bahadur's eyes widened. "But, Captain—"

"No buts," Fuchs snapped. "You want off this ship, there's your ticket back to orbit. Get in."

Eyeing his two companions uneasily, Bahadur protested, "None of us knows how to navigate, sir."

"It's all preset," Fuchs said, iron-hard. "I'll handle the launch sequence from the bridge. The pod is programmed to boost above the atmosphere and establish itself in orbit. I'll tell *Truax* to pick you up. When they go back to Earth you'll go with them."

The woman said something in swift, rasping tones.

Fuchs laughed harshly. "That's entirely correct. I'll tell *Truax* that you are mutineers and murderers and you're to be kept in custody for trial."

The three of them chattered among themselves for a few moments, more frightened than angry.

"It's up to you," Fuchs said. "You can get up to *Truax* right now or you can stay and obey my orders."

Bahadur asked meekly, "If we stay and obey orders, there will be no trial later?"

Fuchs looked up into his pleading eyes. "I suppose I could forget your pathetic little attempt at mutiny. And we can log Sanja's death as suicide."

"Captain!" I objected.

He ignored me and kept his eyes locked on Bahadur. "Well?" he demanded of the crewman. "What's it going to be?"

Bahadur glanced swiftly at his two companions. I wondered how much English they knew, how well they were following this exchange.

Drawing himself up to his full height, Bahadur at last decided. "We will stay, Captain."

"Will you?"

"Yes, Captain."

"And you'll follow all my orders?"

"Yes, sir."

"With no grumbling? No complaints?"

"Yes, Captain."

"All three of you?" Fuchs waved a finger to include the two others. "There'll be no more . . . suicides?"

"We are agreed, Captain, sir," said Bahadur. The other two nodded glumly.

Fuchs smiled broadly at them. But there was no humor in it. "Good! Excellent! I'm glad we're all agreed."

They started to smile back. I wanted to say something, to object to his simply forgetting about Sanja's murder. But before I could form the words, Fuchs's smile evaporated.

"I'm afraid I'm going to have to give you three some very difficult tasks, you know," Fuchs went on. "Each of you will have to
take double watches now, to make up for Sanja's death."

Their faces fell.

"And all the EVA work we'll have to do in preparation for
reaching the ground, that'll be your job, too."

The two others looked toward Bahadur. His eyes had gone so
wide I could see white all the way around the pupils.

"And of course, once we get down to the surface I'll need a volunteer to test the excursion craft. You'll be that volunteer, Bahadur."

The man backed away several steps. "No, Captain. Please. I
cannot—"

Fuchs stalked toward him. "You said you would follow my
orders, didn't you? All my orders? You agreed to that just a
minute ago."

"But I am not . . . that is, I don't know how—"

"You either follow my orders or get off my ship," Fuchs said,
his voice as cold and sharp as an ice pick. "Or would you rather we
had a trial here and now for Sanja's murder?"

"Captain, please!"

It was uncanny. This big, broad-shouldered man was holding
out his hands pitifully, begging for mercy from the short, snarling
captain who confronted him like a pugnacious badger spitting defiance at a confused, frightened hunting dog.

"What's it going to be, Bahadur?" Fuchs demanded.

He looked at his two companions. They seemed just as frightened and confused as he was.

"I'm going to make your life into an unending hell, Bahadur,"
Fuchs promised. "You'll pay for Sanja a hundred times a day, you
can count on that."

"No," Bahadur whimpered. "No."

"Then get off my ship!" Fuchs snarled, jabbing a hand toward
the open hatch. "And take your two accomplices with you."

Bahadur just stood there, totally whipped. I thought he was
about to break into tears.

"Now!" Fuchs snapped. "Obey or leave. Make up your mind
now."

It was the woman who decided. Silently she went to the hatch
and started climbing down into the escape pod. The other crewman
followed her. Bahadur watched them, then shambled past the captain
and disappeared down the shaft that connected to the escape pod.

Fuchs went over to the hatch and kicked it hard. It swung over and clanged shut.

"Seal it," he ordered me. "Before the sniveling little shits change their minds."

Shaking inside, I touched the key that sealed the hatch. Fuchs had orchestrated this to the last detail. He wanted Bahadur and his two fellow mutineers off his ship and he maneuvered them into going.

Wordlessly he tramped back to the bridge, with me trotting along behind him. He seemed to radiate fury, now that he no longer had to pretend to be conciliatory with Bahadur.

He relieved Amarjagal of the conn and took the command chair. "Humphries, take the communications console."

My first impulse was to say it wasn't yet time for my watch, but I swallowed that idea immediately. The captain was in no mood for contradictions, not even delays. I went to the comm console; the crewman already sitting there got up, looking slightly puzzled, and left the bridge.

"Give me the escape pod," he said flatly.

There were three pods on the ship, I saw from the display screen. Before I could ask, Fuchs told me, "They're in number one."

I opened the channel. Fuchs spoke to them briefly in their own language, then called out, "I'm initiating the separation sequence in five seconds."

I tapped the timer. It clicked down swiftly.

"Separated," said the other technician on the bridge, in English.

Before I could ask any questions, the technician reported, "Ignition. They're heading into orbit."

"Put them on the main screen, Humphries," Fuchs commanded.

It took me a few seconds to figure it out, and then I saw Bahadur's tense, sweaty face on the screen. He was pressed back into his chair by the acceleration of the pod's rockets. The two others were sitting slightly behind him. There were four empty chairs in view, as well.

"You're on course for orbit," Fuchs said to them.

"I understand, Captain," Bahadur answered.

Fuchs nodded and turned off his image.

I asked, "Should I notify *Truax* that—"

"No!" he snapped. "We will make no contact with *Truax*. It's bad enough Marguerite is querying their medical files. No contact!"

"But, sir, how will they know that the escape pod is in orbit? How will they make rendezvous?"

"That's Bahadur's problem. The pod has communications equipment. He'll call *Truax* soon enough, never fear."

"Are you sure? Sir?"

He gave me a sour look. "What difference does it make?"

I turned my attention back to my duties. In a few moments, though, Fuchs said, "Give me their course and position."

The graphic showed their trajectory curving up from our altitude, through the sulfuric acid clouds and levelling off above the cloud deck into a slightly elliptical orbit around the planet. I punched up *Truax*'s position. They were orbiting on the other side of Venus, out of direct contact.

Puzzled, I punched up the extended orbital positions for the pod and *Truax*. They would be on opposite sides of the planet for a dozen orbits before the pod would inch close enough to *Truax* for rendezvous maneuvers to be started.

I told Fuchs about the problem.

He shrugged. "They have enough air to last," he said.

"What about electricity?" I asked.

He frowned at me. "If Bahadur has the wits to unfold the pod's solar panels and align them properly, they'll have all the power they need. Otherwise they'll have to go on the pod's internal batteries."

"Will that last long enough, Captain?"

"That's not my problem."

"In all fairness, sir, we should notify *Truax*—"

"If we do, I'll have to report that those three people are mutineers and murderers."

"That's better than letting them die in orbit! Sir."

"They won't die in orbit," Fuchs said calmly. "They won't even make it to orbit."

"What do you mean?"

He pointed a finger toward the screen on my console that displayed their trajectory. "Put that plot on the main screen."

I did, and Fuchs leaned forward in his chair slightly, studying the graph. "I don't think they'll get through the clouds fast enough to avoid being chewed up by the bugs," he muttered.

"They'll only be in the clouds for twenty minutes or so," I said.

"Yes," he said slowly. "That pod has a pretty thin skin, though. It ought to be interesting."

I watched in fascinated horror as the blinking cursor that represented their pod crawled slowly, ever so slowly, along the curve that represented their trajectory. They were solidly in the clouds now. I remembered how *Hesperos* had been eaten away by the aerobacteria. But that had taken days; the escape pod would be in the clouds only for minutes, less than half an hour.

It would have been better to fire it straight up and get out and above the clouds as quickly as possible, I thought as I stared at the screen. But to establish orbit the pod had to be moving parallel to the planet's surface. The only way to do that was to follow a curving course, up and over, like the lob of a ball that's being thrown completely around the world.

No, I told myself. You could fire straight up, and once at a high-enough altitude, make a course change that moves you into a parallel with the ground. But that would take much more rocket propellant than the pod could carry. They had to get through the clouds more slowly. I only hoped that it was fast enough.

I glance over at Fuchs. He was staring at the screen, too, but grinning slightly. He reminded me of a Roman emperor watching gladiators battle to the death in the arena. Which one will die? Will those three poor miserable people in the escape pod make it to orbit, to safety?

I wondered why I cared. They had killed Sanja. They would have killed Fuchs, too. And me. They were mutineers and murderers. Yet I was worried about them, hoping that they would get through their ordeal alive.

Fuchs had no such conflicts. He had known they'd have to get through the clouds; he had remembered the bugs. He hadn't forgiven them for their crimes. This was his kind of justice.

The yellow message light started blinking at me. I clamped on the headset and pulled the microphone close to my lips. Then I touched the key that put the message on the small screen on the right side of my console.

Bahadur's face was frantic. "We are losing pressure!" his voice wailed in my ear. "The bugs are destroying the seal around our main hatch!"

"Put that on my screen," Fuchs commanded before I could turn to inform him.

I did. Bahadur's chest was heaving, his hands waving up and down. "The bugs! They are eating away at us!"

Fuchs said nothing.

"We must do something!" Bahadur screeched. "Pressure is falling!"

Behind him the other crewman and the woman were sitting tensely, safety harnesses crisscrossed over their chests, their faces grim and accusing.

"There's nothing to be done," Fuchs said, his voice cold and hard. "Just hang on and hope that you get through the clouds before the seal fails."

The woman burst out in a long string of sibilant words.

Fuchs shook his head. "I can't save you. Nobody can."

"But you must!" Bahadur was on the verge of hysteria, his eyes popping, chest heaving, hands windmilling in the air. If he hadn't been strapped into his seat, I thought, he would have been running around the pod's cramped little compartment like a madman. "You must!" he kept repeating.

"Turn off the sound," Fuchs said to me.

I reached for the keyboard, hesitated.

"Turn it off!" he snarled.

I tapped the key. Bahadur's frantic pleading cut off, but we could still see his face and the panic in his eyes.

There was no telemeter link between the pod and *Lucifer.* We had no way of monitoring the conditions inside their compartment. But I watched the terror on their faces as their pod flew through the bug-laden clouds. I was holding my breath, I realized, staring alternately at them and the graph showing their progress through the clouds.

The blinking white cursor inched toward the upper edge of the cloud deck slowly; seconds seemed to stretch into hours. All the while Bahadur and his two companions were goggle-eyed and stiff with horror, their mouths screaming silently, their hands windmilling with frustration and panic.

Then they broke through the clouds. The cursor climbed above the top of the cloud deck, into clear space.

"They've made it!" I shouted.

Fuchs replied sardonically, "Have they?"

"They're establishing orbit," I said.

"Good," said Fuchs.

Bahadur was still wide-eyed, I saw, his chest heaving. But in a few moments he'll realize that he's safe, I thought.

Instead, his face turned blood-red. His eyes bulged and then— exploded. Blood burst from every pore in his skin. The two others, as well.

"Explosive decompression," Fuchs said flatly. "The bugs must have chewed through enough of their hatch seal to weaken it too far to hold the air inside their pod."

With a strangled cry, I snapped off the video imagery.

"Turn off the graph, as well," Fuchs said calmly. "It doesn't matter where their pod is now."

I couldn't move my hands. I squeezed my eyes shut, but still the picture of those three people bursting into showers of blood filled my mind.

"Turn it off!" Fuchs growled. "Now!"

I did. The screen went blank.

Fuchs took a deep breath, ran a hand across his broad jaw. "They had a chance. Not much of one, I admit, but they had a chance."

"Yes, they certainly did," I heard myself say.

He glared at me.

"You knew it all along. You knew they couldn't make it through the clouds. You sent them to their deaths."

He shot to his feet. I saw his fists clench and for a moment I thought he was going to haul me out of my chair and beat me senseless. I felt myself cringing inwardly and tried my best not to let it show.

Instead, Fuchs stood there for a few undecided moments, then turned and stalked out of the bridge. Before I could say or even think anything else, one of the other crewmen came in and took the conn.

CONFLICT

finished my watch, went off duty, and stood another watch, all without seeing a trace of Fuchs. He was in his quarters the entire time as the ship spiraled lower and lower, deeper into Venus's hot, dense atmosphere.

Between watches I checked on the ship's pumps, which were now manned by the propulsion engineer who had doubled as Sanja's assistant, the Mongol named Nodon. Strong and agile as a young chimpanzee, he was wiry, all bone and tendon, with a wispy black moustache and ornamental spiral scars on both his cheeks that were meant to make him look fierce. But Nodon was at heart a gentle person. It was impossible for me to guess his age; even though he had probably never been able to afford rejuvenation therapy, he could have been anywhere from thirty to fifty, I thought. Unlike the other crewmen, he spoke English rather well and didn't hesitate to converse with me.

He had been born in the Asteroid Belt, the son of miners who had fled their home in Mongolia when the Gobi desert engulfed the grasslands on which the tribes had lived since time immemorial. He had never been to Earth, never set foot on the Mother World.

We were in the main pump station, one level below the bridge and captain's quarters. Kneeling on the metal mesh deck plates, I could feel the throb of the engines, separated from the pump bay by nothing more than a thin partition. Nodon was explaining how the pumps could be powered by hot sulfur dioxide from the heat exchangers.

"It saves electrical power for those systems that cannot run on heat," Nodon was saying, patting the round metal pump housing as if it were a faithful hound.

"But the nuclear generator provides plenty of electricity, doesn't it?" I asked.

He nodded and smiled cheerfully. "Yes, true. But when the world outside gives us so much free energy, why not accept the gift? After all, we are guests in this world. We should be grateful for anything it offers to us."

A different attitude, I thought. I began to ask him more about the pumps when a shadow fell over Nodon's face. Literally. His smile vanished. I turned and saw the captain standing behind us.

"Learning the pumps, eh? Good."

I couldn't say that he looked cheerful; Fuchs never seemed to show good humor. But he wasn't glaring or angry. My little outburst up on the bridge the day before had apparently been forgotten. Or more likely, I thought, tucked away in memory for later retrieval.

Nodon and I both scrambled to our feet.

Fuchs clasped his hands behind his back and said to me, "When you're finished here, Humphries, report to the observation center. We have several radar images to check on."

"Yes, sir," I said.

"Teach him well, Nodon," he said to the youth. "Once he learns the pumps, I can bring you up to the bridge."

"Yes, sir, Captain!" Nodon said, beaming.

I grew weary of Nodon's explanations long before he did. He seemed truly to be in love with the pumps, their importance to the ship's performance, their intricacies, their nuances, every weld and part and vibration of them.

I thought I could learn just as much from the computer's files on the pumps, but I patiently endured Nodon's smiling, eager dissertation for seemingly endless hours.

At last I excused myself and went up the ladder to the main deck. The observation center was up in the nose, but there was something else that I wanted to do first.

I went down the passageway to the sick bay. It was empty, so I walked down to Marguerite's door and tapped at it. No reply. I rapped harder.

"Who is it?" came her muffled voice.

"Van."

No response for several moments. Then the door cracked open. "I was sleeping," she said.

"May I come in? Just for a couple of seconds?"

She slid the accordion-fold door all the way and I stepped into her quarters. The bed was rumpled, but otherwise the compartment looked neat and orderly. Marguerite had pulled on a pair of wrinkled, faded coveralls. I realized that my own were not all that clean and sweet.

"What do you want, Van?" she asked tightly.

It was the first time we'd been alone in a while. She looked tired, hair tousled, her eyes puffy from sleep, but still very beautiful. The lines of her cheek and jaw would have inspired any sculptor, I thought.

"Well?"

"I'm sorry I disturbed you," I began.

"That's all right," she said, a little more lightly. "I had to get up anyway; someone was pounding at my door."

My brows knit with confusion. "But I was . . . oh, I see! It's a joke."

"Yes," she said, smiling a little. "A joke."

"I wanted to ask if you were able to get my medical records from *Truax*."

She nodded and gestured toward the laptop computer sitting open on the compartment's desk. "Yes, no problem."

"And?"

"And what?"

"Can you synthesize the enzyme for me?"

Marguerite sighed wearily. "Not yet. Probably not at all."

"Why not?" I demanded.

Frowning, she asked, "How much biochemistry do you understand?"

With a shrug I admitted, "Very little."

"I thought as much." She sighed again. Or perhaps it was a stifled yawn. "I have the formula for your enzyme. The computer file gave me the complete breakdown for it: all the amino acids and the order in which they need to be put together."

"So what's the problem?" I asked.

"Two problems, Van. One is getting the proper constituents; most of the factors have to come from someone's blood."

"Well, you can get Fuchs's blood, can't you?"

"The second problem," she went on, ignoring my comment, "is

the equipment. We simply do not have the necessary equipment for this kind of biochemical synthesis."

"Can't you rig something together?"

She scowled at me. "What do you think I've been trying to do for the past day and a half? Why do you think I've been pushing myself so hard I started to fall asleep in the sick bay an hour ago and came back here for a nap?"

"Oh. I didn't realize . . ."

She focused her jet-black eyes on mine. "I'm trying, Van. I'm working as hard as I can on it."

"I appreciate that," I said.

"Do you?"

"I don't want to have to keep getting transfusions from Fuchs. I don't want to be obligated to him for my life."

"But you are."

"I am what?"

"Obligated to him for your life."

"Because of a couple of transfusions?"

Marguerite shook her head. "That, and much more."

"What do you mean by that?"

She looked as if she was on the verge of answering me, but then she said, "Nothing. Forget it."

"No, tell me."

Marguerite shook her head.

"I don't owe Fuchs anything," I said, feeling anger welling up in me. "The man's a monster."

"Is he?"

"I had to sit on the bridge and watch him kill three of the crew," I snapped.

"He executed three murderers."

"He toyed with them the way a cat plays with a mouse. He tortured them."

"He saved your life, didn't he?"

"All he's done is what you forced him to do."

"No one forced him to rescue us from your ship," Marguerite answered hotly.

"No. He was trying to save your mother, not me."

"He loved her!"

"And now he's loving you," I yelled.

Marguerite slapped me. It stung.

"Get out of my quarters," she said. "Get out!"

I scowled at her, feeling the heat of her fingers against my cheek.

Pointing to her mussed-up bed, I growled, "At least it's good to see that you sleep by yourself once in a while."

Then I left quickly, before she slapped me again.

SEARCHING

t's about time you got here," Fuchs said to me when I arrived at the observation center, up in the ship's nose.

"Sorry to be late, sir," I apologized. "I had to stop at—"

"When I give an order I expect it to be obeyed at once, Humphries, without any delays. Understand me?"

"Yes, sir."

It was just as cramped as ever in the observation center, with all the sensors crammed into the compartment. With Fuchs in there it seemed crowded to the point of bursting. *Lucifer's* nose tapered to a rounded point, glassed in with thick quartz ports that could be shuttered when necessary. They were unshielded now and I could see the seething barren surface of Venus, far below us.

Fuchs stood in the midst of all the instruments and computers like a heavy dark thundercloud, hands clasped behind his back, eyes taking in the unending panorama of devastation below.

"She looks so beautiful from a distance," he muttered, "and so desolate up close. Like quite a few women I've known."

From Fuchs, that was an unexpected burst of humor.

"You knew Marguerite's mother, didn't you?" I asked.

He looked at me and huffed. "A gentleman doesn't discuss his women, Humphries."

That ended *that* line of conversation.

Gesturing to the bleak rocky landscape below, Fuchs said, "Radar's picked up several returns that are apparently metallic. We've got to decide which one is your brother's wreckage."

There were no chairs in the observation center; no room for them. The sensors were mounted in the bulkhead and decking; their computers lined a shelf that stood at shoulder height. So we remained standing as we reviewed the computer files of the various radar images. Most of them were little more than glints, either random artifacts in the programming or natural projections of rock that gave sharp radar reflections similar to bare metal.

But wherever there were mountains I saw strong radar reflections indicating metal, starting at roughly nine thousand meters. It reminded me of snowcaps on the mountains of Earth: below that nine-thousand-meter line was bare rock, above it, the Venusian equivalent of snow, bare metal.

"The atmosphere's cooler up at the altitude by about ten degrees or so," Fuchs told me. "There must be some kind of chemical change in the rock at that temperature and pressure."

"But what could it be?" I wondered.

He shrugged. "That's for Venus to know, and us to find out—someday."

Out of curiosity I called up the computer's file of radar reflectivities. The metallic returns from the upper slopes of the mountains might have been any of several metals, including iron sulfide: pyrite, "fool's gold."

I stared hard at the distant peaks as we cruised through the hot, turgid air. Mountains coated with fool's gold?

Then a new worry hit me. "If *Phosphoros*'s wreckage is on a mountainside above the 'snow line,'" I mused aloud, "its radar return will be lost in the reflection from the metal."

Fuchs nodded somberly. "Pray that they hit the ground below nine thousand meters."

As we drifted across the baking hot landscape of bare rocks and metal-coated mountains, I saw a sharp spike on the graph the computer screen was displaying.

"What's that?" I said, sudden excitement quickening my pulse.

"It's nothing," Fuchs answered, with barely a glance at the screen.

"That can't be a glitch in the system," I insisted.

"I agree," Fuchs said, looking up at the graph, "but it's too small to be the wreckage of *Phosphoros*."

"Too small? The return's peak is like a signal beacon."

He tapped the screen with a knuckle. "The intensity is high, granted. But the extent of the return across the ground is too small to be a ship."

"Maybe it's part of the wreckage," I insisted. "The ship probably broke up into several chunks."

But Fuchs was already speaking into the computer's input mike, "Correlate the displayed radar return with known artifacts on the surface."

VENERA 9 appeared on the bottom of the screen in blocky white alphanumerics.

"The first spacecraft to return photographic images from Venus's surface," Fuchs said.

"Heaven and hell," I breathed, awestruck. "That thing has been sitting down there for a hundred years!"

Fuchs nodded. "I'm surprised there's anything left of it."

"If we could recover it," I heard myself thinking aloud, "it would be worth a fortune back on Earth."

Fuchs focused the ship's full battery of telescopes onto the remains of the old Russian spacecraft, while ordering me to make certain the electronic image enhancers were up and running.

It took almost half an hour to get a decent image on our computer screen, but fortunately *Lucifer* was drifting slowly in the sluggish lower atmosphere. The slant range between us and Venera 9 actually decreased slightly while we brought the optics into play.

"There she is," Fuchs said, almost admiringly.

It looked very unimpressive to me. Not much more than a small round disc that had sagged and half collapsed on one side to reveal the crumpled remains of a dull metal ball beneath it, sitting on those baking, red-hot rocks. It reminded me of an old-fashioned can of soda pop that had been crushed by some powerful hand.

"You're looking at history, Humphries," Fuchs said.

"It's so small," I said. "So primitive."

He gave a snorting laugh. "It was the height of technology a century ago. A marvel of human ingenuity. Now it's a museum piece."

"If we could get it to a museum . . ."

"It would probably crumble to dust if anybody touched it."

I wondered about that. In that hot, high-pressure atmosphere of almost pure carbon dioxide, the metal of the ancient spacecraft had held up astoundingly well. That told me that the atmosphere down there wasn't as corrosive as we'd expected. Perhaps the sulfuric acid and chlorine compounds we had found in the clouds did not exist down near the surface; at least, not in such high concentrations.

All to the good, I thought. That meant that the wreckage of Alex's *Phosphoros* should be easier to spot. And maybe his body was still fairly intact, after all.

Fuchs was already scanning through the computer's files for

other radar returns. We were close enough only to one of them to use the telescopes. When their electronically enhanced images appeared on the display screen my heart jumped.

"That's wreckage!" I shouted. "Look . . . it's strewn along the ground."

"Yes," he agreed, then muttered into the computer's input microphone.

NO CORRELATION, the screen showed.

"But that's got to be *Phosphoros!*" I said excitedly. "Look, you can see—"

"*Phosphoros* went down a thousand kilometers farther west," Fuchs said, "near Aphrodite Terra."

"Then what . . ." I stopped myself. I realized what we were looking at. The wreckage of *Hesperos*. My ship. We had been blown far off course by the subsolar wave and now we were just about back where we had been when *Hesperos* broke up.

Fuchs was manually typing in something, and sure enough, the screen displayed HESPEROS with the date when she went down.

I stared at the wreckage. Rodriguez was down there. And Duchamp and Dr. Waller and the technicians. Looking over at Fuchs I saw that he was deep in thought, too, as he gazed at the screen. He was brooding about Duchamp, I guessed. Had he loved her? Was he capable of loving anyone?

He seemed to shake himself and pull his attention away from the screen. "Unfortunately, *Phosphoros*'s wreckage is now over on the night side of the planet. The optics aren't going to be much use to us."

"We could wait until it swings back into the daylit side," I suggested.

He sneered at me. "You want to wait three or four months? We don't have supplies to last another two weeks down here."

I had forgotten that the Venusian day is longer than its year.

"No," Fuchs said, with obvious reluctance, "we're going to have to find your brother's wreckage in the dark."

Great, I thought. Just simply great.

So we sailed slowly through that hot, turgid atmosphere, sinking lower all the time, closer to the baked rocks of the surface.

It was difficult for me to keep track of time. Except for the regular rounds of my watches on the bridge and with Nodon at the pumps, there were no outward cues of day and night. The ship's lighting remained the same hour after hour. The views outside, when I went to the observation center, seemed unchanged.

I ate, I slept, I worked. My relationship with Marguerite, such as it had been, was in a shambles. Except for Nodon, who was hell-bent on teaching me everything I had to know about the pumps so that he could be promoted to the bridge, the rest of the crew regarded me as a pariah or worse, a spy for the captain.

Strangely, Fuchs was my only companion, yet even he grew distant, distracted. For long periods of time, whole watches in fact, he was absent from the bridge. And when he did take the command chair he seemed distracted, his attention focused somewhere else, his mind wandering. Often I saw that he was chewing on those pills of his. I began to wonder if his drug habit was getting the better of him.

Finally I couldn't stand it any longer. Taking my courage—or perhaps my self-esteem—in my hands, I went to the sick bay and faced Marguerite.

"I'm worried about the captain," I said, without preamble.

She looked up from the microscope she'd been bending over. "So am I," she replied.

"I think he's addicted to those pills he takes."

Her eyes flashed, but she shook her head and said, "No, you're wrong. It's not that."

"How do you know?" I demanded.

"I know him much better than you do, Van."

I suppressed the angry retort that immediately sprang to mind and said merely, "Well then, is he sick?"

With another shake of her head, she said, "I don't know. He won't let me examine him."

"Something's definitely wrong," I said.

"It might be the transfusions," said Marguerite. "He can't give so much blood and not feel the effects."

"Have you made any progress on synthesizing the enzyme?"

"I've gone as far as I can," she said. "Which isn't far enough."

"You can't do it?"

Her chin went up a notch. "It can't be done. Not with the equipment we have here."

I saw the flare of irritation in her eyes. "I didn't mean to suggest that you were at fault."

Her expression softened. "I know. I shouldn't have bristled. I suppose I've been working too hard at this."

"I appreciate your trying."

"It's just that . . . I know what to do, I even know how to do it—in theory, at least. But we don't have the equipment. This is a sick bay, not a pharmaceutical laboratory."

"Then, if we don't get back to *Truax* quickly . . ." I let the words fade away. I didn't want to admit where they were leading.

But Marguerite said it for me. "If we don't get back to *Truax* in forty-eight hours you'll need another transfusion."

"And if I don't get it?"

"You'll die within a few days."

I nodded. There it was, out in the open.

"But if the captain does give you a transfusion," Marguerite went on, "he could die."

"Not him," I snapped. "He's too hateful to die."

"Is he? Is that what you think?"

I had touched on a sensitive nerve again. "What I mean is that he won't allow himself to die just to keep me alive."

"Is that what you think?" she repeated, more softly.

"Certainly," I said. "It wouldn't make any sense. I surely wouldn't kill myself over him."

"No," Marguerite said, almost in a whisper, "you wouldn't, would you?"

"Why should I?" I growled.

"You're jealous of him."

"Jealous? Of him?"

"Yes."

Before I had time to think it over I answered, "Yes, I'm jealous of him. He has you, and that makes me angry. Furious."

"Would it change your attitude if I told you he doesn't have me?"

"I wouldn't believe you," I said.

"He doesn't."

"You're lying."

"Why should I lie?"

I had to think a few moments about that. "I don't know," I replied at last. "You tell me."

"I'm not sleeping with him," Marguerite said. "I've never slept with him. He's never asked me to sleep with him."

"But . . ."

"He may have been attracted to my mother once, many years ago. I remind him of her, of course. But he's a different man now. Your father changed him."

"He was in love with my mother, too," I snapped. "Or so he said."

"He told me that your father killed her."

"He's a liar!"

"No," said Marguerite. "He might be wrong, but he's not lying. He's convinced that your father killed your mother."

"I don't want to hear that."

"He believes your father had your mother murdered," Marguerite said, her voice edged in steel.

I couldn't stand it. I turned on my heel and fled from the sick bay.

But even as I ran, her words echoed in my mind: *I'm not sleeping with him. I've never slept with him. He's never asked me to sleep with him.*

FANTASY

knew it was a dream even while I was dreaming it.

Marguerite and I were making love, slowly, languidly, on the beach of some undiscovered island beneath a big gibbous tropical Moon. I could feel the warm sighing breeze coming in off the ocean, hear the soft thrumming of the surf along the coral reef that ringed the lagoon.

There was no one else on the island, no one else in the world as far as we were concerned. Only the two of us, only this timeless place, this haven of tenderness and passion.

Far, far away, though, I heard a distant voice calling my name. It was barely a whisper at first, but it grew more urgent, stronger, more demanding. I realized at last that it was Marguerite whispering in my ear, her breath warm and alive against my bare skin.

"He killed her," she whispered, so softly I could hardly make out her words. "He killed your mother. He murdered her."

"But why?" I begged her to answer me. "How could he kill her? Why would he do it?"

"You know what it's like to feel jealousy. You've felt the rage that boils inside."

"Yes," I admitted. "I know. I've felt it."

"He has the power to give vent to his fury. He has the power to destroy people."

And there was Fuchs standing over us, snarling, "I'll kill you! Just as I killed Bahadur and all the others!"

Marguerite had vanished. Our tropical island had disappeared. We were standing on the hellish surface of Venus, standing in nothing more than our coveralls on those searing hot rocks, breathing that poisonous air, ready to fight to the death.

NODON'S STORY

I awoke with a start and sat up on my bunk like a jack-in-the-box popping up. I was soaked with sweat, my coveralls a soggy, smelly mess.

The digital clock set into the partition at the foot of the bunk told me it was time to start another watch at the pumps. Sliding my battered shoji screen back, I saw that the other crew members were getting ready for duty, too. They quite conspicuously ignored me, turning their backs to me as I stepped out of my compartment.

Only Nodon, smiling broadly, paid any attention to me. He seemed very pleased with my understanding of the pumping system. He was looking forward to leaving the pumps to me and being promoted to the bridge.

"You will handle everything by yourself this watch," he told me, with a crooked little grin, as we headed for the main pumping station. "I will observe only."

I nodded and focused my attention on the dials and gauges that monitored the pumping system. It seemed odd, when I thought about it, but Nodon did almost all the talking between us. Where he was concerned, I was the taciturn, dour one, hardly ever speaking. An ancient scrap of wisdom drifted through my memory, something to the effect that when it comes to learning, it's best to keep one's mouth shut and ears open.

The pumps chugged along smoothly enough, although I saw that one of them was beginning to overheat. I had to take it off-line and bring the backup into action.

Then I had to disassemble the ailing pump to find the cause of its overheating. A gas bearing had clogged slightly, causing enough friction to send the pump's temperature rising. With Nodon watching over my shoulder, I pulled the bearing out and began the laborious task of cleaning it while Nodon watched me intently.

"The captain," I said to him as I worked. "How long have you known him?"

"All my life," he replied. "He was a great friend to my father even before I was born."

I shook my head. "I have a difficult time imagining him as a friend to anyone."

Nodon nodded somberly. "But you did not know him when he was a happy man. He was very different then. The war changed him."

"War?" I looked up from the pump-bearing parts scattered on the deck.

Nodon told me about the Asteroid War. I had read about it in history classes, of course, and seen all the videos: the struggle between competing corporations to gain major shares of the asteroid mining business. The histories told of the economic competition, and how major corporations inevitably bought out most of the small, independent miners and prospectors.

But Nodon was there, and he saw a savagely different kind of conflict. The term "war" was not a metaphor; the corporations hired mercenary troops to hunt down the independents and kill them. Out there in the eternal darkness of deep space battles were fought between spacecraft armed with lasers originally designed to bore through nickel-iron asteroids. Men in spacesuits were shredded with rapid-firing flechette guns. Women, too. Neither side made any distinctions. It was a war of annihilation.

Lars Fuchs was a leader of the independents, a strong and brave young man who had built up a small but highly successful company of his own. He was smart, as well: too wily to be captured by the mercenary troops who combed the Belt to find him. He led the counterattack, raiding the corporate facilities on Ceres and Vesta, battling the mercenaries ceaselessly, driving up the corporations' costs and the mercenaries' body counts, driving men such as my father to rage and desperation.

Fuchs was on the verge of winning the Asteroid War when my father—Nodon told me—crushed him. Not with troops, not with death-dealing weapons, but with a single slender woman. Fuchs's wife. My father's corporate security forces captured her and threatened to kill her. Fuchs surrendered, even though he knew they would murder him as soon as he handed himself over. Instead, though, his wife made a deal with my lecherous father—who had quickly become enamored of her beauty. She offered to marry my father if he let Fuchs live.

That is how my mother returned to Earth to become Martin Humphries's fourth and final wife. And Lars Fuchs remained in the Asteroid Belt, a broken man, robbed of his company, his leadership, and of the woman he had loved. The Asteroid War ended then with the corporations' victory. Independent miners ceased to exist, although a few prospectors still roamed through the vast reaches of the Belt, under contract to the corporations. Fuchs became a rock rat, one of the prospectors who lived at the sufferance of the almighty corporations, a bitter man, hard and burning with inner rage.

"Then he heard of this prize being offered to recover the remains of your brother," Nodon said, his voice soft and faraway with old memories. "He jumped at the chance! It was a cosmic irony to him. That is how he described it: a cosmic irony."

By now I had cleaned the bearing and was putting the pump back together.

"How did he build this ship, then?" I asked. "If he had no money, no resources."

Nodon smiled gently. "He had friends. Friends from the old days, survivors of the war, men and women who knew him and still respected him. Together, they built this ship, out there in the Belt. In secret. I helped, you know. It was our way to get back at the corporations, our pitiful way to gain just a little bit of revenge against men like your father."

I closed the pump covering and started it up. It thrummed to life immediately. Nodon and I both beamed with satisfaction as the gauges showed it working in its normal range.

"And this crew?" I asked. "They all came from the Belt, too?"

His pleased smile evaporated. "Yes, from the Belt. But most of them are scum. Very few people were brave enough to join his crew."

"Venus is a very dangerous place," I said.

"Yes, that is true. But what they were afraid of was to be seen helping Captain Fuchs. It was one thing to help build his ship, deep in the Belt, unseen by prying eyes. But to openly join his crew? Very few had the courage to do that. He had to hire cutthroats like Bahadur."

The memory of poor Sanja dead in his bunk flashed through my mind. And of Bahadur, exploding into a shower of blood.

"Do not think badly of the captain," Nodon told me. "He is a man who has suffered much."

At the hands of my father, I added silently.

MAKING HEADWAY

We were sinking lower and lower as we drifted slowly toward the planet's nightside. It was a planned decrease in altitude that Fuchs calculated would bring us above the eastern highlands of Aphrodite Terra, where *Phosphoros* most probably lay. I only hoped Alex's ship had come to rest low enough so that we could spot it against the bright radar reflections of the mountain's upper slopes.

I felt the need for a shower after my shift at the pumps but didn't have the time. Instead I merely pulled on a clean set of coveralls, popped my pile of ripe-smelling ones into the automated laundry unit, and then hurried up to the bridge.

Fuchs frowned at me as I took over the comm console, but said nothing. I couldn't help staring at him. If I had been in his place, if I had gone through what he'd gone through, how would I feel about having Martin Humphries's son aboard my ship? Why didn't he just let me die? What was going on in that angry, bitter mind of his?

Toward the end of the watch, a call came through from the heat-exchange station. I slipped the receiver plug into my ear and tapped into the translator program.

"Captain, sir, it will be necessary to shut down the central unit for maintenance now," the technician was saying. The computer's flat unemotional translation took all the expression out of the message, but I could hear the technician's guttural, growling dialect in the background.

I swiveled my chair slightly so I could see Fuchs's face reflected in one of my empty screens. He frowned sourly.

"It is necessary, Captain, sir, if we are to avoid a failure of the main heat exchanger," the technician went on.

"I understand," Fuchs said. "Proceed."

"Should I alert the crew—"

"You do your maintenance job," Fuchs snapped. "I'll handle the crew."

"Yes, sir."

To me, Fuchs called, "Humphries, put me on the ship's intercom."

"Yes, sir," I said, with a crispness I did not really feel.

"This is the captain speaking," Fuchs said. "We're going to get a little warmer for a few hours while one section of the main heat exchanger is down for maintenance."

He thought it over for a moment, then said, "That is all."

As I closed the intercom circuit, he ordered me, "Get Dr. Duchamp onscreen, Humphries."

I got no answer from her quarters. She was in the sick bay.

"You heard my warning about the heat?" Fuchs said to her image on his main screen.

"Yes, Captain," she said. "I'm in the sick bay, preparing for heat-related complaints."

"Good," he said. "Don't let anyone go off duty unless they've collapsed with heat prostration. Understand me?"

Marguerite's lips curved slightly. "You don't want me to . . . what's the word? Mollycoddle?"

Fuchs grunted.

"You don't want me to mollycoddle the crew," Marguerite finished.

"That's right," he said. "No pampering."

"Yes, Captain."

It was probably my imagination but it seemed to get hotter in the bridge almost immediately. Or could it be my anemia? I wondered. No, fever had never been a symptom I'd experienced, I told myself. The temperature in here is rising. And fast.

We were down to within ten kilometers of "sea level," the arbitrary altitude the planetary scientists had picked as a baseline for measuring the heights of Venus's uplands and the depths of her craters. The Aphrodite Terra region rose a bit more than three klicks from its surrounding plains, so we had plenty of leeway in altitude. Aphrodite Terra was the size of Africa, and most of it looked fairly rugged on our radar maps. Finding the wreckage of one lost spacecraft was not going to be easy.

For the first time, my mind began to picture what we looked like: a minuscule metal pumpkinseed floating in the dark, still, thick atmosphere of Venus; a tiny artifact from a distant world bearing fragile creatures who needed liquid water for their existence, drifting slowly through a murky soup hot enough to boil water three or four times over, groping our way across this strange, barren, alien landscape, seeking the remains of others of our own kind who had perished in this harsh, inhospitable place.

It was madness, pure and simple. No one but a madman would come here and try this. No one but a maniac such as Fuchs could look out at that blasted, scorched landscape where the rocks were hot enough to melt aluminum and find a fierce kind of *beauty* there. I should have been home, in my house by the gentle sea, where I can walk out in the open green hills and breathe the cool, wine-sharp air, brisk and free and safe.

Instead, here I was, locked in a metal womb with a tyrant who was by any unbiased judgement as insane as Nero or Hitler, comparing himself to Satan incarnate, defying man and nature alike and telling himself it was better to be supreme *here,* in this hell, than to serve some other master back on Earth or out in the Belt.

And I was just as crazy, undoubtedly. Because in my own foolish, haphazard way I had worked just as hard to be in this place and—I shook my head with the realization of it—I was just as determined to play this game until the last, bitter moment.

That moment would end in death, I knew. Either for me or for Fuchs. For the first time in my life, I resolved that I would not be the one to die. I would not be the passive little Runt. I would not let others steer my life, not my father, not my frailties, not even my illness. I was going to survive, no matter what I had to do. I swore it to myself.

Which was easy enough to do, within my own mind. Making it work in the real world was another matter entirely.

But I was determined, for once, to make it work, to make something of myself, to be equal to the love and trust that Alex had shown me.

Suddenly the yellow message light beneath my main screen began blinking urgently. I tapped the keyboard and the display screen spelled out: INCOMING MESSAGE FROM *TRUAX.*

Swiveling in my chair, I called out, "Captain, we have—"

"So I see," he said. "Put it on my main screen, but under no circumstances are you to acknowledge receiving it. Understand me?"

"Understood, sir."

One of *Truax*'s technicians appeared on the screen; she looked puzzled, intent.

"*Truax* to *Lucifer*. Our sensors have just detected a seismic disturbance of some kind in the Aphrodite region. It might be a volcanic eruption. Please acknowledge."

Volcanic eruption? I immediately remembered Professor Greenbaum and Mickey, their theory about Venus's surface overturning.

The technician's face was replaced by a radar display of the western end of Aphrodite. A blinking red dot marked the site of the disturbance.

"That's nearly a thousand kilometers from our position," Fuchs grumbled. "No problem for us."

I started to say, "But it might be—"

"Maintain course and speed," Fuchs said, ignoring me and clicking off the display.

"Should I tell *Truax* we received their message, sir?" I asked.

"No. No contact."

"Sir," I tried again, "that eruption might be the beginning of a major tectonic upheaval."

He scowled at me. "Then we'd better get to the *Phosphoros* pretty damned quick, hadn't we?"

NIGHTSIDE

On Earth, nights are usually cooler than days because the Sun is not beaming its heat down onto the ground. On Venus this is not so. It makes no difference if the Sun is overhead or not, the thick sluggish cloud-topped Venusian atmosphere carries the Sun's heat all the way around the planet, while Venus's slow, ponderous rotation gives that soupy hot atmosphere plenty of time to spread its heat all across the world from pole to pole.

So we sweated and grew ever more irritable in the heat as we slowly groped toward the upland of Aphrodite Terra. The heat exchanger came back on line, but still it grew hotter inside the ship. We were floating through an atmosphere as dense as an earthly ocean thousands of meters below the surface. The temperature outside our hull went past two hundred degrees Celsius, then past three hundred.

Still we descended into the murk. My life became a monotonous routine of watches on the bridge, watches at the pumps, and a few hours to eat, wash, and sleep. Nodon was indeed promoted to the bridge, but Fuchs did not free me from my shifts at the comm console. I still was pulling double duty.

I began to feel the first faint tendrils of my old weakness. A slightly dizzy feeling if I moved my head too suddenly. A trembling in the legs, as if they were threatening to fold under me when I walked. I wished I could feel the chill that once accompanied my anemia; a chill would have felt good in the mounting heat.

I fought off the symptoms as much as I could. Mind over matter, I told myself. Sure. But even the mind is based in matter, and

when the blood supplying that matter lacks red cells, the mind itself
will soon enough collapse.

Marguerite must have been concerned, because Fuchs ordered
me to take a medical checkup and I was certain he wouldn't have
thought of that without her prodding him.

"Your red cell count is sinking fast," she said unhappily.
"You're going to need another transfusion right away."

"Not yet," I said, trying to sound brave. "Give him a chance to
recover from the last one."

"Don't you think—"

"I don't want to kill him," I snapped, trying to sound as coldly
callous as the captain himself. "I need him alive."

Marguerite shook her head, but said nothing.

During my watches on the bridge I tapped into the comm console's translation program and eavesdropped on the crew in their
various workstations. Plenty of griping about the heat. Several men
reported to the sick bay, complaining of dizziness or exhaustion.
The women seemed to take the growing heat better than the men, or
perhaps they were merely more stoic.

It was getting *hot.*

I wondered if Fuchs still was bugging the ship, or if he felt that
his punishment of Bahadur had cowed the rest of the crew sufficiently to eliminate the possibility of mutiny.

He seemed moody, distracted, his mind focused on other things
rather than the immediate problems of steering this submersible dirigible toward its ten-billion-dollar destination. It appeared to me
that Fuchs was concentrating his attention on something in the
future—or perhaps something from his past. And he was chewing
those damned pills of his constantly.

Lucifer ran well enough. Except for the mounting heat inside
the ship, all systems were performing within expected limits. The
crew worked fairly smoothly despite their grumbling; after all, they
knew that their lives depended on their doing things right. Literally.

I began to study the radar imagery as we groped along the
planet's nightside. There was little else for me to do, except log
incoming messages from *Truax* that were never answered or even
acknowledged. The volcanic eruption had subsided, they told us.
The Aphrodite region was seismically quiet once more, like the rest
of the planet. I felt decidedly relieved at that.

We were creeping pretty much along the equator, making slow
headway in the massively turgid atmosphere by using our engines
to force us through the soup. There was no wind to speak of, just a

slow, steady current flowing outward from the subsolar region, barely five kilometers per hour. Our engines easily compensated for that.

The elegance of the engines pleased me in a cerebrally aesthetic way. We were using the heat of the planet's own atmosphere to drive the turbines that ran the big paddle-bladed propellers that pushed us through the thick, hot air.

But each meter of altitude we lost meant the air was thicker and hotter. Heat rejection was becoming a problem. The crew nursed our heat exchangers along, mumbling worriedly over them more and more.

Fuchs paid almost no attention to their fears. His thoughts were obviously elsewhere. I kept searching the radar scans, looking for signs of wreckage down on the surface. I found three strong glints, but they were all far too small to be *Phosphoros*. Only one of them matched the known landing sites of earlier spacecraft probes, though. I wondered what the other two were, and found myself wishing we had enough daylight to use the telescopes.

I became fascinated with that strange, stark, utterly hostile landscape drifting below us. Even off-duty I made my way to the observation center up in the ship's prow to stare for hours on end at the radar imagery unfolding before my eyes. I began to understand Fuchs's fascination with this alien scenery, glowing red-hot in the darkness of night. It really was like looking down at the surface of hell, a barren, blasted, wretched expanse of total devastation, without a drop of water or a blade of grass, without hope or pity or help for pain.

"It's incredible, isn't it?"

I nearly hopped out of my skin. I'd been staring so intently at the radar images and the dull, stygian, sullen glow coming through the observation ports that I hadn't heard Marguerite come up behind me.

She didn't notice how startled I was; all her attention was on the views through the ports. The ruddy light from the surface made her face seem mysterious, exotic.

"It's terrifying and fascinating, both at the same time," she said in a near whisper. "Horrible and beautiful in its own deadly way."

I said, "More horrible than beautiful."

"What's that?" She pointed to the screen that displayed the radar imagery.

It showed a set of circular fractures, as if something gigantic had smashed the rocky surface like an enormous hammer.

"That's called a corona," I said. "An asteroid hit there; a big one. And look here, see these pancake features? Volcanoes, set off by the heat when the asteroid struck."

"As if it weren't hot enough down there already," Marguerite murmured.

"I wonder how old that corona is?" I asked myself more than her. "I mean, we don't know very much about how fast erosion works down on the surface. Did that asteroid hit recently or was the impact a hundred million years ago?"

"There's a lot to learn, isn't there?" she said.

"Not on this trip. We won't be able to do much science. We're here for the money this time around."

Marguerite gave me a strange look. "Do you expect to come back?"

I almost shuddered. But I heard my mouth blabbing, "Maybe. There really is a lot to learn. Greenbaum believes the whole surface of the planet is going to boil over, sooner or later. Maybe I can use some of the prize money to endow—" And then I stopped short, realizing that it was going to be Fuchs who got the prize money, not me.

Marguerite took a step closer to me, close enough to touch my shoulder with her hand. "Van, you have to start thinking about how much of . . . I mean, what condition your brother's body will be in."

"Condition?"

"There might not be much left to recover," she said, very gently.

"There's no oxygen down there to decompose his body," I mused aloud. "No bacteria or other scavengers."

"He was in the ship's escape pod, wasn't he? Sealed in?"

"Yes, that's the last word he sent out."

"Then he was in an oxygen atmosphere when he went down."

"But still . . ." I wanted to think that Alex's body would be preserved, somehow, waiting for me to carry it back home.

Marguerite had no such illusions. "There's the heat," she said. "And the pressure. Under those conditions even carbon dioxide becomes corrosive."

I hadn't considered that before. "You think he'd be . . . totally decomposed?"

"Temperatures that high destroy the chemical bonds that hold proteins together," she said.

"But he'd be in a spacesuit," I speculated. "In the escape pod. If he had time enough . . . he knew the ship was going down. . . ."

"Even so," Marguerite said.

"Do you think there might not be anything? Nothing at all?"

"It's a possibility. As you said, we simply don't know enough about the conditions on the surface, how they effect protein-based tissues."

If there had been a chair or even a stool in the observation port I would have slumped onto it. My legs felt rubbery, my insides a jumble.

"Nothing at all," I muttered.

Marguerite fell silent.

I gazed out onto that hellish landscape, then turned back to her. "To come all this way and find . . . nothing."

"There'd be artifacts, of course," she said. "Parts of the ship. Wreckage. I mean, you could certainly prove that you'd reached his ship, what remains of it."

"You mean Fuchs could prove it."

"Either way."

I almost wanted to laugh. "I can just see my father refusing to pay Fuchs because he failed to bring back my brother's remains."

"You don't think he'd do that, do you?"

"Don't I? It would be the final joke in this whole ridiculous farce."

"It's not really funny, is it?" she said.

But the more I thought about it, the more poetically absurd it all seemed. "Fuchs would tear my father's head off."

"I don't think so," Marguerite countered.

"Oh no? Him with his violent temper?"

"He doesn't have a violent temper," she said.

"The hell he doesn't!"

"He uses violence very deliberately. It's part of his way for getting what he wants. He's perfectly cool about it. Ice cold, in fact."

I didn't believe a word of it. "That's crazy," I said.

"No, it's the truth."

I stared at her for several long moments, watching the glow of Venus's searing heat playing across the planes of her cheeks, the curve of her jaw, striking sparks in her jet-black eyes.

"All right," I said. "I'm not going to argue with you about it. You know him better than I do."

"Yes," Marguerite replied. "I do."

I took a deep breath and turned away from her. Marguerite seemed willing to call an armistice, as well.

"Are those cliffs?" she asked, pointing to the screen that displayed the forward-looking radar imagery.

It took me an effort to shift mental gears. I studied the screen for a few moments, gathering my wits.

"Yes," I said, finally recognizing what the radar was showing. "Those cliffs mark the edge of Aphrodite Terra. That's where the *Phosphoros* went down, most likely."

CONTACT

slept like a dead man, thankfully without dreams. But when I awoke I felt just as tired as I had when I'd crawled into my bunk. Exhausted. Drained.

The crew's quarters were hot. The entire ship was uncomfortably hot, soggy, pungent with human sweat and the enervating inescapable heat that was seeping in from the torrid blanketing atmosphere outside our hull. The bulkheads felt warm to the touch, despite the ship's cooling system. The deck felt slippery, slimy to my bare feet.

At first I thought my exhaustion might have been the symptoms of my anemia coming back. But as I showered and shaved, with a trembling hand, I realized that it was emotional exhaustion as much as the anemia or the heat. My emotions were being whipsawed; it was more than I could deal with.

Marguerite claimed she was not sleeping with Fuchs, yet she seemed tied to him more strongly each time I spoke with her.

There might not be anything left of Alex for us to recover, and even if there were it would be Fuchs claiming the prize money when we got back, if we got back, not me.

I needed Fuchs's blood to stay alive, yet the transfusions were endangering his health. He was obviously not his old powerful, self-confident self. Something was gnawing at him. Were the transfusions sapping that much of his strength? Or was he feeling some form of guilt over the deaths of Bahadur and the two other mutineers?

I couldn't imagine Fuchs feeling guilt over anything, nor allowing himself to slowly die by giving his blood to me—especially to the son of Martin Humphries, the man he hated more than anyone else.

But Fuchs was weakening, whether it was physically or emotionally or a combination of the two. And that frightened me more than anything else. I realized that I would have preferred to see him at his old tyrannical, demanding self than to watch him sinking into moody, listless malaise. I needed him, we all needed him, to run *Lucifer.* Without Fuchs, the crew would up-ship and leave Venus for good.

Without a strong and vigorous captain, I'd be defenseless against the crew. If I tried to keep them from leaving they would slit my throat just as they'd murdered Sanja.

And without Fuchs to protect her, what would happen to Marguerite?

No wonder I felt overwhelmed and exhausted. And helpless.

I was in the galley, trying to get some breakfast down my throat while the sour body smells of my crewmates were making me gag, when the intercom blared, "MR. HUMPHRIES REPORT TO THE CAPTAIN'S QUARTERS AT ONCE."

The others sitting around the crowded galley table glared at me. I gladly dumped my meal into the recycler and hurried down the passageway to Fuchs's compartment.

It seemed slightly cooler in his quarters, but that was probably because there were only the two of us in the compartment. He was sitting on his rumpled bed, tugging on his boots.

"How are you feeling?" he asked as soon as I closed the sliding door behind me.

"All right," I said warily.

"Marguerite tells me you need another transfusion."

"Not just yet, sir."

He got to his feet and went to the desk. His face wore a sheen of perspiration.

"I thought you'd like to see the latest radar pictures," he said, pecking at his desktop keyboard.

The wall screen lit up. I saw the rugged mountains of Aphrodite and, down in the narrow sinuous cleft, the bright scintillations of a strong radar return.

My heart leaped, "The *Phosphoros?*"

Fuchs nodded, his face somber. "Looks like it. Has the right profile."

I stared at the screen. The wreckage of my brother's ship. Whatever was left of Alex was down there, waiting for me to recover it.

"He could have picked a worse spot," Fuchs muttered, his eyes also fixed on the screen, "but not by much."

"That's a pretty narrow valley," I said.

Nodding, Fuchs muttered, "On Earth there would be devilish air currents threading through that valley. Here, well . . . we just don't know."

The mountains looked raw, new, even in the radar image: sharp and jagged, as if they had been thrown up only recently. Those mountains couldn't be new, I thought. Not if Greenbaum and Cochrane were right, and Venus's plate tectonics had been locked up solid for the past half billion years. Vulcanism was also a puzzle. There were plenty of volcanoes to see, but none of them appeared to be active. Yet *something* had to be pumping sulfur compounds into the clouds, and volcanic eruptions seemed the only reasonable source for the sulfur. But in the century or so that probes had been observing Venus, none had ever seen a volcano erupt. Except for the eruption that *Truax* reported, and that scared me to the marrow with visions of Greenbaum's theory erupting in our faces.

I knew that a mere hundred years is less than an eyeblink when it comes to geological processes such as plate tectonics and vulcanism, but still—Earth and Venus are almost exactly the same size. Earth's interior is still bubbling hot; given such a similar mass and size, Venus's interior must be just as hot. Hardly a year goes by on Earth without some of that interior heat forcing its way to the surface in a major volcanic eruption. If there were no volcanoes blasting out boiling lava and steam for a whole century on Earth, the geologists would go insane.

Yet for the hundred or so years that spacecraft had been observing Venus there had been no recorded volcanic eruptions, until now. Why? Was Greenbaum right? Was Venus's crust getting hotter and hotter, edging toward the moment when all the surface rocks actually begin to boil into molten lava? Was it all going to blast right into our faces?

"Come with me," Fuchs said, snapping me out of my terrifying thoughts.

Turning away from the wall screen, I saw that he was already at the door and already scowling at me in his old impatient way. I almost felt glad.

He led me aft along the central passageway, then down a ladder into a small, bare compartment. A heavy hatch was set into its deck. Fuchs worked the control panel on the bulkhead, and I realized the hatch opened onto an airlock. He clambered down into it, then after a moment or so, popped his head up above the level of the deck again.

"It's all right, Humphries. There's pressure on the other side. Come down here."

I stepped to the lip of the hatch and saw that he had opened the airlock's bottom hatch and was starting to crawl through it. I climbed down the rungs set into the circular wall of the airlock. The metal was shining, new, hardly used. There was a ladder extended below the bottom hatch and I went down, one rung at a time, and planted both my feet on the deck.

Turning around, I saw that we were in a small chamber, something like a hangar or a narrow boathouse.

And sitting there, filling most of the chamber's space, was a sleek, arrow-shaped craft of gleaming white cermet. Its pointed nose was transparent. Its flared back end was studded with a trio of jet nozzles.

"What do you think of it?" Fuchs asked, actually grinning at the sight of the vehicle.

"Rather small," I said.

"One man, that's all it'll hold."

I nodded. Walking slowly around her, I could see several manipulator arms folded tightly against the vehicle's sides. I also saw the name that Fuchs had stencilled on the side of the ship: *Hecate.*

He saw the questioning look on my face. "A goddess of the underworld, associated with witchcraft and such."

"Oh."

"This ship will take me to the surface of hell, Humphries. You see the allusion?"

"It's a little rough," I said.

He huffed. "I'm only an amateur poet. Go easy on your criticism."

"This ship will maneuver on its own?" I asked. "It won't be tethered to *Lucifer*?"

"That's right. No tethers. *Hecate* will move independently."

"But—"

"Oh, I know you had a regular bathysphere on your ship. It wouldn't have worked."

That nettled me. "The best designers in the world built that bathysphere for me!"

"Yes, of course," Fuchs sneered. "And you were going to hover your *Hesperos* over the wreckage and lower your armored bathysphere to the surface."

"Right. And the tether connecting us would also be an umbilical that carried my air and electrical power and coolant."

"So I gathered. Did you think anyone—Duchamp or Rodriguez or God and his angels—could keep your mother ship hovering in place over the wreckage for more than ten minutes at a time? You'd be swinging back and forth in that stupid 'sphere like a pendulum."

"No!" I snapped, with some heat. "We did simulations that showed we could pinpoint the ship's position. The air's so dense down there that hovering is no problem."

"Maybe in a nice open plain with plenty of elbow room, but could you hover precisely in that snaky valley where the wreckage is?" Fuchs scoffed. "What did your precious simulations show you about that?"

I glared at him, but I had to admit, "We didn't do a simulation of those conditions."

"But those are the conditions we actually face, aren't they?" he gloated.

"Do you really expect this vehicle of yours to get you safely down to the surface and back?"

With a confident sweep of his hand, Fuchs answered, "*Hecate* was designed after the submersibles that oceanographers use back on Earth. They get to the bottom of the deepest Pacific trenches, ten kilometers and more below the surface. The pressure down there is six times worse than the pressure here on the surface of Venus."

"But the heat!"

"That's the big problem, right enough," he said easily. "*Hecate* doesn't have enough room for heat exchangers and the cooling equipment we're using on *Lucifer*."

"Then how—"

"*Hecate*'s hull is honeycombed with piping that carries heat-absorbing fluid. Even the observation ports are threaded with microducts."

"But what good does that do?" I demanded. "Just moving the heat from one area of the ship to another doesn't help much. You've got to be able to get rid of the heat, get it off-ship."

He broke into a wide, wolfish grin. "Ahh, that's the elegant part of it."

"So?"

"Most of *Hecate*'s mass is ballast: ingots of a lead-based alloy. A very special alloy, one we developed out in the Belt just for this purpose. Quite dense. Melts at almost precisely four hundred degrees Celsius."

"What's that got to do with anything?"

"It's simple," Fuchs said, spreading his hands. "So simple that your brilliant designers didn't think of it."

He looked at me expectantly, like a teacher I remember from prep school who always thought I was better prepared for the day's lesson than I actually was. I turned away from Fuchs, feeling my face twisting into a frown of concentration. A metal alloy. What was the point of carrying ingots of metal for ballast when you're going down to the surface—

"It's hot enough down there to melt lead," I heard myself say.

"Right!" Fuchs clapped his hands in mock applause.

"But I don't see . . ." Then I caught on. "The alloy ingots absorb the heat inside the ship."

"Precisely! And I vent the molten metal off-ship, thereby getting rid of the heat they've soaked up."

"But that will only work for as long as you still have ingots on board."

"Yes. The calculations show I can spend one hour on the surface. Maybe I can stretch it to seventy, seventy-five minutes. But not longer."

"It's . . ." I searched for a word . . . "ingenious."

"It's ingenious if it works," he said gruffly. "If it fails then it was a crazy idea."

I had to laugh at that.

But he was looking past me, past *Hecate* and this tight little chamber.

"I'm going down there, Humphries, down into the pit of hell. I'll be the first man to reach the surface of Venus. Live or die, no one will ever be able to take that away from me. The first man in hell."

My jaw fell open. He was looking forward to it, relishing the idea. Nothing else mattered to him. He was totally focused on it, eyes burning, lips pulled back in an expression that might have been a display of ecstacy or a snarl of defiance. And he was not chewing any pills, either.

"Ironic, isn't it?" he went on, glowing with expectation. "We finally reach a peak of knowledge where we've virtually eliminated aging, banished death. We can live and stay young as long as we like! And what do we do? We fight our damnedest to reach the surface of hell. We risk our foolish necks on escapades that only a madman would undertake! There's human nature for you."

I was speechless. There were no words in me to equal his fierce, maniacal intensity.

At last he shook his head, pulled himself together. "Okay, come along. I don't have more time to waste on this." He jabbed a thumb toward the ladder that led up into the airlock.

As we made our way back to his quarters I wondered why he had bothered showing me *Hecate* at all. Was it pride? Did he want me to admire the little ship, and the thinking that had gone into it? His thinking, of course.

Yes, I thought as we neared the bridge, he wanted to show off to somebody. To me.

And he certainly seemed to be his old, strong self again. Not a shred of uncertainty or infirmity in his appearance. He was looking forward to piloting *Hecate* down to the surface of Venus.

Then it struck me. He brought me down there not merely to show off his ship. He wanted to gloat over it, to show me how much smarter and stronger he was than I, to rub my nose in the fact that he was going to go down to the surface and claim the prize money while I sat up here in *Lucifer* like a hapless, helpless dimwit.

My hatred for him boiled up again. And to tell the truth, I enjoyed the emotion.

I served my watch on the bridge and then made my way back to the main pumping station. Fuchs had the ship circling above the wreckage now, some five thousand meters above the jutting peaks that surrounded whatever was left of my brother and his ship.

I had been fighting off the growing alarm signals that my body was sending to my brain. All through my watch at the pumps I felt the tingling and weakness in my legs slowly spreading to my arms. My vision went slightly blurry, no matter how hard or often I rubbed at my eyes. It took a conscious effort to lift my rib cage and breathe. I even began to feel chilled, fluttery inside.

I stuck it out for the duration of my watch, but I knew I couldn't last much longer without help. Like a drunk trying to prove he's still in command of his faculties I walked stiffly up the passageway, past the bridge, past Fuchs's quarters and then Marguerite's, heading for the sick bay.

She wasn't there. The sick bay was empty. I felt so wiped out that I wanted to crawl up onto the table and close my eyes. But maybe I'd never open them again, I thought.

She had to be somewhere. If my brain had been functioning right I would have used the intercom system to track her down. But

I wasn't reasoning very well. She had to be somewhere, that much I knew. Perhaps in her quarters.

I forced myself back down the passageway and rapped on her door. It rattled, but there was no answer. She *ought* to be here, I said to myself, nettled. I slid the door open; it was unlocked. Her quarters were empty.

Where in the seven golden cities of Cibola could she be? I raged to myself.

Fuchs's quarters! That's where she is. She claims she's not sleeping with him but she's in his quarters, just the two of them by themselves together.

It was only three or four steps to Fuchs's door. I didn't bother to knock. I yanked on the door and it slid open easily.

He was on the bed, half naked. And she was bending over him.

REVELATIONS

Marguerite must have heard me as I stepped into Fuchs's compartment. She turned her head. The expression on her face was awful.

"He's had a stroke," she said.

I realized that she was fully dressed. Tears were running down her face.

"He came off the bridge and called me here," she said, all in a rush. "The instant I came in he collapsed. I think he's dying."

The first thing that flashed through my mind, I'm ashamed to say, was that I needed Fuchs alive for another transfusion. The second, even worse, was that if he died I could drain all his blood and use it; that would be enough to keep me going until we got back to *Truax*. I felt like a vampire, but those were my thoughts.

Fuchs opened his eyes. "Not dying," he growled. "Just need . . . medication." His speech was slurred, as if he were drunk.

"Medication?" I asked.

Fuchs raised his left hand slightly and pointed shakily toward his lavatory. His right arm lay inertly by his side.

Marguerite got up from the bed and rushed to the lavatory.

"Kit . . ." Fuchs called weakly after her. "Under . . . the sink . . ."

I wasn't feeling all that strong myself, so I dragged up a chair and plopped into it, facing Fuchs on the bed.

The right side of his face was pulled down slightly, the eye almost closed. It might have been my imagination, but that side of his face seemed gray, washed out, almost as if it had been frozen.

"You don't . . . look so good," he said, weakly.

"Neither do you."

He made a sardonic rictus of a half smile and murmured, "Two of a kind."

Marguerite came back with a small black plastic case. She already had it open and was reading from the printout on the display screen set into the back of its lid.

"I'm going to inject you with TPA," she said, her eyes on the screen.

Fuchs closed both eyes. "Yeah . . ."

"TPA?" I asked stupidly.

Fuchs tried to answer. "Tissue plasmino . . ." He ran out of strength.

"Tissue plasminogen activator," Marguerite finished for him as she slapped a preloaded cylinder into the metal syringe from the medical kit. "It will dissolve the clot that's blocking the blood vessel."

"How can you be sure—"

"Clot buster," Fuchs said, his words blurred as if his tongue wasn't working right. "Works . . . every time."

I saw in the open medical kit that Marguerite had dropped on the bed beside him that several loops where cylinders had once been stored were now empty.

"How many times has this happened to you?" I blurted.

He glowered at me.

"He's had several mini-strokes," Marguerite said as she pressed the microneedle head of the syringe against Fuchs's bare biceps. Its hiss was barely audible. "This one's the worst yet, though."

"But what's causing it?" I asked.

"Acute hypertension," Marguerite said. Fuchs turned his glower on her.

I was stunned. "What? High blood pressure? Is that all?"

"All?" Marguerite snapped, her eyes suddenly blazing. "It's causing these strokes! It's killing him!"

"But blood pressure can be controlled with medication," I said. "Nobody dies of high blood pressure."

Fuchs laughed bitterly. "Very reassuring . . . *Doctor* Humphries. Feel better . . . already."

"But . . ." I was confused. Hypertension was something you treated with pills, I knew. That was the pills he'd been chewing! If he had the medication he needed, though, why was he having strokes?

"The medication controls the blood pressure only up to a

point," Marguerite said, a little more calmly. "But it doesn't do anything about the root causes."

"Does that mean I'm going to come down with it, too?" I asked. After all, I was getting his blood; did his disease come along with it?

Fuchs's expression turned to contempt, or perhaps it was disgust. He started to shake his head.

"Not from the transfusions," Marguerite said. "It's not carried by the blood."

"But doesn't his medication help?" I asked.

"It helps, but not enough to counteract the stress he's under."

"Stress?"

"Do you think captaining this ship isn't stressful?" she demanded. "Do you think dealing with this crew has been easy?"

"Not the stress," Fuchs mumbled. "The rage. How do you stop . . . the rage? Inside me . . . every minute . . . every day . . ."

"Rage," I echoed.

"Medication . . . can't control it," he said weakly. "The fury inside . . . the hate . . . even my dreams . . . nothing can control it. Nothing."

The rage. That boiling anger within him was what drove Fuchs. His hatred of my father. His blazing frustrated fury seethed within him like those red-hot rocks of hell below us, burning, boiling, waiting to burst loose in a torrent of all-consuming vengeance.

Every minute, he'd said. Every hour of every day. All those years with that hot relentless rage burning inside him, eating away at him, twisting his life, his being, his every moment waking or sleeping, into a brutally merciless torment of hate and implacable fury.

It was killing him, driving his hypertension relentlessly, pushing his blood pressure to the point where the microscopic capillaries in his brain were bursting. He always seemed in complete control of everything and everyone around him. But he couldn't control himself. He could keep the rage hidden, bottled up within him, but now I saw what a merciless toll it was taking on him.

"It's a vicious circle," Marguerite went on, as she pulled out one cylinder from the syringe and pressed in another. "The medication loses effectiveness so he increases the dosage. But the cause of his hypertension is still there! The stresses are getting worse, and so are the strokes."

He was suffering strokes. This tough, hard-handed captain was suffering from blockages in the blood supply to his brain. I stared at him with newfound awe. A normal person would be hospitalized for at least a few days, even with the mildest kind of stroke. I wondered what it felt like, how I would react.

I didn't want to find out.

"What are you doing now?" I asked.

She nodded toward the little display screen as she prepared the syringe. "VEGF to stimulate blood vessel growth and then an injection of neuronal stem cells to rebuild the damaged nerve tissue."

I had asked enough dumb questions, I thought. Later on I checked and found that vascular endothelial growth factor made the body build bypass blood vessels to reroute the circulation around the vessel damaged by the clot. Stem cells, of course, had the potential to build any kind of cells the body required: brain neurons, in this case, to replace those damaged by the stroke.

"If we had proper medical facilities we could treat him and get his pressure down to normal," Marguerite was muttering as she pressed the microneedle syringe home. "But here aboard ship—"

"Stop talking about me in the third person," Fuchs grumbled.

We sat and watched him for long, silent minutes. Vaguely I recalled reading that hypertension makes the blood vessels thicken and stiffen, which raises the blood pressure even more, and so on and so on. It can lead to strokes, I remembered, and even heart failure, all kinds of ailments. Fortunately, if you catch a minor stroke quickly enough, you can prevent most of the long-term damage to the brain. Or so I seemed to remember.

At last Fuchs struggled up to a sitting position. Marguerite tried to make him lie back down, but he pushed her hands away.

"It's all right," he said, his speech stronger, surer. His face was back to its usual color. "The clot buster worked. See?" He lifted his right arm and wiggled his fingers. "Almost back to normal."

"You need rest," Marguerite said.

Ignoring her, Fuchs pointed a thick finger at me. "The crew isn't to know about this. Not a hint of it! Understand me?"

"Of course," I said.

"Are you going to tell him the rest?" Marguerite asked.

His eyes went wide. I had never seen Fuchs look startled before, not even when he was flat on his back from the stroke, but he did at that instant.

"The rest of what?" I asked.

"You're going to make the flight down to the surface," Fuchs said.

"Me?"

"Yes, you. You're relieved of your duties on the bridge. Spend the time in the simulator, learning how to pilot *Hecate*."

My jaw must have dropped open.

"You're a qualified pilot," he said. "I read that in your résumé."

"I can fly a plane, yes," I said, then added, "on Earth." It never occurred to me to ask when and how he saw my résumé.

"Don't think you can claim the prize money because you actually go to the surface," Fuchs added. "I'm still the captain of this ship, and that prize is mine. Understand me? Mine!"

"I don't care about the prize money," I said. My voice sounded hollow, far away.

"Oh no?"

I shook my head. "I want to find my brother."

Fuchs looked away, glanced up at Marguerite, then back at me.

"Very noble," he mumbled.

But Marguerite said, "That's not what I meant."

He said nothing. I sat there like a sack of wet laundry, feeling physically exhausted, emotionally coiled tight, my mind jumping and jittering. How can I pilot *Hecate* with only a few hours of simulator time as training? No matter, I'll do it. I'll get down to what's left of *Phosphoros* and Alex. I'll do it. I will.

"You need another transfusion, don't you?" Fuchs asked gruffly.

"You can't!" Marguerite cried.

"Don't you?" Fuchs repeated sternly to me.

"Yes," I answered, "but in your condition . . ."

He made a dismissive gesture with one hand. "In my condition another transfusion will be helpful. It'll lower my blood pressure, won't it, Maggie?"

Her eyes flashed sudden anger, but then she half-smiled and nodded. "Temporarily," she said.

"You see?" Fuchs said, with mock geniality. "It's a win-win situation. We both gain something."

"That still isn't what I meant," Marguerite said to him, so softly I barely heard her.

Fuchs said nothing.

"It would be better if he heard it from you," she said.

He shook his head.

"If you don't tell him, I will."

"He won't believe you," he said sourly. "He won't believe me, either, so forget about it."

I spoke up. "I don't like being talked about in the third person any more than you do, you know."

"He's your father," Marguerite said.

I blinked. I couldn't have heard her correctly. She couldn't have said what I thought she had. My ears must be playing tricks on me.

But the look on her face was utterly somber, completely serious. I turned my eyes to Fuchs. His features seemed frozen in ice, hard and cold and immobile.

"It's the truth," Marguerite said. "He's your father, not Martin Humphries."

I wanted to laugh at her.

"I was born six years after my mother left him and married my father," I said. "If you're implying that she had an affair while she was married to my father . . ." I couldn't finish the sentence, the very thought of it made me so furious.

"No," Fuchs said heavily. "Your mother wasn't that kind of woman."

"That's right," I snapped.

He glanced at Marguerite, then said to me, "We were really in love, you know." His voice was gentler than I had ever heard it before. Or perhaps he was simply exhausted from the ordeal he'd just gone through.

"Then why did she leave you?" I demanded, even though Nodon had told me why.

"To save my life," he said, without an instant's hesitation. "She agreed to marry your father as the price for his letting me live."

"That's . . . unbelievable," I said.

"You don't believe that your father's had people killed? You never heard of the Asteroid War, the battles the corporations fought to drive out the independent prospectors?"

"In school . . ."

"Yes, I'm sure they told you all about it in your fancy schools. They taught you the official, sanitized version, nice and clean, no blood, no atrocities."

"You're getting off the subject," Marguerite said.

"If my mother hadn't seen you for six years before I was born, how can you claim to be my father?" I challenged him.

He let out a deep, painful sigh. "Because when we were living together we had some of her ova fertilized with my sperm and then frozen."

"Frozen?"

"We were going to have a family," Fuchs said, his voice low, his eyes looking into the past. "As soon as I got my mining company up and running, we were going to have children."

"But why freeze the embryos?" I demanded.

"Zygotes," he corrected. "They weren't embryos yet, merely fertilized eggs that hadn't begun to divide."

"Why go to all the trouble—"

"Because I had to spend so much time in space," he explained. "We wanted to avoid the risk of radiation damage to my DNA."

"But then she married my father."

"To save me."

"She married him."

"But she never had a child by him," Fuchs said. "I don't know why. Maybe he'd gone sterile. Maybe she wouldn't sleep with him once she found out that instead of killing me he destroyed me financially."

Marguerite said, "She had herself implanted with a fertilized egg and you were the baby she bore." Nodding toward Fuchs, she added, "His son."

"How did you know I'm your son?" I insisted.

"I didn't. Not until Marguerite started looking for a way to produce the enzymes you need. She ran DNA scans on both of us."

"I don't believe it," I said.

Marguerite glared at me. "Do you want me to show you the DNA scans? Why do you think his blood type is compatible with yours?"

"But—she waited six years?"

"I don't know why she did it or why she waited," Fuchs said. "She was heavily into drugs by then, I know that much. Living with your father turned her into an addict."

I had no reply to that.

With another groaning sigh, he went on, "Anyway, she got one of the fertilized ova and had herself implanted. He must have realized it wasn't his child as soon as he found out that she was pregnant. . . ."

"And he killed her," I said.

"She died in childbirth, didn't she?" Marguerite asked.

"He probably tried to kill you both," Fuchs said.

"He's always hated me," I said, in a whisper.

Marguerite added, "Your anemia came from her blood, while she was carrying you."

"He's always hated me," I repeated, feeling empty inside, hollow. "Now I know why."

"Now you know it all," Fuchs said.

I looked at him as if seeing him for the first time. I was about his height, although my build was much lighter, much slimmer than his. My face was nothing like his, probably much more like my mother's. But his ice-blue eyes were not far from the shade of my own.

My father. My biological sire. Martin Humphries was not my begetter, he was only my caretaker, the man who had wanted me dead, the man who belittled and scorned me all my life.

"Do you really think he killed my brother?" I wondered aloud.

Fuchs sank back down on the bed, as if all this had suddenly become too much for him to bear.

"Do you think he killed Alex?" I repeated, raising my voice.

"You'll find out when you're down on the surface, going through his ship's wreckage," Fuchs said. "You'll either get your answer there, or you'll never know."

SIMULATIONS

left Fuchs's quarters like a sleepwalker and stumbled down to the virtual reality chamber, to start my hurried training for piloting *Hecate.*

My mind was spinning. Fuchs was my biological father? My mother had loved him so much that she bore his baby even though she was married to Martin Humphries? Yes, I realized, that would be entirely possible. Probable, even. She didn't want a child by Martin Humphries, that was clear. For six years she lived with him, allowed him to shame her with his womanizing, make a mockery of their marriage. Talk about trophy wives! My mother was his prize, the living symbol of his victory over Lars Fuchs. Her life must have been a pit of hell.

And here was Fuchs, my biological father, dying of the stresses that drove him. Obviously he wanted his revenge on my foster father, and just as obviously for all the years of my life he knew there was no way he could touch Martin Humphries, no way he could make Humphries suffer as he himself had suffered, no way he could make Martin Humphries pay for the death of my mother, the woman he loved, the woman who sacrificed her life to save his.

Until this idiotic Venus prize. Once Fuchs heard that Martin Humphries was offering that ten-billion-dollar prize he recognized his chance to score at least a little of the vengeance he had nursed for more than a quarter of a century.

As I slowly pulled on the protective suit that I was to wear in *Hecate,* I went over and over what little I knew about my own origins, wondering who and what I could believe.

Why did she do it? Why did my mother flaunt her love for

Fuchs after six years of marriage to my . . . to Martin Humphries? She must have known how it would enrage him. Perhaps that was why she did it; to hurt him, to strike back at him, to humiliate him in the only way she could.

And he killed her. Did she know he'd go that far? Did she care? She must have protected me, somehow. Must have seen to it that I was safe from his malice, from his hatred.

Yes, she made certain I was physically safe even though she couldn't protect her own life. Or perhaps she didn't care about herself. Perhaps his killing her was a release for her, an end to the pain that had filled her life.

Yet Martin Humphries did not kill me. I was probably cared for by people my mother had chosen. Or, more ironic still, probably it was my terrible physical condition that saved my life. For my first few months I was maintained in a special medical facility while my various birth ailments kept me hovering on the brink of death. Perhaps Martin Humphries figured that I would die of my own accord; he wouldn't have to bother with me, after all.

But I survived. I lived. How that must have tormented him! Me, the constant reminder that no matter how wealthy he was, no matter whom he could buy or sell, whom he could destroy financially or murder outright, I had survived. Me, the weakling, the Runt, the child sired by the one man in the solar system that he hated the most, I lived under his own roof.

He made my life as hellish as he dared. Did Alex know the entire story? Was Alex standing between me and my foster father's murderous wrath? When Alex had his shouting match with his father, just before he left for Venus, was the fight about politics—or about me?

There was only one way for me to find out; only one person in the entire solar system knew what had really happened. Martin Humphries. I had to face him, confront him, get the truth out of him. And to do that, I had to survive this journey to the surface of Venus. I had to go through hell to get back to learn the facts of my own existence.

"Are you asleep down there?" Fuchs's acrimonious voice snarled in my earphones.

That snapped my attention to the job at hand. He must be back on the bridge, I told myself, back in command. Until his next stroke.

"I'm suited up and entering the VR chamber," I said into my helmet mike.

"Okay," he replied. "The *Hecate* simulation is ready whenever you are."

"Good," I muttered as I clomped to the hatch that opened into the virtual reality chamber.

The special protective suit included most of the features of a regular spacesuit, of course, although to me it looked more like the cumbersome rigs worn by deep-sea divers in those ancient days before the invention of scuba gear. Heavy metal helmet with a tiny faceplate, bulky armored torso, arms and legs of thick cermet, boots that felt as if they weighed a ton apiece. The entire suit was honeycombed with tubing that circulated coolant, of course. Actually the tubes carried a true refrigerant and the backpack that I would have to wear included a miniaturized version of the type of cryostat used in physics labs to liquify gases such as hydrogen and helium.

So I shambled through the hatch like some old video monster, the servomotors on the suit whining and wheezing away with every plodding step I took. Without the servos I'd never have had the muscular strength to move my arms and legs.

The VR chamber was a blank-walled compartment. One of the crew had put in a bunk, which would serve as a crude simulation for the couch in *Hecate*'s cockpit. The virtual reality stereo goggles were resting on the bunk, together with a set of data gloves and slippers. It took me several minutes to open the faceplate of my helmet and hook the goggles over the bridge of my nose, even longer to worm on the gloves and work the slippers over my clumsy boots. Fuchs grumbled impatiently every moment of the time.

"The way you're going at it, it'd be easier on my blood pressure for me to pilot *Hecate* myself," he complained.

That was the first time I'd ever heard him mention his blood pressure in front of the crew. He must have been truly disturbed by my slowness.

"I'm getting onto the couch now," I said, once I had closed the faceplate again.

"About time," he muttered.

Once I was stretched out prone on the couch my vision suddenly began to swirl giddily, flashes of color flicking on and off. For an instant I thought this was some new symptom of my anemia, but then the flashing ended as abruptly as it had started and I was looking at *Hecate*'s control panel. The virtual reality simulation had kicked in; my goggles were showing what I'd see when I actually was piloting the little ship.

Above the panel I saw the strewn wreckage of *Phosphoros,* torn and twisted sections of the ship's metallic hull. A computer-graphics illusion, I knew, generated for the VR program. But it looked very real to me, fully three-dimensional.

My imaginary *Hecate* was hovering three kilometers above the illusory wreckage of *Phosphoros,* so my virtual instruments told me. I could see nothing inside the wreck, because we had no idea of what to expect in there. My task was to learn how to bring *Hecate* smoothly down to the wreckage, search its interior for any sign of Alex's remains, and then get safely back to *Lucifer* again.

The ship's controls were simple enough. The computer did most of the work. I merely ran my gloved fingertips over the touchpads in the control panel and the ship responded almost instantly. Whoever had designed the control system had done an admirable job; it all worked intuitively. Right hand controlled pitch and yaw, left hand controlled roll. When you wanted to go left you moved your right index finger leftward along the touchpad. When you wanted to pitch the nose down, you slid your forefinger down the pad. The right foot pedal controlled the thrusters at the ship's tail; the left pedal worked her fins, which pivoted like the diving planes of a submarine.

Simple. But not easy.

I won't tell you how poorly I did, at first. My clumsy attempts at piloting had Fuchs swearing and me sweating.

"You're overcorrecting," he would shout into my earphones.

Or, "Too steep! You're coming in too steep!"

It took more than a dozen tries before he was satisfied enough to let me descend down to the wreckage. Then I practiced working the waldoes, the glovelike implements that controlled the manipulator hands outside the hull. Again, it was simplicity itself in principle. Whatever motions your fingers made were reproduced faithfully by the mechanical hands outside. Again, it was devilishly difficult in practice to get the feel of those manipulators, to learn how to work them deftly enough to pick up a scrap of twisted metal or a piece of shattered equipment.

By the time Fuchs finally agreed to end the VR session I was soaked with perspiration and gasping for breath.

"Meet me in the sick bay," he said as I wearily picked myself up from the bunk that had served as the virtual *Hecate*'s couch.

Nodon came to the VR chamber to help me out of the heat suit. A good thing, too. I don't think I could have done much more than lift the heavy metal helmet off my head.

"How long was I in there?" I asked, panting, as he tugged the suit's heavy torso up and over my head.

"One full watch, almost," he said.

Nearly eight hours. No wonder I was exhausted.

A sly grin cracked his thin, almost fleshless face. "Captain said you did very well," he confided.

"He did?"

"Oh yes. He said you didn't wreck the ship once. Almost! But no wreck."

Faint praise from Fuchs was like a Nobel Prize from anyone else, I thought.

"He also said not to tell you," Nodon added, his smile turning into a boyish grin.

Marguerite was in the sick bay with Fuchs when I got there.

"I don't think we should go through with this transfusion," she said. "You've just suffered a serious stroke and—"

"And he's not going out in *Hecate* with his damned anemia gnawing at him," Fuchs snapped. He was sitting on the narrow examination table, Marguerite standing beside him.

"But your condition . . ." Marguerite objected.

He made a grisly smile for her. "Your ministrations have worked wonders. I'm fine."

She could be just as stubborn as her mother, though. Marguerite insisted on doing a scan of Fuchs's brain before proceeding with the transfusion. I stood in the hatch of the crowded sick bay, feeling tired and weaker every second, while she made him lie down, fixed the scanner to his head, and ran off a reading.

Watching him lying there, his eyes closed while the scanner buzzed softly, I realized anew that this man was my father. It was hard to accept that, even though I knew it was true. I mean, it's one thing to know something is true intellectually, up in the front of your brain. But to *feel* it, to accept it down in your guts, that's something else entirely.

He's my father, I said silently to myself over and over again. This man who can be so brutal at one moment and then quote poetry a moment later, this bundle of contradictions, this wounded snarling animal is my father. I'm made from his genes.

I believed it, but still I had no real feeling for Fuchs—except a grudging respect and a healthy amount of outright fear.

The scanner stopped its buzzing. Marguerite removed it from Fuchs's head while the main display screen on the bulkhead began building up a three-dimensional view of his brain. We all peered at the image intently, even though I really didn't know what I was supposed to be looking for.

"See?" Fuchs said, sitting up again as he pointed to the false-color image of his own brain. "No permanent damage."

The image looked like a normal brain to me; all of it tinged a sort of bluish gray. No alarming areas of red, which I presumed was the color that would be used to show damage.

"New blood vessels are developing," Marguerite said, cautiously. "But the area where the blockage occurred isn't fully repaired yet."

With an impatient shake of his head, Fuchs said, "It's too small to matter. I feel fine. Take a liter of my blood and my pressure will go down to normal."

"A liter!" Marguerite's eyes flashed wide. "Not even half that much."

Fuchs chuckled. He had been joking, I realized. He had a strange sense of humor, dealing with people's lives, including his own.

Rolling up his sleeve and lying back down on the table, he growled, "Come on, get it over with."

I sat in the chair Marguerite had jammed in next to the table and closed my eyes. I couldn't stand to watch anyone get a needle jabbed into his flesh, especially me.

I went back to my bunk in the crew's quarters and slept very soundly. If I dreamed, I don't remember it. When I awoke, I felt strong, refreshed.

Then I realized that in a few hours I would be donning that heavy heat suit again and crawling into the real cockpit of the actual *Hecate*.

I would be going down to the surface of Venus, the first live human being to do so. Me! Alone down there where the rocks are red-hot and the air is so thick it can crush a spacecraft into crumpled wreckage.

To my surprise, I wasn't terrified. Oh, there were butterflies in my stomach, true enough. I didn't feel like one of those ultracool adventurers you see on video. I fully realized that there was a fine chance that I'd die out there, beside my brother.

But most of those butterflies inside me were from anticipation. To my utter surprise, I was looking forward to this! I told myself I was a fool, but it didn't matter; I *wanted* to go, *wanted* to be the first living human being to reach the hellhole surface of Venus, *wanted* to get down there and search for Alex's remains.

I forced myself to picture my home in Majorca and the cool, lovely blue sky and sea. And Gwyneth. My friends. My life before this mission to Venus had shattered everything. It all seemed pale and senseless now. Pointless. Mere existence, not living.

Even as I began to pull on the heat suit, with Nodon and bulky, sulky Amarjagal helping me, I couldn't help thinking, I'm alive! I'm doing something real, something that's never been done before, something that matters in the ongoing development of the human race.

A voice in my head warned sardonically, What you are doing is very likely to kill you.

And the other side of my mind quoted Shakespeare: We owe God a death . . . he that gives it this year is quits for the next.

In other words, I had gone slightly crazy.

HECATE

hings started going wrong right from the start.

Hecate's actual cockpit was different from the VR simulation's. The differences were subtle, but significant.

For one thing, the foot pedals that controlled the thrusters and diving planes were a couple of centimeters too far away for my boots to reach comfortably. I had to stretch my legs and point my toes to get a solid contact with the pedals. In those Frankenstein boots I had to wear, that was a guaranteed method of developing leg cramps. Or foot cramps. Or both.

The layout of the controls was the same, thank goodness, but *Hecate* didn't respond to the controls in the same smooth, clean fashion as the virtual reality sim. As I went through the checklist, lying there prone in the heat suit and sweating bullets even before the ship was released from *Lucifer*'s hold, it seemed to me that there was a slight lag between my touching a control and the response from the ship's systems. It was only a tiny hesitation, but it was noticeable—and annoying.

I was wondering if there was some way to speed up the ship's response even while we went through the checklist and started the separation countdown.

In my helmet earphones I heard Fuchs ask perfunctorily, "T minus two minutes and counting. Any problems?"

"Uh, no," I said, quite unprofessionally. "Everything's pretty good here."

He caught the doubt in my voice. "Pretty good? What does that mean?"

The countdown would go into automatic mode at T minus one

minute, we both knew. This was no time to try to fiddle with the control responses.

"Nothing, forget it. Ready for separation sequence."

Silence from the bridge, until the computer's synthesized voice came on, "T minus one minute. Separation sequence engaged."

"Right," I said.

"T minus fifty seconds. Internal power on."

I heard pumps start chugging. The instrument panel flickered for an eyeblink, then its lights steadied. I knew my suit's cooling system was working, I could hear the tiny fan in my helmet buzzing. Yet I was already drenched with cold sweat. Nerves. Nothing but nerves.

"T minus thirty seconds. Bay hatch opening."

Through *Hecate*'s thick hull and my own suit's heavy insulation I heard the low rumble of the hatch swinging back slowly. From my position, flat on my belly in *Hecate*'s pointed nose, I looked down at the thick quartz panel set into the floor of the cockpit just below the instrument board. All I saw was the inside of my stupid helmet. I had to twist my head and crane my neck to see the window through the tiny faceplate of my helmet.

And there it was, the sullen, incandescent surface of Venus, glowing like a sea of molten lava. I could *feel* that heat boiling up at me, clutching for me. I knew it was my imagination; we were still several kilometers above the surface, yet I felt the hot breath of the planet smothering me.

I stared at those red-hot rocks as the countdown ticked away.

"Three . . . two . . . one . . . release," said the computer's impassive voice.

With a heart-stopping bang the latches that held *Hecate* firmly in their grip suddenly released and I was falling through the thick, still air of Venus toward its distant hard surface. I was frozen with terror, paralyzed as I felt my stomach surging up into my throat. It was like dropping down the longest elevator shaft in the universe toward a blazing hot furnace. But slowly, slowly as in a nightmare.

Fuchs's voice crackled in my earphones:

> "Hurled headlong flaming from th' etheral sky,
> With hideous ruin and combustion, down
> To bottomless perdition . . ."

And he laughed. Laughed!

That broke my terrified paralysis. I kicked at the pedals, ran my fingers across the controllers, struggled to get *Hecate* leveled off and gliding properly.

"Pull her nose up," Fuchs commanded. "Don't dive her! Get your speed right and she'll sink at her natural rate."

"Right," I said, kicking the pedals and working the touchpad controls as furiously as I could.

"You're overcontrolling her!" he shouted so loud in my earphones it made me wince.

I was desperately trying to get the feel of the controls. They didn't respond the way the VR sim did. I got a flash of memory from the first time I tried to ride a horse and realized that this substitute for an automobile had a mind of its own; it did not respond mechanically to my steering.

"I should've gone down myself," Fuchs was grumbling.

Slowly I was getting the feel of the controls, but a glance at the course profile indicator on the panel showed me I was far off my intended speed and angle of descent. The dive-plane control felt especially stiff; the pedal barely budged even when I tried to kick it.

The flight plan was for me to spiral down toward the *Phosphoros*'s wreckage, while Fuchs kept *Lucifer* circling overhead some three kilometers up. I was scanning the wreckage with every instrument aboard *Hecate,* which wasn't really all that much: radar, infrared, and optical sensors. The infrared was practically useless, swamped by the enormous heat flow from the surface.

Greenbaum's theory of planetary upheaval popped into the front of my mind. What if Venus decided to overturn its surface right now, at this precise time? A volcano had erupted less than a thousand kilometers from here. What if everything down there suddenly began to melt and all the stored heat that's been trapped deep below ground suddenly comes bursting out? Murphy's Law on a planetary scale. After five hundred million years of waiting, the planet decides to blow off its surface while I'm there. I'd be roasted in a minute; not even *Lucifer* could escape the catastrophe.

That's not going to happen, I told myself sternly. Put it out of your mind. I remembered the gloomy look on Greenbaum's face when he admitted that there was practically no chance that the cataclysm would happen while we were there to observe it—or be incinerated by it, more likely.

"Stay on the profile!" Fuchs snapped.

I was struggling to do just that, but I wasn't succeeding fast enough to avoid stirring his wrath. Gritting my teeth, I traced my fingertips across the touchpads, feeling more like a child playing with a magnetic sketching toy than an intrepid astronaut making the first controlled descent to the surface of Venus.

"Where's your imagery?" Fuchs demanded.

I saw from the control panel that I hadn't switched on the channel that telemetered the pictures that *Hecate*'s sensors were getting.

"On its way," I said, imitating the clipped tone of astronauts I remembered from old videos.

I put the optical camera view on my own screen, right in front of my face. Now I could see why Fuchs was complaining; it showed nothing but bare hot rocks. It should have been focused on the wreckage.

Gradually I smoothed out *Hecate*'s flight, got the ship on course. I wasn't using the thrusters, they weren't needed until I had to lift from the surface, so I put both my booted feet on the pedal that controlled the diving planes. It was a little easier to work them that way. Sure enough, my calf muscles started cramping, hard enough to make me want to scream from the pain. But I kept at it, grimly determined to get down to the wreckage and find what was left of my brother's body.

In a way it really was like riding a horse. *Hecate* had a will of her own, and I had to learn to deal with it. The controls were terribly stiff and slow to respond, but little by little I got the feel of them, and focused the sensors on the wreckage below. It wasn't anything like flying; Venus's atmosphere was so thick that my descent was more like a submarine groping for the bottom of the ocean.

There wasn't much to see, at first. *Phosphoros*'s gas envelope had collapsed atop most of the ship's gondola. I could only see one end of the gondola sticking out from beneath the warped, twisted metal. Huge sections were missing, eaten away, it looked like. They must have spent even more time in the bug-laden clouds than we had in *Hesperos,* with disastrous results.

As I edged lower, I began to see the characteristic charring-like streaks along what little of the gondola was visible beneath the crumpled gas envelope. The envelope itself was smudged and streaked with the dark char stains from the bugs in the clouds. *Phosphoros* wasn't sabotaged, I realized. It didn't have to be. Those aerobacteria destroyed my brother's ship just as they destroyed my own.

Then I noticed something strange. Curving lines were crisscrossed over the wreckage, a dozen or more thin lines almost like twine or string looped around a package. I wondered what they were. Nothing I remembered from the design drawings or pictures of *Phosphoros* showed strapping or any other kind of structural supports strung across the gas envelope.

Curious.

"Spiral in tighter," Fuchs commanded. "Stay focused on the wreckage."

"That's what I'm trying to do," I said, feeling testy.

"Don't *try,*" he sneered. "Do!"

I snapped, "You come and do it if you don't like the way I'm handling it!"

He went silent.

I could see the wreckage in more detail as I descended cautiously through the thick air. It was clear enough; no haze or dust in the air. But the pressure was so high that it was like peering through seawater. Things were distorted, twisted.

At first I couldn't tell which end of the gondola was sticking out from beneath the collapsed envelope, but as I got closer I recognized it was the forward section. It had split open like an overcooked sausage, ripped right down the middle. I saw plenty of charring streaks that the aerobacteria had left on the outer surface of the hull. The insides looked strangely bare and empty.

With a sudden gasp of hope I saw that the compartment where the escape pod had been housed was empty. Had Alex gotten away? Had he used the pod to ride up into orbit?

Then I realized that it made no difference if he had; it was more than three years since *Phosphoros* went down. He couldn't be alive even if his pod had made it to orbit. Besides, there had been absolutely no radio messages from the escape pod, not even an automated beacon.

Then, to seal the question, I saw the pod. It had rolled a few dozen meters from the rest of the wreckage, coming to rest against a big, hot, glowing rock the size of a suburban house.

And several of those strange dark lines went across the bare rock to the escape pod. They were too straight to be cracks in the surface, and they came from too many different angles to be the track of the pod's rolling across the rocky surface.

"What are those lines?" Fuchs asked.

"That's what I'd like to know," I said.

"They seem to radiate outward from the escape pod."

"Or to come together at the spot where the pod came to rest," I corrected.

"Impact cracks?" he mused.

"There's more of them crisscrossed over the gas envelope," I said.

"Can't be cracks, then."

"Right," I answered. "But what are they?"

"Go find out."

"Right."

"We're using up a lot of fuel, keeping station above you," he said. That was Fuchs's way of telling me to hurry up.

"I'll be on the surface in a few minutes," I said. Inwardly, I was trying to decide if I should put *Hecate* down alongside the pod or next to the wreckage of the ship's main body.

"Check out the pod first," Fuchs said, as if he could read my mind. "Then you can lift and shift over to the gondola."

"Right," I said again. I realized it had been some time since he'd insisted on my addressing him as "sir" or "captain." Did he respect me now as an equal? Or was it the father-son relationship? That was tricky. It was just as wrenching for him to find that I was his son as it was for me to learn he was my father. Neither one of us was prepared to handle that load of emotional freight.

Something flickered in the corner of my eye.

"What was that?" Fuchs snapped.

"What?"

"That light."

I scanned the control panel, looked through the observation port in the deck. Everything seemed to be functioning properly.

"What light?"

"On the horizon," he said, his voice hesitant, uncertain. "In the east."

Trying to remember which way was east, I looked through the forward port. Far off on the horizon there was a glow lighting the grayish-yellow clouds. It pulsed, brightened.

"Sunrise?" I guessed.

"Too soon," said Fuchs. "Besides, the sun rises in the west."

That's right, I said to myself. Then what was the light in the east?

"Wait," Fuchs said. "We're getting a message from *Truax*."

What would *Truax* be sending? I wondered. A warning, the other side of my mind answered. Yes, but a warning about what?

It only took a few moments to get the answer.

Fuchs's voice came back into my earphones. "It's another volcanic eruption."

"Another eruption?"

"Nothing to worry about. It's four hundred kilometers away."

I swallowed hard and tried not to think about Greenbaum. But in my imagination I could see the glee on his face. This might well be only the second Venusian volcano blast in half a billion years. And he'd be getting data from us on it!

Unless we got killed first.

ERUPTION

stared too long at that sullen pinkish glow on the horizon, thinking about volcanoes and Greenbaum and the whole surface of the planet below me opening up and frying me with the stored heat of half a billion years suddenly released into my face.

Two volcanoes within days of each other meant either that Greenbaum was wrong or that Venus was beginning to boil over.

"You're spraying the wreckage!" Fuchs shouted in my earphones.

"What?"

"The exhaust!" he yelled, exasperated. "You're letting it spray over the wreckage."

The molten metal from *Hecate*'s heat sink, I realized. The ship was spitting the melted alloy out from its rear, carrying the built-up heat away from me. Venusian guano, I thought wryly. It was settling over the wreckage.

"Point her nose properly!" Fuchs demanded. "You're covering up the whole blasted wreck!"

He was excited, up there. Hovering high above me in *Lucifer,* Fuchs must have felt completely frustrated at having to sit on his bridge and watch my clumsy efforts to do what he thought he could perform flawlessly.

I wondered what that was doing to his blood pressure as I fought to orient *Hecate* so that I spiraled ever closer to the wreckage without burying it under the ship's excretion of molten alloy.

Could that be the strange lines crisscrossing the wreckage? I wondered. But a quick look at the scene below me showed it was not. Those lines were thin and mostly quite straight, although some of them curved here and there—rather gracefully, actually. *Hecate*'s hot droppings clearly splashed when they hit the ground, forming bright new-looking puddles of liquified metal.

Some of the droppings had spattered one end of the crushed gas envelope. Nothing important had been covered by the alloy, I saw. Fuchs was getting worked up over very little, it seemed to me.

I blinked sweat from my eyes as I worked *Hecate* lower and lower. And then I saw something that made my eyes pop wide.

One of those lines moved. No, more than one. Several of them whipped across the oven-hot rocks to converge on the splashes of alloy that had dropped from *Hecate*.

"You only have fifty-five minutes left on the heat sink," Fuchs's voice warned, a bit more calmly now.

"Did you see that?" I yelled, excited, more puzzled than afraid. "Those lines moved!"

"Moved?"

"Yes! Didn't you see them?"

"No."

"They went to the alloy puddles," I said, almost shouting, trying to convince him.

Fuchs was silent for a few moments, then he replied, "I don't see any movement."

"But I saw them move! And fast, too! Like lightning."

"You can attend to that later," he said, his voice betraying his doubts about my powers of observation. "Get to the escape pod. The clock keeps ticking."

The plan was to use the manipulator arms to open up the escape pod and see if Alex had made it inside successfully. But if he had retreated into it as his ship went down, wouldn't it be better to leave it sealed and bring it up in its entirety? That way, if he really was inside, his body would remain protected from the Venusian atmosphere; at least, as much protection as the pod could give.

"Can *Hecate* lift the whole pod, intact?" I asked into my helmet mike.

No response for a few moments. Then Fuchs asked, "How much does it weigh?"

"I have no idea," I admitted. "A ton or so, I guess."

"Very precise," he said acidly.

"How much can *Hecate* carry?"

Another pause. I imagined him hurriedly scanning the computer files. It was getting hot in the cockpit, despite the heat sink and the ship's cooling system. Really hot. My suit was sloshing with sweat. I felt as if I were lying facedown on a big, soaking-wet sponge.

"*Hecate* can lift four tons," Fuchs replied at last, "once the ballast is off-loaded."

"That should be more than enough to take the pod," I said.

"Right," he agreed. "Should be enough space in the cargo bay to hold it, too."

"All right, then. I'm going to inspect the gondola first and then bring up the pod intact."

Marguerite's voice came through. "Even if your brother was in the pod, Van, there's practically no chance that any organic matter could survive this long."

I was almost close enough to the ground to touch it. The heat was getting ferocious.

"You mean there won't be any physical remains of his body," I said to Marguerite.

"Yes, I'm afraid that's what you've got to expect," she said. "Even if he got into the pod."

Nodding inside my helmet, blinking stinging sweat out of my eyes, I replied, "I'm still going to go for returning the whole pod. Is that all right with you, Captain?"

Fuchs immediately answered, "Okay. Proceed."

Edging *Hecate* toward the burning hot rocks, feeling the glare of the heat on my face even through the ship's thick ports and my helmet, I worked carefully, slowly to keep the ship's tail end pointing away from the wreckage.

"We read ten meters," Fuchs said tensely.

"Ten meters, right."

I had the radar altimeter displayed on the observation port, so I could see the ground inching up toward me and the altitude numbers at the same time.

"Five meters . . . three . . ."

I felt a short of crunching, grinding sensation as the landing skids beneath little *Hecate*'s hull grated across the bare rocks. Very little noise. Then the ship lurched to a stop.

"I'm on the ground," I said. I should have been exultant, I suppose, but instead I was almost exhausted from tension and the searing, overpowering heat.

"Word is being telemetered back to Earth," Fuchs said. "You've touched down on the surface of Venus."

A moment of triumph. All I felt was hot, sopping with sweat, and anxious to get the job done and get out of this hellish furnace.

"I'm activating the manipulators," I said, touching the stud on the control panel that powered up the remote grippers and the outside flood lamps.

Then all the lights went out. The control panel blacked out completely and the steady background hum of electrical equipment died away.

I damned near wet myself. For a breathless moment I was completely in the dark, except for the angry glow of Venus's red-hot rocks, just on the other side of my observation port. I could hear my pulse thudding in my ears.

And then a really scary noise: a kind of a thump, light but definite, as if someone had dropped a cable across the top of the ship.

Before I could say anything, the auxiliary power came up. The control panel glowed faintly. The pumps gurgled somewhere in the back of the ship. Fans whined to life again.

"Power's out," I said, surprised at how steady my voice sounded.

Fuchs sounded worried. "Must be an overload from the manipulator motors."

"And the floodlights," I added.

"Shut them down and try to restart the main batteries."

I did that and, sure enough, the ship powered itself up nicely. I blew out a breath of relief.

Then I realized that if I couldn't use the manipulators there was no point being down here by the wreckage.

A very powerful urge to light off the thrusters and get up and away almost overcame me. I actually had both boots on the thruster pedal before I realized it.

But I stopped and fought back the itch to flee. Think, dammit, think! I raged at myself. There's got to be a way to fix this.

"We're scanning your telemetry," Fuchs said, his voice sounding edgy in my earphones. "Looks like the servo motors in the manipulators are drawing almost twice as much power as they were designed to do. Might be from the heat."

"Listen," I said, my mind racing, "what if I put the manipulators and lamps on the backup power system? The auxiliaries can power the arms and lights while the main batteries run everything else."

After a moment's hesitation, Fuchs replied, "Then you'd be without backup power if the main goes out again."

"It's a risk," I admitted. "But we've got to do *something*. There's no sense being down here without the manipulators working."

"You could get trapped down there!" Marguerite chimed in.

"I want to try it," I said. "Tell me how to reset the manipulators."

"You're sure you want to do this?"

"Yes! Now stop wasting time and tell me how to get the manipulators on the auxiliary system. And the lamps."

It seemed to take hours, but actually within less than ten minutes I had the manipulators powered up from the backup electrical system while the rest of the ship ran as normal on the main batteries. The floodlights seemed dimmer than they had been in the VR simulation, but still bright enough to light the area that the arms would be working in.

"All right," I said at last. "I'm going to poke into the gondola now."

"Okay," said Fuchs.

That's when I found out that my hands wouldn't fit into the waldoes while I had my gloves on.

I could have screamed. I wanted to pound the control panel with my fists. They had fit all right in the virtual reality simulator, but here aboard the real *Hecate* the cursed-be-to-hell-and-back waldo fittings were too tight for me to get my hands into them while I was wearing the heat suit's gloves.

It was the servomotors on the gloves' backs, I saw. Those spiny exoskeletons that powered the gloves and boosted my fingers' natural strength jutted out from the backs of the gloves about two centimeters or so, just enough to prevent me from sliding my hands into the waldoes that controlled the manipulator arms and grippers.

The clock was ticking. I was running out of alloy ballast to keep the ship barely livable, running out of time.

"What's going on down there?" Fuchs demanded. "What's the holdup?"

"Wait a second," I mumbled. No sense telling him what the problem was; neither he nor anyone aboard *Lucifer* could do a cursed thing about it.

I hesitated only a moment longer, then started to pull off the gloves. The air inside the cockpit was at Earth-normal pressure, there was no danger of decompression, as there would be if I'd been in space. It was hellishly hot, though. And if *Hecate*'s hull got punctured, I'd be dead meat without my suit fully sealed up.

So be it. I yanked both gloves off and stuck my hands into the waldoes.

"Ow!" I yelled involuntarily. The metal was *hot*.

"What's the matter?" Fuchs and Marguerite asked simultaneously.

"Bumped my hand," I lied. The metal of the waldoes was hot, all right, but I could stand it. At least, it would take a while before the skin of my hands started to blister.

It was like pushing my fingers into boiling water, but I gritted my teeth and began to work the manipulators. The arms reacted sluggishly, not at all the way they did in the simulator, but I got them extended and gripped the torn edge of the gondola in their metal pincers.

"I'm opening up the gondola. Looking inside," I reported.

"Get the camera lined up with the manipulators," Fuchs snapped.

I pulled my left hand out of its waldo and blew on it, then worked the camera control, slaving it to the manipulators. Wishing I had the time to rip the servomotors off my gloves, knowing I didn't, I stuck my hand back into the waldo. It was like having your face wrapped in a steaming hot towel, except that the waldo didn't cool off. If anything, it was getting hotter.

The remote arms peeled back the thin metal of the gondola. Actually, the metal broke away, snapping like brittle panes of glass. Inside I saw two spacesuits still hanging limply in their open lockers. The helmets were on the deck, though, rather than on the shelves above the suits. The inner airlock hatch was ajar. Another suit was draped over the bench in front of the lockers, a pair of boots sitting precisely where a person's feet would be while he or she began putting on the suit.

But there were no human remains to be seen. Nothing but a whitish powder sprinkled here and there.

And a strange, pencil-thin wire or cable of some sort running up and over the broken side of the hull and down along the center of the deck. It disappeared into the darkness beyond the pool of light from *Hecate*'s floodlamps.

That's when I heard it. A dull, low growling noise, like the rumble of distant thunder, but longer, more insistent, growing louder and stronger until I could see the ground beneath *Hecate*'s skids shaking.

Earthquake? It couldn't be! It was *Hecate* itself that was shaking, rattling, skidding across the oven-hot rocks with a brittle piece of *Phosphoros*'s hull clamped in its manipulator pincers. I could see the wreckage skittering away from me as I banged around inside *Hecate*'s cockpit, rolling and sloshing on my belly while the ship skidded across the ground as if some giant hand were shoving it along.

"Full power!" I heard Fuchs yelling, whether to me or his own crew I couldn't tell. "Maintain trim!"

Then with a smashing impact that nearly tore my insides apart *Hecate* hit something and tilted dangerously up on one skid.

And everything went black.

TIDAL WAVE

I must have been unconscious for only a few moments. My head had slammed against the inside of my helmet when *Hecate* banged against whatever it was that stopped our skidding across the landscape.

That low-pitched thundering was still shaking the ship, but except for a throbbing pain in my head there seemed to be no major damage. The panel was lit, no indications of hull puncture. I almost laughed to myself; if the hull had been punctured I wouldn't be alive to read the panel, not with my gloves off.

". . . the volcanic eruption," Marguerite was saying in my earphones, her voice tight with fear. "It's blown us away from your position."

"I got pushed around, too," I said, surprised at how calm my voice sounded.

"Are you all right?"

"I think so . . ." I was scanning the control panel. No red lights, although several were in the amber. I raised my head to look through the forward port. *Phosphoros*'s wreckage was several hundred meters away now.

"What the hell happened?" I snarled.

"That volcano eruption," she explained. "The glow we saw off on the horizon."

"You mean it's pouring out lava?"

Marguerite's voice was a little softer now, less tense, but only a little. "It's too far away to threaten you, Van. That's no worry."

No worry for them, I thought, up in the air.

"But the explosion sent a pressure wave through the atmosphere," she went on, "like an underwater tidal wave. It blew *Lucifer* almost upside down and pushed us at least a dozen kilometers away from you. The captain's struggling to get the ship trimmed again and back into position above you."

"I've been pushed along the ground like a dead leaf in a gale-force wind," I said.

Fuchs's voice came on. "We're heading back toward you, but it's taking all the power the engines can give to push against this pressure wave. Get set to lift as soon as I give the command."

"I have to get the escape pod."

"If you can," he said. "When I give the order to lift you pull out of there, whether you have the pod or not."

"Yes, sir," I said. But to myself I added, As soon as I have the pod in my grip.

Marguerite's voice returned. "He's got his hands full piloting the ship. It's like riding against a hurricane up here."

I nodded, checking over the control panel again. Everything seemed all right. But was it?

"This is the first time any human has eye-witnessed a volcanic eruption on Venus," Marguerite said. She sounded pleased.

I remembered Greenbaum and felt a tremor of near-hysteria quivering inside me. Are these eruptions the beginning of the cataclysm that Greenbaum had predicted? Was the ground beneath me going to open up and swallow me in boiling magma?

Get away! a voice in my aching head screamed. Get the fuck out of here and back to safety!

"Not without the pod," I muttered grimly.

"What?" Marguerite asked instantly. "What did you say?"

"Nothing," I snapped. "I'm going to be too busy to talk with you for a while."

"Yes. I understand. I'll monitor your frequency, in case you need anything."

Like what? I asked silently. Prayers? Last rites?

I nudged the thruster pedal, to lift off the ground enough so I could make my way back to the wreckage. Nothing happened. I pushed against the bar harder. The ship still wouldn't move. I could hear the thrusters whining, but no motion.

Taking a deep breath, I considered what choices I had. I punched the ballast release, and felt a clunk rattle through the ship as a block of the heat-absorbing alloy was ejected from its bay. That lightened the ship, but it cut down on the time I could stay on the surface without burning to a crisp.

I tried the thrusters again. The ship quivered but did not rise off the ground. Is something holding me down? I wondered.

Something slithered over the ship's hull. I could hear it, sliding, scratching across the metal skin above me. The sound made me shudder with fright.

This was no time for half measures. Either I got away from here or I fried, and pretty soon, too. So I tromped on the thruster pedal with both boots, really kicked it hard. The thrusters suddenly howled and *Hecate* lurched up off the ground and wobbled into the air a good hundred meters.

I fought madly to get control of her. For a moment I thought she would flip over onto her back and nosedive into the ground. But *Hecate* came through. My fingers played across her control pads madly and she responded, straightened out, and pointed her nose toward the wreckage once again.

When we settled down on the rocks I saw that *Hecate* tilted badly over on her left, as if the landing skid on that side had been crushed or ripped away. No matter, I thought, as long as the hull is still intact.

I had put her down alongside Alex's escape pod. Now I had to slide my blistered fingers back into those damnable waldoes and get the manipulators working again.

I did it, although the pain forced tears from my eyes. I made the metal pincers firmly grip the handholds on the escape pod's surface, locked them on, and then gratefully withdrew my fingers from the waldoes. For a few moments I simply lay there, awash in perspiration, my fingers sizzling with pain. I pictured myself swimming in the Arctic ocean, playing among ice floes. My hands still hurt.

I should have pulled my gloves back on, that would have been the smart thing to do. The cautious, safety-minded thing to do. But my scorched hands burned too much even to consider it.

"I've got the pod," I reported, "and I'm ready to lift."

For a heart-stopping moment there was no reply. Then Marguerite's voice came through. "The captain estimates we'll be in place above you in ten minutes."

I let out an inadvertent whistle. They must have been blown a long way off position.

"I'm lifting now," I said. "I'll hover at two kilometers' altitude until you give the order for rendezvous."

A much longer delay before she answered. I had no desire to stay down on the surface a nanosecond longer than I had to.

Fuchs's voice came on. "Okay, but keep below two klicks. The *last* thing we want is a midair collision."

"Agreed," I said. But I thought, No, the last thing I want is to be stuck down here in this oven.

Trying to use my fingernails on the control pads, to avoid touching them with my seared skin, I began to set up the ship's controls for liftoff.

Then my eye caught something strange. As if anything in this landscape of hell wasn't strange.

But some of those lines that had crisscrossed the wreckage had moved again. I was certain of it. In fact, as I stared, goggle-eyed, one of them rose up off the wreckage and wavered in the air like an impossibly thin arm beckoning for help.

And then another. And another.

"They're alive!" I screeched.

"What?"

"Look!" I babbled. "Look at them! Arms, tentacles, feelers—whatever they are, they're alive!"

Marguerite said, "We're barely close enough to see you and the wreck. What are you talking about?"

"Look at the camera imagery, dammit!"

"It's grainy . . . the picture's breaking up too much . . ."

I tried to calm down and describe what I was seeing. The arms—if that's what they were—were all up and waving slowly back and forth in the sluggish current of thick, hot air.

"There can't be anything alive down there," Marguerite insisted. "The heat—"

"Put your telescope on them!" I yelled. "All your sensors! They're alive, dammit! Probably the main body lives deep underground, but it sends feelers, antennas, *something* up to the surface."

"It's hotter underground than it is on the surface," Fuchs growled.

"I see them!" Marguerite's voice jumped an octave higher. "I can see them!"

"What are they doing?" I wondered aloud. "Why are they waving around like that?"

"They weren't doing that before the tidal wave passed through?" Marguerite asked.

"No, they were lying on the ground. Most of 'em were draped over the wreckage."

"And now they've raised themselves . . ." Her voice trailed off.

I had forgotten about raising the ship, staring out the port and watching something that should have been impossible. Was there some other explanation? Could they be something that isn't living?

"Feeding tubes," Marguerite said at last. "Perhaps they're taking in nutrients carried in the air from the volcanic eruption."

"But why here? Why haven't we seen them anywhere else on the planet?" I asked.

"We haven't looked this closely at any other area on the surface," she replied.

I recalled, "They were draped across the wreckage."

"The bugs up in the clouds ate metal ions," said Marguerite.

"Like vitamins. You said they needed the metal ions the way we need vitamins."

"And maybe this underground organism also needs metallic ions," she said.

"It sensed the wreckage!" We were jumping to conclusions, I knew in the back of my mind. But they seemed to fit what we were seeing.

"Is the pod marked in any way?" she asked, her voice rising again with excitement. "Any scars where the feeding tubes might have been eating on the metal?"

Before I could look, Fuchs's voice came through, dry and cold. "You have exactly seven minutes' worth of alloy left. Play at being a biologist once you're back up here, Humphries."

That was like a douse of cold water. "Right," I said. "I'm starting liftoff procedure *now*."

After all, I had the pod in my grip and Marguerite must have every sensor aboard *Lucifer* focused on those feeding arms, or whatever they were. Time to get back to safety.

I quickly scanned the control panel one more time, then pushed on the thruster pedal. The engines whined to life, the ship shuddered—but didn't budge one centimeter off the ground.

CAPTURED

'm stuck!" Inside the helmet, my voice sounded like a terrified shriek.

"What do you mean, stuck?" Fuchs demanded.

"Stuck!" I hollered. "The goddamned ship isn't moving!"

"Wait . . . the telemetry shows everything functioning okay," he said. "Thrusters on full."

"But I'm not moving!"

Silence from *Lucifer*. I pressed both boots against that damnable thruster bar. I really kicked it hard, again and again. The thrusters growled and *Hecate* shuddered, but I didn't budge off the ground. How many minutes were left for the heat rejection system? When the alloy ran out the heat inside the cockpit would build up and cook me within minutes.

"All your telemetry checks out," Fuchs said, an edge in his voice.

"Fine," I retorted. "Then why doesn't the ship move?"

"We're trying to get the telescopes on you. It's not easy, that damned tidal wave is still making the air turbulent up at this level."

For a mad instant I thought I might crawl out of *Hecate* and get into the escape pod that was still lodged in the manipulator arms and use its escape rockets to blast off into orbit.

Great plan, I said to myself. *If* your suit would keep you alive outside the ship, which it can't, and *if* you could get into the pod before you roast to death, which you couldn't, and *if* the pod's escape rockets would work, which they probably wouldn't.

"Well?" I shouted. "What are you doing up there?"

Marguerite replied, "We have you on-screen now." Her voice was shaky; she sounded as if she were on the verge of tears.

"And?" I demanded.

Fuchs said, "Four of those feeding arms are wrapped around *Hecate*. They must be holding you down."

I don't know what I said. It must have been atrocious because Fuchs snapped, "Calm down! Hysteria won't help."

"Calm down?" I screeched. "I'm trapped here! They're *feeding* on the ship!"

"You've tried full power?" Fuchs asked.

"What do you think I'm doing down here?" I raged. "Of course I've applied full power!"

"They're holding you down!" Marguerite stated the obvious.

"What do I do?" I demanded. "What do I do?"

"They're strong enough to hold the ship down even when the thrusters are firing at full power," Fuchs said, also stating the obvious. Or perhaps he was thinking out loud.

"They must all be connected underground," Marguerite said. "It must all be one gigantic organism."

Wonderful. I'm about to be killed and she's spinning biological theories.

I heard that slithering noise again. It was the feeding tubes, the arms that were holding me down. They were eating the ship's hull! They were going to break into the cockpit and eat me! I wanted to scream. I should have screamed. But my throat was frozen with terror. Nothing but a thin squeak came out of my mouth.

"We can't get down to him," Fuchs was saying. "We don't have the time to attach a tow line and pull him loose."

"We don't know if we could pull him loose even if we could attach a line," Marguerite said.

They were talking about me in the third person. As if I weren't able to hear them. As if I were already dead. They thought they were running through possible ways of saving me, but to me it sounded as if they were making excuses for letting me die alone down on the rocks.

My mind was churning, working harder than I had ever worked before. Awash with sweat, lying prone in *Hecate*'s cramped cockpit, trapped and alone on the surface of hell, I realized that only one person in the universe could help me, and that was me myself.

How did those feeder arms find me so fast? They were draped over the old wreckage, including the escape pod. But they wrapped themselves around me within minutes.

"Marguerite!" I yelled into my helmet microphone. "The arms that were on *Phosphoros*'s wreckage? Are they still there? Are they still waving in the air?"

A moment's hesitation, then she answered, "No. They've extended from the wreckage to your ship."

"How many of them are on me?"

"Four . . . no, there's five of them now."

Great. I'm attracting them like flies to garbage. They left the old wreckage for the new meat. But why? Why leave the food they've been grazing on for more than three years now?

Think! I screamed silently at myself. The only advantage you might possibly have over this Venusian monster is your brain. Use it!

Why leave the wreckage for me? What sensory organs did they have that told them fresh meat had arrived?

They sensed the metal ions that surged through the air on the volcano's tidal wave, I remembered. They can sense metal ions even at very low concentrations, the way a human being can sense the nutrients he needs in food: it tastes good.

"Marguerite!" I called again. "Are the arms laid out straight across the ground? Straight from the old wreckage to *Hecate*?"

"No," she said. "They curl and twist . . . it looks as if they followed the trail of the alloy you pumped out. Yes! They run along the splashes of alloy on the ground and follow it to your ship."

That's what interested them: the alloy I'd been excreting.

"I've got to eject the ballast," I shouted with the realization of it. "All of it! Now!"

"You can't eject all the ballast," Fuchs said testily. "It's your heat sink."

I yelled, "It's their picnic food! It's what's attracting them to me!"

"But your cooling system will overload!" Marguerite cried.

"I've only got a couple of minutes before they break the hull apart! I've got nothing to lose!"

Fuchs's voice, tight with tension, said, "Lower left screen on your main panel. Touch the ballast icon."

"I know. I know."

I jabbed at the panel, suppressing a yelp of pain. Even the panel was so hot it burned to touch it. A short menu appeared. Thank god the electronics still worked, despite the heat. But how long would they work once I had tossed the heat sink alloy overboard?

No matter. I was going to fry down here anyway unless I could move those feeder arms off the ship.

My fingertips were scorched, so I used a knuckle to touch the ballast-eject command. I heard the ejector springs bang, rattling the ship.

"Tell me what they're doing," I said, fighting to keep my voice level.

Fuchs said heavily, "The ingots fell just a meter or so from the tail of your ship."

"Are the arms moving?"

"No."

A new fear cut through me. How much damage had the arms already done to the ship's hull? They'd been eating on the metal for only a few minutes, I knew, but was that long enough to weaken the hull's integrity? If I actually could shake loose of them, would *Hecate* fall apart when I applied the thrusters again?

"Any motion?" I asked.

The temperature in the cockpit was soaring. My suit gave me some measure of protection, but still I felt as if I were being roasted alive. The control panel seemed to waver before my eyes. The plastic was starting to melt.

"Anything?"

Marguerite said, "One of them is moving . . . I think."

I could hear the pumps in my suit gurgling madly, trying to carry away the heat that was swiftly building up. But there was no place to carry the heat. It was everywhere, all encompassing, smothering me, boiling me in my own juices.

"Definitely moving!" Marguerite said breathlessly.

"How many . . . ?"

"Two of them. Now a third—my god! They move so fast!"

"Fire the thrusters," Fuchs commanded.

Everything was swimming, melting. I felt dizzy.

"Fire the thrusters!" he roared. *"Now!"*

I wedged my burned hands against the melting plastic of the control panel and pressed both boots against the thruster bar as hard as I could. The thrusters growled, rumbled. The ship shook.

I realized it wouldn't be enough. I was still pinned down, helpless, unable to move.

Then she broke loose! *Hecate* lurched forward, shuddered, then shot up from the ground so hard I was pushed back painfully inside my suit.

Fuchs was yelling commands in my earphones. I saw the ground whipping past and then receding. It should feel cooler, I thought stupidly. It ought to feel cooler.

But it didn't. It was still so hot I was suffocating, boiling inside the protective suit. I wanted to rip it off and be free of it. I think I might actually have started to unfasten the helmet.

Then the ground beneath me opened up. A gigantic crack pulled the solid rock apart with a grinding, terrifying roar that sounded like the howling of all the demons of hell baying at me. Frozen into immobility, stupefied, I stared down into the blinding glare of white-hot magma that blasted a wave of heat up through the thick turgid atmosphere.

Hecate shot up like a dandelion puff caught in the searing blast of a rocket's fiery exhaust. Bouncing and shuddering in the blazing breath from the planet's deep interior, I stared down petrified into the mouth of hell.

What was left of poor old *Phosphoros* tumbled into the widening pit. I saw it melting as it fell deeper into the infernal heat. But the thought that welled up in my mind was, That tentacled monster must be tumbling down into hell, too. Good! Die, you bastard. Go to hell, where you belong.

RETRIEVED

The thrusters' throttle bar jammed in the wide-open position while *Hecate* soared up and away from the white-hot fissure yawning below me. Fortunately they ran out of fuel within a few seconds. Otherwise the ship would have risen up like a rocket-driven artillery shell and arced halfway around Venus, then fallen back to splatter on the surface. As it was, little *Hecate* shot up from the surface like a scalded cat, her nose pointed toward the clouds thirty-some kilometers above.

The temperature cooled off to a "mere" four hundred degrees as *Hecate* soared upward. I was groggy, exhausted. All I wanted to do was close my eyes and sleep. But Fuchs wouldn't allow that. He bellowed in my earphones, screaming and roaring at me. His bawling, blaring voice became more insistent, penetrating into my mind, shaking me out of my heat-induced daze.

"Answer me!" he snarled. "Don't you die on me, don't you take the easy way out. Wake up! Snap out of it!"

It took me several moments to realize that he wasn't raging at me. He was pleading. He was begging me to stay awake and alert, to save myself, not to die.

My eyes were still staring with fascinated horror at the mammoth fissure burning below me. The pit of hell, I thought. I'm looking into the pit of hell. And I understood what Fuchs's mind was like, inside. The burning rage. The fury that he had pent up within him. It was enough to kill any ordinary man. It was a wonder it hadn't killed him already.

"Answer me, damn you," Fuchs was demanding, urging, cajoling. "I can save you, but you've got to give me some help, dammit."

It was still burning hot inside *Hecate* and I felt as weak and limp as an overcooked strand of spaghetti.

"I'm . . . here . . ." I said. My voice was little more than a rasping exhausted whisper.

"Good!" he snapped. "Now listen to me. You're coasting about fifteen klicks above the ground. You're out of fuel and gliding like a soarplane. I'm coming up after you, but *Lucifer* can't reach you fast enough unless you help."

Fast enough for what? Then I realized, fast enough to get me before I died.

I looked out the forward port and saw that *Phosphoros*'s escape pod was still in the manipulator arms' grip.

"I've got . . . the pod," I said. "You'll win the prize . . . no matter what happens . . . to me."

"Idiot!" Marguerite's voice screeched. "He's trying to save your life!"

That popped my eyes open.

"Pay attention," Fuchs said, almost soothingly. "You've got to do some flying. Your control surfaces should still be working."

"Yes . . ."

He started giving me instructions, his voice calm but imperative, trying to get me to swing around in a great descending arc so that he could bring *Lucifer* up close enough to take me aboard.

I'm not that good a flier, I told myself tiredly as I tried to understand his commands and respond to them. I'm no jet-jockey. What does he expect of me? Why doesn't he leave me alone? Why is he doing this?

The memory of Marguerite's shrill voice answered my question: *"He's trying to save your life!"*

"You're overcorrecting," Fuchs said sharply. "Pull the nose up or you'll dive back into the ground."

"I'm trying . . ."

It was a good thing that all I had to do was slide my fingers across the control pads. It wasn't easy, though; my fingers were burned and blistering so badly that I used my knuckles against the pads. The controls were much livelier than they'd been down close to the surface. Up at this altitude the air was about ten times thicker than Earth's at sea level. *Hecate* was operating in a regime somewhere between a submersible and a soarplane.

The ship was trembling, shaking almost like a living creature swimming through the thick, oven-hot air. I realized that holding the spherical pod up in front of her was not helping her aerodynamics. I could fly more easily if I released the pod. But I shook my head inside the helmet. Whatever's left of Alex was inside that pod, I was certain of it. We're going through this together, big brother, I said to him silently. We live or die together, Alex.

Suddenly Fuchs yelled, "No, no, no! Level off! Use the horizon as your guide. Keep your nose on the horizon."

That wasn't as easy to do as he thought. The air was still thick enough to distort long-distance vision. The horizon wasn't flat. It curved upward conspicuously, like a bowl, like the meniscus of a thick liquid in a narrow glass.

"The body of your ship will provide lift if you maintain the proper attitude," Fuchs said, more calmly. Then he added, "And speed. You've got to maintain speed, too."

Hecate was soaring along now; still shaking, vibrating, but gliding on a more or less even keel. I felt giddy from the heat, my mouth dry, every muscle in my body screaming with pain.

"Attitude and speed determine altitude," Fuchs was saying, almost as if he were reciting an ancient formula. "You're doing well, Van."

"Thanks," I mumbled.

"Stay with it."

"I don't know . . . if I can stay . . . conscious much longer," I stammered.

"You've got to!" he snapped. "There's no alternative. You've got to keep awake and pilot your ship, otherwise we won't be able to make rendezvous."

"I'm trying."

"Then try harder! Stay awake."

"It's hot—"

"Just a few minutes more," Fuchs said, suddenly coaxing, almost pleading. "Just a few minutes more."

I blinked my eyes. Far off against that baking-hot horizon I saw a dark spot moving. We were still on the nightside of Venus, but the glow from the ground was bright enough for me to make out a dot against the sullen yellow-gray clouds above me. It couldn't be anything else except *Lucifer.*

Or eyestrain, that sardonic voice in my head sneered. Or even a hallucination.

Fuchs's voice crackled in my earphones again. "I can't see you visually yet but we've got you on radar. Maintain your current speed and attitude, but turn left ten degrees."

"Ten degrees?" I blinked at the control panel. It seemed blurred, baffling.

"Turn left. I'll tell you when to stop."

I slid my knuckles across the control pads, slowly, carefully, my failing eyes on that dark spot off along the curving horizon.

"Too far! Hold it there! Hold it. I'll adjust our course to match yours."

All I wanted to do was sleep. Collapse. Die. It didn't matter anymore. I didn't care. But then I remembered why I was here, what I had promised myself that I'd do. Very well, I said to whatever gods were watching over me, if I die it won't be because I gave up.

Just at the moment, as if in answer to an unvoiced prayer, *Lucifer* lit up like a Christmas ornament. Running lights came to life all along her teardrop-shaped body and began blinking on and off, like a welcoming beacon.

Whatever reserves of adrenaline or moral fiber or just plain stubbornness that remained in me rose up. I still ached from scalp to toes, still felt as weak as a newborn kitten, my suit was still sloshing with perspiration and the heat was suffocating me. But I kept my eyes open and my burned hands on the control pads despite the heat, trying my best to hold the speed and attitude that Fuchs wanted.

Then he said, "Now comes the hard part." And my heart sank.

"You've got to lose a little altitude and a lot of speed, so you can pass beneath us where we can grab you."

I remembered that rendezvous was such a tricky maneuver in the simulations that I had botched it more often than not, and that had been with *Hecate* flying on her own power. I was piloting a glider now; I had used up all the thrusters' fuel trying to break free of those arms that were holding me down on the surface.

"You'll only get one shot at this," Fuchs warned, "so you've got to do it right the first time."

"Understood," I said, my voice a dry, harsh cough.

"I'd do this with the automatic controls from here in *Lucifer*," he added, "but your systems aren't responding to my signals."

"Must be damaged," I said.

Fuchs said, "Maybe the heat." But I remembered *Hecate* slamming into a boulder or something when the tidal wave first struck. Most likely the antennas for the remote-control receivers were damaged then.

"Okay now," Fuchs said. I could hear him taking a deep breath, like a man about to start an impossibly difficult task. "Diving planes down five degrees."

I knew where the diving plane control was. I had to stretch my leg to get the toe of my boot on the left pedal. My foot cramped horribly, but I think the pain actually helped to keep me awake. The digital display read minus one, minus two . . .

Abruptly I heard a tearing, grinding noise and *Hecate* flipped over onto her back so hard I was banged against the overhead in the narrow cockpit.

I must have screamed, or at least yelled out something. Fuchs was bellowing in my earphones but I couldn't understand his words. The ship was spinning madly, slamming me around inside the cockpit like the ball in a jai-alai game bouncing off the walls. My head rattled inside the heavy metal helmet; despite the padding I saw stars and tasted blood in my mouth.

One thought came screeching through my pain, one lesson I had learned in the simulations. The stabilizing jets. *Hecate* had a set of small cold-jet units placed at her nose, tails, and along the sides of the hull. I started to reach for the bright yellow pad that would fire them, then realized that all this had started when I'd moved the diving planes. I'd have to bring them back to neutral before the jets could stabilize the ship's spin.

I saw a glaring red light blinking at me from the control panel. One of the diving planes had not responded to my command. That's what flipped *Hecate* into this spin. It must have been damaged down on the surface, bent or broken against that boulder.

Fuchs was still roaring at me, but I concentrated every gram of my will on the control panel. Bracing myself against the constant slamming around caused by the ship's spin, I brought the diving plane back to its neutral position and then fired the stabilizing jets.

For a moment I thought *Hecate* would tear herself apart. But the spinning slowed and then stopped. The ship was under my control again.

And diving straight for the ground.

"Pull up! Pull up!" Fuchs was bellowing. "Get her nose *up!*" His voice was hoarse, scratchy.

"Trying," I croaked.

The smaller control surfaces seemed to work all right. *Hecate* swooped up in a zoom that dropped my stomach far behind me.

Following Fuchs's painfully rasping commands I made *Hecate* climb back up almost to his altitude, then slowly coasted toward

Lucifer. Staying away from the diving planes, I jinked and jerked my ship raggedly closer and closer. My strength was fading fast. It was so damnably hot, and whatever reserves of adrenaline I had been riding on were totally spent now.

Looking up through the forward port I saw *Lucifer* looming bigger and bigger, its lights still winking and blinking insanely. Its cargo bay doors swung open and the grappling arms extended down toward me. I lowered my manipulators slightly so I could get a better view of the grapples.

"Velocity looks good," Fuchs was saying, almost crooning like a father lulling his baby to sleep. It would be good to sleep, I thought. Then I realized again that he was my father. Did he have any paternal feelings for me? Until a day or so ago he despised me as the son of his deadliest enemy. Now he was guiding me back to safety.

"Hold it there," he said softly.

I couldn't hold it. *Hecate* wasn't an inanimate object but a ship alive in the sluggish winds and currents of Venus's thick hot air. She had a soul of her own, and I was not her master, only an exhausted, terrified mortal trying to get this willful creature to go along with me for just a few moments more.

"Nose up."

Automatically I moved my scorched hands against the control pads.

"Little more . . . little more . . ."

Hecate began to shake again, more violently this time, bucking like a stubborn bronco that didn't like the way she was being handled.

"Don't let her stall!" Fuchs shouted. "Drop the nose a bit!"

Lucifer's cargo bay loomed before me, with the grappling arms dangling, reaching. It looked to me as if I was going to crash into them.

"Another few meters," Fuchs coaxed.

"I . . . can't. . . ." Everything was fading, melting, running together like watercolors in the rain. It would be wonderful to feel the rain, I thought, to stand in the cool gentle rain of Earth and feel blessed water splashing on my face, running across my burned and aching body.

I heard the clang of metal against metal at precisely the moment I blacked out.

THE ESCAPE POD

He's coming out of it."

Those were the first words I heard: Marguerite's voice, brimming with expectation.

I opened my eyes and saw that I was back in *Lucifer*'s sick bay, flat on my back, looking up at the curving metal overhead. I felt too weak to turn my head, too exhausted even to speak.

Then Marguerite came into my view, leaning over me, smiling slightly.

"Hello," she said.

I tried to say hello to her but nothing came out except a moaning croak.

"Don't try to speak," she said. "It'll take a while before the fluids rehydrate you properly."

I managed to blink my eyes, too weak to nod. I could see several intravenous tubes on either side of the table on which I lay. The thought of having needles puncturing my skin normally made my flesh crawl, but the fluids in those tubes looked like nectar and ambrosia to me.

"Your hands will be fine in a few hours," Marguerite told me. "The ship's medical supplies included enough artificial skin to hold you until we get back aboard *Truax* and regenerate your own skin tissue."

"Good," I whispered.

She moved to one of the IV drips and stabbed a finger at its control box. "I'm taking you off the analgesics now, but let me know if you're in pain."

"Only . . . when I breathe," I joked feebly.

It took her a moment to realize I was joking. Then she broke into a grin. "Humor is a good sign, I think."

I nodded weakly.

"Are you hungry?"

"No," I said, then I realized it wasn't so. "Yes. A little." In truth I was too tired to eat, but my stomach did feel empty.

"I'll get you something easy to digest."

When she came back, carrying a small tray, I asked, "How long have I been unconscious?"

Marguerite glanced at the digital displays against the bulkhead. "Seventeen hours, a little more."

"The pod?"

"It's in the cargo bay, still in *Hecate*'s arms," she said. Then she touched a button and the table raised up behind my head slightly. Marguerite picked up a plastic bowl from the tray, sat on the edge of the table, and spooned up something from a bowl. "Now eat this."

It must have been broth of some sort, although it was bland and so tasteless that I couldn't tell what it was supposed to be. But it was very pleasant having her spoon-feed me. Very pleasant indeed.

"Where's Fuchs?" I asked.

"The captain's on the bridge, plotting our ascent back up to orbit so we can rendezvous with *Truax*."

"We'll have to go through the clouds again. The bugs . . ." I didn't finish the sentence. I didn't have to.

"He's trying to estimate the amount of damage they did on the way in," Marguerite explained as she ladled another spoonful of soup for me, "so he can work out our best rate of ascent to minimize their effect."

I swallowed, then nodded. "Once we're in orbit we'll be all right, then."

Marguerite nodded back. "The bugs can't survive in vacuum." Then she added, "I hope."

I must have looked startled, because she laughed and said, "Only joking. I've tested them in a vacuum jar. Their cells burst just the way ours would if we didn't wear spacesuits."

"Good." We started talking about the creatures that I'd run into down on the surface. Was it a single organism with many tentacle-like arms, or several different creatures?

"Whatever it was, it's dead now. It went down to hell when the fissure opened up."

Marguerite shook her head slightly. "Not entirely. There was a fragment of one arm stuck on *Hecate*'s back when you returned. It must have been torn off when—"

I gasped. "A piece of the monster?"

"Less than a meter long," she answered, nodding. "Its outer shell is a form of silicone, quite strong yet flexible. And heat-resistant."

"Silicone," I muttered. Yes, that made sense. Then I asked her, "What about its innards? What could possibly stay alive at such high temperatures?"

Marguerite said, "I'm working on that. It seems to be made of sulfur compounds, very complex, molecules no one's ever seen before; a totally new kind of chemistry."

"You'll get a double Nobel," I said. "First the bacteria and now this."

She smiled down at me.

"Too bad it got killed," I said, although inwardly I still felt glad that it had fallen into the white-hot fissure.

"There must be more than one of them. Nature doesn't make merely one single copy of a species."

"On Earth," I countered. "This thing might be one single organism. Maybe it's spread itself all across the planet."

Her eyes widened.

"That's going to make the surface even more dangerous than we thought," I added.

"Unless the whole surface erupts the way Professor Greenbaum expects it to."

"That'd be a pity," I heard myself say. "It would kill everything, wouldn't it?"

Marguerite hesitated, then answered, "I wonder."

"Based on sulfur compounds, you said."

"It's the first form of life we've found that isn't dependent on water."

"Life's much more varied than we thought."

"And much tougher."

I shuddered. "Tell me about it. It came close to killing me."

"The main body must be deep underground, and it sends those arms up to the surface to feed, like shoots of a tree."

"Feed on what?"

She shrugged. "Organic material raining down from the clouds?" she guessed.

"Is there any organic material falling out of the clouds?"

Marguerite shook her head. "None that I can find. If the bugs in the clouds sink toward the surface when they die, they must be totally decomposed by the heat long before they reach the ground."

"Then what do those things on the ground eat?" I asked again.

"I haven't the foggiest notion," she admitted. "That's why we've got to come back and study them more closely."

The idea of returning startled me for a moment, but then I understood that we had to. Someone had to. We have an entire new world to explore here on Venus. A whole new form of biology.

"What are you smiling about?" Marguerite asked.

I hadn't realized I was smiling. "My brother Alex," I said. "We wouldn't have discovered any of this if he hadn't come to Venus."

Marguerite's face took on a somber expression. "Yes, I suppose that's true."

"That's his legacy," I said, more to myself than her. "His gift to us all."

Marguerite left after a while and I drifted into sleep. I know that I dreamed, something about Alex and my fa—Martin Humphries, that is; but when I awoke the memory of it faded from my conscious grasp like a tantalizing will-o'-the-wisp. The more I tried to remember the dream, the flimsier its images became, until the whole thing disappeared like a mist evaporated by the morning sun.

I saw that all the IV drips had been disconnected, and wondered how long I'd been asleep. I expected Marguerite to pop into the sick bay; she would probably be carrying a beeper that sounded off when the sensors monitoring me told her I had awakened. But I lay there for a good quarter of an hour all by myself; she didn't show up. Probably working on the arm *Hecate* had carried back from the surface.

Nettled by her neglect, I pulled myself up to a sitting position. My head throbbed a little, but that was probably from the pounding I'd taken when *Hecate* had gone into its spinning nosedive. I was totally naked beneath the thin sheet and I could see no clothes anywhere in the cramped confines of the sick bay.

That made some sense, I thought. The coveralls I'd worn in *Hecate* beneath the protective suit must have been rank with sweat.

I swung my legs off the table and stood up warily, keeping one hand on the edge of the table. Not bad. A bit wobbly, but otherwise all right. I wrapped the sheet around my middle and proceeded with as much dignity as I could toward my bunk in the crew's quarters.

Nodon and several others of the crew were sitting around the common table when I got there. They leaped to their feet as I padded in, newfound respect shining in their eyes.

I accepted their plaudits as graciously as I could while clutching the sheet to my waist with one hand, thinking to myself that being a hero of sorts is rather pleasant. Then I went to my bunk and slid the privacy screen shut.

Six sets of coveralls and underwear were laid out neatly on the bunk, freshly laundered. They had even put out matching sets of slipper socks. A show of appreciation for my retrieving the escape pod? Or had Fuchs simply ordered them to do it?

I dressed, and Nodon insisted on escorting me to the bridge. Amarjagal was in the command chair. Fuchs was in his quarters, I was told. But when I went down the short stretch of passageway to his door, Marguerite was already heading toward me.

"We should inspect the pod," she said, her face somber.

I drew in a breath. "Yes, you're right."

"Are you up to it?"

"Of course," I lied. Every muscle and joint in my body still ached. My head felt as if it weighed eleven tons. My hands were stiff with the glossy artificial skin she had grafted onto them; the stuff made my hands feel like I was wearing a pair of gloves that were just a half size too small.

But I wanted to get to the pod. My heart was trip-hammering. Whatever was left of Alex must be in that big metal sphere, I knew. My brother. No, he wasn't my brother. Not biologically. But he'd been my big brother all my life and I couldn't think of him in any other way. What would I find in the pod? What would be left of the Alex who'd loved and protected me for as long as I could remember?

As we clambered down the ladder toward the cargo bay, Marguerite said, "We'll have to put on spacesuits. He's pumped out all the air in the bay."

Surprised, I snapped, "Why?"

"Vacuum's clean," she replied. "He wanted as low a level of contamination as possible."

"Where is he, anyway?" I demanded. "Why isn't Fuchs here? Doesn't he care what's inside the pod?"

She hesitated a heartbeat before replying, "He's in his quarters plotting our trajectory back into orbit. I told you that before."

"Still? How long does it take to plot a trajectory? The computer does all the work."

Marguerite answered simply, "He's working out the trajectory and he said he doesn't want to be disturbed."

We got to the cargo bay level. There was a locker with four spacesuits alongside the bay's personnel hatch.

As we began to pull on the suits, Marguerite said, "Your flight in *Hecate* took a lot out of him, you know."

Ahah! I thought. Aloud, I said to Marguerite, "So, he's resting, then."

Again that little hesitation. Then she said quietly, "Yes, he's resting."

We checked each other's suits once we had buttoned up inside them, going down the checklist programmed into the computers built into the suit wrists. It seemed a bit odd, speaking through the radio to someone standing only a meter away, but the bubble helmets muffled our voices so much we would have had to shout to make ourselves heard.

Once we went through the airlock and into the cargo bay I saw what a battering poor old *Hecate* had endured. She sat lopsidedly on the deck, one landing skid and its support struts crumpled beneath her hull. The hull itself was scratched and dented, long gouges of metal torn away. I walked slowly around the ship, staring at the damage. The diving plane on her left side was simply gone, nothing there but an ugly gash where it should have been. That entire side was badly banged in; that must have been where she'd slammed against the boulder.

I reached out and patted her poor old pitted flank with a gloved hand. The ship had kept me alive, but she would never fly again.

"You're treating it as if it's alive." Marguerite's voice came through my earphones, sounding surprised.

"You're damned right," I said, startling myself at how strong a bond I felt with this broken heap of metal.

In the cargo bay's bright lighting I could see Marguerite's face through the fishbowl helmet. She was smiling at me.

"She'll find a good home back on Earth," Marguerite said. "I'm sure the Smithsonian will want her for one of their museums."

I hadn't thought of that. The idea pleased me. *Hecate* had served well; she deserved a dignified resting place.

My walk around the battered little ship ended at the escape pod, still clutched in *Hecate*'s mechanical arms. The sphere looked like some relic from a bygone century, heavy and crusted with handgrips, a singular circular hatch, a cluster of rocket tubes here, a mini-forest of stubby antennas there. It was more than twice my height in diameter, solid and thick. No portholes anywhere that I could see.

Marguerite pointed to a boxlike metal contraption off by the far bulkhead. "We'll have to get the portable airlock set onto the pod's hatch," she said.

Obviously she had been thinking out this job, step by step, while I had been wrapped up in the emotional turmoil of wondering what to expect once we looked inside.

So we rolled up the portable airlock. The pod's hatch was too low to the deck for the airlock to connect against it.

"We'll have to move it," Marguerite said.

She went to the power cables stored against the cargo bay bulkhead while I climbed back into *Hecate*'s cockpit. It seemed somehow roomier than before, even though the spacesuit I was wearing must have been almost as bulky as the heat-protection suit I'd been in.

The control panel's plastic had not melted, as I thought it had. That must have been due to blurry eyesight and more than a little panic.

"Power's connected," Marguerite reported as the control panel lit up before my eyes. Gingerly I maneuvered the manipulator arms until the pod's hatch was lined up with the portable airlock. Then I shut down *Hecate*'s systems, but not before I gave her control panel a gentle pat and whispered, "Good girl."

I was getting positively maudlin, I thought. But it felt appropriate. It even felt good.

Once I climbed out of *Hecate,* Marguerite and I connected the airlock to the hatch, then tested the seals to make certain that the air inside the pod would not escape into the cargo bay.

"I think we're ready to open the hatch," she said at last.

I nodded inside my helmet, my insides quivering.

Handing me a small case of sensors, Marguerite said, "These are to analyze the air inside the pod. I'll bring the other sensors with me."

"You know how to handle them," I said. "Why don't you bring them?"

"You should go first," she said.

Yes, I thought. She's right. Alex was my brother. It's my place to go in there first.

Nodding again, I ducked into the coffin-sized airlock. I found myself licking my lips nervously. I saw that the indicator light was red; the airlock was already in vacuum, so that when I opened the pod's hatch, no contaminating atmosphere would mix with the air inside.

I had to open the hatch manually, since we did not want to power up the pod's internal systems. We didn't even know if the systems would come on-line, after more than three years of baking on the surface of Venus. The manual control was stiff, but the servo-motors on my gloves and the arms of my suit multiplied my muscular strength by a factor of five or more. Slowly, grudgingly, the little wheel turned as I grunted and strained with both hands.

The hatch cracked open. Inside my spacesuit I couldn't feel the puff of air that must have sighed out into the airlock. We'll pump it back into the pod afterward, I told myself. There wasn't room in the airlock to pull the hatch open all the way, but it swung back enough for me to get into the pod.

Picking up the sensor case, I lifted one booted foot and stepped over the sill of the circular hatch. It was very dark inside, of course. I switched on my helmet lamp and saw two bodies sprawled on the metal deck.

No, not bodies, I immediately told myself. Spacesuits. Fully sealed spacesuits. The two people, whoever they were, had had enough time to get into their suits before the final disaster struck them.

Both suits looked strangely crumpled, shriveled, as if the bodies inside them had melted away. More than three years in the roasting heat of Venus, I thought. The monomolecular fabric of the suits looked oddly gray, discolored. I understood why. They had been baking in the scorching heat of Venus for more than three years. It's a wonder that the fabric didn't burn up entirely, I thought.

Their suits may have been filled with an Earth-normal mix of oxygen and nitrogen at first, but that searing heat would break down any organic molecule and force who knows what kind of hellish chemistry inside the suits. It would turn the suits into slow-cooking ovens.

God! The enormity of their death agonies struck me like a hammer between my eyes. Baking to death, literally cooked inside their own suits. How long did it take? Did they undergo hours or days of that torture or, once they realized what they faced, did they cut off their airflow and asphyxiate themselves?

There were tears in my eyes as I bent over awkwardly in my own suit to examine the names stenciled onto the suits' torsos: L. BOGDASHKY, said the one closest to me. I had to step over it to read the other name: A. HUMPHRIES.

It was Alex. Or what was left of him.

Fighting back an almost overpowering feeling of dread, I peered into the tinted visor of Alex's helmet, more than half expecting to see a skull leering at me. Nothing. The helmet looked empty. I pushed my own fishbowl right up against the visor so my lamp could shine into Alex's helmet. There was nothing inside to be seen.

"Is that him?" Marguerite asked, in a hushed voice.

Startled, I turned to see her standing behind me.

I said, "It was him. It was."

THE CYCLE OF DEATH

There is a powerful difference between knowing something intellectually, up in the front of your brain, and seeing the truth of it with your own eyes. I had known Alex was dead for more than three years, yet when I finally saw that shriveled, seared spacesuit, saw his name stenciled on its chest, saw that his helmet was empty, I knew finally and utterly that Alex was dead.

"I'm sorry, Van," Marguerite said gently. "For what it's worth, I know what it's like."

I nodded inside my helmet. She had lost her mother. I'd lost the man who'd been a brother to me all my life.

But there was no time to mourn him.

"We've got to get inside the suits and see if there's any organic material still remaining," Marguerite said. To her, this was not a personal loss, not a tragedy like her mother's death. This was a problem in biology, a chance to learn something new, an opportunity for adding to the human race's store of knowledge.

"When bodies are cremated in high-temperature furnaces," she told me, "there are always bits of bone and teeth in the ashes."

"Even when they've been burned for more than three years?" I asked.

"We won't know until we've opened the suits and looked," she said firmly.

It would be best to open the suits in vacuum, she said. That would keep the level of contamination down as low as possible.

So, keeping my sorrow to myself, I started to help Marguerite pump the air out of the pod, to turn it into an airless biology labora-

"I'll rest when we reach orbit," he said. "Now get to your duties: Van, to the bridge; Marguerite, back to the cargo bay and that pod. It's my ticket to ten billion dollars."

We both stood up, but Marguerite said, "I'm going to the sick bay and you should come with me."

"Later. Once we're in orbit."

"Your strokes are getting worse each time!" she railed at him. "Don't you understand that? It's only a matter of time before you have a fatal one! Why won't you let me help you? I can bring your blood pressure down, put you on blood thinners. . . ." She ran out of words, and I saw tears brimming in her eyes.

Fuchs struggled to his feet, or tried to. He got halfway up, then sank back into his chair again. "Later," he repeated. "Not now." And he waved us toward the door.

Outside in the passageway I whispered to her, "Nobody dies of strokes anymore!"

"Not if they have proper medical care," Marguerite agreed. "But I don't have the experience or the facilities or even the proper medical supplies to take care of him. And he's too stubborn even to let me do what little I can for him."

"He's got to run the ship, I suppose."

She shot me a furious glance. "That Amarjagal woman can run the ship! But he doesn't trust her to get us through the bugs. He doesn't trust *anyone!*"

Before I could think of what it meant, I said, "He'll trust me."

"You?"

"I'll take over as captain," I heard myself say, as if I believed it. "You get him down to the sick bay and do what you can for him."

She stared at me disbelievingly. "You can't . . ." But she didn't finish the sentence because I was already stepping back to the captain's door and rapping on it.

Without waiting for him to answer, I slid the door back and strode into his quarters. "Captain, I—"

I stopped dead in my tracks. He was still in his chair, but bent facedown over the desk. Unconscious. Or dead.

BACK IN THE CLOUDS

helped Marguerite lug Fuchs's comatose body down to the sick bay. She had been tearful when she'd been arguing with him, but now she was dry-eyed and all business.

"You'd better get to the bridge," she told me, once we had him lying on the table.

"Right," I said.

But Fuchs opened one eye slightly and pawed at the sleeve of my coveralls. "Tell . . . Amar . . ." His voice was terribly slurred, his face twisted into a grisly rictus of pain.

"Don't worry," I said, grasping his shoulder. "I'll take care of everything."

"The bugs . . . sharp angle . . . of ascent."

I nodded as reassuringly as I could. "I know. I'll get the job done."

"You did . . . okay . . . down on . . . surface."

I forced a smile. Praise from him was vanishingly rare. "Thanks." Then on impulse I added, "Father."

He tried to smile back but he couldn't. He mumbled something, but his voice was too slurred for me to understand what he said.

For an awkward moment I simply stood there, my hand on his shoulder. Then his eyes closed and the medical monitors that Marguerite was setting up began wailing shrilly.

"Get out of my way," she hissed urgently.

I beat a retreat to the bridge.

Amarjagal was still in the command chair, looking tired herself.

"When's the next watch due on duty?" I asked.

Her grasp of the English language was minimal. I asked her

again, slower and louder. Her eyes barely flicked to the digital clock on the display panel. "Forty-two minutes."

"And when do we enter the top cloud deck?"

Again she had to translate my words in her head before she could answer, "One hour and one half."

I went to the comm console and, leaning over the shoulder of the crewman sitting there, punched up the translation program. He glared up at me but said nothing.

"Amarjagal," I said, thinking as I spoke, "I will relieve you for one hour. Take a break and then get back here before we enter the last cloud deck."

My words were repeated to her in her own language by the computer's synthesized voice. Then she asked a question.

"What right do you have to give orders?" the synthesized voice said, without inflection.

"I'm taking command of the ship," I said, looking straight at her.

She blinked, then blinked again when the computer translated my words. "But where is the captain?"

"The captain's in sick bay," I said. "I'm speaking for him. You'll have the helm when we enter the clouds again, under my command."

Amarjagal stared at me for a long wordless moment, digesting the computer's words, her stoic face and dark eyes revealing nothing.

"You are not the captain," she said at last.

"I am the captain's son," I said. "And I will act for him while he's in sick bay. Is that understood?"

I hadn't the faintest idea of how she'd react. She simply stared at me, apparently digesting what I had just said, thinking it over, trying to figure out how she should react to this new situation. She had been loyal to Fuchs when Bahadur mutinied. If she accepted my command now, I thought, the rest of the crew would follow her lead. If she wouldn't, then we'd have chaos—or worse, another mutiny.

At last she said in English, "Yes, sir." And she got up from the command chair.

I tried not to let the relief I felt show in my face, but my insides were quivering madly. For the first time in my life, I took the seat of authority. Deep in the back of my mind that self-critical voice was warning me that I was going to screw everything up. But I remembered that I had indeed gone down to the surface and recovered Alex's remains. I was not a helpless, inexperienced, spoiled kid anymore.

Or so I hoped.

The two other crew members on the bridge eyed me warily but said nothing. Not that I could have understood them if they did speak. They watched Amarjagal leave the bridge, then turned back to their consoles in stony silence.

I called up the ship's planned flight profile. As I suspected, Fuchs had set *Lucifer* for the steepest possible ascent through the bug-laden clouds to get us past the danger as quickly as possible. *Lucifer* was essentially a dirigible, an airship that floated through Venus's thick atmosphere propelled by small engines whose main task was to maintain headway against any currents of wind the ship encountered. We could not force our way up through the final cloud deck; we had to climb, venting the gas in our envelope until it was down to vacuum so it could rise to the top of the atmosphere.

We had a set of rocket engines, but they were to be used only after we cleared the topmost cloud deck, to push us on up into orbit. I checked the figures in the computer's flight program. If we fired those rockets too soon we would not establish an orbit around Venus, we would merely fling *Lucifer* into a long ballistic trajectory that would arc back into the clouds halfway around the planet. Once in orbit, though, there was a nuclear propulsion module waiting to power our flight back to Earth. Fuchs had dropped it off in a parking orbit on the way into Venus's clouds.

So above all else, I had to resist the urge to light off the rockets. Fire them too soon, and we would doom ourselves to stay in Venus's atmosphere until the bugs chewed through the hull or the heat got us or our food ran out. A life sentence in hell. And not a long one, at that.

I was worried about those bugs. They had destroyed both Alex's ship and mine. Although Fuchs had bragged about how *Lucifer*'s overdesign had gotten him through the bugs without crippling damage, I wondered how much more of the bugs' attack the ship could take.

Was there anything else I could do? Coat the hull with something the bugs wouldn't or couldn't eat? I hadn't the faintest idea of what that might be, and even if I knew there wasn't much that we could do in less than ninety minutes.

How much damage had *Lucifer* sustained on the way in? I riffled through the captain's files and then the computer's maintenance and safety programs, finding nothing. Either Fuchs didn't get a chance to check the damage or the data were stored somewhere else in the files.

I wanted to ask the crewman running the communications system, but he didn't understand English. I called up the translation program and tried to make him understand what I needed. He stared hard at me, frowning with concentration, then turned back to his keyboard. A stream of data began pouring across the main display screen. Perhaps it was the data I sought, perhaps it was something else entirely. Either way, I couldn't understand a bit of it.

Amarjagal came back to the bridge and I got out of the command chair. Using the language program, I asked her about data on damage to the ship.

"We did check for damage," the computer's voice translated. "Hull integrity was not breached."

"But how much damage was done?" I demanded, feeling frustrated at this laborious process of translating from one language to the other. Time was ticking away. I thought that I should bring Nodon up to the bridge to translate for me.

"Not enough to breach the hull," came her answer.

I went from frustration to exasperation. "Is there any way to assess how much more damage we can take before the hull is breached?"

Amarjagal puzzled over that for what seemed like half an hour, then replied simply, "No."

So we were about to climb into that bug-infested cloud deck, more than fifteen kilometers thick from bottom to top, without the faintest idea of how much damage the hull had sustained during the first trip through or how much more damage we could take before the hull cracked open.

Holding back my anger and frustration, I said to Amarjagal—to the computer, really—"Rig the ship for the steepest ascent possible."

"Understood," she said back to me.

I left the bridge in a black fury. We were heading blindly into danger, without any idea of how to protect ourselves. But halfway down to the sick bay another thought struck me: What difference does it make? I almost laughed aloud at the realization. We're going back into the bugs and there's not a damned thing we can do about it. We're simply going to have to get through them as quickly as we can, and let the chips fall where they may.

Deep in my gut I was still totally dissatisfied with the situation. But up in my brain I adopted a fatalist's pose: Whatever happens, happens. If you can't do anything about it, that's it.

Yet something inside me refused to accept the situation. Something was gnawing at me the way the bugs would soon be chewing on our hull. There must be *something* we can do! But what?

Fuchs was unconscious when I reached the sick bay, and Marguerite was staring at the monitors along the bulkhead as if she thought that if she looked at them long enough, hard enough, they would show her what she wanted to see. The monitors weren't whining any danger signals, at least, although I realized that might be because Marguerite had turned the alarms off.

"How is he?' I asked.

She jerked back, startled. She'd been studying the monitors so hard she hadn't noticed me.

"I've got him stabilized, I think. But he's sinking. It's slow, but he's losing it. Brain function isn't returning, despite the hormone injections."

"You're doing everything you can," I said, trying to soothe her.

But Marguerite shook her head. "He needs more! If I could talk to one of the medical centers on Earth—"

"Why not?" I said. "We can establish a comm link through *Truax*."

"He gave orders forbidding any contact, remember?"

I pushed past her and banged the comm unit on the bulkhead. "Amarjagal, I want a comm link with *Truax* immediately! Medical emergency."

It took a few moments, but she replied, "Yes, sir."

Turning back to Marguerite, I grinned. "Rank hath its privileges. And powers."

She didn't bother to say thank you. She immediately started telling *Truax*'s communication tech what she needed. At least they both spoke English and there was no translation problem between them.

I headed back for the bridge as the ship's intercom blared, "RIG FOR STEEP ASCENT. STORE ALL LOOSE ARTICLES SECURELY. ALL HATCHES WILL SHUT IN THIRTY SECONDS."

On impulse, I went past the bridge and sprinted along the passageway to the observation center, up in the nose. Through the thick windows I saw the underside of the cloud deck coming up fast. Then the ship began angling upward steeply. I almost toppled over; I had to grab one of the sensor packs Marguerite and I had installed to keep my balance.

It was going to be a wild ride, I thought, as I made my way cautiously back to the bridge, like stepping down a steep gangplank.

Nodon was at the comm console when I got to the bridge, Amarjagal in the command chair. She started to get up, but I waved her back.

"You have the con, Amarjagal," I said as I took the chair beside her. "You can handle this much better than I could."

If my words pleased her, once the computer translated them, she gave no indication.

Nodon said to me, "Sir, the captain of *Truax* is sending many questions. Some of them are addressed to you personally, sir."

I hesitated, then replied, "Tell *Truax* we'll talk with them after we establish orbit. For now, I want only the medical channel to remain open."

"Yes, sir," said Nodon.

So I belted myself into the chair beside Amarjagal as *Lucifer* angled steeply into the last layer of clouds between us and the relative safety of space. It's strange, I thought: I had always considered space to be a dangerous environment, a vacuum drenched with hard radiation and peppered with meteoroids that could puncture a ship's hull like high-powered bullets. But after our stay on Venus, the cold empty calm of space looked like heaven itself to me.

The topmost cloud deck is the thickest of Venus's three, and we seemed to be approaching it at a crawl. I watched the main screen's display of our planned ascent trajectory, a long curving line through an expanse of gray that represented the clouds. The blinking cursor that marked our position seemed to barely move toward the underside of the cloud deck. The bugs were going to have plenty of time to gnaw on our hull. I remembered what they did to Bahadur and his cohorts in the escape pod.

There had to be *something* more that we could do to get through the clouds. Thoughts whirled through my mind, flashing like kaleidoscope images. Bahadur. The escape pod. Our rocket engines. The acceleration that rocket thrust produces.

On impulse, I popped the tiny display screen up from the arm of my chair and called up the rocket propulsion program. How much extra rocket propellant were we carrying? Could we use the rockets to push us through the clouds and still have enough left to establish orbit once we were clear of the cloud deck?

No, I saw. The margins were too thin. It would be too much of a risk.

"Approaching dayside," the navigation technician called out, in English.

Amarjagal nodded wordlessly. Then she turned to me. "We will face the superrotation winds again," she warned.

"Understood," I said, imitating the clipped professional talk of the crew.

I turned my attention back to the display screen and called up alternative trajectories. Maybe . . . no, nothing. All the programs had us lighting up the rockets only after we had cleared the bug-laden cloud deck.

On a hunch, I checked the rocket engines' specs. They could run for five times longer than the brief burst Fuchs had programmed. I asked the computer to show a trajectory that minimized thrust and maximized burn time. Once the numbers appeared on my screen, I asked for a correlation with our ascent trajectory.

Yes! If we lit the rockets now, as we entered the clouds, they would push us through the cloud deck in twelve minutes and still produce enough thrust to establish us in orbit. Barely.

To me, getting through those waiting bugs in twelve minutes was infinitely better than spending twelve hours in the clouds.

"Amarjagal," I called to her, "look at this." And I put the new trajectory on her main screen.

She frowned at the display, brows knitted, the corners of her mouth turned down. But she grasped what I was showing her, that I could clearly see. After a few moments she turned to me and said, "It does not leave us any reserve for orbital maneuvering."

"Oh," I said, feeling crushed. We'd have to be able to maneuver once we got into orbit, to make rendezvous with the rocket engines that would take us back to Earth.

Amarjagal's frown softened. "The nuclear module has maneuvering jets."

I blinked at her. "We could get it to maneuver to us?"

She nodded. "If necessary."

"Then let's do it!" I said.

"This is not the trajectory your father planned," she pointed out.

"I know," I said. "But I'm in charge now."

For a long moment she said nothing, merely staring at me with those expressionless dark eyes. Then she nodded and said the best two words I'd ever heard.

"Yes, sir."

We were already in the clouds before she finished making the changes to the guidance and propulsion programs. I imagined I could hear the bugs chewing on our hull.

Amarjagal spoke into her lip mike in her own language, and the computer's flat voice boomed through the ship: "PREPARE FOR TWO-GEE THRUST IN ONE MINUTE."

I gripped the armrests of my chair, expecting to be flattened into it as we lit off the rockets. But it wasn't anywhere near as dramatic as I'd envisioned. The ship shuddered, trembled under the sudden acceleration, but except for the muffled roar of power, lighting off our rockets' engines was something of an anticlimax, really.

Until I glanced over at the screen that showed our progress. We were sailing through the clouds beautifully, that cursor rising through the gray region like a rocket-propelled cork popping up to the surface of the sea.

I grinned at Amarjagal and she actually smiled at me.

At last the cursor showed that we had cleared the cloud deck. No alarms ringing. The trajectory plot showed we were on course for rendezvous with the rocket pack. We had made it through the bug-infested clouds. I exhaled a huge sigh of relief.

"I'd like to see the forward view," I said to Amarjagal.

She nodded her understanding and said a brief word to Nodon. The main screen showed the dark expanse of infinity, speckled with stars. I smiled gratefully.

"Rear view, please," I said.

Now I could see Venus again, those swirling cloud tops brilliant with sunlight. We're safe, I said silently to the goddess. We've come through the worst you can throw at us.

That's when the superrotation wind gripped us. The ship lurched like a prizefighter who'd just taken a punch to the jaw. But I laughed aloud. Go ahead, I said to Venus, blow us a farewell kiss.

BEYOND DEATH

stayed on the bridge while Amarjagal fought us through the superrotation winds, the ship bucking and shuddering like a thing alive. I could see on the trajectory display that we were being pushed off course, but there was nothing we could do about it except hope that once we reached orbit, the nuke module waiting to propel us back to Earth would be close enough to make rendezvous with us.

The fact that we were accelerating at two gees, rather than passively floating like a dirigible, actually helped. *Lucifer* climbed past the superrotation winds in record time. The jouncing and bouncing died away, but the ship still rattled under the thrust of her rockets.

All of a sudden the engines cut off. One instant we were shaking like a racing car on a rough track with the muted rumble of the rockets in our ears. Half a blink later the noise had snapped off and everything was as smooth as polished glass.

We were in orbit. In zero gravity. My arms floated up off the arm rests and my stomach crawled up into my throat.

Amarjagal was speaking to the technicians on the bridge in their own language. It was crucial that we make rendezvous with the nuclear module; otherwise we'd be stuck in Venus's orbit.

But there was something even more important for me to do. Unstrapping from my chair, I flung myself toward the hatch. I had to find a lavatory *now,* or throw up all over the bridge.

The nearest toilet was in Fuchs's quarters. Even in my state of misery I hesitated a moment before barging in. But only a moment. I was really sick, and I knew he was down in the sick bay with Marguerite. I spent a miserable half hour upchucking into the plastic bowl. Every time I thought I was finished, it took only a slight movement of my head to bring on the nausea all over again.

But then I heard the intercom report, "RENDEZVOUS ESTABLISHED. BEGINNING SPIN-UP TO ONE GEE."

I staggered over to Fuchs's bed and almost instantly fell asleep.

When I awoke, everything seemed normal. All my internal organs were in their proper places and I could turn my head without making the world swim about me.

I sat up cautiously. I lifted one of the captain's pillows and let it drop to the floor. It fell normally.

I laughed. Amarjagal must have successfully rendezvoused with the nuclear module and now we were spinning at the end of the connecting tether, creating an artificial gravity inside *Lucifer*. Artificial or not, it felt wonderful.

I got out of bed and went down to the crew's quarters, where I showered and dressed in fresh coveralls. Feeling rested and relaxed, knowing that we would soon be getting my medical supplies from *Truax* and then heading back to Earth, I strolled down to the sick bay.

One look at Marguerite's face erased the smile from my face.

"He's dead," she told me.

Fuchs lay on the narrow table, his eyes closed, his face gray and lifeless. The monitors were silent, their screens dark.

"When?" I asked. "How long ago?"

She glanced at the digital clock. "Five—six minutes. I just finished disconnecting the monitors."

I stared down at his lifeless body. My true father. I had barely had the chance to know him and now he was gone.

"If we'd been on Earth," Marguerite said, her voice full of self-reproach, "if we'd had some *real* medical doctors instead of me . . ."

"Don't blame yourself," I said.

"He could have been saved," she insisted. "I know he could have been saved. Or even preserved, frozen, until they could repair the damage to his brain."

Cryonics, she meant. Freeze the body immediately after clinical death in the hope of correcting whatever caused its death and eventually reviving the patient. It had been done on Earth. Even at Selene, on the Moon, people had used cryonics to survive their own death.

A wild idea popped into my mind. "Freeze him, then. And quickly!"

Marguerite scowled at me. "We don't have the facilities, Van. It's got to be done—"

"We have the biggest, coldest freezer of them all, right outside the airlocks," I said.

Her mouth dropped open. "Put him outside?"

"Why not? What's going to harm him out there?"

"Radiation," she answered. "Meteoroids."

"Put him in a spacesuit, then. That'll give him some protection."

"No, it would take too long. He's got to be frozen quickly."

"One of the escape pods, then," I said. "Open its hatch to vacuum. It'll cool down to cryogenic temperature in minutes."

I could see the wheels turning inside her head. "Do you think . . . ?"

"We're wasting time," I said. "Come on."

It was an eerie sort of funeral procession, Marguerite and I carrying Fuchs's body down the passageway and ladders, through an airlock, and into one of the escape pods. We were as tender with him as we could be, a strange sort of treatment for a man who had spent so much of his life seething with hate, burning for revenge. But I knew the devils that drove him, I had glimpsed the fury and agony they had caused, and I felt nothing but regret for the life of frustrated rage he had led, a man of enormous strength and enormous capabilities whose life had been wasted utterly. My father. My true father.

We put him down on the narrow decking between empty seats inside the second of our three escape pods. It occurred to me that we ought to say some words of ritual, but neither Marguerite nor I knew any. Death was rare, back on Earth, and although Fuchs might be clinically dead, we hoped there would be a chance to revive him.

"I remember something," Marguerite said as we stood looking down at him, both of us puffing from the exertion of carrying him.

"What?"

"I remember it from a video I saw, about old-time sailing ships. Something about, 'in sure and certain hope of resurrection . . .' Something like that."

I felt suddenly irritated. "Come on," I snapped. "Let's get out of here and open the outer hatch so he can freeze down."

So we started our two-month journey back to Earth with a dead man lying in one of the ship's escape pods, its outer hatch open to the cryogenic cold and vacuum of space.

It was exactly a week after we broke orbit around Venus and started home that Marguerite told me about Alex's remains.

I'd had a long meeting with the captain of the *Truax,* answering as many of his questions as I deemed proper. Then we'd transferred my medical supplies to *Lucifer* and our two ships started Earthward on their separate trajectories.

I'd appropriated Fuchs's quarters. I was hesitant about moving into the captain's compartment, at first, but it seemed like the logical thing to do. If I were to keep the respect of Amarjagal and the rest of the crew, I could hardly remain in my old bunk in the crew's quarters. I wanted them to know that I was in charge, even if I let Amarjagal run the bridge most of the time. So I moved into the captain's cabin.

There wasn't much ship's business for me to attend to. The crew was happy to be alive and heading home; they were already spending the huge bonuses Fuchs had promised them, in their imaginations. In a few cases, more than imagination was involved. I allowed them to communicate with Earth, and I think some of them spent so freely over the electronic links that they'd actually be in debt by the time we landed.

I was busy talking with Mickey Cochrane and flocks of other scientists, showing them the data and video we had collected on Venus. Perhaps "talking with" is the wrong phrase. Even light waves needed more than nine minutes to travel the distance between *Lucifer* and Earth. We could not have conversations; one side talked and the other side listened. Then we reversed positions.

I was surprised that Professor Greenbaum didn't get involved, until Mickey told me that he had died.

"Died?" I gasped with surprise. "How?" I could understand people getting killed in accidents, or dying because they didn't get proper medical treatment in time, like Fuchs. But Greenbaum must have been in the center of a great university. What on earth could have killed him?

Mickey couldn't hear my blurted question, of course. She simply went on, "The official cause of death was renal failure. But it was really just old age. He never took rejuvenation therapy and his internal organs simply wore out."

How could a man allow himself to die when he didn't have to? I simply could not understand the man's way of thinking. Life is so precious . . .

"He died a happy man, though," Mickey added, with a smile. "Your telemetry data about the volcanic eruptions convinced him that he was right, and Venus is starting an upheaval phase."

I wondered if she thought so, too. When it came my turn to talk, I asked her. Nearly twenty minutes later her reply reached my screen.

"We'll see," she said, noncommittally.

It was shortly after that "conversation" with Mickey that Marguerite came to my compartment, looking very serious, very somber.

"What is it?" I asked, gesturing her to a seat in front of the desk. I'd been reading one of Fuchs's crumbling old books, something about gold mining in the Yukon nearly two centuries ago.

"Your brother," she said, sitting tensely on the front few centimeters of the chair.

My heart clenched in my chest. "Is there anything left of Alex? Anything at all?"

"There was a fine, powdery residue inside his spacesuit," Marguerite said.

"Ashes."

"Yes. Ashes."

It all flashed before my eyes again: Alex trapped inside the escape pod, broiling alive on the merciless surface of Venus. How long did it take? Did he open his visor and let death come quickly?

As if she could read my thoughts, Marguerite said, "His suit was intact. Apparently he remained in it until the heat overcame him."

I sagged back in the swivel chair.

"He . . ." Her voice faltered, then she swallowed hard and resumed, "he left a message for you."

"A message?" Every nerve in me jangled.

Marguerite reached into her coverall pocket, took out a slim data chip, and reached across the desk to hand it to me. I saw that it had "Van" scrawled across it.

"It was in a thigh pouch of his suit. I presume it's a message," she said. "I haven't run it."

I held the chip in the palm of my outstretched hand. This is all that's left of Alex, a voice in my mind told me.

Marguerite got to her feet. "You'll want to look at it in private," she said.

"Yes," I mumbled. It was only when she reached the door that I thought to add, "Thank you."

She nodded once, then left, gently closing the door behind her.

How long I sat there staring at the chip, I don't know. I think I was afraid to run it, afraid to see my brother dying. I knew that he wasn't really my brother, not genetically, but there was no other way that I could think of Alex. He'd been my big brother all my life, and now I realized that he was thinking of me in the last agonized moments of his life.

Had he known that his father was not my father? Unlikely, I thought. Martin Humphries would never tell anyone, not even his much-loved son, that he'd been cuckolded by his most hated enemy.

With enormous reluctance, I clicked the chip into the desktop computer. Strangely, I noticed that my hand was steady. My insides weren't jumpy, either, not anymore. I felt glacially cold, almost numb, the only emotion I felt a consuming desire to learn what Alex wanted me to know in his last moments of life.

The computer screen lit up and there was Alex, his face barely discernable behind the visor of his helmet. The picture was weak, grainy. He was inside the escape pod, sitting in front of its communications console in his sealed spacesuit.

"I don't know if this will ever get to you, little brother," he said. "I'm afraid I've made a mess of this mission."

The audio quality was poor, but it was Alex's voice, a voice I thought I'd never hear again. Tears sprang to my eyes. I pawed at them as he continued speaking.

"Van, there's something in the topmost cloud deck of Venus that's eroded *Phosphoros*'s gas envelope so badly that we've sunk down to the surface. I've tried to contact Earth, but it looks as if whatever it is that's destroyed us knocked out the communications antennas, too."

I caught myself nodding, as if he could see me.

"I don't know if this chip will ever get to you. I imagine the only way it could would be for someone to come down to the surface of Venus and find the wreckage, and I doubt that anyone would be foolhardy enough to try that for a long, long time."

Not unless they were offered a ten-billion-dollar prize, I thought.

"Van, the night before I left I told you that I wanted to help the Greens by bringing back imagery of a world where greenhouse warming has run amok. Well, that's been a bust, too. A total fiasco."

A burst of electronic snow nearly blotted out the picture on the screen, but Alex's voice continued, scratchy and weak.

"There's no relationship between what's happened here on Venus and what's happening on Earth. Just no relationship at all. The two planets might have started out with the same conditions, but Venus lost almost all its water very early. Where Earth built up oceans, Venus was so hot that almost all its water boiled off into space right away, billions of years ago."

He was speaking rapidly now, as if afraid that he wouldn't be able to tell me everything he wanted me to know.

"There's no way to compare Earth's greenhouse warming with conditions here on Venus. No way. The Greens are going to be very disappointed; they won't be able to use Venus as an example of what will happen on Earth if we don't stop our greenhouse warming."

He coughed suddenly. The picture cleared slightly, and I peered as hard as I could, trying to make out his face behind the visor.

"The pod's systems are breaking down," Alex said, his voice almost calm. Not quite, but he wasn't the least bit panicky. I imagine he realized there was nothing at all that could be done to save him.

"Getting really hot now . . . really . . . broiling." The screen went blank for an instant, then a faint, grainy picture came on again.

No! I screamed silently. Don't go away, Alex! Don't die! Talk to me. Tell me—

"Failed," Alex said, sounding sadder than I had ever known him to be. "I've failed . . ."

His voice faded out. I waited for more, but the audio gave me nothing except a background hiss. Then the picture winked out completely.

I sat staring at the blank screen, listening to the hiss of the speakers. Then even that sound stopped. I could hear nothing but the background hum of the computer itself.

Alex's final thoughts were about failure. With his last breath he believed that he had failed, Venus had defeated him, his bright hopes for helping the Greens to reverse the greenhouse warming of Earth had died on the hellish surface of Venus, along with his crew, along with himself. My brilliant, handsome, charming, laughing big brother died thinking of himself as a failure.

And thinking of me. He hadn't addressed his last message to his father. Or to the Greens. He wanted to speak to me! He wanted to confess to me his final thoughts, his last realizations.

I looked up from the dead screen, leaned my head back against the padded chair, and saw in my mind the times Alex and I had shared. They seemed so pitifully few, a handful of moments in our two lives.

I resolved to do better.

A NEW LIFE

called Marguerite to my compartment. She slid the door back less than a minute later, and I realized she must have been in her own quarters, next to mine. Then I glanced at the desktop clock. It was past midnight, more than five hours since she'd handed me Alex's chip. I'd been sitting at the desk for more than five hours.

"I woke you," I said.

She almost smiled. "No, I don't dress that quickly."

She still wore the coveralls she'd been wearing earlier.

"You couldn't sleep?" I asked.

"I was working," Marguerite said, taking one of the chairs in front of the desk. "Thinking, really."

"About what?"

"Your brother."

"Oh."

"He must have loved you very much."

"I loved him, too," I said. "I think he's the only person in the solar system I've ever loved."

"So we've both lost the ones we loved the most," Marguerite said, her voice low.

"Your mother," I remembered.

She nodded once, tight-lipped, holding on to her emotions.

I stared at Marguerite. How like her mother she looked, yet she was a very different personality.

"Marguerite, how much . . . material is there in my brother's remains?"

She blinked at me, puzzled.

"Enough to get a good sampling of his DNA?" I asked.

"For cloning?" she asked back.

"For cloning," I said.

She looked away from me for a moment, then returned her gaze to meet mine. "It won't work, Van. I've already checked that. The heat was too much, too long a time. It dissociated all the polypeptides, all the long-chain molecules. The nucleic acids, everything . . . they were all broken apart by the heat."

My heart sank.

"There's nothing we can do," Marguerite said.

"He thought he was a failure," I told her. "My brother died thinking he'd accomplished nothing."

"I don't understand."

So I explained to her about the Greens and Alex's hope of using Venus to convince the people of Earth that they had to take drastic steps to avoid a disaster on Earth from global warming.

Once I finished, Marguerite said, "Yes, the Greens will be dismayed, all right. Crushed. They were counting on making Venus a visible example. They wanted people to think of the greenhouse warming every time they looked up and saw Venus in the sky."

I shook my head. "That's not going to work. The scientists like Mickey and the others will have to tell them the truth, that Venus's greenhouse and ours have nothing to do with each other."

"Your father will be very pleased."

I looked up sharply at her.

"He and his kind will trumpet the news, won't they? He even sacrificed his son to learn that Venus has nothing to tell us."

"But that's the good news," I heard myself say. Whisper, almost.

"Good news for your father," Marguerite countered.

"No," I said, my voice louder, stronger, as I realized the truth of it. "No, it's *bad* news for my father and good news for the rest of us."

She leaned forward slightly in her chair. "What do you mean?"

"The greenhouse warming on Earth has no relationship to the runaway greenhouse on Venus!" I said, almost jubilant.

"And that's good news?"

I jumped up from my chair and came around the desk. "Of course it's good news! It means that what's happening on Earth isn't the inexorable workings of nature, as it was on Venus. It's man-made!"

"But the scientists—"

I grasped Marguerite by the wrists and pulled her out of her chair. "The scientists have been telling us for nearly half a century that human actions are causing the global warming. We've been pouring greenhouse gases into the atmosphere by the gigaton."

"But the industrialists have claimed the warming is part of a natural climate cycle," Marguerite said, almost bemused at my sudden enthusiasm.

"Right. But now we have the imagery of Venus, where nature has produced a *real* greenhouse . . . and we can show that it's nothing like what's happening on Earth!" I was so excited I wanted to dance across the cabin with her.

Marguerite shook her head, though. "I don't see how that helps the Greens."

I laughed. "Let my father and his friends trumpet the news that Venus and Earth are two completely different cases. Let them tell the world that Venus's greenhouse has no relationship to what's happening on Earth.

"And how does that help the Greens?"

"Because we'll come back and say, 'Yes! You're right. Venus is a natural disaster. . . . Earth is a *man-made* disaster. And what humans do, they can undo!'"

Marguerite's eyes flashed with understanding. She broke into a wide, warm smile. "If human actions are causing the greenhouse, then human actions can fix it."

"Right!" And I wrapped my arms around her and kissed her soundly. She didn't object. She kissed me just as hard, in fact.

But then she pulled back slightly and said, "Do you realize what you're getting yourself into?"

"I think so. I'm going to be an even bigger disappointment to my fa—to Martin Humphries. He'll go ballistic. Maybe he'll even attain escape velocity."

"You're going to become the spokesman for the Greens," she said, quite seriously.

"I guess I am."

"That's a heavy responsibility, Van."

I shrugged and nodded, without letting her out of my arms.

"Some of the Greens' leaders won't trust you. Other will be jealous of you. There's a lot of politics inside the movement, let me tell you. A lot of knives in the dark."

I realized what she was telling me. "I'll need someone to guide me, to protect me."

"Yes, you will."

"My father's people will be after my scalp, too. They can play very rough."

She looked directly into my eyes. "Are you certain you want to take on all this?"

I didn't hesitate for a nanosecond. "Yes," I said. Then I added, "If you'll come with me."

"Me?"

"To be my guide, my protectress."

An odd expression came over her beautiful face. The corners of her lips curled up slightly, as if she wanted to smile, but her eyes were dead serious.

"The mother of my children," I added.

Her jaw fell open.

"I'm a very wealthy man," I said, still holding her about the waist. "I don't have any really bad habits. I'm in reasonably good health, as long as I get my medication."

"And?" she prompted.

"And I love you," I said. It wasn't exactly true, and we both knew it. Neither one of us knew what love really was, but we'd been through so much together, there was no one on Earth—no one in the solar system, actually—whom I was closer to.

"Love is a big word," Marguerite whispered. But she snuggled closer in my arms and rested her head on my shoulder.

"We'll learn all about it," I whispered back. "Starting now."

I wasn't prepared for the enormous interest the news media showered upon me. As soon as we established orbit around the Moon I was deluged with requests for interviews, docudramas, biographies. They wanted me to appear on global net shows, to star in an adventure series! I was a celebrity, asked to sit next to media stars and politicians and make appearances everywhere.

Politely but firmly I turned them all down, giving the news media nothing except the highlights of our expedition—which was dramatic enough to keep viewers all through the Earth-Moon system riveted to their screens night after night for a week.

I granted interviews, of course, but very selectively. In each interview I stressed the idea that Venus's greenhouse was completely different from Earth's, that the Earth's warming was largely the result of human actions, and that humans could stop the greenhouse if they were willing to make the necessary changes. The Greens at first were furious; I received loud demands to "recant" my heretical (to them) views. I even got threats. But as my message began to sink in, some of the Green leaders started to realize that what I was saying could be beneficial to them, very helpful to their political stance. I still got threats from angered fanatics, but the leadership began to use my interviews as ammunition in their campaigns.

Meanwhile I handed all our data over to Mickey Cochrane, who flew up to *Lucifer* while we were still in lunar orbit, quarantined until the medical inspectors determined that we were not bringing alien diseases back home with us.

Of course we were carrying samples of the Venusian aerobacteria and the fragment of the feeding arm from the creature on the surface, which enormously complicated our quarantine period. Mickey and her fellow scientists were overcome with joy at the samples and all the data about Venus that we had brought back with us. I was offered an honorary membership in the International Academy of Science. Marguerite received a full membership, and hints that a special Nobel Prize would eventually be awarded to her.

One of my chores while we waited in parking orbit was to contact Gwyneth, who was still living in the flat in Barcelona.

She looked as exotic and beautiful as ever. Even on the wall screen of my compartment aboard *Lucifer,* her tawny eyes and rich, full lips made my pulse throb faster.

But after a few moments of chat, I told her, "I'm deeding the flat to you, Gwyneth. It will be yours, free and clear."

She didn't look surprised. She accepted it as if she'd expected as much.

"This is good-bye, then," she said. It wasn't a question.

"I'm afraid so," I said, surprised that I didn't feel any pain. Oh, perhaps a little twinge, but none of the pangs of separation that I thought I'd suffer.

She nodded slightly. "I thought as much. I've been watching your interviews on the news. You've changed, Van. You're not the same person anymore."

"I don't see how I could be," I said, thinking of all that I'd been through.

"You're going to see your father soon?" It was her parting shot, with just enough of a barb in it to tell me that she was far from pleased at my ending our relationship.

"I'm going to see . . . him just as soon as they lift quarantine on my ship," I said.

She smiled slightly. "To claim your ten bill."

"Yes, that," I replied. "And a few other things."

SELENE CITY

I t took two weeks for the assorted medics and biologists to agree that *Lucifer* and her crew posed no threat to the human population of Earth and Moon.

Once they finally cleared us, I sent Marguerite to my house on Majorca, telling her, "I've got to see Martin Humphries before I go home."

"Can't you do this by videophone?" Marguerite asked. "Or you can set up a virtual reality meeting."

"No," I said. "This has to be face-to-face, him and me. On his turf."

So I went down to Selene City.

I was ushered into the sitting room of his residential suite in the Hotel Luna, and told, "Mr. Humphries will be with you shortly, sir."

I walked across thick carpeting to the room's actual window. Above-ground buildings were rare on the Moon; windows even rarer. I stared out at the rich glowing crescent of Earth hanging in the darkness outside. There was a stubby black telescope by the window, mounted on a slim tripod. I squinted through the eyepiece, searching for Connecticut, where the family home had been.

The sprawling house was in jeopardy from the swelling Connecticut River; as sea levels rose the entire valley was slowly being drowned by the encroaching waters of Long Island Sound. I swung the 'scope toward Majorca, but it was off on the limb of the globe, barely discernable. The Majorca house was safe enough, up on its hilltop, but the seawall protecting Palma was already crumbling, threatening the city.

It had taken more than a century for global warming to begin causing such disasters. It would take more than a century to correct them, I knew. We had long decades of toil and struggle ahead of us, but I was certain that we had the knowledge and the tools to eventually succeed.

"So there you are, stargazing."

I straightened up and turned at the sound of his sarcastic voice.

"Hello," I said, "Mr. Humphries."

He didn't look a bit different from the last time I'd seen him in the flesh, at his hundredth-birthday bash. Tall, straight carriage, slim. Dark, form-hugging suit with slightly padded shoulders. And those hard, cold eyes.

"Mr. Humphries?" If he was taken aback by the formality of my address to him, he hid it well. He crossed the room and sat on the upholstered sofa beneath an electronic reproduction of some garish neoclassical painting, Delacroix, I think: horse-mounted bedouins in swirling robes racing across the desert with long rifles in their hands.

"You're not my father," I said flatly.

He didn't blink. "Fuchs told you that?"

"DNA scans proved it."

He let out a breath. "So now you know."

"I know why you had my mother murdered," I said.

That popped his eyes wide. "She died of a drug overdose! She did it herself. It was suicide, not murder."

"Was it?"

"I loved her, for Christ's sake! Why do you think I hounded Fuchs until he gave her up? I loved her, she was the only woman I ever loved, damn her to hell and back!"

"Very loving words," I sneered.

He jumped to his feet, face red, hands jittering agitatedly. "I wanted her to love me, but she never did. She wouldn't let me touch her! And then she went and had a baby—*his* baby!"

"Me."

"You."

"That's why you've hated me all these years," I said.

He gave a short, barking laugh. "Hated you? No, that's too active a word. I loathed you, you miserable little Runt. Every time I saw you I saw the two of them laughing at me. Every day of your life was another reminder that she couldn't stand my guts, that she loved that bastard Fuchs, not me."

"So that's why you set up this Venus mission, to get me to kill myself."

He seemed startled by the thought. "Kill you? Hah! Who cared about you? Who the fuck would've thought that you, the weakling, the cowardly pitiful Runt, would take up my challenge? Nobody in his right mind would've expected that. You surprised the hell out of me, let me tell you."

"Then why . . .?" All of a sudden I saw the truth.

Martin Humphries nodded, understanding the dawning light in my eyes. "It was to kill Fuchs, of course. He was way out in the Belt, where his fellow rock rats protected him. Besides, I promised your mother that I wouldn't go after him, and despite what you think I kept my promises to her. Despite everything, I let the son-ofabitch live."

"Until you got the idea for the Venus prize. It was a trap, all along."

"Once Alex was killed I couldn't hold back anymore. I wanted that bastard Fuchs *dead*! So I dangled ten billion dollars' worth of bait and, sure enough, he came after it."

"And so did I."

Something of his old smirking expression crept back across his face. "That was a bonus. I never expected you, of all people, would take the challenge. But I figured, what the hell, Venus will kill both of you. Father and son."

"But I survived."

He shrugged. "I got what I was after. Fuchs is dead. Damned good and dead."

"Maybe not," I said.

He stared at me.

"We froze his body. Marguerite Duchamp is bringing together the world's top cryonics people to see if he can be revived."

Martin Humphries staggered back a few steps, his face ashy white, and plopped down gracelessly on the sofa.

"You son of a bitch," he whispered, pronouncing each word distinctly. "You fucking traitorous son of a bitch."

I suppose I should have enjoyed the look of utter shock and confusion on him, but I felt no sense of victory, no joy of triumph. Only a kind of disgust that he could hate a man—two men, actually—so deeply.

"I've come here to ask you a question," I said, feeling cold and implacable inside. "One question."

His eyes narrowed.

"Did you have Alex's ship sabotaged? Are the rumors true?"

"No!" he snapped, fists clenching. "Alex was my son, my

flesh and blood! Not like you. He was part of *me!* How could I harm him?"

I believed him. I felt the steely hatred gripping my heart fade a little. I realized that I wanted to believe him, despite everything. I did not want to go through my life thinking that he had murdered Alex.

"All right, then," I said quietly. "Then it's over."

"Is it?" Looking up at me, he said, "You think I'm going to let you get your hands on my ten billion now? After what you've done?"

"I already have my hands on it," I said. "I contacted your lawyers as soon as we established lunar orbit. The money's still in escrow. All that's needed is my signature."

"And mine!" he snapped.

"You'll sign."

"Like hell I will!"

"If you don't, the news media get the whole story. You, Fuchs, my mother, me—the entire story. They'll love it."

"You . . . you . . ." He ran out of words.

Heading for the ornate desk in the far corner of the room, I said, "I'll be going Earthside as soon as I leave here. I've got to start organizing the next expedition to Venus."

"The next . . . ?"

"That's right. We've learned how to survive even on the planet's surface. Now we're going back to begin the *real* exploration."

Martin Humphries shook his head, whether in wonder or sorrow or disbelief I neither knew nor cared.

"You'll be able to sign the escrow papers electronically," I told him. "Your lawyers have already agreed to that. You won't have to leave Selene."

"Get out of my sight!" he snarled.

"Nothing could please me more," I said. "But I want to leave you something, something you've bought and paid for."

He glared at me as I slipped a data diskette into his desktop computer.

"Here's Venus," I said.

All the room's walls, even the windows, were smart screens. Suddenly they all showed the glowering red-hot surface of Venus, the views that little *Hecate*'s cameras had recorded. I punched out all the overhead lights; Martin Humphries sat, sagging and defeated, as the sullen red anger of Venus enveloped him. I could almost feel the heat as I stood by the desk.

Walking slowly to the door, I watched as the wall screens

showed the wreckage of *Phosphoros* scattered across those baking rocks, with those strange feeding arms stretched over it. Martin Humphries sat transfixed, actual perspiration breaking out on his forehead.

I grasped the door handle and waited. The ground opened up, a white-hot fury of lava swallowing the wreckage, burning, destroying, melting everything it touched with its incandescent rage.

I left Martin Humphries sitting there, staring into the blinding fury of Venus.

I left him in hell.

As I headed toward the rocket port and the shuttle that would take me back to Majorca, back to Marguerite, I wondered if Alex had left samples of his sperm before he ventured off on his space missions. It would have been the prudent thing to do, if he'd intended to someday marry and have children. A protection against the radiation levels that could be encountered in space during a solar storm. Alex was a prudent man; I felt certain that he had sperm samples tucked away safely, perhaps in the Connecticut house.

I wondered how Marguerite would feel when I asked her to carry his cloned zygote. Would she do that for me? It was a lot to ask, I knew. We'd have children of our own, of course, but first I wanted to bring Alex back.

I wondered how it would feel to be his big brother.

WOMEN,
FOOD,
AND
HORMONES

WOMEN, FOOD, AND HORMONES

A Four-Week Plan to Achieve
Hormonal Balance, Lose Weight,
and Feel Like Yourself Again

Sara Gottfried, MD

Houghton Mifflin Harcourt
Boston ▪ New York
2021

Library of Congress Cataloging-in-Publication Data
Names: Gottfried, Sara, author.
Title: Women, food, and hormones : a 4-week plan to achieve hormonal balance,
lose weight, and feel like yourself again / Sara Gottfried, MD.
Description: Boston : Houghton Mifflin Harcourt, 2021. |
Includes bibliographical references and index.
Identifiers: LCCN 2021004079 (print) | LCCN 2021004080 (ebook) |
ISBN 9780358345411 (hardcover) | ISBN 9780358578437 | ISBN 9780358578840 |
ISBN 9780358346210 (ebook)
Subjects: LCSH: Reducing diets. | Ketogenic diet. | Low-carbohydrate diet. | Menopause —
Popular works. | Middle-aged women — Health and Hygiene — Popular works.
Classification: LCC RM222.2 .G6817 2021 (print) | LCC RM222.2 (ebook) |
DDC 613.2/5—dc23
LC record available at https://lccn.loc.gov/2021004079
LC ebook record available at https://lccn.loc.gov/2021004080

Book design by Chrissy Kurpeski

Printed in the United States of America
1 2021
4500833039

Carrot Cake Shake recipe adapted from Kelly LeVeque; Tahini Bread, Cauliflower Ceviche, Halibut with Almond Crust recipes courtesy of Nathalie Hadi; Tofu Masala Soup recipe courtesy of Anu French, MD; Shakshuka, Crispy Cucumber Salad with Tahini Dressing, Tahini Dressing; Kimchi, Shirataki, and Bok Choy Bowl; Lemon-Herb Mojo, Slow-Cooker Chicken, Nut-Crusted Chicken Fingers, Almond-Coconut Macaroons, Chocolate-Avocado "Ice Cream," Avocado-Lime Sorbet recipes adapted from *Brain Body Diet* by Sara Gottfried, MD; Egg-Avocado Bake, Mayonnaise, Ranch Dressing, Seaweed Salad, Kale and Caesar Salad, Alkaline Broth with Collagen, Chicken Bone Broth, Beef Bone Broth, Salmon and Avocado Bowl with Miso Dressing, Black Cod with Miso, Braised Turmeric-Cinnamon Chicken, Beef and Vegetable Stew, No-Bake Coconut Love Bites, Dark Chocolate–Coconut Pudding recipes adapted from *Younger* by Sara Gottfried, MD.

CONTENTS

PART I

Understanding Women, Food, and Hormones

INTRODUCTION:
The Language of Hormones

Few things on earth are as misunderstood as women, food, and hormones.

I've seen it again and again in my practice: women come to me feeling overtired, cranky, frazzled, and—inevitably—lamenting the extra pounds they've put on despite their best efforts to exercise and eat right. More often than not, these issues start when women enter their midthirties. My patients notice that it's harder to maintain a healthy weight. Those holiday pounds are harder to shave off, even with January's discipline. The diet plans that worked in the past don't seem to work anymore. Even more disheartening, diets that work for male co-workers and partners don't seem to work the same for them.

My patients are often surprised when I explain that the solution to their symptoms can't be found by counting calories or clocking miles on the treadmill, but by learning to speak the language of hormones.

I know what you're thinking: *hormones?* Yes, hormones.

As a board-certified physician who has been practicing medicine for more than twenty-five years, and precision medicine for the past fifteen, I can tell you without a doubt that you cannot achieve true health without achieving hormonal health and balance. I can help you do just that, using science that honors your body.

What does that mean, exactly? When your diet and lifestyle support your hormones, your hormones will support you. It's like a cool breeze on a hot summer day when your food tells your body to burn fat and promote health. You flip a metabolic switch, and your body is transformed. This is particularly welcome after age thirty-five, when the scale gets harder to budge!

What makes the scale stick? Your metabolism is grinding to a halt. Your metabolism is the sum of all of the biochemical reactions in your body, including those related to your hormones, that dictate how you feel and determine how fast or slow you burn calories. Metabolism is the foundation of your health, today and tomorrow. When you learn to speak the language of hormones, you can improve metabolism, lose fat, and finally maintain a healthy body weight by burning rather than storing fat. At the same time, you resolve nagging, unpleasant symptoms like fatigue, cravings, moodiness, insomnia, and a weak immune system. Too many health plans don't work because they are designed by men, for men, and not for women's complex hormonal needs. I'm going to show you how to achieve this ultimate goal in a way that *honors your unique female biology.*

WHAT TO EAT?

Many of my patients want to know what to eat to stay healthy, but they feel confused. I don't blame them: there's so much conflicting information out there. And over time, the answer has changed. In the 1980s, fat was villainized; later, sugar. As fasting protocols became all the rage, the focus shifted from *what should I eat* to *when should I eat.* Very often my patients come to me having tried these various plans, only to find they just gained weight, or they are so overwhelmed with choices, they stay in the same food rut because they aren't sure which plan is right for them.

What *not* to eat is easy. The truth is, a powerful link exists between consumption of processed food, weight gain, and poor immunity. More than half of Americans' caloric intake now comes from ultraprocessed foods: chips, soda, cookies, candy, and other Frankenfoods. The results are plain to see. Not only did the United States fare worse than many other countries during the COVID-19 pandemic, but also our rates of weight gain, obesity, diabetes, cardiovascular disease, cancer, and depression are high. The food we eat sets us up to be extraordinarily unhealthy, making us vulnerable to chronic disease and to viruses like COVID-19.

My answer to this age-old question of what to eat? *Eat for your hormones.*

Food is the backbone of the hormones you make. When it comes to your health and metabolism, food is medicine. I'm going to clear up the confusion about what's healthy and what's not and give you all the support you need to be successful. I'll share a proven plan that's designed to meet your hormonal needs and help you reclaim your health in four weeks.

To start, consuming healthy fat is especially critical to long-term hormone balance. Healthy fat makes you feel more satisfied, and it slows down or eliminates the spikes in blood sugar that can make you accumulate fat. You need moderate protein — not so much that it turns into sugar, but not so little that your muscles start to break down. Some guidelines you've likely heard about before are important too, such as avoiding sugar and excess refined carbohydrates, enjoying healthy fats like extra-virgin olive oil and avocado oil, and even following fasting protocols. I've integrated these strategies into a single cohesive approach I call the Gottfried Protocol, which will allow you to switch your metabolism from stuck and inflexible to unstuck and flexible. As you do so, you'll lengthen your health span (that is, your healthy life span), support your immune system, and improve your overall health.

HOW NUTRITION AND I EVOLVED TOGETHER

I didn't learn the answers to these food queries at Harvard Medical School or the University of California at San Francisco, where I served my internship and residency in obstetrics and gynecology. In fact, during my medical education, nutrition and lifestyle approaches to health were tolerated but never championed. Yet this lack of interest was a scientific contradiction that has since been evolving. We now know that better diet and lifestyle are the most important drivers of disease prevention and reversal for the people who are willing to commit to them. Science has documented the evidence for this fact many times over, though the discoveries have been largely ignored by mainstream medicine.

Look no further than the hormone insulin. You've probably heard about it. Insulin's primary job is to move glucose into your cells, thereby lowering the glucose in your blood. It's a key hormone in the treatment and prevention of diabetes. The scientific literature demonstrates that dietary and lifestyle approaches to diabetes — a condition in which cells become numb to the hormone insulin — work better than medications,[1] perhaps because they don't disrupt normal biochemistry and instead help an individual return to a state of homeostasis, or balance. Yet few physicians (myself included) learned how to use nutritional intervention or how to guide changes to behavior and lifestyle.

As a result, I had to teach myself how to do these things. Fortunately, I had an ideal patient, one who struggled with multiple hormone problems: *me*. My personal struggle to balance my hormones has informed my career as a physician and writer. I come to this topic as a doctor and scientist, but also as a case study.

In medical school, I was taught to advise patients to exercise more and eat less if they wanted to lose weight. When I followed that advice, I made my hormone imbalance worse because the essential role of metabolic hormones, and how they function in women, was missing from the equation. In my thirties, I began to battle depression, premenstrual syndrome, and belly fat. I wrestled with my weight because my levels of testosterone, growth hormone, estrogen, and progesterone were too low, and my insulin and cortisol were too high. That made me get stressed about the small stuff. I'd work out for hours with nothing to show for it on the bathroom scale or in my musculature. I was on a mostly vegan diet, and I wasn't getting the healthy fat I needed to synthesize these hormones in my body. Seemingly overnight, my triceps area became flabby. There were longitudinal lines on my nails, and I noticed weird fatty "cushions" at my knees. *What?!* Worst of all, I felt frazzled and overwhelmed much of the time; I lacked inner peace. If you're like me or my patients, you may not notice that your hormones are off kilter. Instead, you may observe difficulty with sleeping, with losing the baby weight, or with low sex drive. Maybe your workouts don't seem to have an impact.

After being offered an antidepressant and the birth control pill to address my afflictions, I just felt they were not the right treatment. Then, with a simple blood test, I discovered my hormones were out of balance. As I corrected my hormones, I learned they were the root cause of my troubles. I began seeing hormone imbalance in nearly all of my patients who were medicated by their well-meaning doctors. I wrote several books about how to balance hormones: *The Hormone Cure, The Hormone Reset Diet, Younger,* and *Brain Body Diet.* However, I didn't fully connect the dots between hormones, food, and metabolic flexibility until now. My goal is to save you time in finding a solution. I uncovered what worked, and what didn't, to get my hormones back in the target zone, burn fat, and lose weight. You can too.

Thankfully, the culture of medicine is changing. Science and technology are advancing. My practice has evolved, thanks to these recent developments.

Today I help my patients personalize the way they eat in order to balance their hormones. I do this through the practice of *precision medicine.* Defined by the National Institutes of Health as an emerging approach to disease treatment and prevention, precision medicine takes into account individual variability in genes, environment, and lifestyle.[2] Its practitioners use every means possible: wearable sensors like watches, rings, and continuous glucose monitors; nutrient trackers, Bluetooth body-composition scales in the bathroom at home, and food log apps; stress tests, stress hormone tests, heart rate variability, and other measures of recovery; genetic and epigenetic panels; home lab testing (yes, including poop tests), finger pricks, and computation to analyze these complex data flows. This is a collaborative process involving the patient and other clinicians; we share a common dashboard documenting health and progress.

Do you need to go that far in order to lose weight and get healthier? Not necessarily. But the information and experience that I picked up over the past five years while guiding patients through my protocols are now streamlined into the book you're holding and the four-week program you will learn. This is the foundation for *Women, Food, and Hormones.*

NOT A ONE-SIZE-FITS-ALL PROGRAM

As described by the medical journal *The Lancet,* we are witnessing an "overabundance of information — some accurate and some not — that makes it harder for people to find trustworthy sources and reliable guidance when needed."[3] Unproved theories and so-called miracle cures contribute to today's infodemic, the flood of misinformation regarding the reasons for our obesity epidemic and the metabolic catastrophe following in its wake. The situation is complicated by the fact that diet programs don't work the same way for every person and that many such programs have been created by men and tested on male bodies, not female ones.

The fact that you have a unique biology can get lost in the media hype around the latest diet craze. Bear with me for a quick "science moment." Let's consider the diet trend now most frequently searched for online. This is the ketogenic diet — or "keto," as it has been affectionately nicknamed — a very low carbohydrate diet that puts the body in a state of ketosis, which means it is burning fat instead of sugar. Very few authors of books promoting the keto diet or its practitioners are paying attention to the contradictory outcomes reported by researchers. For example, the diet may not be the best choice for some people at risk for cancer or already battling it.[4] According to limited studies, ketones produced by the body when on a ketogenic diet may be associated with progression of cancer, metastasis, and poor clinical outcomes.[5]

Based on the scientific data, the ketogenic diet is not a one-size-fits-all quick fix. It's more of a mixed bag: On classic keto, some women lose weight. Some develop better focus, or perhaps avoid certain types of cancer. On the other hand, some women develop thyroid dysfunction. Some find the diet physically stressful, though they may not consciously notice this; nonetheless, stress-related hormones may block weight loss. For just under half of the women on a ketogenic diet, changes to menstrual hormones and loss of the monthly cycle occur; the quality of studies reporting these results is, however, uneven. Some women actually *gain* weight on diets like keto, and for the most part, no one is warning them about the effects on hormones.

Given this range of results—from the impressive to the potentially harmful—anyone considering a ketogenic diet needs to have a medical doctor in her court. We need medical doctors to make sense of the contradictory information, to help women follow protocols proven to work, and to keep them safe.

AN ANTIDOTE TO THE INFODEMIC

I am a physician-scientist who practices precision medicine. I am a clinical assistant professor of integrative medicine and nutritional sciences at Sidney Kimmel Medical College, Thomas Jefferson University, located in Philadelphia, Pennsylvania. There I also serve as the director of precision medicine at the Marcus Institute of Integrative Health.

In *Women, Food, and Hormones,* I will teach you the scientific basis of hormone balancing by changing what, how, and when you eat, using the Gottfried Protocol. You'll see hundreds of citations from peer-reviewed journals to document my statements about the key hormones of metabolism—you will meet them all shortly.

But I'm getting ahead of myself. You'll get to know the names and functions of the key hormones very soon, and how they work together to create an extraordinary symphony in your body—or deafening alarm bells. Learning how each instrument, each hormone, works and what you can do to encourage the beautiful music that comes from balanced hormones is so empowering. When your hormones work in harmony, you won't just look better — you'll also feel better.

If you go to a conventional doctor for treatment of symptoms of hormone imbalance, you will likely receive a prescription for a pill. The doctor may try to tell you that lifestyle changes aren't enough. But that's not what I've found. In fact, as a leader in the integrative, precision, and functional medicine movement, I believe that lifestyle changes are the best hope for a comprehensive solution. Lifestyle choices, starting with food, play a huge role in hormonal balance, and by extension, your total health. In this book, you'll be learning more about the latest scientific breakthroughs concerning hormones and your health. You'll find out how to reset your hormones with your fork and glass in Part 2, which covers the how-to of the Gottfried Protocol.

The Gottfried Protocol is not some fad diet, but rather a science-based approach to health for women. If you've read my previous books, you know that I'm not easily sold on the latest trends. In *Brain Body Diet*, I question the keto diet's value as a weight-loss plan for women. Since writing *Brain Body Diet*, I've pored over the studies published on the subject each year. After two failed attempts at trying to follow keto the classic way, I came up with an approach that worked for me and can work for most women. Then I taught my patients how to do it and watched hundreds of them achieve their weight-loss goals and sustain a healthy weight by using a modified ketogenic diet paired with designed support detoxification and fasting. My approach takes into account individual differences and female physiology.

Throughout this book, I provide general advice that has worked for many of my patients. But not everyone is the same. A ketogenic diet, the supplements I recommend, or other aspects of the system I suggest here may not be appropriate for women (or men) who have certain medical conditions, medical histories, or unique sensitivities.

And of course I cannot give individualized medical advice in this book. It's never a bad idea when starting a new diet or health plan to talk with your physician and health team to make sure the plan is right for you.

WHY IT'S NOT THE SAME FOR WOMEN

Even though women are more likely than men to carry some extra pounds with no health risks, women face more societal pressure to be thin. In my medical practice, I've seen the private suffering of women of all shapes, sizes, races, and ethnicities who struggle to meet our culture's unrealistic standards when it comes to weight. I've learned that even women who aren't overweight are often battling body-image issues and unhealthy relationships with food.

I want you to know that anyone, regardless of body type, can be healthy and strong and feel energized. While many men and women turn to keto, for example, because they are hoping to lose weight, I believe the goal should be health, not weight loss for the sake of weight loss. Nevertheless, we have to wonder why women's bodies respond to food differently than men's do.

In this book, I expose the keto paradox: Why does classic keto help men lose weight and cause some women to gain it? Why does classic keto reverse some diseases and exacerbate others? When does keto clear inflammation, and when does keto cause it? I keep finding the same answer: *hormones!*

High-fat, low-carbohydrate diets cause weight loss for many reasons, but probably not quite in the way you're thinking. Many people think, *If I go keto, I can eat lots of satisfying fat, lose weight, and fit into that cute dress I wore in college.* Well, maybe. The classic ketogenic diet, as practiced most commonly today, doesn't work for many women (and the cute dress stays in storage) because the ketogenic process is misunderstood and therefore not managed for success. Most people think that a low-carb diet causes weight loss simply because eating fewer carbs reduces insulin levels and burns fat. If it worked like that, switching from regular soda to diet soda would cause weight loss, but it doesn't; if you replace one hormonal calamity (sugar) with a potentially worse one (artificial sweeteners), your hormonal messaging gets thrown further out of whack. A common result of switching to diet soda is weight *gain*.[6] Furthermore, if you starve your body of carbohydrates over the long term, you may lose weight, but unfortunately this may cause additional problems, ones that have given the classic keto diet a bad rap.

I have seen up close the frustration the classic keto diet can cause. I meet a large number of "keto refugees" in my office and in my online courses. Some women are too stressed to perform classic keto successfully (stress affects hormones, as discussed on page 30), or they don't get the carbohydrates they need to promote normal hormonal regulation. They gained weight on keto, or didn't lose weight, or started to doubt the high-animal-fat and high-calorie food plan. They've experienced more inflammation and more mood crashes, and they even whisper about the dreaded keto crotch (if you need to ask what that is, consider yourself lucky). They are wondering why butter in their coffee and fat bombs (a popular keto dessert) aren't making them feel or look great, although their husbands or their male co-workers claim success with them.

The truth is, classic keto has mostly been studied in men, and it needs to be modified for many women in order to be successful.

We aren't totally sure why women respond to keto differently.[7] But experts have some ideas. Hormones play a primary role. There's the stress gap — the fact that women are twice as likely to suffer from stress, anxiety, and depression. Women more commonly experience thyroid problems and autoimmunity. Women are more sensitive to carbohydrate restriction and calorie restriction than men are; these restrictions may activate an alarm that shuts down menstruation and increases inflammation — and may explain why so many women on keto lose menstrual regularity. Experts suggest that, compared to men, women are more likely to experience a plummet in blood sugar. Maybe a combination of these issues causes the problem.

There is one thing we know for sure: your hormones dictate your success or lack thereof on the classic ketogenic diet. You won't see the results you want if you don't factor hormones into the equation. I go into more depth about these hormones — and include questionnaires to help you determine whether your hormones are in balance — in Part 1.

We all have these hormones. We may have different levels at one age versus another, or one woman may have more or less compared to another. These hormones juggle function a bit differently (for instance, you need both growth hormone and testosterone for bone strength, but they strengthen the bone in different ways), but all of them are influenced by what we eat.

For example, studies show that higher fat in the diet, and polyunsaturated fatty acids specifically (the fat found in many nuts, flaxseed, and fish), contributes to increased concentration of testosterone in women. (More details are in the Notes.)[8] Once again there is a gap in the research: the effect of the ketogenic diet on testosterone has not yet been studied in healthy women.

When losing weight, men have something known as the *testosterone advantage*. Because their testosterone levels are typically ten times higher than those of women and testosterone is responsible for increasing muscle mass, men have more muscle and burn calories faster. When they diet, using the keto plan or something else, men tend to lose weight faster than women. Only for men has the ketogenic diet been shown to raise testosterone, improve lean body mass, and decrease fat mass.[9] In other words, men may get a double testosterone advantage with classic keto. They start off with higher testosterone levels, then the ketogenic diet and the resulting boost to testosterone help them burn more fat and build more muscle, so they drop weight and look better faster.

While higher levels of testosterone may give men an edge, lower testosterone and higher estrogen levels may put some women at a disadvantage and lead to slower or lower results. On the other hand, estrogen has many positive influences on the body, no matter a woman's age. It is the main reason why we have a lower rate of heart disease than men do before age fifty-two, and why we tend to store fat around our hips and thighs, a far healthier place than the waist for these reserves. Fortunately, you don't need to know your exact levels of these hormones, unless you prefer that level of precision. I will guide you, based on your questionnaire results, to customize the protocol so that it works for you.

HOW I CAN HELP YOU, WOMAN TO WOMAN

The Gottfried Protocol is designed to sidestep the keto paradox with a program that's tailor-made for a woman's body. You will be able to sustain a lower weight while eating a healthy quantity of high-quality carbs, resulting in better hormone balance and more fat loss.

We all need help. This book is designed to help you reconnect your food with your hormones so you feel whole and at peace with your body and your food: no longer at war, no longer feeling flabby or sluggish and wondering why nothing works. The strategies and case studies in this book are body positive. The goal is not to get skinny but rather to regain the healthiest possible version of you. It works, if you do it right. And there's rigorous science behind it.

My promise: I'll put *science first* to help keep you safe. I'll help you decide whether the Gottfried Protocol is right for you, and whether you'll need a few personal workarounds to ensure success. I won't tell you to eat fake food that works over the short term but doesn't create long-term freedom around food and a healthy gut, and I won't advise anything that is not supported by good evidence. I'll assist you in determining your carb threshold, or how long your leash needs to be — each day, each week, each month — so that you can have a piece of cake at your son's birthday party and occasionally enjoy a splurge when at a dinner party with friends. I'll help you avoid the yo-yo roller-coaster of weight loss and regain that plagues many women.

Keeping you informed and safe is not a promise I take lightly. This is not a pledge to get you skinny in one week, with no effort on your part. That's a potentially dangerous fantasy.

Instead, I will give you easy-to-implement tools to customize the Gottfried Protocol for your own body, so that you can achieve all the benefits: burn fat, reduce inflammation, fight cancer, balance hormones and gut bacteria, improve neurological diseases, and even increase life span. I am offering you a proven solution, supported by research and hundreds of success stories, mine included.

MEET THE HORMONES

In this book, you will discover a new way to eat for your hormones. Hormones decide what the body does with the fuel you eat. Your hormones exist in delicate balance, playing alongside one another like instruments in an orchestra. Throughout the day, your hormones fluctuate in rhythm, going up and down like crescendos in a symphony. Each hormone is like a specific instrument that must play on time, at the right volume, and in the correct cadence. In combination, your hormones create a beautiful harmony, which serves as your stable sense of well-being and grace.

What are the hormones of metabolism? Thousands have been detected and researched, but the key hormones we'll focus on are insulin, cortisol, leptin, ghrelin, thyroid, estrogen, testosterone, and growth hormone. Metabolic hormones are involved in thousands of micro communications and processes in the body. To name a few, hormones are involved in satiety (leptin, insulin), hunger (ghrelin, cortisol), female qualities (estradiol), more masculine qualities (testosterone, the most abundant hormone in women, and involved in vitality, muscle mass, and agency), and fat burning (insulin, growth hormone, and cortisol). These are the hormones that govern your response to food, but the relationship is bidirectional.

Metabolic hormones regulate your response to food, and in turn, food regulates metabolic hormones. Insulin is the most influential. It's like a bouncer at a club that either opens the door to glucose or not. If the bouncer doesn't open the door to usher in the glucose, the glucose in your blood rises and over time can lead to insulin block and fat accumulation. That's the central problem of insulin resistance, and it can be identified way before a diagnosis of diabetes.

We won't get mired in explaining every hormone in detail, as it's not necessary to get the Gottfried Protocol to work for you. What's important to know is that these hormones are at work in the background, either helping you lose weight and feel great, or not.

Writing about hormones is about telling the truth, especially the difficult truths about being female and over the age of thirty-five. The levels of many hormones start to drop in our twenties (testosterone, DHEA), thirties (growth hormone, progesterone), and forties through fifties (estrogen). At the same time, other key metabolic hormones, insulin and leptin (and its cousin, ghrelin, the hunger hormone), can rise. These combined hormonal shifts can make life feel more difficult. Why?

- Metabolism slows down yet appetite increases, which means belly fat accumulates seemingly overnight, increasing inflammation. Your weight climbs.
- The liver, the primary organ that regulates fat loss, loses reserve. It is busy metabolizing hormones, clearing toxins, dealing with your latest alcoholic beverage, adjusting cholesterol levels, trying to sort out what fuel you are eating now (carbs? protein? fat?), and generally trying to run the show for the rest of the body.
- The rest of the gut, including the intestines, suffers too. Your gut is involved in regulating your hormones. Most of my patients have one or more problems with their gut that can impede fat loss, such as an imbalance of gut microbes (dysbiosis) or leaky gut syndrome (increased intestinal permeability, which can occur when the tight junctions between the cells lining the small intestine become disrupted).
- On a related note, most of my patients have a substantial *fiber gap*. What you eat has a major influence on the microbes in your gut, a relationship known as the host-microbe interaction. You need the right prebiotic fibers to feed the benevolent bugs, thereby improving immune function and hormone balance. You may not be getting enough of these key fibers.[10]

When you follow the Gottfried Protocol, you'll specifically address each of these challenges, from metabolism to gut health. Your healthy population of gut microbes will increase, and we'll say good-bye to the ones that may be hanging on to fat and inflammation.

WHAT IS THE GOTTFRIED PROTOCOL?

The hormone-balancing Gottfried Protocol has three tenets: detoxification, nutritional ketosis, and intermittent fasting. After experimenting with the Gottfried Protocol for the past five years, I've discovered the essential sequence of these three tenets to activate fat loss for women over the age of thirty-five.

- **Detoxification.** Activating your body's detoxification pathways is essential to prevent the problems that women commonly experience in ketosis, so we do that first. Why? Detoxification clears out your liver and eliminates any recirculating, tired hormones that are clogging up your metabolism.
- **Nutritional ketosis.** You enter nutritional ketosis when you follow a food plan that is low in carbohydrates, moderate in protein, and high in fat. I have adjusted the classic ketogenic diet to make it more effective at restoring insulin levels in women and helping you lose weight. To cut a long story short, you will be (1) eating more plants; (2) consuming tablespoons of extra-virgin olive oil, the occasional spoonful of medium-chain triglyceride oil (associated with weight loss, improved satiety, and removal of alcohol), prebiotics, and probiotics; and (3) tracking net carbs, among other macronutrients. You will use your macronutrients to calculate your ketogenic ratio, and then measure your glucose-ketone ratio (more about this in Part 2). Success on a ketogenic diet is multifaceted — part of it is psychological. The diet's fat-burning power often results in weight loss, improved lean body mass, and increased metabolic rate in a short time, which in turn inspires continuing adherence to the plan and then more improved outcomes. Nonetheless, pitfalls exist, and I will teach you how to avoid them. (See page 18 for a graphic illustrating how the ketogenic diet works.)

- **Intermittent fasting.** This type of fasting means you don't eat for twelve to twenty-four hours in a single day. Data show that intermittent fasting is particularly effective at encouraging weight loss because it improves the balance of many hormones (including insulin, ghrelin, leptin, and afternoon cortisol) and leads to metabolic switching, as reviewed recently in the venerable *New England Journal of Medicine*.[11] (Metabolic switching is when you use fasting and other techniques to suppress insulin and glucose to a level that triggers a switch from burning carbohydrates to burning fat in the body.) Fasting helps regulate inflammation, increases brain function so you feel sharper, lowers blood pressure, and may modulate leptin so you feel more satisfied.[12] Still not convinced? Intermittent fasting helps with cholesterol levels (see details in the Notes).[13] Perhaps most important, I've found intermittent fasting to be extremely effective in aiding women over the age of thirty-five to lose fat and feel better; about 95 percent of my patients are successful at it.

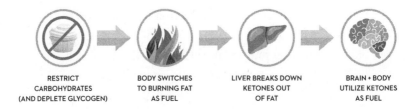

| RESTRICT CARBOHYDRATES (AND DEPLETE GLYCOGEN) | BODY SWITCHES TO BURNING FAT AS FUEL | LIVER BREAKS DOWN KETONES OUT OF FAT | BRAIN + BODY UTILIZE KETONES AS FUEL |

WHY METABOLIC FLEXIBILITY MATTERS TO YOU

Earlier, I defined metabolism as the sum total of chemical reactions that determine how you feel and the speed with which you burn fuel. Understanding the speed of your metabolism is important, but another significant yet often overlooked aspect of metabolism is its *flexibility*. Before you start restricting carbs and deprive yourself perhaps unnecessarily, find out how metabolically flexible you are. Carbs are not the enemy, but lack of metabolic flexibility just might be.

What is metabolic flexibility? It's the ability to adapt to changes in metabolic demand,[14] like when you eat an apple (rich in healthy carbohydrates) versus a slab of salmon (rich in healthy fat), or when you go for sixteen hours without eating and your body needs to burn fat to create fuel. If you have diabetes, are obese, or have an "apple-shaped" body, with more fat at the waist than the hips, then it's likely you have metabolic inflexibility. Metabolic flexibility exists on a spectrum, ranging from normal metabolic flexibility to inflexibility. Indicators that inflexibility is setting in include rising blood-glucose levels, insulin resistance (when insulin starts to rise in the blood), prediabetes, early damage to blood vessels, abnormal lipids, hypertension, and obesity.

Metabolic inflexibility is a major issue affecting many people: according to the Centers for Disease Control, obesity rates continue to rise.[15] Up to 38 percent of the US population has prediabetes.[16] Even people with a normal weight, or who are overweight but not obese, might have metabolic inflexibility. (This doesn't just affect how you fit into your clothes; excess weight is linked to difficulty in fighting illnesses like coronavirus and may make you less responsive to vaccination.[17]) The good news is that if you are metabolically inflexible, or on your way to inflexibility, we can reverse the condition with precision medicine to improve the way you eat, move, think, and sleep.

The Gottfried Protocol will put you on the path to metabolic flexibility: low fasting blood sugar after an overnight fast and mild ketosis from producing a small amount of ketones (a sign that you are burning fat), normal blood sugar after eating, and a normal waist-to-hip ratio. You won't crave the crappy carbs anymore. In short, food freedom!

YOU ARE NEVER A LOST CAUSE

You are never too old to balance your hormones. Yet on social media and elsewhere, I hear women say, "I'm in menopause — it's too late for me." Not true. Many of the hormones addressed, especially insulin, growth hormone, testosterone, and estrogen, are modulated by food, detoxification, ketosis, and timing of meals. There is no upper limit on the best age to achieve hormonal balance.

Similarly, you are never a lost cause. Even if you've been frustrated by a lack of results and feel like your metabolism is the slowest of your life, you can still make progress—I have the case studies to prove it—though it may take longer. You might lose a pound per day initially, like Lara, age forty-five, did in the first five days, or more slowly, like Lotus, age fifty-one—but Lotus now has lost 39 pounds, even though she had a slow metabolism at the start of the Gottfried Protocol. Keep the long view.

Fortunately, you can successfully follow the evidence-based Gottfried Protocol, get your metabolic hormones back on track, and lose weight regardless of whether you are omnivore, pescatarian, vegetarian, or vegan.[18] I've included recipes and sample meal plans to mix and match, so that you can hit your daily targets and be triumphant.

If you chase symptoms with medication, you are less likely to heal than if you chart a new path with the lifestyle medicine of the Gottfried Protocol. You can wipe the slate clean and create hormonal homeostasis. You'll come to love and value your body in a whole new way, and you'll be inspired to eat this way because you feel so good and your health problems resolve. Baggage, trauma, and self-sabotage will become a thing of the past.

LET'S ADD LIFE TO YOUR YEARS

Losing fat after age thirty-five is not about discipline so much as *what to eat, when to eat it, and how your food talks to your hormones.* Most people don't realize that hormones drive metabolism. When your hormones start to get imbalanced after age thirty-five, following certain rules will help you avoid a thickening waist and greater risk of heart disease, diabetes, and cancer. I'll share with you more about my story in Chapter 1, and throughout the book, you'll meet other women who've followed the Gottfried Protocol, encountered a new way to eat in order to feed their hormones, and experienced fat and weight loss.

I'll give you a proven way to enter mild ketosis that will activate your get-me-lean hormones, reverse inflammation, and give you peace of mind. The Gottfried Protocol is based on my own small clinical study with ten overweight and obese women before and after following a ketogenic diet. I used a personalized approach with an N-of-1 design, which arguably produces the highest-quality scientific evidence. In this method of doing research, each individual is the focus of a separate case study. [19]

When you learn the basics of what to eat and when, and how your food talks to your hormones, you can create a hormonal symphony that makes you feel energized throughout the day, without those 4 p.m. dips. You'll burn fat instead of storing it at your waist, where it increases your risk for most chronic diseases. You'll fit into your clothes, so that picking an outfit will take ten seconds, not ten hours — because all of your clothes will look great. You'll feel physically, psychologically, and emotionally satisfied, so you won't eat two dinners every night because you feel like you deserve it. You'll have more time for the things you love. You will learn to eat in a manner that works for your hormones, that connects the dots between nutrition and hormones for your body, and that adds way more life to your years.

1

THE TRUTH ABOUT WOMEN, HORMONES, AND WEIGHT

Grant me the serenity to accept
the hormones I cannot change,
the courage to change the ones I can,
and the wisdom to tell the difference.

I call this the Serenity Prayer for Hormones. Why invoke a prayer? If you've ever experienced hormone-induced weight gain, inexplicably gained 5 pounds right before your period, or suffered from PMS or sleepless nights, thanks to shifting hormones, then you probably understand.

Our hormones rule our bodies, dictating how we think, feel, and look. And while I can't turn back the clock to give you the hormones you had in your early twenties (and the fast metabolism that came with them), the good news is that we have science-based guidelines to bring key hormones back into balance. My goal with this book is to empower you to do so. And that's what the Serenity Prayer for Hormones is all about.

I learned the hard way that people, particularly women, with endocrine dysfunction—a hormone imbalance known for certain common signs and symptoms—tend to struggle the most with their weight. These are my patients with the most stubborn weight-loss resistance. Throughout the book, you'll hear stories about them and my online followers and how they were able to turn frustration into success. I suspect you'll relate to more than a few.

The good news is that we can do something about it too, starting with your fork. We now know what works to resolve hormone imbalances, especially in women over the age of thirty-five. The key is to begin with food, because what you eat is the backbone of every hormone you make. Your food choices may seem inconsequential in the moment, but every bite determines the balance of hormones, the health of your gut and nervous system, the function of your blood vessels, and the strength of your immune system.

Here is the Serenity Prayer in action:

Melissa and I were in my medical office, reviewing her hormone tests. Melissa reported subtle changes in her periods, which suggested she had begun the perimenopausal transition. At age thirty-eight, Melissa was about 30 pounds overweight, with a waist circumference of 40 inches, and she told me she had tried absolutely everything to lose weight. She looked me straight in the eye and said, "Just tell it to me straight. Explain *what I can change* and *what I can't* with my hormones. I know that as I get older, there's a limit to how much I can course-correct. If I make the changes you suggest, will I lose weight? Do I have hormone issues that are beyond repair?" She sighed heavily for the second time.

No! Your hormones are not beyond repair. Like most patients in my practice who are overweight, obese, or just have to work incredibly hard to maintain a healthy weight, Melissa struggles with hormone imbalances. (The telltale physical sign for Melissa, besides the changes in her period, was her apple shape—a common term for larger midsections, with a waist circumference divided by hip circumference that is above 0.85. In Melissa's case, her waist-to-hip ratio was 0.92.) After a round of medical detective work, we found problems with insulin and thyroid—two of the most common hormone imbalances that make it hard to lose weight. In my experience, insulin is the worst, but thyroid and sex hormones are close behind and interrelated.

For the third time, Melissa sighed heavily. According to Chinese traditional medicine, this is a sign of liver qi (pronounced "chee") stagnation, and to my mind, a clue that her hormones were not in balance.

The Liver, Hormones, and Traditional Chinese Medicine

Though I'm not a practitioner of traditional Chinese medicine (TCM), I've learned a lot over the years from studying its ancient precepts. According to TCM, liver qi stagnation (LQS) is often linked to all sorts of hormonal imbalance, beginning with premenstrual syndrome and irregular cycles, but by the time a woman reaches perimenopause, there are likely several patterns at play. The liver in TCM is defined by function and is not equivalent to the anatomical organ known in Western medicine as the liver. The life force of the liver, known as qi, can stagnate as a result of stress or anxiety. When qi flows properly, things are in harmony and function properly, but when flow is blocked, problems occur.

Liver qi is responsible for movement of qi through the body, so when it becomes stagnant, women may experience mood swings, frustration that erupts easily, constipation, premenstrual syndrome, and irregular periods, among other problems. (Learn more about what my acupuncturist, Emily Hooker, has to say about liver qi stagnation in the Notes.)[1]

Do you struggle with hormone imbalance affecting your weight? Take the following questionnaire to see.

Metabolic Hormone Questionnaire

Do you have or have you experienced any of the following symptoms in the past six months?

- Have you been steadily gaining weight since the birth of a child, perimenopause, or menopause?
- Do you experience high stress or chronic low-grade stress? Sweat the small stuff?
- Do you have high blood pressure, now defined as systolic blood pressure greater than 120 or diastolic blood pressure over 80?[2]
- Is your body mass index 25 or higher? Use an online calculator to determine your BMI, or use this formula: BMI = weight ÷ height². If you used kilograms and centimeters, you have your result. If you used pounds and inches, you need to multiply the result by 703. For example, for a woman who is 150 pounds with a height of 64 inches, BMI = (150 ÷ 64²) × 703 = 25.7.
- Have you ever gained 3 to 5 pounds overnight? Or 5 to 7 pounds with menstruation?
- Are you fatigued at any point during the day, despite adequate rest?
- Do you notice thinning head hair, loss of outer third of eyebrows, puffy face, dry and coarse skin, constipation, lack of energy, intolerance of cold, infertility, heavy menstruation, carpal tunnel syndrome, or any combination of these?
- Do you feel like something blocks you from losing weight, no matter what you try?
- Do you struggle to adhere to a diet? As in, you know what to do but you cannot stick to a plan over the long run, and so you lose the same 5 to 10 pounds over and over again?
- Do you eat very clean but don't feel that the bathroom scale reflects it?

- Do you experience food cravings, particularly for sweets, chocolate, cheese, or bread?
- Have you tried a strict ketogenic diet, but it didn't work for you? You didn't lose the weight as expected, you didn't experience mental clarity, you hit a plateau, or you gained weight?
- Do you have a diagnosis of Hashimoto's thyroiditis, celiac disease, rheumatoid arthritis, multiple sclerosis, systemic lupus erythematosus, psoriasis, or some other autoimmune disease?
- Has your appetite increased? Do you find yourself still hungry after a normal-sized serving of food that previously satisfied you?
- Has your blood sugar been rising? Is your fasting blood sugar greater than 85 mg/dL, which I consider out of the optimal zone? Or is it greater than 99 mg/dL, in the prediabetes or diabetes range, based on tests taken by your health-care practitioner?
- Have you experienced more difficulty sleeping through the night since giving birth or perimenopause, are you feeling more stress, or all of the above?
- Do you have extra fat in your abdomen? Is your waist circumference greater than 35 inches for women, or greater than 40 inches for men? (Another way to measure it is a waist-to-hip ratio greater than 0.85 in women, or greater than 0.90 in men.)
- Examine the skin around your neck and where you have folds in the skin, such as your axilla (armpits). Do you see darkening of the skin and a velvet-like texture, known as acanthosis nigricans?

Interpreting Your Score

If you answered yes to five or more of the questions above, you probably have a hormone imbalance affecting your weight and metabolism. If this is you, don't panic. First of all, you're not alone. My practice is full of women with hormone imbalances. Overall, about 80 percent of them score 5 or higher, and lab testing confirms that one or more metabolic hormones are out of balance. My personal score was 10 before I designed the Gottfried Protocol for metabolic hormones, so if your score is high, don't fret.

Fortunately, you found this book. My goal is to identify the root cause of your imbalance and resolve it. (If you are experiencing excessive or severe symptoms, be sure to consult a health-care practitioner.) Continue reading this chapter to learn more about the connection between hormones and weight gain, and how to optimize diet to achieve weight loss.

FIVE PRINCIPLES
OF WOMEN + WEIGHT

In my late thirties, I gave birth to my second daughter and my hormones went crazy. I lost my ability to manage my weight easily. In hindsight, this was probably caused by a combination of toxic stress, my borderline blood sugar issues during pregnancy, the demands of motherhood, and getting older. But the experience shifted my career from general OB/GYN to precision medicine, with emphasis on understanding the intersection of women, hormones, and weight. Not every woman goes through a period of crazy hormones, but many do.

As I mentioned in the introduction, your hormones are like your own internal symphony orchestra, playing music to your cells 24/7. If your inner song is in rhythm and harmony, you'll be resilient and metabolically flexible. Or, if it's like mine at age thirty-nine, it can sound like noise: the clarinet is too soft, the cello is too loud, and the beat is off. It may seem like you're doing everything right with your diet and workouts, but the results don't show. Conducting the symphony may seem to be out of your control, but the truth is, you have more power than you realize to bring your hormones into harmony by changing your lifestyle.

Here are the five principles I discovered that will keep your hormonal symphony in tune.

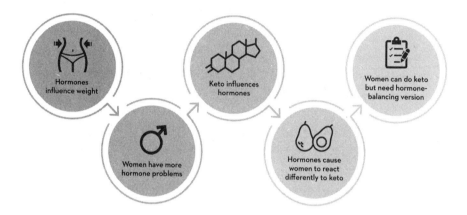

1. Hormones influence weight.
2. Women have more hormone problems than men do.
3. The ketogenic diet influences hormones.
4. Because of their hormones, women react differently to the ketogenic diet than men do.
5. Women can follow a ketogenic diet, but they do better with a hormone-balancing version, such as the Gottfried Protocol.

I will walk you through the details of each of these principles so that you can get your hormones back on beat and holding it all together—and lose weight for good.

1. Hormones influence weight.

Several hormones are involved in the control of weight, fluid retention, and the amount of fat carried on the body. It's the fat, particularly visceral fat at your waist, that concerns me most. In this section, I want to connect the dots between your fat, your hormones, and your health once and for all.

Which hormones? The list is long: insulin, cortisol, thyroid, testosterone, estrogen, progesterone, growth hormone, and leptin. (The diagram below details several of these hormones and where they are produced in the endocrine system, the set of glands that produces the various hormones that circulate throughout your body.) The hormone imbalance that rises to the top is insulin block (also known as insulin resistance), which causes the body's cells to become numb to insulin. Then the pancreas needs to make more and more insulin to do the job of pushing glucose into cells. Insulin block is closely tied to weight gain and visceral fat.[3]

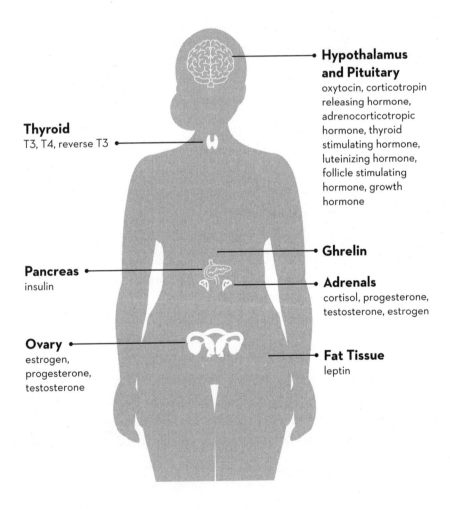

Hypothalamus and Pituitary
oxytocin, corticotropin releasing hormone, adrenocorticotropic hormone, thyroid stimulating hormone, luteinizing hormone, follicle stimulating hormone, growth hormone

Thyroid
T3, T4, reverse T3

Ghrelin

Pancreas
insulin

Adrenals
cortisol, progesterone, testosterone, estrogen

Ovary
estrogen, progesterone, testosterone

Fat Tissue
leptin

Hormones are chemical messengers — think of them as text messages sent around your body. They request certain functions, like stabilizing your mood, making your skin moist, building muscle at the gym, and telling you to eat more. When they are in order, you can reach a healthy weight and maintain it. You can sleep well at night and wake up refreshed. You don't feel cranky, anxious, and fat.

Back to the symphony analogy for hormones — the official conductor of the orchestra is your brain, particularly the parts known as the hypothalamus and the pituitary gland. Your brain communicates to your other endocrine organs, like your adrenal glands (brass), ovaries (testes in men; woodwinds), thyroid (percussion), and fat (strings). But the conductor is vulnerable. Poor eating, too much drinking, and excess stress will affect its function.

When the conductor is on top of its game, well fed and resilient, hormones remain in balance and the music is wonderful. Your usual strategies for weight loss will tend to work, just as I found was the case early in my thirties, before I had kids. When the conductor is off kilter, so are your hormones. They may individually conspire against weight loss, and even cross-talk to make matters worse. For example, Melissa's thyroid problems didn't occur in isolation. Her elevated insulin levels and fat deposits made her thyroid function worse.[4] Then, to make matters more unfair, being overweight increased her chances of developing more thyroid problems.[5] Fortunately, the Gottfried Protocol helps your brain conduct the symphony with ease and grace, so your body can return to a state of balance and health.

There are many common endocrine problems that lead to *weight-loss resistance,* including thyroid imbalances and insulin block, and they can be caused by a myriad of factors, including high stress and chemicals in the environment — found in body products, cleaning supplies, and food — that disrupt specific hormones. Plus, what you eat can affect your hormones, as we'll discuss in the next chapter.

2. Women have more hormone
problems than men do.

Straight talk: compared to men, women have more hormone imbalances, leading to higher rates of anxiety, depression, and insomnia.[6] The unpleasant symptoms of hormone imbalance create a cascade of additional problems, particularly when it comes to weight loss. For example, sleeping less than six hours or more than nine is associated with metabolic syndrome, a constellation of belly fat, insulin block, blood sugar problems, high blood pressure, and lipid issues.[7]

As a physician and a woman, I'm all too familiar with the vicious cycle of body dissatisfaction, stress, and weight gain. Women who struggle with extra weight, even a small number of pounds, often find themselves locked in a battle with their body. Maybe you can relate? It's no wonder women experience more body dissatisfaction than men do. In advertisements, media such as TV programs and movies, and well-intended comments from family members and friends, we're told from a young age that we need to be thin and beautiful, no matter the cost.

When we are socialized to internalize this ideal, we do a thing that academics call *self-objectification,* making us more likely to experience body shame and dissatisfaction. This means we internalize an observer's view of our body as an object that must be evaluated on the basis of our looks, resulting in frequent and habitual monitoring of our outward appearance.[8] Women are more likely than men to do this. Women who self-objectify are more likely to have disordered eating.[9] Objectification sells products,[10] but self-objectification has a higher cost; that is, the internal battle that so many of my female patients experience.

In a sad, ironic twist, this self-objectification can lead to higher stress levels, even more hormone imbalance, and then weight gain. Many of my patients feel like they are more stressed than ever — and they aren't alone. Women experience higher levels of stress than men do, as shown in the American Psychological Association's annual stress survey. In 2020, it was reported that more women than men feel that now is the lowest point in the country's history that they can remember. (Maybe men are paying less attention?)

This stress affects our health—and our hormones. Most women are unaware of their hormone imbalances. But even before menopause, women are more vulnerable to them. The most common endocrine disorders affecting women before menopause are problems with testosterone, insulin, and thyroid.[11] The most common cause of hypothyroidism in the United States is Hashimoto's thyroiditis, an autoimmune disease that is *five to ten times* more common in women than men.

Then additional hormonal shifts come with age and menopause, when women more commonly experience low estrogen, testosterone, and growth hormone. Since estrogen is involved in many activities, including appetite arousal and food intake,[12] loss of hormones like estrogen can trigger weight gain. The main estrogen that regulates the female body is estradiol. See the illustration for how estrogen changes as women age, leading to wild fluctuations in perimenopause that can increase appetite.

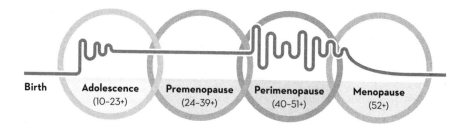

| Birth | Adolescence (10–23+) | Premenopause (24–39+) | Perimenopause (40–51+) | Menopause (52+) |

On the other hand, when overweight or obese women lose fat, growth hormone increases.[13] The good news is that you set off a virtuous cycle: you are more able to recover after exercise, heal from an injury, boost metabolism, and then you burn more fat, and growth hormone rises more. Success!

Just knowing that hormones can block weight loss, and that women are more likely to experience hormone imbalance, is part of the solution. And my protocol is designed to bring your hormones back into balance with a modified ketogenic diet.

3. The ketogenic diet influences hormones.

Here's what's good about the keto diet—a low-carbohydrate, moderate-protein, high-fat diet—when it comes to hormones. It is one of the most effective strategies to repair insulin, the main hormone involved in weight gain, general misery, and cardiovascular disease, which is the number-one killer of both men and women.

The trouble is that keto has the potential to adversely affect other hormones, including cortisol, thyroid, and estrogen. Chronic elevations in cortisol are associated with lots of problems, including oxidative stress (the rust of aging that accumulates in our cells), cholesterol problems, poor vascular function, platelet clumping, plaque buildup in the arteries[14]—and increased visceral fat, the problem I worry about the most, in terms of your health.[15] In men, consuming carbohydrates reduces cortisol production.[16] Likewise, restricting carbs may *increase* cortisol production, unless you know how to avoid it.

Estrogen may get out of balance in people who eat a "lazy keto" diet, like fast-food burgers wrapped in lettuce with bacon on top, and forget to eat sufficient vegetables to feed good microbes in the gut. Healthy estrogen balance relies on a healthy ecosystem of microbes. People who eat more animal products, like meat and cheese, but skimp on vegetables risk a rise in the levels of misbehaving members of the estrogen family.

4. Because of their hormones, women react differently to classic keto than men do.

We've already talked about the keto paradox, so you know that the traditional keto diet doesn't always work for women. We still need more studies that explore how keto influences women's hormones, but some possible reasons for differences in outcomes have arisen in the research.

First, keto may not provide enough carbs for women—carbs help mitigate the stress response, lower cortisol, boost growth hormone, and support thyroid function. Second, women and men also differ in terms of how and where their body fat is stored, in their hormonal production, and in their brain responses to signals regulating weight and distribution of body fat. Women tend to store energy as fat in the subcutaneous space under the skin, whereas men are more likely to store energy as fat in their belly. Think "hourglass" or "pear" figure versus "dad bod" and beer bellies. This is called *partitioning*—women tend to partition fat in their subcutaneous space and become fat in the lower body (hips, butt, thighs), and men partition fat in their abdomen, in and around their abdominal organs.

Men have 50 percent more lean body mass and 13 percent lower fat mass than premenopausal women do.[17] Men, perimenopausal women, and menopausal women accumulate more fat in their belly than premenopausal women do, resulting in an "apple" body shape and a greater risk of developing complications associated with obesity.[18] For premenopausal women, fat tends to be deposited in the lower body: the hips, butt, and thighs.[19] Starting in perimenopause, the period of time when menstruation changes as your ovaries run out of high-quality eggs, women become more like men in that they tend to store fat at the waist. As you'll learn in Chapter 5, when you take your own measurements, we want the waist-to-hip ratio to be less than 0.85 for women (and less than 0.90 for men). A high waist-to-hip ratio predicts a risk for many problems, including insulin resistance and heart attack.[20]

Third, when it comes to insulin and the risk of diabetes, men and women are different.[21] Overall, healthy premenopausal women are more sensitive to the hormone insulin than men are—that means we need lower amounts of insulin than men do to lower blood glucose levels. We have lower rates of metabolic syndrome, at least before menopause.[22] Unfortunately, our advantage over men disappears when blood glucose climbs.[23] That's the position I found myself in five years ago, as I started to enter perimenopause. For a variety of reasons involving stress and insufficient sleep, I stored more fat. It seemed like overnight my subcutaneous fat nearly doubled—especially on my hips and legs.

I developed prediabetes, with a fasting glucose between 100 and

125 mg/dL. As my visceral fat increased, I couldn't zip my jeans, a very sad affair that tends to kick off in perimenopause, as the body begins the transition to menopause, which usually starts at about age forty-seven. Estrogen levels decline, the rate of fat gain doubles, and lean body mass declines — these gains and losses continue until two years after the final menstrual period.[24] Changes in fat partitioning during perimenopause reflect hormonal changes in women, and are confirmed in animal models of menopause.[25] Body fat, waist circumference, and waist-to-hip ratio increase during the menopausal transition except in women who take hormone therapy.[26]

Alcohol consumption and exercise play an important role in weight gain for most women.[27] Applying the rule of partitioning, our fat deposits shift from making us hourglasses and pears to apples with more belly fat.[28] It's not just a problem of vanity: women gain an average of 5 pounds over three years of the menopausal transition, and 20 percent *gain 10 pounds or more.* No wonder I couldn't zip my jeans! The weight gain is associated with a greater risk of heart disease, high blood pressure, total cholesterol, low-density lipoprotein cholesterol, triglycerides, and fasting insulin.

Fourth, keto can also affect the thyroid gland. Some people develop thyroid problems such as lower triiodothyronine (T3) or thyroxine (T4) levels, which are suggestive but not diagnostic of hypothyroidism.[29] Many women feel the change as symptoms: constipation, cold hands and feet, and hair loss.[30] Given the risk of thyroid dysfunction with a classic keto diet, I recommend modifying keto with the Gottfried Protocol and having your thyroid levels checked every six months until further research clarifies the effects. Fortunately, I have not seen any thyroid issues arise with my protocol.

For people with epilepsy, following the classic ketogenic diet is associated with menstrual irregularity and constipation.[31] We do not know if the same is true for people without epilepsy on the ketogenic diet, though fecal volume (the amount of stool you produce) may decline. It may be especially important for women to keep their bowels moving regularly in order to obtain the benefits of keto, since regular bowel movements are tied tightly with the balance and detoxification of estrogen.

Finally, a diet low in carbohydrates can also negatively impact a woman's sleep.[32] Nearly all hormones are released according to the circadian rhythm, the natural daily rhythm that both dictates your sleep cycle and is influenced by it. When sleep becomes disrupted because of the keto diet or another factor—a problem more common to women than men—other hormones may become disrupted. Disrupt the rhythm, disrupt the hormones. Not surprisingly, sleep disruption is connected to more visceral fat at the waist.[33]

In the only study of the ketogenic diet suggesting a benefit for women that does not apply to men, female rats on a ketogenic diet didn't lose bone mass, but male rats did.[34] Of course, we need to replicate these data in humans before drawing firm conclusions.

5. Women can follow a ketogenic diet, but they do better with a hormone-balancing version such as the Gottfried Protocol.

The primary reasons women don't seem to benefit equally from a ketogenic diet are related to hormones, which can influence effective detoxification, stress and cortisol, thyroid function, hunger and food addiction, and blood sugar levels.

The Gottfried Protocol is a modified keto diet that works better for women. It includes a detox component, a modified carb count, and more vegetables and fiber for a more alkaline diet.[35] In my experience with patients, the Gottfried Protocol contributes to healthy gut function, improved hormones, and significant fat loss. Plus, my patients are not hungry. Finding a plan that works is important, especially when you consider that dietary change could prevent half of all chronic diseases.[36]

Here's an example of how a change in diet affects our health. You see, our bodies have been becoming more acidic since our hunter-gatherer years. Since the agricultural revolution (starting ten thousand years ago) and the industrial revolution (starting two hundred years ago), soils have become increasingly depleted in minerals that we need, such as calcium, magnesium, iron, manganese, copper, and zinc. Standard diets likewise have less magnesium, fiber, and potassium, as compared to sodium; chloride has increased in comparison to bicarbonate. The result is that the food most of us are eating may induce metabolic acidosis: the body's delicate balance between acid and base shifts to the acid side, causing higher blood pressure (see details in the Notes).[37]

All these changes result in a greater risk for kidney stones, which may occur more frequently for people on "lazy keto."[38] Low carb with high protein isn't the right answer; instead, you need to eat more vegetables and other specific foods that boost magnesium, fiber, and potassium. A more alkaline diet that's rich in vegetables will improve hormones like growth hormone, increase levels of vitamin D, help your bones, and reduce muscle loss.[39] That's what you get with the Gottfried Protocol.

I've wondered over the years if the decreased insulin and glucose that we see as a result of the ketogenic diet, or even during fasting, when you go for some period of time without eating (such as fourteen to sixteen hours), might be perceived as a greater alarm in women as compared to men — meaning it sets off warning signals in the female body that something is wrong. I suspect that for women in perimenopause, this alarm might be more sensitive, perhaps requiring gentler methods (like a shorter fasting window of 13 to 14 hours). I have not yet found clear evidence supporting my observations with the ketogenic diet on this point, but fasting for forty-eight hours does seem to trigger a major stress response in overweight premenopausal women (it activates the sympathetic nervous system, producing the fight-flight-freeze response).[40] In contrast, men who do weight lifting (another stressor) experience increased calm, relaxation, reduced blood pressure, and a feeling of being well rested (the parasympathetic activity known as the rest-and-digest response).[41]

Putting it all together, my approach gets my patients pooping and detoxing; adding more carbs, nonstarchy vegetables, and plenty of fiber; and aiming for a more gradual insulin-fixing process, so that we don't shock the female body into a fat-storing panic. You'll get all the details in Part 2.

That's exactly what happened with Melissa. A blood test indicated that she was low in a hormone called DHEA, which is a precursor to testosterone, and low in the mineral magnesium. Her body composition test showed high levels of visceral fat, as reflected in a waist circumference of 39 inches. Other tests showed that she had multiple risk factors for cardiovascular disease, including her cholesterol levels: a rising LDL and a low HDL. She started the Gottfried Protocol — first, we got her pooping, detoxing, and correcting her insulin. Her initial goal was to lose 5 pounds only. Progress with weight loss was slow at first, but steady, and to date she has lost 17 pounds. Even more important, her glucose is now normal and her cholesterol panel is heading in the right direction.

Is Keto Right for Me?

In this book I will be sharing a well-formulated ketogenic diet, one that is designed with women's issues and hormones in mind. If you have a history of medical conditions (such as gallbladder problems or no gallbladder, cardiovascular disease, or a history of kidney stones), or if you've been told to stay away from high-fat diets, you will want to check with your doctor before starting this diet. You may need additional guidance to try the Gottfried Protocol, such as which specific oils to use if you have gallbladder problems. Absolute and relative contraindications are discussed later in the book, but please ask your clinician for help if you are unsure about any detail.

Highlights

In this chapter, we covered the key precision-medicine principles for women, hormones, and metabolism.

▶ You learned about how hormones influence weight and which hormones are the most important to know about and to target.

▶ You discovered that women have more hormone problems than men do, and that over the age of thirty-five and during perimenopause, major changes occur that can make your body resistant to weight loss.

▶ Women and men differ in terms of how their endocrine system directs fat storage and in their brain responses to signals regulating weight and body fat distribution. You learned that women partition fat more in their subcutaneous space and may become fat in the lower body (hips, butt, thighs — the "pear" shape), whereas men partition fat in their abdomen, in and around their abdominal organs — the "apple" shape. In perimenopause, women may become more like men, with higher insulin levels, lower estrogen levels, weight gain, and fat gain at the waist — hence, more apple-shaped. Polycystic ovary syndrome and insulin resistance can cause the shape too.

▶ We discussed how the ketogenic diet can address these hormonal changes, but that women react differently to keto. The Gottfried Protocol takes this into account. Specifically, women need to be pooping daily to detoxify and reset their hormones, they need more fiber and nonstarchy vegetables, and they need to pay attention to how carbohydrate restriction might be affecting stress and cortisol levels. You can do the ketogenic diet, but you will react best if you follow the modified version that I cover in Part 2. It will help you optimize your hormones and set yourself up for permanent weight loss.

Fortunately, you can apply the principles of precision medicine to customize your own weight-loss program. In the next few chapters, we will cover a few other hormones in detail, including growth hormone and testosterone, and connect the dots between what you eat and the hormonal symphony.

2

HOW GROWTH HORMONE KEEPS YOU LEAN

When my patient Carrie turned forty-three, she noticed several un-welcome changes. She felt like the normal dewiness of her skin and volume of her muscle had changed, and she showed me photographic evidence on her smartphone. Throughout her life, she felt generally calm and collected; now she had bouts of anxiety. Her energy was lower. It was harder to recover from a night of poor sleep or a work-out. Looking in the mirror, she saw more sagging skin and less mus-cle. Even more frustrating, she'd gained stubborn extra pounds since having kids, mostly concentrated at her waist, but none of her usual diet tactics were working. Determined to get to her goal weight of 130 pounds, she explained that a typical day followed a standard "mom" diet formula: oatmeal with fruit for breakfast, multiple cans of diet soda, a small salad at lunch, and a take-out dinner, washed down with a few glasses of wine. Low calorie — well, except for all that wine.

I asked about her sleep, and she confessed that she was going to bed later than she used to, more like 11 p.m. or midnight, after stream-ing video with her partner, and her sleep was not as solid. When I ex-amined Carrie, I noticed saggy cheeks and thin lips. I agreed that overall she didn't have much muscle tone, considering her age and how much she worked out at the gym.

Perhaps you can relate to Carrie's struggles. You may even think that her complaints are the unavoidable results of aging, but I disagree. I suspected that hormones were to blame for her recent weight gain, her challenge with the scale, her frustrating drop in energy, and her body's general lack of definition. In fact, a hormonal switch was to blame — that is, the toggle between "let's burn fat" and "let's store fat," controlled in her body by several key hormones.

Carrie was surprised to hear that her daily food choices weren't helping her lose weight because they were activating the wrong hormones. At first my concern about a faulty hormonal switch barely registered with her. Then a simple blood test confirmed that I was right, which meant that Carrie's "mom" diet was effective at packing on more pounds, not helping them come off, and it was exacerbating her hormone imbalance. Let me explain.

HORMONES:
THE MISSING KEY

A hormone is a substance that regulates function in the body. It is produced in the body and transported in fluids such as the blood in order to tell a distant cell what to do. Hormones can be inside the body (endogenous) or made in a lab from animals or plants and given to someone (exogenous), in over-the-counter form or by prescription. Hormones influence behavior, mood, muscle mass, energy, and metabolism. They drive what you are interested in and want to focus on, like eating or burning fat or having sex. Often, hormones are cited to disparage or dismiss women, as in *"You're hormonal! Get it together!"* In reality, hormones influence our behavior, and our behavior can influence our hormones. First, let's see how hormones work and then what we can do about them.

Hormones That Influence the Body's Fat Management

Three hormones play a key role in the hormonal switch that can take you from storing fat to burning fat.

Growth hormone stimulates growth and cell regeneration. As a kid, it makes you taller. As an adult, it keeps your muscles lean by building muscle and burning fat. Unfortunately, growth hormone declines slowly as you age, beginning around age thirty, especially if you experience a lot of stress, eat carbs throughout the day, sit too much, and don't exercise enough.

Testosterone is the most abundant hormone in both men and women, and it plays a central role in functions similar to those of growth hormone, including building muscle and burning fat. Testosterone is now recognized as a multitasking hormone in women, involved in keeping metabolism strong and libido healthy. Like growth hormone, it declines in your thirties but drops more precipitously in perimenopause and menopause.

Insulin regulates the amount of glucose in your blood. In healthy folks, when the pancreas detects that too much glucose is in the bloodstream, insulin signals muscles, the liver, and other tissues to absorb it and convert it to energy. If you eat excess carbohydrates or don't manage stress well, insulin becomes blocked and glucose rises in the blood, and at high levels it can be toxic. This is called insulin resistance: your cells become numb to the insulin message. This condition is a precursor to diabetes (prediabetes) and can lead to greater hunger and more fat storage, particularly at the belly.

Growth hormone is a build-you-up hormone, meaning that it plays a key role in building muscle and keeping bones strong, while simultaneously breaking down fat. It's central to weight loss, and problems with growth hormone may be less recognized in women compared to men. Growth hormone made you became taller as a child. For adults, growth hormone is still involved in growth and repair, including bone mineralization, protein synthesis, cellular growth, and fat breakdown. We have naturally lower levels of growth hormone as we age. Production peaks in early adulthood but then declines by 1 to 3 percent per year after age thirty—a decline that's much more precipitous than that of other hormones, and therefore may be more noticeable.[1] Many of my female patients notice the telltale signs of a fat, droopy abdomen and loss of muscle tone. One thirty-seven-year-old patient with low growth hormone calls it the "melted candle" look.

It's relatively easy to test your growth hormone levels. To confirm my suspicion of Carrie's low growth hormone, we ordered a blood test that's a proxy for growth hormone, called IGF-1, and we found she was, indeed, low. (IGF-1 is a growth factor produced by the liver when stimulated by a rise in growth hormone. IGF-1 is easier to measure than growth hormone.)

Testosterone functions overlap with growth hormone in that it builds muscle and boosts metabolism. Both growth hormone and testosterone are multitasking hormones, performing more than one job in the body. For example, testosterone can boost your mood and sense of confidence while helping you build muscle in the gym, and it helps your thyroid work better. (You will learn more about testosterone and how to activate it for weight loss in the next chapter.)

BOOSTING GROWTH HORMONE

You might wonder if you can just take a pill to boost your growth hormone and watch the pounds melt off your middle. Unfortunately, no. But when we look at the factors that determine your growth hormone—age, sex, diet, nutrition, food timing, sleep, and exercise—you'll soon realize that many of these are within your power to manipulate to your advantage.

The goal with the Gottfried Protocol is to get your hormones, including the essential growth hormone, back into balance. You don't want growth hormone to dip too low, or you may feel prematurely old, like Carrie. You may feel frail before your time, and even note a loss of brain power.[2] But you also don't want to crank growth hormone up too high as it may be associated with a greater risk of cancer. You want it to be in balance, and eating the right food, in the right quantities, and at the right time are the most important drivers.

Growth Hormone Questionnaire

Do you have or have you experienced any of the following symptoms in the past six months?

- Do you notice signs of premature aging, such as a sagging face, thin lips, droopy eyelids, or wrinkles?
- Do you feel less inner peace or calm than in the past? Have you experienced more anxious feelings that lack a specific cause?
- Is your height normal, but you're beginning to hunch over?
- Examine your hands. Do you notice thinning muscles, such as reduced muscle tone at the palm of the hands, especially just beneath the thumb and under the little finger?
- When you pinch the skin at the back of the hand for 3 seconds, does your skin immediately snap back, or is it delayed? (This is also a test for dehydration.)
- Look at your nails. Do you see striae, or longitudinal lines?
- Do you have increased stretch marks on the abdomen?
- Do you have more belly fat than in the past, especially at your waistline?
- Are your inner thighs saggy?
- Do you have fatty cushions (fat deposits) above the knees?

- Are you experiencing more difficulty in performing common daily tasks?
- Are you noticing a change in emotional reactions? Are you more reactive than you used to be, giving sharp verbal retorts to comments that may not have bothered you in the past?
- Do you feel colder than others while at the same ambient temperature? Do you need to wear socks to bed? (In medicine, we refer to this issue as cold intolerance.)
- Are you noticing that your muscles are less pronounced than they used to be? When you exercise regularly, do you notice less of a muscle response or a loss of strength?
- Have you been diagnosed with osteopenia (less bone density compared to your peers) or osteoporosis? Have you been diagnosed with a fracture?
- Have you noticed diffuse thinning of body hair?
- Are you noticing that your quality of life has declined?
- Is your sleep light or disrupted? Are you going to bed later than usual? (The first three to four hours of sleep each night are the time when you produce the highest levels of growth hormone.)

Please note: If you are experiencing excessive worry that interferes with relationships, work, or other aspects of your life, it's time to talk to a licensed mental health professional or doctor about whether you have an anxiety disorder.

Interpreting Your Results

If you answered yes to five or more of the questions above, you may have low growth hormone. Don't panic — it's easy to reverse low growth hormone if you get help sooner rather than later. Read on to learn more about low growth hormone, its root cause, and how the Gottfried Protocol can help.

THE SCIENCE OF
LOW GROWTH HORMONE

If science makes you run for the hills, here's the short version of what depletes growth hormone: *lack of sleep, lack of exercise, tons of stress,* and *munching on carbs all day long.* Hmmm, sounds like my thirties. Now, you may still be in denial and think to yourself, "No, not me," but let's take a deeper look. Mothering two kids led to profound sleep deprivation for me and probably bottomed out my growth hormone. When I went back to work after having each kid, I was basically sedentary and running on stress (that is, high cortisol). Who had time for the luxury of exercise? I felt almost constantly hypoglycemic, so each day was a blur of many things that cranked up my blood sugar: fruit, energy bars, and chips.

Growth hormone is a crucial hormone that—among its numerous roles—keeps you lean and energized. When everything is in check, growth hormone works harmoniously with your hormones cortisol and adrenaline to burn fat and build muscle. As mentioned earlier, growth hormone is a component of the hormonal switch between burning glucose to burning fat.[3] We'll be discussing this hormonal switch in greater detail in this chapter and the next few, as we cover the jobs of three hormones: growth hormone, testosterone, and insulin. For now, it's important to know that sometimes the switch gets stuck in the "store fat" position because the body perceives too much stress due to deadlines, restricted calories or other famine signals, overexercise, insufficient sleep, or toxins.

High levels of growth hormone, as measured by blood levels of IGF-1, are associated with better cognitive function.[4] Most people think that hormones like growth hormone gradually decline with age, and that's true to a certain extent. But I've found that the drop is more precipitous in my female patients who struggle with their weight and have loads of stress. In fact, the level of growth hormone that you had when you were an adolescent (that's ages ten to nineteen, according to the World Health Organization) was *eight hundred times* the level of other hormones, such as the one that regulates thyroid hormone production or the hormone that helps control ovulation.[5] (I know, *eight hundred* seems like a typo—it's not!) I imagine that because production is so high and then drops so exponentially, during early middle age it can hit some of us especially hard.

You may wonder why you should care about growth hormone. Here's the skinny. **When growth hormone (and other hormonal) levels are optimal, you can enjoy benefits including fat loss or easy weight maintenance, increased energy and stamina, and more.** Trouble starts when hormones become unruly or your body stops making sufficient growth hormone. Studies show that impaired levels can increase fat, break down muscle, decrease energy[6]—and generally make life miserable. Low growth hormone is even one of the markers for frailty as you age.[7] Here are some other symptoms of growth hormone deficiency:

- Reduced lean body mass
- Increased abdominal obesity
- Increased insulin resistance, leading to prediabetes and type 2 diabetes
- Decreased muscle mass
- Hypertension (high blood pressure)
- High triglycerides (high levels of a type of fat in the blood)
- Anxiety and depression
- Fibromyalgia
- Decreased bone density

GROWTH HORMONE IN WOMEN

Women make growth hormone differently than men do. Before menopause, women tend to have higher levels of it.[8] As is the case for a few other hormones, you don't make it continuously, but rather you produce growth hormone in pulses—and mostly at night, while you sleep. Men have longer periods of time between pulses of growth hormone; women produce it more continuously, with only short intervals between those pulses.[9] IGF-1 levels are lower in women compared to men after age fifty — perhaps this is because women are more than twice as likely to suffer from insomnia.[10] Another difference is related to exercise. When men and women engage in anaerobic exercise (intense, shorter exercise, such as burpees, box jumps, and sprints, which break down glucose without oxygen), women produce higher levels of growth hormone as a result.[11] And peak production occurs twice as soon in women (20 minutes after exercise) compared to men (40 minutes after exercise). We can use that to our advantage to boost growth hormone and lose fat!

If growth hormone is such a good thing, and we all make less as we age,[12] why do some people experience a more dramatic drop than others? Besides the factors already mentioned (eating too much sugar, not exercising enough, experiencing a great deal of stress, and so forth), too much belly fat and a decline in sex hormones (examples: estrogen, testosterone) can contribute to the drop.

Though you cannot control your chronological age, you can control belly fat. Abdominal fat plays more of a factor in growth hormone decline than age does, according to one study in the *Journal of Clinical Endocrinology and Metabolism*. This is true even for people who are not obese.[13]

GROWTH HORMONE AFFECTS OTHER HORMONES TOO

Growth hormone, cortisol, and insulin are interconnected, and when they go haywire, problems ensue. For instance, one study found that overweight adolescent girls with high cortisol and low growth hormone stored more belly fat and had increased insulin resistance,[14] setting the stage for obesity and diabetes. Combine stress, poor sleep, and inadequate growth hormone levels with a diet high in sugar and processed foods, and you've got a formula for feeling lousy, lethargic, and out of juice. Here are the other hormone imbalances that may impact growth hormone and contribute to metabolic inflexibility.

- **Insulin block.** In this condition, insulin is no longer able to push glucose efficiently inside a cell, and the cell becomes numb to the effects of insulin; this is common in children and adults with growth hormone deficiency.[15]
- **Leptin.** Adults who lack growth hormone have higher levels of leptin, the hormone that tells you to stop eating. These higher levels indicate leptin block, and folks who experience this often feel hungry all the time.[16]
- **Estrogen.** As women age and estrogen declines, growth hormone declines.[17] Estrogen, among its many other jobs, suppresses appetite. That's why women over forty often need a new strategy to get growth hormone in balance.
- **Testosterone.** Adults who are low in growth hormone make less DHEA, the hormone that is the precursor (building block) to testosterone.[18] (Chapter 3 will cover the androgen family, including DHEA and testosterone.)
- **Others.** Additional hormones that influence growth hormone are mentioned in the Notes, including but not limited to thyroid hormone, luteinizing hormone, and follicle stimulating hormone.[19]

MEET MOLLY

Molly was a forty-nine-year-old patient who came to my preci-sion medicine practice because her mood felt flat, sort of "blah" and muted, and her body felt pudgy. Normally she was a high-energy, life-of-the-party type, so this was new for her. Her internist, after ad-ministering a single thyroid test (thyroid stimulating hormone or TSH, the typical screening test for low thyroid function), told her she was just getting older. More extensive testing revealed several hor-mone issues: not only was her IGF-1 low, indicating low growth hor-mone, but her thyroid function was borderline slow (as measured by multiple tests, covered in the Notes).[20] Her levels of testosterone and estrogen had decreased but were "normal" for menopause, and her fasting insulin was creeping up. With my guidance, Molly began a new food plan that included morning whey protein shakes, detoxification, and intermittent fasting. I initiated a low dose of thyroid medication. Within eight weeks, her IGF-1 was up by 32 percent, she had gained 2 pounds of muscle, she had lost 12 pounds of fat, and best of all, her energy was back.

HOW TO FIX THE GROWTH HORMONE DEFICIT

Let's correct your whispering growth hormone and muscle loss. Here is my prescription for what to do. You'll find recipes, meal plans, and the support you need in Part 2.

- **Eat healthy protein.** You can raise IGF-1 by eating protein, particularly proteins rich in the amino acid called methionine. The goal is balance; you want to get the right amount of protein for you — not too much and not too little. However, many of the studies of protein consumption are limited to men. According to one, for men of ages forty to seventy-five, both animal and vegetable proteins raise IGF-1;[21] in a smaller study of men, only red meat increased it.[22] In women, higher protein intake has been associated with higher levels of IGF-1, but the association was limited to animal protein and did not apply to vegetable protein.[23] Other research in athletes shows that whey protein shakes are particularly helpful at raising IGF-1 and testosterone,[24] boosting IGF-1 in postmenopausal women,[25] and increasing muscle mass in older folks.[26] Think foods like grass-fed, grass-finished beef (from pasture-fed cows never fattened with grain, which increases inflammation); SMASH fish (salmon, mackerel, anchovies, sardines, and herring); whey protein shakes; and pastured eggs and chicken. Carrie drank a whey protein shake every morning during her workout (about 10 minutes into weight lifting) and added SMASH fish most days of the week. For dinner, she alternated poached eggs with grass-fed, grass-finished beef twice per week.

- **Eat healthy fats.** Omega-3s have been shown to raise growth hormone in animal studies.[27] If you have increased belly fat and insulin and blood sugar problems—a common driver of weight gain, inflammation, and even breast cancer—your body may be producing more of the type of fats that make you inflamed and resistant to weight loss.[28] Consuming a healthy mix of omega fats can help your body be more sensitive to insulin and keep the fat-burning switch in the "on" position. Not surprisingly, eating more omega-3s as found in flaxseed and SMASH fish, which creates a higher ratio of omega-3s to omega-6s, has been shown to reduce breast cancer by 27 percent.[29] Add medium-chain triglyceride (MCT) oil and chia seeds to your smoothie, and macadamia nuts and avocado oil to your salad. Top it off with a square of dark chocolate. I provide more information on what and how much to eat in Part 2.

- **Fast.** You may have heard about the fasting diet trend. Multiple studies show that intermittent fasting increases growth hormone.[30] An animal experiment suggested that fasting is more likely to stimulate the fat-burning benefit of growth hormone,[31] which is why a 14/10 protocol (fourteen hours of overnight fasting, and ten hours for your eating window—for instance, stop eating by 6 p.m. and then eat breakfast at 8 a.m. each day) is part of the Gottfried Protocol. One study found a twenty-four-hour fasting period boosted growth hormone at an average of 1,300 percent in women and almost 2,000 percent in men.[32] It's not fair—I know! But research shows there is a benefit to fasting for both men and women, even if men see a greater increase in growth hormone.

- **Exercise.** Exercise raises growth hormone and IGF-1, and the more strenuous, the greater the effect.[33] Personally, I raised my IGF-1 by 53 percent over eight weeks with high-intensity interval training. I became interested in exercise as a way to boost IGF-1 when a friend taught me about high-intensity interval training, using a method of maximal effort for 60 to 75 seconds followed by 1 to 2 minutes of rest, for a total of eight rounds. (See "Raising IGF-1 with Exercise" on page 56 for details.) IGF-1 mediates many of the beneficial effects of exercise on brain health and function.

- **Take a sauna.**[34] Sauna bathing for 30 to 60 minutes raises growth hormone up to 140 percent after a single session.[35]
- **Put down the wine (and other alcoholic beverages).** If your growth hormone is out of balance, alcohol may lower it further.[36] While on the Gottfried Protocol, abstain from drinking. Think of alcohol as liquid sugar—it goes directly to the liver and can be converted into fat. Unless you're at your goal weight and body fat, avoid alcohol. It will clog your liver, hinder detoxification, and make you puffy and resistant to weight loss.
- **Consider supplements.** Some key supplements can help increase growth hormone; they include vitamin D (aim for serum vitamin D level 60 to 90 ng/mL) and creatine (15–20 g/d for five days, thereafter 3–5 g/d), which have been shown to help men and women with declining muscle mass.[37] Vitamin D is a hormone that has over four hundred jobs in the body and has been shown in twenty-five randomized trials to reduce risk of viral infection.[38]
- **Can I just get a growth hormone shot?** You may wonder why you can't just take a growth hormone prescription and top off your low levels. Unfortunately, long-term studies of growth hormone administration show conflicting safety results, so the Food and Drug Administration has very strict guidelines. In a nutshell, injecting yourself with growth hormone is not something I recommend due to side effects, including joint pain, swelling, carpal tunnel syndrome,[39] and cancer, particularly of the breast, colon, and prostate.[40] As you will learn in Chapter 6, if weight loss is still elusive on the Gottfried Protocol, you may want to discuss with your physician a prescription for peptides that help boost growth hormone, known as growth hormone *secretagogues.*[41]

Raising IGF-1 with Exercise

When I was forty-six, I used exercise to raise my blood level of IGF-1 from 219 to 334 ng/mL in an N-of-1 experiment. It wasn't a huge commitment; it was 20 minutes, four days per week, to be exact. Let me explain.

I've been exercising for years. Not because I love it but because I need it for my brain and weight. I heard from a friend about something called "Sprint 8" and decided to try it. Sprint 8 is a system for high-intensity interval training (HIIT) that's super-efficient, with eight rounds of burst training interspersed with recovery at your usual moderate level of exercise.

Here's how I did it. I didn't perform any other exercise, just Sprint 8 four times per week.

- Jog at moderate pace for 3 to 5 minutes. I have a genetic tendency toward an Achilles injury, so I warm up for 5 to 10 minutes first and always stretch my Achilles. For me, a moderate jogging pace is a 12-minute mile, or 5 miles per hour on a treadmill.
- Sprint all out for 30 seconds, so hard you can't go more than 30 seconds.
- Recover for 75 to 90 seconds. If you have trouble with math or have more time to spare, I encourage going for 90 seconds.
- Lather, rinse, repeat. Repeat the sprint for a total of eight cycles.
- Cool down at your moderate pace.

After six weeks, I retested my IGF-1 and it had risen to 334, an increase of 53 percent. My weight was about the same, but at the time, I didn't have weight to lose. My body fat was lower. My waist circumference decreased. *It worked!*

Carrie raised her IGF-1 by 40 percent over four weeks by following the Gottfried Protocol and consequently lost 15 pounds, including 12 pounds of fat. In the next chapter, you'll learn more about testosterone, a close cousin of growth hormone with overlapping functions — and another metabolic hormone you can activate to lose fat more easily.

Highlights

Growth hormone is one of the top metabolic hormones with a prominent role in weight, health, and fitness.[42]

- ▶ Keeping growth hormone balanced helps maintain your body fat, lean muscle mass, bone, tendons, and brain function. It also builds your brain, skin, hair, internal organs, and bones.
- ▶ Having too much growth hormone is associated with cancer risk, which is why you want to use diet and other targeted lifestyle interventions to keep this hormone in balance rather than taking a prescription shot.
- ▶ The key with growth hormone is balance — you don't want too little, and you don't want too much.

3

TESTOSTERONE:
It's Not Just for Men

Nicole made a telehealth appointment because, at age forty-four, she was experiencing middle-age spread. She pointed to her flabby muscles — and no amount of time in the gym seemed to help. She grabbed a fistful of what she considered to be too round of a belly, and then pointed to her back fat, or "hate handles," as she called them. The increased belly and back fat were new.

I am careful to normalize body fat. We need it to make hormones, and we need healthy fat in our diet to build hormones. Having cholesterol levels that are not too high and not too low drive hormonal, mental, and physical health. Eating healthy fat does not make us fat. On the other hand, visceral fat is part of that worsening continuum from metabolic flexibility to inflexibility that I mentioned — that's why I measure it in all of my patients.

When I asked about her mood, she confided that she felt more fearful about her future, less assertive at work. She told me about other woes: night sweats, hemorrhoids, sciatica, a recent bone screening showing osteopenia (age-related bone loss), not cooking at home as much and eating cereal for dinner, less interest in physical activity. When we got to her sexual history, I asked about sex drive. Nicole shifted uncomfortably in her seat and replied: "Near zero." Finally, I asked about her values and how that related to the reason she made her appointment. She told me she wants to be healthier, add more years to her life, and experience more of the wonderful things life has to offer.

We measured her waist at 36 inches, and weight at 144 pounds (at 5 feet 2 inches tall, her body mass index or BMI was in the overweight range at 26.3, and her body fat was in the obese range at 33 percent). Her hormones were sputtering in perimenopause. When we ran a few blood tests, most striking were her low testosterone and DHEA levels. I knew exactly what to do to help her.

You likely know testosterone (known as "T" for short) as the *male* sex hormone. But women make T too. We don't have testes like men do, so we make it in our ovaries, as well as in cells within the adrenal glands, fat, skin, and brain.[1] Overall, healthy men have ten to twenty times the levels of healthy women, but while men have more, T is the *most abundant biologically active hormone* in women. Yes, T is more abundant in the female body than even estrogen. You have receptors for T throughout your body, from the brain to the breast to the vagina and many places in between. In fact, given women's lower level of T compared to men's, you might even say that women are exquisitely sensitive to it.

Most women have plenty of T — and its precursor, DHEA (see the box on page 64) — until their twenties, when their levels begin to decline.[2] That's one reason why young women typically have a lot of energy, sex drive, and confidence, as well as muscle and bone strength, and don't have as hard a time keeping their weight in the normal range. T is a build-you-up hormone, like growth hormone, meaning that it aids in the construction of the body — from bones to muscles to skin — and simultaneously breaks down fat. But T has an even broader job description. While it's involved in body composition and muscle mass, it also plays a central role in sex drive, mood, and well-being. Women require adequate levels to feel vital and lean, cell to soul.

That's why, as women age and their T plummets, many of them experience a reduction in energy, sex drive, strength, the ability to maintain a healthy weight, and that basic feeling of health and vitality. My clinical experience confirms this: In my patients, women at age forty have half the level of T of women in their twenties, and many of them have complaints like Nicole's.

To determine if your T levels may be low, fill out the following questionnaire.

Testosterone Questionnaire

Do you have or have you experienced any of the following symptoms in the past six months?

- Do you have a normal female pattern of body hair, but the hair is thinning – particularly under your arms and in the pubic area?
- Do you notice signs of premature hair loss on the head, at the temples (sides of the forehead)?
- Do you like physical activity and sports, but your interest has been fading recently?
- Have you experienced intense emotional stress or trauma as an adult?
- Are you a long-distance runner or do you engage in other regular endurance exercise?
- Has your sex drive declined gradually since your twenties?
- Is your clitoris less sensitive than it used to be, which makes stimulation to orgasm take longer or require more effort?
- Is vaginal intercourse painful or irritating?
- Do you feel more passive, or less likely to take risks in daily life?
- Do you feel more fragile and excessively sensitive

to difficulties, as if your resistance to stress is diminished?

- Do you feel depressive or tend to cling to a negative point of view?
- Are your muscles reduced in volume, tone, and strength?
- Have you noticed more cellulite and/or varicose veins?
- Is your skin thin, dry, and/or easily sunburned?
- Are you experiencing more joint pain, particularly low back pain?
- Do you have dry eyes?
- Have you lost height? Become more hunched over with your posture?
- Is your body scent diminished?
- Do you have fat accumulation at the breasts, waist, and/or hips?

If you answered yes to five or more of the questions above, you may have low T, and I recommend you proceed as if you do. You can raise low T with lifestyle changes like diet and exercise if you get help early. If you wait until too late, the only option may be to discuss T replacement with a trusted and well-educated clinician who can discuss the risks and benefits. If you are uncertain or want additional confirmation, consider getting tested for T, through a blood or urine test. Suggested labs are mentioned in the Notes, which are commonly ordered by most conventional gynecologists.[3]

LOW T IN WOMEN

While low T is a well-recognized problem in men, the implications of T deficiency — and the benefits of T therapy — in women have long been the subject of debate. Many doctors don't think about T when female patients complain of low energy, low sex drive, flab (as in Nicole's case), weight gain, or an inability to lose weight in the ways that used to work when they were younger. There are many other surprising symptoms of low T in women, from bonier hands to a less sensitive clitoris (see the questionnaire for a more complete list), which can be uncomfortable, embarrassing, inconvenient, or just depressing, and they can begin to surface in women as early as their midthirties.

So why are doctors so oblivious at best, or dismissive at worst, concerning low T in women? Why do many of them fail to test for it? A dearth of publicized research means that many physicians have no idea that levels decline steeply during a woman's reproductive years, especially for those who undergo removal of their ovaries (called oophorectomy, this is sometimes performed along with a hysterectomy to treat or prevent ovarian cancer).[4] Also, most physicians don't recognize the benefits of identifying and treating women who are suffering with low T. But even if doctors think of low T as a possible problem, test for it, and want to treat it, there are currently no FDA-approved treatments for low T in women. They have to wing it, or prescribe something off-label, or prescribe something that hasn't been well tested in women, and that can be something a lot of doctors hesitate to do.

While you may not get the kind of response you would like from your doctor, and while controversy continues to exist regarding T therapy for women who are deficient, fortunately, there are solutions available for you. Therapeutic lifestyle intervention — especially dietary factors — can help significantly boost your levels of androgens (the so-called male hormones, including T and its precursor, DHEA) when you are low.

In the Androgens Family, Testosterone Is the Star

T is one type of androgen. Androgens are so-called "male" hormones (*andro-* is a Greek term for "man") that are present in higher concentrations in men than women. They are responsible for male sexual development, sperm count, and sex drive, as well as secondary sexual characteristics like muscle and bone growth, facial and body hair growth, and a deep voice. They can also influence energy and mood.

The other androgens besides T include androstenedione, dihydrotestosterone (DHT), dehydroepiandrosterone (DHEA), and dehydroepiandrosterone sulfate (DHEA-S). Each of these is complexly related to different actions in the body. For example, DHT is linked to balding, and DHEA is a hormone that is used to make both T and estrogen and is also related to immunity, mood, cognition, strength, and aging (or *not* aging — it is sometimes called the "anti-aging hormone"). DHEA-S is involved in the onset of puberty in youth and in stress throughout life; also, it can be a factor in the onset of dementia in old age.

Just as men have a lot of androgens and some (but a much smaller amount) estrogens, women have a lot of estrogens and a much smaller amount of androgens. (As mentioned, we still have more T in total amount than estrogens.) Both sexes need both types of sex hormones. When women experience decreasing levels of androgens with age, they tend to experience reduced sex drive, feel more tired, and just don't feel as well as they once did, even if they can't pinpoint specific symptoms. (In men, since T is used to create the estrogen called estradiol, decreased T often leads to decreased estrogen, which is linked to increased body fat and weaker muscles.)

THE SCIENCE OF
LOW TESTOSTERONE
IN WOMEN

There are a number of reasons why low T is common in women. For one thing, your body naturally makes less T as you get older, but natural menopause has less of an effect on T levels than you might think — the drop in T typically precedes menopause by many years. There is a dramatic 50 percent reduction between ages twenty and forty, and DHEA drops even more precipitously than T as you age.[5] The exception is surgical menopause — when your ovaries are removed, T plummets.[6] Otherwise, the loss of T is gradual and not dramatic with menopause. Another potential cause of low T: the birth control pill. It raises sex hormone binding globulin (SHBG), which is like a sponge that carries T around the body and tends to lower your free T levels.[7]

While lower T can be a natural thing, what I've found in my practice to be one of the biggest contributors to unnaturally low levels of T in women is lifestyle — especially diet.

Another common reason for low T is a medication: statins for high cholesterol. Not only that, but statins deplete many phytonutrients (see the list in Notes).[8] The television ads suggest statins are a panacea, but the truth is that they are a very common cause of declining T, and even a severe form of muscle breakdown called rhabdomyolysis. Most of the research has focused on men, but the effect applies to women as well.[9]

Why you have low T can help you determine your solution, but similar to the research on growth hormone, much of the research on raising T with diet and other lifestyle factors comes from studies on men. Still, we can take much of what we already know about how to increase T and apply it to *you*. I've done this with my patients and seen great results.

WHY TESTOSTERONE IS
IMPORTANT FOR WOMEN

I've already hinted at why you want and need T, but let's look more closely at what else it can do for you.

If you're trying to get leaner and lose more body fat, T is an important ally. It is the hormone that creates a weight-loss edge for men. It generally helps men build more muscle mass and gives them a higher resting metabolic rate — that is, men tend to burn more calories at rest than women do. Since women produce less T than men, we have less muscle mass and a lower metabolic rate — which is why men lose weight and gain muscle more easily than women do. I suspect this is why the ketogenic diet, which involves higher fat, moderate protein, and low carbohydrate intake, tends to work better for men, according to my research. The Gottfried Protocol follows a ketogenic framework but is adapted for women, together with detoxification and fasting.

Wishing you were in the mood more often? T and the other androgens are the main hormones that fuel sex drive in both men and women, and T levels are positively linked with the ability to have an orgasm.[10] Women with low DHEA have a higher likelihood of low sexual desire at all ages from eighteen to seventy-five (though some with low DHEA have a normal sex drive).[11] According to other studies, the free level of T — or "free" T, meaning, the amount that is biologically available to bind to receptors, the way a lock fits into a key — matters more than total T, which is calculated as free T plus the amount of T bound to carriers in the blood.[12] Of course, T isn't the only factor in a healthy libido. For women, context is also very important — that includes relationship satisfaction, emotional support, self-esteem, optimism, the presence of pain, contentment, and life satisfaction.[13] However, there is no denying that T and other androgens play a role in translating those emotional elements into a physical response.

Not feeling so cheerful lately? T may also be involved in mood and cognition, though data on this possibility are more limited.[14]

DHEA (that precursor to T) may also be a remedy for severe stress, as measured by cortisol levels. The way DHEA supplements seem to reduce the effects of the stress response after severe trauma may mean it could be a therapy to reduce risk of post-traumatic health problems and even death.[15]

If fertility is a concern, you may be interested to hear that DHEA and T are being explored in assisted reproduction, especially for women with aging eggs.[16] That's an area of research to keep an eye on.

Feeling sluggish and wondering if your thyroid is to blame? Androgens to the rescue yet again. Healthy T levels help regulate the conversion of inactive thyroid hormone (T4) to active thyroid hormone (T3), which can increase thyroid hormone levels that so often decline as women age, but that are also too low in many younger women, for a variety of reasons. A thyroid hormone boost can help you reenergize, so that you can again experience that light and springy feeling.

Maybe you, like Nicole, just want to get healthier in general. Studies show that impaired T levels are associated with several serious health conditions that involve the immune system, inflammation, and glucose problems, including depression, breast cancer, obesity, type 2 diabetes, and Alzheimer's disease.[17]

In the breast, as an example, T may decrease the abnormal growth of cells and density of the breast on a mammogram, but if too much T is converted to estrogen, the risk of breast cancer may rise.[18] For mood, women with low T may benefit from topping off their T with a prescription.[19] It's a case of delicate balance.

TOO MUCH T

As you can see, T is a boon to women's health in multiple significant ways. However, too much of a good thing is not such a good thing, and with androgens, more is not necessarily better. As with all hormones, balance is everything. Excess T in women is a top reason for infertility, irregular periods, and cardiovascular disease. It could also contribute indirectly to breast cancer risk. T, as you may recall, is converted from DHEA, and then converted to a type of estrogen called estradiol.[20] Too much of this specific type of estrogen could put you at greater risk for breast cancer. Ideally, you want a healthy balance between protective androgens like T (and its precursor DHEA), which may reduce your risk of breast cancer, and stimulatory estrogens like estradiol, which may raise your risk of breast cancer.

Too much T also raises your risk of diabetes and obesity, as can occur with polycystic ovary syndrome (PCOS), a condition in which T levels are abnormally high. PCOS is a complex condition that may be difficult to diagnose, but most women who have it share certain metabolic and mental health symptoms. (See Notes for additional information.)[21] Up to 75 percent of women with PCOS are overweight. While losing weight is hard enough for most people, women with PCOS have an even harder time, probably because of their high insulin levels, which trigger the body to hoard fat. High insulin increases hunger and carbohydrate cravings, making a tough situation even more difficult.

When you have too much T circulating in your bloodstream (as with PCOS), it can stimulate your hair follicles to thicken and grow, resulting in increased growth of body and facial hair. Hirsutism, or excess hair growth, in a male pattern, is present in 80 percent of women with excess androgens. Another marker that's important in dealing with PCOS is a deficiency of SHBG (the sponge that soaks up free T). Women with PCOS who have low levels of SHBG are at greater risk of the metabolic issues I just mentioned, such as blood sugar imbalances.[22]

What helps with PCOS from a dietary perspective? Low-carb[23] and ketogenic diets,[24] which may help to rebalance T when it's too high.

Again, balance is the key. When T (and other hormone) levels are optimally balanced, you can enjoy benefits like fat loss, increased energy and stamina, higher libido, easier orgasms, lower disease risk, more confidence, and a buoyant mood.

The goal with the Gottfried Protocol is to get your hormones back into balance, and that includes T. You want the right amount — not too little, and not too much. If T drops too low, you may feel apathetic and flabby. But you also don't want T to climb too high, as that can put you at risk for conditions like PCOS.

WHAT YOU CAN DO ABOUT LOW TESTOSTERONE

In order to boost low T levels, the first and most important step you can take is to *improve your diet*—and not just generally, but in some very specific ways. First, let's look at the foods that science has linked with low T in men. In my experience, these foods likely have the same effect in women. You will notice that the lists below are in line with ketogenic principles—cut the carbohydrates, consume moderate protein, and get healthy fats in your diet. The foods associated with lower T are as follows:

- Bread, both refined and whole grain.
- Pastries, and all similar foods made with flour.
- Sugar-sweetened beverages. Consumption of sugar-packed drinks is significantly associated with low serum T in men of ages twenty to thirty-nine in the United States.[25] A single serving of a sugar and protein drink lowers T by 19 percent in overweight and obese boys,[26] and a single oral glucose load drops T by 25 percent in men.[27]
- Coffee. Both caffeinated and decaffeinated coffee decrease T in a randomized trial involving women; men, by contrast, experienced a rise in T after drinking caffeinated coffee.[28] A study in premenopausal women confirmed these results,[29] while a separate study in postmenopausal women showed that drinking caffeine as coffee or other caffeinated beverages is associated with lower bioavailable T.[30] However, data from an observational study are contradictory, showing potential benefits and drawbacks to caffeine.[31] (Randomized trials are less likely to be biased, and they are considered a higher level of evidence compared to observational studies.)
- Diet beverages.

- Dairy products (milk, yogurt, cheese, ice cream, and so forth).
- Desserts in general (in other words, foods with a lot of sugar).
- Restaurant food.[32]

Now let's look at foods and behaviors associated with higher T, more muscle mass, and less visceral fat:

- Homemade food. Make your kitchen the best restaurant around.
- Dark-green vegetables.
- Sufficient but not excess protein (about 0.75 to 1.0 grams per pound of lean body mass—less if you are sedentary and more if you are very active with exercise).
- Exercise, for men. Keto has been shown to raise T in men who exercise.[33]
- Certain herbs, including fenugreek, tribulus, and ginkgo biloba dry extracts, shown to improve T levels. These herbs have been studied in combination to help boost low sex drive among women.[34] Studies suggest that fenugreek[35] and tribulus[36] may be helpful when taken individually as well. These herbs are available at your local health food store.
- Detoxification and removal of endocrine disruptors.

How Much Protein Do You Need?

I'm a fan of moderate protein intake because excess protein gets converted into sugar in the body, driving up your insulin, driving down your T, and potentially making you store more fat. Moderate protein means 3 to 4 ounces of wild-caught fish. Two eggs, a few times per week. One ounce of nuts or seeds. (For more details, see Chapter 5.) For instance, a woman weighing 130 pounds, with 100 pounds of lean body mass, should eat about 85 to 100 grams of protein each day, or enough to preserve lean body mass. Athletes may need more protein to maintain or increase muscle mass.

Bisphenol A and Testosterone

One of the worst culprits when it comes to blocking T is the androgen disruptor bisphenol A (BPA). Not only does BPA mess with the balance of T in your body,[37] it acts as an obesogen — a foreign chemical linked to unwanted weight gain that attaches to insulin or leptin receptors.[38] Is BPA involved in the low T that I see in my patients who are premenopausal and menopausal, in lockstep with less muscle mass, more anxiety, more depression, and a slower metabolism? We don't yet know because studies of BPA have mostly focused on its adverse effects on women who want to become pregnant and/or have polycystic ovary syndrome.

Beyond targeting individual foods that science has linked with low or high T, the Gottfried Protocol is my own secret weapon for balancing androgens, along with all the other hormones, for maximum health and vitality. In Chapter 5, I'll share a detailed plan to address key metabolic hormones—the Protocol is a combination of detoxification, ketosis, and intermittent fasting, adapted for women.

You may be thinking, "Uh, Dr. Sara, that sounds like a lot. I'm too busy." I get it, but you probably don't have time to cart around your extra 15 pounds either, or muddle through daily fatigue, or take on the downstream health problems that an unhealthy lifestyle can cause. The effort you put into this plan now will save you time—and possibly save your health—later.

Other Ways to Boost T

Besides eating the right foods, there are other things you can do to boost T. One is to take the supplement DHEA, which as you may remember is the precursor to T, and it is sometimes used to increase T levels. For example, new research suggests that adding DHEA may maintain T levels for women on the birth control pill.[39] However, the use of DHEA is controversial because of limited information as to its long-term safety. A Cochrane database systematic review of twenty-eight randomized trials suggested that DHEA may modestly improve low sex drive, but other outcomes are lacking. Plus, so-called "androgenic" side effects are common,[40] such as oily hair and skin, acne, excessive sex drive, aggression, excessive clitoris swelling or sensitivity, excessive muscle development, male-pattern hair loss, and excess body hair. Still, given the lack of other options for raising T, I do sometimes recommend DHEA as a supplement to my patients who are unable to raise their T sufficiently with other lifestyle changes.

You might wonder if you could just start taking T in order to help the pounds melt off your middle. Or perhaps you wonder about T pellets injected under the skin. Well . . . though there are several forms of FDA-approved T treatments available to address low T in men, we lack proof that they are safe for women, which is why the FDA has not approved a T formulation for women. For now, I suggest avoiding T supplements as a treatment for women unless absolutely necessary. Hopefully, the research will catch up soon. In the meantime, commit to dietary and lifestyle changes to achieve T balance. It's safer, and still effective, without the potential side effects.

Let's go back to Nicole, from the beginning of the chapter, and her complaints of low muscle tone and sex drive, and see how she fared when she tried the Gottfried Protocol. She focused first on detoxification, then ketosis, and then added intermittent fasting. As you will see in Chapter 5, I prefer an overnight fast of fourteen to sixteen hours, but you can work your way up to it slowly. Nicole got into ketosis immediately—after her first fourteen-hour overnight fast, her blood ketones were 2.0 mmol (0.5 or greater is diagnostic of mild ketosis, which is the goal on my food plan) suggested that her metabolic flexibility would be relatively easy to restore. Within one week, her ketones were consistently at 1.0 to 2.0 mmol, suggesting that her body successfully and rapidly adapted to fat burning. After four weeks, she dropped 3 inches off her waist and 8 pounds off her weight. At that time, we found that her measures of free and total T were better, but still borderline low. I added supplemental DHEA, at a dose of 5 milligrams per day, which she purchased online. (DHEA does not require a prescription in the United States, but I recommend taking it only after consultation with an experienced clinician.). After eight weeks, she went from weighing 144 pounds down to 130, and her body fat decreased from 33 to 25 percent—giving her a normal and healthy body mass index of 23.8. She lost a total of 4 inches off her waist. Her T and DHEA went back into the normal range. Nicole felt mentally focused, her libido improved, and she was back to enjoying sex regularly. She felt healthier than she had in years—it was as if she got her body back, and her life.

Highlights

▶ Testosterone (T) is a key hormone associated with weight, vitality, strength, and sex drive.

▶ Healthy men have more T than healthy women, but T is the *most abundant biologically active hormone* in women. Yes, you have more T than even estrogen.

► When women have low T, they may experience many different symptoms, such as increased weight and body fat, decreased muscle mass, declining mood, and faltering sex drive.

► Women can also have too much T, typically as part of polycystic ovary syndrome (PCOS). We need T in balance in order to function at our best.

► We know much more about low T in men than in women, but while we wait for more research, you can focus on food, lifestyle, and supplements to improve your production of T as well as other key androgens.

4

THE KETO PARADOX

Jen is a thirty-seven-year-old woman with a stressful job in technology. She and her fiancé wanted to lose weight before their wedding, so they would look great in their photos. After hearing about the so-called miraculous ketogenic diet, they decided to try it together. Jen's main goals were to lose 15 pounds, feel trim in her wedding dress, and gain more mental clarity for planning the event. Now that you know a lot more about hormones and how they differ between men and women, can you guess what happened?

That's a trick question because first, in order to predict the outcome, you need to understand exactly what a ketogenic diet is, how it works, and why results can sometimes be paradoxical.

KETOSIS 101

The ketogenic diet you've probably heard so much about is a low-carbohydrate, moderate-protein, high-fat diet that isn't actually new. Its first clinical application dates to more than a century ago, when it was used as a treatment for children with epilepsy. It did indeed seem like a "miracle cure" (though I would never describe anything we do in medicine as a "miracle") because in many cases, it *stopped or signifi-*

cantly reduced the children's seizures. About 10 to 20 percent of kids were *super responders*—they improved dramatically and early in the ketogenic process compared to other kids, and some were able to get off their seizure medication.[1] More recently, people with other neurological issues, such as multiple sclerosis, Parkinson's disease, and Alzheimer's disease, have used the ketogenic diet with success that has been reported anecdotally (there isn't yet much research on this subject).[2] Although scientists don't completely understand why this diet seems to have a beneficial effect on neurological conditions, the primary theory is that it's the ketones (also called ketone bodies).

Normally, the human body (and especially the human brain) burns sugar for energy. We get this sugar from the carbohydrates we eat (and secondarily, from the protein). When carbohydrates are drastically reduced, however, the body turns to fat for fuel instead of sugar. It does this by triggering the liver to release ketones, which the body and brain can burn and use for energy. Remember, burning fat instead of sugar is part of ketosis. We probably developed this ability early in human history, to survive the seasons when carbohydrates from fruits and vegetables were scarce or nonexistent. At such times, animal fat became a critical source of fuel, and our bodies figured out how to use it.

The brain in particular seems to thrive when fueled by ketones, not sugar. This may be why ketones (and a ketogenic diet) seem to benefit people with brain issues. Because it's easier for the body to burn sugar than ketones, burning ketones for fuel seems to induce weight loss: it takes more energy and burns more fat. Initially, weight loss was considered a side effect of ketosis (the state of burning fat instead of sugar), rather than its primary purpose.

The reason why the ketogenic diet leads to weight loss is that when you are in ketosis, you are literally burning your fat stores as fuel. When you switch to eating fewer carbs and more fat, your body recognizes that this is a new scenario. When it runs out of sugar (and glycogen, which is your liver's store of "carb energy"), your body discovers that it can rely on plenty of dietary fat coming in. This keeps your body from sensing any lack of incoming energy. There is no famine—it's just a different kind of fuel. Your body adapts, becoming metabolically flexible, and the fat on your body starts to burn away.

Getting your body to flip the switch from burning carbohydrates to burning fat offers fascinating health benefits: mental focus, better memory and attention, less inflammation, and, as I've already mentioned, weight loss. Overall, a ketogenic diet may be an easier path to weight loss because it helps you feel more satisfied than calorie-restricted diets do. Eager to lose weight, many people have been jumping on the keto bandwagon. Recently it has become a very big trend.

That all sounds great, right? But before you empty your produce bin into the trash or stock up on a year's supply of bacon, here's a reminder: *the ketogenic diet has mostly been studied in men and works quite well for them.* Women, on the other hand, tend not to do so well on this diet. There are exceptions—some women do great on keto—but in general, a man and a woman (like Jen and her fiancé) can go on an identical keto diet and get completely different results.

As we touched on earlier, keto may also not be healthy for people with different health issues. That's why if you have a history of any disease, you should speak with your physician before trying keto. If you have cancer or a history of cancer, discuss keto with your oncologist. While the majority of research on the ketogenic diet in cancer is favorable,[3] one animal model suggests that keto may worsen a certain form of cancer called acute myeloid leukemia, as published in the journal *Nature*.[4] On the other hand, most cancer cells feed on sugar, so keto may be an important tool that's synergistic to multimodal cancer prevention and treatment, though further trials are needed to explore this possibility. The bottom line: it's complicated! Keto needs to be personalized to each woman's situation. (See "Is Keto Safe for Me?" for further information on absolute and relative contraindications to the ketogenic diet.) If you have questions about keto related to particular health conditions, such as gallbladder issues or a history of kidney stones, discuss them with your healthcare professional.

Is Keto Safe for Me?

How can you tell if the keto diet is safe for you?[5] A ketogenic diet is not safe for people who have congenital health conditions that make them unable to metabolize fatty acids. These conditions include pyruvate carboxylase deficiency, porphyria, and other fat metabolism disorders. Other health conditions that may be worsened by a ketogenic diet include pancreatitis, active gallbladder disease, impaired liver function, and poor nutritional status. It also may not be appropriate for people who have undergone gastric bypass surgery, people with a history of abdominal tumors or cancer, and those with a history of kidney failure. Those who have type 1 diabetes should avoid keto. Furthermore, I do not recommend keto for women who are pregnant or breastfeeding because of the lack of safety data.

There are also rare metabolic conditions that contraindicate the keto diet, such as carnitine deficiency (primary), carnitine palmitoyltransferase (CPT) I or II deficiency, carnitine translocase deficiency, beta-oxidation defects, mitochondrial 3-hydroxy-3-methylglutaryl-CoA synthase (mHMGS) deficiency, medium-chain acyl dehydrogenase deficiency (MCAD), long-chain acyl dehydrogenase deficiency (LCAD), short-chain acyl dehydrogenase deficiency (SCAD), long-chain 3-hydroxyacyl-CoA deficiency, and medium-chain 3-hydroxyacyl-CoA deficiency.

When in doubt, check with your doctor. It's never a bad idea to speak with your physician or health team before starting a new dietary plan. And be sure to keep up-to-date on the research as more indications and contraindications emerge, based on the latest scientific evidence.

Keto and the Male Bias in Research

It's perhaps not surprising that women are more likely to have problems on keto, given that the bulk of the data on the ketogenic diet comes from men.[6] Some of the studies performed on men include evaluation of hunger and appetite for weight loss[7] or the time line of changes in satiety and appetite[8] in overweight and obese men;[9] studies in athletic men;[10] cardiovascular blood tests[11] in healthy men; and ketogenic tests in male (but not female) mice.[12] Similarly, low-carb diets have been mostly tested on men.[13] A small handful of ketogenic trials for weight loss have included women, but they made up less than 20 percent of the participants.[14]

This gender gap isn't unique to research on keto — or, more broadly, research on diet and nutrition. In most realms of medicine, women have historically been underrepresented in clinical research, or even left out entirely. It wasn't until the early 1990s that a federal law was passed requiring that studies funded by the National Institutes of Health (NIH) include women. Furthermore, it wasn't until 2014 that the NIH began requiring that animal studies include both sexes. *Seriously?* And it's still not routine for researchers to analyze their results by gender. Since women are not merely men with ovaries, we can't (and shouldn't) extrapolate the results of research on men to predict results in women. If we did, we would be ignoring fundamental biological differences, such as how female hormones interact with the rest of the female body, and we would be dismissing the profound endocrinological transitions that women undergo and men don't, such as pregnancy, nursing, perimenopause, and menopause.

What's more, applying something as influential as a dietary prescription to women without an adequate scientific basis can affect health and weight loss in ways that can be dangerous. Not only may women assume their failure to lose weight and feel better is their fault (and feel resentful toward their keto-

> successful male friends and partners), but they could end up with more risk factors for chronic disease, such as high cholesterol, inflammation, high stress, diabetes, and weight gain.

What's up? Why does keto help most men lose weight but cause some women to gain it? Furthermore, why does keto reverse some diseases, such as high blood sugar and high blood pressure, yet exacerbate others? When does keto clear inflammation, and when does keto cause it?

I've been taking care of women since 1994, but over the past ten years a large number of "keto refugees" have visited my office and participated in my online courses. I have seen up close the frustration they experience with keto—and by now, I feel like I've seen it all. Women tell me they gained weight on keto and ask if it's because of the calorie-dense food plan or the generous amount of animal fat. They experience more inflammation, their joints ache, and they wonder why they don't feel or look as great as their husbands or male co-workers using the same diet plan. They get stressed or start their period and come out of ketosis.

We aren't totally sure why women respond to keto differently than men do,[15] but I can make an educated guess, based on what I've seen in my practice (and you've read about in the past three chapters): *it's the hormones.* From a hormonal perspective, it's logical that a diet low in carbs and high in fat would have a different effect on men than on women. As you learned in the previous chapter, the endocrine system, and the hormones it produces, responds differently to fat, carbs, and protein, and since women and men have very different hormonal profiles, of course their bodies and hormones will react to a ketogenic diet differently.

So let's go back to Jen and her fiancé. What do you think happened when they both changed to a food plan low in carbs, moderate in protein, and high in fat?

HORMONES, FAT STORAGE, AND THE (DIET) BATTLE OF THE SEXES

As you may have guessed by this point, Jen's fiancé quickly lost weight: 12 pounds in the first ten days on keto. Jen, on the other hand, *gained weight* almost immediately and noticed no change at all in her brain fog. This was not what she expected. Frustrated and disillusioned, she gave up on keto. But when you keep hearing how great something is, it's hard not to give it another try. Jen began to wonder if she had "done keto right." After all, she admittedly hadn't been tracking her carb, protein, and fat grams (her macronutrients, or "macros"), so maybe she wasn't hitting the right ratios.

Six months later, Jen tried keto again. This time, she faithfully kept a log of her food in order to stick to the proper macronutrient rations that she'd read about online: 10 percent carb, 20 percent protein, and 70 percent fat. But now she had a new problem: she was always hungry. Keto is meant to kill your appetite, so Jen couldn't understand why that wasn't happening. Her fiancé wasn't hungry. He'd have some bacon and eggs and feel great (and then be down another pound!). But that feeling of satisfaction never kicked in for Jen, and things got even worse during her period, when she craved chocolate cake. After one month, she didn't feel any different (other than constantly dreaming about bread and doughnuts), and while she hadn't gained any weight, she hadn't lost any either. Frustrated again, she quit. When she finally came to see me, Jen told me all about her disappointing experience, and I reassured her that she was definitely not the only woman to struggle with keto. Then I told her not to give up hope just yet.

Why is this happening to so many women? What is it about female hormones that respond so differently to keto? First of all, it's helpful to look at the science of dieting in general. Women are already, sorry to say, at a disadvantage when it comes to weight loss. Studies have demonstrated that on a diet, men lose more weight than women do.[16] One study showed that they lost twice as much weight and three times as much fat mass when compared to women on a diet.[17] Men seem to lose more belly fat (the more dangerous visceral fat), while women tend to lose more subcutaneous fat (the less harmful type).[18] That translates to more metabolic improvement in men (the rate at which their bodies transform food into fuel).

The differences go even further. Men tend to be less likely to be aware of their weight or dissatisfied with their weight, and they are less likely to even try to lose weight — and of course, when they did try, according to one study, they were 40 percent more likely than women to lose and maintain a weight loss greater than 10 pounds and increase their exercise over the course of one year.[19]

By contrast, women are more likely to want a lower body weight than men do and consistently have higher levels of body dissatisfaction.[20] Unrealistic societal norms and the multi-billion-dollar dieting industry affect women more than men. There is even a ripple effect related to income. Waist circumference is negatively correlated with wages for women but not for men. *No obesity measure correlates with men's earnings.*[21] Clearly, women experience a greater burden when it comes to weight loss.

Weighty Issues

Another issue that women face more commonly than men do is food addiction and other eating disorders. Overeating is the most common one. Women have a fourfold greater risk of being addicted to food — we are more likely to eat for emotional reasons, positive or negative, or because we feel overly stressed. That means that for us, giving up the cupcakes may not be a straightforward undertaking. This factor makes compliance with any diet, let alone a low-carb diet, more challenging. As a woman, I know these pressures well, and I have internalized many of them. Together we will keep an eye on health, not just appearance, because that's my primary job as a precision medicine physician.

It all seems terribly unfair, I know. And it is! But it is also one of the main reasons why I developed the Gottfried Protocol and wrote this book. I want to help level the playing field with an accessible, user-friendly approach that can help women succeed on keto as well as men do. The Gottfried Protocol works *with* your hormones, instead of forcing on your body a program that wasn't tested on women or designed with your body chemistry in mind. When you are able to get healthy on your own terms, you'll gain the confidence, clarity, energy, and good health that will enable you to thrive.

THE SCIENCE OF FEMALE HORMONES AND KETO

Before I explain why your hormones will work well with the Gottfried Protocol, let's take a deeper dive into why female hormones don't work with traditional keto diets. Let's start with Jen. Jen's ketogenic diet "failures" and the ensuing frustrations were likely due to her hormones and unresolved inflammation. To confirm this, the first thing I did was order some tests. We discovered that Jen had several issues:

1. Jen had a high level of cortisol in her urine, which mirrored her concern that she was under a lot of stress. Many women of Jen's age experience high perceived stress and become so accustomed to the feeling that they don't even realize it's a problem. But chronic stress can be a primary cause of brain fog, concentration issues, high blood pressure, and subclinical hypothalamic-pituitary-adrenal dysfunction (so-called adrenal fatigue, a term I don't like). Remember that Jen was eating low-carb. Since high-quality whole-food carbohydrates like greens and multicolored vegetables can promote healthy adrenal function and stabilize cortisol levels, I suspected her diet could be exacerbating her stress.

2. She had high blood sugar, in the range that indicated prediabetes, a condition in which blood sugar is above

normal but not quite at diabetes level. Prediabetes is generally considered to be a warning that diabetes is imminent without treatment; it is a telltale sign of metabolic inflexibility. (See Notes for laboratory criteria.[22]) Prediabetes is common in overweight women and even in some women who are not overweight but can no longer process carbohydrates efficiently or who have become insulin resistant. High blood sugar can also cause concentration issues and a general feeling of being unwell. It's also a risk factor for heart disease, although some women have no symptoms (but all the risks). Jen was surprised that she could have high blood sugar while eating low-carb, but for some women, certain types of fat can actually trigger high blood sugar.[23] I've seen this in Jen as well as other patients. Low carb doesn't always mean lower blood sugar — saturated fat may raise blood sugar levels, perhaps due to inflammation.

3. Jen's thyroid, T, and growth hormone were borderline low. I suspected this was also a function of her low-carb diet, since carbohydrates can also promote healthier thyroid and estrogen function in many women.

4. Another test showed that Jen had chronic inflammation. We hear a lot about inflammation, usually in the context of its being a bad thing that can contribute to weight gain. Typically, that means the immune system is having a dysfunctional response to a perceived injury or infection. But because there's a lot that's misunderstood about inflammation, it's helpful to unpack the concept. There are two types: a short-term type of inflammation, called acute, and a long-term type of inflammation, called chronic. Acute inflammation occurs when you cut yourself or sprain an ankle or get an infection, and in such a case the acute inflammation (immune response) is good — the region becomes swollen and red as your white blood cells swarm in and fight for your healing. Jen, however, showed evidence of chronic inflammation (an immune response that won't resolve), as indicated by a high level of c-reactive protein

in her blood. Sometimes this is caused by too much saturated fat in women,[24] though the science is still evolving and suggests that lifestyle factors, such as exercise, may play a role.[25]

This list gives you a sense of the specific ways in which a typical ketogenic diet won't work very well for women with hormonal imbalance. Traditional keto may be too low in carbohydrates for women with a hormone imbalance, since carbs help mitigate the stress response and lower cortisol. They also boost growth hormone and support thyroid function.

Another issue is inflammation, specifically chronic inflammation. Chronic or unresolved inflammation is problematic and can have a variety of causes. Sometimes it's due to an immune response that never turns off, like a light left on in a room. That can occur when you eat inflammatory foods (refined carbohydrates, sugary drinks, certain fried foods), or because of exposure to toxins, chronic stress, excess visceral fat, and even autoimmune diseases like Hashimoto's thyroiditis. Chronic and unresolved inflammation is nothing to mess around with as it can lead to other consequences, such as heart disease, Alzheimer's disease, cancer, and depression.

One study showed that the shift into ketosis, by which fat is burned preferentially during exercise, takes longer to kick in for women as compared to men. Men tend to burn fat more easily, and they burn it at a lower intensity than women. I believe this is because women's bodies not only tend to need more carbs and hang on to fat for a variety of reasons (including fertility, though the problem persists and may worsen after menopause), but because women tend to have a more inflammatory response to certain fats. Because of this, their bodies resist the switch to fat burning longer than men's bodies do. That inflammatory response from fats can also elevate blood sugar, as it seemed to have done with Jen.

What's Your Metabolotype?
Apple, Pear, or Celery?

Where a woman stores her fat seems to be a good predictor of how her physiology behaves — storing fat predominantly in the abdominal area carries with it the same metabolic risks that it does for men, especially those who have obesity. However, many women with obesity and "pear-shaped" fat stores are actually *protected* from metabolic and cardiovascular diseases.

We can call these different metabolic types *metabolotypes*. Beyond the apple (extra fat at the waist) and the pear (extra fat at the hips and thighs — that's me!), there's the celery (no extra fat). These are the lucky women who just don't gain weight. They have a fast metabolism no matter what. Lifelong athletes often fit into this category — my youngest sister is one of them. She just never struggles with her weight, even after reaching age forty and having two kids.

On the other hand, women are also much more efficient at storing fat compared to men. After eating a high-calorie, high-fat meal, women with pear-shaped fat distributions store more of the fat in the gluteo-femoral region — the good old butt and thighs. As I mentioned in the Metabolic Hormone Questionnaire in Chapter 1, you can determine if you have an apple or pear shape by measuring your waist-to-hip ratio. If your waist measurement divided by your hip measurement is greater than 0.85 for women, or greater than 0.90 for men, you have an apple shape.

Whether you have an apple or pear metabolotype, there is a way to customize the Gottfried Protocol for you. In my experience, apples need more detoxification, fewer carbs (at least temporarily, for four weeks), deeper ketosis (where you are producing significant levels of ketones from burning fat, defined as greater than 1.0 mmol/L), and intermittent fasting. (Remember Melissa from Chapter 1? She has reduced her waist-to-hip measurement from 0.92 to 0.88, and is on her way to better health and lower risk of metabolic syndrome, diabetes, and heart disease. Small changes can truly aggregate to major transformation.) Pears can get away with lighter ketosis (where you are producing a mild amount of ketones from burning fat, defined as a level of 0.5–1.0 mmol/L) but also respond well to intermittent fasting. In Part 2, we will perform measurements to check your metabolotype, and I'll provide additional prescriptions to personalize the Gottfried Protocol.

So, what's the verdict? Is keto out for Jen (and for you)? Definitely not. While classic keto may not work for most women, I've found that with certain work-arounds specifically designed for a woman's body and hormonal profile, keto *can absolutely* work for women. What's more, women with either the apple or the pear shape can succeed with a well-formulated ketogenic diet—the trick is the "well-formulated" part.

THE GOTTFRIED PROTOCOL: A PROGRAM FOR METABOLIC FLEXIBILITY

Watching how these symptoms, test results, and reactions to keto have played out in my practice has formed the foundation for my plan. Over the past decade, I've tackled the keto paradox with a smart, safe protocol that, based on my research, has been proved to work for women. Now I'm sharing it with you.[26] I'm going to give you an evidence-based way to enter mild ketosis that activates your get-me-lean hormones, reverses inflammation, and provides you with peace of mind regarding safety and effectiveness. You'll learn the tips and tricks that I've discovered while taking care of women on keto, such as when you might need a few blood tests and how to prep meals so keto works in your busy life. Here are other key features of this female-centric plan:

1. Detoxifying before and during keto, which can balance hormones by freeing up your endocrine system from the onslaught of a toxic load.
2. Understanding which dietary adjustments to make based on your body type.
3. Layering in specific carbohydrates that feed the beneficial microbes in the gut (your microbiome) and also the endocrine system in a way that further balances hormones.
4. Incorporating intermittent fasting into your regimen, which can keep you in mild ketosis with a slightly higher carbohydrate intake.
5. Timing your largest and smallest meals the right way, so you never end up starving and overeating.

In Part 2, I'll guide you through the complete four-week protocol, with recommendations for personalizing the ketogenic diet for your situation, body type, and lifestyle — just as I do with my precision medicine patients. We will cover the do's and don'ts of the protocol, and I'll provide a troubleshooting guide, shopping list, and recipes that I developed in my own kitchen. Along the way, I'll share scientific breakthroughs that will help you succeed, such as how to make up your sleep debt, which has been shown to simultaneously help multiple hormones, including insulin, cortisol, ghrelin, and leptin.[27]

And what about Jen? She followed the very same plan I outline in this book. She started on the Gottfried Protocol, eating more organic vegetables than she did in the first two (unsuccessful) rounds of keto, along with supplements that addressed an overburdened liver — that is, a liver that doesn't detoxify chemicals efficiently, which may contribute to inflammation and foil attempts at weight loss.

Next, Jen added intermittent fasting to the plan. She ate between 8 a.m. and 6 p.m. and went to bed earlier. After two weeks of adjusting to intermittent fasting without hijacking her cortisol, she progressed to a 16:8 protocol, which means that she ate between 10 a.m. and 6 p.m. She stopped eating three hours before she went to sleep. After an overnight fast, she was ready for a healthy breakfast with some whole-food carbs, such as avocado on keto toast.

Jen prepped meals on the weekend, so that her refrigerator and freezer were stocked with nourishing soups and snacks that fed her gut microbes, lowered her insulin, and were rich in plant-based fats — yet made it easy to stick to the plan during the busy workweek. (See the recipes in Chapter 9.) She restricted animal-based fats to less than 30 percent of her daily total fat intake but continued to enjoy wild meats, such as a bison burger wrapped in lettuce or grass-fed beef such as filet mignon on the grill, and she cooked with ghee, olive oil, and avocado oil.

She learned about medium-chain triglycerides (MCTs) — a special type of fat you'll read about in Chapter 5 — that helps produce ketones, boost fat burning, and ignite brain function. (The "medium-chain" refers to how the carbon atoms are arranged in their chemical structure — most fats in a typical diet are long-chain triglycerides.) MCT oil can help you stay in ketosis (fat-burning mode), even if you add a few more carbs to your diet. Jen added MCTs to her salads and smoothies, along with macadamia nuts as a snack, and she ate more fatty fish at dinner.

In four weeks, she lost 12 pounds, most of it fat, and she felt better than she had in years. Her prediabetes and brain fog disappeared. *Success!* She was delighted. And she's kept the weight off. For long-term maintenance, she cycles in and out of the Gottfried Protocol, a mashup of a low-carb Mediterranean diet and detoxification, ketosis, and intermittent fasting.

Before Jen started the Gottfried Protocol, we got clear about her values. I asked her to write a personal value statement regarding her goals, hormones, and weight. Here is Jen's statement:

Scary diseases run in my family, like diabetes and heart disease. I believe that I will not develop these diseases if I choose a lifestyle that won't allow them to take hold. That means being careful with what I eat and how much alcohol I drink. I want to be fit and lean so that I fit into my wedding dress, but beyond that, I want to show up for my marriage as the healthiest version of myself. My relationship is my highest value — my relationship to my husband and myself. My career is next, and I have to be the best version of myself to be successful and create financial independence. All of these values stem from my health.

Jen used her personal values statement as a simple framework to guide her behavior during the four weeks of the Gottfried Protocol. She wrote her statement on a sticky note, placed it on her bathroom mirror, and reread it while brushing her teeth and flossing. It became a lighthouse for her, a beacon in the sunshine and storm of life.

You, like Jen, *can* be successful on a ketogenic diet. In Part 2, you'll learn exactly how. This protocol is designed for a new generation of women seeking health, a good life with the occasional carb, and a closet full of clothes that fit. In the following pages, I'll give you all the tools you need to burn stubborn fat, gain energy, clear that brain fog, and lower your chances of developing a chronic disease. All this awaits you, and the answer, after all, really can be keto. But it's not going to be a man's keto. It's going to be all yours.

Highlights

Ketogenic diets have many proven benefits, including mental focus, reduced appetite, and weight loss, although most studies of the diet have focused on men.

▶ We must deal with the keto paradox: the diet that works well for men often doesn't work well for women.

▶ Though we do not completely understand the sex and gender differences in diet effectiveness, fat distribution, and fat type between men and women, the answers seem to be rooted in the differences in hormones.

▶ The reasons women don't generally seem to benefit from the traditional ketogenic diet have to do with hormones, which can influence detoxification, stress and cortisol, thyroid function, hunger and food addiction, and low blood sugar.

► Eating crappy carbs can spike your insulin and blood sugar, leading to insulin block and fat accumulation. Alternatively, eating more healthy fat makes you feel satisfied, and it slows down or eliminates the rise in blood sugar rise that many foods cause.

► This book describes a modified ketogenic diet and lifestyle plan specifically formulated for women and personalized to your particular body type. You *can* succeed at keto!

PART II

The Four-Week
Gottfried Protocol

5

HOW TO START
AND WHAT TO EAT

Are you ready to change the way you look and feel, not just by improving the fit of your skinny jeans today but by improving the expression of your genes for the rest of your life? It all starts with your food and how it communicates with your hormones—changing your diet gives you the true power to reset your hormones and amplify fat loss. It's the change you've been waiting for: major improvements in health and wellness that I witness daily in my patients. I'm sharing them with you now. You've learned about the important hormones in the symphony, and now you're ready to orchestrate greater metabolic flexibility.

Though changing food habits can be remarkably difficult, it's well worth it: the hormonal changes you'll enjoy will be dramatic. I have evidence-based tactics to help you overcome the challenge of changing what you eat; I'll share these proven techniques in this chapter and beyond. This chapter covers the nuts and bolts you'll need to prepare for the first week of the protocol—and the first week of your new, healthier life.

HOW CHANGE STARTS

For the Gottfried Protocol, limiting carbohydrates over the short term will instigate a change in the body's hormonal messaging. After four weeks, we'll increase slow-burn carbohydrates over the long term to prevent difficulties that some people experience on extreme keto diets.

This time line is based on sound scientific reasoning. First, we want your hormones to scream loud and clear that it's time to raid the reserves, empty the pantry, and prepare the body for a state of equilibrium rather than fat storage. Cutting out carbohydrates is the best way to inspire this message, but we want to do it in a way that is easy on your body and optimizes hormonal balance. To do this, the Gottfried Protocol starts with a detox, then activates the powerful weight-loss power of traditional ketogenic diets, and finally harnesses the health-boosting and disease-resistant qualities of the Mediterranean diet for the long term. The Protocol features a three-stage, four-week program with a built-in self-assessment so you can adjust the program depending on how your unique body responds. Here's a rundown of the features that make the Gottfried Protocol different from other plans:

- Detoxification early in the process to support the body as it rids itself of stored toxins as fat is melted off.
- Scaled carbohydrate recommendations, beginning with the most restrictive, to encourage hormones to signal fat burning and a metabolism that supports long-term weight loss.
- Increasing slow-burn carbohydrate consumption in the second and third phases (Transition and Integration) to avoid the potential long-term issues associated with extremely low-carb diets.

This plan has been carefully constructed to work with a woman's body in a healthy and effective way. This approach includes these key benefits:

- Significant reduction of abdominal fat, which reduces inflammation and helps sustain growth hormone balance. Remember, in Chapter 1 we talked about how increased abdominal fat plays a greater role than age does in the decline of growth hormone. Perhaps even more important, for our goals, growth hormone levels are *improved* with weight loss.[1]
- Monitoring your unique body to see how you respond to a low-carbohydrate diet. Not everyone will respond in the same way, and you'll want to be able to adjust the Gottfried Protocol to make sure it is right for you.

FOOD HABITS
CAN BE CHANGED

Okay, I get it—all of this sounds great in theory. But I know what you're wondering: let's get down to the details. What exactly does this change of diet look like . . . and how hard will it be?

For many people, food is more than just fuel: it has a powerful emotional and psychological hold over us. Does the crunch of chips dipped in guacamole remind you of a perfect summer day? (Are you thinking "Where's my margarita?") Does a gooey-fluffy chocolate croissant arouse memories of a trip to France? Maybe it's simply a hearty bowl of pasta that takes you back to happy times around the family table growing up? Whatever your personal favorites, I get it: the power of food is rooted in memory, good times, and the strong desire to re-create the sensation associated with these positive experiences.

Memories can be both dangerous and instructive when you head into a new diet. Over the past five years, scientific research has been shedding light on how memory plays a powerful role in a range of risky behaviors, including use of hard-core drugs, binge eating, compulsive use of video games, excessive consumption of alcohol, use (and misuse) of marijuana, compulsive shopping, and constant internet surfing. The culprit, as revealed in this research, is not always the activity or substance, but rather the type of decision making involved. What was once a conscious decision to engage in an activity has been transformed into a subconscious one by means of what researchers call *habit memories*.[2] A multidisciplinary team of scientists from universities around the globe theorizes that rogue habit learning is one of the keys to explaining the entire process of addictive behaviors.[3]

Think of habit memories as a mental bias that makes changing food behaviors especially tough.[4] Fortunately, according to the latest research, we can learn how to overcome this type of mental interference and improve our decision making. We can extinguish habit memories.[5]

I believe women are particularly vulnerable to habit memories, and they can create unique challenges related to our hormones, metabolism, and weight loss. The research confirms my hunch.[6] Full disclosure: I used to be one of those women. My habit memory was eating chocolate chip cookies with my grandmother as a kid. Cookies were a source of comfort for me, and my go-to treat when stressed, until I learned better ways of soothing myself, like texting or calling a friend, doing yoga, practicing meditation, and exercising. I learned how to rewrite habit memories in order to honor my female biology, and so can you.

This means that when you're looking at a simple choice—like whether to have a cup of herbal tea or a pint of ice cream after dinner —your deepest desires and decision making may be based on habit memories. And we know what your habit memory would choose! However, your hormones see the situation differently. Every food you eat becomes a real-time driver of function, such as good health and high energy levels—or dysfunction, such as a thickening waistline or a depressing number on the bathroom scale. Fortunately, your taste buds turn over every two weeks, so as you enter ketosis and start losing weight, you will form new memories of healthy foods that support your lean hormones.

BUT FIRST . . . WHY?

One of the best ways to change your food habits is to get clear on your personal values and write a statement expressing them. This statement can become a touchstone that you return to over the next four weeks and beyond. It doesn't have to be complicated: simply write a few bulleted points or sentences about *why* you want to lose weight and how this desire relates to your beliefs and values. Be specific about the people and situations that make you feel most alive. Here are a few prompts:

- My goals for weight loss are . . .
- The reason I want to lose weight is . . .
- This is important to me because . . .
- So that I can . . .

In Chapter 4, I shared Jen's personal value statement. When I asked Lara to create one, she shared a poignant story:

> The day before I started the Gottfried Protocol, I was with my children and we were taking slow-motion videos of us each blowing dandelion seeds. When I saw the videos of me in profile view, I just wanted to cry. I deleted the videos. My mom never wanted to be in a picture because she was ashamed of her appearance, even though she was thin and beautiful. I don't want to miss out on those family moments and memories, and I want to feel confident about showing up in those family photos. And I want to make sure I'm modeling healthy attitudes about body image to my kids.

From this story, Lara wrote the following personal value statement:

> To be the best version of myself, to honor my power to determine my health destiny by combatting my genetic risk for diabetes and Alzheimer's disease through a healthy lifestyle, to appreciate life

and people for the gifts that they are, and to help others fully realize their potential in life and health.

Before you embark on this plan, take some time to write your own personal value statement. Think about what you're hoping to achieve — and, most important, *why* these goals matter to you. This values statement will keep you motivated as you embrace this new way of eating and living: and it will be a reminder you can turn to again and again over the coming weeks, whenever you need motivation.

From Dr. Sara's Case Files

Caroline is a forty-four-year-old woman who lost 50 pounds following the Gottfried Protocol. Once I showed her the basics, she was off and running. When I first met her, she was 5 feet, 8 inches tall, and weighed 200 pounds. She lost 35 pounds in her first six months of cycling through the Gottfried Protocol, and 15 more pounds over the next six months. Her main tips for success are to have a freezer full of soups and stews, to make lunch the main meal of the day (and not just a tiny salad, but a satisfying meal with plenty of plant-based fat), and to avoid snacks. Most important were meal prep and storing food in the correct portion sizes. When she fit back into her high school jeans, she explained that her hormones were back on track too: her heavy periods (a sign of estrogen dominance) had resolved, and her night sweats (a sign of insulin block and possibly fluctuating estrogen) had disappeared. She had renewed energy for exercising outside, including jogging with her dog.

HOW FOOD AND HORMONES COMMUNICATE

As we get started on the course for better hormonal and metabolic function, let's connect the dots between your food and your hormones. Once you understand how food directly impacts your hormones (and hence your weight), we will dive into the how-to, and I'll share the four-week hormone reset that has helped hundreds of women take charge of their health. In this next section, you'll get actionable advice and specific dietary guidelines so that you can put your newfound knowledge into practice.

Savory tortilla chips, a freshly baked pastry, and comforting pasta are wildly different foods, right? Not if you ask your hormones or your metabolism. All of those foods, once eaten, turn into pretty much the same thing: processed carbohydrates mixed with fat that hold almost zero nutritional value yet trigger a boatload of inflammation. If I eat one serving of these foods (and it's hard for me to stop at just one), I can guarantee that my weight will be up the next day. For your hormones, these favorite foods transform into something far more sinister—a message that tells your body to store fat.

I know it's not easy to give up some of your favorites—after all, these foods are connected to habit memories. We have emotional and psychological connections with our childhood favorites and our go-to comfort foods. Not to mention that they taste good! Say you are going down the buffet line. Where you expect to see the label "Fettuccine Alfredo," you see one that says "Store-More-Fat-Hormone Pasta." Would you take a serving?

To your hormones, food isn't flavor, texture, and happy memories; to your hormones, food is information. The complex conversation between food and hormones is the main reason why the ketogenic diet works differently for women versus men. In Part 1, you read about how hormones work and how different aspects of food influence them—now is the time to eat in a way that honors and respects these crucial food-hormone connections.

Here's the beautiful part: because food is information, we can use food choices to communicate with our hormones in the way we desire. Once you learn the language of hormones, you'll be able to guide the conversation. If you're carrying extra weight or body fat, it's almost certainly because those hormones have been receiving very little in the way of encouragement. So now we're going to use food to tell them, loud and clear, that this is their time to thrive.

To do this, the Gottfried Protocol progresses through stages, each one allowing more satisfying and less restrictive food selections.

OVERVIEW OF THE FOUR-WEEK GOTTFRIED PROTOCOL

After years of leading women through a ketogenic diet designed to honor their hormones, I realized that most of us need to think of keto as a short-term pulse, not a long-term diet involving lifelong restricted eating. Trial and error have shown that four weeks may be the ideal length for a ketogenic pulse for women. After you complete your first four-week pulse, I'll show you how to rotate in and out of keto, using intermittent fasting and carb cycling so that you can gain all of the hormone benefits of keto without the problems that so many women face. The key point is to commit to four weeks (Prep plus Implementation) of eating in a way that serves you, followed by another phase (Transition) in which we test your carb limit and see your response to immune-triggering foods. Here is the basic time line:

Preparation	Implementation	Transition
20–25 grams of net carbs and detoxification. Keep a ketogenic ratio of 2:1. Get your bowels moving so you can mobilize fat!	20–25 grams net carbs per day, and add intermittent fasting (14/10 to 16/8). Continue a ketogenic ratio of 2:1.	Start to add net carbs slowly, 5 grams at a time, and heading toward a ketogenic ratio of 1:1 for the long term, or until you repeat the diet.

- **Preparation (seven days).** This week sets the foundation for your body to release toxins as the Gottfried Protocol starts melting fat. Toxins are pollutants, synthetic chemicals, heavy metals, and endocrine disruptors that are stored in fat tissue, mess with your hormones, and make you store excess fat. (This release of toxins is one of the reasons why many people feel lousy on traditional ketogenic diets.) To put it less delicately, you must be pooping every day to clear out the toxins and process the healthy fat you'll be burning. You'll take a detox questionnaire to guide you as you improve your detoxification pathways. You'll be eating more of the vegetables known for their toxin-binding capacity, such as bok choy, broccoli, broccoli sprouts, cauliflower, and kale. Along the way, we will wrangle with those fat-storing hormones (such as cortisol, insulin, and leptin), which have been running the show, by introducing intermittent fasting, which is covered in the next chapter. Third, we will jump-start growth hormone, testosterone, and other metabolic hormones by feeding you the dietary sources needed to produce more of them.

- **Implementation (twenty-one days).** This three-week period is designed to trigger weight loss while boosting energy, gut health, and metabolic hormones, so it will include the right amount of slow-burning carbohydrates. The focus will be on dialing in the right amount of variety, nutrient density, and quantity of food for you.

At the end of twenty-eight days, you'll complete a self-assessment to help you adjust the protocol by finding your body's optimal macronutrient balance, which will encourage healthy weight loss.

- **Transition (variable).** Once you've completed the core four-week program, you'll begin the process called Transition. This is when you will slowly add back some key good carbs, in increments of 5 grams every three days. This stage includes additional detoxification support to help your body rid itself of the toxins released from fat over the previous weeks. Most important, Transition is a time of celebrating your new body, the improved communication between your diet and hormones, and even a new set of healthier habit memories. Where's my cheesy zoodle ragu? Yum!

Look, I know this may seem like a lot of detail to keep track of, or it may sound complicated. But don't stress; we will go through this one step at a time. And you'll find that these baby steps add up to major transformation. You might be thinking—can't I just take a drug? Or start peptides to boost my growth hormone? Or take up kickboxing? I wish it were that simple, but the truth is that food is the primary driver of your weight and health. Dial in the food, and we can dial in the weight that is the healthiest for you.

Getting Started in Three Steps

1. Know How Your Hormones React to Your Food
2. Be the Guinea Pig
3. Count Your Macros

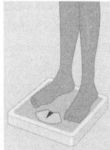

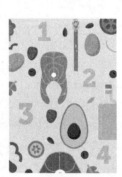

Know How Your Hormones React to Your Food

Be the Guinea Pig

Count Your Macros

THE BASICS, STEP BY STEP

Before we get into the specific foods for each stage, let's consider the basics, one step at a time.

Step 1: Know How Your
Hormones React to Your Food

The first step is to consider how your hormones interpret food as information. The best example is sugar (that is, refined carbohydrate — see the box "Understand Your Macronutrients"), which sends one of two messages. If your hormones determine that your body needs the sugar at that moment, your hormonal system will communicate to your metabolism that the sugar should be packaged up as blood glucose and released into the bloodstream to be burned. However, if your hormones determine that your body doesn't need the sugar (and, by the way, it *never* needs the 152 pounds of table sugar, plus additional refined carbohydrates, that Americans tend to eat each year), your hormonal system will signal to the body's energy-processing system (metabolism) that the sugar (or carbs) should be converted to fat and stored.

Based on this concept, it might seem that if we ate only the amount of sugar and carbs that we need to burn each day, we wouldn't gain weight, right? Energy in, energy out. In a perfectly working body, that would be true, but who has one of those? Many of us have spent a lifetime abusing our hormones with fast-burning carbohydrates, so our systems get stuck in store-the-sugar mode.

The interplay between metabolism, hormones, and food intake is incredibly complex and not well understood, but we do know that certain foods trigger hormonal messages that cause the body to pack on weight — exactly what you don't want. Other foods trigger hormonal messages that tell the body to burn the fat reserves — exactly what you do want. We also know that not everyone responds the same way to food messages; as you learned in Chapter 3, sex and even gender differences can be profound. Not only that, but individual differences owing to genetics, food sensitivities, and toxic load can be even greater. (Regarding genetic response to food, the gene-environment interface can modulate ketones, cholesterol, cognitive function, weight loss, and how you adapt to fat burning, which we will cover later.) The way that food and your body interact is just like conversation: context and audience are everything. Comment to your best friend about your bad boss while exercising at the gym, and you both get a good laugh; say the same thing to your co-workers during a team meeting and you might find yourself looking for a new job.

Understand Your Macronutrients

The Gottfried Protocol is a four-week program with a specific macronutrient pattern: low carbohydrate, moderate protein, and high fat. Carbs, protein, and fat are all different forms of fuel for the body — here's a quick refresher on their functions, along with an overview of targets to hit for success on this plan.

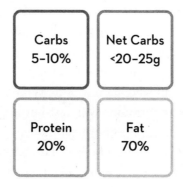

Carbs	Net Carbs
5–10%	<20–25g
Protein	**Fat**
20%	70%

Carbs

- Carbs turn into sugar in your body.
- These nutrients provide 4 calories of energy per 1 gram.
- Your need for carbs depends on your exercise level. For example, women at the higher end of the range, those avid, high-intensity exercisers who work out six hours per week or more, should eat about 35–50 grams of carbs each day.
- Carbs are important! Don't malign them: we need carbs for optimal thyroid and adrenal function. But too much isn't a good thing either. We need to determine your carb limit for

weight loss and hormone balance: high enough to support the thyroid and adrenal glands but low enough to repair your levels of insulin, leptin, growth hormone, and testosterone.

Net Carbs

- Net carbs are simply the carbohydrates absorbed by the body.
- Calculate net carbs for whole foods by taking the total carb count and subtracting the grams of fiber.[7]
- Aim for 25 grams of net carbs each day. This is essential, especially for women, to feed the microbiome and to stay in balance while on a ketogenic diet. (Read more on page 121.)

Protein

- Protein helps build and repair muscle, but it can turn into sugar (via a process called gluconeogenesis) if you eat too much of it.
- It provides 4 calories of energy per 1 gram.
- Aim for 50–75 grams of protein per day. Some of my patients need to remain at the lower end of the limit (50–60 grams) to avoid problems with blood sugar and stay in ketosis.

Fat

- Fat helps you make healthy hormones.
- It provides 9 calories of energy per 1 gram.
- Aim for 60 to 90 grams of healthy fat per day.

Step 2: Be the Guinea Pig

This plan provides a solid framework to follow, but it's also designed for personalization. The key to using the messaging power of food to your advantage is to pay attention to your unique body's response as you use the program. The goal is to learn how to speak to *your* hormones, practicing the principles of precision medicine, in order to lose weight and overcome unhealthy habit memories.

First, we have to reprogram your hormonal messaging system to tell your body to burn fat reserves rather than add to them. This is where personalized nutrition becomes really important—for example, you will define the daily carbohydrate level that works best to support your health. If you have insulin block or carb intolerance, getting the sugar and carbs down will be key to your success. You may not know if these are issues are relevant to you unless you've been previously diagnosed with prediabetes or if you struggle with weight loss (by detecting excess deep belly fat through body composition testing, the lab testing described in the Notes, or stalling in your weight-loss efforts on the Gottfried Protocol.)[8] Many people with insulin block have to temporarily limit even healthy carbs, such as certain fruits and starchy vegetables. We will personalize your intake of protein and fat too, but carbs come first.

Second, we want to measure your results accurately, so you can be accountable to yourself and continue on the path to success. It's all too easy to fall back on subjective measures of progress. For example, here's how my mind works sometimes: If I wear pants that make me feel fat, if I am grumpy after a poor night's sleep, or if I catch a view of myself in the mirror that I don't like, I might be tricked into believing that I have failed at weight loss and come down with a case of the "f*ck its." (More on this in the next chapter.) On the other hand, a flattering comment or a long hike might make me think I deserve to cheat on my program. But if I measure progress through clear metrics, my assessment won't be based on my mood or my clothing choices but on a series of inarguably objective data points. (That's where measuring your progress and personalizing your program come in.)

Before starting the program, measure your waist circumference, hip circumference, and weight. You can then calculate your body mass index (BMI) based on your weight and height—the healthy goal is a BMI of 18.5 to 24.9 m/kg^2. For women who aren't satisfied with this range, I get it: studies show that the ideal BMI of 22–24.9 is associated with the lowest risk of premature mortality.[9] You can also divide waist circumference by hip circumference to get your waist-to-hip ratio. Follow these steps:

- Measure your waist at the height of your belly button.
- Measure your hips by finding the largest circumference while holding the measuring tape level.
- Measure your weight first thing in the morning, on an empty stomach, ideally after you've pooped (that is, completely evacuated your bowels).
- Record these measurements in the "Measuring Success" table. This table includes room for additional stats that you may want to track, such as your net carbs or fasting blood sugar.
  - Your waist-to-hip ratio is your waist circumference (in inches or centimeters) divided by your hip circumference (measured in the same units).
  - You can determine your BMI with a calculator you can find online or with this formula: BMI = weight ÷ height². If you use kilograms and centimeters, you have your result. If you use pounds and inches, you need to multiply the result by 703. (See Notes for more details, including an online calculator.)[10] For example, for a woman who weighs 155 pounds with a height of 5 feet 4 inches (64 inches total), BMI = $(155 ÷ 64^2) \times 703 = 26.6$ m/kg².
  - Your metabolotype may vary over time. If your waist-to-hip ratio is greater than 0.85 (the measure is 0.9 for men), you have an apple metabolotype. If your waist measures 2 inches or more than your hips measure, you are definitely an apple. If your hips are larger than your waist and your BMI is 25 or greater, there's a good chance you have a pear metabolotype. If your BMI is less than 20 and your waist measures less than your hips, there's a good chance you have a celery metabolotype. (Bust size, whether large or small, doesn't really matter in terms of metabolism. We are primarily interested in your waist-to-hip measurement.) Write your metabolotype in the space provided in the table — it may change over the four weeks of the program!

Measuring Success: Before and After Measurements

	Before	After
Waist (inches or centimeters)		
Hips (inches or centimeters		
Weight (pounds or kilograms)		
Waist-to-hip ratio (WHR)		
Body mass index (BMI)		
Metabolotype		
Other		

For more advanced measurements, see the Notes.[11]

Finally, "being the guinea pig" means testing whether you're making ketones. As you'll learn in the next chapter, it's the best way to measure your success with getting into ketosis.

Step 3: Count Your Macros

This part gets confusing for a lot of people, so let's make it as painless as possible. I'm going to teach you how to count your macros in a foolproof way (refer back to "Understand Your Macronutrients" on page 106). Then, after you complete the four-week program and enter Transition, you'll have the high fat and moderate protein dialed in, so you can simply track your net carbs going forward and define your personal limit.

I know this seems like a lot of work, but trust me: it's worth the investment. I failed keto until I took these steps and followed them carefully. Then I taught other women, such as Amy, how to do it too.

The key is to figure out the ketogenic ratio of your diet, so that you can reset your hormones. (And remember, this diet has been specifically designed for women's unique needs.) I'm going to walk you through the formula to calculate the ketogenic ratio over the next pages, but don't stress if this seems overly complicated at first. To make it easier, the specific food details in this chapter include sample meals!

Learning how to count macros is the best way to make sure your diet is activating ketones and improving your hormonal balance. You'll be shifting what you eat away from refined carbohydrates and toward healthy fats and certain proteins, which will increase the ketogenicity of your food—meaning that your body's ability to make ketones will improve because of the foods you eat.

Here's the basic formula for the ketogenic ratio:[12]

$$\text{Ketogenic Ratio} = \frac{\text{ketogenic factors}}{\text{anti-ketogenic factors}} = \frac{\text{fat (grams)}}{\text{carbs (grams) + protein (grams)}}$$

I want you to eat a ketogenic ratio of 2 ketogenic factors to 1 anti-ketogenic factor. That means you'll eat 2 grams of fat for every 1 gram of carbohydrate and protein combined. Most therapeutic applications of the ketogenic diet (such as those used for treatment of epilepsy) are more aggressive, asking for a ketogenic ratio of 4:1. That's tough to do if you want to eat a nutritionally sound food plan that includes vegetables; it requires a diet that is 90 percent fat and 10 percent a combination of protein and carbohydrates. I find that this type of keto diet may be too severe for many women.

Let's see what this looks like in real life. Say you are having scrambled eggs with spinach for breakfast. Here's how you calculate your ratio: 2 eggs contain about 12 grams of protein and 10 grams of fat. So you scramble 2 eggs in a pan with 1 tablespoon of olive oil (14 grams of fat) and add ¼ cup of spinach (contains less than ¼ gram of protein, less than ¼ gram of carbs, and less than ¼ gram of fiber — I'm going to call that a wash, or "0"). So the net, if you add these together, is 24 grams of fat in your scrambled eggs, with 12 grams of protein and carbs. That's 24:12, or the 2:1 ratio that we are seeking.

$$\text{Ketogenic Ratio} = \frac{\substack{\text{ketogenic factors} \\ \text{24 (fat from the eggs and oil)}}}{\substack{\text{anti-ketogenic factors} \\ \text{12 (protein from the eggs)}}} = \frac{\substack{\text{fat (grams)} \\ 2}}{\substack{\text{carbs (grams) + protein (grams)} \\ 1}}$$

Protein is more complicated. As you know, when the body gets more protein than it needs, the liver converts the extra protein into glucose in a process called gluconeogenesis. That's why the Gottfried Protocol is a *moderate protein* diet. (Read more details in the Notes.)[13]

This ratio will work if you follow an important rule: *you must not eat excess calories.* We all know that calories are not the only important part of a diet, but if you want to burn the fat you've stored at your waist, you need to follow the ketogenic ratio and make sure you don't eat more calories than you expend.[14] Fortunately, I can help you with that by specifying portion sizes with sample meals. I also provide more information on how to troubleshoot and avoid pitfalls in this chapter and the next.

You'll stick with this ketogenic ratio of 2:1 for three weeks, and then we will back off to a ketogenic ratio of 1:1 for the final week as we transition to a balanced low-carb food plan.

Read on for my goof-proof rules.

THE DO'S AND DON'TS OF COUNTING YOUR MACROS

I'm going to make calculating the macronutrients (macros) of the ketogenic diet ridiculously simple. You have three main macros: fat, protein, and carbohydrates. We'll start with fat.

- **Do eat healthy fat.** Fat is the most calorie-dense of the macronutrients. Each gram of fat contains 9 calories, but not all sources of fat are created equal. There is still a lot of debate about the health benefits of saturated fat, so I want you to focus primarily on eating plant-based sources of fat, listed on page 117, and to limit saturated fat from animal sources.
- **Do eat moderate amounts of protein.** Each gram of protein contains 4 calories. You need to limit protein so that you stay in a ketogenic ratio of 2:1. See page 120 for healthy protein choices.
- **Do eat limited carbohydrates.** Each gram of carbohydrate has 4 calories, but once again, not all carbs are created equal. There is an optimal number of carbs that will allow you to lose weight, and we want to stay under it. This threshold is your *personal carb limit.* You can define it through trial and error, or you can take my advice (based on helping patients for the past thirty years), and stick to a limit of 20 to 25 grams of net carbs per day. (Not surprisingly, this is the same amount of net carbs that has been found to be the limit for healthy ketosis dating back to the 1970s.)[15] Most people who start a classic ketogenic diet restrict carbs (especially nonstarchy fibrous vegetables) too much, and the result is that their fiber count drops severely, from an average

of 28 grams to 6 grams per day.[16] Most keto programs use total carbs instead of net carbs, and usually aim for 20 to 35 grams per day. But that doesn't work for most women: we need fiber to support our hormones, especially estrogen and insulin, in order to keep them working best for weight loss. That's why it's important to learn how to track your net carbs each day.

- **Do limit net carbs to less than 25 grams per day.** Net carbs are the carbohydrates that are absorbed by the body. To calculate the net carbs in whole foods, subtract the grams of fiber from the total number of grams of carbs. I want you to limit processed foods, but even I eat them occasionally. (See examples in the Notes.)[17] NOTE: Your goal from Day 1 through Day 28 is to keep your net carbs below 25 grams per day. Practice this by recording your net carbs before Day 1 on your tracker, so you get the hang of it. To implement this strategy, plan ahead. Don't make the mistake of eating a meal and then checking the macros afterward — it's too late. Plan your menu a day in advance, and calculate the macros ahead of time. Say I plan to eat Avo Toast (see recipe on page 204). I'll toast one piece of keto bread (4 net carbs), mash one-third of an avocado (1 net carb), schmear it on the bread, and then drizzle 1 tablespoon of olive oil over top. The meal, a common breakfast for me, has a total of 5 net carbs and keeps me full for four to five hours.

- **Don't drink alcohol on Days 1 through 28.** I think of alcohol as liquid sugar. Women can't tolerate alcohol as well as men; they develop alcohol-related health problems at lower doses than men do. Alcohol interferes with the metabolism of estrogen and increases the risk of breast cancer.[18] And skipping your glass of wine may do more for your mental health than drinking it, according to a study published in 2019.[19] Alcohol has 7 calories per gram, so it's more calorie-dense than protein or carbs. Here's worse news: if you're carb intolerant, alcohol will kick you out of ketosis. *Alcohol blocks fat burning.* And that same quality that makes you feel more relaxed makes you more prone to second-guess your commitment and eat off the plan. If you are serious about weight loss, stay away from alcohol for at least three weeks. You can add it back during Transition if you must, and then you can see if you can stay in ketosis and continue to lose weight. If introducing alcohol causes a plateau in weight loss, back off from the sauce.

Here is a cheat sheet you can use to plan every meal during your first four weeks:

- Minimum fat: 20–40 grams
- Maximum protein: 10–20 grams
- Maximum net carbs (total carbs less total fiber): 7–10 grams, but less is preferable

If you are carb intolerant or insulin resistant, you may need to keep your carb limit even lower. (I cover this topic in the next chapter, where we talk about troubleshooting.) How do you know? Your waist is 35 inches or more as a woman, or 40 inches or more as a man. You are hungry most of the time because your appetite hormones are confused. Fat burning is close to impossible, and you are resistant to weight loss.

From Dr. Sara's Case Files

"Thank you! I loved this program. It was a keto jumpstart for me. I've always wanted to try keto, and now I did. I lost 6 pounds [in the first ten days] on the program (and I didn't even work out because I am nursing an injury). Thank you!"
— *Amy, age forty-two and member of our online Gottfried Protocol Program*

BECOME A BELIEVER (AND A TRACKER)

Let's say somebody came up to you and said, "I'll bet you $1,000,000 that you won't lose weight if you replace your rice crackers, granola bars, bagels, and pasta with bacon, avocados, cheese, and eggs."

Would you take the bet?

There was a time I wouldn't have, but now I would.

By the time you finish reading this chapter, I'm thinking you'll take that bet too. You now understand about restricting carbs the right way (that is, not dropping them too low and making sure they are the slow-burning type found in certain vegetables and a limited range of fruits). Putting this knowledge into action will allow your body to switch from burning sugar to burning fat as fuel. This produces ketones, which are especially supportive of brain function and stable energy for women over the age of thirty-five, when they start to hit early perimenopause.

I know this might feel like a lot of information to process, but I promise you, the hormone corrections and the pounds lost on the scale will make it worth this investment in your health. While attaining a healthy weight is important, it's not the only goal — we want to get you to a place of happier hormones, improved gut function, lower inflammation, restful sleep, more energy, and clearer thinking.

For the next four weeks, think of your food as a way for you to talk with your body. You're going to become fluent in the language of your hormones. The first word in this language is *fat,* the good kind. We're going to fight fire with fire or, more precisely, we're going to fight fat with fat.

Preparation	Implementation	Transition
20–25 grams of net carbs and detoxification. Keep a ketogenic ratio of 2:1. Get your bowels moving so you can mobilize fat!	20–25 grams net carbs per day, and add intermittent fasting (14/10 to 16/8). Continue a ketogenic ratio of 2:1.	Start to add net carbs slowly, 5 grams at a time, and heading toward a ketogenic ratio of 1:1 for the long term, or until you repeat the diet.

The Gottfried Protocol Timeline

FROM MACROS TO MEALS: WHAT TO EAT ON THE GOTTFRIED PROTOCOL, AND WHY

Okay, now you've got the basics down — but how do they translate to your plate and what you eat each day?

The Gottfried Protocol Loves Healthy Fat

Many of the hormones that we are trying to balance by means of the Gottfried Protocol are derived from cholesterol (a type of bodily fat found in all cells), so it makes sense that fat communicates best with your hormones. On the Gottfried Protocol, 60 to 70 percent of your diet will come from fat, mostly from plant-based sources, so it is critical to include fats with each meal. Eating more fat means you'll feel more satisfied (so you'll be more likely to stick with the program and not cheat). But keep in mind that fat is not "one size fits all." Some of my patients can have 2 tablespoons of coconut oil per day, and others hit a weight-loss plateau with that much saturated fat. Just as with carbs, when it comes to fat, you have to be the guinea pig and see what works best for you. Experiment with the following foods to expand your repertoire of healthy fats:

- **Avocado.** Sliced and placed on a salad, with lime juice drizzled over the top, or whipped as a base for creamy keto smoothies, avocados are a nutritional powerhouse. But before you go avo crazy, see How to Rock the Guac (page 124) for guidance on how much to enjoy.
- **Chocolate and cocoa.** You can have limited amounts of dark chocolate (90 percent cocoa solids or higher allowed), but consider going broader and using pure cocoa as a spice in savory dishes such as Mexican mole — delicious as a sauce for meat dishes.
- **Coconut.** Use 1 tablespoon per day of coconut oil during the twenty-eight-day program. See how you respond to it. In one study, coconut oil increased inflammation, as measured by blood

levels of something called endotoxin, whereas fish oil and cod
liver oil decreased inflammation, and the effect of olive oil was
neutral.[20] This is a great example of precision medicine — we
need to understand what works best for you by finding the oils
that reduce your inflammation.

- **Olive oil.** Use organic extra-virgin olive oil, and add it to
  virtually any dish. One of my mentors, Mark Houston, MD,
  recommends 5 tablespoons per day.

- **Nuts.** The best ketogenic varieties are macadamia nuts, walnuts,
  almonds, and pecans. Limit nuts to one serving, or 28 grams,
  per day. The heart-healthy and cancer-preventing benefits
  come at a dose of 12–30 grams per day, so take care not to eat
  too many.[21] For susceptible people, nuts can irritate the gut and
  trigger inflammation, owing to compounds like phytates and
  tannins, which can make them difficult to digest. You may notice
  gas, discomfort, or bloating after eating them. If you have an
  intolerance to nuts, skip them.

- **Seeds.** Sunflower, pumpkin, sesame, hemp, and flax — add these
  seeds to salads and other meals for a tasty crunch that is sure to
  satisfy some of those old habit memories.

- **Medium-chain triglyceride oil.** Take inspiration from Jen and
  add MCT to salads, smoothies, and vegetable dishes. Why?
  MCTs are a form of saturated fatty acid that is missing from
  the modern diet and has been shown to improve cholesterol
  profiles and to lower levels of fasting glucose and diastolic blood
  pressure.[22] Because it is efficiently used as energy, it is less likely
  to be stored as fat, so it can help support your weight-loss goals.[23]
  Specifically, taking MCT may help you eat less for the next forty-
  eight hours.[24] (More scientific details are in the Notes.)[25] Most
  women can tolerate ½ to 2 tablespoons per day. Too much may
  trigger diarrhea or make weight loss stall because of the caloric
  density. Personally, I aim for 1 tablespoon (20 grams) to 1.5
  tablespoon (30 grams) per day in my shake or salad — 30 grams
  is the dose with the most positive proven effects.

One note of caution: As you start to plan your meals, the most important thing to keep in mind is to avoid that deadliest combination —high fat together with high carbs. This duo can increase inflammation, block insulin, and add to stored fat. Scientific studies show that a meal which includes saturated and trans fats, paired with refined carbohydrates, raises alarm bells in the body and significantly increases the risk of cardiovascular disease.[26] For the nerds like me who like to know more, this mechanism is described in greater detail in the Notes.[27]

Your Daily Dose of Nuts

Nuts are brimming with vitamins, minerals, unsaturated fat, and antioxidants. They mostly consist of fat (about 50 to 75 percent), with a moderate amount of protein, making them an ideal keto food on the run. Research shows that people who eat their daily ounce of nuts (28 grams) minimize certain health risks: a 29 percent reduced risk of heart disease, a 24 percent lower likelihood of death from respiratory disease, and an 11 percent lower likelihood of death from cancer, according to the *New England Journal of Medicine.*[28]

Nuts are also dense in calories, so we need to get the dose right: high enough to reduce your risk of disease and support your transition to ketosis, but low enough that you aren't getting too many calories or irritating your gut.

Here is a rough guideline for that daily ounce:

- 30 pistachios
- 20 almonds
- 20 hazelnuts
- 15 macadamias
- 15 pecans
- 9 walnuts
- 2 tablespoons of pine nuts

Eat Protein
in Moderation

We've talked a lot about why you need to avoid excess protein; protein should make up 20 percent of your daily calories, but not all protein is created equal. Eating a factory-farmed beefsteak and its constituent inflammatory hormones, antibiotics, xenoestrogens, arachidonic acids, and omega-6 fats sends a fire-alarm message of inflammation to your hormones. Eating a grass-fed bison steak, with its clean protein and omega-3 fats, fuels your body and your hormones in a healthy way. In my opinion, the two meats shouldn't even be considered part of the same food group.

It is especially important to choose organic protein whenever possible because toxins that are rampant in conventionally raised meat confuse hormonal signaling, getting in the way of the clear message you're trying to send to your hormones during the Gottfried Protocol. Organic vegetables tend to have about 30 percent less pesticide residue[29] and reduce your exposure to antibiotic-resistant bacteria by a third, compared to conventional varieties. Good protein choices include the following items (in order of preference, starting with plants):

- Nuts (macadamia nuts, walnuts; see the list in "Your Daily Dose of Nuts").
- Seeds (pumpkin, flax, hemp).
- Eggs (from cage-free chickens).
- Wild-caught fish (varieties that are low in heavy metals, such as salmon, mackerel, sardines, trout).
- Shellfish (crab, mussels, oysters, scallops, shrimp).
- Free-range poultry (higher in omega-3 fats), preferably dark meat, with skin on.
- Organ meats (from free-range, grass-fed sources).
- Grass-fed beef and wild game (maximum of twice per week), including beef jerky with no added sugar.

- Pork (free of antibiotics and hormones, at a maximum of twice per week — avoid if weight increases) — choose pork chops, pork ribs, and pork rinds (I add chopped pork rinds to my salads as an alternative to croutons).

Understand Carbs:
The Body's False Energy

Carbohydrates are likely today's most confusing dietary element, trumping even cholesterol in the mixed-message department. Carbohydrates are a critical part of a diet that ensures optimal human function; however, for the past century, with the invention of factory food, carbohydrates all too often form the basis of an entire day's food plan. We've been drowning in carbohydrates, so our hormones are dismally out of balance. Their only recourse, when presented with another load of carbohydrates, is to tell the body to convert it to sugar and store it.

One reason for the carbohydrate confusion is that carbohydrates include a huge range of foods: everything from organic squash to angel food cake. And there are vast, contradictory messages about what to do with carbs. Ask a hundred nutritionists, and you'll get a wide spectrum of answers.

The Dietary Guidelines for Americans recommends that people consume 300 grams of carbs per day. I find this WAY off the mark for most people, particularly women over the age of thirty-five, who have waning levels of testosterone and growth hormone. Your optimal carb levels largely depend on the message you want to send to your hormones, your activity level, and whether you are male or female. Even the diet with the strongest scientific proof for preventing heart disease — the Mediterranean diet — recommends that 25–50 percent of daily calories come from carbohydrates. For an 1,800-calorie-per-day diet, that's 112 to 225 grams of carbohydrates, which is still too high. No wonder I started gaining weight on a Medi diet after age thirty-five!

The variance in carbohydrate recommendations doesn't mean they're all always wrong. If you're riding in the Tour de France and burning 5,000 calories each day, 300 grams will provide only about half of what you need. However, if you're like most Americans, living on highly processed simple carbohydrates laced with toxins for most of your life and eating more than you burn, you may need to reboot your daily carb consumption at an order of magnitude well below what the Dietary Guidelines recommend. After extensive research and experience with helping my patients work on weight loss, I find that a temporarily restrictive approach to carbohydrates, starting with 35–50 grams per day, and a maximum of 25 net carbs, is most effective.

What do 25 grams of net carbohydrate look like? When it comes to carbohydrate-dense grains, it's about the equivalent of a small pancake, ¾ of a cup of cooked pasta or rice, or most of a small bagel. My friend Jo, who loves carbs, asked me: did I mean individually or all together? Sorry, Jo: individually. Each of these options, too small to be satisfying, would complete your daily limit, so it's best to avoid them on the four-week program. Carbs also hide in sugars — ½ cup of sorbet or 1 cup of ice cream contains about 30 grams of carbs. (I know, right? We spent all those years opting for sorbet instead of ice cream to be healthier, yet as it turns out, sorbet has double the carbs!) You'll feel fuller from eating up to 30 grams of vegetables containing carbohydrates, which translates to about 8 cups of broccoli or cauliflower.

You're going to reduce carbohydrates over the short term, but increase fiber in order to beat your fat hormones and improve fat loss. Lowering net carbohydrates is the best method to reset your hormones — and we will do it by gently fasting and detoxifying, a topic we'll cover in the next chapter.

Go Big on Veggies, Small on Fruit

The Protocol calls for myriad vegetables prepared with olive oil, but since we're limiting carbohydrates, particularly during the four-week program of the Gottfried Protocol, avoid starchy vegetables, including potato, corn, peas, winter squash, turnips, and beets. These can be reintroduced during the Transition phase.

For other vegetables, eat both raw and cooked varieties (cooking makes some nutrients more bioavailable, while destroying others), and prioritize vegetables that assist with detoxification, such as these:

- Leafy greens (arugula, kale, Swiss chard, collard greens, spinach, lettuces).
- Cauliflower, bok choy, broccoli, brussels sprouts, asparagus, bell peppers, onions, garlic, eggplant, cucumber, celery, summer squashes, zucchini, radishes, cabbages.
- Mushrooms.
- Limited starchy vegetables: jicama, pumpkin, winter squash during the Transition phase.

Sugars lurk in fruits in the form of fructose, so avoid most fruits during the four-week program. That said, certain fruits are lower in net carbs than others and are okay to include in small portions. (When you transition to eating more carbs during Transition, you can try adding small portions of low-glycemic fruits such as berries.) Gottfried Protocol–friendly fruits include these:

- Lemons.
- Limes.
- Olives.
- Tomatoes.
- Avocados. (Note that avocado is listed as a healthy fat, yet it's a fruit. See "How to Rock the Guac" so you don't get too much. The right amount for one serving is somewhere between ¼ and ½ of an avocado for most of my patients until they reach their weight goal.)

Use Dairy with Care

Although dairy can be a significant source of healthy fat, there are reasons to use restraint. Some dairy products are high in natural lactose sugar. In randomized trials, increased dairy consumption is not associated with weight loss unless calories are decreased,[30] which usually occurs on a ketogenic diet because it is more satisfying and does result in weight loss. Calories matter, but hormones may matter more. Calories are less of a priority than getting your hormones back in balance. That means you can consume dairy, but not with abandon. Provided you are not dairy sensitive (that is, intolerant of casein, the main protein in milk) or lactose intolerant, and the dairy product is organic and sourced from grass-fed cows, you may include these healthy sources of fat:

- Butter.
- Hard cheeses.
- Other sugar-free and low-lactose dairy products.

Avoid high-lactose dairy products, including milk and ice cream.

How to Rock the Guac

Before you whip up an avocado smoothie with a side of avocado slices dipped in guacamole, consider this: when I was trying keto for the first time to get back to an optimal weight, I overindulged in avocado, thinking it was a healthy fat that could be eaten without limit. Avocado is good for you, but only if eaten in the right amounts. Keep in mind that a whole avocado contains a significant amount of fat *and* carbs, so limit the amount to ¼ to ½ avocado per day. I'd rather have you eat a variety of diverse foods than use most of your daily carb allowance on avocado.

Nutrition information on the California Avocados website is based on the FDA-selected portion size for the food (⅓ of a medium avocado).[31] Since it's really easy to eat a whole avocado if you're not careful, this avocado nutrition table is adjusted for a whole medium-sized avocado, so you can see what you're getting if you do overindulge:

By the numbers, if you eat a whole avocado, you're consuming a third of your daily carb allowance, which doesn't leave much room for other nutritious carbohydrate foods. Be careful with avocado, at least until you've reached your healthy weight goal, which for most of my patients means achieving a BMI between 20 and 24.9.

AVOCADO NUTRITION FACTS

One medium avocado contains 3 servings

Total fat	24 g
Saturated fat	3 g
Trans fat	0 g
Polyunsaturated fat	3 g
Monounsaturated fat	15 g
Cholesterol	0 g
Sodium	0 g
Total carbohydrate	12 g
Dietary fiber	9 g
Total sugar	0 g
Added sugars	0 g
Net carbohydrates	3 g
Protein	3 g

GET SPICY

It's been said that variety is the spice of life, and any nutrition plan will be more successful if it includes more palate-pleasing options. With that in mind, consider the following ways to add variety and flavor to your diet while still speaking the language of hormones:

- Dark chocolate (90 percent cocoa solids or higher).
- Unsweetened vinegars.
- Unsweetened coffee and tea.
- Unsweetened mustards.
- Spices: ginger, garlic, cayenne pepper, turmeric, cardamom, chili, fennel.
- Herbs: rosemary, parsley, cilantro, red clover, burdock root.

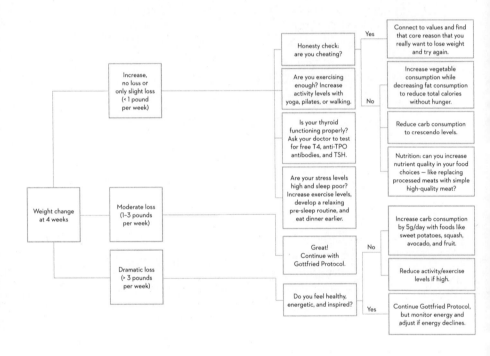

SUGAR: THE WRONG
HORMONAL MESSAGE

You know how fickle communication can be in a relationship, right? You say the right words twenty times in a row, and everything is flourishing. But then you slip up, say the wrong thing once, all hell breaks loose, and you destroy all the goodness. If the relationship has been solid for many years, it can handle the damage. However, if you slip up during those first few months of dating, it can spell the end.

Hormonal communication is no different. If you have a long history of supporting your hormones, a little sugar isn't going to hurt. But if you're like most women, and your metabolic hormones have been battered for decades by excess sugars, stress, and toxins, they need a good long stretch of virtuous communication. Think of the four-week Gottfried Protocol like those first delicate but thrilling months in a new relationship — don't send the wrong message.

With that in mind, here is the most destructive word in the language of the Gottfried Protocol: *sugar!*

I know I'm not the first to tell you sugar is bad, but when it comes to metabolic hormones, sugar is worse than you probably realize. Growth hormone is the ultimate metabolic hormone, and sugar is poison for it. Is it really that bad? Maybe even worse. Growth hormone improves insulin action,[32] and while clinical growth hormone deficiency is considered a rare condition, even minor alterations of growth hormone secretion are associated with metabolic and growth disorders.[33] When it comes to control of blood sugar, growth hormone does a job similar to that of cortisol and insulin,[34] but it does not cause the imbalances associated with these other two more famous hormones. Insulin and cortisol are aggressive and powerful, and they can overshoot easily, whereas growth hormone is more of a sensitive, New Age, likes-to-snuggle type. If you overload your system with sugar and stress, like so many of us do every day of our lives, cortisol and insulin dominate the dance floor while growth hormone plays wallflower.

This means you can't optimize growth hormone if you're indulging in double chocolate brownies, raising your blood sugar and inviting insulin to rise excessively. Dance with insulin for too long, and other hormones like growth hormone lose hope and become out of balance as your waist measurement expands. In healthy people, insulin blocks the release of growth hormone, and the hormone disruption may be even worse for people with obesity.[35] Eliminate added sugar from your diet, limit natural sugar, and, for the Preparation and Implementation phases of the Gottfried Protocol, avoid even seemingly healthy higher-sugar-content whole foods like bananas, grapes, and many other fruits. If you're insulin resistant, consider limiting these foods over the long term, until your insulin is repaired. Focus instead on healthy fats, anti-inflammatory proteins, and high-fiber foods like leafy greens and low-glycemic fruits (avocados, olives, coconut).

Sugar hides everywhere, so avoiding it isn't easy. During the four-week Gottfried Protocol, avoid sugar, even in its so-called healthy forms as listed here:

- Whole and refined grains and flour products.
- Added and natural sugars in food and beverages.
- Starchy vegetables like potatoes, corn, and winter squash. (Potatoes and squash can be added in limited amounts, such as 1–2 ounces, in the Transition phase.)
- Fruits other than those on the allowed list, unless factored into daily total carb consumption.
- All fruit juices.
- Legumes, including beans, lentils, and peanuts.
- Alcohol.

WHAT DOES A MEAL WITH 70 PERCENT FAT LOOK LIKE?

Before we get into the meal possibilities, consider this: there are two ways to look at the question of what a meal with 70 percent fat looks like. First, what does it look like on the table, and second, what does it look like on you? The second part is maybe the more important, so I want to give you an objective data point from which to watch improvement happen: weight and waist circumference. And I'm going to start by giving you a lesson in how to properly collect these data points.

INTEGRATION:
GET YOUR DETOX ON

Why do the Preparation and Transition stages of the Gottfried Protocol include detoxification? Because detoxification and weight loss are inseparable, particularly for women. Detoxification is commonly the missing piece when it comes to creating a hormone-balancing ketogenic diet.

Fat is where the body squirrels away toxins (remember obesogens like BPA, the artificial chemicals that disrupt hormones and contribute to obesity?) when the natural detoxification system exceeds capacity. As fat is burned, the toxins are released into the bloodstream to be broken down and eliminated from the body; during rapid weight loss, the rate of toxins released from fat accelerates.[36] We need a way to keep removing the toxins, especially when more get released during weight loss. (I share more advanced detox strategies in Chapter 6 for people with stubborn weight gain.)

The Three Phases of Detoxification

The body handles detoxification in three distinct phases: in phase one, the liver uses enzymes to break down harmful substances into a state that the body can handle; in phase two, the now-separate components of the compound are made soluble in water; and in phase three, they are eliminated from the body via urine, feces, or sweat. If you want to learn more about the phases of detox, refer to the Notes.[37] We will be focusing on phase three, so that you can promptly get rid of toxins released from fat.

To accomplish this goal, we'll use foods that bolster detox capacity. Despite being touted as a tool for weight loss, some food-detox programs have not demonstrated lasting results, but I'm going to show you how to do it correctly, so that you don't regain the weight.[38] That's why I've combined detoxification with ketogenic recommendations in a gentle, staged process. Look for opportunities to consume the following foods:

- **Clean, lean protein.** Without sufficient dietary protein, your liver cannot complete phase two detoxification, during which toxins are excreted.
- **Foods rich in fiber.** Among its many roles, fiber binds BPA and other toxins, helping your body excrete them. Smart high-fiber choices include avocados, olives, and nonstarchy vegetables. You can add supplemental fiber to shakes (see the Recipes). In the Transition phase of the Protocol, you can add back organic berries (no more than ¼ cup serving per day) and legumes (only in small portions, and none at all until the end of Implementation).
- **Foods rich in sulfur.** Detoxification pathways require this mineral, which is abundant in cruciferous veggies (broccoli and cauliflower among them, especially broccoli sprouts), onions, barnyard eggs, and garlic.
- **Healthy fat.** Inflammation forces your body to hoard toxins and contributes to nearly every disease on the planet. Wild-caught fish and flaxseed or chia seeds are among the many anti-inflammatory fatty foods that help your body detoxify.
- **Filtered water.** Among its many duties, water helps eliminate toxins and boosts cellular energy, tissue structure, and nutrient processing. Choose filtered water (use a simple carbon filter or get more fancy with reverse osmosis) so you're not flooding your body with more pollutants, like the heavy metals and other potentially harmful substances common in tap water. Drink more than you did before starting the diet because we are here to *change things* in your body. Further, dehydration is one of the two most common complications of the ketogenic diet (the other is gastrointestinal upset) during the first month.[39] You should hydrate like an athlete, particularly during the first two to three weeks. Increased hydration will support detoxification and reduce the issues known to be associated with ketogenic diets and other weight-loss programs, while giving you the best chance of sustaining the benefits of the program over time. Add electrolytes to your

water (see my favorite keto-friendly brands in the Resources). Aim for 60 or more ounces per day of filtered water, which will make you get up to urinate once an hour.

ADJUST FOR YOUR METABOLOTYPE

As mentioned in Chapter 4, whether you have an apple or pear metabolotype, there is a way to personalize the Gottfried Protocol for you. Women with an apple metabolotype need more detoxification, fewer carbs (at least temporarily, for four weeks), and deeper ketosis (by which you produce significant amounts of ketones, measured as greater than 1.0 mmol/L in the blood). (In the next chapter, you will learn how to check for ketosis.) Be sure to follow the basic guidelines for detoxification in this chapter as well as the more advanced strategies described in Chapter 6. Aim for 20 grams or fewer net carbs per day to start. Add intermittent fasting, with the goal of a fourteen-hour overnight fast starting twice per week.

Pears can get away with lighter ketosis (in which the body is producing ketones from burning fat in smaller quantities, measured at 0.5–1.0 mmol/L in the blood) but respond well to intermittent fasting. Try consuming 25 or fewer net carbs per day, and add intermittent fasting every night for fourteen hours. This is particularly helpful for women over forty who are in perimenopause or menopause and feel like all their fat migrated to their hips and butt.

This customization, together with the troubleshooting suggestions and plateau busters in the next chapter, provide powerful tools to help you progress toward wellness.

A SAMPLE DAY ON
THE GOTTFRIED PROTOCOL

Making more food at home will give you the greatest success with weight loss. Eating out is associated with diabetes and weight gain,[40] so do your best to curb the dine-in or take-out habit and replace it with nutritious homemade meals. Not a cook? No need to stress. I will show you how to become a master of meal assembly.

On Day 1, you'll eat 70 percent fat and limit your carbs to a huge salad. In the next two chapters, we'll get into each phase of the Gottfried Protocol in detail, but for now, here are some examples of what meals might look like at the breakfast table, at both a sit-down lunch and a grab-and-go quick one, and at dinner, including an out-on-thetown evening of fine dining and a home-cooked meal.

Breakfast

Sit down: Keto granola with coconut milk (2 net carbs total, in grams).

On the run: Avocado on keto toast (6 net carbs). (See recipe for Avo Toast, page 204.)

Lunch

Home cooked: 6 ounces brussels sprouts sautéed with 3 ounces grass-fed brisket, and a small side salad with detoxifying greens such as watercress and broccoli sprouts.

On the run: By the start of Implementation, you'll have a soup to grab from the freezer. When you're starting the Protocol, try to avoid fast food, but if you have no other option, here are a few suggestions. Get a salad with guacamole and your choice of protein from Chipotle Mexican Grill (they have a keto salad listed under their lifestyle bowls — but avoid tortillas, tortilla chips, and corn). Or get a burger wrapped in lettuce and skip the french fries.

Dinner

Home cooked: 6 ounces mashed cauliflower with turkey meatballs and truffle oil, plus a side salad.

On the town: A wide range of meals can fit the plan if you tiptoe around the carbs and low-quality fats. Ask for salad, a side of avocado, or steamed nonstarchy vegetables (I usually order a "double") as a substitute for the carbs. Ask for a side of olive oil and fresh lemon for salad dressing. Avoid dessert, sauces, and glazes, and always ask if sugar is used in the preparation of a dish.

See Chapter 9 for more than sixty Gottfried Protocol recipes, along with Seven-Day Meal Plans for a variety of dietary preferences, including vegetarian and vegan. See Resources for product recommendations.

Dr. Sara's Secret Keto Weapon: Soups

Soups add diversity, comfort, and convenient nutrition to a ketogenic diet. They make great leftovers for a meal the next day or a grab-and-go lunch pulled from the freezer. When you are wringing your hands because you're tired and can't think of what to eat for dinner, you'll be happy that you made a batch of Chicken-Ginger Soup, Tofu Masala Soup, Creamy Goddess Greens Soup, or a simple vegetable soup. Just pull a jar out and defrost it.

My other favorites are a keto version of the hearty Greek meal-in-a-bowl called Avgolemono (chicken soup with lemon and riced cauliflower), chicken zoodle soup, and in the summer, Gazpacho — mine is heavy on the cucumbers and avocado. You'll find these recipes and more in Chapter 9, along with time-saving tips and suggested products that will make meal prep manageable and the results delicious.

I cook my soup bases on Sunday, and stock the refrigerator and freezer for the week. Get creative with nonstarchy vegetables in a base of bone broth or vegetable broth. When you reheat the base, add fish, shellfish, meat, more vegetables, and extra-virgin olive oil.

FINAL SENDOFF:
IT'S ONLY FOUR WEEKS!

At this point, you may be thinking that it's all too much—you just want to eat a cupcake and call it a day. Don't put off your health and hormones for another minute. Yes, this plan is asking you to change the way you eat. And yes, you will need a high level of precision to hit the right ketogenic ratio. Don't let this worry you. Remember: we are talking about only four weeks, and I'm providing you with all of the support you need for success.

Before you panic and reminisce about all of the food habit memories you can't enjoy anymore, I have good news: I provide a hormone-benefiting version of each of these carb-laden treats. We will swap the chips for keto crackers, lose the croissant but enjoy keto bread with nut butter, and swap pasta for shirataki noodles (made from Japanese konjac root, with zero net carbs). Over the past few years, I've found the swaps that satisfy my cravings without telling my hormones to nosedive, and I'm so excited to share them with you.

Now you understand that if your hormones aren't balanced, no amount of dieting or exercise will work. And now you know what to do to fix it. Following the steps and the macros that we cover in this chapter and applying it to your next meal is your first big leap into getting your hormones back on track, by getting your food on board. Balanced hormones + less hunger = weight loss. Let's do this!

Highlights

- ▸ Get your food to send the right information to your hormones.
- ▸ Don't let habit memories bring you down. Replace unhealthy habit memories with keto swaps that will form new, health-supporting habit memories (see Resources for more ideas).
- ▸ Familiarize yourself with the three steps — understand the hormone-food connection, be the guinea pig, and count your macros — before you begin Day 1.

▶ Remember: we are pulsing to a ketogenic ratio of 2:1 (fats in proportion to protein plus carbs, all in grams) for four weeks, and then we will back off to a ketogenic ratio of 1:1.

I've included all of the resources you need for success, including troubleshooting tips, recipes, meal plans, and product recommendations.

6

DETOXING, CIRCADIAN FASTING, AND TROUBLESHOOTING

Now that you understand how most diets can make women crash hormonally, and you are armed with macronutrient targets and the 2:1 ketogenic ratio, we are ready to fine-tune your fat loss. Together we will find your sweet spot, so you'll feel satiated as your hormones settle into place, the belly fat shrinks, and you lose weight. This creates the orchestra that plays the music of life to your 60 to 90 trillion cells. In this chapter, I'll share with you the lessons I learned the hard way so that you'll be spared the trial and error in accelerating hormone balance. Armed with the tips and tricks in this chapter, you can leapfrog into trial and success.

Some of my patients are like Lara, who lost 5 pounds in the first five days and entered ketosis, firmly crossing the line from "overweight" (BMI 25–30) to "normal" (BMI less than 25.0) *Five days!* She went on to lose another 4 pounds by the end of week two, but then hit a plateau. I'll show you what worked for Lara, and what can work for you if you encounter resistance to weight loss — a phenomenon that is unfortunately very common for women over thirty-five. But with science-backed solutions, it can be overcome.

Lara's experience is very common on the Gottfried Protocol.

When you reduce carbohydrates, you initially lose weight fast because carbohydrates drag water with them. But then weight loss may slow down as the body gets adjusted to burning fat. This is known as becoming keto-adapted, or fat-adapted. Lara is 5 feet, 8 inches tall and began the program at 165 pounds, giving her a BMI of 25.1 kg/ m² (mildly overweight). Our first goal for Lara was to lose 5 pounds of mostly fat mass. She accomplished that goal. Ultimately, her goal is to weigh 145 pounds, with a healthy BMI of 22. You'll hear more about her progress with busting her plateau and the "what next?" answers that really help when you need to keep burning fat despite the slowdown.

Here are the questions we'll answer:

- What reasonable weight-loss goals can you achieve and sustain with the Gottfried Protocol?
- Is detoxification proceeding successfully?
- How do you accelerate hormonal repair by layering in circadian-based intermittent fasting?
- What are the top seven pitfalls to avoid?

Most of all, keep in mind one of my mottos: imperfect action trumps perfect inaction (something I paraphrased from President Harry Truman). You can start late, start over, try and fail, and ultimately try and succeed. All those micro decisions I'm asking you to make will add up to a major transformation. That's been my own experience in developing and refining the Gottfried Protocol. Don't aim for perfection — it is the enemy of good. I only ask that you stay on the path and be kind to yourself. Hang in there long enough to let your hormone, gut, and brain circuits catch up.

SET REALISTIC GOALS

As you enter nutritional ketosis, set small goals. I like to begin with 5 pounds of weight loss, with preserved muscle mass. The best way to track this is by measuring your weight daily after your morning bowel movement (if you are not having a bowel movement every morning, see the detox troubleshooting guide later in the chapter). Measure your waist at belly-button level weekly, using the technique described in the last chapter. If you are losing fat and preserving muscle mass, your weight will decline and your waist circumference will decrease. (See the Notes for more advanced techniques.)

What's a reasonable amount of weight loss? There are many factors to consider: age, resting metabolic rate (how fast or slow you burn calories), baseline hormones, activity level, stress, and how much weight you have to lose to get to your goal BMI.

My recommendation is to aim ultimately for a BMI of 18.5 to 24.9, but to break it down into steps. If your BMI is above 24.9, begin with the goal of losing 5 percent of your weight or 5 pounds of mostly fat. Why? It's a manageable goal that has been shown to have a beneficial effect on health, particularly for those with polycystic ovary syndrome (PCOS) — the most common type of metabolic disturbance that women experience.

Lara, who began the Gottfried Protocol at 165 pounds, had lost 5 pounds by Day 5. She lost 5 percent of her weight (8.25 pounds) by Day 12 of the Protocol. By Day 22, she was down 10 pounds, with a total weight of 155 pounds. One month later, she weighed 150 pounds.

Like Lara, you probably gained weight gradually. The average woman gains 2 pounds per year from age sixteen to age thirty-six.[1] Scientists have shown that this weight gain is subtle, representing as little as 20 extra calories per day, likely combined with wayward activity of hormones like cortisol and insulin. That means we need to lose the pounds gradually too, for this important reason: rapid weight loss is rarely sustainable. Go slow. I know you're desperate to lose weight — I've been there too. But your palate, your brain circuits (including your set point, the way your brain regulates body fat within a narrow range, similar to a thermostat, based on food intake and exercise), your gut (from the taste receptors in your mouth to the stretch receptors in your stomach), and your hormones have been hijacked by years, if not decades, of adulterated food and an environment that promotes fat storage (known as an obesogenic environment). We can fix this problem. If you follow my guidelines, you'll have to complete this process only once.

To improve your outcome, I recommend that you perform the Gottfried Protocol with a friend. We know that accountability can improve results. When I succeeded in my third attempt at keto, I texted my weight every morning to a friend, and she did the same. We kept each other motivated and engaged through daily connection and our affirming words of support!

Q&A WITH DR. SARA

Q: *Can I have a cheat day?*

A: No. Keto isn't like diets that allow for a cheat day. You must eat at least a 2:1 ketogenic ratio to get the hormonal benefits of a ketogenic diet. Furthermore, most of my patients find it easier to follow a strict diet, 100 percent of the time, rather than 95 or 98 percent. I've been there myself, plus science backs up this principle. Dairy is a common ingredient in cheat meals, and it can kick you out of ketosis by raising insulin (see the next chapter, on food intolerances). One day of sugar and flour, and the sugar cravings and morphine-like substances derived from gluten and casein (very sedating and addictive opioids called gluteomorphins and caseomorphins) are back in charge. Don't do it. Four weeks of strict, 100 percent adherence will get you the best results.

KEEP MEASURING

In addition to tracking your macronutrients (fat, protein, total carbs, net carbs), daily weight, and weekly waist circumference, we will layer in measuring ketones. Here's something I constantly communicate to my patients: what you measure improves. You direct your intentions and attention toward measurement, and it will help you reach your goal.

Many people take two to seven days to enter ketosis after starting my Protocol. I highly recommend testing yourself for ketones, an important metric, because if weight loss stalls, you will have the data to pinpoint why.

Back in the days of the Atkins diet, people would pee on a test strip to check for ketones in the urine. This can work initially, but once you become keto-adapted, you are less likely to continue spilling ketones into your urine. I recommend a blood ketone monitor that measures beta-hydroxybutyrate; it may be the most important ketone when you're in ketosis and has many benefits in terms of improving metabolism. When you are firmly in ketosis during Implementation, your blood ketones should measure 0.5 to 3.0 millimolar (mmol/L). A blood ketone level that is less than 0.5 mmol/L indicates that the body is not in ketosis.

No other diet has a metric that tells you if you're doing it effectively. Isn't that cool? The best way to check your ketones and glucose levels is to do so at the same time each day (see Resources for devices that measure both). For most busy women, that's first thing in the morning, after measuring your weight. I measure while drinking a large glass of filtered water since we all tend to wake up dehydrated, particularly when in ketosis. Getting into the testing habit will make the final week, Transition, easier, as you start to test for your personal carbohydrate limit. Additionally, I like to check glucose two hours after I eat (also called postprandial or meal glucose), as that can better identify a different type of problem with insulin than fasting glucose alone can.

Q&A WITH DR. SARA

Q: My ketones were 0.3 mmol/L on Day 1, then 0.7 mmol/L on Day 3. Then I started my period, and now my ketones are 0.4 mmol/L on Day 7. Is this normal?

A: This is an example of why you might need a food log, in which you track your weight and ketones each morning, along with every food and drink that you consume. In the same log, you can track your macronutrients and net carbs. I urge my patients to keep a log as an online spreadsheet and to share it with me for troubleshooting, as needed. The best way to unravel why you fell out of ketosis is to review your log and take note of patterns. Some of my patients crave more carbohydrates before their period and pop out of ketosis when they consume more than 20 to 25 net carbs per day. Similarly, we can use the log to identify the foods that help you enter a deeper state of ketosis.

TRACK YOUR GLUCOSE KETONE INDEX (GKI)

A biomarker is a measure that tells you if something in particular is happening in your body. GKI is a biomarker that can help you track your progress on the Gottfried Protocol—it's one of the best indicators of your metabolic state. GKI shows the relationship between your ketone levels and your glucose levels, measured by a simple formula: dividing your blood glucose level (must be in the units mmol/L) and your blood ketone level (mmol/L).

Originally developed as way of tracking progress with cancer treatment,[2] measuring GKI can help us track whether both variables —glucose and ketones—are collectively heading in the right direction. In medicine, this measure is also used for patients with diabetes, obesity, Alzheimer's disease, Parkinson's disease, epilepsy, insulin resistance, and traumatic brain injury. For weight loss, the GKI is the most helpful single biomarker that I use to track a patient's success with the Gottfried Protocol — it is far more helpful than tracking glucose and ketones independently, since daily life, stress, activity, and nutrition may interfere with individual measurements. We are looking for trends.

Generally, I recommend a GKI of 1–3 to address problems with obesity, insulin resistance, circadian health, sleep, and weight loss. A GKI of 3–6 is still helpful for repairing insulin block, and a GKI of 6–9 still has weight-loss benefits.

How to Calculate Your GKI

[Glucose (mg/dL)/18]/ketone (mmol/L)

If you are outside the United States, use this calculation, which is more direct: glucose (mmol/L)/ketone (mmol/L).

If you are in the United States, you need to use a correction of 18.0 to convert the glucose reading from mg/dL to mmol/L units.

KEEP UP THE DETOXIFICATION

To deepen and accelerate the balancing of hormones that occurs with the ketogenic diet, continue the detoxification. We want to keep refreshing your liver detoxification pathways so that you can clear the toxins released as you burn more fat. Here are many practical ideas to assist you.

Detox and Food

- Eat more cruciferous vegetables. You use the very same receptor on cells for environmental toxins that you use for cruciferous vegetables, so you can crowd out the toxins by eating them.[3]
- Eat sulforaphane daily. This nutrient is found in the highest concentrations in cruciferous vegetables (broccoli, brussels

sprouts, cabbage, cauliflower, kale, radishes). It helps multiple liver detox pathways and has been found to improve leaky gut.

- Keep eating green leafy vegetables, zucchini, cucumber, and eggplant. Vegetables trigger a cleanup of the immune system. Most of my patients can eat these vegetables without limit and do not need to bother counting them; the same finding is reported by other keto researchers.[4] However, you must continue counting your other macronutrients, particularly those vegetables not listed here, protein, and fats.

- Track all macros. My hope is that you will completely eliminate processed foods, but if not, count those macros religiously as well.

- Avoid toxins whenever possible, particularly genetically modified foods and wine (which you aren't drinking during the four-week cycle anyway); they contain glyphosate, the most common herbicide.[5] Glyphosate inhibits growth hormone and will work against your fat-loss goals. Read more in the Notes about a supplement that may help repair the gut after glyphosate exposure.[6]

- Avoid *obesogens,* chemicals that can disrupt your body's hormones and make you fat. These man-made environmental chemicals can cause weight to increase.[7] Obesogens include some medications (for example, selective serotonin reuptake inhibitors, or SSRIs), pesticides, and xenobiotics like bisphenol A (BPA), a known obesogen. Unfortunately, it's tough to completely avoid these chemicals. Endocrine disruptors exist in plastic bottles, printed receipts, metal food cans, detergents, foods, toys, and skin care products. One animal study found that BPA suppresses growth hormone and release.[8] It disrupts the microbiome, the environment of gut bacteria that is crucial to our health, influencing how we absorb nutrients and experience cravings and even moods.[9] One healthy option is to eat more probiotic food and consider taking probiotics, which may help decrease the effects of BPA and other toxins; this has been shown to be the case in studies of animals.[10]

- Consider your home, work, and even vacation environments more broadly. Are any obesogenic, meaning they promote weight gain and are not conducive to weight loss? (See the following "Q&A with Dr. Sara.")

- Eat these for the best source of support for the liver: cruciferous vegetables (notice the theme), shiitake mushrooms, turmeric, and rosemary. Berries provide important nutrients to support liver function too, but you will need to make sure that when eating them in the first four weeks of the Gottfried Protocol, you follow the 2:1 ketogenic ratio with your macros. Most of my patients wait to eat berries until Day 29, during Transition. That is when we'll look more closely at gradually increasing carb intake and seeing how you respond.

Q&A WITH DR. SARA

Q: *What actions can I take to detoxify obesogenic environments?*

A: You don't just have to eliminate toxins in your food; living or working in a toxic environment can be just as harmful for your health and your waistline. What do I mean by a toxic environment? It can come in many forms. Maybe it's an office culture that encourages ordering take-out rather than bringing in your own healthy lunch. Or spending time with loved ones who prefer to watch TV while consuming a bag of tempting, carb-loaded snacks. Come up with creative ways to circumvent these potential pitfalls, and reclaim your space. For example, take a walk at lunch or after dinner, or keep fresh celery sticks handy in the fridge for when you crave some "crunch."

Detox and Bowel Movements

- Be sure you are completely evacuating your bowels at least once or twice per day. That means you don't feel like there's still any stool that's stuck in your colon or rectum.
- Eat and drink the right stuff. To keep your gut moving, you will require sufficient hydration, high-fiber vegetables, and possibly a magnesium supplement.
  - Drink plenty of filtered water, at least half of your body weight (measured in pounds) in ounces. So, for Lara at 165 pounds, that's 77.5 ounces of filtered water each day. By the way, her weight loss improved when she increased to 90. She adds keto-friendly (no sugar) electrolytes.
  - Eat high-fiber vegetables plus 25 grams of lettuce daily (see Recipes for a list of ideas, from romaine to red leaf).
  - Add 1–2 tablespoons of ground flaxseed to a shake bowl (see Recipes) or shake.
  - Include 1–2 tablespoons of MCT oil with each meal.
  - Consider taking a magnesium supplement. More than half of US adults are low in magnesium, a condition that can block many hormone pathways and harm your health.[11] I aim to get my Gottfried Protocol patients to 800 milligrams per day, but you can find the right dose for you by starting at 200–300 milligrams and slowly increasing the amount. Note that magnesium supplements may interact with certain medicines, and may not be appropriate for those with diabetes, intestinal disease, heart disease, or kidney disease. Please speak with your health care provider if you are taking medicines or have one of these conditions.

Q&A WITH DR. SARA

Q: *I am following all of your recommendations, but I'm still not having a bowel movement every day. What else can I do?*

A: A daily bowel movement is healthy and detoxifying. I have a lot of patients with constipation, and it can take a while to normalize the transit time of food as it travels through your gut. I think of this list of actions – drinking more filtered water, getting your nonstarchy veggies, adding flaxseed and MCT to your meals, and taking magnesium – as the basics. Just like a shampoo for your hair, you want to keep up a consistent pattern of lather, rinse, repeat. Some of my patients improve their transit time by adding the Ayurvedic herb triphala, either in powder form (mixed with water) or as a capsule, to their list of supplements. Other common causes of constipation include toxic stress, thyroid problems, and missing micronutrients. If you get up to 800 milligrams of magnesium, plus you are doing all of the other activities, I recommend that you consult with a functional medicine clinician to further evaluate your gut.[12]

Detox and Sweating

- Exercise to the point of sweating, which will help you excrete toxins. I am obsessed with this combination: two-thirds lifting with heavy weights, even at home, and one-third cardio. However, exercise tends to make me ravenously hungry, so I use a kitchen scale to measure my food. Exercise moves your lymphatics, which helps with detoxification. Overall, the goal is sweat.

- Another way to sweat is to soak in a hot bath with Epsom salts. Begin an hour or more before you expect to fall asleep. Let's just say I order Epsom salts by the 32-pound bucket, and that amount will carry you through the Gottfried Protocol. I add 4 cups of Epsom salts, about 1–2 cups of baking soda, a few drops of at least two essential oils (a mix, on repeat, is spruce and frankincense) and then I soak in the hottest water I can tolerate for 20 minutes or more. (My dose of Epsom salts has increased since I wrote about them in *The Hormone Reset Diet*.) Then I lie in bed over a towel while I continue sweating, and I read a favorite book. This is another way to restore magnesium, and it's delightfully relaxing before sleep. Think of it as a hormone-balancing alternative to a cocktail — one that actually helps you relax while improving your sleep.

- Try a sauna. I can't say enough about its benefits. It's another way to sweat without the exercise and the increase in appetite that can result. In today's world, where so many toxins seem unavoidable, a sauna is one way of removing them. Installing a sauna in your home is a sound investment — you'll pay for it when you sell your house, and it will keep your brain and body clear of certain toxins. The data on sauna use for detoxification support contain gaps, but the findings are sufficient to get my nod of approval.[13]

- Explore additional supplements to support the liver:
  - N-acetyl cysteine (NAC) helps protect the liver from damage and may regulate female hormones.[14] For some women with PCOS, it may improve insulin levels,[15] though not for all.[16] Dose: 600 milligrams twice per day.
  - Milk thistle has been shown to decrease liver inflammation and lower blood glucose in diabetic patients.[17] Dose: 140 milligrams three times daily for forty-five days.
  - Turmeric extract has been shown to protect against liver injury, help patients with fatty liver, improve total and low-density cholesterol, and possibly reduce blood glucose and body mass index (BMI).[18] Dose: 500 milligrams per day.

Other Lifestyle Changes

- Become a super sleeper. Quality sleep is important for detoxification as well the production of growth hormone and testosterone. Your body produces growth hormone during deep sleep, so aim for seven to eight and a half hours of total sleep each night, and, if you track it, about 90 to 120 minutes of deep sleep. Develop a bedtime ritual that includes removing screens for the last hour, and avoid eating at least three hours before bedtime.

- Rise above toxic stress. We are all so tense and inflamed. My method to unwind and reset is yoga, including daily meditation. I write about stress relief in all of my books because stress hormones tend to block fat loss, and it will serve you well to find effective ways to become stress resilient. No method is good or bad or better; the key is to find what's right for you. I suggest trying yoga or a meditation app, like Calm or Headspace or Ten Percent Happier. For certain people, yoga or meditation or mindfulness feels alien or they cannot sit still. That's okay. Try it anyway. I think of yoga as a fundamental key to reset your body's endocrinology, whereby you replace negative hormones with more positive ones. Less cortisol and insulin, more testosterone, oxytocin, and growth hormone.

Q&A WITH DR. SARA

Q: *I've been stressed and have started craving and eating more carbs again. What can I do?*

A: We've all been there. I call it carb creep. When you start to eat excess carbohydrates (that is, over your limit), you may also notice fluid retention, and the scale can climb because of more water weight. I see this commonly in patients who eat take-out food or eat out at restaurants, where carbs are often hidden in the food. Weight can spiral up over time, and you can gain 5 pounds or more until you identify and address the problem. Don't let that happen.

Here's are the questions that I ask my patients: Are you tracking every food and drink you consume? Are you weighing yourself every morning and measuring your ketones and GKI? What you measure improves. Are you calculating net carbs for every meal, before you eat it? Are you covering the basics by drinking plenty of filtered water, avoiding sugar and alcohol, and eating lightly steamed non-starchy vegetables? Are you making signature meals and soups? (See Recipes.) Are you moving, pooping, and sleeping? Do you have an accountability partner to whom you text or email your daily progress and with whom you troubleshoot challenges? On a deeper level, take an abdominal breath, and make a list of things you can do besides eat carbs when you feel stressed. Here's my list: text a friend, call one of my sisters, go for a walk, hop on the exercise bike, swing a kettlebell twelve times, do ten burpees, talk to my husband, breathe deeply or meditate for 5 minutes, drink a glass of filtered water, read a book, or take a nap.

If you notice carb creep, nip it in the bud right away by recommitting to the basics of the Gottfried Protocol.

CIRCADIAN-BASED INTERMITTENT FASTING: AN EASY, HEALTHY HABIT

I tried keto twice for fat loss before I got it to work for my hormones. As I look back on what I did wrong, it all looked right from the outside. I was eating macros in the desired range: 70/20/10. I entered ketosis. But the first time, I ate too much fat—probably too many saturated fat calories for me (butter in my coffee, liberal amounts of bacon and cheese in my diet). The second time, I didn't eat enough vegetables, and my gut microbes suffered. I didn't mop up the toxins first. I was eating breakfast, lunch, and dinner, plus snacks in between. Oh, and I didn't stop drinking alcohol—that's a longer story, but I've got several hacks for you in this chapter if you can't imagine life without your nightly glass of wine!

The third round of ketosis worked: I lost 20 pounds of mostly fat. What was different: circadian-based intermittent fasting, a focus on detoxification, and eating in a way that honors female hormones, including giving up alcohol. Leveraging this combination of factors, the Gottfried Protocol is a weight-loss accelerator.

Intermittent fasting is a back door to ketosis, because most people produce ketones after sixteen or so hours of fasting. When you eat within a window that leverages circadian rhythm, your body will be more aligned with the release of nearly every hormone that you produce. This means that if you start eating several hours after the sun rises (ideally after a fasted workout) and stop eating a few hours before the sun sets, you will be working with and not against how the human body, male and female, evolved to eat—with extended periods of metabolic rest. Now we work longer days and use artificial light at night, so our eating patterns less and less resemble the way they evolved. The worst-case scenario for your metabolic hormones is for you to eat a big meal and then go to bed, yet that's what most people do. For the benefit of your hormones, you need to be in a state of fasting every night when you go to bed.

Of all the programs I have utilized with thousands of patients in my clinic over twenty-five years, time-restricted eating is the easiest behavioral modification to encourage weight loss, especially for women. In a 2019 University of Illinois at Chicago study, obese adults lost about 3 percent of their body mass by adhering to a 16:8 diet.[19] The plan was simple: the participants limited their food intake to only eight hours per day. And they fasted for the other sixteen.

When you combine circadian-based intermittent fasting with eating ketogenic food, you produce more ketones faster, which can aid weight loss. You can get the Gottfried Protocol benefits without hunger or deprivation by closing your kitchen after dinner, thereby creating an approximate fourteen-to-sixteen-hour window during which you shift into fat-burning, insulin-and-growth-hormone-optimizing mode. (Don't worry: most of that fasting will occur while you sleep.)

Your effort will be rewarded with optimal levels of insulin and growth hormone (and other hormones), fat loss, increased energy and stamina, and other health benefits. Achieving *mild* ketosis through a sixteen-hour overnight fast increases mental acuity, lowers blood sugar, resets insulin block, triggers autophagy (clearing out of damaged cells), repairs DNA, and regulates mTOR (the gene involved in your health span, or healthy life span).

The Science of Circadian-Based Intermittent Fasting

Studies of humans and animals indicate that circadian-based intermittent fasting has the following benefits:

- Reverses weight gain.[20]
- Restores the normal expression of genes involved in diet-induced obesity, especially in models of postmenopausal obesity.[21]
- Improves blood sugar (heals insulin block).[22]
- Lowers cardiometabolic risk.[23]
- Reduces risk of breast cancer and other cancers.[24]
- Markedly reduces aging.[25]
- Turns white fat into more metabolically favorable brown fat, so that you burn more calories.[26]
- Reshapes gut microbiota in favor of obesity-protective bacteria (for example, *Oscillibacter, Ruminococcaceae*), and contributes to microbiota diversity, a universal hallmark of health.[27]
- Improves the metabolic consequences of a disrupted circadian clock.[28]
- May help the brain ward off neurodegenerative diseases like Alzheimer's, other forms of dementia, and Parkinson's, while improving mood and memory.[29]

And intermittent fasting does all of this without curbing calories or requiring a specific dietary strategy![30]

Some of you may succeed with a rapid dive into intermittent fasting. I advise most of my female patients to ease into it, however, since it can be stressful for the body, and we don't want to raise cortisol levels by adding more stress. Here's how to do it.

HOW TO EASE INTO
INTERMITTENT FASTING

1. Start with tracking your normal food pattern, and introduce time-restricted eating with an overnight fast of twelve to fourteen hours on nonconsecutive days — and a corresponding eating window of twelve to ten hours, respectively — with *adaptive exercise only* (Pilates, yoga, walking) on those days. You can do this on Day 1 or begin at any time during the four-week Protocol. The sooner you start, the sooner you will see more hormonal benefits.

2. During this gradual ramping up, eat more of your carbs at breakfast in the morning, if possible, because that is when we are more insulin sensitive and can burn the carbohydrates as fuel. Eat low carb at dinner — this is a great time to eat fish or take omega-3 supplements to help you feel satisfied longer. Keep within your total carb and net carb limits each day.

3. Fast for three or more hours before bedtime, as this is the most insulin-resistant time of day.

4. Consume only healthy noncaloric drinks in the morning. Black coffee or tea first thing are okay and do not break your fast. There is debate as to whether calories, such as a tablespoon of cream in your coffee, break the fast. The most conservative approach is to stick to water, black coffee, or green tea, with nothing added.

5. Break your fast in the morning with nutrient-dense food. This is when I eat keto Avo Toast or a green smoothie packed with vegetables, nuts, and seeds.

6. Continue to follow the Gottfried Protocol dietary recommendations from the previous chapter: Eat whole, minimally processed foods prepared at home whenever possible. Avoid added sugar, refined flour, and trans fats. Maximize vegetable intake. Healthy fats are encouraged, along with moderate protein.

7. During maintenance, work up to a 16:8 approach: a sixteen-hour overnight fast and an eight-hour eating window. For instance, eat at 10 a.m., finish by 6 p.m., and eat no food between 6 p.m. that day and 10 a.m. the next day.

8. You can pick your own feeding window as long as it allows for a sixteen-hour overnight fast. Most of my patients find it easiest to track this with an app. Working women or those who socialize a lot at dinner often prefer a later eating window, say, noon to 8 p.m. (Note that some women need to stick to 14:10 for one week before extending to 16:8 if sixteen hours feels stressful or too long at first. You can ease into it.)

9. Time the taking of your early morning and bedtime probiotics to help to boost the anti-obesogenic bacteria and reduce the obesogenic bacteria (in, for example, the *Lactobacillus* family).

10. Continue circadian-based intermittent fasting past the four-week Gottfried Protocol if you've got more than 15 pounds to lose.

Daily Checklist for the Gottfried Protocol

- Bowel movement.
- Weight recorded.
- Blood ketones and glucose tested to determine GKI.
- Circadian-based intermittent fasting.
- Sweating (daily body movement — fasted workouts are best — and an Epsom salt bath or a sauna five days per week).
- Hydration with added no-sugar electrolytes to support kidney function, reduce risk of kidney stones, and prevent "keto flu."
- Continual detoxification through eating vegetables, avoiding toxins, and encouraging balanced liver function.

Q&A WITH DR. SARA

Q: *I have (fill in the blank with a medical condition). Can I do the Gottfried Protocol?*

A: Unfortunately, it is not possible to cover in this book every possible medical condition and whether it contraindicates ketosis. Also, I cannot give specific medical advice outside an established patient-physician relationship. Instead, I encourage you to consult with a member of your health-care team, such as your primary care physician. The contraindications to the ketogenic diet that I discuss in Chapter 4, both in the text and the Notes, are a start. But to find out what will work specifically for you, it's best to get advice from medical professionals who know you.

THE TOP SEVEN THINGS THAT GO SIDEWAYS ON THE GOTTFRIED PROTOCOL

Because I've been using this program with patients, I've encountered many common problems that can derail success. Here's what to look out for and how to respond:

1. **You eat too many calories.** When I first tried keto, I had difficulty achieving my macros, so I starting drinking my coffee with butter and MCT oil. I was consuming too much fat and eating beyond my metabolic ceiling. You may overeat because you are leptin resistant and you do not feel full, even in ketosis. (You can check for this by measuring your leptin level in the blood. If above 8 ng/dL, leptin resistance may be driving you to overeat.) The solution is to eat foods that are lower in calorie density. Greens (such as salads) have 100 calories per pound. Vegetables, 200 calories per pound. Meat has 800 calories, bread 1,500, and chocolate 2,500 calories per pound. Calorie-

dense foods activate the reward system.[31] Eat more greens and vegetables, and less meat.

2. **You keep drinking alcohol.** Do you want to burn fat, improve your sleep, and clear your brain, or do you want to drink your glass of wine? I'll wait here while that reality check sinks in. In my experience, alcohol will kick you out of ketosis. And it certainly disrupts most of your hormones. Take 1–2 teaspoons of MCT in the afternoon to avoid that first glass of wine. Based on anecdotal reports, it seems to raise healthy short-chain fatty acids in the body, which may make you feel more satisfied when you prepare for dinner.[32]

3. **You have a slow metabolism.** We know that women with a higher BMI and slower metabolic rate (the rate at which you burn calories at rest) take longer to lose weight and may be more likely to experience plateaus. Improving hormonal balance may take longer, but it may help with boosting metabolic rate. You may want to seek professional help to measure your resting metabolic rate and test hormones.

4. **You experience constipation.** This is a common side effect of ketosis. I've seen patients retain or gain 2 to 5 pounds due to constipation, even when they are having a partial bowel movement each morning. The problem may be incomplete bowel evacuation. Try the techniques listed on page 146 if this happens to you.

5. **You have trouble getting into ketosis.** Or perhaps you get into ketosis but come back out of it. There can be several reasons for this, including eating too much protein. The amount of protein you ate ten or twenty years ago may no longer be the right amount for you. If, in my fifties, I ate the same level of protein that I did when I was in my thirties, I would have high blood sugar now. Other common foods that may spike your blood sugar and lower your level of ketosis are dairy products, alternative sweeteners, alcohol, and packaged foods. (Recently, I used a tooth whitener from my dentist, which popped me out of ketosis and caused my fasting glucose to rise to the 110

mg/dL range, which is where I used to be back when I had prediabetes.) For optimal therapeutic benefits, I'd like for you to get in and stay in ketosis for four weeks. When in doubt, test. The best way to know if a food is suppressing ketosis is to test your ketones and glucose before and after eating the food. I like to test before eating it and again one hour after, and once more two hours later. See more detail in the next chapter, where we further discuss how to identify your trigger foods and determine your personal carb limit.

6. **You have a high level of carb intolerance.** You may need to drop total carbs further, down to 5 percent of total calories per day. True, I've given you all the reasons why this may not be good for your hormones, but the kingpin hormone is insulin, and we need to get that hormone straightened out first.

7. **You come down with a case of the "f*ck its."** Oh, I've been there. Maybe you're constantly hungry because steady ketosis hasn't yet kicked in (probably due to item 5 or 6 in this list). Maybe your metabolism is on the slow side, so weight loss is more gradual than you want. Maybe you're sick of diet culture or berating yourself over eating too much. The goal here isn't to make you unhealthfully thin; instead, the objective is to swap your badly behaved hormones for hormones that optimize your health and help you accomplish your long-term vision for yourself. For me, that means a healthy BMI, with good muscle tone and all the clothes in the closet fitting well. Getting dressed is simple. Food is neutral. I can go four to six hours between meals, with steady blood sugar and energy. I've waited most of my life for this level of freedom and security, and I want that for you too.

Nine Plateau Busters

If your weight seems stuck going up and down within a 2- to 3-pound range and won't drop after five to seven days, consider trying one of these:

1. Resistance training. Aim for two-thirds weight training and one-third cardio. Lift heavy weights. Building muscle will raise your resting metabolic rate. Bonus: exercise when you first wake up, before your eating window opens.

2. Using a food scale. Weighing your food will keep you honest and on track.

3. Mitochondrial support. I recommend taking L-carnitine first thing in the morning to help transport triglycerides to your mitochondria, where fat is burned.

4. Cryotherapy. This is exposure to cold air or water. I go to a local cryotherapy center. Or you could take an ice bath (a cold bath with ice) for 20 minutes twice per week. Some people prefer cold showers.

5. Troubleshooting net carbs. If you're not losing weight, drop your net carbs below 20 grams per day to combat carb intolerance or insulin resistance. Consider getting a blood test to look at fasting insulin, glucose, and hemoglobin A1C. The good news is that once you use this food plan to reverse your carb intolerance, you will be able to eat more carbs without gaining weight.

6. Restricting calories. Try doing this temporarily, for one to two days.

7. Extending fasting. Go for 18:6 or even 20:4.

8. Adding insulin sensitizers. These supplements may improve the function of insulin and improve fat loss. (See page 159 for details about keto-supportive supplements.)

9. Adding growth-hormone-boosting peptides. They require a prescription and a responsible prescriber, but they may help when nothing else is working.

What if you can't get into ketosis? Here are good strategies to kick your body into ketosis if you're not getting there:

- Try cryotherapy (see Plateau Busters).
- Add fat, like extra-virgin olive oil.
- Restrict calories, or fast for fourteen to sixteen hours to flip the metabolic switch to the fat-burning mode.
- Incorporate MCT oil (40 grams per day can induce ketosis).
- Try additional blood sugar support (see the box below for details about keto-supportive supplements).

What if you're constipated? Regular bowel movements are key to your success. Here are some great tricks to help you avoid or do away with constipation, a common issue for women on keto plans:

- Hydrate adequately.
- Eat high-fiber vegetables plus 25 grams of lettuce daily (any type of lettuce; see Recipes for ideas).
- Consume one quarter of an avocado.
- Eat ground flaxseed.
- Take MCT oil.
- Add a magnesium supplement.

Keto-Supportive Supplements

Evidence from scientific studies shows that these supplements help resolve inflammation. Consider them in addition to the supplements I mentioned previously to support the liver.

- **Alpha-lipoic acid** is a fatty acid made by your body, and I recommend it in supplement form to encourage weight loss and improve insulin sensitivity; solid evidence points to its effectiveness in preventing cell damage in the body.[33] I prescribe this supplement for prediabetes, diabetes, aging skin, lipid problems, cataracts, glaucoma, and other health issues. It enhances insulin sensitivity, lowers glucose, and reduces advanced glycation end products (AGEs, harmful substances formed when protein or fat combine with sugar in the body).[34] It can help you with age-related loss in glutathione, the master antioxidant. Alpha-lipoic acid improves mitochondria. (See Resources; there are two forms, or isomers, which have different properties, and I recommend R-lipoic acid because it is more biologically active than S-lipoic acid. Alpha-lipoic acid supplements tend to include the "R" and "S" forms in a 50:50 ratio.) A dose of R-lipoic acid is 100 to 200 milligrams per day, with 2–4 milligrams of biotin per day as well, to prevent the biotin depletion that can occur with long-term use of lipoic acid.

- **Balanced omegas** — you need to be well oiled to resolve inflammation.[35] I recommend taking a blend of different omegas, including alpha linoleic acid, eicosapentaenoic acid (EPA), docosahexaenoic acid (DHA), which are omega-3s, and gamma linoleic acid, a healthy omega-6. Therapy with just one of these may create an imbalance in your fatty acid pathway. For my patients, I track the ratio of omega-3 to omega-6 because higher ratios are associated with lower risk of disease (or conversely, we seek lower ratios if looking at the ratio of omega-6 to omega-3), including breast cancer.[36] See Resources for further information.

- **Berberine** has been shown to lower blood sugar and inflammation, and to modestly reduce weight.[37] Dose: 500 milligrams, three times per day.

- **Specialized proresolving mediators (SPMs)** are a recent discovery that may help with the chronic inflammation of insulin resistance and obesity, though randomized trials have not been performed.[38] See Resources for dosing details.

- **Spirulina** is a type of blue-green algae that I add to my shakes, as you will see in the Recipe section. A dose of 500 milligrams twice per day (or the approximate equivalent in your daily shake) is associated with lower weight and appetite. Spirulina is anti-inflammatory and detoxifying.

Common Hormone Imbalances: PCOS and Breast Cancer

The most common hormone imbalance that I see in my medical practice is polycystic ovary syndrome (PCOS), affecting 20 to 30 percent of my patients. Women with PCOS are the most resistant to weight loss because they are battling multiple hormone problems at once: insulin block, leptin resistance, low adiponectin (a hormone derived from fat that protects against insulin resistance, diabetes, and atherosclerosis), high testosterone and DHEA, high cortisol, high aromatase, and, as a result, dysestrogenism (known colloquially as "estrogen dominance"). They have signs of unresolved inflammation, like belly fat, and blood tests showing high cRP, interleukin-6, and TNF-alpha, which raise aromatase and put weight loss even further out of reach.

Back in 2013, I recommended a low-carb diet full of whole foods and polyphenols to address PCOS, as that was the most well proven approach at the time, and this was further validated since the publication of my book *The Hormone Cure*.[39] Fortunately, we now have more data to support a hormone-balancing ketogenic diet for women struggling with PCOS, with studies showing weight loss and improved hormones, from insulin to testosterone.[40]

What about breast cancer, the dreaded disease that affects one in eight women within the course of a lifetime? PCOS has many risk factors that overlap with those of breast cancer, and the hormonal pattern in PCOS may be implicated in the development of breast cancer: specifically, wayward insulin.[41] (Studies that try to correlate PCOS with breast cancer are mixed — some positive[42] and some negative[43] — though the negative studies failed to make appropriate statistical adjustments.) Meta-analyses show a definitive link between PCOS and endometrial cancer, another hormonally mediated type of cancer.[44] The takeaway is that the hormone-balancing keto reset is a well-documented way to address metabolic dysfunction, the root cause of both PCOS and breast cancer.

Highlights

- ► In this chapter, you learned to layer in deeper detoxification and periods of metabolic rest by fasting each night for fourteen to sixteen hours.
- ► Together we can troubleshoot the most common problems that arise on a hormone-balancing ketogenic diet to maintain the four-week pulse and keep you burning fat and losing weight.
- ► You gained weight gradually, and you will lose weight gradually. Go slowly. Keep the long view. Aim for long-term weight loss and maintenance. You'll have to do this only once if you do it right.
- ► You don't have to be perfect — stress resulting from perfectionism raises cortisol and insulin, and can block weight loss — but you can't quit. Not now, not before you receive all the demonstrated benefits of a well-formulated ketogenic diet that balances your hormones and makes you feel more alive.
- ► Reread Chapter 5 and this chapter for the support you need. Go to my Instagram (Instagram.com/saragottfriedmd) to ask questions and be part of the community of Gottfried Protocol warriors.

7

TRANSITION

You did it! You spent four weeks reorganizing, recovering, and restoring your hormones to create metabolic youth. You followed the rules and made it to Day 29. I've been there myself, and I know that road can be challenging. Your hormone levels, hormone receptors, and transportation of hormones in your body are all improved, and as a result you've lost weight and feel like yourself again. It's a process of deconstructing the old version of your body and reconstituting it in a superior way. Congratulations!

Preparation	Implementation	Transition
20–25 grams of net carbs and detoxification. Keep a ketogenic ratio of 2:1. Get your bowels moving so you can mobilize fat!	20–25 grams net carbs per day, and add intermittent fasting (14/10 to 16/8). Continue a ketogenic ratio of 2:1.	Start to add net carbs slowly, 5 grams at a time, and heading toward a ketogenic ratio of 1:1 for the long term, or until you repeat the diet.

The Gottfried Protocol Timeline

I've seen over the years in my practice that getting your hormones back in balance is one of the best actions you can take to promote long-term health and to feel incredible. Still, most people don't realize that making a significant lifestyle change, even for a pulse of four weeks, presents a major psychosocial challenge. Your partner probably complained or gave you an eye roll. Maybe you're weary of making multiple meals for others at home and along with yours. You probably want to skip meal prep on Sunday. By this stage of the program, I hope you realize the pounds lost don't matter as much as your mindset — your self-directed attitude and thoughts. Most important, how do you feel? On Day 29, I expect that you feel triumphant, regardless of whether your progress with weight loss was big or small. I agree: it was the tiny steps you took each day that added up over four weeks to major transformation.

The intention of the Gottfried Protocol is to change the conversation between your food and hormones. By Day 29, you've started a new conversation between your hormones and fat to make you leaner and healthier. You are creating metabolic flexibility, the ability of your body to efficiently switch between using carbs and fats as fuel, based on your need and available nutrients. The whole point is to not be trapped in the metabolically inflexible state of burning carbs 24/7. Maybe your brain fog cleared up, your night sweats and hot flashes are ebbing, or your PCOS symptoms are improving. You're now burning more fat and feeling hopeful and encouraged about weight loss.

So, what's next?

During Transition, you will be burning both fat and carbs to meet your body's energy demand, and we will define the upper and lower limit of the amount of carbs that works best for you, for continued fat burning. Transition takes about a week or two, and it will provide a lifetime of benefits.

MEET LOTUS, AGE FIFTY-ONE

Lotus is a busy physician who went on the Gottfried Protocol to deal with her growing waistline, slowing metabolism, and worsening cholesterol levels. Before we met, her hormones had felt like a hot mess for many months. Previously, she suffered from endometriosis and underwent a hysterectomy and ovary removal in 2019. She had all the symptoms of perimenopause: weight gain, hot flashes, night sweats, brain fog, and mood swings. Her thyroid function was slow; she had prediabetes. At a height of 5 feet, 4 inches, and a weight of 163 pounds, she had an overweight body mass index of 28. Combined with a low metabolic rate (a calculated basal metabolic rate of 1,406 calories/day), this meant slower progress with the Gottfried Protocol, but Lotus prevailed. She had tried a ketogenic diet before, but it didn't work — she felt she never had effective guidance or the right mindset. After I explained the Protocol and walked her through the guidelines I share in this book, she felt ready.

Three weeks later, Lotus was making great progress. All of her perimenopausal symptoms were gone, a result I see frequently because those symptoms are driven by hormones — not just estrogen and progesterone but insulin too.[1]

After four weeks, Lotus was down to 154 pounds (and had a lower BMI of 26) and felt a renewed sense of grace, like she had a new lease on life. She kept to her 2:1 ketogenic ratio with mostly vegetarian Indian food. (I include several of her recipes in Chapter 9.) When she checked her labs before and after the Gottfried Protocol, her leptin and testosterone were normal, her blood sugar was improved, her total cholesterol had dropped, and her good cholesterol was the best it had been in twelve years. Progress!

We still need to work on her fitness, muscle mass, and growth hormone to build on her amazing gains. Our new goal became to get her BMI to less than 24.9 and to increase growth hormone with weight training. Meanwhile, at the time of this writing, she has lost 39 pounds, her weight is 124 pounds, she has a BMI of 21.3, and her GKI is consistently 2–3. Now our goal is maintenance, with added carbs and more exercise. She has her energy back and has found a new balance and joy.

HANDLE YOUR
TRANSITION WITH CARE

Like Lotus, you'll take on the final task in the Gottfried Protocol, which is to protect your new hormones by slowly transitioning to a more balanced food plan. As I mentioned in the introduction, the Gottfried Protocol is a therapeutic pulse to right your hormones, not a long-term diet. We just don't have enough data related to women to recommend it for an extended period.

I know you are eager to be done, but I urge you to move through this final stage with great patience and grace. In this chapter, I will teach you how to gradually increase your carbohydrates while staying on the edge of ketosis. The Gottfried Protocol is a food plan meant to be followed for four weeks, and a maximum of six months continuously, before easing into a more evidence-based, balanced, and anti-inflammatory food plan, such as the Mediterranean diet. (I will cover this transition in this chapter.)

If you finish your four weeks of the Gottfried Protocol and then on Day 29 splurge on 200 grams of carbs, you will lose the sacred opportunity to learn the upper and lower limit of the carb threshold that works for you. Reintroduce additional carbs slowly, and be patient. If you return to all the old carbs you used to eat, you will both lose this opportunity and gain back the weight you lost.

The Transition phase of adding back carbohydrates may take you nine days, or it may take you longer. Everyone is unique. Don't skimp on it. Don't race through it with a plate of nachos and multiple rounds of margaritas. Take the time you need to collect data on yourself and then integrate this information. I will take you by the hand and show you how to do it methodically, based on my latest experience with transitioning off a ketogenic food plan over the past several years. The goal is to be like Lotus, who has transitioned to a mostly vegetarian and balanced diet with more carbs and less fat, yet continues to stay in mild ketosis and lose weight. Despite many health challenges, like a slow metabolic rate and a BMI in the overweight range, Lotus is down 39 pounds from when she started. She feels hopeful for the first time in years, which empowers her to keep working for better health.

RULES OF ENGAGEMENT FOR TRANSITION

Our main goal of Transition is to define your carb limit so that you can determine an upper limit on the carbohydrates you can eat each day and not gain weight. In the process, you will learn about digestion, absorption, focus, mood, energy, performance, sleep, self-care, and health versus disease. We all have our own carb threshold for weight loss. The healthier you get, the higher the number. These rules of engagement will help you define your personal carb limit to enable you to maintain healthy hormones and continue to lose weight.

- **Define your carb limit.** This will be the number of daily net carbs under which you will continue to lose weight and over which you may begin to gain weight.
- **Continue measuring ketones.** Stay in mild ketosis either with the food that you eat, or with circadian fasting, or ideally, with both. Keep up the detoxification: this has been shown to improve metabolic flexibility by relying less on glucose and more on ketones. Over the long term, mild ketosis is one of the best ways to improve health span, the period of time you are free of disease and feeling your healthiest.[2]
- **Transfer to an anti-inflammatory diet.** I recommend a carb-adjusted version of the evidence-based Mediterranean diet (more details later in this chapter). You will be able to manage your weight successfully because you'll know your personal carb limit, and if you need to continue to lose weight, you'll repeat the four-week pulse of the Gottfried Protocol after you finish Transition. Armed with your carb limit, you can continue to lose weight by staying below it.

- **If you fall out of ketosis, get back in as soon as possible.** If you are still craving more carbs or processed food, it can take longer than twenty-eight days to adapt to ketosis and rid yourself of cravings. Just because you're in ketosis doesn't mean all cravings disappear. For some of my patients, it takes a few days, but for others, it can take months. Of course, you are not defined by the number on the bathroom scale or the size of your dress. You are defined by your daily choices, particularly what you do when faced with a challenge. Think of indulging a craving as a challenge, nothing more, nothing less. I like to have a plan for when I fall off the wagon — and I'll share my best strategies with you later in this chapter.

- **Keep your motivation in mind.** Remember why you embarked on the Gottfried Protocol: to change your relationship to carbs and to fix your hormones. We all know the allure of carbs. One bite may feel soothing, but the truth is, most forms of carbohydrate — whether it's popcorn, starchy foods (rice, potatoes, root vegetables), fructose (fruit sugar), lactose (milk sugar), or sugar itself (and its cousins: honey, maple syrup, and even some sugar substitutes) — turn into glucose in the gut. Excess carbs are the root cause of hormone imbalance for many people. Unfortunately, the more you eat, the more you want. Stand firm as you test your carb limits, and follow the plan I describe in this chapter. Keep in mind that when you overeat carbs, you convert your body back into a fat-storing machine. Avoid the hormonal mess that leads to diabetes and metabolic syndrome by carefully titrating your own personal carb limit.

DEFINE YOUR CARB LIMIT

The Gottfried Protocol starts you at a carb limit of 20 to 25 net carbs per day. For the first three days of Transition, increase your net carbs by 5 grams. It may take up to three days to notice a change in your weight or other measures (listed below). If your weight stays the same or decreases, after three days add another 5 grams, and track how your body responds over the next three days.

For example, if you were eating 20 grams of net carbs per day for the four weeks of the Gottfried Protocol, then for Days 29–31, eat 25 grams of net carbs. If you stay in ketosis and your weight stays stable or continues to decrease, then on Days 32–35, eat 30 grams of net carbs. On Days 36–39, eat 35 grams of net carbs. Track your weight, blood sugar, and ketones each day. When your weight increases, you've reached your personal carb limit.

Your blood ketones will probably decrease as you reach your carb limit. When you fall out of ketosis (blood ketones less than 0.5 mmol/L) and your weight loss stops, you have reached your personal carb limit. Dial your daily carb limit to less than this threshold.

What carbs should you add first? I recommend adding starchier vegetables first, then low-sugar fruits such as berries, along with legumes and hummus. Be very careful with potatoes, grains, and dairy until your personal carb limit is well defined.

What Determines Your Personal Carb Limit?

- Current weight.
- Gender.
- Health and lifestyle.
- Genetics and epigenetics (how the genes talk to your cells).
- Glucose and ketones.
- Hormones like insulin, cortisol, growth hormone, leptin.
- Age.
- Metabolic flexibility.
- Foods you eat — before and during the Gottfried Protocol.
- Stress level.
- Gut function.
- Level of physical activity.
- Medications.

Signs That You've Exceeded
Your Personal Carb Limit

- **Increase in weight.** Normally weight can fluctuate by about 1 pound per day when hormones are stable. If you are having a daily bowel movement and your weight increases by 2 pounds or more over the next seventy-two hours, you've crossed your current carb limit.
- **Rise in glucose (fasting glucose greater than 85 mg/dL) and decline in ketones (less than 0.5 mmol/L).** This represents a fasting glucose-ketone index greater than 10.
- **Fatigue.** When you go past your carb limit, you may feel exhausted, like you need a nap. Depending on when you consume the extra carbs, fatigue could occur in the morning, afternoon, or evening, or all day long. Usually the fatigue occurs after the meal with excess carbs.
- **Brain fog.** Overconsumption of carbs may cause difficulty with focus or concentration. This is one of the most common symptoms of insulin resistance.
- **Mood swings.** Excess carbs can make you feel depressed or tired.
- **Bloating.** Eating over your personal carb limit may cause intestinal gas.

How Much Is 5 Net Carbs?

Okay, now you know the plan—here's what those 5 net carbs look like on your plate:

- 2 ounces of butternut squash. I cut fresh squash into cubes and store them in the freezer so I can steam small amounts at a time.
- ½ of a sweet potato (1.75 ounces), which has about 8 net carbs; aim for 1 ounce only.
- ¼ cup of blueberries, which contains about 4 to 5 net carbs.
- ¼ cup of black beans, which contains 5.8 net carbs, so eat a little less (approximately 1 ounce).

- 1 ounce cashews (28 grams), or about 18, which contain 7.7 grams of net carbs. I'll do the math for you: eat 11 cashews to get 5 net carbs.
- 1 piece of keto bread (my favorite has 4 net carbs; see Resources).

CHECK FOR FOOD INTOLERANCES

Consider testing certain foods to see if you are intolerant to them by measuring whether they block your ketone levels. Many foods trigger ketone dips or glucose spikes for some people but not for others. These are common culprits:

- Dairy products.
- Grains.
- Gluten.
- Egg.
- Alcohol.
- Artificial sweeteners.
- Legumes.
- Almond or coconut flour.
- Rice.
- Prepackaged foods.

One of the best ways to tell if you're reacting to a specific food is to measure your ketones and glucose before and after you eat it. It's a three-test process (described in the next section), but it's worth the extra effort because once you know which food is getting in your way, you can eliminate it from your diet. Why does this matter? Because food intolerances can lead to weight-loss resistance and autoimmune disease. The most frequent food intolerances found in a recent study of a hundred people with autoimmune conditions were casein, cow's milk, wheat, gliadin (a type of protein in gluten), egg whites, and rice.[3]

I know what you're thinking: what about your bones? Dairy may not do your body good, despite the marketing messages from the

Dairy Council. A new study found that dairy products do not prevent age-related bone loss or fractures in women over age forty.[4] Great sources of calcium include many of the Gottfried Protocol foods, like cruciferous vegetables (collard greens, broccoli, and kale), eggs, greens (such as spinach), and sesame seeds. Also, I tell my patients to maintain healthy levels of vitamin D (serum levels of 50–90 ng/mL) to ensure bone strength and to let this vitamin handle the approximately 399 jobs it does for us, such as immune system modulation.

A note about alcohol: When you've been off alcohol for three or more weeks, your liver is clean and fresh. Drinking will hit you harder than before. If you choose to reintroduce alcohol, start with half a serving, such as about 2.5 ounces of wine.

CONTINUE MEASURING KETONES

As you become more keto-adapted, you will continue to improve your metabolic flexibility and become more efficient at burning both carbs and fat. In Transition, keep tracking your macronutrients (fat, protein, total carbs, net carbs), daily weight, weekly waist circumference, ketones, and potentially your glucose-ketone index (GKI).

We can use GKI to track your body's response to an increase in carb intake. We want your ketones to continue to be 0.5 to 3.0 millimolar per liter (mmol/L). A blood ketone level that is less than 0.5 mmol/L means the body is not in ketosis.

During Transition, I measure my ketones and glucose first thing in the morning after weighing myself, and again after eating a test food of extra net carbs. Like me, you can check postprandial GKI one and two hours after you eat to test for food intolerances (read on for more details on this).

As we discussed, GKI is one of the best indicators of your metabolic state. Continue to aim for a GKI of 1–3 to address obesity, insulin resistance (block), and weight loss. A GKI of 3–6 is still helpful for repairing insulin block, and a GKI of 6–9 still has weight-loss benefits.

MEASURING FOR
FOOD INTOLERANCES

To tell if you're reacting to a specific food as a food intolerance or sensitivity, perform the following three-step process:

1. Measure your fasting (or preprandial, "before meal") glucose and ketones; this should be done at least three hours after your last meal. Then determine your GKI. This is your baseline.
2. Eat or drink the food in question. It's best if you eat only this food, such as a serving of yogurt, cheese, or beans.
3. Measure your glucose and ketones again 60 minutes and then 120 minutes later. Calculate the GKI.

How to interpret the results: Avoid foods that cause your blood glucose to rise more than 30 mg/dL from baseline to the 60-minute result or prevent it from returning to baseline after two hours. Ideally your glucose should be between 90 and 115 mg/dL. Limit or avoid foods that cause a drop in ketones of 0.5–1.0 mmol/L, or less than 0.5 mmol/L, or a GKI greater than 10, or some combination of these results.

BENEFITS OF THE
MEDITERRANEAN DIET

The Mediterranean diet is an ancient way of eating that evolved in the region of the Mediterranean Sea, particularly Italy and Greece, which boast the healthiest and longest-lived populations in the world. As you transition from the four-week Gottfried Protocol to a Mediterranean diet, you will have many more food options, and you can modulate the amount of carbs you consume each day (since you know your personal carb limit) by eating just below your limit.

These are the foods featured in the Mediterranean diet:

- Plant-based whole foods (nuts, seeds, vegetables, fruits, legumes, grains).

- Moderate consumption of fish, seafood, and dairy.
- Limited red meat and other meat products.
- Olive oil as the main source of fat and cooking oil.
- Low-to-moderate consumption of alcohol, mostly red wine (as my patients are quick to point out).

Indigenous edible plants and herbs from the region include olives, borage, chard, capers, lupines, asparagus, watercress, mallow, thistle, grapes, beets, tigernut, parsley, cumin, coriander, fennel, oregano, rosemary, sage, lemon balm, savory, fenugreek, bay leaf, saffron, and mushrooms. Other plants originated in Asia (rice, fruits like apples, raspberries, plum, quince), Africa (artichoke, millet, okra, melons), and the Americas (corn, peanuts, tomatoes, peppers, eggplant).[5]

Multiple randomized trials have shown the health benefits of a Mediterranean diet for risk reduction of cardiovascular disease,[6] metabolic syndrome,[7] type 2 diabetes,[8] obesity,[9] cancer[10] (including breast cancer),[11] cognitive decline,[12] and other neurodegenerative disease like Alzheimer's[13] and multiple sclerosis.[14] Specifically, for the best blood sugar control in diabetes, the Mediterranean diet and the low-carb diet are equally effective at reducing glycated hemoglobin (known as a blood test called hemoglobin A1C) and weight, together with providing the greatest benefit in high-density lipoprotein (the "good" cholesterol).[15]

Personally, I gain weight on a classic Mediterranean diet because I have a low personal carb limit. If that's the case for you, focus during Transition on a low-carb Mediterranean diet, limiting grains and fruit and loading up on vegetables, nuts, seeds, fish, and seafood.

Alcohol: My Opinion

My opinion on alcohol is not popular. But the truth is, the very thing that we hope to get from alcohol — relaxation, relief from the stress of a busy day — is getting robbed from us. Most patients I guide through the Gottfried Protocol are eager to get back on booze. Most patients I talk to about transitioning to the Mediterranean diet interrupt me to sing the praises of red wine. I urge caution because that eagerness may signal a sticky relationship to alcohol, which may slow down or even halt your progress with hormone balancing and ketosis.

What does alcohol do to the body? Two glasses of Chardonnay contain more than 6 grams of carbs, and after being on the wagon for four weeks, your liver is clearer and alcohol can take it down, making you buzzed faster. Alcohol raises cortisol, which may then disrupt your sleep. This has a knock-on effect on insulin. We know that one night of bad sleep makes you more insulin resistant the next day. Higher cortisol may disrupt the regular insulin signal. If you are chronically disrupting it by consuming a moderate amount of alcohol, that will lead to more insulin resistance. Add to that high stress, not getting enough exercise to make your muscles hungry for glucose, and you start to get a compounded problem with insulin.

Simply put, alcohol can harm your hormones.[16] Alcohol is a neurotoxin. After ages thirty-five to forty, the blood-brain barrier (BBB) gets thinner, so alcohol hits harder and hangovers linger longer. Additionally, alcohol can alter the BBB by changing the normal function of your tight junctions. A leaky blood-brain barrier is linked to multiple problems, such as memory issues, multiple sclerosis, stroke, and Alzheimer's disease. Plus, alcohol is a carcinogen that increases a woman's risk of breast cancer, even at the modest dose of three servings per week.

Alcohol wreaks havoc on the liver, your primary detox organ. Alcohol is the toxin that goes to the front of the line in liver metabolism. It's like a triage system. Ridding alcohol from your system is your liver's top priority. That means that all the other toxins we are exposed to that we can't avoid — such as air pollutants and pesticides — get pushed to the back of the detox line when alcohol is around.

Half of US adults drink alcohol, and 10 percent have alcohol use disorder (AUD). Women get buzzed and drunk faster than men, even when adjusted for body weight, because we have more fat and less water, and there are other variations based on the menstrual cycle. Historically, alcohol misuse and AUD have been more common in men than women. However, recent data from the past ten years show we are catching up. The alcohol industry specifically targets women in their marketing campaigns and wants to normalize alcohol consumption, so that you feel it is a core part of feeling good and connected to others.

Binge eating is associated with AUD,[17] so if you want to correct your hormones and feel your best, limit or eliminate the alcohol. I encourage you to assess your relationship with alcohol honestly and reconsider whether it is good for your health, particularly after age thirty-five. Don't fall for the lie that Big Alcohol is telling you and that perhaps your friends have internalized.

KEEP DETOXING

By Day 29, you will have cleared out many toxic fats by following the Gottfried Protocol. Consuming healthy fats like olive oil, avocado oil, nuts, and seeds—along with fiber—will help you flush out the liver and gallbladder and rid toxic fats (from trans fats, fried foods, and excessive saturated fat) from your body. The job of the gallbladder is to break down fats after a meal. Eating healthy fat will trigger the hormone cholecystokinin to nudge the gallbladder to collect bile and release it into the intestines to improve digestion of fat. If you have had your gallbladder removed or have gallbladder issues, you may find that you digest MCT oil best because it is broken down more easily.

Some of my patients continue to have occasional constipation, and I repeat the same recommendations:

- Aim to evacuate fully your bowels a minimum of once (or twice) per day.
- Drink plenty of water, and add no-sugar electrolytes.
- Eat high-fiber vegetables, including lettuces and cruciferous vegetables.
- Add ground flaxseed and/or MCT oil to each meal.
- Take your magnesium — most of us are low, so I try to get my Gottfried Protocol participants up to 800 milligrams per day.
- Continue exercising and sweating — they will help you maintain your fat loss.

CONTINUE CIRCADIAN-BASED INTERMITTENT FASTING

You've now had firsthand experience in how effective intermittent fasting is, and, if you're like most of my patients, you probably find that it's a relatively easy lifestyle shift to make. That should be motivation enough to continue intermittent fasting through Transition and beyond. Your commitment will be met with improved insulin, growth hormone and other hormones, fat loss, and increased energy, vitality, and focus.

Throughout Transition, continue with the sixteen-hour overnight fast for about two to five days per week. Some of our Gottfried Protocol participants do it every night to keep their blood sugar, insulin, and ketosis in the optimal range. Hormones are released on a circadian rhythm, and you can keep yours releasing correctly by getting 10 minutes of morning light before 10 a.m., which helps raise melatonin at night and strengthens your hormonal rhythm. I do this with

Decision Tree for Transition

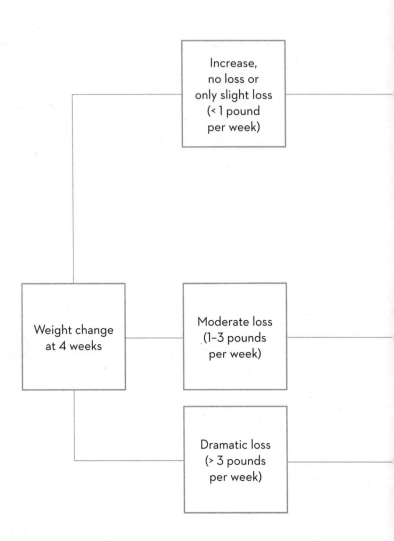

Honesty check:
are you cheating?

Yes → Connect to values and find that core reason that you really want to lose weight and try again.

Are you exercising enough? Increase activity levels with yoga, pilates, or walking.

No →

Increase vegetable consumption while decreasing fat consumption to reduce total calories without hunger.

Is your thyroid functioning properly? Ask your doctor to test for free T4, anti-TPO antibodies, and TSH.

Reduce carb consumption to crescendo levels.

Are your stress levels high and sleep poor? Increase exercise levels, develop a relaxing pre-sleep routine, and eat dinner earlier.

Nutrition: can you increase nutrient quality in your food choices — like replacing processed meats with simple high-quality meat?

Great! Continue with Gottfried Protocol.

No →

Increase carb consumption by 5g/day with foods like sweet potatoes, squash, avocado, and fruit.

Reduce activity/exercise levels if high.

Do you feel healthy, energetic, and inspired?

Yes → Continue Gottfried Protocol, but monitor energy and adjust if energy declines.

a dog walk most mornings. Continue circadian-based intermittent fasting past the four-week Gottfried Protocol if you've got more than 15 pounds to lose.

WHAT TO DO AFTER FALLING OFF THE WAGON

Look, it happens. Maybe it was a holiday splurge or a birthday celebration. At some point, you may find that you've overindulged in foods that take you out of ketosis and make you gain weight. When that happens, get back on the path as soon as possible. Return to your personal carb limit and aim below it. I advise my patients to plan their recovery meals in advance—Gottfried Protocol–compliant meals that will help you regain a sense of balance. To avoid further temptation and get back on track, make a contract with yourself. Start implementing it the day after your overindulgence. Here is a simple outline you can use:

Personal carb limit   _____

Eating window   _____

Breakfast   _____

Lunch   _____

Dinner   _____

Exercise goal   _____

Weight the next day _____

LAST THOUGHTS ON TRANSITION

As a final sendoff, remember to feed and nurture yourself. Have you taken my advice to find your favorite ways to hit the pause button? Found an app that supports you? Sometimes I need a daily reminder to reconsent to this process. I feel too busy to slow down, but we need to slow down in order for healing to occur. All healing takes place in the parasympathetic nervous system, where relaxation, deep belly breathing, and chilling out are the focus.

I believe the body is on loan from a Higher Power, so don't you want to take every measure to care for it? I know I do, and that's what I hope for my patients and tribe. That includes metabolic flexibility — your capacity to adapt to burning carbs or fat based on fuel availability.

Continue aiming for a BMI of 18.5 to 24.9 kg/m², but remember to break it down into modules. We discussed Lara's modules for weight loss in the last chapter; her initial goal or module was to lose 5 pounds of mostly fat in order to get her BMI to less than 24.9 kg/m².

For Lotus, the first module was the same as Lara's: to lose 5 pounds of mostly fat. The second module was to complete four weeks of the Gottfried Protocol, in which she lost a cumulative total of 12.5 pounds. The third module was to get her BMI under 24.9 during Transition while slowly switching to a lower-carbohydrate Mediterranean diet. In Transition, Lotus began to back off from the ketogenic ratio of 2:1 so we could see how her body (and weight) would respond to incrementally higher carb levels; this occasionally put her into a ketogenic ratio of 1:1. She even enjoyed a small piece of chocolate cake at her daughter's birthday celebration, but she got right back on plan with her next meal — and has lost a total of 33 pounds. A reasonable goal is to be like Lotus and continue to lose 3 to 5 pounds of mostly fat per month after you complete the Gottfried Protocol.

What's it worth to have the healthiest version of your body? I place the highest value on it, a higher value than the slight awkwardness of declining noncompliant food or alcohol when I'm visiting with friends, or the temptation when my daughter orders pizza. You won't feel your best if you are chronically inflamed, overwhelmed, depleted, or stressed. Take the time to perform Transition carefully and methodically in order to reach a level of health and vigor that you may not have known was possible for you.

Highlights

► In this chapter, we discussed reintroducing small doses of carbohydrates in order to define your personal carb limit. Take it step by step, or 5 grams of net carbs at a time, to determine your threshold for weight loss going forward.

► You may also choose to reintroduce alcohol and see how you respond to it, but be cautious and lower your dose — your liver pathways are now clear and alcohol will hit harder.

► Watch out for foods that spike your blood sugar or take you out of ketosis by tracking your glucose-ketone index. When you identify problem foods and eliminate them, you set yourself up for long-term hormonal balance, healthy fat burning, and the best symphony for your cells.

► Keep troubleshooting the most common issues in order to solidify the progress you've achieved with four-week Gottfried Protocol pulse.

► Remember that you gained weight gradually, and you will lose weight gradually. Go slow with Transition. Keep your eyes focused on long-term weight loss and maintenance.

► If you need ongoing support or a daily check-in, return to Chapters 5 and 6, and this chapter. Reread them as often as necessary.

► The Gottfried Protocol is not just another diet. It's a tool that allows you to get to know yourself on a deeper level, hormones and all, if you will allow it. It will teach you so much about how your food talks to your hormones, and vice versa. This increased self-awareness, intimacy, and knowledge will serve you for the years and decades to come.

8

INTEGRATION

Done! *Hurray!* In just over four weeks, you solved an enormous problem, one you may not have even known you had. You changed the food on your plate, changed the hormones in your tissues, and as a result, changed your life for the better. I am delighted because the investment you've made in your hormonal symphony will pay dividends for the rest of your life. Regardless of the symptoms you had when you first started this program — crossing a line with your weight, energy, infertility, stubborn belly fat, prediabetes, hot flashes, night sweats, moodiness, anxiety, insomnia, poor stamina — you can now go forward with knowing how foods impact your hormones and body. Consequently, you are now experiencing the benefits of a well-tuned orchestra and improved metabolic flexibility.

Now it's time to create a plan for the rest of your life that integrates hormonal balance. I'm here to cheer you on and provide guidance. I've learned over the years that there's no magic formula that keeps your weight exactly where you want it. Instead, it's the repetition of the little steps provided in this book that add up over time to major transformation. Commit to those steps, because small steps taken consistently are the most impactful. Repeat the Gottfried Protocol if and when symptoms of hormone imbalance recur (refer to pages 26–28 for the questionnaires), when you begin having trouble again with sugar cravings, or when you gain 5 pounds.

As you now know, the goal is metabolic flexibility, the healthy metabolic state in which the body shifts efficiently between the two main fuels: glucose and fat. When you perform intermittent fasting or restrict carbs, your body burns fat. When you eat more than your personal carb limit (defined in Chapter 7), your body burns glucose, setting up cravings for more and triggering fat storage. Insulin runs the show, but now that insulin is in a more balanced state, you can shift easily and rapidly, depending on which fuel is available and appropriate. When insulin is in the healthy range after completion of the Gottfried Protocol, the body can more easily switch between fat and glucose as fuel. I'll repeat: *the point of it all is metabolic flexibility.*

You may have been stuck before the Gottfried Protocol in a pattern of glucose burning from eating sugar or excess carbs, elevated insulin, and even insulin block. Over time, that can lead to other hormone imbalances and serious health problems, as we've discussed.

When food and hormones are out of whack, life is tough, even cruel and inhumane. It can turn us into numbed-out automatons going through the motions of daily experience. It can make us vulnerable to disease. That's especially true during a time of crisis. It can make challenging times feel daunting and frightening, or you may feel nothing at all. Maybe you've experienced significant grief. Maybe you got sick during the pandemic, or faced a different harrowing medical diagnosis. Maybe you gained the "quarantine 15" or have put on weight because of a stressful job. Maybe you lost someone you love, or a job. Taking a prescription pill may seem like the right answer, or at least an easy one.

Here's what I can tell you after a few decades of studying how pharmaceuticals compare to lifestyle changes: lifestyle changes are more effective than almost any prescription. The trick is making sure your values are in the right place, and being resolute about what is truly important to you. No more self-sabotage or internal debates, because you have the deciding vote with your next set of choices, from what's in your grocery cart to what's on your plate. When you can clearly state your values, your behavior aligns with them. The process becomes simple and empowering.

Remember what matters to you

In this final chapter, I want to take a moment to connect to your own desire for change. It's like an internal compass, pointing you toward your next actions, connections with people and places and ideas, and personal codes of conduct. That compelling desire or drive can only come from you. As you consider your desire to improve your metabolic health, I want to praise your success so far and accept any of your weaknesses, false starts, backsliding, or plateaus — all in an atmosphere of collaboration rather than confrontation, judgment, or belittlement.

By this point in *Women, Food, and Hormones,* you have a good sense of your priorities and values regarding food, hormones, and health. You know what your ideal fat mass and weight should be, and how you want your clothes to look and feel. Let's make these ideas more explicit and integrate them more thoroughly into our lives. Why? Because when you take the ambiguity out of what you value most and act in accordance with those values, life becomes simpler, more fun, and definitely more fulfilling. Trust me, life in congruence with your highest values is more like vacation. You are pulled forward by a strong, undeniable vision for yourself. Life is less about control, or the illusion of control that many of us use to cope with fear. Do you ever feel like weight loss is a matter of control? It's not. That's an illusion. Fear and control are not effective for long-term weight loss and health. Instead, long-term success is about valuing your metabolic hormones, metabolic flexibility, and health above all else, and eating in a way that is congruent with your values.

Revisit the personal value statement you wrote back in Chapter 5. Just as your metabolotype may change from apple to pear (or maybe even to celery!), your value statement may evolve to integrate fresh ideas and insights based on your experience. See if your personal value statement needs any editing. (If you skipped the exercise the first time, no problem — go back to Chapter 5 and write it for the first time. It can still be a compass going forward to help you maintain progress.) You may want to amend it by adding certain numbers, like the maximum weight you will allow before repeating the Gottfried Protocol or the minimum muscle mass you envision for yourself as you age.

IT'S NEVER TOO LATE TO BALANCE YOUR HORMONES

At the beginning of the book, I explained that it's never too late to get your metabolic hormones in order. You now have that enviable clean slate — you are in hormonal homeostasis. While following the Gottfried Protocol, you invested in detoxification, so your liver is no longer maxed out. You can easily fast and heal your body with fourteen to sixteen hours of metabolic rest to induce gentle ketosis. Hopefully, I've empowered you to apply what you know about the food-hormone connection so that you can solve or avoid the problems that are so prevalent in women after age thirty-five, from insulin resistance to diabetes, breast cancer, and heart disease.

You are not stuck with the hormones that you have, even if your doctor has dismissed your concerns or told you there's nothing you can do. The endocrine system, like all parts of the body, is malleable: it can keep growing, learning, storing new memories, and changing itself and the function of the body, often regardless of age and previous issues. You can always get the orchestra back on track. That's the promise and benefit of precision medicine. You want to keep your endocrine system interacting with your inner and outer world, as well as your gastrointestinal, neurological, and immune systems. You want to create balance across the cohesive whole of your body, and food is the great integrator. This level of attention to your food and hormones will keep you in a sound body and mind for years to come.

MAINTAINING
A BALANCED YOU

Your task going forward is to keep up the measurement — that is, the regular assessment of your weight, waist and hip measurements, and maybe your fat mass. Decide now, and add to your personal value statement this new line in the sand. If you cross that line because of a cheat day or a birthday celebration, do another pulse of the Gottfried Protocol for one to four weeks. For example, after vacation, I will sometimes follow Implementation for one week to get back on track. Or maybe you have a special event that's six weeks away — you could follow the program for the length of time that you need. However, I do not recommend staying in ketosis for longer than six months because of the limited safety data, particularly for women.

Pick your favorite meals from the past few weeks and make them part of your regular repertoire. Keep working your favorite practice and let it work you.

No doubt you will encounter challenges. Challenges are inevitable, but hormone imbalances are not. Build your resilience: continue feeding your healthy gut microbes by eating plants — and a lot of them, a pound per day. Keep monitoring your blood sugar and ketones after you complete the Gottfried Protocol, maybe every other day for a few weeks, and then once per week if you're stable and in the target zones. Maintain or grow your lean body mass by tracking it at least every quarter or yearly (more often if you are gaining weight) and by performing the exercise combination (two-thirds weight lifting to one-third cardio) that's been shown to be best for cardiovascular health. Sweat more: walk in the forest, practice yoga, or visit a sauna. Cultivate friendships with people who eat mindfully, so you can upgrade your habits and health span together.

You've already made great strides in balancing your hormones; now you want to maintain your progress. Over time, the commitment you make to your favorite Gottfried Protocol practices will aggregate into a habit, and eventually, a sense of integrity and freedom.

We started this book with the analogy of a cool summer breeze for food-based hormonal balance. My hope is that this final chapter adds further motivation, like the wind at your strong back as you move forward toward health and healing. Over the years, I've learned that staying motivated is a process. The weight loss, clarity, peace, equanimity, happiness, and mental focus of the Gottfried Protocol will energize you and keep you motivated, even more so than when you began, if you allow it.

LIVE YOUR VALUES

When it comes to hormones and body mass, I know what I want. I want to be that woman with sparkling eyes and effusive energy who is changing the conversation about hormones, who is a champion of others, and who practices what she preaches in a loop of integrity. I want to continue to be a leader in the new paradigm of medicine, which includes taking inventory of implicit bias, racial disparities, and health inequities, and promoting anti-racist policy and policy makers. Privately, I want to be emotionally connected with my family and friends, not distracted by thoughts of my thighs or bathroom scale or what to wear. I can't be whole if I'm thinking about whether I have a thigh gap. I want to nurture others. My values are a compass for who I want to be in the world and how I integrate research, studying, synthesis, writing, and teaching. This particular combination of values and roles nourish me, cell to soul.

James Baldwin, the American novelist, playwright, essayist, poet, and activist, wrote the following words: "I have always been struck, in America, by an emotional poverty so bottomless, and a terror of human life, of human touch, so deep that virtually no American appears able to achieve any viable, organic connection between his public stance and his private life." I agree. That's why we need to reach beyond the boundaries of our lives and get very intentional about our highest values and how they can map our life roles. And I hope that includes your unique biology as a woman, particularly your hormones.

Now it's your turn. How can you continue to refine your values and live in accordance with them, so that you avoid emotional poverty? This condition disrupts hormones in a way that food may not help. On the other hand, I've learned recently from a friend that the voids we experience in life can point to our most essential values. Whatever is missing, such as emotional nurturing of ourselves and others, can direct us to the complementary value that creates fulfillment. Personally, I recently left a job because it restricted my freedom to teach the content that matters most to me and also took me away from my family. It showed me how highly I value freedom, autonomy, and family life. Voids create values. What voids are you experiencing? Consider health, body size, your emotional life, your sense of security, the congruence between your public life and private life. Balance requires many inputs — and a prescription for the rest of your life to keep your head, heart, and hormones in balance.

PLEASE HELP
SPREAD THE WORD

Lifestyle choices, starting with food, play a huge role in hormonal health, and by extension, a person's total health. Together we need to raise the bar. We have a long way to go — please help spread the message by talking to your doctor and other health-care professionals about the topics in this book and the evidence-based Gottfried Protocol.

Tell your loved ones, especially your mothers, sisters, and daughters, that there is another way to handle the symptoms of hormonal craziness, fat accumulation, and weight gain. Chat with your friends and hair stylist about what you discovered about your own body while following these tenets. In many ways, you are your own best doctor. Share your story of challenge and success with me and others on social media. Help me spread the word. Serving others is good for the hormones. Please help me get the best information out to people who still suffer and desire change.

CLOSURE

For most of you, the Gottfried Protocol will provide a food-hormone framework that will allow you to reclaim your health and body, making big significant progress over four weeks.

Even though hormones can sometimes be vulnerable, prone to being pulled out of balance by modern lifestyle choices and exposures, the Gottfried Protocol will help you live in a happy, energized, and high-performance state in which food and hormones act as allies. That means there are ongoing, rich, deep conversations occurring between food, metabolic hormones, gut health (including the gut lining, the liver, the microbiome and its microbiota, and the immune system), heart and vascular system health, brain health, mitochondrial health, and fat (subcutaneous and visceral). Without those conversations, we can too easily fall back to the default setting, which we don't want. Avoid it.

Remember too that you've now got a comprehensive food plan in your back pocket — not a restrictive, short-term means to an end but a personalized dietary regimen that you've just tested on yourself. You also launched important daily habits that will help you govern life — in short, the broader precision-medicine protocol that will keep your hormones in homeostasis for the win. All of these new skills and habits, combined with what you've learned by following the Gottfried Protocol, provides closure on past dysfunction and new data to support a fresh start.

Lifestyle medicine is the most effective solution for the hormone dysfunction that we may face as women. Let your lifestyle choices lift you up rather than take you down. We find our own way amid the noise of the diet culture and the anti-diet culture. Ultimately, we get to make a decision about what to do with our food and our bodies. I support you in your decisions. You can get to a place of peace with your hormones and weight while still taking steps to become the healthiest possible version of yourself. Remember, your hormones are an orchestra, and there are no solo acts. There is only an integrated whole.

Finally, I hope you go beyond fixing your metabolic hormones to create a balanced, soulful existence. By creating balance between the sympathetic (fight-flight-freeze) and parasympathetic (rest-and-digest) nervous systems, the hypothalamic-pituitary-adrenal axis, and the endocrine glands, and by favoring positive thoughts and feelings about the body—you restore homeostasis. The only way to achieve it that I know of is with comprehensive lifestyle medicine, not the next prescription pill. It's the small daily choices that will influence your ability to return to balance. Lifestyle factors powerfully affect hormones, and vice versa. Leverage the malleability of your endocrine system and become stronger at the broken places. Your body will be at one with itself. You will get healthier and maybe reverse disease. Your body will learn to rewire itself to serve you and your highest values.

9

RECIPES AND MEAL PLANS

Now for the fun — and delicious — part! In this chapter, you will find my favorite recipes and meals, which will set you up for success on the Gottfried Protocol. The emphasis is on real whole foods and generous portions of healthy fats in order to restore hormone levels to optimal ranges. Whenever possible, use organic ingredients.

Small amounts of sea salt or kosher salt are suggested as seasoning while in ketosis, as long as you are avoiding processed food that is high in sodium and do not have a condition that warrants sodium restriction (examples include salt-sensitive high blood pressure, impaired kidney function, and increased calcium losses in the urine, but check with your doctor if you are unsure). When you restrict carbohydrates, your body excretes excess fluid, and sodium leaves with it. To make sure you have sufficient sodium levels, sprinkle a little sea salt (approximately ⅛ teaspoon) on your food.

As you will find, I've learned how to modify many popular dishes to make them keto-friendly, so you won't feel deprived or miss your favorite flavors and meals. You can see what I've done and then apply the same process to your most beloved meals.

SHAKES

I make a shake most mornings after a fourteen- to sixteen-hour fast and a workout (I exercise in a fasted state). My typical workout is two-thirds heavy weights and one-third cardio, but sometimes it's just slow-flow or restorative yoga. Consuming a functional shake is a great way to break a fast with dense nutrients, sufficient protein, and a small amount of carbs to restore the body. These are my favorite Gottfried Protocol shakes, but honestly, there is an infinite number of combinations that you can make from the following recipes, which are merely guides. The first recipe is a template that you can alter to suit your particular tastes and hormone-based requirements. Generally, I aim for 7 to 10 net carbs per meal to stay under my limit of 25 net carbs per day. I recommend using filtered water for all shake recipes. (For more on why filtered water is important, see page 130.)

The Basic Gottfried Protocol Shake for Ketosis

This great go-to shake is a perfect way to break your fast.

Serves 1

> *Liquid:* 6–8 ounces filtered water or favorite liquid (such as unsweetened almond, coconut, or cashew milk)
> *Vegetables:* ½–1 cup kale, spinach, mixed greens, and/ or 1 scoop Reset360 Super Greens or another organic greens powder
> *Shake powder (optional):* 1–2 scoops of a shake powder that provides a ketogenic ratio of 1:1 or better.
> *Fat:* ¼ of an avocado, 1–3 tablespoons flaxseed, 1–3 tablespoons soaked chia seeds (or other nuts or seeds), ½–1 tablespoon medium-chain triglyceride (MCT) oil or avocado oil, nut butters, or cacao nibs
> *Boosters:* 1–2 scoops supplemental fiber such as Reset360

Daily Fiber or another source of fiber, spirulina or chlorella, dark cacao powder, or cinnamon

Ice: 6+ ice cubes

1. In the jar of a high-speed blender, combine ingredients and whip to desired consistency.

Creamy Green Chia Shake

I like to keep extra greens stacked in glass containers in my freezer so I can easily add them to shakes as desired. This shake is a delicious and nutritious way to get extra greens into your diet. Note that I soak the chia seeds in the morning before my workout, so there is plenty of time for the soluble fiber to soak up to ten to twelve times its weight in water, creating a gel-like consistency that makes the shake creamier. Drinking a shake containing this chia water increases satiety and can help with rebalancing hormones.

Serves 1

4 ounces filtered water
2–3 tablespoons chia seeds, depending on desired thickness
2–3 ounces frozen kale
1/3–1/4 of an avocado, pit and skin removed
1/2 cup unsweetened coconut milk (or other unsweetened nut milk)
1 scoop or 1/2 serving of Reset360 Keto Thrive powder in vanilla
1/2–1 tablespoon MCT oil
6+ ice cubes
Optional: 1 scoop organic greens powder
Optional: 1–2 scoops supplemental prebiotic fiber

1. In the jar of a high-speed blender, soak chia seeds in filtered water for about 20 minutes before adding other ingredients. Whip to desired consistency.

Pumpkin Spice Shake

Fresh pumpkin has more carbs than several other vegetables, but it provides many important nutrients, including vitamin A, lutein, and zeaxanthin, all of which may help protect your eyesight. For this recipe, you can roast a small (4–6 pound) pumpkin in the oven at 400 degrees F for about 30 to 45 minutes. Split the pumpkin in half and sprinkle with sea salt. Allow to cool, then store the pumpkin in the refrigerator for up to three days or in the freezer for up to three months.

Serves 1

> 4–6 ounces filtered water
> ¼ cup pumpkin puree
> ½ teaspoon cinnamon
> ½ teaspoon allspice
> ½ teaspoon nutmeg
> ¼ teaspoon cloves
> Tiny peel of fresh ginger
> ½ cup unsweetened coconut milk (or other unsweetened
>   nut milk)
> 1–2 scoops of a ketogenic shake powder in vanilla
> ½–1 tablespoon MCT oil
> 6+ ice cubes
> Optional: 1–2 scoops supplemental prebiotic fiber

1. In the jar of a high-speed blender, combine ingredients and whip to desired consistency.

Post-Workout Shake

I started using cranberries in my shakes during the COVID-19 pandemic when all the other frozen fruit was sold out. Turns out cranberries tend to be neglected, but they are a nutrient powerhouse, with only 4 net carbs per ½ cup. They add tartness and color to a shake, and it's a good idea to aim for a variety of colors in your diet to help support immune resilience. Research shows that brightly colored vegetables and fruits are superior to most supplements in modulating immune function.

Serves 1

> ¼–½ cup cranberries
> ½ cup unsweetened coconut milk (or other unsweetened nut milk)
> 1 scoop or ½ serving ketogenic shake powder in vanilla
> ½–1 tablespoon MCT oil
> Handful of nuts (such as macadamia nuts, or others listed on page 119, no more than 28 grams)
> 6+ ice cubes
> Optional: 1–2 scoops supplemental prebiotic fiber

1. Place all ingredients in the jar of a high-speed blender and whip to desired consistency.

Iced Coffee Collagen Shake

This shake is a great way to get going in the morning — even when made with decaffeinated coffee. Think of it as a more nutritious version of a latte.

Serves 1

> 4 ounces unsweetened coffee or decaffeinated coffee, frozen
>> into cubes
> ¼–⅓ of an avocado, pit and skin removed
> 1 cup unsweetened coconut milk (or other unsweetened
>> nut milk)
> 1 scoop or serving of collagen or ketogenic shake powder
>> in vanilla
> ½ teaspoon Ceylon cinnamon
> ½–1 tablespoon MCT oil
> Handful of nuts (such as macadamia nuts, or others listed on
>> page 119, no more than 28–30 grams)
> 6+ ice cubes
> Optional: 1–2 scoops supplemental prebiotic fiber

1. Place all ingredients in the jar of a high-speed blender and whip to desired consistency.

Almond Butter–Cacao Nib Shake

This shake is like a liquid version of chocolate-almond bark.

Serves 1

> 6 ounces unsweetened almond milk
> 2 tablespoons chia seeds
> 1–2 scoops ketogenic shake powder
> 1–2 tablespoons almond butter
> ½–1 tablespoon MCT oil
> Handful of nuts (such as macadamia nuts, or others listed on
>> page 119, no more than 28–30 grams)
> 6+ ice cubes

Optional: 1–2 scoops supplemental prebiotic fiber
Optional: top with chopped almonds (1 teaspoon) and cacao
    nibs (1 teaspoon)

1. Soak chia seeds in almond milk for 20 minutes. Place seeds, milk, and remaining ingredients in the jar of a high-speed blender and whip to desired consistency.

Dragon Fruit Shake

I've been experimenting with low-carb fruits like pitaya (dragon fruit). The amount in this shake does not change my blood sugar levels — it represents 5 net carbs.

Serves 1

    1 cup unsweetened coconut milk (or other unsweetened
        nut milk)
    2 tablespoons chia seeds
    2 scoops ketogenic shake powder in vanilla
    1 scoop Reset360 organic greens powder or ½ cup frozen
        greens such as spinach or kale
    ½–1 tablespoon MCT oil
    6+ ice cubes
    Optional: 50 grams pitaya (dragon fruit) or other low-carb fruit
    Optional: 1–2 scoops supplemental prebiotic fiber

1. Soak chia seeds in milk for 5–10 minutes. Place all ingredients in the jar of a high-speed blender and whip to desired consistency.

Golden Milk Shake

Golden milk, or turmeric milk, is an anti-inflammatory drink that has been part of Indian food culture for many centuries. You will absorb the inflammation-fighting benefits of turmeric more readily if you combine it with fat.

Serves 1

> 1 cup unsweetened coconut milk (or other unsweetened nut milk)
> 1 scoop ketogenic shake powder in vanilla
> ½–1 tablespoon MCT oil
> Golden mix: 1 teaspoon turmeric powder, ½ teaspoon Ceylon cinnamon, ½ inch freshly grated ginger root or ½ teaspoon powdered ginger, and ¼ teaspoon ground cardamom
> 6+ ice cubes
> Optional: 1–2 scoops supplemental prebiotic fiber

1. Place all ingredients in the jar of a high-speed blender and whip to desired consistency.

Dark Chocolate–Sea Salt Shake

For the chocolate lover!

Serves 1

> 1 cup filtered water or unsweetened coconut milk (or other unsweetened nut milk)
> Handful of nuts (such as macadamia nuts, or others listed on page 119, no more than 28 grams)
> 2 scoops ketogenic shake powder in chocolate
> 1–2 scoops supplemental prebiotic fiber
> 1 tablespoon flaxseed
> ¼ teaspoon vanilla extract

1 tablespoon MCT oil
6+ ice cubes
Optional: 1–2 scoops supplemental prebiotic fiber
Optional: ⅛ teaspoon of coarse sea salt

1. Place all ingredients except salt in the jar of a high-speed blender and whip to desired consistency. Optional: sprinkle with sea salt.

Carrot Cake Shake

This recipe is adapted from one created by my friend Kelly LeVeque, a celebrity nutritionist and bestselling author.

Serves 1

1 cup unsweetened almond milk
1–2 scoops ketogenic shake powder in vanilla
1 ½ teaspoons ground cinnamon
1 tablespoon almond butter
1 tablespoon flaxseed
½ cup chopped raw carrots (about 4 net carbs)
½ cup frozen riced cauliflower (about 1.5 net carbs)
Optional: handful of spinach

1. Place all ingredients in the jar of a high-speed blender and whip to desired consistency.

Deep Green Shake

This shake is packed with detoxifying greens.

Serves 1

> 1 cup filtered water or unsweetened coconut milk (or other unsweetened nut milk)
> ½ cup of frozen dark leafy greens (spinach, kale, or the like)
> Handful of nuts (such as macadamia nuts, or others listed on page 119, no more than 28 grams)
> 2 scoops ketogenic shake powder in vanilla
> 1 tablespoon flaxseed
> ½ teaspoon cinnamon
> ¼ teaspoon vanilla extract
> ½–1 tablespoon MCT oil
> 6+ ice cubes
> Optional: 1 scoop organic greens powder
> Optional: 1 teaspoon spirulina
> Optional: 1–2 scoops supplemental prebiotic fiber

1. Place all ingredients in the jar of a high-speed blender and whip to desired consistency.

BREAKFASTS

Green Egg Scramble

I keep bamboo bags of greens in my freezer to throw into a shake or a sauté. Make your life easier by stocking up with bags of shredded brussels sprouts, spinach, radicchio, kale, and cabbage.

Serves 1

> 2 tablespoons extra-virgin olive oil
> 1 cup shredded greens, such as brussels sprouts, spinach,
>   radicchio, kale, or cabbage
> 2 pastured eggs, whisked
> 1–2 tablespoons fresh herbs such as basil, parsley, or thyme
> ¼ of an avocado, peeled and chopped

1. Sauté greens in olive oil over medium heat until softened. Place bed of greens on a plate. Scramble eggs in remaining oil; add herbs after eggs are set. Top greens with eggs and avocado, and serve immediately.

Avo Toast

Creamy and satisfying avocado smashed onto well-toasted keto bread is a divine quick meal. I make it by first spreading extra-virgin olive oil and peeled, smashed garlic onto the toast before adding the mashed avo, but there are endless variations.

Serves 1

> 1 piece keto bread (about 4 net carbs) — see Tahini Bread recipe (page 206) and Resources
> 1 garlic clove, peeled and crushed
> 1 tablespoon extra-virgin olive oil
> ¼ of an avocado, pit and skin removed
> Fresh lemon juice
> Sea salt
> Optional toppers: chopped herbs (cilantro, dill, parsley), chopped radish, sliced tomato, Pesto (see recipe on page 223), chimichurri, a poached or fried pastured egg, pickled red onion, seeds (pumpkin, sunflower), red pepper flakes

1. Toast bread. Rub the garlic clove on bread, and drizzle with olive oil. Mash avocado in a bowl and spread onto toast. Top with lemon juice and sea salt, to taste. If desired, add another optional ingredient.

Coffee Cake

I love this bread! You have to commit to taking only one serving — the aroma while it's baking is very tempting. I find that certain sugar substitutes like stevia tend to make me overeat, so I measure my serving and then walk away from the rest of the loaf. Note that I developed this recipe when I was deeply into ketosis. If you have taste buds trained to a crappy carb diet, this keto coffee cake may not taste right to you. But if you're in ketosis, it will taste divine. The flax meal, rich in omega-3s, will help balance your omegas.

Serves 12 to 15

> 1 cup filtered water
> 1/2 cup flax meal
> 1/2 cup coconut flour (can substitute almond flour)
> 1/2 teaspoon fine Himalayan pink salt
> 1 teaspoon baking soda
> 1/2 cup grass-fed butter, plus more to grease the pan (can substitute ghee or coconut oil)
> 1 teaspoon almond extract
> 1 teaspoon ground cinnamon
> 3 pastured eggs
> 1 tablespoon apple cider vinegar
> 3–4 drops liquid stevia (use plain, or consider English toffee flavor)
> 1/3 cup stevia chocolate chips (total 3 net carbs)
> Optional: fresh lemon zest

1. Preheat oven to 350 degrees F. Grease a loaf pan with butter, ghee, or coconut oil.
2. Combine water with flax meal in a small bowl and set aside.
3. In a medium bowl, whisk or sift together coconut flour, salt, and baking soda. Whisk in melted butter, then add eggs and moistened flax mixture. Mix in vinegar, stevia, and chocolate chips. Add lemon zest, if desired, to taste.
4. Place mixture in the greased loaf pan and bake for 40–45 minutes, until the top is browned. Let loaf cool on a rack for 15–30 minutes. To serve, cut into 12 to 15 slices. Store in the refrigerator or freezer.

Tahini Bread

Tahini (sesame paste) is an excellent choice on the Gottfried Protocol because the macronutrient ratio of fat, protein, and carbs is 76:10:14. Tahini is low in net carbs (about 1.8 net carbs per tablespoon).

Makes 1 loaf

> 1 ½ cups tahini
> 4 eggs
> 1 ½ tablespoons apple cider vinegar
> ¾ teaspoon baking soda
> ½ teaspoon salt
> 1 tablespoon sunflower seeds, plus 1 teaspoon for topping
> 1 tablespoon sesame seeds, plus 1 teaspoon for topping
> 1 tablespoon chia seeds, plus 1 teaspoon for topping
> 1 tablespoon pumpkin seeds, plus 1 teaspoon for topping

1. Preheat oven to 350 degrees F, and line a loaf pan with parchment paper.
2. Mix all ingredients until well combined and pour into prepared pan.
3. Sprinkle with reserved teaspoon of each seed, and bake until loaf is slightly brown on top, and firm.

Courtesy of Nathalie Hadi

Frittata with Spinach, Eggplant, and Pine Nuts

I cook this frittata in a cast iron pan to get a small dose of iron along with the stellar amino acid profile of pastured eggs. If you eat dairy-free, you can make this without the heavy cream.

Serves 4

> 1 cup Japanese eggplant, cut into ½-inch rounds and then into
> ½-inch cubes
> Sea salt
> 2 tablespoons extra-virgin olive oil
> 1 cup spinach
> 6–8 pastured eggs
> ¼ cup heavy cream
> 2 tablespoons parsley, chopped
> 2 tablespoons pine nuts, toasted

1. Preheat oven to 350 degrees F. Sprinkle eggplant with sea salt. Sauté eggplant in olive oil over medium heat (don't let it smoke) for about 15 minutes. Add spinach and sauté for 1 more minute. Whisk eggs with heavy cream and pour into pan. Place pan in oven and bake for 20 minutes or until eggs are set. Top with parsley and toasted pine nuts.

Shakshuka

This Middle Eastern dish, pronounced "shahk-shoo-kah," is traditionally served for breakfast, but you can eat it anytime. It can be served
with a small amount of yogurt, kefir, or tahini, which is the lowest in net
carbs. Traditionally, shakshuka contains tomato paste, but I removed it
because of its sugar content.

Serves 2 to 4

> 2 tablespoons grape-seed oil
> 1 large yellow onion, chopped
> 1 red or green bell pepper, chopped
> 1 small hot pepper, deseeded and chopped
> 4 garlic cloves, smashed and chopped
> 2–3 cups ripe tomatoes, chopped
> 2 teaspoons cumin
> 1 teaspoon salt
> 1 teaspoon ground pepper
> 2 cups spinach
> 4 large pastured eggs
> Optional: ½ cup feta cheese
> Optional: ¼ cup fresh parsley, chopped

1. In a large deep pan, heat the oil over medium heat and sauté the
   onions until brown. Add the peppers and garlic. Cook for about 5
   minutes until soft, then add the tomatoes, cumin, salt, and pepper.
   Cover and cook on low heat for another 5 to 10 minutes, stirring often.
2. Add the spinach, and let the vegetables simmer for another 10 to
   15 minutes until you've made a thick sauce. Feel free to taste and
   adjust the seasonings.
3. Once the sauce has thickened, make four small wells in it, in the
   pan. Carefully crack each egg and place one into each of the wells.
   (It's easier if you crack each egg individually into a glass and gently
   pour it into the sauce.) Make sure that the yolks do not break. The
   egg whites should spread out over the sauce; use a fork to swirl the
   whites if needed.
4. Once you've added all the eggs, cover the shakshuka and heat for 5
   to 10 minutes, until the egg whites have cooked. The yolks should

remain slightly soft. Remove from the stove and top, if desired, with feta and fresh parsley. Enjoy this dish while it's hot!

Adapted from Brain Body Diet *by Sara Gottfried, MD*

Egg-Avocado Bake

Avocados are the quintessential ketogenic plant-based food. Halved avocados are a great container for other nutrient-dense foods like an egg or crabmeat. Avocados come in many sizes, so you can scale the recipe for the size of the freshest avocados you can find and, as we discussed earlier, take care not to eat too much avocado each day. Pro tip: put a couple of drops of hot sauce or whatever condiment you like in the hole before you add the egg.

Serves 2 people per avocado

Avocados, halved, pit and skin removed
Eggs (1 egg per avocado half, meaning 2 per whole avocado)
Optional: hot sauce, Pesto (see recipe on page 223), chimichurri
Salt and pepper to taste
Optional: cilantro, scallions, hot chilies, greens as toppings

1. Scoop out some of the flesh (about 1 tablespoon) of an avocado half, so there is a hole big enough for an egg. Repeat with remaining avocado halves.
2. Put the avocado halves in a small baking dish. You want them to be snug, so they don't tip over. It helps to nestle the avocados in pie weights, dried beans, or coarse salt to keep them standing up straight. Crack one egg at a time into a small ramekin or glass. Slide the egg carefully into the hole of an avocado half; repeat for each half. Season avocado halves with salt and pepper, and drizzle any desired condiments over them. I like to use a little Pesto or chimichurri here. Bake at 450 degrees F for 10 to 12 minutes, or until egg whites are set but the yolks are still a little runny.
3. Douse with greens or other toppings (cilantro, scallions, and hot chilies are all delicious options!).

Adapted from Younger *by Sara Gottfried, MD*

SALADS

Basic Green Salad

When you make salads, rotate the greens — romaine, red romaine, butterhead, oakleaf, red Lolla Rossa, mesclun, endive, radicchio, spinach, kale, watercress, cabbage, Swiss chard, collard greens, and so on — from day to day. Add any available raw or steamed vegetables, including bell peppers, broccoli, or cauliflower, for example. We know that extra-virgin olive oil is very heart-healthy, so think of salads as a prebiotic vehicle for it. I aim for 4 to 5 tablespoons of extra-virgin olive oil per day — on salads, steamed vegetables, keto bread, and shirataki noodles.

Serves 2 to 4

> 1 tablespoon shallot, peeled and chopped
> 1 tablespoon red wine vinegar (or another no- or low-carbohydrate vinegar like Champagne vinegar or apple cider vinegar)
> 2 cups torn or chopped greens, such as romaine or butter lettuce
> 1 cucumber, chopped (I do not peel if organic)
> ½ cup bell pepper, sliced
> ½ cup broccoli sprouts (or any type of sprouts: alfalfa, sunflower, mung bean, radish, cress, fenugreek, or the like)
> ¼ cup carrots, grated
> ½ cup cherry tomatoes, sliced in half
> 2–3 tablespoons extra-virgin olive oil
> 1 tablespoon sunflower seeds
> 2 tablespoons fresh thyme, chopped
> Optional: add ¼ cup grated cheese (such as Parmesan or Asiago, or vegan cheese), another healthy protein (such as nuts, shrimp, wild salmon), or a combination

1. In a small bowl, soak chopped shallots in red wine vinegar. In a large bowl, combine all the other vegetables.
2. Blend vinegar and shallots with olive oil. Toss this dressing with vegetables, coating them well. Top with sunflower seeds, fresh thyme, and any optional additions.

Little Gem Salad

Little Gem lettuce has a flavor somewhere between that of romaine and butter lettuce. If you can't find this variety, use half of a heart of romaine instead.

Serves 2 to 4

> 2 cups Little Gem lettuce, torn
> ½ cup jicama, sliced
> ¼ cup red onion, sliced
> ¼ cup poblano chili pepper, chopped
> ½ of an avocado, halved, pitted, peeled, and sliced
> 1–2 tablespoons almonds, chopped
> 2 tablespoons extra-virgin olive oil
> 1 tablespoon Champagne vinegar
> 2 tablespoons pumpkin seeds
> 2 tablespoons cilantro, chopped
> Optional: small amount of queso fresca (literally "fresh cheese," usually a mixture of cow and goat cheese), such as cotija or Oaxacan cheese
> Optional: moderate amount of protein (2–3 ounces), such as a chicken thigh or drumstick, salmon, low-mercury tuna, or shrimp

1. In a large bowl, combine all ingredients through almonds. Separately, combine olive oil and Champagne vinegar, then drizzle on top of salad, and toss. Top with pumpkin seeds, cilantro, and optional protein.

Chopped Greens and Marcona Salad

The Marcona almond, known as the "queen of almonds," is imported from Spain. These almonds are shorter and rounder than the California variety. I buy them blanched, roasted in olive oil, and sprinkled with sea salt from the grocery store or online.

Serves 2 to 4

> 2 cups greens (such as romaine, mesclun, endive, radicchio, spinach, kale, or the like), chopped
> ½ cup jicama, chopped
> ¼ cup Manchego cheese, chopped
> 2–3 tablespoons Marcona almonds, chopped
> 2–3 tablespoons extra-virgin olive oil
> 1 tablespoon Champagne vinegar (or red or white wine vinegar, or apple cider vinegar)

1. Combine all ingredients through almonds. Whisk olive oil and Champagne vinegar, and toss with salad.

Tea Leaf Salad

You can purchase organic laphet fermented tea leaves online or at some grocery stores. Or just omit them from the recipe.

Serves 2 to 4

> 1 cup romaine lettuce, chopped
> 1 cup green or purple cabbage, chopped
> ½ cup cherry tomatoes, sliced in half
> 1 red bell pepper, sliced
> Tea Leaf Dressing (recipe follows)
> 1-2 tablespoons sunflower seeds
> 1-2 tablespoons sesame seeds
> Optional: peanuts, cooked yellow split peas

1. Place the romaine lettuce in a shallow bowl and top with vegetables. Toss with Tea Leaf Dressing, then top with sunflower and sesame seeds.

Tea Leaf Dressing

> ¼ cup white vinegar
> ¼ cup loose green-tea leaves (such as sencha) or laphet fermented tea leaves, packed in olive oil
> ¼ cup organic sesame oil
> ¼ cup avocado oil
> ½ tablespoon fish sauce
> Juice of ½ lemon
> 1 tablespoon fresh ginger, minced
> 1 garlic clove, smashed and minced

1. Add ingredients to the jar of a high-speed blender and whip until smooth.

Crispy Cucumber Salad
with Tahini Dressing

Kohlrabi, or German turnip, is another cruciferous vegetable that aids in detoxification. It can be eaten raw or lightly cooked.

Serves 2 to 4

> 2–4 Kirby, English, or Persian cucumbers, thinly sliced (I do not peel if organic)
> 2 kohlrabies, thinly sliced
> 1 fennel bulb, thinly sliced
> ½ of a jicama, chopped
> ½ cup red onion, finely chopped
> 1 cup fresh cilantro, chopped
> 3–4 tablespoons Tahini Dressing (recipe follows)
> 2 tablespoons pumpkin seeds

1. In a large bowl, combine the cucumber, kohlrabi, fennel, jicama, and onion. Add the cilantro, and toss well with Tahini Dressing. Top with pumpkin seeds.

Adapted from Brain Body Diet *by Sara Gottfried, MD*

Tahini Dressing

Tahini is made from either hulled or unhulled sesame seeds. Unhulled seeds have a more distinct, bitter flavor, whereas hulled seeds are nuttier and make for creamier tahini. Unhulled whole sesame seeds have more calcium, yet hulled seeds are still quite rich in calcium and other nutrients. It's a question of personal preference. You can use this dressing with Crispy Cucumber Salad or as a topping for grilled chicken or roasted vegetables.

> 1 cup 100 percent pure ground tahini (made of sesame
>   seeds only)
> ½ cup filtered water, room temperature or warmed
> ¼ cup extra-virgin olive oil
> ¼–½ cup fresh lemon juice
> 3–4 garlic cloves, smashed and finely chopped
> Dash of salt
> Dash of black pepper

1. Place the ingredients through garlic in a sealable container, and shake well until fully combined. The mixture should turn from a paste into a white sauce. Add more water or lemon juice until the dressing reaches your preferred consistency and flavor. Season with salt and pepper.

Adapted from Brain Body Diet *by Sara Gottfried, MD*

"Taco" Salad

This version of the taco salad is dense with nutrients, without losing the yum factor. The onion in the ground meat and the Pico de Gallo (recipe follows) adds prebiotic fiber to promote healthy microbiota in the gut. I prefer Pico de Gallo to salsa in this salad because it's chunkier, crunchier, and less runny.

Serves 4 to 6

> 1 pound of grass-fed, grass-finished ground beef (may substitute pastured ground chicken, turkey, or pork)
> 1 medium yellow onion, chopped
> 1 tablespoon extra-virgin olive oil
> 1 teaspoon ground cumin
> 1–2 heads romaine lettuce, torn into bite-sized pieces
> 1 red cabbage, sliced and diced
> 1 avocado, pitted, peeled, and chopped
> 2 Persian cucumbers, coarsely chopped (I do not peel if organic)
> 8 ounces cheddar cheese, grated (I like raw-milk cheddar, medium sharp; a nondairy cheese can be substituted)
> Pico de Gallo (recipe follows)
> Keto Taco Dressing (recipe follows)
> Optional: ½ cup full-fat sour cream (can substitute crème fraîche or full-fat plain yogurt), fresh herbs, chopped avocado

1. Prepare the meat first. In a medium saucepan, add olive oil and most of the chopped yellow onion (reserve 2 tablespoons for Pico de Gallo). When onion is softened, add ground meat and work with a wooden spoon to break into small crumbles. Cook until meat is brown throughout, then add cumin.
2. Assemble Pico de Gallo.
3. Create a bed of romaine lettuce and red cabbage (about 4–8 ounces per person). Cover with ground meat (3–4 ounces for women, 5–6 ounces for men). Add remaining ingredients in layers; top with grated cheese and, if desired, a dollop of sour cream or other topping option. Add Pico de Gallo and Keto Taco Dressing to taste.

Pico de Gallo

¼ cup tomatoes, chopped
3 scallions, chopped
Chopped fresh chilies (or ½ teaspoon chipotle powder)
Juice of 1 lime
1 tablespoon chopped fresh cilantro

1. Combine ingredients in a small bowl.

Keto Taco Dressing

1–2 fresh chipotle peppers or ½ teaspoon chipotle powder
Juice of 1 lemon
2 tablespoons extra-virgin olive oil

1. Whip ingredients in the jar of a high-speed blender until smooth.

Torn Greens with Ranch Dressing

My family loves to spoon this delicious Ranch Dressing over grilled romaine hearts or use it as a dip for cucumber slices. By the way, why tear salad greens? Because it increases their nutrient density.

Serves 2 to 4

> 2–8 cups romaine lettuce, kale, spinach, or other greens, torn
> 1 cup Mayonnaise (recipe follows, or purchase a brand made
>   with avocado oil)
> Ranch Dressing (recipe follows)

Mayonnaise

> 1 cup avocado oil, extra-virgin olive oil, or a mixture
> 1 yolk from a pastured egg
> 1 tablespoon Dijon mustard
> Juice of ½ lemon
> ½ teaspoon salt

1. Place all ingredients in a narrow container or jar. I use the mixing cup that came with my immersion blender, but a half-pint jar works well too. Place the head of the immersion blender at the bottom of the jar and turn the blender on. The bottom of the jar should quickly emulsify (you'll see it turn white and thick). Slowly move the immersion blender up toward the top of the jar as the mixture emulsifies. If any oil slips back down into the jar, simply move the head of the blender down to mix it in, then continue lifting the blender up toward the surface until all the oil is incorporated and the mixture is thick. This process takes 1 to 2 minutes.

2. This Mayonnaise will keep covered in the refrigerator up to 1 week, depending on the freshness of your egg.

From Younger *by Sara Gottfried, MD*

Ranch Dressing

¼ cup coconut milk
1 teaspoon apple cider vinegar
1 teaspoon onion powder
1 garlic clove, finely minced
1 teaspoon dried dill or 1 tablespoon fresh, minced
2 teaspoons dried parsley or 2 tablespoons fresh, minced
1 tablespoon dried chives or 3 tablespoons fresh, minced
Salt and pepper to taste

1. Add these ingredients to 1 cup of Mayonnaise. Stir until well combined. Add coconut milk as needed to thin the mixture. Season with salt and pepper to taste. Pour the dressing over the torn greens, and toss.
2. Ranch Dressing will keep for 1 week, covered, in the refrigerator. It will thicken as it chills.

Adapted from Younger *by Sara Gottfried, MD*

Seaweed Salad

Seaweed is high in essential minerals, including iodine, calcium, iron, copper, magnesium, manganese, molybdenum, phosphorus, potassium, selenium, vanadium, and zinc. Some seaweed salads that can be bought premade include added sugar or not-so-great oils and vinegars. Here's one that's cleaned up, ready to spruce up your thyroid function.

Serves 2 to 4

> 2 ounces dried wakame (or a seaweed mix)
> 1 small daikon radish, julienned
> ½ English cucumber, julienned (I do not peel if organic)
> 1 tablespoon extra-virgin olive oil
> 1 teaspoon sesame oil
> Juice of half a lime or half a lemon
> 2 teaspoons fresh ginger juice
> 1 tablespoon tamari (gluten-free soy sauce)
> 4 tablespoons walnut or avocado oil
> ½ teaspoon stevia, or to taste
> Pinch of sea salt
> Optional: toasted sesame seeds, crushed roasted nori, diced avocado

1. Soak seaweed in cold water for about 5 minutes, until it's rehydrated and no longer tough. Rinse and drain. If there are any large pieces, chop them. Combine the seaweed, daikon, and cucumber in a medium bowl.
2. To make the dressing, mix the remaining ingredients in a small bowl. Add dressing to seaweed mixture, toss, and let sit for a few minutes for the dressing to be absorbed. Add optional toppings if desired, and eat salad with chopsticks.

Adapted from Younger *by Sara Gottfried, MD*

Kale and Caesar Salad with "Raw Parmesan"

A dairy-free version of the classic. If you want to get a jump-start on preparing this salad, make the dressing ahead of time. It will keep for twenty-four hours in the refrigerator.

Serves 4 to 6

> 1 bunch lacinato kale
> 2 heads romaine lettuce
> 1 cup cherry tomatoes, halved
> ½ cup cashews, soaked for 2 hours or more
> ¼ cup hemp
> ¼ cup nutritional yeast
> Juice of 2 lemons
> 1 garlic clove, crushed
> ½ teaspoon sea salt or pink Himalayan salt
> ⅓ cup filtered water
> ⅓ cup extra-virgin olive oil
> Optional topping: "Raw Parmesan" (recipe follows)

1. Destem the kale, then finely chop the leaves. Rinse, spin in a salad spinner, then pat dry. Place kale in an extra-large bowl. Tear the romaine into bite-size pieces. Rinse, spin in a salad spinner, then pat dry. Add lettuce to the bowl of kale. You should have roughly 2 to 3 cups of chopped kale and 4 to 6 cups of torn romaine. Fold in cherry tomatoes.

2. To make the dressing, rinse and drain the cashews. In a blender or food processor, combine the cashews and the remaining ingredients. Blend until smooth. Add the dressing to the greens, and toss until coated. If needed, add salt to taste, and toss again. If desired, sprinkle salad with "Raw Parmesan" and serve.

"Raw Parmesan"

½ cup macadamia or cashew nuts, not soaked
1 teaspoon nutritional yeast (or more, to taste)
Optional: pinch of garlic powder

1. Grate the nuts, or process them in a food processor. Add remaining ingredients, and mix or process until combined.

Adapted from Younger *by Sara Gottfried, MD*

Cauliflower Ceviche

Cauliflower may be the most versatile vegetable in the Gottfried Protocol.

Serves 2 to 4

1 head of cauliflower
1 small red onion, diced
3 tomatoes, diced
2 red chilies, diced
½ cup cilantro, chopped
Juice of 5 lemons
Sea salt and pepper
1 tablespoon extra-virgin olive oil

1. Steam whole cauliflower for 5 minutes. Cut into small pieces.
2. Mix cauliflower, vegetables, and cilantro in a big bowl. Add lemon juice, salt, and pepper to taste, and combine well. Leave in refrigerator to marinate for 30 minutes. Drizzle with olive oil, and serve.

Adapted from Nathalie Hadi

SAUCES AND SALSAS

Keep keto boredom at bay! These sauces and salsas are great to have on hand in the refrigerator, so that you can add zing to your meals, along with healthy extra-virgin olive oil and other phytonutrients.

Chermoula (Moroccan Green Sauce)

2 garlic cloves, peeled and crushed, then chopped
¼ cup extra-virgin olive oil
¼ cup parsley, chopped
½ cup cilantro, chopped
1 teaspoon paprika
½ teaspoon cumin
Juice of 1 lemon
Sea salt to taste

1. Pound garlic with a mortar and pestle. Add herbs and remaining ingredients, then mix well.

Pesto

I love pesto made with a wide range of greens. Certainly basil and pine nuts are the classic base, but you can use my template in this recipe and apply chard, kale, arugula, and any other greens, and combine them with any of your favorite nuts. Delicious on shirataki noodles or keto toast!

2 garlic cloves, peeled, crushed, and chopped
2 tablespoons of nuts, such as pine nuts, walnuts, or almonds
2 cups greens, such as basil, or kale or chard with stems cut away
½ cup Parmigiano-Reggiano, grated
¼ cup extra-virgin olive oil

1. Process garlic and nuts in a food processor. Add greens and olive oil, then add cheese last, and process again.

Pepita Salsa

I love this salsa on flaxseed crackers (available at grocery stores and on-line) or keto bread.

½ cup roasted pumpkin seeds
½ cup extra-virgin olive oil
¼ cup cilantro
1 tablespoon white wine vinegar

1. Combine ingredients in the jar of a high-speed blender and whip until smooth.

SOUPS AND BROTHS

Alkaline Broth with Collagen

Give yourself a nonsurgical facelift with this collagen boost. This broth is delicious to sip, hot or cold, when you feel like you need a little something extra.

Serves 2 to 12

> 1–2 cups of three of the following vegetables, roughly chopped: celery, fennel, green beans, zucchini, spinach, kale (destemmed), chard (destemmed), carrots, onion, garlic, cabbage
> ½–1 teaspoon spice (such as cumin or turmeric)
> Filtered water (enough to cover the vegetables)
> Optional: 1 tablespoon powdered collagen protein (Bulletproof and Great Lakes are good brands)

1. Place vegetables and spices in a large soup pot, and cover with filtered water. Bring to a boil, then simmer on low for 30 to 45 minutes. Strain the broth, and set vegetables aside for another use. Whisk in the powdered collagen protein, if using.

Adapted from Younger *by Sara Gottfried, MD*

Avgolemono (Lemon-Chicken Soup with Riced Cauliflower)

In college, avgolemono was my favorite Greek comfort soup. I've adapted this version with riced cauliflower, but I've seen other recipes that use sesame seeds. This recipe has about 5–6 net carbs per serving.

Serves 4

> 4 tablespoons extra-virgin olive oil
> 1 yellow onion, finely chopped
> 6 celery stalks, minced
> 3 cups riced cauliflower
> 4 cups Chicken Bone Broth (see recipe on page 227)
> 2 pastured eggs, at room temperature and beaten
> 4 pastured chicken thighs, cooked and shredded
> Juice of 1 lemon
> Salt and pepper to taste
> Optional: lemon zest, chopped parsley

1. In a Dutch oven or stockpot, heat olive oil over medium heat. Stir in onion and celery, and cook until translucent. Add riced cauliflower and Chicken Bone Broth, and stir to combine. Remove soup from heat, and cool for at least 10 minutes.

2. Remove ¼ cup of stock, place in a bowl, and whisk the eggs into it energetically, so that the egg whites do not curdle. Very slowly whisk this egg-stock mixture into the remaining cooled stock. Add chicken, stir, and gently reheat. Season with salt and pepper. Serve immediately, with a squirt of the fresh lemon juice; top with lemon zest and parsley, if using. This soup can be kept in the refrigerator for 3–4 days or stored in the freezer, in an airtight container, for 3 months.

BONE BROTHS

Bone broth is rich in collagen, a protein needed for healthy skin, teeth, and nails. Your body's production of collagen declines with age, which is why those wrinkles, neck wattles, and weak joint cartilage can catch up with us. For our family, making bone broth is the most convenient way to get collagen into our food plan. If the process sounds disgusting, just start with chicken bones, filtered water, and a slow cooker — the slow cooking breaks the collagen down into gelatin. You'll be amazed. You can use the broth recipes when broth is called for in other dishes in this chapter. Expect cooking your own broth to take several hours. You can also purchase powdered bone broth at the grocery store or online.

Chicken Bone Broth

Serves 2 to 12

> Bones, feet, and neck from 1 chicken
> 2 small onions or shallots, roughly chopped
> 1 head garlic
> 1 teaspoon peppercorns
> 1 or 2 bay leaves
> 2 tablespoons sea salt
> 2 tablespoons apple cider vinegar
> 4 quarts filtered water
> 1 bunch fresh herbs, such as tarragon, per serving

1. Put all the ingredients except the fresh herbs into a large stockpot and let sit for an hour. Bring the broth to a boil, and get rid of any foam that rises to the top. Cook on a very low flame for 8 to 12 hours. Let cool. Separate the meat (if any) from the bones. Strain the broth. Allow to cool, and place in glass jars, leaving 1 to 2 inches of space at the top to prevent breakage of the glass. Keep in the refrigerator for up to 4 days, or freeze.

2. To serve, warm a serving of strained broth to the desired temperature (do not boil). Wash the fresh herbs, and add a large handful for extra minerals and taste.

Adapted from Younger *by Sara Gottfried, MD*

Beef Bone Broth

Serves 2 to 12

> 2 pounds (or more) femur bones from grass-fed cattle, or other bones from a healthy source
> Optional: 2 feet from pastured chicken, for extra gelatin
> Filtered water (enough to cover contents)
> 2 tablespoons apple cider vinegar
> 1 onion, roughly chopped
> 2 carrots, roughly chopped
> 2 stalks celery, roughly chopped
> 1 tablespoon or more sea salt
> 1 teaspoon peppercorns
> Optional: additional herbs or spices, to taste
> 2 cloves garlic, roughly chopped
> 1 bunch parsley, roughly chopped

1. If you are using raw bones, especially raw beef bones, it improves flavor to roast them in the oven before making the broth. Place them in a pan, and roast for 30 minutes at 350 degrees F. Then put the bones, including the chicken feet, if using, in a 5-gallon stockpot. Pour the filtered water over the bones, and add the vinegar. Let sit for 20 to 30 minutes. The acid from the vinegar helps make the nutrients in the bones more bioavailable.

2. Add onions, carrots, and celery to the pot. Season with salt, peppercorns, and additional spices or herbs, if using. Bring the broth to a boil. Once it has reached a vigorous boil, reduce heat to a simmer, and keep the broth simmering until it is done.

3. During the first few hours of simmering, remove the impurities that float to the surface. A frothy or foamy layer will form and can

be easily scooped off with a big spoon and thrown away. I typically check the broth every 20 minutes for the first two hours to do this. Bones from grass-fed, healthy animals produce far fewer impurities than bones from conventionally raised animals.

4. During the last 30 minutes, add the garlic and parsley.
5. Remove broth from the heat, and allow it to cool. Strain the broth, using a fine-mesh strainer to remove all the bits of bone and vegetable. Store cooled broth in quart-sized glass jars (leave 1–2 inches of space at the top to prevent breakage of the glass) in the refrigerator for up to four days, or in the freezer to use later.

Adapted from Younger *by Sara Gottfried, MD*

Fish Bone Broth

Bone broth detoxifies and nourishes the kidneys, according to traditional Chinese medicine. Fish stocks made from fish heads have thyroid-strengthening properties. For this recipe, do not use bones from oily fish, such as salmon, because the broth will stink up the whole house! Use only non-oily fish, such as sole, turbot, rockfish, or my favorite, snapper. I use this broth as a base for shirataki noodles and vegetables such as purple cabbage, broccoli, and bell peppers.

Serves 2 to 12

> 3 quarts filtered water
> 2 pounds fish heads and bones (fish heads alone will suffice)
> ¼ cup raw, organic apple cider vinegar
> Himalayan or Celtic sea salt to taste

1. Place water and fish heads and bones in a 4-quart stockpot. Stir in vinegar while bringing the water to a gentle boil. As the water rolls and bubbles, skim off any foam that rises to the surface. It is important to do this because the foam contains impurities and off flavors. Reduce heat to a simmer, and cook broth for at least 4 hours but no more than 24. Add salt at the end of cooking, to taste. Cool and then strain the broth into containers for refrigeration. Freeze what you will not use in one week.

Chicken-Ginger Soup with Cabbage "Pasta"

Get creative by substituting vegetables for pasta. Good candidates include cabbage (as in this recipe), hearts of palm, and spiralized zucchini (also known as zoodles).

Serves 4

2 tablespoons extra-virgin olive oil (or coconut oil)

1-inch piece of fresh ginger (or more, if you like it spicy), washed, peeled, and diced

1 medium yellow onion, diced

2–4 cloves of garlic, crushed and sliced

2 quarts filtered water

4 pastured chicken thighs, bone in

¼ green cabbage, finely shredded (a chiffonade)

2 tablespoons MCT oil

Sea salt and pepper

Optional: fresh cilantro or tarragon, torn, as garnish

1. Prepare the base. Heat the olive oil in a large soup pot over medium heat, and add the ginger, onion, and garlic. Cook for 5 minutes, stirring, until onion is translucent. Add water and chicken, and bring to a boil. Continue simmering for 30 minutes or until the chicken is thoroughly cooked.

2. Remove ginger and chicken. Shred the chicken and return it to the soup. Season with salt and pepper to taste.

3. To serve, place a bed of cabbage (about ½ cup) in each bowl. Ladle soup over cabbage. Top with ½ tablespoon of MCT oil and fresh torn herbs, if using.

4. Store soup base in the freezer for up to one month or in the refrigerator for 3–5 days.

Gazpacho

A refreshing summer soup, made keto with extra-virgin olive oil.

Serves 4 to 6

2–3 green, red, and yellow peppers, seeded
1–2 cucumbers (I do not peel if organic)
1 red onion, peeled and diced
1 avocado, halved, pitted, peeled, and chopped
1 cucumber, diced
3 medium heirloom tomatoes, diced
2 garlic cloves, smashed and diced
2 tablespoons fresh lemon juice
2 tablespoons apple cider vinegar
2 tablespoons each chopped basil, parsley, and cilantro
1 cup extra-virgin olive oil
Optional: a clump of fresh crabmeat as topping

1. Place peppers and cucumber(s) in the jar of a high-powered blender and puree. In a bowl, combine this mixture with the remaining ingredients, and chill for 3–4 hours. Gazpacho keeps in the fridge for up to 5 days.

Sorrel Soup

Easy to Make Vegan or Vegetarian

Serves 4, hot or cold

> 8 ounces unsalted grass-fed butter
> 2 yellow onions, diced
> 4–6 garlic cloves, smashed and diced
> 10 cups fresh sorrel leaves, rinsed, with stems removed
> 4 cups Chicken Bone Broth (see recipe on page 227) or
> vegetable/vegan broth
> 1 cup fresh Italian flat-leaf parsley
> 2 teaspoons grated nutmeg
> Pinch of cayenne pepper
> Himalayan sea salt and black pepper to taste
> 1 cup full-fat sour cream or crème fraîche
> Optional: fresh chopped chives for garnish

1. Melt the butter in a soup pot over medium heat. Add the onions and garlic and cook, covered, until tender and translucent, about 15 minutes. Add the sorrel, cover, and cook until it is completely wilted, about 5 minutes.
2. Add bone broth, parsley, nutmeg, and cayenne, and bring to boil. Reduce heat, cover, and simmer for 50 minutes. Add salt and pepper to taste.
3. Transfer soup in batches to a blender, and puree until smooth. If serving hot, return soup to pot and heat slowly over low heat, stirring constantly. If serving cold, transfer to a glass or stainless steel bowl, cover, and chill at least 4 hours in the refrigerator. Ladle into bowls and garnish with sour cream or crème fraîche and chives, if using.

French Onion Soup

A twist on the classic to support the microbiome.

Serves 4 to 6

1–2 tablespoons grape-seed oil

3 large yellow or white onions, quartered and thinly sliced

6 cups vegetable broth, or 4 cups filtered water plus 2 cups
Chicken Bone Broth (see recipe on page 227)

2 cups greens (kale, chard, or spinach), thinly sliced

1 bay leaf

½ cup fresh thyme, chopped

Sea salt to taste

1 teaspoon fresh ground pepper

½ cup grated vegan cashew-nut cheese or nutritional
yeast flakes

¼ cup green onions, chopped

1. Heat the grape-seed oil in a large pot, and cook the onions until
they are soft and browned.
2. Add the broth, greens, and bay leaf. Season soup with thyme, salt,
and pepper. Simmer over low heat for 1 hour.
3. To serve, top each bowl of soup with cashew nut cheese or
nutritional yeast flakes and green onions.

Thai Coconut-Chicken Soup (Tom Kha Gai)

Easy to Make Vegan or Vegetarian

Kaffir lime leaves are sometimes hard to find. The zest and juice of one lime can be substituted. You can make this soup without chicken, and instead of fish sauce, use vegetarian broth and tamari.

Serves 6 to 8

> 2 stalks lemongrass
> 1 large piece of Chinese ginger, peeled and chopped
> 2 cloves garlic
> 10–12 kaffir lime leaves
> 2 whole cardamom pods
> 6 cups Chicken Bone Broth (see recipe on page 227)
> 1 pound pastured chicken breast or thighs, cut into
>   1-inch pieces
> 1 cup chopped shiitake mushrooms
> 1 13.5-ounce can unsweetened coconut milk
> 3 tablespoons fish sauce
> Chili oil and cilantro leaves for serving

1. Remove base of lemongrass stalks with a sharp knife, and discard tough outer layer.
2. Chop lemongrass stalks into 2-inch pieces and toss into a blender with the chopped ginger, kaffir lime leaves, and garlic cloves. Pulse a few times until ingredients form a pulp. Add blended ingredients plus 2 cardamom pods to large stockpot over medium-high heat, cooking for 1 to 2 minutes, until fragrant. Add Chicken Bone Broth. Once it's boiling, reduce heat to low and simmer for 20 to 30 minutes, to allow flavors to infuse. Strain the broth through a fine sieve into a large clean pan.
3. Add chicken and mushrooms to broth, and simmer for 20 to 25 minutes, until chicken is cooked through. Remove from heat. Stir in the coconut milk and fish sauce. Garnish with chili oil and fresh cilantro leaves.

Tofu Masala Soup

This delicious soup contributed to Dr. Anu French's success on the Gottfried Protocol.

Serves 4

> 1 tablespoon ghee
> ½ red onion, chopped
> 2 cloves garlic, minced
> 1-inch piece of ginger
> 2 tablespoons olive oil
> 1 cup sliced portabella mushrooms
> ½ bell pepper, chopped
> 1 cup cherry tomatoes, sliced
> ½ teaspoon turmeric powder
> ½ teaspoon garam masala
> 3 cups veggie broth
> 1 cup bok choy, roughly chopped
> 6 ounces extra-firm tofu, cut into cubes
> Salt to taste

1. Add ghee to a large soup pot, and sauté red onions, garlic, and ginger until onions are translucent.
2. Add 1 tablespoon of the olive oil, then the mushrooms, bell pepper, tomatoes, turmeric, and garam masala, and sauté 5 minutes. Add the broth to this mixture and allow to come to a brief boil, then add bok choy and tofu. Add remaining 1 tablespoon olive oil. Add salt to taste. Simmer for another 10 minutes.

Courtesy of Anu French, MD

Creamy Goddess Greens Soup

This soup is delicious hot or cold. Make extra for lunch the next day. Easy to make vegan or vegetarian.

Serves 4 to 6

2 tablespoons coconut oil
3 cups cauliflower florets, chopped
6 asparagus spears, chopped
2 large shallots, thinly sliced
2 cloves garlic, smashed and roughly chopped
1 cup arugula
1 cup broccoli rabe florets
½ cup watercress leaves
3 cups organic vegetable or free-range chicken broth
¾ cup coconut milk
3 tablespoons lemon juice
¼ teaspoon cayenne pepper
1 teaspoon dried rosemary
2 tablespoons extra-virgin olive oil
Salt and pepper to taste

1. Heat coconut oil in a large soup pot over medium heat. Add cauliflower, asparagus, shallots, and garlic, and cook until cauliflower is tender and shallots are translucent.
2. Reduce heat to low. Stir in arugula, broccoli rabe, and watercress. Keep stirring over low heat until leaves have brightened.
3. Add broth.
4. Working in batches, transfer soup to a blender, and puree until smooth.
5. Return to pot over low heat. Stir in coconut milk, lemon juice, cayenne, rosemary, olive oil, salt, and pepper.

MAIN DISHES

Tahini-Sesame Noodles

When I'm on the Gottfried Protocol, one of my favorite swaps for pasta is shirataki noodles, or "miracle noodles," made from konjac root, an excellent source of prebiotic fiber. Konjac root is the source of glucomannan, a type of fiber that has been shown to be associated with weight loss. Konjac grows in Japan, China, and Southeast Asia. *Shirataki* is Japanese for "white waterfall," a reference to the noodles' translucent appearance. It comes in a variety of noodle shapes, from fettuccine to angel hair, and in the shape of grains of rice. (See Resources for the brands that I use.) This calorie-free, carb-free food is 97 percent water and 3 percent glucomannan. It absorbs sauces very well — just be sure to rinse it well in a colander with warm filtered water before using.

Serves 2

> 2 tablespoons tahini
> Juice of 1 lemon
> 4 tablespoons MCT oil or extra-virgin olive oil
> 2 teaspoons sesame oil
> 1 tablespoon tamari
> 1 cup of chopped or ribboned vegetables of your choice (I love broccoli, purple cabbage, and zoodles — noodles made from zucchini)
> 1–2 packages of shirataki noodles, fettuccine style, rinsed in warm water

1. Combine tahini with lemon juice, MCT oil (or olive oil), sesame oil, and tamari. Whisk until smooth. In a large bowl, create a bed of shirataki (you don't need to cook them — just rinse in warm water), add the vegetables, and top with the tahini mixture. Toss and serve.

Kimchi, Shirataki, and Bok Choy Bowl

If you want to avoid cooking with oil, you can steam the vegetables instead of sautéing them and add the olive oil before serving.

Serves 2

> 2 tablespoons extra-virgin olive oil
> 14 ounces (2 packages) vermicelli-style shirataki noodles
> 4 cups baby bok choy, thinly sliced
> 2 Japanese eggplants, thinly sliced (about 2 cups)
> 2 tablespoons sesame seeds
> 2 cups greens (kale, chard, or spinach), thinly sliced
> Kimchi to taste
> 1 tablespoon organic sesame oil
> 1–2 tablespoons extra-virgin olive oil

1. Over medium heat, sauté half the shirataki noodles (1 package), baby bok choy, and Japanese eggplant in olive oil (alternatively, you could steam them). Sprinkle with sesame seeds.
2. Assemble all ingredients in a pretty bowl: greens and uncooked shirataki on the bottom, sautéed mixture in the middle, and kimchi on the top. Drizzle with sesame oil and olive oil.

Adapted from Brain Body Diet *by Sara Gottfried, MD*

Vegetable "Fettuccine" Alfredo

The "fettuccine" noodles in this recipe are made of vegetables. Unlike the traditional heavy Alfredo sauce, the one in this recipe relies on Brazil nuts to provide substance and texture. It's fine to vary the amounts of vegetables as you prefer.

Serves 4

2 extra-large turnips, spiralized
1 cup carrots, shredded
2 cups lacinato kale, destemmed and shredded
6 tablespoons Brazil nut butter (or ½ cup Brazil nuts)
6 tablespoons water
2 tablespoons apple cider vinegar
2 tablespoons tamari
Sea salt to taste

1. Combine the turnips, carrots, and kale in a large bowl. To make the sauce, blend the rest of the ingredients in the jar of a high-speed blender. Pour about ¼ cup of the sauce over the vegetables, adding more if you need it, to create an even coating. Store the leftover sauce in the refrigerator for up to 3 days.

Salmon and Avocado Bowl with Miso Dressing

Serves 4

> 4 6-ounce salmon fillets (or steelhead trout, which has a
>   similar taste)
> 1 or 2 lemons, sliced in half for rubbing
> Sea salt
> 2 teaspoons fresh lime juice
> 2 teaspoons white miso
> 2 teaspoons filtered water
> ¼ teaspoon freshly ground pepper
> 3 tablespoons extra-virgin olive oil
> 6 cups romaine lettuce, torn
> 1 avocado, peeled and diced
> ¾ cup cucumber, sliced (I don't peel if organic)
> ½ of a red bell pepper, thinly sliced
> ¼ cup walnuts, toasted

1. Preheat the broiler. Place the oven rack about 6 inches from the broiler. Line a baking sheet with foil.
2. Arrange the salmon fillets on the sheet, skin side down. Rub them with lemon and season with sea salt. Broil until the salmon is just cooked through, 7 to 10 minutes (depending on thickness). Remove the skin from each fillet. Chop salmon into generous bite-size pieces.
3. While salmon is cooking, prepare the dressing: In a small bowl, whisk together the lime juice, miso, water, and pepper. While whisking, slowly pour in the extra-virgin olive oil.
4. In a large bowl, combine cooked salmon with lettuce, avocado, cucumber, and red bell pepper, and toss. Divide among four plates. Drizzle 1 tablespoon of the miso dressing over each salad. Top with walnuts and serve.

Adapted from Younger *by Sara Gottfried, MD*

Grilled Salmon Steaks with Lemon-Herb Mojo

Can you tell I love salmon? It's my top choice for resolving inflammation by means of your fork.

Serves 2

> 8 ounces salmon steak
> Sea salt and pepper for seasoning
> 1 teaspoon sesame or grapeseed oil
> 1 cup Lemon-Herb Mojo (recipe follows)

1. Preheat oven to 450 degrees F. Season salmon with salt and pepper and place on foil with sesame or grapeseed oil. Bake salmon until cooked through, approximately 12 to 15 minutes. Plate with a generous serving of Lemon-Herb Mojo.

Lemon-Herb Mojo

This sauce is superb on salads, roasted vegetables, chicken, or fish.

> Juice of 2 lemons
> 3–4 tablespoons avocado oil or extra-virgin olive oil
> 2–3 garlic cloves, roughly chopped
> ½ of a red onion, roughly chopped
> ½ cup fresh cilantro or parsley
> Sea salt to taste

1. Place all the ingredients in a food processor. Pulse to combine until you've created a fragrant, well-blended sauce.

Adapted from Brain Body Diet *by Sara Gottfried, MD*

Halibut with Almond Crust

I love making this dish with halibut from Alaska, where I attended high school. You can substitute salmon or other fish fillets that will hold up to the almond coating.

Serves 6

> 6 halibut fillets, approximately 3 to 6 ounces each
> Sea salt and pepper
> 1 teaspoon grape-seed oil
> 1 cup chopped blanched almonds
> ¼ cup chopped fresh parsley
> 1 tablespoon lemon zest
> 1 pastured egg, beaten

1. Preheat oven to 400 degrees F. Sprinkle halibut with salt and pepper. Mix almonds, parsley, and lemon zest in a shallow dish. Brush fillets with egg and press into almond mixture to coat.
2. Oil a baking sheet, and place halibut on top. Bake until cooked and crust is brown, about 12 to 15 minutes, depending on the thickness of fillets.

Adapted from Nathalie Hadi

Black Cod with Miso

If you're tired of salmon at this point, consider black cod, also known as sablefish. It has as much omega-3 fat as salmon.

Serves 2

> 2 tablespoons regular olive oil (not extra-virgin, which has a
>   lower smoke point)
> ½ cup white miso paste
> 3 tablespoons tamari
> Optional: 1 tablespoon erythritol sweetener or few drops of
>   stevia (optional)
> 1 pound (2 to 4 fillets) black cod
> Avocado oil for pan

1. To make marinade, mix the olive oil, white miso paste, tamari, and sweetener, if using, in a container and set aside. Clean the fillets and pat them dry. Place the fillets in the container, coat them with the marinade, cover, and refrigerate overnight.
2. Preheat the oven to 400 degrees F. Remove the fish from the fridge and scrape off the marinade. Coat a cast iron skillet with avocado oil, and heat at medium-high. Add the fish, and brown, about 2 minutes per side.
3. Transfer the fillets to the oven and bake until flaky, about 10 minutes.

Adapted from Younger *by Sara Gottfried, MD*

Braised Turmeric-Cinnamon Chicken

Divine comfort food. Pro tip: It's all about the two-hour simmer. Don't cut it short. This dish is delicious served over riced cauliflower and steamed spinach.

Serves 4 to 6

> 1 whole chicken with skin, chopped into 8 pieces (or substitute chicken thighs)
> Sea salt to taste
> Freshly ground pepper
> Ground cinnamon
> Turmeric
> 2 tablespoons olive oil
> 1 medium to large yellow onion, chopped
> 4 cloves garlic, chopped
> 2 cinnamon sticks
> 1 14-ounce can whole peeled Italian tomatoes (no sugar added)
> 1–2 cups Chicken Bone Broth (see recipe on page 227)
> Fresh mint and parsley to garnish

1. Wash and dry chicken pieces. Season all over with salt, pepper, and a light sprinkling of ground cinnamon and turmeric.
2. Coat a large pot with olive oil and place over medium heat. When oil is heated, sear chicken pieces for 1 minute on each side, until the skin is browned. Remove chicken pieces from pan and set aside.
3. Lower heat to medium-high and add onions. Stir for 1 minute or until soft, then add garlic. Let cook for another minute, until translucent. Add cinnamon sticks, tomatoes, and broth, and season with salt and pepper. Stir and bring to simmer. Add chicken pieces back into the pot, submerging them in the liquid. Simmer for about 2 hours uncovered, shaking the pan from time to time to move the chicken around, until meat is falling off the bone.
4. Garnish with mint and parsley, and serve.

Adapted from Younger *by Sara Gottfried, MD*

Slow-Cooker Chicken

I love the simplicity of this meal in a pot. Just five ingredients, plus wa-ter. You could probably use an Instant Pot (mine is still in the cabinet, untouched). To make sure the chicken is cooked all the way through, make sure the internal temperature gets to 165 degrees at some point during the cooking. This is the perfect nourishing soup to eat when you don't feel well.

Serves 4 to 8

> 3 large onions, thinly sliced
> 4–8 cups filtered water (enough to cover chicken)
> 1 pastured whole chicken
> 1 onion, chopped
> 1 cup celery, chopped
> 1 cup carrots, chopped
> Optional: 2 cups spiralized zucchini

1. Assemble the sliced onion, water, and chicken in a slow cooker. Cook on high for 4 to 6 hours or on low for 6 to 8 hours. Add water, if necessary, to keep chicken covered. Add celery and carrots for the last hour of cooking. If desired, add spiralized zucchini as an alternative to noodles.
2. After soup is fully cooked, remove chicken and shred. Place some in the bottom of each soup bowl. Ladle broth and veggies over chicken, and serve.

Adapted from Brain Body Diet *by Sara Gottfried, MD*

Nut-Crusted Chicken Fingers

A crowd-pleaser for both kids and adults. The chicken fingers can be placed on top of a salad or served with a sauce (try the recipe for Pesto on page 223, or use chimichurri or your favorite low-carb hot sauce).

Serves 2 adults or up to 4 children

> ½ cup ground nuts (macadamia nuts, almonds, or walnuts)
> ¼ cup ground flax
> ¼ cup sesame seeds
> 1 large pastured egg
> 1 8-ounce pastured boneless skinless chicken thigh, cut
>   into strips

1. In a small bowl, combine the ground nuts, flax, and seeds. In a separate bowl, beat the egg. Place the strips of chicken in the egg to marinate for 5 minutes, flipping the strips to coat as needed.
2. Preheat the oven to 350 degrees F. Cover a large baking tray with parchment paper.
3. Once the chicken is coated well in egg, carefully press each strip into the nut mixture, making sure it is well coated on both sides. Then place the coated chicken on the baking tray. Do not crowd the pieces.
4. Bake for about 20 minutes. Remove the chicken from the oven. Turn the chicken pieces and return them to the oven for another 15 to 20 minutes, until fully cooked and golden.

Adapted from Brain Body Diet *by Sara Gottfried, MD*

Beef and Vegetable Stew

This is one of the hearty soups that prevented hunger cravings for me, leading to success the third time I tried a ketogenic diet.

Serves 6 to 12

> 4 tablespoons coconut oil (expeller-pressed)
> 8 cloves garlic, minced
> 2 pounds stew meat from grass-fed beef, cut into bite-sized pieces
> 1 large yellow onion, chopped
> 5 carrots, chopped
> 5–7 stalks celery, chopped
> 1 cup butternut squash, cubed
> Optional: 1 cup red wine (preferably organic; note the alcohol will burn off while cooking)
> 6 bay leaves
> 3 sprigs fresh thyme or 1/2 teaspoon dried
> 1 sprig fresh rosemary or 1 teaspoon dried
> 1 teaspoon smoked paprika
> 2 quarts Beef Bone Broth (see recipe on page 228)
> Sea salt and pepper to taste
> Optional: 1–2 tablespoons almond butter, to thicken

1. In a heavy stockpot, heat the coconut oil over medium-high heat. Add garlic and meat, and cook until the meat is browned, but be careful not to burn the garlic. Add the vegetables and stir until they are mixed in well with the meat (you may need to add more oil). Add the red wine and cook for 5 to 8 minutes to allow the alcohol to cook off, so it doesn't affect ketosis. Add spices. Stir to combine. Add broth.

2. Cover and bring to a boil, then lower heat to simmer for 1 hour. Taste for salt and seasoning. If you want a thicker stew, add the optional almond butter. Provided the veggies are done, the stew is now ready to eat. But if left to cook at a very low heat for 3 to 4 hours, it will be even tastier.

Adapted from Younger *by Sara Gottfried, MD*

VEGETABLES

Baked Jerusalem Artichokes with Thyme and Lemon

Jerusalem artichokes are full of prebiotic fiber.

Serves 4 to 6

> 1 ½ cups heavy cream or crème fraîche
> Juice of 1 lemon
> 2 garlic cloves, peeled, smashed, and chopped
> 1 handful of fresh thyme, chopped
> ½ cup Parmesan, grated
> 2 ¼ pounds Jerusalem artichokes, peeled and sliced like a pencil
> 1 slice keto bread, toasted
> Extra-virgin olive oil

1. Preheat oven to 425 degrees F. In medium bowl, mix cream, lemon, garlic, half of the thyme, and most of the Parmesan. Add artichokes and stir to combine.
2. Use food processor to pulse toasted keto bread into crumbs. Add remaining thyme and Parmesan to the food processor and combine. Place artichokes in a gratin dish. Sprinkle with the dry topping and drizzle with olive oil. Bake 30 minutes.

Roasted Eggplant

I love the delicate taste of Japanese eggplant, but you can substitute other varieties, such as the teardrop-shaped American or the rounded European. For a sauce, try this chapter's recipe for Tahini Dressing or Chermoula.

Serves 2 to 4

> 4 Japanese eggplants, sliced into rounds on the diagonal, approximately ½ inch thick
> Spray olive oil or coconut oil
> Sea salt and pepper to taste

1. Preheat oven to 350 degrees F. Set eggplant slices on a parchment-lined baking sheet and spray with oil. Roast until tender, about 15 to 20 minutes. Season with salt and pepper, and serve with the sauce of your choice.

Steamed Artichokes

Don't be intimidated by the work of cooking and eating artichokes. It's a divinely flavorful vegetable to include in the Gottfried Protocol. The options for dipping will add flavor, along with a dose of healthy fat. If you'd like, make your own mayonnaise (see the recipe for Mayonnaise on page 218), or keep a good brand in your refrigerator (see Resources).

Serves 2 to 4

> 2–4 medium artichokes
> 2–4 cloves of garlic, to taste
> 1 bay leaf
> Juice of 1 lemon
> 2–4 tablespoons mayonnaise, melted butter, or ghee,
>   for dipping

1. Trim artichokes — cut off top inch and stem, and use kitchen shears to clip the tips of the pointy leaves. Make sure that the bottom of each artichoke is flat; trim as needed.
2. Fill a pot with several inches of cold water, and add garlic, bay leaf, and lemon juice. Place a steamer basket in the pot and add artichokes. Make sure the water doesn't rise above the bottom of the basket, so that the artichokes steam rather than boil. Cover the pot, bring water to a boil, then reduce heat to a simmer. Steam until the leaves can be plucked easily from the artichoke — about 20 to 30 minutes.
3. To eat: Starting at the base of the artichoke, pluck one leaf at a time. Dip it in mayonnaise or another fat, then pull the base of the leaf through your teeth to scrape away the delicious fleshy part. Continue the process, one leaf at a time. When you come to the fuzzy center, which sits on top of a meaty core known as the heart, scrape away the fibrous fuzz to get to the heart. The edible disk that remains is the best part.

DESSERT

Keto Pumpkin Custard

This may sound like a holiday dessert, but it's scrumptious at any time of year.

Serves 4 to 6

> 15 ounces canned pumpkin puree (or roast your own, as explained on page 196)
> 2 large pastured eggs
> 1 cup heavy cream
> ¼ cup granulated erythritol sweetener
> 1 ½ teaspoons pumpkin pie spice
> ½ teaspoon salt
> 1 teaspoon vanilla extract
> Optional: 1 teaspoon xanthan gum

1. Preheat oven to 350 degrees F. Place 4 to 6 ramekins (or small shallow bowls) in a large pan with high enough sides to hold a water bath. Fill a kettle with water, and set to boil.
2. In a large mixing bowl, combine pumpkin puree, eggs, cream, sweetener, spice, salt, vanilla, and xanthan gum, if using. Whisk together until smooth.
3. Divide the mixture among ramekins. Place the whole pan of ramekins into the oven, and then carefully fill the pan with hot water until the water reaches halfway up the sides of the ramekins. (Or, if you prefer, you can fill the pan before putting it in the oven.)
4. Bake for 40 minutes or until set (an inserted knife should emerge mostly clean). Carefully remove the ramekins from the water bath (I use kitchen tongs with rubber bands wrapped around the end of each tong, to get a good grip), and allow custard to cool on a wire rack. Store in the refrigerator.

No-Bake Coconut Love Bites

These are a healthy alternative to fat bombs! I use organic vanilla extract.

Serves 12 to 20

> 3 cups unsweetened shredded coconut
> 6 tablespoons coconut oil
> ½ cup xylitol or erythritol sweetener
> 2 teaspoons vanilla extract
> ½ teaspoon Himalayan sea salt
> Optional toppings: shredded coconut, unsweetened cocoa powder, finely chopped nuts, dark chocolate with stevia — melted for piping or drizzling

1. Put all ingredients (except toppings) into a food processor or blender. Combine until the mixture is blended and sticks together. (Note: If you are using a high-powered blender like a Vitamix, do not turn your machine on high as it may melt the batter.) Remove the mixture from the blender or food processor and form into desired shapes. I usually make balls with a melon scooper.
2. Decorate with toppings as desired. I use a plastic bag with a tiny hole cut in the corner to pipe the chocolate, or you can just drizzle it. You can also leave them plain.
3. Leave to firm up at room temperature on a plate or other hard surface.

Adapted from Younger *by Sara Gottfried, MD*

Almond-Coconut Macaroons

A keto update of the Passover favorite.

Serves 6 to 12

> 1 cup almond or coconut flour
> 2 cups unsweetened shredded or flaked coconut
> Optional: 1 teaspoon cocoa powder
> 2 large pastured eggs
> ½ teaspoon salt
> ½ teaspoon vanilla extract
> ½ teaspoon cinnamon powder

1. Preheat oven to 300 degrees F.
2. In a large bowl, mix together the almond flour and shredded coconut. Add the cocoa powder, if using. In a separate bowl, beat together the eggs.
3. Pour the eggs into the flour mixture. Add salt, vanilla, and cinnamon.
4. Wet your hands and form little balls of batter. Pat them tightly together. Place the macaroons at least 1 inch apart on a baking tray lined with parchment paper.
5. Bake for about 15 to 20 minutes, or until cookies are golden in color.

Adapted from Brain Body Diet *by Sara Gottfried, MD*

Dark Chocolate–Coconut Pudding

I eat dessert only twice per week, and this recipe truly satisfies.

Serves 4

> 2 cups coconut milk (reserve 2 tablespoons for dissolving gelatin)
>
> 1 tablespoon high-quality unflavored powdered gelatin (a form of collagen that is soluble only in hot liquid)
>
> 3–4 ounces dark chocolate (90 percent cocoa solids), chopped into small pieces
>
> ½ teaspoon vanilla extract
>
> Pinch of sea salt

1. Reserve 2 tablespoons of the coconut milk. Heat the rest on low in a heavy-bottomed pot.
2. In a separate small pan, mix the reserved coconut milk with the gelatin, and stir over low heat for a few minutes until dissolved; set aside. In the heavy-bottomed pan, add the dark chocolate to the coconut milk and whisk constantly until it melts completely and mixture is smooth.
3. Add the gelatin mixture to the chocolate mixture by slowly pouring it in as you whisk. (If you put it in all at once, the mixture will get clumpy.) Turn off the heat and whisk in the vanilla extract.
4. Pour the pudding into bowls or cups, and chill for at least 2 hours, or until set. Garnish with a pinch of sea salt and serve.

Adapted from Younger *by Sara Gottfried, MD*

Chocolate-Avocado "Ice Cream"

For those who love the frozen stuff — this alternative is much more nutritious.

Serves 2 to 4

1 avocado, halved, pitted, peeled, and chopped
1 can (13 ½ ounces) full-fat coconut milk
½ cup unsweetened cocoa powder
¼–½ cup erythritol sweetener or monk fruit extract
½ cup filtered water
2 teaspoons vanilla extract
½ teaspoon sea salt

1. Place the avocado and coconut milk in a food processor or blender and combine. Add the remaining ingredients and blend for about 2 minutes, until smooth. You may need to stop partway and scrape down the sides. Freeze the "ice cream" using one of these methods:

MACHINE METHOD

2. Place mixture in the container that came with your ice cream machine, and put in the refrigerator for 2 hours, to set up before freezing. Then prepare and freeze according to the manufacturer's instructions.

HAND METHOD

Place mixture in a freezer-safe container and freeze for 1 hour. Over the next 3 to 4 hours, remove the mixture from the freezer every 20 minutes and whisk it slightly, to prevent it from getting too icy. It should thicken after each whisking until it's firm enough to scoop.

3. Prior to serving, let the "ice cream" thaw a little, for 5 to 10 minutes.

Adapted from Brain Body Diet *by Sara Gottfried, MD*

Avocado-Lime Sorbet

Refreshing and light.

Serves 2 to 4

> 2 ripe avocados, halved, pitted, peeled, and chopped
> 2 cups unsweetened almond milk (or filtered water, if you
>   prefer a lighter taste and icier texture)
> ¼–½ cup xylitol or erythritol sweetener or monk fruit extract
> 2 tablespoons fresh lime juice
> 1 tablespoon lime zest
> ½ teaspoon sea salt

1. Place the ingredients in a food processor or blender and combine until smooth. Freeze the sorbet using one of these methods:

MACHINE METHOD

2. Chill the container that came with your ice cream machine, then place the mixture in it. Prepare and freeze according to the manufacturer's instructions.

HAND METHOD

Place the mixture in a freezer-safe container and freeze for 1 hour.

3. Over the next 3 to 4 hours, remove the mixture from the freezer every 20 minutes and whisk it slightly, to prevent it from getting too icy. It should thicken after each whisking until it's firm enough to scoop.

4. Best if eaten within 24 hours.

Adapted from Brain Body Diet *by Sara Gottfried, MD*

MEAL PLANS

Omnivore

	Day 1	Day 2	Day 3	Day 4	Day 5	Day 6	Day 7
Breakfast	Iced Coffee Collagen Shake (page 198)	Green Egg Scramble (page 203)	Deep Green Shake (page 202)	Shakshuka (page 208)	Avo Toast (page 204)	Carrot Cake Shake (page 201)	Almond Butter–Cacao Nib Shake (page 198)
Lunch	Little Gem Salad (page 211), moderate protein (chicken, salmon, low-mercury tuna)*	Slow Cooker Chicken, spaghetti squash (leftover)	Sorrel Soup (page 232), Nut-Crusted Chicken Fingers (leftover)	Crispy Cucumber Salad with Cilantro-Tahini Dressing (page 214)	Baked Jerusalem Artichokes with Thyme and Lemon (page 248), smoked salmon	Thai Coconut-Chicken Soup (leftover)	Chopped Greens and Marcona Salad (page 212), Gazpacho (page 231)
Dinner	Slow Cooker Chicken (page 245), spaghetti squash, artichoke	Avgolemono Soup (page 226), green salad, Nut-Crusted Chicken Fingers (page 246)	"Taco" Salad (page 216)	Beef and Vegetable Stew (page 247), green salad	Thai Coconut-Chicken Soup (Tom Kha Gai) (page 234)	Salmon with Almond Crust (see variation, Halibut with Almond Crust, page 242), riced cauliflower	Egg-Avocado Bake (page 209), avocado, green salad

* Reminder: I recommend 10–20 percent of calories from carbohydrates, 20 percent of calories from protein, and the remaining 60–70 percent from fat.

Pescatarian

	Day 1	Day 2	Day 3	Day 4	Day 5	Day 6	Day 7
Breakfast	Dark Chocolate–Sea Salt Shake (page 200)	Keto granola, nut milk	Shakshuka (page 208)	Almond Butter–Cacao Nib Shake (page 198)	Golden Milk Shake (page 200)	Green Egg Scramble (page 203)	Avo Toast (page 204)
Lunch	Little Gem Salad (page 211), moderate protein (chicken, salmon, low-mercury tuna)	Shirataki noodles, Pesto (page 223)	Kale and Caesar Salad with Raw "Parmesan" (page 221), Grilled Salmon Steaks (leftover)	Tahini-Sesame Noodles (leftover)	Torn Greens with Ranch Dressing (page 218), smoked salmon	Basic Green Salad (page 210), Roasted Eggplant (page 249), Fish Bone Broth (page 229)	Crispy Cucumber Salad with Cilantro-Tahini Dressing (page 214)
Dinner	Frittata with Spinach, Eggplant, and Pine Nuts (page 207)	Grilled Salmon Steaks with Lemon-Herb Mojo (page 241)	Tahini-Sesame Noodles (page 237)	Salmon and Avocado Bowl with Miso Dressing (page 240)	Black Cod with Miso (page 243), riced cauliflower, medium green salad	Roasted fish, Chermoula (page 223), leftover vegetables	Halibut with Almond Crust (page 242)

Vegetarian

	Day 1	Day 2	Day 3	Day 4	Day 5	Day 6	Day 7
Breakfast	Carrot Cake Shake (page 201)	Keto granola, nut milk	Dragon Fruit Shake (page 199)	Green Egg Scramble (page 203)	Basic Gottfried Protocol Shake for Ketosis (page 194)	Avo Toast (page 204)	Shakshuka (page 208)
Lunch	Little Gem Salad (page 211), 2 poached eggs	Tahini-Sesame Noodles (page 237)	Frittata (leftover)	Torn Greens with Ranch Dressing (page 218)	Kimchi, Shirataki, and Bok Choy Bowl (page 238)	Seaweed Salad (page 220)	Sorrel Soup (page 232)
Dinner	Tea Leaf Salad (page 213)	Frittata with Spinach, Eggplant, and Pine Nuts (page 207)	Tofu Masala Soup (page 235)	Gazpacho (page 231)	Egg-Avocado Bake (page 209)	Vegetable "Fettuccine" Alfredo (page 239)	Baked Jerusalem Artichokes with Thyme and Lemon (page 248)

Vegan

	Day 1	Day 2	Day 3	Day 4	Day 5	Day 6	Day 7
Breakfast	Iced Coffee Collagen Shake (page 198)	Keto granola, nut milk	Deep Green Shake (page 202)	Almond Butter-Cacao Nib Shake (page 198)	Basic Gottfried Protocol Shake for Ketosis (page 194)	Carrot Cake Shake (page 201)	Golden Milk Shake (page 200)
Lunch	Little Gem Salad (page 211)	Tahini-Sesame Noodles (page 237)	Avo Toast (page 204)	Crispy Cucumber Salad with Cilantro-Tahini Dressing (page 214)	Seaweed Salad (page 220)	Sorrel Soup (page 232)	French Onion Soup (page 233)
Dinner	Cauliflower Ceviche (page 222)	Tofu Masala Soup (page 235)	Gazpacho (page 257)	Vegetable "Fettuccine" Alfredo (page 239)	Baked Jerusalem Artichokes with Thyme and Lemon (page 248)	Kimchi, Shirataki, and Bok Choy Bowl (page 238)	Roasted Eggplant (page 249)

RESOURCES

APPS

- Zero and MyCircadianClock for intermittent fasting.
- Lifesum (use the keto setting) or MyFitnessPal for macronutrients.
- Calm, Headspace, Ten Percent Happier for meditation.
- Peloton and Glo-Yoga for yoga and meditation.

DEVICES

You don't need all of these. Most important are the Renpho scale and Keto-mojo.

- Renpho scale — a Bluetooth body-composition scale. I want you to lose fat and preserve muscle mass, and this $30 scale will help. It may not be the most accurate, but the trends over time can be helpful.
- Blood ketone monitor — Keto-mojo and Precision Extra.
- Glucose monitor — Precision Xtra Blood Glucose and Ketone Monitoring System and Contour next EZ. Both require that

you prick your finger for a drop of blood, and the meters plus supplies are available at drugstores and online. I prefer the Precision because it allows you to also check your blood ketones, and both glucose and ketones may be helpful to monitor while on the Gottfried Protocol.

- Continuous glucose monitor: Abbott FreeStyle Libre, DexCom.
- Oura ring — for sleep, exercise, and recovery tracking.
- Apolloneuro.com — a wearable wellness device for stress relief.
- Urine ketone strips — I don't use them, but some people like them.

TESTS TO CONSIDER

These are tests that I commonly order in my precision medicine practice. You might want to discuss them with your physician or physical trainer.

- Body composition.
- Resting metabolic rate.
- Exercise performance, such as VO2 max.
- Continuous glucose monitoring.
- Laboratory testing.

You can also order your own clinical laboratory tests from Wellnessfx.com and Yourlabwork.com.

Here are additional genomic and biomarker tests that I recommend. For the following tests, I recommend that you review results with a functional medicine clinician, even for the direct-to-consumer testing:

Genomic testing

3x4 Genetics https://www.3x4genetics.com/

DNA Life https://www.dnalife.healthcare/

Genomind https://www.genomind.com/

Genova Diagnostics https://www.gdx.net/

DetoxiGenomic Profile: www.gdx.net/core/sample
-reports/DetoxiGenomics-Sample-Report.pdf

EstroGenomic Profile: www.gdx.net/core/support-guides/
Estro-Genomic-

Gut, microbiota, and microbiome testing

Gastrointestinal Microbial Assay Plus (GI-MAP) by
Diagnostic Solutions Lab, https://www.diagnosticsolutionslab
.com/tests/gi-map

GI360 Microbiome Profile by Doctor's Data, https://www
.doctorsdata.com/gi-360/

GI Effects by Genova, https://www.gdx.net/product/gi-effects
-comprehensive-stool-test

GutBio by Onegevity, https://www.onegevity.com/
products/gutbio

Organic Acids Test by Great Plains Laboratory, https://www.
greatplainslaboratory.com/organic-acids-test

Hormone testing

Dried urine test for comprehensive hormones (DUTCH) by
Precision Analytical https://dutchtest.com

Complete Hormones test by Genova: www.gdx.net/product/
complete-hormones-test-urine

Essential Estrogens by Genova: www.gdx.net/product/essential
-estrogens-hormone-test-urine

Micronutrient testing

NutrEval by Genova. This test documents micronutrient
deficiencies and heavy metals in the blood and urine and

provides information about personalized supplementation need for antioxidants, amino acids, B vitamins, digestive support, essential fatty acids, and minerals. www.gdx.net/product/nutreval-fmv-nutritional-test-blood-urine

Metabolomix by Genova. This test provides many of the same features as the NutrEval but can be performed at home with blood spot and urine specimens. https://www.gdx.net/product/metabolomix+nutritional-test-urine

Micronutrient Test by Spectracell. This test is preferred by my mentor, Mark Houston MD, for assessing cellular deficiencies and insufficiencies relevant to cardiovascular disease. https://www.spectracell.com/micronutrient-test-panel

KITCHENWARE

Cast iron skillets. These are my go-to pans for cooking. A little iron will scrape off and get in your food, so make sure you do not have excess iron in your body before using.

Enameled cast iron. I bought my first Le Creuset enameled cast iron Dutch oven from a used cooking store in San Francisco when I was an intern in medicine back in 1994. My collection continues to serve most every need, particularly for making bone broths and soups that cook for hours to days.

GreenPan. Ceramic nonstick, toxin-free cookware featuring the Thermolon coating, free of toxins like perfluorooctanoic acid (PFOA), per- and polyfluroalkyl substances (PFAS), lead, and cadmium. Dishwasher- and metal utensil–safe.

ScanPan. Environmentally progressive nonstick pans made in Denmark and free of PFOA and PFOS, the toxins in Teflon, yet these pans provide a durable nonstick surface. The Classic Fry Pan is the most versatile pan in my collection (9.5 inch/24 cm).

Vitamix. I buy a new Vitamix about once every three years, when my ice cubes no longer blend to smooth. It is unparalleled in blending performance. Certified reconditioned blenders are available at their website.

FOOD

Success on the Gottfried Protocol requires creativity and innovation in finding swaps for refined carbs like pasta, rice, cereal, and bread. Here are my favorite swaps:

- Bread becomes keto bread, which is denser (see Recipes for Tahini Bread on page 206 and Coffee Cake on page 205, or check out the brand recommended on the next list).
- Cereal becomes keto granola (see brands that follow).
- Crackers become flackers or vegetable crudités (celery sticks, sliced zucchini, radishes, sliced carrots, sliced squash).
- Pasta becomes spiralized zucchini, squash, turnip, or other vegetables (see Recipes), or shirataki or konjac (see brands that follow).
- Rice becomes riced cauliflower or shirataki rice.
- Brownies become keto brownies.
- Cookies become keto cookies.
- Potato chips become oven-baked pork rinds — they can also be ground up as a swap for breadcrumbs or panko.

Keto bread: Make your own, or buy Base Culture Original Keto Bread (Baseculture.com), which has 4 net carbs per slice (8 grams of carbs, 4 grams of fiber, 6 grams of fat, 4 grams of protein). Made from water, eggs, almond butter, flaxseed, arrowroot flour, psyllium husk, almond flour, and apple cider vinegar, it's grain-free, gluten-free, preservative-free, and dairy-free. I keep several loaves in my freezer for making grilled cheese or vegan cucumber sandwiches, or I add nut or seed butter for a quick snack.

Brownies: I love the High Key Brownie Baking Mix in Blondie Original (1 net carb) or Chocolate Chip Fudge (2 net carbs). Be attentive to serving size!

Cereal: For cold cereal, choose a keto granola with less than 5 net carbs per serving. (Be sure to weigh out the serving, as they should be small yet are nutrient dense.) My favorite brands include Low Karb Cacao (3 net carbs) made with almonds, pecans, and coconut, and Cinnamon Pecan (2 net carbs). Other brands include Julian Bakery Keto Granola in Peanut Butter Cinnamon (3 net carbs) or High Key Cinnamon Almond (2 net carbs). For warm cereal, I like High Key Keto Instant Hot Cereal in Cocoa Almond or Strawberries and Cream (both 2 net carbs).

Chocolate: I like the Chocolate Zero keto bark and dark chocolate peanut-butter cups. I keep Lily's sugar-free chocolate chips on hand and mix them with 1 tablespoon of nut butter.

Flax crackers: My favorite crackers are made from flax and are available at flackers.com. (I also use Forti-Flax premium ground flaxseed by Barlean's in my shakes and my keto Coffee Cake recipe.)

Vegetables: I keep hardy vegetables in the refrigerator (broccoli, kale, bok choy, celery, collard greens, eggplant, and lettuce, especially romaine). Some I keep in the freezer (broccoli, riced cauliflower, and greens such as kale, spinach, and collards). For travel, I use Poshi packets of asparagus and French beans, packed in vinegar and extra-virgin olive oil, and ready to eat. I also travel with Urban Remedy sour cream and chive kale chips, and a low-carb Rainbow salad, both vegan (Urbanremedy.com).

Salmon: I travel with packets of smoked salmon (less than 1 carb) or salmon jerky (0 carbs) from Alaska Smokehouse (wwgormet.com).

Tuna: I like Safe Catch Elite wild tuna, sustainably wild-caught and tested for mercury. I like the chili-lime flavor and travel with packets of these.

Snacks: If you like a crunchy, salty snack, consider High Key Goat Cheese snack bags. I travel with these too. I have a casein intolerance but can tolerate these in rotation (every four days or so). Another choice is Epic Oven Baked Pork Rinds. These come in a variety of flavors — I like chili-lime or Himalayan salt. I've tried vegan options, but they are too high in carbs for me. I travel with grass-fed beef jerky and beef sticks, including the New Primal Sea Salt Beef Thins.

SUPPLEMENTS

Alpha-lipoic acid: I like Stabilized R-Lipoic Acid Supreme by Designs for Health.

Balanced omegas: I like EFA-Sirt Supreme from Biotics Research because it has a balanced blend of the essential fatty acids EPA, DHA, and GLA, together with mixed tocopherols, specially formulated to be high in gamma (γ)-tocopherol. You can also make your own mix of EPA and DHA (I take 4 grams per day), and add either GLA (I like Metagenics and take 2–3 grams per day) or separately from evening primrose oil (6 percent GLA), borage oil (24 percent GLA), or black currant oil (17 percent GLA).

Electrolytes: I use Designs for Health Electropure (0 grams carbs), ½ teaspoon in 8 to 12 ounces of filtered water.

Medium-chain triglyceride chews: When you are first starting on keto, these chews can help get you into ketosis more quickly and improve focus and energy. Many of my patients find them helpful in the afternoon to prevent alcohol cravings. I use them when traveling. I recommend Designs for Health KTO-C8

MCT Oil Chews with 500 mg caprylic acid, in strawberry/watermelon flavor.

Specialized pro-resolving mediators: In the United States, there are two companies that manufacture SPMs with high-quality standards: Designs for Health and Metagenics. I recommend either brand. Follow the instructions on the bottle for dosage.

ACKNOWLEDGMENTS

There are innumerable people to thank, and I am sure I will miss many. Deep gratitude to my patients and cases for this book; they keep me humble and curious about why fat loss is so challenging as we age.

I'm grateful to the friends and colleagues who generously helped me clarify and organize my thinking: Drs. Rachel Abrams, Erin Amato, Anthony Bazzan, Melissa Blake, Sheldon Cohen, Anu French, Victoria Hall, Mark Houston, Laura Konigsberg, Daniel Monti, Myles Spar, and Will Van Derveer. Special thanks for the outstanding editing by Pamela Walter. While writing this book, I was moved by a timely lecture on the role of axiology, or the study of values, and how values motivate behavior change. The talk was given by Keith Kurlander, cofounder (along with Dr. Will Van Derveer) of the Integrative Psychiatry Institute. Thank you, Keith, for connecting the dots between values and behavior change!

My extraordinary agent, Celeste Fine, continues to lead me forward with tremendous grace, insight, and wit.

Once I embarked on a book about women, food, and hormones, I couldn't have done it without my extraordinary editorial, design, social media, and launch teams: Deb Brody, Topher Donahue, Maya

Dusenbery, Nathalie Hadi, Sharon Kastoriano, Eve Minkler, Sarah Pelz, Emma Peters, Shara Alexander, and Kevin Plottner. Special thanks to our digital and tech team: Kenny Gregg and Barry Napier.

I am grateful to the woman who helps create calm in our home: Leslie Murphy.

Thank you to my loving family, including my brilliant daughters, who keep me honest about feminism, intersectionality, and body-positive language. I'm grateful to my dog daughter, Juneau, for reminding me that it's time to play. Thank you to my beloved parents, Albert and Mary.

Heartfelt thanks to Johanna Ilfeld, PhD, one of my best friends and fitness partner, who read draft after draft with abiding affection, irreverence, and wisdom; and David Gottfried, my husband, life partner, and greatest love.

NOTES

INTRODUCTION:
THE LANGUAGE OF HORMONES

1. Diabetes Prevention Program Research Group, "10-Year Follow-Up of Diabetes Incidence and Weight Loss in the Diabetes Prevention Program Outcomes Study," *The Lancet* 374, no. 9702 (2009): 1677–86; R. B. Goldberg et al., "Targeting the Consequences of the Metabolic Syndrome in the Diabetes Prevention Program," *Arteriosclerosis, Thrombosis, and Vascular Biology* 32, no. 9 (2012): 2077–90; Diabetes Prevention Program Research Group, "Long-Term Effects of Lifestyle Intervention or Metformin on Diabetes Development and Microvascular Complications over 15-year Follow-Up: The Diabetes Prevention Program Outcomes Study," *The Lancet Diabetes & Endocrinology* 3, no. 11 (2015): 866–75.

2. P. Garrido et al., "Proposal for the Creation of a National Strategy for Precision Medicine in Cancer: A Position Statement of SEOM, SEAP, and SEFH," *Clinical and Translational Oncology* 20, no. 4 (2018): 443–47; G. Gonzalez-Hernandez et al., "Advances in Text Mining and Visualization for Precision Medicine," *Biocomputing* 23 (2018): 559–65; C. A. L. Wicklund et al., "Clinical Genetic Counselors: An Asset in the Era of Precision Medicine," *American Journal of Medical Genetics, Part C: Seminars in Medical Genetics* 178, no. 1 (2018): 63–67; "Precision Medicine," *National Institutes of Health,* https://olao.od.nih.gov/content/precision-medicine, accessed September 18, 2020.

3. "The Truth Is Out There, Somewhere," *Lancet* 396, no. 10247 (2020): 291.

4. T. N. Seyfried et al., "Role of Glucose and Ketone Bodies in the Metabolic Control of Experimental Brain Cancer," *British Journal of Cancer* 89, no. 7 (2003): 1375–82; L. M. Rodrigues et al., "The Action of β-hydroxybutyrate on the Growth,

Metabolism, and Global Histone H3 Acetylation of Spontaneous Mouse Mammary Tumours: Evidence of a β-hydroxybutyrate Paradox," *Cancer & Metabolism* 5, no. 1 (2017): 4–17; C. Bartmann et al., "Beta-hydroxybutyrate (3-OHB) Can Influence the Energetic Phenotype of Breast Cancer Cells but Does Not Impact Their Proliferation and the Response to Chemotherapy or Radiation," *Cancer & Metabolism* 6, no. 1 (2018): 8; M. Chen et al., "An Aberrant SREBP-Dependent Lipogenic Program Promotes Metastatic Prostate Cancer," *Nature Genetics* 50, no. 2 (2018): 206–18; G. Kolata, "High-Fat Diet May Fuel Spread of Prostate Cancer," *The New York Times*, January 16, 2018, https://www.nytimes.com/2018/01/16/health/fat-diet-prostate-cancer.html, accessed August 15, 2018; J. Sremanakova et al., "A Systematic Review of the Use of Ketogenic Diets in Adult Patients with Cancer," *Journal of Human Nutrition and Dietetics* 3, no. 6 (2018): 793–802.

5. G. Bonuccelli et al., "Ketones and Lactate 'Fuel' Tumor Growth and Metastasis: Evidence That Epithelial Cancer Cells Use Oxidative Mitochondrial Metabolism," *Cell Cycle* 9, no. 17 (2010): 3506–14; U. E. Martinez-Outschoorn et al., "Ketones and Lactate Increase Cancer Cell 'Stemness,' Driving Recurrence, Metastasis, and Poor Clinical Outcome in Breast Cancer: Achieving Personalized Medicine Via Metabolo-Genomics," *Cell Cycle* 10, no. 8 (2011): 1271–86.

6. S. E. Swithers, "Artificial Sweeteners Produce the Counterintuitive Effect of Inducing Metabolic Derangements," *Trends in Endocrinology & Metabolism* 24, no. 9 (2013): 431–41.

7. J. S. Volek et al., "Cardiovascular and Hormonal Aspects of Very-Low-Carbohydrate Ketogenic Diets," *Obesity Research* 12, no. S11 (2004): 115S–123S; J. S. Volek et al., "Comparison of Energy-Restricted Very-Low-Carbohydrate and Low-Fat Diets on Weight Loss and Body Composition in Overweight Men and Women," *Nutrition & Metabolism* 1, no. 13 (2004): 1–13; H. M. Dashti et al., "Long-Term Effects of Ketogenic Diet in Obese Subjects," *Molecular and Cellular Biochemistry* 286, no. 1–2 (2006): 1–9; G. Ruaño, "Physiogenomic Analysis of Weight Loss Induced by Dietary Carbohydrate Restriction," *Nutrition & Metabolism* 3, no. 1 (2006): 3–20; K. Durkalec-Michalski et al., "Effect of a Four-Week Ketogenic Diet on Exercise Metabolism in CrossFit-Trained Athletes," *Journal of the International Society of Sports Nutrition* 16, no. 1 (2019): 16.

8. The higher fat intake in women was in the setting of relatively high carbohydrate intake (51 percent of total calories per day), not a ketogenic diet. S. L. Mumford et al., "Dietary Fat Intake and Reproductive Hormone Concentrations and Ovulation in Regularly Menstruating Women," *The American Journal of Clinical Nutrition* 103, no. 3 (2016): 868–77.

9. J. M. Wilson et al., "The Effects of Ketogenic Dieting on Body Composition, Strength, Power, and Hormonal Profiles in Resistance Training Males," *The Journal of Strength and Conditioning Research* (2017); A. R. Kuchkuntla et al., "Ketogenic Diet: An Endocrinologist Perspective," *Current Nutrition Reports* 8, no. 4 (2019): 402–10.

10. When it comes to healthy gut microbiota, what matters is the type, quality, quan-

tity, and origin of the food. Gut bugs utilize nutrients in the food you consume for basic biological functions (such as regulating the immune system) and then create metabolic outputs that impact your physiology—including energy balance, glucose signaling, inflammation, and fat loss. One of the most important nutrients for a healthy microbiome is microbiota-accessible carbohydrates, such as prebiotic fiber. The key to success on the Gottfried Protocol is to get sufficient quantities of these specific carbs and to feed the good bugs.

F. Bäckhed et al., "The Gut Microbiota as an Environmental Factor That Regulates Fat Storage," *Proceedings of the National Academy of Sciences of the United States of America* 101, no. 44 (2004): 15718–723; M. Rescigno, "Intestinal Microbiota and Its Effects on the Immune System," *Cellular Microbiology* 16, no. 7 (2014): 1004–13; L. Geurts et al., "Gut Microbiota Controls Adipose Tissue Expansion, Gut Barrier, and Glucose Metabolism: Novel Insights into Molecular Targets and Interventions Using Prebiotics," *Beneficial Microbes* 5, no. 1 (2014): 3–17; B. O. Schroeder et al., "Signals from the Gut Microbiota to Distant Organs in Physiology and Disease," *Nature Medicine* 22, no. 10 (2016): 1079–89; K. Makki, "The Impact of Dietary Fiber on Gut Microbiota in Host Health and Disease," *Cell Host & Microbe* 23, no. 6 (2018): 705–15.

11. R. de Cabo et al., "Effects of Intermittent Fasting on Health, Aging, and Disease," *New England Journal of Medicine* 381, no. 26 (2019): 2541–51.

12. Note that intermittent fasting increases neurogenesis, the ongoing growth and development of new nerve cells (that is, neurons, which contribute to functions like learning, emotional regulation, and memory). B. Malinowski, "Intermittent Fasting in Cardiovascular Disorders—An Overview," *Nutrients* 11, no. 3 (2019): 673; A. L. Mindikoglu, Intermittent Fasting from Dawn to Sunset for 30 Consecutive Days Is Associated with Anticancer Proteomic Signature and Upregulates Key Regulatory Proteins of Glucose and Lipid Metabolism, Circadian Clock, DNA Repair, Cytoskeleton Remodeling, Immune System, and Cognitive Function in Healthy Subjects," *Journal of Proteomics* 217 (2020): 103645; S. H. Baik et al., "Intermittent Fasting Increases Adult Hippocampal Neurogenesis," *Brain and Behavior* 10, no. 1 (2020): e01444.

13. Intermittent fasting decreases total cholesterol, LDL-cholesterol (known colloquially as the "bad" type), and serum triglycerides. It reduces fat accumulation in the liver and fat tissues. G. M. Tinsley et al., "Effects of Intermittent Fasting on Body Composition and Clinical Health Markers in Humans," *Nutrition Reviews* 73, no. 10 (2015): 661–74; A. Bener et al., "Effect of Ramadan Fasting on Glycemic Control and Other Essential Variables in Diabetic Patients," *Annals of African Medicine* 17, no. 4 (2018): 196; A. R. Rahbar et al., "Effects of Intermittent Fasting During Ramadan on Insulin-like Growth Factor-1, Interleukin 2, and Lipid Profile in Healthy Muslims," *International Journal of Preventive Medicine* 10, no. 7 (2019): 1–6; S. Ebrahimi et al., "Ramadan Fasting Improves Liver Function and Total Cholesterol in Patients with Nonalcoholic Fatty Liver Disease," *International Journal for Vitamin and Nutrition Research* (2019).

14. B. H. Goodpaster et al., "Metabolic Flexibility in Health and Disease," *Cell Metabolism* 25, no. 5 (2017): 1027–36

15. https://www.cdc.gov/media/releases/2020/s0917-adult-obesity-increasing.html, accessed September 29, 2020.

16. N. Stefan et al., "Causes, Characteristics, and Consequences of Metabolically Unhealthy Normal Weight in Humans," *Cellular Metabolism* 26, no. 2 (2017): 292–300; N. Stefan et al., "Obesity and Impaired Metabolic Health in Patients with COVID-19," *Nature Reviews Endocrinology* (2020): 1–2.

17. S. Y. Tartof, et al. "Obesity and Mortality Among Patients Diagnosed With COVID-19: Results from an Integrated Health Care Organization," *Annals of Internal Medicine* (2020): M20-3742; W. Dietz et al., "Obesity and Its Implications for COVID-19 Mortality," *Obesity (Silver Spring)* 28, no. 6 (2020): 1005; A. Simonnet et al., "High Prevalence of Obesity in Severe Acute Respiratory Syndrome Coronavirus-2 (SARS-CoV-2) Requiring Invasive Mechanical Ventilation," *Obesity (Silver Spring)* 28, no. 7 (2020): 1195–99; Erratum in *Obesity (Silver Spring)* 28, no. 10 (2020): 1994; B. M. Popkin et al., "Individuals with Obesity and COVID-19: A Global Perspective on the Epidemiology and Biological Relationships," *Obesity Reviews* (2020) Aug 26:10.1111/obr.13128.

18. L. Gupta et al., "Ketogenic Diet in Endocrine Disorders: Current Perspectives," *Journal of Postgraduate Medicine* 63, no. 4 (2017): 242–51.

1. THE TRUTH ABOUT
WOMEN, HORMONES, AND WEIGHT

1. My outstanding acupuncturist, Emily Hooker, provides the following insights about traditional Chinese medicine (TCM) and hormones in women: "While traditional Chinese medicine texts do not explicitly acknowledge perimenopause, female life cycles are thought to occur in seven-year phases, with 42 being the age that the shao yang (gallbladder, associated with liver) begins to decline. That said, they also assert that a woman's hair turns white in that phase, which seems dated and potentially lifestyle-based. Just as you write that cortisol dysregulation is at the root of many patterns, this can be said of LQS, and yes, sighing is definitely an indication that there's a LQS component.

Over time, LQS has the potential to cause a host of other imbalances, often beginning with spleen qi deficiency. This could be at the root of any metabolic issue, though seldom as a singular diagnosis. Either way, that has no bearing on the accuracy of your assessment of Melissa, who certainly presents with LQS. Incidentally, I am seeing a 44-year-old female patient at the moment with a nearly identical picture. Her cortisol levels are high, progesterone and testosterone are low, thyroid is underactive, and she also gained about 20 pounds within the past year. Her TCM diagnosis is liver qi stagnation with spleen qi and yang deficiency causing dampness." To learn more from Emily, go to emilyhookeracupuncture.com.

2. P. K. Whelton et al., "ACC/AHA/AAPA/ABC/ACPM/AGS/APhA/ASH/ASPC/NMA/PCNA Guideline for the Prevention, Detection, Evaluation, and Manage-

ment of High Blood Pressure in Adults: Executive Summary: A Report of the American College of Cardiology/American Heart Association Task Force on Clinical Practice Guidelines," *Hypertension* 71, no. 6 (2018): 1269–1324.

3. B. V. Howard et al., "Insulin Resistance and Weight Gain in Postmenopausal Women of Diverse Ethnic Groups," *International Journal Obesity and Related Metabolism Disorder* 28, no. 8 (2004): 1039–47; O. T. Hardy et al., "What Causes the Insulin Resistance Underlying Obesity?" *Current Opinion Endocrinology, Diabetes, and Obesity* 19, no. 2 (2012): 81–87; H. U. Moon et al., "The Association of Adiponectin and Visceral Fat with Insulin Resistance and β-Cell Dysfunction," *Journal of Korean Medical Science* 34, no. 1 (2018): e7; J. Fatima et al., "Association of Sonographically Assessed Visceral and Subcutaneous Abdominal Fat with Insulin Resistance in Prediabetes," *Journal of the Association Physicians of India* 67, no. 4 (2019): 68–70.

4. J. Rezzonico et al., "Introducing the Thyroid Gland as Another Victim of the Insulin Resistance Syndrome," *Thyroid* 18, no. 4 (2008): 461–64; C. Anil et al., "Metformin Decreases Thyroid Volume and Nodule Size in Subjects with Insulin Resistance: A Preliminary Study," *Medical Principles and Practice* 25, no. 3 (2016): 233–36; C. Sallorenzo et al., "Prevalence of Pancreatic Autoantibodies in Non-Diabetic Patients with Autoimmune Thyroid Disease and Its Relation to Insulin Secretion and Glucose Tolerance," *Archives of Endocrinology and Metabolism* 61, no. 4 (2017): 361–66; P. Zhu et al., "Thyroid-Stimulating Hormone Levels Are Positively Associated with Insulin Resistance," *Medical Science Monitor* 24, no. 1 (2018): 342–47; U. Mousa et al., "Fat Distribution and Metabolic Profile in Subjects with Hashimoto's Thyroiditis," *Acta Endocrinologica* 14, no. 1 (2018): 105–12; X. Zhang et al., "Effect of Insulin on Thyroid Cell Proliferation, Tumor Cell Migration, and Potentially Related Mechanisms," *Endocrine Research* 44, nos. 1–2 (2019): 55–70; X. He et al., "Role of Metformin in the Treatment of Patients with Thyroid Nodules and Insulin Resistance: A Systematic Review and Meta-Analysis," *Thyroid* 29, no. 3 (2019): 359–67.

5. A. Verma et al., "Hypothyroidism and Obesity? Cause or Effect," *Saudi Medical Journal* 29, no. 8 (2008): 1135–38; R. Song et al., "The Impact of Obesity on Thyroid Autoimmunity and Dysfunction: A Systematic Review and Meta-Analysis," *Frontiers in Immunology* 10, no. 1 (2019): 2349.

6. R. C. Kessler et al., "Lifetime and 12-Month Prevalence of DSM-III-R Psychiatric Disorders in the United States," *Archives of General Psychiatry* 51, no. 1 (1994): 8–19; R. C. Kessler et al., "Posttraumatic Stress Disorder in the National Comorbidity Survey," *Archives of General Psychiatry* 52, no. 12 (1995): 1048–60; M. Altemus et al., "Sex Differences in Anxiety and Depression Clinical Perspectives," *Frontiers in Neuroendocrinology* 35, no. 3 (2014): 320–30.

7. L. Fan et al., "Non-linear Relationship Between Sleep Duration and Metabolic Syndrome: A Population-Based Study," *Medicine (Baltimore)* 99, no. 2 (2020): e18753.

8. B. L. Fredrickson et al., "Objectification Theory: Toward Understanding Women's

Lived Experiences and Mental Health Risks," *Psychology of Women Quarterly* 21, no. 2 (1997): 173–206; C. Rollero et al., "Self-Objectification and Personal Values: An Exploratory Study," *Frontiers in Psychology* 8, no. 1 (2017): 1055; R. Kahalon et al., "Experimental Studies on State Self-Objectification: A Review and an Integrative Process Model," *Frontiers in Psychology* 9, no. 1 (2018): 1268.

9. L. M. Schaefer et al., "Self-Objectification and Disordered Eating: A Meta-Analysis," *The International Journal of Eating Disorders* 51, no. 6 (2018): 483–502.

10. L. Cheng, "The Commercialization of Female Bodies in Consumer Society," *Journal of Humanity* 9, no. 1 (2015): 123–25.

11. M. P. J. Vanderpump, "The Epidemiology of Thyroid Disease," *British Medical Bulletin* 99, no. 1 (2011): 39–51; R. Hoermann et al., "Recent Advances in Thyroid Hormone Regulation: Toward a New Paradigm for Optimal Diagnosis and Treatment," *Frontiers in Endocrinology* 8, no. 1 (2017): 364; A. G. Juby et al., "Clinical Challenges in Thyroid Disease: Time for a New Approach?" *Maturitas* 87, no. 1 (2016): 72–78.

12. D. M. Roesch, "Effects of Selective Estrogen Receptor Agonists on Food Intake and Body Weight Gain in Rats," *Physiology & Behavior* 87, no. 1 (2006): 39–44; A. L. Hirschberg, "Sex Hormones, Appetite, and Eating Behaviour in Women," *Maturitas* 71, no. 3 (2012): 248–56; L. Asarian et al. "Sex Differences in the Physiology of Eating," *American Journal of Physiology-Regulatory, Integrative, and Comparative Physiology* 305, no. 11 (2013): R1215–67.

13. G. D. Miller et al., "Basal Growth Hormone Concentration Increased Following a Weight Loss Focused Dietary Intervention in Older Overweight and Obese Women," *The Journal of Nutrition, Health, & Aging* 16, no. 2 (2012): 169–74.

14. M. Devaki et al., "Chronic Stress-Induced Oxidative Damage and Hyperlipidemia Are Accompanied by Atherosclerotic Development in Rats," *Stress* 16, no. 2 (2013): 233–43; S. N. Kales et al., "Firefighters and On-Duty Deaths from Coronary Heart Disease: A Case Control Study," *Environmental Health* 2, no. 1 (2003): 14; M. Kumari et al., "Chronic Stress Accelerates Atherosclerosis in the Apolipoprotein E Deficient Mouse," *Stress* 6, no. 4 (2003): 297–99; H. E. Webb et al., "Stress Reactivity to Repeated Low-Level Challenges: A Pilot Study," *Applied Psychophysiology Biofeedback* 36, no. 4 (2011): 243–50.

15. P. M. Peeke et al., "Hypercortisolism and Obesity," *Annals of New York Academy of Science* 771, no. 1 (1995): 665–76; S. Paredes et al., "Cortisol: The Villain in Metabolic Syndrome?" *Revista da Associacao Medica Brasileria (1992)* 60, no. 1 (2014): 84–92; J. Q. Purnell et al., "Enhanced Cortisol Production Rates, Free Cortisol, and 11beta-HSD-1 Expression Correlate with Visceral Fat and Insulin Resistance in Men: Effect of Weight Loss," *American Journal of Physiology Endocrinology and Metabolism* 296, no. 2 (2000): E351–57; A. Tchernof et al., "Pathophysiology of Human Visceral Obesity: An Update," *Physiological Reviews* 93, no. 1 (2013): 359–404.

16. M. J. McAllister et al., "Exogenous Carbohydrate Reduces Cortisol Response

from Combined Mental and Physical Stress," *International Journal of Sports Medicine* 37, no. 14 (2016): 1159–65.

17. C. J. Ley et al., "Sex- and Menopause-Associated Changes in Body-Fat Distribution," *The American Journal of Clinical Nutrition* 55, no. 5 (1992): 950–54.

18. L. M. Brown et al., "Central Effects of Estradiol in the Regulation of Food Intake, Body Weight, and Adiposity," *The Journal of Steroid Biochemistry and Molecular Biology* 122, nos. 1–3 (2010): 65–73.

19. Ley et al., "Sex- and Menopause-Associated Changes."

20. Q. Cao et al., "Waist-Hip Ratio as a Predictor of Myocardial Infarction Risk: A Systematic Review and Meta-Analysis," *Medicine* 97, no. 30 (2018); V. A. Benites-Zapata VA et al., "High Waist-to-Hip Ratio Levels Are Associated with Insulin Resistance Markers in Normal-Weight Women," *Diabetes Metabolic Syndrome* 13, no. 1 (2019): 636–42.

21. B. Tramunt et al., "Sex Differences in Metabolic Regulation and Diabetes Susceptibility," *Diabetologia* 63, no. 3 (2020): 453–61.

22. V. Regitz-Zagrosek et al., "Gender Aspects of the Role of the Metabolic Syndrome as a Risk Factor for Cardiovascular Disease," *Gender Medicine* 4 (2007): S162–77; E. Gerdts et al., "Sex Differences in Cardiometabolic Disorders," *Nature Medicine* 25, no. 11 (2019): 1657–66.

23. S. V. Ahn et al., "Sex Difference in the Effect of the Fasting Serum Glucose Level on the Risk of Coronary Heart Disease," *Journal of Cardiology* 71, no. 2 (2018): 149–54.

24. G. A. Greendale et al., "Changes in Body Composition and Weight During the Menopause Transition," *JCI Insight* 4, no. 5 (2019).

25. A. M. Goss et al., "Longitudinal Associations of the Endocrine Environment on Fat Partitioning in Postmenopausal Women," *Obesity (Silver Spring)* 20, no. 5 (2012): 939–44; S. Ballestri et al., "NAFLD as a Sexual Dimorphic Disease: Role of Gender and Reproductive Status in the Development and Progression of Nonalcoholic Fatty Liver Disease and Inherent Cardiovascular Risk," *Advances in Therapy* 34, no. 6 (2017): 1291–326.

26. J. R. Guthrie et al., "Weight Gain and the Menopause: A 5-Year Prospective Study," *Climacteric: The Journal of the International Menopause Society* 2, no. 3 (1999): 205–11.

27. S. L. Crawford et al., "A Longitudinal Study of Weight and the Menopause Transition: Results from the Massachusetts Women's Health Study," *Menopause (New York, N.Y.)* 7, no. 2 (2000): 96–104.

28. S. C. Ho et al., "Menopausal Transition and Changes of Body Composition: A Prospective Study in Chinese Perimenopausal Women," *International Journal of Obesity (2005)* 34, no. 8 (2010): 1265–74.

29. F. Fery et al., "Hormonal and Metabolic Changes Induced by an Isocaloric Isoproteinic Ketogenic Diet in Healthy Subjects," *Diabète & Métabolisme* 8, no. 4 (1982): 299–305; E. Kose et al., "Changes of Thyroid Hormonal Status in Patients

Receiving Ketogenic Diet Due to Intractable Epilepsy," *Journal of Pediatric Endocrinology & Metabolism* 30, no. 4 (2017): 411–16; Y. J. Lee et al., "Longitudinal Change in Thyroid Hormone Levels in Children with Epilepsy on a Ketogenic Diet: Prevalence and Risk Factors," *Journal of Epilepsy Research* 7, no. 2 (2017): 99–105.

30. For a complete list of hypothyroid symptoms, see pages 30–31 and Chapter 9 of my book *The Hormone Cure: Reclaim Balance, Sleep, Sex Drive, and Vitality Naturally with the Gottfried Protocol* (New York: Simon and Schuster, 2013).

31. J. Sirven et al., "The Ketogenic Diet for Intractable Epilepsy in Adults: Preliminary Results," *Epilepsia* 40, no. 12 (1999): 1721–26.

32. R. M. Kwan et al., "Effects of a Low Carbohydrate Isoenergetic Diet on Sleep Behavior and Pulmonary Functions in Healthy Female Adult Humans," *Journal of Nutrition* 116, no. 12 (1986): 2393–402.

33. A. A. Prather et al., "Poor Sleep Quality Potentiates Stress-Induced Cytokine Reactivity in Postmenopausal Women with High Visceral Abdominal Adiposity," *Brain, Behavior, Immunity* 35, no. 1 (2014): 155–62; S. K. Sweatt et al., "Sleep Quality Is Differentially Related to Adiposity in Adults," *Psychoneuroendocrinology* 98, no. 1 (2018): 46–51.

34. In this research study of the ketogenic diet in rats, investigators used microcomputed tomography and histomorphometry analyses on the distal femur. They found trabecular bone volume, serum IGF-I, and the bone formation marker P1NP were lower in male rats fed a low-carb, high-fat diet. A. Zengin et al., "Low-Carbohydrate, High-Fat Diets Have Sex-Specific Effects on Bone Health in Rats," *European Journal of Nutrition* 55, no. 7 (2016): 2307–20.

35. G. K. Schwalfenberg, "The Alkaline Diet: Is There Evidence That an Alkaline pH Diet Benefits Health?" *Journal of Environmental and Public Health* 2012, no. 1 (2012): 727630.

36. B. E. Millen et al., "The 2015 Dietary Guidelines Advisory Committee Scientific Report: Development and Major Conclusions," *Advances in Nutrition* 7, no. 3 (2016): 438–44; Q. Qian, "Dietary Influence on Body Fluid Acid-Base and Volume Balance: The Deleterious 'Norm' Furthers and Cloaks Subclinical Pathophysiology," *Nutrients* 10, no. 6 (2018): 778.

37. Acid and alkaline refer to pH: acids have a low pH of less than 7, and alkaline has a high pH of more than 7. The pH of blood is 7.4, but foods can leave an acidic or alkaline ash. L. Frassetto et al., "Diet, Evolution and Aging—The Pathophysiologic Effects of the Post-Agricultural Inversion of the Potassium-to-Sodium and Base-to-Chloride Ratios in the Human Diet," *European Journal of Nutrition* 40, no. 5 (2001): 200–213; M. Konner et al., "Paleolithic Nutrition: Twenty-Five Years Later," *Nutrition in Clinical Practice* 25, no. 6 (2010): 594–602. J. R. Buendia et al., "Longitudinal Effects of Dietary Sodium and Potassium on Blood Pressure in Adolescent Girls," *JAMA Pediatrics* 169, no. 6 (2015): 560–68; A. Sebastian et al., "Postulating the Major Environmental Condition Resulting in the Expression of Essential Hypertension and Its Associated Cardiovascular Diseases: Dietary Im-

prudence in Daily Selection of Foods in Respect of Their Potassium and Sodium Content Resulting in Oxidative Stress-Induced Dysfunction of the Vascular Endothelium, Vascular Smooth Muscle, and Perivascular Tissues," *Medical Hypotheses* 119, no. 1 (2018): 110–19.

38. S. T. Reddy et al., "Effect of Low-Carbohydrate High-Protein Diets on Acid-Base Balance, Stone-Forming Propensity, and Calcium Metabolism," *American Journal of Kidney Diseases* 40, no. 2 (2002): 265–74; E. H. Kossoff et al., "Dietary Therapies for Epilepsy," *Biomed Journal* 36, no. 1 (2013): 2–8.

39. L. Frassetto et al., "Potassium Bicarbonate Reduces Urinary Nitrogen Excretion in Postmenopausal Women," *The Journal of Clinical Endocrinology & Metabolism* 82, no. 1 (1997): 254–59; L. Frassetto et al., "Long-term Persistence of the Urine Calcium-Lowering Effect of Potassium Bicarbonate in Postmenopausal Women," *The Journal of Clinical Endocrinology & Metabolism* 90, no. 2 (2005): 831–34; J. A. Wass et al., "Growth Hormone and Memory," *The Journal of Endocrinology* 207, no. 2 (2010): 125–26; G. K. Schwalfenberg, "The Alkaline Diet: Is There Evidence That an Alkaline pH Diet Benefits Health?" *Journal of Environmental and Public Health* 2012, no. 1 (2012): 727630.

40. R. Solianik et al., "Two-Day Fasting Evokes Stress, but Does Not Affect Mood, Brain Activity, Cognitive, Psychomotor, and Motor Performance in Overweight Women," *Behavioural Brain Research* 338, no. 1 (2018): 166–72.

41. R. Solianik et al., "Effect of 48H Fasting on Autonomic Function, Brain Activity, Cognition, and Mood in Amateur Weight Lifters," *Biomed Research International* 2016, no. 1 (2016): 1503956.

2. HOW GROWTH HORMONE KEEPS YOU LEAN

1. J. D. Veldhuis et al., "Somatotropic and Gonadotropic Axes Linkages in Infancy, Childhood, and the Puberty-Adult Transition," *Endocrine Reviews* 27, no. 2 (2006): 101–40; J. D. Veldhuis, "Aging and Hormones of the Hypothalamo-Pituitary Axis: Gonadotropic Axis in Men and Somatotropic Axes in Men and Women," *Ageing Research Reviews* 7, no. 3 (2008): 189–208.

2. E. Corpas et al., "Human Growth Hormone and Human Aging," *Endocrine Reviews* 14, no. 1 (1993): 20–39; A. Bartke, "Growth Hormone and Aging: Updated Review," *The World Journal of Men's Health* 37, no.1 (2019): 19–30.

3. S. Perrini et al., "Metabolic Implications of Growth Hormone Therapy," *Journal of Endocrinological Investigation — Supplements* 31, no. 9 (2008): 79–84; S. Perrini et al., "Abnormalities of Insulin-like Growth Factor-I Signaling and Impaired Cell Proliferation in Osteoblasts from Subjects with Osteoporosis," *Endocrinology* 149, no. 3 (2007): 1302–13; K. R. Short et al., "Enhancement of Muscle Mitochondrial Function by Growth Hormone," *The Journal of Clinical Endocrinology & Metabolism* 93, no. 2 (2008): 597–604; N. Møller et al., "Effects of Growth Hormone on Glucose, Lipid, and Protein Metabolism in Human Subjects," *Endocrine Reviews* 30, no. 2 (2009): 152–77.

4. L. I. Arwert et al., "The Relation Between Insulin-Like Growth Factor I Levels

and Cognition in Healthy Elderly: A Meta-Analysis." *Growth hormone & IGF Research* 15, no. 6 (2005): 416–422.

5. U. J. Lewis, "Growth Hormone: What Is It and What Does It Do?" *Trends in Endocrinology & Metabolism* 3, no. 4 (1992): 117–21; M. B. Ranke et al., "Growth Hormone — Past, Present, and Future." *Nature Reviews Endocrinology* 14, no. 5 (2018): 285–300.

6. F. Mourkioti et al., "IGF-1, Inflammation, and Stem Cells: Interactions During Muscle REGEneration," *Trends in Immunology* 26, no. 10 (2005): 535–42; C. P. Velloso, "Regulation of Muscle Mass by Growth Hormone and IGF-I," *British Journal of Pharmacology* 154, no. 1 (2008): 557–68, M. E. Molitch et al., "Evaluation and Treatment of Adult Growth Hormone Deficiency: An Endocrine Society Clinical Practice Guideline," *The Journal of Clinical Endocrinology & Metabolism* 96, no. 6 (2011): 1587–609.

7. A. L. Cardoso et al., "Towards Frailty Biomarkers: Candidates from Genes and Pathways Regulated in Aging and Age-Related Diseases," *Ageing Research Reviews* 47, no. 1 (2018): 214–77.

8. G. Vab den Berg et al., "An Amplitude-Specific Divergence in the Pulsatile Mode of Growth Hormone (GH) Secretion Underlies the Gender Difference in Mean Growth Hormone Concentrations in Men and Premenopausal Women," *Journal of Clinical Endocrinology and Metabolism* 81, no. 7 (1996): 2460–67; J. O. Jørgensen et al., "Sex Steroids and the Growth Hormone/Insulin-like Growth Factor-I Axis in Adults," *Hormone Research in Paediatrics* 64, Suppl. 2 (2005): 37–40.

9. G. Norstedt et al., "Secretory Rhythm of Growth Hormone Regulates Sexual Differentiation of Mouse Liver," *Cell* 36, no. 4 (1984): 805–12.

10. F. Roelfsema et al., "Growth-Hormone Dynamics in Healthy Adults Are Related to Age and Sex, and Strongly Dependent on Body Mass Index," *Neuroendocrinology* 103, nos. 3–4 (2016): 335–44; J. P. Span et al., "Gender Difference in Insulin-Like Growth Factor I Response to Growth Hormone (GH) Treatment in Growth Hormone–Deficient Adults: Role of Sex Hormone Replacement," *Journal of Clinical Endocrinology Metabolism* 85, no. 3 (2000): 1121–25.

11. A. Eliakim et al., "Effect of Gender on the Growth Hormone-IGF-I Response to Anaerobic Exercise in Young Adults," *Journal of Strength and Conditioning Research* 28, no. 12, (2014): 3411–15.

12. M. Russell-Aulet et al., "Aging-Related Growth Hormone Decrease Is a Selective Hypothalamic Growth Hormone–Releasing Hormone Pulse Amplitude Mediated Phenomenon," *The Journals of Gerontology, Series A: Biological Sciences and Medical Sciences* 56, no. 2 (2001): M124–29.

13. N. Vahl et al., "Abdominal Adiposity and Physical Fitness Are Major Determinants of the Age-Associated Decline in Stimulated Growth Hormone Secretion in Healthy Adults," *The Journal of Clinical Endocrinology & Metabolism* 81, no. 6 (1996): 2209–215.

14. M. Misra et al., "Lower Growth Hormone and Higher Cortisol Are Associated

with Greater Visceral Adiposity, Intramyocellular Lipids, and Insulin Resistance in Overweight Girls," *American Journal of Physiology-Endocrinology and Metabolism* 295, no. 2 (2008): E385–92.

15. I. Fukuda et al., "Serum Adiponectin Levels in Adult Growth Hormone Deficiency and Acromegaly," *Growth Hormone & IGF Research* 14, no. 6 (2004): 449–54; R. Stawerska et al., "Relationship Between IGF-I Concentration and Metabolic Profile in Children with Growth Hormone Deficiency: The Influence of Children's Nutritional State as Well as the Ghrelin, Leptin, Adiponectin, and Resistin Serum Concentrations," *International Journal of Endocrinology* 2017 (2017); E. Witkowska-Sędek et al., "The Associations Between the Growth Hormone/Insulin-like Growth Factor-1 Axis, Adiponectin, Resistin, and Metabolic Profile in Children with Growth Hormone Deficiency Before and During Growth Hormone Treatment," *Acta Biochimica Polonica* 65, no. 2 (2018): 333–40.

16. Z. P. Li et al., "Study of the Correlation Between Growth Hormone Deficiency and Serum Leptin, Adiponectin, and Visfatin Levels in Adults," *Genetics and Molecular Research: GMR* 13, no. 2 (2014): 4050–56.

17. J. D. Veldhuis et al., "Distinctive Inhibitory Mechanisms of Age and Relative Visceral Adiposity on Growth Hormone Secretion in Pre-and Postmenopausal Women Studied Under a Hypogonadal Clamp," *The Journal of Clinical Endocrinology & Metabolism* 90, no. 11 (2005): 6006–13.

18. Li et al., "Study of the Correlation Between Growth."

19. The complete list of hormones that are involved in regulating growth hormone and/or IGF-1 include estrogen, cortisol (that is, adrenocorticotropic hormone), thyroid (specifically, the control hormone for thyroid production, thyrotropin releasing hormone), luteinizing hormone, follicle-stimulating hormone, human chorionic gonadotropin (the hormone of pregnancy), insulin, other growth factors (for example, platelet-derived growth factor [PDGF], epidermal growth factor [EGF], and fibroblast growth factors [FGFs]), combined with age, sex, diet, nutrition, and other lifestyle factors. A. Kasprzak et al., "Insulin-like Growth Factor (IGF) Axis in Cancerogenesis." *Mutation Research/Reviews in Mutation Research* 772, no. 1 (2017): 78–104.

20. I recommend a full hormone panel to my patients, including thyroid stimulating hormone or TSH, free T3, free T4, reverse T3, thyroid peroxidase antibodies, and anti-thyroglobulin antibodies. Additional thyroid tests may be indicated, checking on symptoms. See Resources for recommended labs that perform this type of testing without a doctor's orders, but please work with a collaborative health-care practitioner to interpret results.

21. E. Giovannucci et al., "Nutritional Predictors of Insulin-like Growth Factor I and Their Relationships to Cancer in Men," *Cancer Epidemiology, Biomarkers, & Prevention* 12, no. 2 (2003): 84–89.

22. S. C. Larsson et al., "Association of Diet with Serum Insulin-like Growth Factor I in Middle-Aged and Elderly Men," *The American Journal of Clinical Nutrition* 81, no. 5 (2005): 1163–67.

23. M. Holmes et al., "Dietary Correlates of Plasma Insulin-like Growth Factor I and Insulin-like Growth Factor Binding Protein 3 Concentrations," *Cancer Epidemiology, Biomarkers, & Prevention* 11, no. 9 (2002): 852–61.

24. S. M. Phillips et al., "Dietary Protein for Athletes: From Requirements to Optimum Adaptation," *Journal of Sports Sciences* 29, Suppl. 1 (2011): S29–38; M. Huecker et al., "Protein Supplementation in Sport: Source, Timing, and Intended Benefits," *Current Nutrition Reports* 8, no. 4 (2019): 382–396.

25. K. Zhu et al., "The Effects of a Two-Year Randomized, Controlled Trial of Whey Protein Supplementation on Bone Structure, IGF-1, and Urinary Calcium Excretion in Older Postmenopausal Women," *Journal of Bone and Mineral Research* 26, no. 9 (2011): 2298–306.

26. J. M. Bauer et al., "Effects of a Vitamin D and Leucine-Enriched Whey Protein Nutritional Supplement on Measures of Sarcopenia in Older Adults, The PROVIDE Study: A Randomized, Double-Blind, Placebo-Controlled Trial," *Journal of the American Medical Directors Association* 16, no. 9 (2015): 740–47; M. Rondanelli et al., "Whey Protein, Amino Acids, and Vitamin D Supplementation with Physical Activity Increases Fat-Free Mass and Strength, Functionality, and Quality of Life and Decreases Inflammation in Sarcopenic Elderly," *The American Journal of Clinical Nutrition* 103, no. 3 (2016): 830–40; S. Verlaan et al., "Sufficient Levels of 25-Hydroxyvitamin D and Protein Intake Required to Increase Muscle Mass in Sarcopenic Older Adults—The PROVIDE Study," *Clinical Nutrition* 37, no. 2 (2018): 551–57.

27. E. Castillero et al., "Comparison of the Effects of the n-3 Polyunsaturated Fatty Acid Eicosapentaenoic and Fenofibrate on the Inhibitory Effect of Arthritis on IGF1," *Journal of Endocrinology* 210, no. 3 (2011): 361–68.

28. In the omega-3 pathway, several problems can upregulate an enzyme called delta-5-desaturase, which leads to production of more arachidonic acid, an inflammatory fat. These problems include essential hypertension, cardiovascular disease, insulin resistance, obesity, and metabolic syndrome.

    C. Russo et al., "Increased Membrane Ratios of Metabolite to Precursor Fatty Acid in Essential Hypertension," *Hypertension* 29, no. 4 (1997): 1058–63; B. Vessby, "Dietary Fat, Fatty Acid Composition in Plasma and the Metabolic Syndrome," *Current Opinion in Lipidology* 14, no. 1 (2003): 15–19; T. Domei et al., "Ratio of Serum n-3 to n-6 Polyunsaturated Fatty Acids and the Incidence of Major Adverse Cardiac Events in Patients Undergoing Percutaneous Coronary Intervention," *Circulation Journal* 76, (2012): 423–29; K. Inoue et al., "Low Serum Eicosapentaenoic Acid/Arachidonic Acid Ratio in Male Subjects with Visceral Obesity," *Nutrition & Metabolism* 10, no. 1 (2013): 25; E. Warensjö et al., "Fatty Acid Composition and Estimated Desaturase Activities Are Associated with Obesity and Lifestyle Variables in Men and Women," *Nutrition, Metabolism, and Cardiovascular Diseases* 16, no. 2 (2006): 128–36.

29. B. Yang et al., "Ratio of n-3/n-6 PUFAs and Risk of Breast Cancer: A Meta-Analy-

sis of 274135 Adult Females from 11 Independent Prospective Studies," *BMC Cancer* 14, no. 1 (2014): 105.

30. T. J. Merimee et al., "Diet-Induced Alterations of Growth Hormone Secretion in Man," *Journal of Clinical Endocrinology Metabolism* 42, no. 5 (1976): 931–37; K. Y. Ho et al., "Fasting Enhances Growth Hormone Secretion and Amplifies the Complex Rhythms of Growth Hormone Secretion in Man," *Journal of Clinical Investigation* 81, no. 4 (1988): 968–75; H. Nørrelund et al., "Modulation of Basal Glucose Metabolism and Insulin Sensitivity by Growth Hormone and Free Fatty Acids During Short-Term Fasting," *European Journal Endocrinology* 150, no. 6 (2004): 779–87; H. Nørrelund, "The Metabolic Role of Growth Hormone in Humans with Particular Reference to Fasting," *Growth Hormone & IGF Research* 15, no. 2 (2005): 95–122.

31. H. E. Bergan et al., "Nutritional State Modulates Growth Hormone–Stimulated Lipolysis," *General and Comparative Endocrinology* 217–218 (2015): 1–9.

32. B. D. Horne et al., "Relation of Routine, Periodic Fasting to Risk of Diabetes Mellitus, and Coronary Artery Disease in Patients Undergoing Coronary Angiography," *American Journal of Cardiology* 109, no. 11 (2012): 1558–62.

33. R. Gatti et al., "IGF-I/IGFBP System: Metabolism Outline and Physical Exercise." *Journal of Endocrinological Investigation* 35, no. 7 (2012): 699–707.

34. J. Leppäluoto et al., "Heat Exposure Elevates Plasma Immunoreactive Growth Hormone–Releasing Hormone Levels in Man," *The Journal of Clinical Endocrinology & Metabolism* 65, no. 5 (1987): 1035–38; J. Sirviö et al., "Adenohypophyseal Hormone Levels During Hyperthermia," *Endocrinologie* 25, no. 1 (1987): 21–23; K. Kukkonen-Harjula et al., "How the Sauna Affects the Endocrine System," *Annals of Clinical Research* 20, no. 4 (1988): 262–66; K. Kukkonen-Harjula et al., "Haemodynamic and Hormonal Responses to Heat Exposure in a Finnish Sauna Bath," *European Journal of Applied Physiology and Occupational Physiology* 58, no. 5 (1989): 543–50; D. Jezová et al., "Sex Differences in Endocrine Response to Hyperthermia in Sauna," *Acta Physiologica Scandinavica* 150, no. 3 (1994): 293–98.

35. R. Lammintausta et al., "Change in Hormones Reflecting Sympathetic Activity in the Finnish Sauna," *Annals of Clinical Research* 8, no. 4 (1976): 266–71.

36. M. Välimäki et al., "Effect of Ethanol on Serum Concentrations of Somatomedin C and the Growth hormone (GH) Secretion Stimulated by the Releasing Hormone (GHRH)," *Alcohol and Alcoholism* 1 (1987): 557–59; L. Dees et al., "Effects of Ethanol During the Onset of Female Puberty," *Neuroendocrinology* 51, no. 1 (1990): 64–69; M. Välimäki et al., "The Pulsatile Secretion of Gonadotropins and Growth Hormone, and the Biological Activity of Luteinizing Hormone in Men Acutely Intoxicated with Ethanol," *Alcoholism: Clinical and Experimental Research* 14, no. 6 (1990): 928–31; N. Rachdaoui et al., "Pathophysiology of the Effects of Alcohol Abuse on the Endocrine System," *Alcohol Research: Current Reviews* 38, no. 2 (2017): 255–76.

37. A. De Spiegeleer et al., "Pharmacological Interventions to Improve Muscle Mass,

Muscle Strength, and Physical Performance in Older People: An Umbrella Review of Systematic Reviews and Meta-Analyses," *Drugs & Aging* 35, no. 8 (2018): 719–34.

38. A. R. Martineau et al., "Vitamin D Supplementation to Prevent Acute Respiratory Tract Infections: Systematic Review and Meta-Analysis of Individual Participant Data," *British Medical Journal* (2017): 356: i6583.

39. M. R. Blackman et al., "Growth Hormone and Sex Steroid Administration in Healthy Aged Women and Men: A Randomized Controlled Trial," *Journal of the American Medical Association* 288, no. 18 (2002): 2282–92; H. Liu et al., "Systematic Review: The Safety and Efficacy of Growth Hormone in the Healthy Elderly," *Annals of Internal Medicine* 146, no. 2 (2007): 104–15.

40. S. M. Orme et al., "Mortality and Cancer Incidence in Acromegaly: A Retrospective Cohort Study," *The Journal of Clinical Endocrinology & Metabolism* 83, no. 8 (1998): 2730–34; W. E. Sonntag et al., "Adult-Onset Growth Hormone and Insulin-Like Growth Factor I Deficiency Reduces Neoplastic Disease, Modifies Age-Related Pathology, and Increases Life Span," *Endocrinology* 146, no. 7 (2005): 2920–32; A. J. Swerdlow et al., "Cancer Risks in Patients Treated with Growth Hormone in Childhood: The SAGhE European Cohort Study," *The Journal of Clinical Endocrinology & Metabolism* 102, no. 5 (2017): 1661–72.

41. J. Berlanga-Acosta et al., "Synthetic Growth Hormone–Releasing Peptides (GHRPs): A Historical Appraisal of the Evidences Supporting Their Cytoprotective Effects," *Clinical Medicine Insights: Cardiology* 11, no. 1 (2017); J. T. Sigalos et al., "Growth Hormone Secretagogue Treatment in Hypogonadal Men Raises Serum Insulin-Like Growth Factor-1 Levels," *American Journal Men's Health* 11, no. 6 (2017): 1752–57; J. T. Sigalos et al., "The Safety and Efficacy of Growth Hormone Secretagogues," *Sexual Medicine Reviews* 6, no. 1 (2018).

42. B. C. Nindl et al., "Insulin-like Growth Factor I as a Biomarker of Health, Fitness, and Training Status," *Medicine and Science in Sports and Exercise* 42, no. 1 (2010): 39–49.

3. TESTOSTERONE: IT'S NOT JUST FOR MEN

1. C. Longcope, "Adrenal and Gonadal Androgen Secretion in Normal Females," *Clinics in Endocrinology and Metabolism* 15, no. 2 (1986): 213–28.

2. S. L. Davison et al., "Androgen Levels in Adult Females: Changes with Age, Menopause, and Oophorectomy," *The Journal of Clinical Endocrinology & Metabolism* 90, no. 7 (2005): 3847–53.

3. To test your testosterone, I recommend asking your health-care practitioner for a blood test that includes total and free testosterone (that is, the amount that is biologically available to exert effects on your cells). See if they will also measure bioavailable testosterone. You can test DHEA, testosterone, and its downstream hormones in your urine. Next best is to test yourself at the labs that I use for my patients, including WellnessFx.com and DUTCHtest.com. More are mentioned in Resources.

4. Davison et al., "Androgen Levels in Adult Females."

5. N. Orentreich et al., "Age Changes and Sex Differences in Serum Dehydroepian-drosterone Sulfate Concentrations Throughout Adulthood," *Journal of Clinical Endocrinology Metabolism* 59, no. 3 (1984): 551–55.

6. Davison et al., "Androgen Levels in Adult Females"; R. Haring et al., "Age-Specific Reference Ranges for Serum Testosterone and Androstenedione Concentrations in Women Measured by Liquid Chromatography-Tandem Mass Spectrometry," *Journal of Clinical Endocrinology Metabolism* 97, no. 2 (2012): 408–15.

7. C. M. Coenen et al., "Changes in Androgens During Treatment with Four Low-Dose Contraceptives," *Contraception* 53, no. 3 (1996): 171–76; Y. Zimmerman et al., "The Effect of Combined Oral Contraception on Testosterone Levels in Healthy Women: A Systematic Review and Meta-Analysis," *Human Reproductive Update* 20, no. 1 (2014): 76–105; N. Zethraeus et al., "Combined Oral Contraceptives and Sexual Function in Women—A Double-Blind, Randomized, Placebo-Controlled Trial," *Journal of Clinical Endocrinology Metabolism* 101, no. 11 (2016): 4046–53; S. Both et al., "Hormonal Contraception and Female Sexuality: Position Statements from the European Society of Sexual Medicine (ESSM)," *Journal of Sexual Medicine* 16, no. 11 (2019): 1681–95.

8. Statins deplete CoQ10, selenium, selenoproteins, omega 3FA, tocopherols and to-cotrienols, K2, other fat soluble vitamins, Heme A, carnitine, free T3, creatine, copper, and zinc. Practitioners, see IFM Tool Kit at IFM.org for further information. P. H. Langsjoen et al., "The Clinical Use of HMG CoA-Reductase Inhibitors and the Associated Depletion of Coenzyme Q10: A Review of Animal and Human Publications," *Biofactors* 18, nos. 1–4 (2003): 101–11; C. R. Harper et al., "Evidence-Based Management of Statin Myopathy," *Current Atherosclerosis Reports* 12, no. 5 (2010): 322–30; H. Qu et al., "Effects of Coenzyme Q10 on Statin-Induced Myopathy: An Updated Meta-Analysis of Randomized Controlled Trials," *Journal of the American Heart Association* 7, no. 19 (2018): e009835.

9. J. Y. Shin et al., "Are Cholesterol and Depression Inversely Related? A Meta-Analysis of the Association Between Two Cardiac Risk Factors," *Annals of Behavioral Medicine* 36, no. 1 (2008): 33–43; G. Corona et al., "The Effect of Statin Therapy on Testosterone Levels in Subjects Consulting for Erectile Dysfunction," *Journal of Sexual Medicine* 7, no. 4, part 1 (2010): 1547–56; E. J. Giltay et al., "Salivary Testosterone: Associations with Depression, Anxiety Disorders, and Antidepressant Use in a Large Cohort Study," *Journal of Psychosomatic Research* 72, no. 3 (2012): 205–13; G. Roberto et al., "Statin-Associated Gynecomastia: Evidence Coming from the Italian Spontaneous ADR Reporting Database and Literature," *European Journal of Clinical Pharmacology* 68, no. 6 (2012): 1007–11; C. M. Schooling et al., "The Effect of Statins on Testosterone in Men and Women: A Systematic Review And Meta-Analysis of Randomized Controlled Trials," *BMC Medicine* 11, no. 1 (2013): 57.

10. L. Mernone et al., "Psychobiological Factors of Sexual Functioning in Aging Women—Findings from the Women 40+ Healthy Aging Study," *Frontiers in Psychology* 10, no. 1 (2019): 546.

11. S. R. Davis et al., "Circulating Androgen Levels and Self-Reported Sexual Function in Women," *Journal of the American Medical Association* 294, no. 1 (2005): 91–96.

12. R. Basson et al., "Role of Androgens in Women's Sexual Dysfunction," *Menopause* 17, no. 5 (2010): 962–71; S. Wåhlin-Jacobsen et al., "Is There a Correlation Between Androgens and Sexual Desire in Women?" *Journal of Sexual Medicine* 12, no. 2 (2015): 358–73.

13. Mernone et al., "Psychobiological Factors of Sexual Functioning."

14. S. R. Davis et al., "Global Consensus Position Statement on the Use of Testosterone Therapy for Women," *The Journal of Clinical Endocrinology and Metabolism* 104, no. 10 (2019): 4660–66.

15. C. Bentley et al., "Dehydroepiandrosterone: A Potential Therapeutic Agent in the Treatment and Rehabilitation of the Traumatically Injured Patient," *Burns & Trauma* 7, no. 26 (2019).

16. H. E. Nagels et al., "Androgens (dehydroepiandrosterone or testosterone) for Women Undergoing Assisted Reproduction," *Cochrane Database of Systemic Reviews* 11, no. 1 (2015).

17. G. P. Williams, "The Role of Oestrogen in the Pathogenesis of Obesity, Type 2 Diabetes, Breast Cancer, and Prostate Disease," *European Journal of Cancer Prevention* 19, no. 4 (2010): 256–71; J. McHenry et al., "Sex Differences in Anxiety and Depression: Role of Testosterone," *Front Neuroendocrinology* 35, no. 1 (2014): 42–57; F. Saad, "The Emancipation of Testosterone from Niche Hormone to Multi-System Player," *Asian Journal of Andrology* 17, no. 1 (2015): 58–60; L. Y. Hui et al., "Association Between MKP-1, BDNF, and Gonadal Hormones with Depression on Perimenopausal Women," *Journal of Women's Health* 25, no. 1 (2016): 71–77; S. Rovira-Llopis et al., "Low Testosterone Levels Are Related to Oxidative Stress, Mitochondrial Dysfunction, and Altered Subclinical Atherosclerotic Markers in Type 2 Diabetic Male Patients," *Free Radical Biology & Medicine* 108, no. 1 (2017): 155–62; H. O. Santos, "Ketogenic Diet and Testosterone Increase: Is the Increased Cholesterol Intake Responsible? To What Extent and Under What Circumstances Can There Be Benefits?" *Hormones (Athens)* 16, no. 3 (2017): 150–60.

18. X. Zhang et al., "Postmenopausal Plasma Sex Hormone Levels and Breast Cancer Risk over 20 Years of Follow-Up," *Breast Cancer Research and Treatment* 137, no. 3 (2013): 883–92; R. T. Fortner et al., "Premenopausal Endogenous Steroid Hormones and Breast Cancer Risk: Results from the Nurses' Health Study II," *Breast Cancer Research* 15, no. 2 (2013): R19; Endogenous Hormones and Breast Cancer Collaborative Group et al., "Sex Hormones and Risk of Breast Cancer in Premenopausal Women: A Collaborative Reanalysis of Individual Participant Data from Seven Prospective Studies," *The Lancet Oncology* 14, no. 10 (2013): 1009–19; R. Kaaks et al., "Premenopausal Serum Sex Hormone Levels in Relation to Breast Cancer Risk, Overall and by Hormone Receptor Status — Results from the EPIC Cohort," *International Journal of Cancer* 134, no. 8 (2014): 1947–57; R. Glaser et al., "Testosterone and Breast Cancer Prevention," *Maturitas* 82, no. 3 (2015): 291–

95; K. A. Bertrand et al., "Circulating Hormones and Mammographic Density in Premenopausal Women," *Hormones & Cancer* 9, no. 2 (2018): 117–27.

19. J. L. Shifren et al., "Transdermal Testosterone Treatment in Women with Impaired Sexual Function After Oophorectomy," *New England Journal of Medicine* 343, no. 10 (2000): 682–88; R. Goldstat et al., "Transdermal Testosterone Therapy Improves Well-Being, Mood, and Sexual Function in Premenopausal Women," *Menopause* 10, no. 5 (2003): 390–98; E. J. Hermans et al., "Exogenous Testosterone Attenuates the Integrated Central Stress Response in Healthy Young Women," *Psychoneuroendocrinology* 32, nos. 8–10 (2007): 1052–61; K. K. Miller et al., "Low-Dose Transdermal Testosterone Augmentation Therapy Improves Depression Severity in Women," *CNS Spectrums* 14, no. 12 (2009): 688–94.

20. B. C. Trainor et al. "Testosterone Promotes Paternal Behaviour in a Monogamous Mammal via Conversion to Oestrogen," *Proceedings of the Royal Society of London, Series B: Biological Sciences* 269, no. 1493 (2002): 823–29.

21. Metabolic problems associated with PCOS include glucose intolerance, metabolic syndrome, and type 2 diabetes. L. J. Moran et al., "Impaired Glucose Tolerance, Type 2 Diabetes, and Metabolic Syndrome in Polycystic Ovary Syndrome: A Systematic Review and Meta-Analysis," *Human Reproduction Update* 16, no. 4 (2010): 347–63; N. S. Kakoly et al., "Ethnicity, Obesity, and the Prevalence of Impaired Glucose Tolerance and Type 2 Diabetes in PCOS: A Systematic Review and Meta-Regression," *Human Reproduction Update* 24, no. 4 (2018): 455–67.

Mental health problems associated with PCOS include anxiety, depression, body dissatisfaction, and lower quality of life. S. Elsenbruch et al., "Quality of Life, Psychosocial Well-Being, and Sexual Satisfaction in Women with Polycystic Ovary Syndrome," *The Journal of Clinical Endocrinology & Metabolism* 88, no. 12 (2003): 5801–7; M. J. Himelein et al., "Depression and Body Image Among Women with Polycystic Ovary Syndrome," *Journal of Health Psychology* 11, no. 4 (2006): 613–25; L. M. Pastore et al., "Depression Symptoms and Body Dissatisfaction Association Among Polycystic Ovary Syndrome Women," *Journal of Psychosomatic Research* 71, no. 4 (2011): 270–76; A. F. Nasiri et al., "The Experience of Women Affected by Polycystic Ovary Syndrome: A Qualitative Study from Iran," *International Journal of Endocrinology and Metabolism* 12, no. 2 (2014); C. Kaczmarek et al., "Health-related Quality of Life in Adolescents and Young Adults with Polycystic Ovary Syndrome: A Systematic Review," *Journal of Pediatric and Adolescent Gynecology* 29, no. 6 (2016): 551–57.

22. L. J. Moran et al., "Sex Hormone Binding Globulin, but Not Testosterone, Is Associated with the Metabolic Syndrome in Overweight and Obese Women with Polycystic Ovary Syndrome," *Journal of Endocrinological Investigation* 36, no. 11 (2013): 1004–10.

23. X. Zhang et al., "The Effect of Low Carbohydrate Diet on Polycystic Ovary Syndrome: A Meta-Analysis of Randomized Controlled Trials," *International Journal of Endocrinology* 2019, no. 4386401 (2019): 1–14.

24. J. C. Mavropoulos et al., "The Effects of a Low-Carbohydrate, Ketogenic Diet on

the Polycystic Ovary Syndrome: A Pilot Study," *Nutrition & Metabolism (Lond)* 2, no. 35 (2005); G. Muscogiuri et al., "Current Insights into Inositol Isoforms, Mediterranean, and Ketogenic Diets for Polycystic Ovary Syndrome: From Bench to Bedside," *Current Pharmaceutical Design* 22, no. 36 (2016): 5554–57; R. K. Stocker et al., "Ketogenic Diet and Its Evidence-Based Therapeutic Implementation in Endocrine Diseases," *Praxis (Bern 1994)* 108, no. 8 (2019): 541–53 (article in German; abstract available in German from the publisher).

25. L. Chen et al., "Sugar-Sweetened Beverage Intake and Serum Testosterone Levels in Adult Males 20–39 Years Old in the United States," *Reproductive Biology Endocrinology* 16, no. 1 (2018).

26. Note that the drink contained 30 grams of glucose and 30 grams of protein. A. Schwartz et al., "Acute Decrease in Serum Testosterone After a Mixed Glucose and Protein Beverage in Obese Peripubertal Boys," *Clinical Endocrinology* 83, no. 3 (2015): 332–38.

27. Note that the drink contained 75 grams of glucose. L. M. Caronia et al., "Abrupt Decrease in Serum Testosterone Levels After an Oral Glucose Load in Men: Implications for Screening for Hypogonadism," *Clinical Endocrinology* 78, no. 2 (2013): 291–96.

28. N. M. Wedick et al., "The Effects of Caffeinated and Decaffeinated Coffee on Sex Hormone–Binding Globulin and Endogenous Sex Hormone Levels: A Randomized Controlled Trial," *Nutrition Journal* 11, no. 1 (2012): 86.

29. K. C. Schliep et al., "Serum Caffeine and Paraxanthine Concentrations and Menstrual Cycle Function: Correlations with Beverage Intakes and Associations with Race, Reproductive Hormones, and Anovulation in the BioCycle Study," *The American Journal of Clinical Nutrition* 104, no. 1 (2016): 155–63.

30. R. L. Ferrini et al., "Caffeine Intake and Endogenous Sex Steroid Levels in Postmenopausal Women: The Rancho Bernardo Study," *American Journal of Epidemiology* 144, no. 7 (1996): 642–44.

31. D. Hang et al., "Coffee Consumption and Plasma Biomarkers of Metabolic and Inflammatory Pathways in US Health Professionals," *The American Journal of Clinical Nutrition* 109, no. 3 (2019): 635–47.

32. T. Hu et al., "Testosterone-Associated Dietary Pattern Predicts Low Testosterone Levels and Hypogonadism," *Nutrients* 10, no. 11 (2018): 1786.

33. Wilson et al., "The Effects of Ketogenic Dieting."

34. K. Z. de Souza et al., "Efficacy of *Tribulus terrestris* for the Treatment of Hypoactive Sexual Desire Disorder in Postmenopausal Women: A Randomized, Double-Blinded, Placebo-Controlled Trial," *Menopause* 23, no. 11 (2016): 1252–56; F. B. C. Vale et al., "Efficacy of *Tribulus terrestris* for the Treatment of Premenopausal Women with Hypoactive Sexual Desire Disorder: A Randomized Double-Blinded, Placebo-Controlled Trial," *Gynecological Endocrinology.* 34, no. 5 (2018): 442–45; S. Palacios et al., "Effect of a Multi-Ingredient-Based Food Supplement on Sexual Function in Women with Low Sexual Desire," *BMC Women's Health: London* 19, no. 1 (2019): 58.

35. E. Steels et al., "Efficacy of a Proprietary Trigonella Foenum-Graecum L. Of-Husked Seed Extract in Reducing Menopausal Symptoms in Otherwise Healthy Women: A Double-Blind, Randomized, Placebo-Controlled Study," *Phytotherapy Research* 31, no. 9 (2017): 1316–22; S. Begum et al., "A Novel Extract of Fenugreek Husk (Fenusmart™) Alleviates Postmenopausal Symptoms and Helps to Establish the Hormonal Balance: A Randomized, Double-Blind, Placebo-Controlled Study," *Phytotherapy Research* 30, no. 11 (2016): 1775–84; A. Rao et al., "Influence of a Specialized Trigonella Foenum-Graecum Seed Extract (Libifem), on Testosterone, Estradiol, and Sexual Function in Healthy Menstruating Women: A Randomised Placebo-Controlled Study," *Phytotherapy Research* 29, no. 8 (2015): 1123–30.

36. de Souza et al., "Efficacy of *Tribulus terrestris*"; Vale et al., "Efficacy of *Tribulus terrestris.*"

37. T. Takeuchi et al., "Serum Bisphenol A Concentrations Showed Gender Differences, Possibly Linked to Androgen Levels," *Biochemical and Biophysical Research Communications* 291, no. 1 (2002): 76–78; A. Tomza-Marciniak et al., "Effect of Bisphenol A on Reproductive Processes: A Review of In Vitro, In Vivo, and Epidemiological Studies," *Journal of Applied Toxicology* 38, no. 1 (2018): 51–80; Y. Hu et al., "The Association Between the Environmental Endocrine Disruptor Bisphenol A and Polycystic Ovary Syndrome: A Systematic Review and Meta-Analysis," *Gynecological Endocrinology* 34, no. 5 (2018): 370–77; A. Konieczna et al., "Serum Bisphenol A Concentrations Correlate with Serum Testosterone Levels in Women with Polycystic Ovary Syndrome," *Reproductive Toxicology* 82, no. 1 (2018): 32–37.

38. L. Le Corre et al., "BPA, an Energy Balance Disruptor," *Critical Reviews Food Science and Nutrition* 55, no. 6 (2015): 769–77; S. Legeay et al., "Is Bisphenol A an Environmental Obesogen?" *Fundamental & Clinical Pharmacology* 31, no. 6 (2017): 594–609; J. J. Heindel et al., "Environmental Obesogens: Mechanisms and Controversies," *Annual Review of Pharmacology Toxicology* 59, no. 1 (2019): 89–106; B. S. Rubin et al., "The Case for BPA as an Obesogen: Contributors to the Controversy," *Front Endocrinology (Lausanne)* 10, no. 30 (2019).

39. R. H. W. van Lunsen et al., "Maintaining Physiologic Testosterone Levels During Combined Oral Contraceptives by Adding Dehydroepiandrosterone: II. Effects on Sexual Function. A Phase II Randomized, Double-Blind, Placebo-Controlled Study," *Contraception* 98, no. 1 (2018): 56–62.

40. C. S. Scheffers et al., "Dehydroepiandrosterone for Women in the Peri- or Postmenopausal Phase," *Cochrane Database Systemic Reviews* 1 (2015).

4. THE KETO PARADOX

1. E. Vining et al., "A Multicenter Study of the Efficacy of the Ketogenic Diet," *Archives of Neurology* 55, no. 11 (1998): 1433–37; D. R. Nordli et al., "Experience with the Ketogenic Diet in Infants," *Pediatrics* 108, no. 1 (2001): 129–33; K. Tran et al., "Can You Predict an Immediate, Complete, and Sustained Response to the

Ketogenic Diet?" *Epilepsia* 46, no. 4 (2005): 580–82; E. Neal et al., "The Ketogenic Diet for the Treatment of Childhood Epilepsy: A Randomised Controlled Trial," *The Lancet Neurology* 7, no. 6 (2008): 500–506; L. Shah et al., "How Often Is Antiseizure Drug-Free Ketogenic Diet Therapy Achieved?" *Epilepsy & Behavior* 93, no. 1 (2019): 29–31; B. Gilbert, "Benefits and Complications of the Ketogenic Diet for Epilepsy," *Neurology Advisor,* https://www.neurologyadvisor.com/topics/epilepsy/benefits-and-complications-of-the-ketogenic-diet-for-epilepsy/. Accessed November 27, 2019.

2. T. J. W. McDonald et al., "Ketogenic Diets for Adult Neurological Disorders," *Neurotherapeutics* 15, no. 4 (2018): 1018–31; M. Rusek et al., "Ketogenic Diet in Alzheimer's Disease," *International Journal of Molecular Sciences* 20, no. 16 (2019): 3892; G. M. Broom et al., "The Ketogenic Diet as a Potential Treatment and Prevention Strategy for Alzheimer's Disease," *Nutrition* 60 (2019): 118–21; R. Nagpal et al., "Modified Mediterranean-Ketogenic Diet Modulates Gut Microbiome and Short-Chain Fatty Acids in Association with Alzheimer's Disease Markers in Subjects with Mild Cognitive Impairment," *EBioMedicine* 47 (2019): 529–42.

3. H. Y. Chung et al., "Rationale, Feasibility, and Acceptability of Ketogenic Diet for Cancer Treatment," *Journal of Cancer Prevention* 22, no. 3 (2017): 127–134; D. D. Weber et al., "Ketogenic Diet in the Treatment of Cancer — Where Do We Stand?" *Molecular Metabolism* 33 (2020): 102–21.

4. B. D. Hopkins et al., "Suppression of Insulin Feedback Enhances the Efficacy of PI3K Inhibitors," *Nature* 560, no. 7719 (2018): 499–503.

5. A. F. Luat et al., "The Ketogenic Diet: A Practical Guide for Pediatricians," *Pediatric Annals* 45, no. 12 (2016): e446–50; G. Muscogiuri et al., "The Management of Very Low-Calorie Ketogenic Diet in Obesity Outpatient Clinic: A Practical Guide," *Journal of Translational Medicine* 17, no. 1 (2019): 356.

6. A. Johannessen et al., "Prolactin, Growth Hormone, Thyrotropin, 3, 5, 3'-Triiodothyronine, and Thyroxine Responses to Exercise After Fat- and Carbohydrate-Enriched Diet," *The Journal of Clinical Endocrinology & Metabolism* 52, no. 1 (1981): 56–61; L. J. McCargar et al., "Dietary Carbohydrate-to-Fat Ratio: Influence on Whole-Body Nitrogen Retention, Substrate Utilization, and Hormone Response in Healthy Male Subjects," *The American Journal of Clinical Nutrition* 49, no. 6 (1989): 1169–78; J. Langfort et al., "Effect of Low-Carbohydrate-Ketogenic Diet on Metabolic and Hormonal Responses to Graded Exercise in Men," *Journal of Physiology and Pharmacology: An Official Journal of the Polish Physiological Society* 47, no. 2 (1996): 361–71; F. Q. Nuttall et al., "The Metabolic Response to a High-Protein, Low-Carbohydrate Diet in Men with Type 2 Diabetes Mellitus," *Metabolism* 55, no. 2 (2006): 243–51; A. E. Lima-Silva et al., "Low Carbohydrate Diet Affects the Oxygen Uptake on-Kinetics and Rating of Perceived Exertion in High-Intensity Exercise," *Psychophysiology* 48, no. 2 (2011): 277–84; A. Zajac et al., "The Effects of a Ketogenic Diet on Exercise Metabolism and Physical Performance in Off-Road Cyclists," *Nutrients* 6, no. 7 (2014): 2493–508; K. D. Hall et al., "Energy Expenditure and Body Composition Changes After an Isocaloric Ketogenic Diet

in Overweight and Obese Men," *The American Journal of Clinical Nutrition* 104, no. 2 (2016): 324–33; S. Vargas et al., "Efficacy of Ketogenic Diet on Body Composition During Resistance Training in Trained Men: A Randomized Controlled Trial," *Journal of the International Society of Sports Nutrition* 15, no. 1 (2018): 31.

7. A. M. Johnstone et al., "Effects of a High-Protein Ketogenic Diet on Hunger, Appetite, and Weight Loss in Obese Men Feeding Ad Libitum," *The American Journal of Clinical Nutrition* 87, no. 1 (2008): 44–55.

8. S. R. Nymo et al., "Timeline of Changes in Appetite During Weight Loss with a Ketogenic Diet," *International Journal of Obesity* 41, no. 8 (2017): 1224–31.

9. Hall et al., "Energy Expenditure and Body Composition."

10. Vargas et al., "Efficacy of Ketogenic Diet."

11. M. J. Sharman et al., "A Ketogenic Diet Favorably Affects Serum Biomarkers for Cardiovascular Disease in Normal-Weight Men," *The Journal of Nutrition* 132, no. 7 (2002): 1879–85.

12. K. K. Ryan et al., "Dietary Manipulations That Induce Ketosis Activate the HPA Axis in Male Rats and Mice: A Potential Role for Fibroblast Growth Factor-21," *Endocrinology* 159, no. 1 (2017): 400–413.

13. C. M. Young et al., "Effect on Body Composition and Other Parameters in Obese Young Men of Carbohydrate Level of Reduction Diet," *The American Journal of Clinical Nutrition* 24, no. 3 (1971): 290–96; S. B. Hulley et al., "Lipid and Lipoprotein Responses of Hypertriglyceridaemic Outpatients to a Low-Carbohydrate Modification of the AHA Fat-Controlled Diet," *The Lancet* 300, no. 7777 (1972): 551–55; B. Fagerberg et al., "Weight-Reducing Diets: Role of Carbohydrates on Sympathetic Nervous Activity and Hypotensive Response," *International Journal of Obesity* 8, no. 3 (1984): 237–43; J. W. Helge et al., "Prolonged Adaptation to Fat-Rich Diet and Training: Effects on Body Fat Stores and Insulin Resistance in Man," *International Journal of Obesity* 26, no. 8 (2002): 1118–24; J. S. Volek et al., "Body Composition and Hormonal Responses to a Carbohydrate-Restricted Diet," *Metabolism-Clinical and Experimental* 51, no. 7 (2002): 864–70; R. H. Stimson et al., "Dietary Macronutrient Content Alters Cortisol Metabolism Independently of Body Weight Changes in Obese Men," *The Journal of Clinical Endocrinology & Metabolism* 92, no. 11 (2007): 4480–84; A. R. Lane et al., "Influence of Dietary Carbohydrate Intake on the Free Testosterone: Cortisol Ratio Responses to Short-Term Intensive Exercise Training," *European Journal of Applied Physiology* 108, no. 6 (2010): 1125–31; K. Pilis et al., "Three-Year Chronic Consumption of Low-Carbohydrate Diet Impairs Exercise Performance and Has a Small Unfavorable Effect on Lipid Profile in Middle-Aged Men," *Nutrients* 10, no. 12 (2018): 1914; H. S. Waldman et al., "Effects of a 15-day Low Carbohydrate, High-Fat Diet in Resistance-Trained Men," *The Journal of Strength & Conditioning Research* 32, no. 11 (2018): 3103–11; M. M. Michalczyk et al., "Anaerobic Performance After a Low-Carbohydrate Diet (LCD) Followed by 7 Days of Carbohydrate Loading in Male Basketball Players," *Nutrients* 11, no. 4 (2019): 778.

14. L. Stern et al., "The Effects of Low-Carbohydrate Versus Conventional Weight

Loss Diets in Severely Obese Adults: One-Year Follow-Up of a Randomized Trial," *Annals of Internal Medicine* 140, no. 10 (2004): 778–85; I. Shai et al., "Weight Loss with a Low-Carbohydrate, Mediterranean, or Low-Fat Diet," *New England Journal of Medicine* 359, no. 3 (2008): 229–41; N. Iqbal et al., "Effects of a Low-Intensity Intervention That Prescribed a Low-Carbohydrate vs. a Low-Fat Diet in Obese, Diabetic Participants," *Obesity* 18, no. 9 (2010): 1733–38.

15. Volek et al., "Cardiovascular and Hormonal Aspects"; Volek et al., "Comparison of Energy-Restricted"; Dashti et al., "Long Term Effects of Ketogenic Diet"; Ruaño, "Physiogenomic Analysis of Weight Loss"; Durkalec-Michalski et al., "Effect of a Four-week Ketogenic Diet."

16. R. L. Williams et al., "Effectiveness of Weight Loss Interventions — Is there a Difference Between Men and Women? A Systematic Review," *Obesity Review* 16, no. 2 (2015): 171–86.

17. D. J. Millward et al., "Sex Differences in the Composition of Weight Gain and Loss in Overweight and Obese Adults," *British Journal of Nutrition* 111, no. 5 (2014): 933–43.

18. A. Wirth et al., "Gender Differences in Changes in Subcutaneous and Intra-Abdominal Fat During Weight Reduction: An Ultrasound Study," *Obesity Research* 6, no. 6 (1998): 393–99.

19. Men were 64 percent less likely to be aware of their weight ("weight perception"), 61 percent less likely to experience weight dissatisfaction, and 45 percent less likely to attempt weight loss. Men who attempted weight loss were 40 percent more likely than women to lose 10 pounds or more over one year, maintain that loss, and increase exercise. S. A. Tsai et al., "Gender Differences in Weight-Related Attitudes and Behaviors Among Overweight and Obese Adults in the United States," *American Journal of Men's Health* 10, no. 5 (2016): 389–98.

20. A. Furnham et al., "Body Image Dissatisfaction: Gender Differences in Eating Attitudes, Self-Esteem, and Reasons for Exercise," *Journal of Psychology* 136, no. 6 (2002): 581–96.

21. E. Johansson et al., "Obesity and Labour Market Success in Finland: The Difference Between Having a High BMI and Being Fat," *Economics and Human Biology* 7, no. 1 (2009): 36–45.

22. Diagnostic ranges for cortisol and blood glucose. I measure cortisol in blood and urine. I measure glucose in blood and the interstitial space with a continuous glucose monitor. This is how the American Diabetes Association defines prediabetes: borderline glycemia measured by any of three measures — fasting plasma glucose 100–125 mg/dL (5.6–6.9 mmol/L), 2-h plasma glucose 140–199 mg/dL (7.8–11.0 mmol/L), or hemoglobin A1c 5.7–6.4 percent (39–46 mmol/mol).

J. S. Yudkin, "'Prediabetes': Are There Problems with This Label? Yes, the Label Creates Further Problems!" *Diabetes Care* 39, no. 8 (2016): 1468–71; American Diabetes Association, "2. Classification and Diagnosis of Diabetes: Standards of Medical Care in Diabetes — 2018," *Diabetes Care* 41, no. 1 (2018): S13–27.

23. D. E. Laaksonen et al., "Serum Fatty Acid Composition Predicts Development

of Impaired Fasting Glycaemia and Diabetes in Middle-aged Men," *Diabetic Medicine* 19, no. 6 (2002): 456–64; R. M. Van Dam et al., "Dietary Fat and Meat Intake in Relation to Risk of Type 2 Diabetes in Men," *Diabetes Care* 25, no. 3 (2002): 417–24; G. Riccardi et al., "Dietary Fat, Insulin Sensitivity, and the Metabolic Syndrome," *Clinical Nutrition* 23, no. 4 (2004): 447–56; A. Shaheen et al., "A Hypothetical Model to Solve the Controversy over the Involvement of UCP2 in Palmitate-Induced β-cell Dysfunction," *Endocrine* 54, no. 2 (2016): 276–83; M. Mazidi et al., "Dietary Food Patterns and Glucose/Insulin Homeostasis: A Cross-sectional Study Involving 24,182 Adult Americans," *Lipids in Health and Disease* 16, no. 1 (2017): 192; M. Rapoport et al., "Triglycerides, Free Fatty Acids, and Glycemic Control: An Unresolved Puzzle," *The Israel Medical Association Journal* 20, no. 6 (2018): 385–87; A. Julibert et al., "Total and Subtypes of Dietary Fat Intake and Its Association with Components of the Metabolic Syndrome in a Mediterranean Population at High Cardiovascular Risk," *Nutrients* 11, no. 7 (2019): 1493.

24. J. Y. Lee et al., "Saturated Fatty Acids, but Not Unsaturated Fatty Acids, Induce the Expression of Cyclooxygenase-2 Mediated Through Toll-Like Receptor 4," *Journal of Biological Chemistry* 276, no. 20 (2001): 16683–89; J. M. Fernández-Real et al., "Insulin Resistance, Inflammation, and Serum Fatty Acid Composition." *Diabetes Care* 26, no. 5 (2003): 1362–68; K. M. Ajuwon et al., "Palmitate Activates the NF-κB Transcription Factor and Induces IL-6 and TNFα Expression in 3T3-L1 Adipocytes," *The Journal of Nutrition* 135, no. 8 (2005): 1841–46; C. Klein-Platat et al., "Plasma Fatty Acid Composition Is Associated with the Metabolic Syndrome and Low-Grade Inflammation in Overweight Adolescents," *The American Journal of Clinical Nutrition* 82, no. 6 (2005): 1178–84; A. R. Weatherill et al., "Saturated and Polyunsaturated Fatty Acids Reciprocally Modulate Dendritic Cell Functions Mediated Through TLR4," *The Journal of Immunology* 174, no. 9 (2005): 5390–97; S. Santos et al., "Systematic Review of Saturated Fatty Acids on Inflammation and Circulating Levels of Adipokines," *Nutrition Research* 33, no. 9 (2013): 687–95; J. E. Kaikkonen et al., "High Serum n6 Fatty Acid Proportion Is Associated with Lowered LDL Oxidation and Inflammation: The Cardiovascular Risk in Young Finns Study," *Free Radical Research* 48, no. 4 (2014): 420–26; C. Harris et al., "Associations Between Fatty Acids and Low-Grade Inflammation in Children from the MELISSAplus Birth Cohort Study," *European Journal of Clinical Nutrition* 71, no. 11 (2017): 1303–11; D. M. Rocha et al., "The Role of Dietary Fatty Acid Intake in Inflammatory Gene Expression: A Critical Review," *São Paulo Medical Journal* 135, no. 2 (2017): 157–68.

25. L. Arab et al., "Biomarkers and the Measurement of Fatty Acids," *Public Health Nutrition* 5, no. 6a (2002): 865–71; C. Kasapis et al., "The Effects of Physical Activity on Serum C-Reactive Protein and Inflammatory Markers: A Systematic Review," *Journal of the American College of Cardiology* 45, no. 10 (2005): 1563–69; M. Gleeson et al., "The Anti-Inflammatory Effects of Exercise: Mechanisms and Implications for the Prevention and Treatment of Disease," *Nature Reviews*

Immunology 11, no. 9 (2011): 607–15; B. Ruiz-Núñez et al., "Lifestyle and Nutritional Imbalances Associated with Western Diseases: Causes and Consequences of Chronic Systemic Low-Grade Inflammation in an Evolutionary Context," *The Journal of Nutritional Biochemistry* 24, no. 7 (2013): 1183–1201; S. Santos et al., "Fatty Acids Derived from a Food Frequency Questionnaire and Measured in the Erythrocyte Membrane in Relation to Adiponectin and Leptin Concentrations," *European Journal of Clinical Nutrition* 68, no. 5 (2014): 555–60; M. Mazidi et al., "Impact of the Dietary Fatty Acid Intake on C-Reactive Protein Levels in US Adults," *Medicine* 96, no. 7 (2017): e5736.

26. Rodrigues et al., "The Action of β-hydroxybutyrate."

27. G. Beccuti et al., "Sleep and Obesity," *Current Opinion in Clinical Nutrition and Metabolic Care* 14, no. 4 (2011): 402–12.

5. HOW TO START AND WHAT TO EAT

1. T. L. Stanley et al., "Effects of Growth Hormone–Releasing Hormone on Visceral Fat, Metabolic, and Cardiovascular Indices in Human Studies," *Growth Hormone & IGF Research* 25, no. 2 (2015): 59–65.

2. L. R. Squire et al., "Conscious and Unconscious Memory Systems," *Cold Spring Harbor Perspectives in Biology* 7, no. 3 (2015): a021667; J. Goodman et al., "Memory Systems and the Addicted Brain," *Frontiers in Psychiatry* 7 (2016): 24; M. M. Torregrossa et al., "Neuroscience of Learning and Memory for Addiction Medicine: From Habit Formation to Memory Reconsolidation," *Progress in Brain Research* 223 (2016): 91–113; J. Goodman et al., "The Dorsolateral Striatum Selectively Mediates Extinction of Habit Memory," *Neurobiology of Learning and Memory* 136 (2016): 54–62; L. Mang et al., "The Influence of Mood and Attitudes Towards Eating on Cognitive and Autobiographical Memory Flexibility in Female University Students," *Psychiatry Research* 269 (2018): 444–49.

3. E. Patrono et al., "Transitionality in Addiction: A 'Temporal Continuum' Hypotheses Involving the Aberrant Motivation, the Hedonic Dysregulation, and the Aberrant Learning," *Medical Hypotheses* 93 (2016): 62–70.

4. V. Voon, "Cognitive Biases in Binge Eating Disorder: The Hijacking of Decision Making," *CNS Spectrums* 20, no. 6 (2015): 566–73.

5. J. Goodman et al., "Enhancing and Impairing Extinction of Habit Memory Through Modulation of NMDA Receptors in the Dorsolateral Striatum," *Neuroscience* 352 (2017): 216–25.

6. Mang et al., "The Influence of Mood and Attitudes."

7. For whole foods, take total carbs and subtract fiber (in grams) to determine your net carbs. For processed food, subtract fiber (in grams) and sugar alcohol (in grams from total carbs in grams) to determine your net carbs.

8. Laboratory testing for insulin resistance involves both impaired fasting glucose and impaired glucose tolerance. These are the diagnostic criteria of optimal, borderline, prediabetes, and diabetes that I have used in my medical practice based on the best evidence, but you should know that numerous groups, from the

American Diabetes Association to the World Health Organization, use criteria that lack consensus.

- Fasting glucose: optimal 70–85, borderline 86–99, prediabetes 100–125, diabetes greater than 126 mg/dL
- Continuous glucose monitor with optimal average glucose less than 100 and standard deviation less than 15 mg/dL (in my opinion, based on clinical experience and my preferred way to diagnose insulin issues)
- 2-hour postprandial glucose prediabetes 140–199 mg/dL, diabetes greater than 199 mg/dL
- hemoglobin optimal less than 5 percent, borderline 5.0–5.6 percent, prediabetes A1C 5.7–6.4 percent, diabetes greater than 6.4 percent

World Health Organization, "Definition and Diagnosis of Diabetes Mellitus and Intermediate Hyperglycaemia: Report of a WHO/IDF Consultation" (2006): 1–50; N. Bansal, "Prediabetes Diagnosis and Treatment: A Review," *World Journal of Diabetes* 6, no. 2 (2015): 296; W. C. Y. Yip et al., "Prevalence of Pre-Diabetes Across Ethnicities: A Review of Impaired Fasting Glucose (IFG) and Impaired Glucose Tolerance (IGT) for Classification of Dysglycaemia," *Nutrients* 9, no. 11 (2017): 1273; Z. Punthakee et al., "Classification and Diagnosis of Diabetes, Prediabetes, and Metabolic Syndrome," *Canadian Journal of Diabetes* 42 (2018): S10–15; American Diabetes Association, "2. Classification and Diagnosis of Diabetes: Standards of Medical Care in Diabetes—2018," *Diabetes Care* 41, no. 1 (2018): S13–27.

9. A. Hozawa et al., "Association Between Body Mass Index and All-Cause Death in Japanese Population: Pooled Individual Participant Data Analysis of 13 Cohort Studies," *Journal of Epidemiology* 29, no. 12 (2019): 457–63; M. D. Rahman et al., "Trend, Projection, and Appropriate Body Mass Index Cut-Off Point for Diabetes and Hypertension in Bangladesh," *Diabetes Research and Clinical Practice* 126 (2017): 43–53.

10. This online calculator is offered by the Centers for Disease Control: https://www.cdc.gov/healthyweight/assessing/bmi/adult_bmi/english_bmi_calculator/bmi_calculator.html, accessed May 20, 2020.

11. When I am coaching a patient about the Gottfried Protocol, I ask if they want the basic or the advanced approach. For people who have the bandwidth, it can be helpful to measure more advanced metrics, including the following:

- Daily fingerstick for blood sugar and ketones (see Resources for recommended brands, like Keto-mojo and Precision Extra), in order to calculate the glucose ketone index
- Continuous glucose monitor (see Resources for recommended brands)
- Bluetooth body composition scale (see Resources—I use Renpho.)
- Resting metabolic rate
- Exercise performance, such as VO2 max

12. One of the best descriptions of the ketogenic ratio is in this book: Jacob Wilson and Ryan Lowery, *The Ketogenic Bible* (Las Vegas: Victory Belt, 2017), 39–40.

13. Proteins are mixed in their ketogenic effect. Why? Some building blocks of protein, called amino acids, are ketogenic and others are anti-ketogenic. Examples of ketogenic amino acids are leucine and lysine. An example of an anti-ketogenic amino acid is alanine.

14. I. A. Cohen, "A Model for Determining Total Ketogenic Ratio (TKR) for Evaluating the Ketogenic Property of a Weight-Reduction Diet," *Medical Hypotheses* 73, no. 3 (2009): 377–81.

15. Young et al., "Effect on Body Composition."

16. S. H. Duncan et al., "Reduced Dietary Intake of Carbohydrates by Obese Subjects Results in Decreased Concentrations of Butyrate and Butyrate-Producing Bacteria in Feces," *Applied and Environmental Microbiology* 73, no. 4 (2007): 1073–78.

17. To calculate the net carbs in processed foods, subtract the fiber and a portion of the sugar alcohols. So for one-third of a medium avocado, that's 4 grams of carbohydrates, less 3 grams of fiber (4g – 3 g = 1 g), so 1 net carbohydrate. For my favorite brownies, which I recommend in Resources, that's 13 total carbs per each serving of brownie, less 5 grams of fiber, less 7 grams of sugar alcohols (in this case, erythritol and allulose), or 1 net carb.

18. J. Rehm et al., "Alcohol Use and Cancer in the European Union," *European Addiction Research* (2020): 1–8; S. Parida et al., "Microbial Alterations and Risk Factors of Breast Cancer: Connections and Mechanistic Insights," *Cells* 9, no. 5 (2020): 1091.

19. X. Yao et al., "Change in Moderate Alcohol Consumption and Quality of Life: Evidence from 2 Population-Based Cohorts," *CMAJ* 191, no. 27 (2019): E753–60.

20. M. Venkatesh et al., "Dietary Oil Composition Differentially Modulates Intestinal Endotoxin Transport and Postprandial Endotoxemia," *Nutrition & Metabolism* 10, no. 1 (2013): 6.

21. A. Dagfinn et al., "Nut Consumption and Risk of Cardiovascular Disease, Total Cancer, All-Cause and Cause-Specific Mortality: A Systematic Review and Dose-Response Meta-Analysis of Prospective Studies," *BMC Medicine* 14, no. 1 (2016): 207; C. Guo-Chong et al., "Nut Consumption in Relation to All-Cause and Cause-Specific Mortality: A Meta-Analysis 18 Prospective Studies," *Food & Function* 8, no. 11 (2017): 3893–905.

22. M. P. St-Onge et al., "Consumption of a Functional Oil Rich in Phytosterols and Medium-Chain Triglyceride Oil Improves Plasma Lipid Profiles in Men," *The Journal of Nutrition* 133, no. 6, (2003): 1815–20; J. R. Han et al., "Effects of Dietary Medium-Chain Triglyceride on Weight Loss and Insulin Sensitivity in a Group of Moderately Overweight Free-Living Type 2 Diabetic Chinese Subjects," *Metabolism* 56, no. 7 (2007): 985–91; M. P. St-Onge et al., "Medium-Chain Triglyceride Oil Consumption as Part of a Weight Loss Diet Does Not Lead to an Adverse Metabolic Profile When Compared to Olive Oil," *Journal of the American College of Nutrition* 27, no. 5 (2008): 547–52.

23. K. Mumme et al., "Effects of Medium-Chain Triglycerides on Weight Loss and

Body Composition: A Meta-Analysis of Randomized Controlled Trials," *Journal of the Academy of Nutrition and Dietetics* 115, no. 2 (2015): 249–63.

24. T. Maher et al., "A Comparison of the Satiating Properties of Medium-Chain Triglycerides and Conjugated Linoleic Acid in Participants with Healthy Weight and Overweight or Obesity," *European Journal of Nutrition* (2020): 1–13.

25. Here are additional details about MCT.

MCT oil increases ketones by 19 percent and can help flip the metabolic switch from burning glucose to burning fat. (C. Vandenberghe et al., "Medium-Chain Triglycerides Modulate the Ketogenic Effect of a Metabolic Switch," *Frontiers in Nutrition* 7 (2020): 3–6.

Additionally, in limited studies in Alzheimer's disease, some measures of cognition improved with addition of MCT oil to the diet (K. I. Avgerinos et al., "Medium-Chain Triglycerides Induce Mild Ketosis and May Improve Cognition in Alzheimer's Disease: A Systematic Review and Meta-Analysis of Human Studies," *Ageing Research Reviews* [2019]: 101,001), and brain utilization of ketones may double (E. Croteau et al., "Ketogenic Medium-Chain Triglycerides Increase Brain Energy Metabolism in Alzheimer's Disease," *Journal of Alzheimer's Disease* 64, no. 2 [2018]: 551–61).

MCT talks to hormones too and may help you become more insulin sensitive and lower your adiponectin within six weeks, at least according to one small uncontrolled study (D. D. Thomas et al., "Effects of Medium-Chain Triglycerides Supplementation on Insulin Sensitivity and Beta Cell Function: A Feasibility Study," *PLoS One* 14, no. 12 (2019).

26. The mechanism for damage is believed to be through the elevation of bacterial toxins from the gut, known as endotoxemia, for five to eight hours after you eat it. P. Dandona et al., "Macronutrient Intake Induces Oxidative and Inflammatory Stress: Potential Relevance to Atherosclerosis and Insulin Resistance," *Experimental & Molecular Medicine* 42, no. 4 (2010): 245–53; F. Biobaku et al., "Macronutrient-Mediated Inflammation and Oxidative Stress: Relevance to Insulin Resistance, Obesity, and Atherogenesis," *The Journal of Clinical Endocrinology & Metabolism* 104, no. 12 (2019): 6118–28.

27. When you eat saturated or trans fats together with refined carbohydrates, the mechanism for damage is a combination of oxidative stress, unresolved inflammation, endotoxemia, increased expression of SOCS-3 and TLR4, blocking IRS-1 and PI3K pathways inducing insulin resistance, according to personal communication with Mark Houston, MD, and Dandona et al., "Macronutrient Intake."

28. Y. Bao et al., "Association of Nut Consumption with Total and Cause-Specific Mortality," *The New England Journal of Medicine* 369, no. 21 (2013): 2001–11.

29. C. Smith-Spangler et al., "Are Organic Foods Safer or Healthier Than Conventional Alternatives? A Systematic Review," *Annals of Internal Medicine* 157, no. 5 (2012): 343–66; S. Watson, "Organic Food No More Nutritious Than Conventionally Grown Food," *Harvard Women's Health Watch*, September 5, 2012,

https://www.health.harvard.edu/blog/organic-foodno-more-nutritious-than
-conventionally-grown-food-201209055264. Accessed May 6, 2020.

30. A. S. Abargouei et al., "Effect of Dairy Consumption on Weight and Body Composition in Adults: A Systematic Review and Meta-Analysis of Randomized Controlled Clinical Trials," *International Journal of Obesity* 36, no. 12 (2012): 1485–93.

31. California Avocados, "Avocado Nutritional Information," https://www.californiaavocado.com/nutrition/nutrients. Accessed May 6, 2020.

32. S. Kim et al., "Effects of Growth Hormone on Glucose Metabolism and Insulin Resistance in Humans," *Annals of Pediatric Endocrinology & Metabolism* 22, no. 3 (2017): 145.

33. L. A. Frohman, "Growth Hormone," *Encyclopedia of Neuroscience*, vol. 1 (London: Academic Press, 2009).

34. Diabetes Teaching Center at the University of California, San Francisco, "Blood Sugar & Other Hormones," https://dtc.ucsf.edu/types-of-diabetes/type1/understanding-type-1-diabetes/how-the-body-processes-sugar/blood-sugar-other-hormones/

35. R. Lanzi et al., "Elevated Insulin Levels Contribute to the Reduced Growth Hormone (GH) Response to GH-Releasing Hormone in Obese Subjects," *Metabolism* 48, no. 9 (1999): 1152–56; J. Xu et al., "Crosstalk Between Growth Hormone and Insulin Signaling," *Vitamins & Hormones* 80 (2009): 125–53; H. Qiu et al., "Influence of Insulin on Growth Hormone Secretion, Level, and Growth Hormone Signaling," *Sheng Li Xue Bao* 69, no. 5 (2017): 541–56.

36. M. La Merrill et al., "Toxicological Function of Adipose Tissue: Focus on Persistent Organic Pollutants," *Environmental Health Perspectives* 121, no. 2 (2013): 162–69.

37. Your liver processes toxins in two phases. In phase one, it converts fat-soluble toxins into water-soluble substances. At the end of phase two, the liver excretes these water-soluble toxins via urine, stool, sweat, and other body fluids. In a detoxification protocol, this two-step process needs to be managed in the opposite order: optimize phase two before triggering phase one. This is one of the reasons why detoxification and "cleanse" programs are controversial and can make people sick; if toxins are removed from tissues at a higher rate than they are removed from the body, it makes a person feel terrible and can even have severe consequences. Think of it this way: you don't warm up the car in the garage, and then open the garage door to let out the fumes.

38. J. Obert et al., "Popular Weight Loss Strategies: A Review of Four Weight Loss Techniques," *Current Gastroenterology Reports* 19, no. 12 (2017): 61.

39. M. S. Duchowny, "Food for Thought: The Ketogenic Diet and Adverse Effects in Children," *Epilepsy Currents* 5, no. 4 (2005): 152–54.

40. G. Zong et al., "Consumption of Meals Prepared at Home and Risk of Type 2 Diabetes: An Analysis of Two Prospective Cohort Studies," *PLoS Medicine* 13, no. 7 (2016): e1002052.

6. DETOXING, CIRCADIAN FASTING, AND TROUBLESHOOTING

1. M. M. Hetherington et al., "Understanding the Science of Portion Control and the Art of Downsizing," *Proceedings of the Nutrition Society* 77, no. 3 (2018): 347–55.

2. J. J. Meidenbauer et al., "The Glucose Ketone Index Calculator: A Simple Tool to Monitor Therapeutic Efficacy for Metabolic Management of Brain Cancer," *Nutrition & Metabolism* 12, no. 1 (2015): 1–7.

3. Y. Li, "Exogenous Stimuli Maintain Intraepithelial Lymphocytes Via Aryl Hydrocarbon Receptor Activation," *Cell* 147, no. 3 (2011): 629–40.

4. A. Paoli et al., "Effect of Ketogenic Mediterranean Diet with Phytoextracts and Low Carbohydrates/High-Protein Meals on Weight, Cardiovascular Risk Factors, Body Composition, and Diet Compliance in Italian Council Employees," *Nutrition Journal* 10, no. 1 (2011): 112; A. Paoli et al., "Long Term Successful Weight Loss with a Combination Biphasic Ketogenic Mediterranean Diet and Mediterranean Diet Maintenance Protocol," *Nutrients* 5, no. 12 (2013): 5205–17; A. Paoli et al., "Ketogenic Diet and Phytoextracts," *Scientific Advisory Board* 21, no. 4 (2010): 24–29; A. Paoli et al., "Ketogenic Diet Does Not Affect Strength Performance in Elite Artistic Gymnasts," *Journal of the International Society of Sports Nutrition* 9, no. 1 (2012): 34; A. Paoli et al., "Effects of n-3 Polyunsaturated Fatty Acids (ω-3) Supplementation on Some Cardiovascular Risk Factors with a Ketogenic Mediterranean Diet," *Marine Drugs* 13, no. 2 (2015): 996–1009; G. Bosco et al., "Effects of the Ketogenic Diet in Overweight Divers Breathing Enriched Air Nitrox," *Scientific Reports* 8, no. 1 (2018): 1–8; A. Paoli et al., "Effects of a Ketogenic Diet in Overweight Women with Polycystic Ovary Syndrome," *Journal of Translational Medicine* 18, no. 1 (2020): 1–11.

5. Y. Aitbali et al., "Glyphosate Based-Herbicide Exposure Affects Gut Microbiota, Anxiety, and Depression-Like Behaviors in Mice," *Neurotoxicology and Teratology* (2018); I. Argou-Cardozo et al., "Clostridium Bacteria and Autism Spectrum Conditions: A Systematic Review and Hypothetical Contribution of Environmental Glyphosate Levels," *Medical Sciences* 6, no. 2 (2018): 29; C. E. Gallegos et al., "Perinatal Glyphosate-Based Herbicide Exposure in Rats Alters Brain Antioxidant Status, Glutamate and Acetylcholine Metabolism, and Affects Recognition Memory," *Neurotoxicity Research* (2018): 1–12; P. Good. "Evidence the US Autism Epidemic Initiated by Acetaminophen (Tylenol) Is Aggravated by Oral Antibiotic Amoxicillin/Clavulanate (Augmentin) and Now Exponentially by Herbicide Glyphosate (Roundup)," *Clinical Nutrition ESPEN* 23 (2018): 171–83; L. N. Nielsen et al., "Glyphosate Has Limited Short-Term Effects on Commensal Bacterial Community Composition in the Gut Environment Due to Sufficient Aromatic Amino Acid Levels," *Environmental Pollution* 233 (2018): 364–76.

6. J. J. Gildea et al., "Protection Against Gluten-Mediated Tight Junction Injury with a Novel Lignite Extract Supplement," *Journal of Nutrition & Food Sciences* 6, no. 547 (2016): 2; J. J. Gildea et al., "Protective Effects of Lignite Extract Supplement

on Intestinal Barrier Function in Glyphosate-Mediated Tight Junction Injury," *Journal of Clinical Nutrition & Dietetics* 3, no. 1 (2017).

7. A. Di Ciaula et al., "Diet and Contaminants: Driving the Rise to Obesity Epidemics?" *Current Medicinal Chemistry* 26, no. 19 (2019): 3471–82; L. A. Hoepner, "Bisphenol A: A Narrative Review of Prenatal Exposure Effects on Adipogenesis and Childhood Obesity Via Peroxisome Proliferator-Activated Receptor Gamma," *Environmental Research* 173 (2019): 54–68; Rubin et al., "The Case for BPA as an Obesogen"; R. Chamorro-Garcia et al., "Current Research Approaches and Challenges in the Obesogen Field," *Frontiers in Endocrinology* 10 (2019): 167; J. J. Heindel, "History of the Obesogen Field: Looking Back to Look Forward," *Frontiers in Endocrinology* 10 (2019): 14.

8. K. Katoh et al., "Suppressing Effects of Bisphenol A on the Secretory Function of Ovine Anterior Pituitary Cells," *Cell Biology International* 28, no. 6 (2004): 463–69.

9. A. B. Javurek et al., "Effects of Exposure to Bisphenol A and Ethinyl Estradiol on the Gut Microbiota of Parents and Their Offspring in a Rodent Model," *Gut Microbes* 7, no. 6 (2016): 471–85; J. Xu et al., "Developmental Bisphenol A Exposure Modulates Immune-Related Diseases," *Toxics* 4, no. 4 (2016): 23; K. P. Lai et al., "Bisphenol A Alters Gut Microbiome: Comparative Metagenomics Analysis," *Environmental Pollution* 218 (2016): 923–30; L. Reddivari et al., "Perinatal Bisphenol A Exposure Induces Chronic Inflammation in Rabbit Offspring via Modulation of Gut Bacteria and Their Metabolites," *MSystems* 2, no. 5 (2017); Y. Malaisé et al., "Gut Dysbiosis and Impairment of Immune System Homeostasis in Perinatally Exposed Mice to Bisphenol A Precede Obese Phenotype Development," *Scientific Reports* 7, no. 1 (2017): 1–12; J. A. DeLuca et al., "Bisphenol-A Alters Microbiota Metabolites Derived from Aromatic Amino Acids and Worsens Disease Activity During Colitis," *Experimental Biology and Medicine* 243, no. 10 (2018): 864–75; T. R. Catron et al., " Host Developmental Toxicity of BPA and BPA Alternatives Is Inversely Related to Microbiota Disruption in Zebrafish," *Toxicological Sciences* 167, no. 2 (2019): 468–83.

10. K. Oishi, "Effect of Probiotics, Bifidobacterium Breve, and Lactobacillus Casei on Bisphenol A Exposure in Rats," *Bioscience, Biotechnology, and Biochemistry* 72, no. 6 (2008): 1409–15; S. Song et al., "The Anti-Allergic Activity of Lactobacillus Plantarum L67 and Its Application to Yogurt," *Journal of Dairy Science* 99, no. 12 (2016): 9372–82.

11. A. A. Ismail et al., "Chronic Magnesium Deficiency and Human Disease: Time for Reappraisal?" *QJM: An International Journal of Medicine* 111, no. 11 (2018): 759–63; M. S. Razzaque, "Magnesium: Are We Consuming Enough?" *Nutrients* 10, no. 12 (2018): 1863; J. L. Workinger et al., "Challenges in the Diagnosis of Magnesium Status," *Nutrients* 10, no. 9 (2018): 1202.

12. For a list of functional medicine clinicians, go to the "find a practitioner" link at the Institute of Functional Medicine, https://www.ifm.org/find-a-practitioner/. Accessed December 16, 2020.

13. J. Hussain et al., "Clinical Effects of Regular Dry Sauna Bathing: A Systematic Review," *Evidence-Based Complementary and Alternative Medicine* (2018).

14. C. P. Oliveira et al., "N-Acetylcysteine and/or Ursodeoxycholic Acid Associated with Metformin in Non-Alcoholic Steatohepatitis: An Open-Label Multicenter Randomized Controlled Trial," *Arquivos de Gastroenterologia* 56, no. 2 (2019): 184–90; D. Thakker et al., "N-Acetylcysteine for Polycystic Ovary Syndrome: A Systematic Review and Meta-Analysis of Randomized Controlled Clinical Trials," *Obstetrics and Gynecology International* (2015).

15. A. M. Fulghesu et al., "N-Acetyl-Cysteine Treatment Improves Insulin Sensitivity in Women with Polycystic Ovary Syndrome," *Fertility and Sterility* 77, no. 6 (2002): 1128–35; G. Oner et al., "Clinical, Endocrine, and Metabolic Effects of Metformin vs. N-acetyl-cysteine in Women with Polycystic Ovary Syndrome," *European Journal of Obstetrics & Gynecology and Reproductive Biology* 159, no. 1 (2011): 127–31.

16. A. Elnashar et al., "N-Acetyl Cysteine vs. Metformin in Treatment of Clomiphene Citrate–Resistant Polycystic Ovary Syndrome: A Prospective Randomized Controlled Study," *Fertility and Sterility* 88, no. 2 (2007): 406–9.

17. S. Ebrahimpour-Koujan et al., "Lower Glycemic Indices and Lipid Profile Among Type 2 Diabetes Mellitus Patients Who Received Novel Dose of Silybum Marianum (L.) Gaertn.(silymarin) Extract Supplement: A Triple-Blinded Randomized Controlled Clinical Trial," *Phytomedicine* 44 (2018): 39–44.

18. S. Rahmani et al., "Treatment of Non-Alcoholic Fatty Liver Disease with Curcumin: A Randomized Placebo-Controlled Trial," *Phytotherapy Research* 30, no. 9 (2016): 1540–48; Y. Panahi et al., "Efficacy and Safety of Phytosomal Curcumin in Non-Alcoholic Fatty Liver Disease: A Randomized Controlled Trial," *Drug Research* 67, no. 04 (2017): 244–51; R. Goodarzi et al., "Does Turmeric/Curcumin Supplementation Improve Serum Alanine Aminotransferase and Aspartate Aminotransferase Levels in Patients with Nonalcoholic Fatty Liver Disease? A Systematic Review and Meta-Analysis of Randomized Controlled Trials," *Phytotherapy Research* 33, no. 3 (2019): 561–70; F. Mansour-Ghanaei et al., "Efficacy of Curcumin/Turmeric on Liver Enzymes in Patients with Non-Alcoholic Fatty Liver Disease: A Systematic Review of Randomized Controlled Trials," *Integrative Medicine Research* 8, no. 1 (2019): 57–61; A. Ghaffari et al., "Turmeric and Chicory Seed Have Beneficial Effects on Obesity Markers and Lipid Profile in Non-Alcoholic Fatty Liver Disease (NAFLD)," *International Journal for Vitamin and Nutrition Research* (2019).

19. K. Gabel et al., "Effects of 8-hour Time Restricted Feeding on Body Weight and Metabolic Disease Risk Factors in Obese Adults: A Pilot Study," *Nutrition and Healthy Aging* 4, no. 4 (2018): 345–53, https://content.iospress.com/articles/nutrition-and-healthy-aging/nha170036.

20. M. N. Harvie, "The Effects of Intermittent or Continuous Energy Restriction on Weight Loss and Metabolic Disease Risk Markers: A Randomized Trial in Young Overweight Women," *International Journal of Obesity (London)* 35 (2011): 714–27;

S. Gil et al., "A Smartphone App Reveals Diurnal Eating Patterns in Humans That Can Be Modulated for Health Benefits," *Cell Metabolism* 22, no. 5 (2015): 789–98; G. M. Tinsley et al., "Effects of Intermittent Fasting on Body Composition."

21. A. Chaix et al., "The Effects of Time-Restricted Feeding on Lipid Metabolism and Adiposity," *Adipocyte* 4, no. 4 (2015): 319–24; H. Chung et al., "Time-Restricted Feeding Improves Insulin Resistance and Hepatic Steatosis in a Mouse Model of Postmenopausal Obesity," *Metabolism-Clinical and Experimental* 65, no. 12 (2016): 1743–54.

22. A. Chaix et al., "Time-Restricted Feeding Is a Preventative and Therapeutic Intervention Against Diverse Nutritional Challenges," *Cell Metabolism* 20, no. 6 (2014): 991–1005; R. Antoni et al., "Effects of Intermittent Fasting on Glucose and Lipid Metabolism," *Proceedings of the Nutrition Society* 76, no. 3 (2017): 361–68.

23. G. C. Melkani et al., "Time Restricted Feeding for Prevention and Treatment of Cardiometabolic Disorders," *The Journal of Physiology* 595, no. 12 (2017): 3691–700.

24. R. E. Patterson et al., "Intermittent Fasting and Human Metabolic Health," *Journal of the Academy of Nutrition and Dietetics* 115, no. 8 (2015): 1203–12; C. R. Marinac et al., "Prolonged Nightly Fasting and Breast Cancer Prognosis," *JAMA Oncology* 2, no. 8 (2016): 1049–55; L. A. Smith et al., "Translating Mechanism-Based Strategies to Break the Obesity–Cancer Link: A Narrative Review," *Journal of the Academy of Nutrition and Dietetics* 118, no. 4 (2018): 652–67.

25. E. N. Manoogian et al., "Circadian Rhythms, Time-Restricted Feeding, and Healthy Aging," *Ageing Research Reviews* 39 (2017): 59–67.

26. J. T. Haas et al., "Fasting the Microbiota to Improve Metabolism?" *Cell Metabolism* 26, no. 4 (2017): 584–85; R. Kivelä et al., "White Adipose Tissue Coloring by Intermittent Fasting," *Cell Research* 27, no. 11 (2017): 1300–1301; G. Li et al., "Intermittent Fasting Promotes White Adipose Browning and Decreases Obesity by Shaping the Gut Microbiota," *Cell Metabolism* 26, no. 4 (2017): 672–85.

27. S. Eslami et al., "Annual Fasting; The Early Calories Restriction for Cancer Prevention," *BioImpacts: BI* 2, no. 4 (2012): 213–15; A. Zarrinpar et al., "Diet and Feeding Pattern Affect the Diurnal Dynamics of the Gut Microbiome," *Cell Metabolism* 20, no. 6 (2014): 1006–17; A. Chaix et al. "The Effects of Time-Restricted Feeding"; J. L. Kaczmarek et al., "Complex Interactions of Circadian Rhythms, Eating Behaviors, and the Gastrointestinal Microbiota and Their Potential Impact on Health," *Nutrition Reviews* 75, no. 9 (2017): 673–82; Li et al., "Intermittent Fasting Promotes White"; R. E. Patterson et al., "Metabolic Effects of Intermittent Fasting," *Annual Review of Nutrition* 37 (2017): 371–93; E. Beli et al., "Restructuring of the Gut Microbiome by Intermittent Fasting Prevents Retinopathy and Prolongs Survival in db/db Mice," *Diabetes* (2018): db180158.

28. S. Panda, "Circadian Physiology of Metabolism." *Science* 354, no. 6315 (2016): 1008–15.

29. M. P. Mattson et al., "Impact of Intermittent Fasting on Health and Disease Pro-

cesses," *Ageing Research Reviews* 39 (2017): 46–58; B. K. Shin et al., "Intermittent Fasting Protects Against the Deterioration of Cognitive Function, Energy Metabolism, and Dyslipidemia in Alzheimer's Disease-Induced Estrogen Deficient Rats," *Experimental Biology and Medicine* 234, no. 4 (2018): 334–43.

30. M. Hatori et al., "Time-Restricted Feeding Without Reducing Caloric Intake Prevents Metabolic Diseases in Mice Fed a High-Fat Diet," *Cell Metabolism* 15, no. 6 (2012): 848–60.

31. K. M. Pursey et al., "Neural Responses to Visual Food Cues According to Weight Status: A Systematic Review of Functional Magnetic Resonance Imaging Studies," *Frontiers in Nutrition* 1 (2017): 7–18.

32. I learned this hack from Jeffrey Becker, MD, in a lecture he gave at the Integrative Psychiatry Institute, where I am on the faculty. He recommends 1 teaspoon of MCT oil at work, or half a nutrition bar, in the afternoon to help prevent cravings for alcohol.

33. M. C. Houston, "Treatment of Hypertension with Nutraceuticals, Vitamins, Antioxidants, and Minerals," *Expert Review of Cardiovascular Therapy* 5, no. 4 (2007): 681–91; S. T. Sinatra et al., *Nutritional and Integrative Strategies in Cardiovascular Medicine* (Boca Raton, FL: CRC Press, 2015); L. Rochette et al., "Alpha-Lipoic Acid: Molecular Mechanisms and Therapeutic Potential in Diabetes," *Canadian Journal of Physiology and Pharmacology* 93, no. 12 (2015): 1021–27; S. Kucukgoncu et al., "Alpha-Lipoic Acid (ALA) as a Supplementation for Weight Loss: Results from a Meta-Analysis of Randomized Controlled Trials," *Obesity Reviews* 18, no. 5 (2017): 594–601.

34. Rochette et al., "Alpha-Lipoic Acid."

35. K. H. Weylandt et al., "Omega-3 Fatty Acids and Their Lipid Mediators: Towards an Understanding of Resolvin and Protectin Formation," *Prostaglandins & Other Lipid Mediators* 97, nos. 3–4 (2012): 73–82; R. Ramaswami et al., "Fish Oil Supplementation in Pregnancy," *New England Journal of Medicine* 375, no. 26 (2016): 2599–601.

36. Yang et al., "Ratio of N-3/N-6 PUFAs"; C. J. Fabian et al., "Omega-3 Fatty Acids for Breast Cancer Prevention and Survivorship," *Breast Cancer Research* 17, no. 1 (2015): 1–11.

37. M. Houston, *Personalized and Precision Integrative Cardiovascular Medicine* (Philadelphia: Lippincott Williams & Wilkins, 2019); Z. Ilyas et al., "The Effect of Berberine on Weight Loss in Order to Prevent Obesity: A Systematic Review," *Biomedicine & Pharmacotherapy* 127 (2020): 110137; M. Rondanelli et al., "Polycystic Ovary Syndrome Management: A Review of the Possible Amazing Role of Berberine," *Archives of Gynecology and Obstetrics* (2020): 1–8.

38. C. N. Serhan, "Pro-Resolving Lipid Mediators Are Leads for Resolution Physiology," *Nature* 510, no. 7503 (2014): 92–101; C. N. Serhan et al., "Resolvins in Inflammation: Emergence of the Pro-Resolving Superfamily of Mediators," *The Journal of Clinical Investigation* 128, no. 7 (2018): 2657–69; P. C. Norris et al., "Identification of Specialized Pro-Resolving Mediator Clusters from Healthy Adults After

Intravenous Low-Dose Endotoxin and Omega-3 Supplementation: A Methodological Validation," *Scientific Reports* 8, no. 1 (2018): 1–13.

39. C. C. Douglas et al., "Role of Diet in the Treatment of Polycystic Ovary Syndrome," *Fertility and Sterility* 85, no. 3 (2006): 679–88; Gottfried, *The Hormone Cure*, M. McGrice et al., "The Effect of Low Carbohydrate Diets on Fertility Hormones and Outcomes in Overweight and Obese Women: A Systematic Review," *Nutrients* 9, no. 3 (2017): 204; L. Barrea et al., "Source and Amount of Carbohydrate in the Diet and Inflammation in Women with Polycystic Ovary Syndrome," *Nutrition Research Reviews* 31, no. 2 (2018): 291–301; L. Barrea et al., "Adherence to the Mediterranean Diet, Dietary Patterns, and Body Composition in Women with Polycystic Ovary Syndrome (PCOS)," *Nutrients* 11, no. 10 (2019): 2278.

40. Mavropoulos et al., "The Effects of a Low-Carbohydrate"; Gottfried, *The Hormone Cure*; D. Kulak et al., "Should the Ketogenic Diet Be Considered for Enhancing Fertility?" *Maturitas* 74, no. 1 (2013): 10–13; Muscogiuri et al., "Current Insights into Inositol Isoforms"; M. Melanie et al., "The Effect of Low Carbohydrate Diets on Fertility Hormones and Outcomes in Overweight and Obese Women: A Systematic Review," *Nutrients* 9, no. 3 (2017): 204; M. Caprio et al., "Very-Low-Calorie Ketogenic Diet (VLCKD) in the Management of Metabolic Diseases: Systematic Review and Consensus Statement from the Italian Society of Endocrinology (SIE)," *Journal of Endocrinological Investigation* 42, no. 11 (2019): 1365–86; Paoli et al., "Effects of a Ketogenic Diet in Overweight Women."

41. Gottfried, *The Hormone Cure*; M. J. Carvalho et al., "Controversial Association Between Polycystic Ovary Syndrome and Breast Cancer," *European Journal of Obstetrics & Gynecology and Reproductive Biology* 243 (2019): 125–32.

42. A. Balen, "Polycystic Ovary Syndrome and Cancer," *Human Reproduction Update* 7, no. 6 (2001): 522–25; Gottfried, *The Hormone Cure*; C. C. Shen et al., "A Nationwide Population-Based Retrospective Cohort Study of the Risk of Uterine, Ovarian, and Breast Cancer in Women with Polycystic Ovary Syndrome," *The Oncologist* 20, no. 1 (2015): 45; F. Shobeiri et al., "The Association Between Polycystic Ovary Syndrome and Breast Cancer: A Meta-Analysis," *Obstetrics & Gynecology Science* 59, no. 5 (2016): 367–72.

43. Gottfried, *The Hormone Cure*; J. Barry et al., "Risk of Endometrial, Ovarian, and Breast Cancer in Women with Polycystic Ovary Syndrome: A Systematic Review and Meta-Analysis," *Human Reproduction Update* 20, no. 5 (2014): 748–58; M. Gottschau et al., "Risk of Cancer Among Women with Polycystic Ovary Syndrome: A Danish Cohort Study." *Gynecologic Oncology* 136, no. 1 (2015): 99–103; H. R. Harris et al., "Polycystic Ovary Syndrome and Risk of Endometrial, Ovarian, and Breast Cancer: A Systematic Review," *Fertility Research and Practice* 2, no. 1 (2016): 14; D. C. Ding et al., "Association Between Polycystic Ovarian Syndrome and Endometrial, Ovarian, and Breast Cancer: A Population-Based Cohort Study in Taiwan," *Medicine* 97, no. 39 (2018).

44. Gottfried, *The Hormone Cure*; Barry et al., "Risk of Endometrial, Ovarian, and Breast Cancer"; Shen et al., "A Nationwide Population-Based Retrospective";

Gottschau et al., "Risk of Cancer Among Women"; Harris et al., "Polycystic Ovary Syndrome"; Ding et al., "Association Between Polycystic Ovarian Syndrome."

7. TRANSITION

1. R. R. Wing et al., "Weight Gain at the Time of Menopause," *Archives of Internal Medicine* 151, no. 1 (1991): 97–102; G. M. Van Dijk et al., "The Association Between Vasomotor Symptoms and Metabolic Health in Peri- and Postmenopausal Women: A Systematic Review," *Maturitas* 80, no. 2 (2015): 140–47; P. Tuomikoski et al., "Vasomotor Symptoms and Metabolic Syndrome," *Maturitas* 97 (2017): 61–65; S. Sayan et al., "Relationship Between Vasomotor Symptoms and Metabolic Syndrome in Postmenopausal Women," *Journal of International Medical Research* 46, no. 10 (2018): 4157–66.

2. V. D. Longo et al., "Fasting, Circadian Rhythms, and Time-Restricted Feeding in Healthy Lifespan," *Cell Metabolism* 23, no. 6 (2016): 1048–59.

3. F. Coucke, "Food Intolerance in Patients with Manifest Autoimmunity: Observational Study," *Autoimmunity Reviews* 17, no. 11 (2018): 1078–80.

4. T. C. Wallace et al., "Dairy Intake Is Not Associated with Improvements in Bone Mineral Density or Risk of Fractures Across the Menopause Transition: Data from the Study of Women's Health Across the Nation," *Menopause* 27, no. 8 (2020): 879–86.

5. A. Trichopoulou et al., "Healthy Traditional Mediterranean Diet: An Expression of Culture, History, and Lifestyle." *Nutrition Reviews* 55, no. 11 (1997): 383–89; S. Dernini, "The Erosion and the Renaissance of the Mediterranean Diet: A sustainable Cultural Resource," *Quaderns de la Mediterrania* 16 (2011): 75–82; T. I. Gonzàlez, "The Mediterranean Diet: Consumption, Cuisine, and Food Habits," in *MediTERRA 2012: The Mediterranean Diet for Sustainable Regional Development*, ed. F. Mombiela (Paris: CIHEAM Sciences/Presses de Sciences Po, 2012), 115–32; N. R. Sahyoun et al., *Historical Origins of the Mediterranean Diet, Regional Dietary Profiles, and the Development of the Dietary Guidelines* (Totowa, NJ: Humana Press, 2016), 43–56; C. M. Lăcătuşu et al., "The Mediterranean Diet: From an Environment-Driven Food Culture to an Emerging Medical Prescription," *International Journal of Environmental Research and Public Health* 16, no. 6 (2019): 942.

6. M. De Lorgeril et al., "Mediterranean Alpha-Linolenic Acid–Rich Diet in Secondary Prevention of Coronary Heart Disease," *The Lancet* 343, no. 8911 (1994): 1454–59; M. De Lorgeril et al., "Mediterranean Diet, Traditional Risk Factors, and the Rate of Cardiovascular Complications After Myocardial Infarction: Final Report of the Lyon Diet Heart Study," *Circulation* 99, no. 6 (1999): 779–85; R. Estruch et al., "Retraction and Republication: Primary Prevention of Cardiovascular Disease with a Mediterranean Diet," *New England Journal of Medicine* 368 (2013): 1279–90; M. Sotos-Prieto et al., "Assessing Validity of Self-Reported Dietary Intake Within a Mediterranean Diet Cluster Randomized Controlled Trial among US Firefighters," *Nutrients* 11, no. 9 (2019): 2250.

7. J. Salas-Salvado et al., "Effect of a Mediterranean Diet Supplemented with Nuts on Metabolic Syndrome Status: One-Year Results of the PREDIMED Randomized Trial," *Archives of Internal Medicine* 168, no. 22 (2008): 2449–58; M. T. Mitjavila et al., "The Mediterranean Diet Improves the Systemic Lipid and DNA Oxidative Damage in Metabolic Syndrome Individuals: A Randomized, Controlled Trial," *Clinical Nutrition* 32, no. 2 (2013): 172–78; N. Di Daniele et al., "Impact of Mediterranean Diet on Metabolic Syndrome, Cancer, and Longevity," *Oncotarget* 8, no. 5 (2017): 8947–79; M. Finicelli et al., "Metabolic Syndrome, Mediterranean Diet, and Polyphenols: Evidence and Perspectives," *Journal of Cell Physiology* 234, no. 5 (2019): 5807–26.

8. O. Ajala et al., "Systematic Review and Meta-Analysis of Different Dietary Approaches to the Management of Type 2 Diabetes," *American Journal of Clinical Nutrition* 97, no. 3 (2013): 505–16; J. Salas-Salvadó et al., "Prevention of Diabetes with Mediterranean Diets: A Subgroup Analysis of a Randomized Trial," *Annals of Internal Medicine* 160, no. 1 (2014): 1–10; published correction appears in 169, no. 4 (2018): 271–272.

9. Shai et al., "Weight Loss with a Low-Carbohydrate"; F. M. Sacks et al., "Comparison of Weight-Loss Diets with Different Compositions of Fat, Protein, and Carbohydrates." *New England Journal of Medicine* 360, no. 9 (2009): 859–73; C. Haro et al., "Two Healthy Diets Modulate Gut Microbial Community Improving Insulin Sensitivity in a Human Obese Population," *Journal of Clinical Endocrinology Metabolism* 101, no. 1 (2016): 233–42.

10. N. Di Daniele et al., "Impact of Mediterranean Diet on Metabolic Syndrome, Cancer, and Longevity," *Oncotarget* 8, no. 5 (2017): 8947–79.

11. E. Toledo et al., "Mediterranean Diet and Invasive Breast Cancer Risk Among Women at High Cardiovascular Risk in the PREDIMED Trial: A Randomized Clinical Trial," *JAMA Internal Medicine* 175, no. 11 (2015): 1752–60.

12. E. H. Martínez-Lapiscina et al., "Mediterranean Diet Improves Cognition: The PREDIMED-NAVARRA Randomised Trial," *Journal of Neurology and l Neurosurgery Psychiatry* 84, no. 12 (2013): 1318–25; A. Knight et al., "A Randomised Controlled Intervention Trial Evaluating the Efficacy of a Mediterranean Dietary Pattern on Cognitive Function and Psychological Wellbeing in Healthy Older Adults: The MedLey Study," *BMC Geriatrics* (2015): 15:55; C. Valls-Pedret et al., "Mediterranean Diet and Age-Related Cognitive Decline: A Randomized Clinical Trial," *JAMA Internal Medicine* 175, no. 7 (2015): 1094–103.

13. J. E. de la Rubia Ortí et al., "Improvement of Main Cognitive Functions in Patients with Alzheimer's Disease After Treatment with Coconut Oil Enriched Mediterranean Diet: A Pilot Study," *Journal of Alzheimer's Disease* 65, no. 2 (2018): 577–87.

14. S. I. Katz et al., "Randomized-Controlled Trial of a Modified Mediterranean Dietary Program for Multiple Sclerosis: A Pilot Study," *Multiple Sclerosis Related Disorders* 36 (2019): 101403.

15. O. Ajala et al., "Systematic Review and Meta-Analysis."

16. J. L. Steiner et al., "Impact of Alcohol on Glycemic Control and Insulin Action," *Biomolecules* 5, no. 4 (2015): 2223–46; M. B. Esser et al., "Peer Reviewed: Prevalence of Alcohol Dependence Among US Adult Drinkers, 2009–2011," *Preventing Chronic Disease* 11 (2014); R. W. Wilsnack et al., "Gender Differences in Binge Drinking: Prevalence, Predictors, and Consequences," *Alcohol Research: Current Reviews* 39, no. 1 (2018): 57–76.

17. K. Bogusz et al., "Prevalence of Alcohol Use Disorder Among Individuals Who Binge Eat: A Systematic Review and Meta-Analysis," *Addiction* (2020). doi: 10.1111/add.15155.

INDEX

ABOUT THE AUTHOR

Sara Gottfried, MD, is a board-certified physician who graduated from Harvard Medical School and the Massachusetts Institute of Technology, and completed residency at the University of California at San Francisco. Over the past two decades, Dr. Gottfried has seen more than 25,000 patients, and specializes in identifying the root causes underlying her patients' conditions to achieve true and lasting health transformations, not just symptom management. To promote unprecedented health, she is likely to test her patient's DNA and next-generation biomarkers, and then prescribe a personalized lifestyle protocol, using primarily food (not drugs) plus other proven interventions to optimize the gene-environment interface. For each patient, she designs an N-of-1 trial to provide rapid information on whether the personalized prevention plan will improve outcomes. It's not "one method fits all." It's not disease-centered. It's not "fix 'em up and send 'em home." It's a mission to transform health care, one patient at a time.

Dr. Gottfried is a global keynote speaker who practices evidence-based integrative, precision, and functional medicine. She is a clinical assistant professor in the Department of Integrative Medicine and Nutritional Sciences at Sidney Kimmel Medical College, Thomas Jefferson University, and director of precision medicine at the Marcus Institute of Integrative Health. She has published three *New York Times*–bestselling books: *The Hormone Cure, The Hormone Reset Diet,* and *Younger.* Learn more at http://SaraGottfriedMD.com.